The Heart of Texas Collection

A 6-in-1 Edition including
Lonesome Cowboy, Texas Two-Step, Caroline's Child, Dr. Texas, Nell's Cowboy *and* Lone Star Baby

THE HEART OF TEXAS COLLECTION

A 6-in-1 Edition including
Lonesome Cowboy, Texas Two-Step,
Caroline's Child, Dr. Texas,
Nell's Cowboy *and* Lone Star Baby

DEBBIE MACOMBER

Harlequin Books
*Toronto • New York • London
Amsterdam • Paris • Sydney • Hamburg
Stockholm • Athens • Tokyo • Milan
Madrid • Warsaw • Budapest • Auckland*

CONTENTS

Lonesome Cowboy   1
Texas Two-Step   149
Caroline's Child   285
Dr. Texas   419
Nell's Cowboy   553
Lone Star Baby   687

Dearest Friends,

After the success of MIDNIGHT SONS, and those stubborn Alaskan men, Harlequin approached me about doing another six-book series. But where was I going to find heroes to match those strong, endearing bush pilots? The answer wasn't long in coming. I've always had a weakness for cowboys, and no place on earth grows 'em quite like Texas.

So, my friends, here they are: the men and women of Promise, Texas. Situated deep in the Texas hill country. Promise is truly a town with heart, populated by people like you and me—hardworking, proud and just a little sassy. A town with an interesting past and an exciting future.

For the MIDNIGHT SONS series, my husband and I traveled to Alaska. This time around, I conned my editor, Paula Eykelhof, into exploring Texas with me. With a rental car, a map and the sense of direction of a pet rock, Paula and I toured the Texas hill country. We met the people, sampled the barbecues, tasted the wines and gazed endlessly at cowboys. If this wasn't heaven, then we were pretty darn close!

So I invite you to sit back, put your feet up and allow me to introduce you to a few of those Texan cowboys. The men of Alaska started this craziness, but the men in Texas refuse to be outdone. They're just as stubborn, just as ornery, just as proud. And just as lovable.

Enjoy.

Debbie Macomber

THE PEOPLE OF PROMISE
CAST OF CHARACTERS

Nell Bishop: thirty-something widow with a son, Jeremy, and a daughter, Emma. Her husband died in a tractor accident.

Ruth Bishop: Nell's mother-in-law. Lives with Nell and her two children.

Dovie Boyd: runs an antiques shop and has dated Sheriff Frank Hennessey for ten years

Caroline Daniels: postmistress of Promise

Maggie Daniels: Caroline's five-year-old daughter

Dr. Jane Dickinson: new doctor in Promise

Ellie Frasier: owner of Frasier's Feed Store

Frank Hennessey: local sheriff

Max Jordan: owner of Jordan's Towne & Country

Wade McMillen: preacher of Promise Christian Church

Edwina and Lily Moorhouse: sisters. Retired schoolteachers.

Cal and Glen Patterson: local ranchers. Brothers who ranch together.

Phil and Mary Patterson: parents of Cal and Glen. Operate a local B&B.

Louise Powell: town gossip

Wiley Rogers: sixty-year-old ranch foreman at the Weston ranch

Laredo Smith: wrangler hired by Savannah Weston

Barbara and Melvin Weston: mother and father to Savannah, Grady and Richard. The Westons died six years ago.

Richard Weston: youngest of the Weston siblings

Savannah Weston: Grady and Richard's sister. Cultivates old roses.

Grady Weston: rancher and oldest of the Weston siblings

LONESOME
COWBOY

LONESOME
COWBOY

One

Grady had warned her repeatedly. He'd told Savannah that the ghost town was dangerous, that it was a disturbing place. He'd told her over and over not to look for it. And all these years Savannah *had* stayed away. But the more her brother cautioned her, the more convinced she'd become that she had to find it. If for no other reason than the roses. Roses were Savannah's passion—especially old roses, planted before 1867 and now found mostly in cemeteries and abandoned homesteads.

It was because of the roses that she ignored Grady's advice and began to seek out the long-lost town.

After a six-week search, roaming about the rugged Texas hill country, first in the truck, then on horseback and finally on foot with no map and little information, she'd located it. Bitter End. What a strange name, but no stranger than the town itself.

No matter how furious Grady was when he discovered what she'd done, it'd been worth the risk. This certainly wouldn't be the first time she'd defied her older brother. Nor would it be the last. Grady seemed to carry the weight of the world on his shoulders; he rarely smiled anymore. He was as loud and demanding as Savannah was quiet and intense. But her stubbornness was easily a match for his.

Glancing at the truck's speedometer, she pressed her foot to the floor, although it generally wasn't in her nature to rush. However, her chances of escaping Grady's anger were greater if she got back to the house before he returned from his duties around the ranch. Not that she *feared* his anger; she simply preferred to avoid it.

Her brother was so often angry these days, with beef prices dropping and all the other problems associated with running a large cattle ranch. It didn't help that, thanks to Richard, they continued to struggle with debt and financial hardship.

Savannah forced her thoughts away from the unhappy events of six years earlier. It was wrenching enough to have lost both parents in one devastating accident, but Savannah feared that their brother's betrayal, which had followed so soon afterward, would forever taint their lives with bitterness.

"Oh, Richard," she whispered as the truck sped down the winding country road. The pain he'd wrought in her life and Grady's was the kind that even love would never completely heal.

Grady had changed in the years since their parents' tragic deaths—and Richard's betrayal. Finances and other concerns had harassed and tormented him until she barely knew him any longer. Through sheer stubbornness and backbreaking work he'd managed to accomplish the impossible. He's saved the Yellow Rose Ranch, but at a terrible price. Grady had sacrificed himself and his youth to hold on to the land that had been settled by their great-great-grandfather shortly after the Civil War. Or, as her Southern grandmother called it, the War of the Northern Aggression.

Savannah had wanted to help with their finances; after all, she had a college education. It would be a small thing to return to school and take the necessary courses to obtain her teaching certificate. The Promise school board had repeatedly advertised for substitute teachers, and a full-time position was bound to become available within a few years. Grady, however, wouldn't hear of it. He needed her on the Yellow Rose, and Savannah accepted that. She handled the majority of the paperwork, cooked, cleaned the house and did the gardening. She'd indulged her love for roses, started keeping goats and occasionally hand-raised orphaned or abandoned calves. For six years she'd picked up the slack and made a decent life for herself. But compared to Grady, she didn't feel she was doing nearly enough.

Her desire to contribute to the family income had prompted her to establish a mail-order business for her roses, and while Grady had politely listened to her plans, he hadn't encouraged them. Her small venture was just now starting to show a profit, of which Savannah was extremely proud. In the past few months she'd been spending her evenings working on a catalog.

What Grady needed, in Savannah's opinion, was to marry and start a family. At thirty-five he was well past the age most men settled into family life. He probably would've done so long before now if he hadn't been required to dedicate every waking minute to the ranch. She wondered whether it was too late, whether he'd ever get married. Savannah herself had long since given up any hope of marriage and children. Her maternal urges would have to be satisfied by her animals, she told herself wryly. She'd turned thirty-one her last birthday and hadn't dated in the past four or five years. She rarely thought about having a relationship anymore. Men didn't understand her quiet ways or appreciate her strength or gentleness of spirit. It no longer mattered. She was content with her life. She'd learned to take pleasure in small things—the beauty of flowers, the affection of animals, the comfort of a well-ordered house.

Indian paintbrush, bluebonnets and pink evening primroses, all in bloom, lined the twisting road. Savannah loved spring. The scent of the air brought with it the promise of warm weather and new life. Grady and Wiley, the hired hand who'd been with them so many years he was more family than foreman, had assisted in delivering fourteen calves this week and were looking for that many more in the next couple of days.

Savannah glanced at her watch and hoped Grady had been delayed this afternoon. Otherwise he was going to have a conniption, especially when he realized where she'd gone.

Sighing, she turned the familiar bend in the road and caught sight of an abandoned truck parked close to the ditch. Savannah didn't recognize the vehicle; that in itself was unusual. People who didn't know the area hardly ever wandered this far off the beaten path.

The truck had seen better days. The color had faded badly and a large dent in the side revealed a section where rust had eaten a hole the size of a small plate. With the truck parked as it was, fifteen miles outside of town, far from anywhere, Savannah couldn't help wondering if something was wrong. She might have stopped to investigate if she hadn't been in a hurry.

The decision was taken from her a few miles down the road when she saw a cowboy walking, carrying a saddle. Even from this distance she could see how weary he was; he seemed to be favoring one side, limping discernibly. At the sound of her approach, he straightened, shifted the weight of his saddle and stuck out his thumb.

Never in all her life had Savannah stopped for a hitchhiker, but this man, miles from anywhere and walking in the opposite direction from town, must have been spent.

Savannah pulled over and eased to a stop. She opened the door and climbed out. "Is that your truck parked back there?"

"Yes, ma'am," he answered politely. He was tall and wiry, about her age, she guessed. His Stetson rested low on his brow, shading his face from the afternoon sun. When he touched his fingers to the brim in greeting, she noticed that his eyes were pale blue. "I'd be much obliged for a ride."

Although she'd stopped, Savannah hesitated, unsure what to do. "I wasn't headed toward town."

"As far as you'd take me would be appreciated. Your truck's the first vehicle to come along in more'n two hours." He gave her a tired smile. "I'd hoped to find a ranch and use the phone there, but I haven't seen one yet."

Apparently he didn't realize he was walking away from Promise. "I live ten or so miles down the road." Shielding her eyes from the glare of the sun, she pointed toward the Yellow Rose. Riding with her would only take him farther from where he needed to go. She was about to explain as much, then realized he was tired, hurting and probably hadn't eaten a decent meal in hours, if not days. Grady wouldn't be pleased, but . . . She shrugged off the prospect of her brother's wrath.

"If you like, you can stay the night in the bunkhouse and I'll drive you to town in the morning."

She could tell that her offer surprised him; his eyes widened briefly. "That's mighty kind of you, ma'am."

The fact that he called her ma'am made her feel dowdy and old-fashioned. She supposed that was exactly what she was, though. No one had to tell her she looked older than her age. She usually wore full-length dresses rather than the more fashionable shirt and jeans; her mother had encouraged this, saying that dresses complimented her tall willowy figure. She'd grown accustomed to working in them, donning an apron for household chores. Her thick straight blond hair fell down her back, almost to her waist. Grady had teasingly called her a flower child of the sixties, and in some ways, she did resemble a hippie.

"I'm Savannah Weston."

"Laredo Smith." Again he touched the brim of his hat.

"Pleased to meet you," she said, and smiled shyly. "Laredo's an unusual name."

He grinned as if the comment was familiar. "So I've heard." He hitched the saddle higher and added, "My given name's Matthew, but when I was a kid and we moved away from Texas, I wanted to take part of it with me. From that day on I only answered to Laredo. After all these years, I don't know who Matthew is, but Laredo . . . well, it's a comfortable fit and suits me just fine."

Savannah couldn't have said why, but she had the impression that these details weren't something he shared often. She told herself it was silly to feel honored—but she did, anyway.

She must have smiled because he responded with a grin of his own. It amazed her how a simple smile could transform his drained features.

A hint of something warm and kind showed in his sun-weathered face, mesmerizing her for a moment. A little shocked by her own response, Savannah decided she was being fanciful and looked away. Laredo Smith was a stranger and she'd do well to take care.

"If you'd like, you can put your saddle in the truck bed," she offered, and walked to the back to lower the tailgate.

The leather creaked as he lifted it from his shoulder and wearily set it down. He hesitated when he saw the roses and reached out a callused hand toward the fragile buds. Gently he fingered a delicate pink petal.

"There are antique roses, aren't they?" He closed his eyes and breathed in the distinctive perfumed scent of the flowers.

His knowledge surprised her. Few people knew about old roses or had heard the term. In her research Savannah had learned that many of the roses found in Texas were of unknown lineage, recovered from hidden corners and byways in an ongoing search-and-rescue mission—like the one she'd been on that very day. Savannah was well aware that some would describe her as a "rose rustler"; it wasn't how she thought of herself. Her overwhelming motivation was her love of the flowers.

"You know about old roses?" she asked.

"My grandmother had a rose garden and she grew roses passed down by her own grandmother. It must be at least twenty years since I saw one. Where'd you ever find these?"

Her pause was long enough for him to notice. "In an old graveyard," she said. "Near, um, an abandoned town." While it was the truth, it wasn't the *entire* truth, but Savannah didn't dare add any details about the ghost town. Only a few people in Promise had even heard of Bitter End. And although Grady had repeatedly warned her against seeking it out, he'd never told her exactly what was so threatening about the long-deserted town.

Only now did Savannah understand her brother's concerns. The dangers weren't found in the crumbling buildings or the abandoned wells; no, they weren't so easily explained. She couldn't help shuddering as she remembered the sensation of . . . darkness that had come over her when she'd first set foot on the still, silent grounds. Even that didn't adequately describe the emotions she'd experienced. It wasn't a feeling of evil so much as a pressing sadness, a pain and grief so raw that a hundred years hadn't dimmed its intensity.

Knowing little of the town's history, Savannah had felt defenseless and almost afraid. Years earlier, Grady and two of his friends had heard their parents discussing Bitter End, but when Savannah questioned her mother, she'd refused to talk about it. From Grady, Savannah had

learned that the town was said to have been settled by Promise's founding fathers. Why they'd moved, what had happened to prompt the reloca-
tion, was an unsolved mystery. For all she knew, it was something as
mundane as water rights. Although that would hardly account for what
she'd felt. . . .

Despite Grady's warnings, Savannah had found Bitter End and dug
up the old roses in the graveyard, but she hadn't ventured beyond the
fenced area beside the church. She left as quickly as she could. By the
time she made it back to the truck, she was pale and trembling.

She'd driven away without looking back. She hadn't investigated any
of the other buildings, and she was annoyed now for letting the opportunity pass. She might have found more old roses had she taken the time to
search.

"They're beautiful," Laredo said. The light pink bud, perfectly
formed, lay like a jewel in the palm of his hand.

"They truly are exquisite, aren't they?" The sheer joy and excitement
she'd felt on discovering the roses quickened her voice. "I just couldn't
be happier! It's so much more than I hoped to find!"

His gaze held hers and he nodded, seeming to share her enthusiasm.

Warming to her subject, Savannah added, "It's incredible to think
they've survived all these years without anyone to care for them."

Laredo gently withdrew his hand from the rosebud.

"Would you be more comfortable if I rode in the back, ma'am?" he
asked.

"Savannah," she insisted.

The smile returned again, briefly. "Savannah," he echoed.

"You're welcome to ride in front with me."

He climbed slowly into the cab and she could see that the action
pained him considerably.

"I don't suppose you know anyone who's looking for a good wrangler?" he asked.

"I'm sorry, I don't," she said with sincere regret.

He nodded and winced, pressing his hand against his ribs.

"You've been hurt," she said.

"A cracked rib or two," he answered, obviously embarrassed by her
concern. "My own damn fault," he muttered.

"A horse?"

"Not exactly." His voice was rueful, a bit ironic. "I got shoved
against a fence by a bull. You'd think that after all these years working
ranches, I'd know better than to let myself get cornered by a bull."

"My daddy cracked a rib once and he said it left him feeling like he'd been gnawed by a coyote, then dumped over a cliff."

Laredo chuckled. "Your daddy sounds like he's got quite a sense of humor."

"He did," Savannah agreed softly, starting the engine. She knew the tires hitting the ruts in the road would hurt him, so she drove slowly and carefully.

Laredo glanced over his shoulder—to check on his saddle, Savannah suspected. She was surprised when he mentioned the roses a second time. "I never thought to smell roses like those again."

"I'm so glad I found them!" she burst out. "These are the best ones yet." Their scent was sweet and strong and pure, far more aromatic than modern hybrids. These roses from Bitter End were probably White Lady Banks—a rare and precious find.

Savannah talked excitedly about her roses; the cowboy encouraged her, asking interested and knowledgeable questions.

What surprised Savannah was how comfortable she felt with Laredo Smith. They could have talked for hours. Generally when it came to conversation with a man, especially a stranger, Savannah was shy and reticent. The ease with which she talked to Laredo was unprecedented.

It wasn't just roses they talked about, either. Soon Savannah found herself telling him about her gardens at the ranch and the love her mother, Barbara, had for flowers. One topic led swiftly to another. She described Promise and assured him it was a friendly town. He asked about having his truck repaired and she mentioned a couple of reliable garages.

"Oh, my," she said, and held her palm to her mouth.

"Is something wrong?"

"I got to chatting away and almost missed the turnoff for the ranch." Such a thing had never happened before. Then, hardly knowing what she was doing, she glanced over at him and said, "The fact is, Laredo, the Yellow Rose could use an extra hand. If you need a job, we'd be happy to offer you one."

Laredo brightened visibly. "I'm good with horses and I'm willing to work hard."

"Grady'll probably have a few questions for you." She added this second part knowing her brother wasn't going to be pleased with her hiring a stranger. In the past he'd always been the one to do the hiring and firing, but if he took offense, he could discuss the matter with her. Every instinct she possessed told her Laredo Smith was worthy of their trust. Besides, they needed extra help, whether Grady was willing to admit it or not.

Laredo grew quiet, and then she felt his eyes on her. "Since you offered me the job, I think it's only fair to tell you I was fired from my last position." He told her he'd been accused of theft, wrongly accused. He neither cast nor accepted blame. "I may be a lot of things, but a thief isn't one of them. If you change your mind, I'll understand."

"I won't," she said, but the instincts that had felt so right moments earlier wavered like dry grass whipped by a harsh summer wind. "I . . . I appreciate your being honest enough to tell me," Savannah said. Naturally the first thing Grady would want from a stranger, especially one *she'd* taken it upon herself to hire, was references. Well—like everything else about this day—she'd cross that bridge when she came to it.

"You won't be disappointed," Laredo added. "You have my word on that."

A plume of dust followed them as they headed down the pitched dirt driveway leading off the highway. No sooner had Savannah pulled into the yard and turned off the engine than Grady dashed out of the barn and stalked toward her like an avenging angel.

"Just where the bloody hell have you been all afternoon?" her brother demanded, ignoring the shambling black dog that trailed him and nudged the fist clenched at his side.

Savannah inhaled deeply and held her breath while she climbed out of the truck. If she hadn't stopped to pick up Laredo, she might have returned before Grady rode in from the range. Rather than answer his questions, she leaned over and scratched Rocket's ears. The old dog, who'd once belonged to their father, was now well past his prime. He wagged his tail in appreciation.

"You might have left a note." Her brother's ranting continued despite her lack of response.

"I apologize, but—" She wasn't allowed to finish.

"I don't want an apology. I want to know where you were all afternoon." His eyes narrowed on the man beside her. "And I have a feeling I'm not going to like the answer."

It mortified her to have her brother yell at her like this in front of Laredo. "Grady," she said urgently, "perhaps we could discuss this inside."

"You did it, didn't you? Even though I warned you! I *told* you not to look for Bitter End! Doesn't anyone listen to me anymore? I thought you were smarter than this! *Anything* could happen to you up in those hills all by yourself. What's the matter with you, anyway? You should know better than to risk your fool neck over something as ridiculous as a stupid rosebush." His face had turned red with anger.

Disregarding Laredo, her brother advanced toward her. Two steps was as close as he got before her newfound friend moved protectively in front of her, directly in Grady's path.

"Who the hell are you?"

"Grady, this is Laredo Smith," Savannah said evenly, praying she sounded calm and in control. "His truck broke down, and, um, I've offered him a job."

A second of shocked silence followed. "You *what?*"

The anger Grady had shown earlier paled in comparison to the fury that blazed in his eyes now. Savannah didn't acknowledge his outburst. "Dinner's in the Crock-Pot. Chili verde, your favorite."

Grady stared at her, his mouth hanging open, as if he didn't recognize her as his sister.

"I'll have everything ready and on the table in ten minutes. Grady, would you be kind enough to show Laredo to the bunkhouse and ask Wiley to wash up?"

"This is Wiley's poker night," Grady muttered. "But I—"

"So it is," she said, and headed up the porch steps and into the kitchen. Her heart pounced like a prairie rabbit's at the approach of a hawk's shadow. "Then there'll just be the three of us."

It didn't take her long to set the table for dinner. When she heard the door swing open, she squared her shoulders, and turned to greet her brother and Laredo with a wide smile. "I hope you two had a chance to introduce yourselves."

"We didn't get around to exchanging pleasantries," Grady snarled.

"Laredo, I hope you'll forgive my brother," she said, placing the warm tortillas on a plate. "It's clear he isn't in one of his more cordial moods."

"Your brother?" The words slipped from Laredo's lips in a low whisper of surprise.

"The two of us are equal partners in the Yellow Rose Ranch," she said as a subtle way of reminding Grady that she'd had every right to hire Laredo.

Still grumbling under his breath, Grady pulled out a chair and reached for the blue-checked napkin.

"Can I help you with anything, Savannah?" Laredo asked, looking around for something to do.

"There's a cold pitcher of lemonade in the refrigerator," she said, hoping Grady realized it wouldn't hurt him any to lend her a hand now and then. She tried not to be judgmental of her brother, but lately he'd grown so cranky and irritable. It was more than their perpetual money problems, she suspected, but whatever plagued him, he kept to himself. Savannah wished he'd be more open with her, share his troubles, but that wasn't Grady's way. Like their father he kept everything locked inside, preferring to carry the burden of his problems alone. Once again she wished he'd think about marriage. She had the perfect woman in mind.

GRADY WESTON was furious with his sister. He didn't know what had come over her. It wasn't like her to openly defy him, nor had he ever known her to pick up a hitchhiker. And never, not once in all these years, had she taken an active role in the management of the ranch. Yet in one single day, his levelheaded younger sister had not only gone against his express orders, she'd gone and hired him additional help. A stranger, no less!

Grady wouldn't have believed it if he hadn't seen it with his own eyes, heard it with his own ears. Savannah wasn't herself. He frowned at Laredo Smith, instinctively distrusting him. One look told Grady the saddle bum was an outsider, a drifter. Not to be trusted. Yet Savannah had invited the man into their home and their lives like a long-lost relative—*and* offered him employment. The problem with Savannah could be reduced to one simple explanation. She couldn't see the bad in people. She was just too damn trusting.

In spite of that, Grady had often admired Savannah for her common sense. But from all appearances, she'd lost every shred of good judgment she'd ever possessed. All within the space of a single day.

"I can't remember when I've tasted better chili," Laredo said, serving himself a second helping when Savannah passed him the bowl.

She lowered her gaze and Grady watched, amazed as color seeped into her cheeks. "I appreciate the compliment, but Nell Bishop's the one who deserves the credit. It's her recipe."

"My compliments to Nell, then, and to you, too."

Savannah's blush deepened. If it wasn't so pathetic, Grady might have rolled his eyes. The town was full of men who were interested in Savannah, but she hadn't given one of them a lick of encouragement. Not a one. *Then she happens on a complete stranger who doesn't look like he's got two dimes to call his own and she practically faints because he compliments her cooking!*

Grady shoved his plate aside, appetite gone. His day had gone poorly. A calf had died after a desperate struggle to save its life, and he wasn't sure the mother was going to make it, either. He'd had the vet out, and they'd done everything they could, but it didn't look promising. If that wasn't bad enough, he'd found a break in the fence line. Luckily he'd been able to repair it before any of the herd had escaped.

The problems never ended. Day in and day out, he faced one crisis after another, each one heaped on top of all the others. He didn't know what it was to laugh anymore, didn't know what it was to spend a night in town drinking with his buddies. Hell, he couldn't even remember the last time he'd kissed a woman. In six years his life had boiled down to two things—work and worry.

It seemed a million years ago that he'd been young and carefree. Everything had changed for him—and for Savannah—in the course of an afternoon. The life he'd lived before they lost their parents was little more than a vague memory.

After a day like this the last thing he needed was for the one constant, the one sane sensible person in his life, to lose her bearings. Go loco on him. Grady glanced at Savannah and he felt his heart twist with sorrow, frustration, guilt. His sister was as lovely as those roses she cared so much about. She was still young and pretty, although she didn't appear to realize that.

Grady hadn't saved the ranch all on his own, nor was he the only one who'd dedicated his life to building back everything they'd lost. He couldn't have done it without her. Savannah had found a hundred ways to encourage him, lighten his load, and he didn't thank her nearly enough.

Regret settled in the pit of his stomach. He shouldn't have laid into her the way he had when she got home, but damn it all, he'd been worried sick. It wasn't like her to disappear and not tell him where she was going. In the past she'd always been conscientious about that, and with good reason.

Even though the risk of her encountering danger was slim, an accident could always happen. It had to his mother and father. Caught in a flash flood, they'd been swept away in a matter of moments and drowned. Never would he forget the day Sheriff Frank Hennessey had come to deliver the tragic news. So it wasn't that Grady didn't trust Savannah, but her disappearance that afternoon had brought back memories he wished he could forget.

But it was more than the memory of his parents' accident that had distressed him. For three or four months now his sister had been asking him about the ghost town. In the beginning he'd answered her questions and hadn't given her curiosity much thought, but when she persisted, he'd asked her a few questions of his own. That was when she mentioned the old roses. Damn fool woman was willing to risk her neck over something as . . . as unimportant as flowers. If that didn't beat all, he didn't know what did.

Grady had warned her plenty, not that it'd done any good. Hell, he couldn't have found the abandoned frontier town again had he tried. The one and only time he'd ever stepped foot in Bitter End, he'd been about fifteen. Grady and the two Patterson brothers had overheard their parents talking about a ghost town somewhere up in the hills. Without their parents' knowledge the boys had decided to go exploring, to find the place for themselves.

Grady and his friends had set out, thinking it all a grand adventure. As he recalled, they'd spent weeks looking, and when they finally stumbled on the ghost town, it'd spooked them so badly they'd never discussed that day again.

Grady didn't believe in ghosts; he wasn't a superstitious man. But the town was haunted by something he'd been too young to name or understand, something he didn't fully comprehend even now. An unfamiliar sensation had descended on him that day, and not only him, but the others, too. He remembered the silence that had come over them, how they'd whispered to each other as if they were afraid someone could hear. He remembered a feeling of deep sadness and an ambiguous kind of threat. It hadn't made sense then and made even less sense now.

What mattered was his sister, and Grady didn't want her wandering around in the country alone in search of some half-dead flowers. Especially if it meant she was wandering around in Bitter End.

"Would you care for another helping?" Savannah asked Laredo, breaking into Grady's thoughts.

Laredo planted his hands on his stomach and shook his head. "As delicious as it is, I don't think I could manage another mouthful. As I said earlier, this is one of the best meals I've had in years. I hope your brother appreciates what a fine cook you are."

Even from across the table Grady could feel Savannah's pleasure at the other man's remark. It *sounded* genuine, but Grady suspected Laredo Smith was a consummate con man, who knew a good thing when he saw it. It was clear to Grady, if no one else, that Laredo Smith was out to take advantage of his sister. Not that he had a raindrop's chance in hell of doing so as long as Grady lived and breathed. The drifter could sweet-talk some other rancher's sister. He'd get nowhere with Savannah; Grady would personally see to that.

"I'll help with the dishes," Laredo offered.

Grady resisted suggesting that Laredo was laying it on a little thick, but he was already out of Savannah's good graces and she wouldn't appreciate his sarcasm.

"I'll do the dishes later," Savannah said. "It's more important that I take care of the roses."

"I could help you with that," he suggested next, and then, as if qualifying his statement, he added, "My grandmother let me help her."

"That . . . that would be lovely."

Grady couldn't recall the last time he'd seen his sister this flustered. Like a schoolboy eager to please his teacher, Laredo stood and carried his empty plate to the sink.

Grady couldn't allow this to continue. It was time he set the other man straight. "Before this goes any further, you need to know, Mr. Smith, that there's no work for you here."

"Excuse me," Savannah said, her voice rising, "but *I* was the one who hired Laredo."

"I'll be happy to drive you back into Promise myself," Grady volunteered, ignoring his sister. "Would *now* be convenient?"

The two men glared at each other.

"Grady," Savannah protested, but to no avail. He'd tuned her out, unwilling to listen to her arguments.

When she couldn't attract his attention, Savannah tried reaching Laredo. She said his name, but he, too, ignored her, eyes locked with Grady's. The silent battle of wills didn't last long. Slowly Laredo's shoulders relaxed, and he nodded. "Now would be fine."

Grady hadn't expected him to capitulate this easily. If anything, he'd anticipated an argument. Laredo Smith was no fool. The way Savannah had fussed over him at dinner, blushed and made a general idiot of herself, there was no telling how much the drifter could take her for.

"I'll get my saddle."

"No!"

Savannah's cry caught them both off guard. Grady's attention flew to her, as did Laredo's.

Her face was red and her hands had tightened into fists. "If you two had listened to me earlier, I could have cleared this up immediately." She exhaled a long shaky breath. "I was the one who hired Laredo."

"And I said I don't need anyone just now," Grady countered brusquely.

"I didn't say I hired him to help you, Grady. Laredo Smith is working for me."

TWO

Laredo sat on the thin mattress and nursed his aching ribs. They hurt a little less now that the aspirin had had time to take effect. Without asking, Savannah had handed him the pills after dinner, as if she knew intuitively how uncomfortable he'd been. She continued to fascinate him, but it was abundantly clear that her big brother wasn't keen on Laredo hanging around her. Not that Laredo blamed him. If Savannah was his sister, he'd keep a close eye on her, too.

Following dinner, they'd transplanted the old roses she'd found that day. Afterward she'd proudly walked him through the flower garden, telling him the names of various plants, describing their characteristics. She grew azaleas, rhododendrons and many others, some of which he'd never seen before. A hedge of sunflowers separated the flowers from a small herb garden. And then there were her roses.

As she led him down the narrow pathways of her rose garden, she stopped to tell him about each one. It was almost, he thought fancifully, as if she were introducing him to her children. Little pieces of her heart, planted and nourished in fertile ground. From the way her roses flourished, she'd obviously lavished them with love and care.

The rows of old roses were what impressed him most—but no less than Savannah's knowledge of their histories. She was able to tell him where each one had come from and when it was first grown. Gesturing in her enthusiasm, she lost her large straw hat; Laredo stooped to pick it up. She smiled as he returned it, but didn't interrupt her history of the Highway 290 Pink Buttons—small roses with double blossoms. Found in this part of Texas, she told him proudly. Her voice was full of reverence as she spoke of the inherent beauty of the old roses, their perfect scent, their ability to survive.

When they'd finished walking around the garden, she wrote out a list of tasks she had in mind for him. Laredo listened carefully, had her show him where he'd find the supplies he'd need and promised to get started first thing in the morning. He was eager to prove she hadn't made a mistake by hiring him, and that her trust in him had been well placed. *Saying* it was one thing, but the proof was in the results.

In the morning, as soon as he finished dealing with his truck, he planned to be in that rose garden working his fool head off. It wasn't wrangling, wasn't what he knew best, but if he treated the roses with the same respect and appreciation he did a good quarter horse, then he'd do fine.

"Cowboy, you got everything you need?" A froggy male voice cut into Laredo's musings, startling him. He swiveled around to find an older man standing just inside the large bunkhouse. Two rows of beds lined the floor—like an army barracks; at the other end was a door leading to the foreman's private room.

"Wiley Rogers," the foreman said.

"Laredo Smith. And yes, thanks, I'm fine for now. I have some stuff in my truck—clothes and such—but I can get those in the morning." He stood and moved toward the man. They exchanged brusque handshakes.

Rogers had to be sixty if he was a day, with legs bowed from too many years in the saddle. "Hear you're workin' for Savannah," he said with a friendly smile.

Laredo nodded.

The foreman chuckled and rubbed his unshaven jaw, eyeing Laredo carefully. Whatever his opinion, he was keeping it to himself. "If that don't beat all," he muttered, still grinning. "Never thought I'd see the day . . ."

"Beg your pardon?"

"It's nothing," Wiley said. After a moment's reflection he revised his statement. "Actually it *is* something, but you wouldn't understand. Nice meetin' you, Laredo. You need anything else, just give me a holler."

"Thanks, I will." He sat back down on the bed as Wiley retired to his room and closed the door.

Once the lights were out, Laredo lay on his back and stared up at the ceiling, waiting for sleep to claim him. He should've been dead to the world by now. He was exhausted. And for the first time in days the pain in his side had dulled. His belly was full and he had employment, of sorts. He didn't know how long Savannah would find enough tasks to keep him busy, but he didn't imagine this job would last more than a week or two.

As soon as he found out what was wrong with the truck and had it repaired, he'd hit the road. In hindsight, Earl Chesterton had done him a favor by firing him. Although it sure as hell dented his ego to lose that job, especially under those circumstances. His jaw tightened every time he thought about being accused of theft.

But he was determined to look at this as a blessing in disguise—what his grandmother would have called it. Finding himself unexpectedly jobless was just the incentive he needed to head back to Oklahoma and pursue his dream of breeding and selling quarter horses. After talking about it for years, he was actually going to do it. With the bitterness of being fired from the Triple C Ranch came the sweetness of this chance to live his dream. Even knowing it would mean years of sacrifice, the thought of being his own boss and living on his own land excited Laredo.

Intent on sleeping, he closed his eyes and tried to empty his mind. To his surprise a vivid image of Savannah appeared, clear as anything. He studied her a long while, this warm, gentle woman who'd come so fortuitously into his life. She was a comfortable person, and she possessed a kind heart. He liked Savannah Weston, but then it was impossible *not* to like her. In fact—even more than that—he found himself attracted to her. Strongly attracted.

It was years since a woman had captivated him the way Savannah had. She wasn't like other women he'd known. He'd never felt relaxed or easy around the opposite sex, but Savannah brought out his every protective instinct. She was shy but genuine, and he liked that. He liked that a lot. Pretty, too, without being flashy. He sensed that despite her quiet unassuming manner she had courage and strength. She reminded him a bit of the frontier women he'd read about who'd helped tame the territory of Texas. Especially with those long dresses she wore.

Her brother, on the other hand, was another matter. Hardheaded, stubborn, suspicious. Laredo had taken exception to the way Grady spoke to his sister, but it wasn't his place to get involved in their family affairs.

No, sir.

He'd work here while there was work to be had, get his truck back in good running order, then head for Oklahoma as soon as he could arrange it.

That would be the best thing for everyone. For the Westons and for him.

As SHE'D PLANNED days before, Savannah drove into town the next morning. Her errand list seemed endless. Hardware store, library, the grocery. Finally she was hurrying toward the post office. Her last stop. She realized that the urgency to get back to the ranch had more to do with seeing

Laredo again than with any task that waited for her. *Anyone would think you were a schoolgirl!* But she couldn't help the way her heart reacted to the man.

The dinner she planned for that night was Grady's favorite—chicken-fried steak, cream gravy and fresh green beans. A peace offering. He'd barely had a word for her all morning, but then he wasn't communicative at the best of times. Still, there was no mistaking his anger. She'd felt his gaze following her in the kitchen this morning as she'd moved about, preparing breakfast. They'd carefully avoided each other's eyes. Savannah seldom defied her brother, but Grady had left her no option.

Because she'd stood her ground, Laredo was staying. For some reason that made her happier than anything had in years.

Savannah purposely saved the post office till last, hoping Caroline Daniels, the postmistress, would have time to chat. Dovie Boyd, who owned the antique store and the Victorian Tea Room, was just leaving when Savannah pulled into the parking lot. They exchanged cheerful waves.

The interior of the post office was blessedly cool, and Savannah glanced toward the front counter, relieved to see no other patrons. Deciding to pick up her mail first, she found her post-box key and inserted it into the lock. The metal door swung open to reveal Caroline's nose and brown eyes.

"Is it true?" the postmistress demanded.

"True?" Savannah blinked back her surprise at discovering Caroline's face thrust at her though the small opening.

"I thought I was your best friend."

"You are," Savannah said.

"Then one would think you'd have told me about a handsome stranger working at the Yellow Rose."

Savannah felt color explode in her face. Apparently word of her hiring Laredo had already spread through town. In less than twenty-four hours, too! How, she didn't know—didn't even want to know. This was the problem with living in a small town. Nothing was private. Unnerved, she closed the small door and twisted the key, locking it.

"Savannah!" came Caroline's muffled voice.

Reluctantly Savannah unlocked the box and opened the door. "Who told you?" She withdrew the few envelopes from the box and thrust them into her bag.

"Ellie Frasier, and she said he's cute, too."

"Ellie met him?" Savannah asked. Ellie was the daughter of John Frasier, owner of the feed store. She was young and pretty, and she had a lively, fun-loving personality. More than once Savannah had hoped Grady would notice her, seeing as he made weekly trips to Frasier's for grain and such. Savannah had hinted a couple of times that he needn't rush home—that maybe he could invite Ellie out for coffee or a cold beer. Her suggestions had met with a glare and a low growl that said he didn't take kindly to her matchmaking efforts.

"So, is he as cute as Ellie says?"

Savannah's blush deepened and she raised her hand to her face. "I . . . I wouldn't know."

Caroline's chuckle was full of disbelief. "Okay, if you won't answer that, then tell me his name."

No harm there. "Laredo Smith."

"So you were able to talk Grady into hiring another hand. Where'd he happen to meet Laredo?"

This was where the story got difficult. "Grady didn't exactly . . . hire Laredo."

The brown eyes staring at her from the back of her mailbox darkened perceptibly. "What do you mean?"

Savannah sighed. She might as well explain it once and for all and be done with it. "Laredo isn't working for Grady. I'm the one who hired him."

"You?" Those same eyes narrowed. "Meet me up front."

While Savannah had hoped to discuss the events of the day before with Caroline, she'd wanted to bring up the subject of Laredo in her own time. She certainly hadn't expected an inquisition, especially this soon. But lately Caroline had been encouraging her to get out more, mingle. Savannah decided to accept her friend's advice the day Caroline took it herself.

"You've got that look again," Caroline teased when Savannah approached the counter.

"What look?"

"The one that says you're . . . you know, perturbed."

"Well, I am." As far as Savannah was concerned she had every right to feel perturbed, annoyed and downright peeved. The entire town was discussing her life, or soon would be, particularly when it became common knowledge that Laredo Smith worked for her and not Grady. She absolutely deplored gossip and refused to partake in it. She'd never pry into anyone's personal business. Why, she'd been Caroline's best friend for ages, and not once had she asked who'd fathered five-year-old Maggie. If Caroline felt inclined to tell her, then she would, but Savannah would rather die than ask.

"Get over it, Savannah. It isn't every day a handsome stranger wanders into town."

"Laredo didn't exactly wander into Promise." She supposed she'd have to tell Caroline the truth. That'd be preferable to having her hear wild rumors later on.

"I know. His truck broke down. It's the transmission, and with parts and labor it'll be close to fifteen hundred dollars. Plus it's going to take at least ten days for the parts to come in."

Good grief, Caroline knew more about Laredo than she did! "Who told you all that?" Silly question when the answer was obvious. Wiley had mentioned that he was going to help Laredo tow his truck into Powell's Garage that morning. Paul Powell's wife, Louise, did the paperwork and was a known talker. Apparently she'd been at the garage when Wiley and Laredo arrived. To complicate matters, Wiley tended to have a loose tongue himself. Savannah had the sudden urge to sit down with an entire pitcher of iced tea, only she had the feeling that all the iced tea in the world wasn't going to make anything better.

Caroline watched her closely. In a gentler tone of voice she asked, "You hired him yourself?"

"Yes. I've been looking for someone to help me with the garden and—and now that I'm starting to get more orders for my roses, well, it makes sense to hire some help." She could have managed very well on her own, though, and Caroline knew it.

"You like him, don't you, Savannah?"

"Of course I like Laredo. He's kind and thoughtful and . . ." She couldn't continue. "Grady was just awful! Oh, Caroline, I was mortified." She brought one hand to her mouth, remembering the confrontation between the two men after dinner.

"Grady? What else is new?"

"I offered Laredo a job. I shouldn't have done it without talking to Grady first, but he needed the work and you know how I've been after Grady to hire an extra hand."

"So *you* hired him, and Grady didn't appreciate your . . . help."

Savannah looked away. "That's putting it mildly. He insisted he didn't need anyone else and offered to drive Laredo into town that very minute. He made it sound as if he wanted him off our property, the sooner the better. I didn't know Grady could be that rude! I was embarrassed, and angry, so I . . . I stepped in and claimed I'd hired Laredo to work for me."

Caroline's eyes sparked with approval. "I'll bet Grady just hit the roof."

"Put it this way—he wasn't pleased."

Nibbling on her lower lip, Caroline crossed her arms and leaned against the counter. "So, tell me, how'd you meet your new employee?" The questions weren't getting any easier. "I saw him walking down the road," Savannah admitted wryly, "and I . . . I stopped and offered him a lift."

Caroline's eyes widened at this, but she didn't comment. Savannah continued. "He asked about work in the area, and before I could stop myself, I said there was a job on the Yellow Rose."

"Which is why Grady took an immediate dislike to him," Caroline muttered.

She knew Grady almost as well as Savannah did. "That's right. He acted like a jerk for no reason other than the fact that *I* was the one to hire him. Oh, Caroline, I don't think I've ever been more furious with my brother."

"So what happened next?"

A sense of pride and satisfaction came to her rescue, and Savannah started to giggle. "If only you could've seen Grady's face when I told him Laredo was working for me. I thought he was going to explode." To give him some credit, Grady had kept his mouth shut. Instead he'd stormed out of the house like a two-year-old, leaving Savannah and Laredo standing there in awkward silence.

Caroline burst out laughing. "I can see it all now! Oh, Savannah, I'm so proud of you."

"Really?"

"Really. It's about time someone put Grady Weston in his place. Don't get me wrong, I think the world of him, but he's become such a curmudgeon in the last few years. He takes everything so seriously. I can't remember the last time I heard him laugh."

Savannah's heart went out to her brother. What Caroline said was true, but it was only because Grady carried such a heavy load of responsibilities. In only a few years he'd taken the ranch from the edge of bankruptcy and made it viable again. Finances remained tight, but they were no longer in danger of losing the land that had been in the family for generations. Savannah reminded herself of all this every time Grady's behavior distressed her. And it had never distressed her more than last night. His opinion of Laredo—and by extension, her—was so scathing. She knew very well that he considered her "a damned fool"—his favorite epithet—for trusting a stranger.

She lowered her eyes, not wanting Caroline to read her face. "Am I a fool, Caroline?"

"You? You're joking, right?"

"No, please, I need to know. I . . . I'm attracted to Laredo. I've never felt this way about a man. He's not like anyone else. He listens to me, and even though we've barely met, he . . . he understands me better than my own brother does. We spent an entire hour in my garden last night, and he let me tell him about my roses. His grandmother had old roses and he was genuinely interested in what I'm doing."

Caroline's features softened.

"And he's honest. He told me he'd been fired from his last job and why. He didn't have to do that, but he did and I respect him for it." It sounded foolish now, as if everything her brother had said was true.

"What does your heart tell you?" Caroline asked.

Savannah wavered. When she was with Laredo, there was no doubt how she felt, but in the light of cold reality, she was forced to wonder if she really was as gullible and naive as Grady thought. "I'm not sure anymore."

"Why is it so important that you have all the answers right this moment?"

"I don't know, it's just that—"

Caroline laughed. "Be more patient, Savannah. Life has a way of working things out. And for heaven's sake, quit being so hard on yourself! It isn't a sin to be attracted to a man. Why *shouldn't* you be?"

"But . . . oh, Caroline it's been so long since anyone made me feel this way."

"Then I like him already."

"You do?"

"How could I not? He's brought color to your cheeks."

Embarrassed, Savannah raised both her hands to her face.

"He's made your heart smile."

What a nice way of putting it. That was exactly how she felt.

"And I've never seen you look happier."

She *was* happy, Savannah realized. Deliriously so, simply because a kindhearted man had walked in the garden with her and listened as she told him stories about old roses. He'd more than listened; he'd been interested, asking questions, touching her roses with a gentle hand. Savannah had hardly slept the entire night, thinking about their time together.

"I'm too old," she blurted. Of her entire high school graduating class, she was the only one still unmarried. Two were already on their second marriages, Savannah hadn't even managed to fall in love.

"Nonsense! Too old?" Caroline countered. "That's the most ridiculous thing you've ever said."

"Ellie's right—Laredo *is* handsome. Why would he be interested in someone like me?"

"Because you're beautiful, Savannah, inside and out. He'd be a fool not to recognize that. Now stop worrying and just be yourself."

Savannah felt only slightly reassured. Her biggest fear was that she'd made more of this attraction than there was. She'd barely known Laredo twenty-four hours, and yet it felt as if she'd known him all her life. She was afraid this might be some unrealistic fantasy. It didn't seem possible that he could share her feelings.

"Can you still watch Maggie on Monday night?" Caroline asked hopefully, interrupting Savannah's relentless worries.

"Of course," Savannah told her. She enjoyed having the five-year-old over while Caroline did volunteer work as a math tutor. Grady intimidated the little girl, but Maggie was slowly warming to him, and although Grady wasn't admitting it, he'd come to enjoy Maggie's visits, as well.

"When I drop her off, I can meet your Laredo for myself."

Your Laredo. Savannah blushed and smiled. "He might not be there."

"Then I'm going to plant myself in the living room until he shows up. I'm dying to meet this marvel who's made my very dearest friend finally—*finally*—fall for a man."

"I was thinking of asking him to come to church with me on Sunday," Savannah said. Actually the idea had just occurred to her, and she looked to Caroline for confirmation of its worth.

"Great! I can meet him then. And so can everyone else."

Everyone else. Savannah's heart fell. Tongues were sure to wag if she showed up at Sunday services with a man on her arm. Well, let them, she decided suddenly. She'd speak to him about church this very afternoon.

"I DON'T WANT to talk about it," Grady growled at Wiley as they rode back toward the ranch house that afternoon. They'd spent most of the day searching through brush for cows and newborn calves. He was completely drained, mentally and physically. Grady had been up late every night for three weeks, checking on newborn calves in the calving barn. Sleep this time of year was a luxury for any rancher.

Wiley looked offended. "Hey, I didn't say a word."

"That may be, but you're about ready to burst with curiosity, I can tell."

"Seems to me you're wantin' to say your piece, otherwise you wouldn't've mentioned it."

It being Savannah and the hand she'd hired. Even now Grady couldn't believe what she'd done. He had trouble grasping the fact that his own sister could behave like a dithering fool over some saddle bum. But he'd had an even harder time accepting what Richard had done. It'd taken weeks for everything to sink in, and even then, Grady couldn't understand how his own brother could betray them. Only when the bills piled up and the federal government had come after the inheritance tax had he been forced to face the truth. Richard was a bastard, pure and simple. As for Smith . . .

"I don't like him," Grady announced. That was all he intended to say. If Wiley commented, fine. If he didn't, that was fine, too.

"You talkin' about Laredo Smith?"

"Smith," Grady repeated with a snicker. "Mighty convenient surname if you ask me."

"Lots of people called Smith."

"My point exactly," Grady snarled. As a rule Wiley wasn't this obtuse. "I'd bet my snakeskin boots the name's phony."

"He seems like a fine young man to me."

It didn't set well that his friend, his confidant, his foreman would take the other man's side. "What do you mean?"

"He's a real worker. He was up early, wanting to get started in Savannah's garden before I helped tow his truck into town. We had it to Powell's by the time they opened, and Paul took a look at it while we were still there."

"What's wrong with it?" Grady had decided he wanted nothing to do with this hired hand of Savannah's but it was in the best interests of his family to learn what he could.

"Transmission needs to be replaced and the brakes are shot, too. Paul said once he got the parts, he'd have it running in a couple of days."

"Good." Grady suspected the stranger would disappear about the time his truck was repaired.

"He doesn't look like he's got cash enough to pay for it once the work's done."

"What?" Grady groaned.

"You heard me. Why else do you think he was lookin' for a job?"

They headed toward the creek and slipped out of their saddles to allow their horses a long drink of cool water. Grady didn't like the idea of Laredo lingering at the Yellow Rose. He'd seen men like Smith before. Drifters, washed-up rodeo riders, shiftless men with shiftless lives. No roots or families. They spent their money as fast as they earned it without a thought to their next meal, let alone the future. They might work hard, but they also played hard and lived harder. Laredo Smith wasn't the type of man he wanted hanging around his sister, that was for damn sure.

"Find out anything else about him?" Grady asked, kicking a rock with the toe of his boot. His interest was out in the open now, no reason to hide it.

Not waiting for Wiley's reply, Grady climbed back into the saddle with the ease of a man long accustomed to riding.

"I thought you said you didn't want to talk about it."

Grady tossed his foreman a furious look, but Wiley responded with a knowing chuckle. The old man knew he could get away with saying what he damn well pleased, and an angry glower wouldn't change that.

"He let drop a few bits of information on the way into town," Wiley admitted as he, too, remounted. "He's been workin' on the Triple C over in Williamsburg for the last couple years."

Grady had heard of the ranch, which was one of the larger spreads in the Texas hill country. He'd spoken to Earl Chesterton, the owner, a time or two at the district cattlemen meetings, but they were little more than nodding acquaintances. Compared to the Triple C, the Yellow Rose was small stuff.

"You gonna check on him?" Wiley asked in a tone that said he disapproved of the idea.

Grady snorted. "Why would I do something like that? He doesn't work for me, remember?"

"You're the one with all the questions," Wiley pointed out.

"I was curious. You can't blame me for that, especially when all I'm doing is looking out for Savannah." He didn't want to say it out loud, but he was worried about his younger sister. Not once in all these years had she openly crossed him. Not that she didn't have any opinions, and not that she was meek or passive, like some people assumed.

Savannah had ways of making her wishes known. Subtle ways. The fact was, he'd come to recognize that when she baked his favorite peach cobbler, she had something on her mind. She'd wait until after dinner; when he was enjoying dessert, she'd sit down with him, sweetness personified, and ask a few harmless—but pertinent—questions. Slowly she'd lead up to what she really wanted, making her point casually and without fanfare.

Grady always listened, and often her nonconfrontational style worked and he'd change his mind. He considered himself a fair man; if he felt her concern was valid, he acted on it.

Then Laredo Smith arrived, and suddenly his sister's behavior had undergone a drastic change. She'd actually raised her voice to him, and all because of this worthless drifter. Well, she was welcome to Laredo Smith. If she wanted to walk around with her heart dangling from her sleeve, acting like a lovelorn fifteen-year-old, he wasn't going to stop her. By the same token, he wouldn't offer sympathy when a month or two down the road Laredo left her high and dry.

"How old is Savannah now?" Wiley asked. "She's over twenty-one, right?"

"You know damn well how old she is."

Wiley set his Stetson farther back on his head and grinned. "You're right, I do. I was just wondering if *you* did."

Grady frowned. "She's old enough to know better."

"Old enough to know her own heart, too, I'd say."

Grady nudged his gelding, Starlight, into a trot and turned toward the house, following the fence line. He wanted to check that it was secure and ascertain the condition of the windmill and water tank before he headed in for the night.

"Like I said earlier," he announced stiffly, "I don't want to talk about it."

"Then you aren't interested in hearin' what else Smith said."

What Grady wasn't interested in was playing games. He reined in Starlight and turned to look back at the foreman. "You got something to say, then I suggest you say it."

"He's a wrangler."

Grady wasn't impressed. Wranglers were a dime a dozen in Texas.

"We could use a good wrangler. Payin' someone to come in and care for the horses can get downright costly."

"I can take care of them myself."

"Sure, the same way you can deliver calves, plant alfalfa, move herds and everything else all by your lonesome. Hey," he said with a shrug, "it was just a suggestion."

Despite his dour mood, Grady threw back his head and laughed. "Wiley, why do you think I'm paying you the big bucks? Since you're so concerned about my welfare, *you* can be my wrangler from now on. You think we need to take one on full-time? Then I'm naming you the Yellow Rose's official wrangler. You can feed, water, groom and worm the horses from this day forward. Don't forget to take care of the tack, too, while you're at it."

"Quit foolin' around."

"Do I look like I'm fooling?" Grady asked with a broad grin. The expression on Wiley's face was worth a thousand bucks. For the first time in longer than he cared to remember, Grady threw back his head and laughed until his throat felt raw.

SAVANNAH SET THE PLATTER of chicken-fried steak on the oven rack and turned the saucepan of thick cream gravy to simmer. The green beans were tender, and she'd sliced fresh tomatoes from her kitchen garden. An apple pie cooled on the counter. All she needed to do now was stir up a pitcher of lemonade, and dinner would be ready when Grady and Wiley returned.

With a few extra moments on her hands, she decided to step outside. Laredo had been working all afternoon in the hot sun, and knowing he was probably thirsty, she poured him a glass of iced tea. As she walked into the sunshine, she was honest enough to admit that the tea was only an excuse to be with him.

Her gardens had never looked better, but she couldn't find Laredo. He'd been there no more than five minutes ago. Disappointed, she was about to return to the house when she spotted him in the goat pen with Samson and Delilah, her two kids. They were a thank-you gift for the roses she'd given a friend for an anniversary party. Seeing Laredo, she felt her heart go still, and she smiled with pleasure.

Grady had delighted in teasing her about her pets. He called it a silly woman thing, viewing her goats the same way he did her roses. He didn't care one whit about something she dearly loved. Roses were her heart, her joy, her passion. Sometimes Savannah wondered if they could truly be brother and sister, their differences seemed so profound.

Laredo knelt in the grass with the two young goats, petting them, talking to them. Samson, in particular, didn't normally take to strangers, but apparently Laredo was a special case.

Savannah wasn't sure how long she stood there watching. Several minutes, anyway, because the cold glass in her hand had numbed her fingers. Not wanting Laredo to know she'd been spying on him, she returned to the house. She set the glass aside and raised her cold hands to her face, to cool her flushed cheeks.

Incredibly the urge to cry came over her, and she didn't know why. She'd barely exchanged a word with Laredo all day; they'd both been busy with their own chores. And yet Savannah had never felt closer to anyone than she did to him for those few moments, watching him with her goats.

This stranger, this man she barely knew, possessed the ability to touch her soul. Savannah wondered if she'd ever be the same.

Three

Savannah enjoyed listening to Wade McMillen preach. His messages, simple and direct, cut straight to the heart. He was the most unlikely preacher she'd ever seen. A large man, tall and muscular, he looked as though he'd be more comfortable at home herding cattle than delivering sermons. Perhaps that was what made him so popular.

It might have been her imagination, but Savannah felt the curious stares of those around her. The word about her and Laredo was out, she was sure of it. Now everyone in the town knew she—and not Grady—had hired him.

Soon she'd be the subject of speculative comments and whispered questions—if she wasn't already. She felt mortified, but pride helped her hold her head high and look straight ahead. Her mind wandered throughout Wade's sermon, though, something that didn't usually happen. When her thoughts weren't focused on the consequences of her actions, they zoomed with startling ease to Laredo.

She'd wanted to invite him to church and had tried to broach the subject a number of times, but had lost her nerve. Even an invitation to Sunday-morning worship had seemed rather brash. In light of the interest she'd generated, Savannah would be forever grateful that Laredo *wasn't* with her. His presence would've set tongues wagging for sure.

Laredo had worked all day Saturday building trellises, even though she'd insisted she didn't require him to work weekends. He'd brushed aside her protests and pounded and sawed from dawn to dusk. By the end of the day, a long row of freshly painted trellises stood drying in the late March sun.

After dinner he sat on the porch with her until Grady arrived. Her brother's disapproval was evident in everything he said and did. She wanted to plead with Laredo to ignore him, wanted to insist she was her own woman, but again she remained silent.

A coward, that was what she was. Savannah would've given just about anything to find the courage to tell him what was on her mind and in her heart.

Actually, as Caroline had said, she'd done one thing that made her proud. She'd stood up to Grady, and because she had, Laredo was still at the ranch. Challenging Grady was no easy task. His strong personality had quelled braver souls than hers.

The congregation stood, and Savannah reached for the hymnal and opened it to the appropriate page. Her soft voice lifted with those in the choir. She glanced over at Caroline, standing in the front row of the choir in her long white robe. Her friend must have noticed because she acknowledged Savannah with an almost imperceptible wink. Savannah relaxed for the first time since she'd entered the church that morning.

After a closing prayer organ music once again filled the church and the service ended.

Savannah followed Nell Bishop and her two children out of the pew. Jake Bishop had been killed in a freak tractor accident three and a half years ago. They'd always seemed the perfect couple, so deeply in love—a great team, everyone said. Savannah knew life had been difficult for Nell without Jake and she admired the other woman's strength. Nell had refused to leave the ranch, working it herself. When asked why she hadn't sold off the spread and moved into town, Nell had simply explained that keeping the ranch was what Jake would have wanted. Walking with Nell, Savannah felt safe from gossip. The widow was a private person, as she was herself, and would never pry into her affairs.

Louise Powell stood in the vestibule, craning her neck. Savannah strongly suspected the woman wanted to grill her about Laredo.

Savannah wished there was some way she could just vanish.

"Savannah! Savannah, over here!" Louise raised one gloved hand and waved frantically.

It would do no good to avoid her, Savannah decided miserably. If there was one thing she hated more than gossip, it was being the center of attention.

As soon as she reached the vestibule, Louise was at her side. Louise had celebrated her fiftieth birthday in January and hated the thought of being a half a century old. In the weeks since, she'd changed her hairstyle and purchased a new wardrobe, trying for a younger look. Unfortunately she came across as a woman who was obviously fifty and dressed like twenty-five.

"I met your new friend!" Louise exclaimed. Savannah suspected this was Tammy Lee's influence on her. Tammy Lee—Louise's new friend—was a middle-aged divorcée whose reputation could charitably be described as colorful. "What a nice young man." She paused, waiting for Savannah's comment, but when none was forthcoming, she plowed ahead, wrapping her arm around Savannah's waist. "I understand he's working for you." An annoying giggle followed. "Savannah, I wonder if we really know you, after all. I've always thought of you as shy and retiring, but you know what they say about still waters." The girlish giggle returned.

"There's someone I have to see," Savannah said in an effort to escape.

"Laredo?" Louise asked. This was accompanied with a squeeze tight enough to make Savannah wince. "If you run out of work for him, you send him my way, understand?"

"If you'll excuse me, please . . ." Savannah said a little desperately.

The Moorhouse sisters, Edwina and Lily, stepped into the vestibule, distracting Louise. Both were retired schoolteachers. Miss Edwina had been Savannah's first-grade teacher and Miss Lily her third. The two were inseparable and Savannah loved them dearly.

"Good morning," Savannah mumbled as she slipped past the elderly pair.

By the time she walked outside, she felt like gasping for air. Reverend McMillen stood just outside the large double doors and greeted each parishioner by name. Wade had a way of looking at a person and seeing more than the obvious. "Are you okay, Savannah?" he asked, holding her hand between both of his. "You're looking flushed."

"I'm fine. Just a little warm." Her discomfort had more to do with attracting unwelcome attention. All she wanted was to hurry home before someone else had the chance to corner her.

"Savannah! Savannah!" Maggie Daniels, Caroline's five-year-old daughter, raced to her side and proudly offered her a crayon drawing she'd made in Sunday-school class.

"Hi there, Maggie-may. What's this?" Savannah asked, studying the paper. Maggie was her joy, the child of her heart. It had been a shock when Caroline Daniels announced she was pregnant her senior year in college. From the beginning there'd been plenty of speculation about the father of Caroline's child, but Caroline had never said, and no one had ever asked. Caroline's mother, Florence, had served as postmistress in Promise for years, and when she died last spring, Caroline had taken over her duties.

Maggie had apparently transferred her love for her grandmother to Savannah. It made Savannah feel privileged, and she reciprocated the child's feelings a hundred percent. Recently Caroline had relied more and more on Savannah to baby-sit, but she never minded. It was a delight to spend time with the little girl.

"That's Joseph," Maggie explained now, pointing to a lumpish figure in her drawing.

"Ah, I see," Savannah said. "He's wearing his coat of many colors. Look what a good job you've done!"

Maggie glowed with pleasure. She tucked her small hand in Savannah's. "Where's Mommy?"

Savannah was about to ask the same thing. The question was answered soon enough when Caroline exited the side door with the other members of the choir. It generally took her a few moments to hang up her robe and put away the music sheets.

"Mommy, Mommy, look!" Maggie cried, rushing toward her mother, pigtails bouncing. The youngster threw her arms around Caroline as if it'd been a year since they'd seen each other.

"Would you like to join us for brunch?" Caroline asked, lifting Maggie into her arms.

Savannah declined with a quick shake of her head. "I put a roast in the oven before I left."

"Did Louise corner you?" Caroline lowered her voice.

"She tried."

"Hey, give the old biddy something to talk about."

"Caroline!"

"She's jealous, that's all."

"Jealous of what?" Savannah wanted to know.

"Of you. For being young and pretty and having a good-looking man in your life."

"Laredo's not in my life—at least not in the personal sense," Savannah felt obliged to protest—although she wished it wasn't true. She'd like him to kiss her or hold her hand—anything so she'd know he felt the same things she did. Once she'd caught him looking at her and she thought he seemed . . . interested, but she couldn't be sure. If she'd had more experience, she'd know.

"Well, more's the pity," Caroline said with a laugh. "A little romance would do you a world of good."

"What about you?" Caroline was a fine one to talk. Savannah couldn't remember the last time her friend had gone out on a date.

"Me? Romance?" Caroline shook her head. "No, thanks. I've had enough romance to last me a lifetime."

"Oh, Caroline, don't allow one negative experience to sour you for-ever."

Sadness dimmed her eyes, although Caroline made an effort to hide it. "Some people are meant to fall in love, and then there are people like me . . ." Her words faded and she looked away.

Savannah's heart went out to her, but she didn't know what else to say.

LAREDO HEARD Wiley whistling in the back of the bunkhouse. The old coot was certainly in a good mood. By nature the foreman appeared to be an easygoing sort, but this afternoon he was downright cheerful.

Stitching a stirrup, Laredo inserted the needle into the worn leather. No one had asked him to repair the saddle, but he had time on his hands, and keeping himself occupied was better than sitting around doing noth-ing. He wasn't a man who could remain idle long.

Although it was none of his concern, he'd visited the barn and in-spected the horses. They were well cared for and in good health. Widowmaker, the stallion kept for breeding purposes, reminded Laredo of Grady. Man and beast shared the same temperament—although he figured he'd have a better relationship with Widowmaker than he ever would with Grady. Horses instinctively recognized Laredo as a friend. He shared an affinity with them that was the key to his success as a wrangler. From the time he was a toddler he'd enjoyed working with his father and their horses.

One of his fondest childhood memories was of his father holding him high enough to pet and talk to Midnight, a beautiful roan gelding. Mem-ories of his father were few and far between. Laredo had been six when word came that Russell Aaron Smith had been killed in a country with a name he couldn't pronounce. He'd bled to death in a rice field six thou-sand miles from home. Shortly afterward Laredo's mother had moved back with her parents, into the very house where she'd been born, and had never remarried. His grandfather was a good man, patient and car-ing, but he'd owned an office-supply store and didn't understand Laredo's love of the country or his passion for horses.

As a teenager Laredo had started working summers on local ranches. His talent was soon recognized. To please his mother he'd grad-uated from high school, but the instant that diploma had been placed in his hand he was gone. She'd dated Clyde Schneider for years and Laredo had always assumed that once he was out of the picture they'd finally get married, but it hadn't happened.

His mother would love Savannah, Laredo thought, but he hesitated to say anything in his next letter home for fear she'd give the relationship more importance than it warranted. Laura Smith wanted grandchildren and brought up the subject at every opportunity, reminding him that it was time he settled down, started a family. He'd dismissed her heavy hints; he didn't consider himself the marrying kind. Not now, anyway, when he had nothing to offer a woman other than a few hundred dusty acres he'd bought in Oklahoma and a stallion he'd recently spent his life savings to acquire. Laredo was on his way to pick him up. Renegade—the horse he'd pinned his dreams on. The horse he hoped would sire a dynasty of quarter horses. But right now that was all he had—and Savannah Weston deserved a damn sight more. If he was ever in a position to entertain marriage, he hoped he found a woman like her. No, he couldn't mention Savannah to his mother; if he did he'd never hear the end of it.

Wiley broke into song and Laredo gave an involuntary shudder at the off-key rendition of an old Kenny Rogers hit. He couldn't recall the title, but it was some ballad about a woman not taking her love to town. In Wiley's version the words were barely distinguishable, the tune not at all.

When Wiley appeared, his hair was wet and slicked back, his boots polished. He wore a tan suede jacket and string tie with a turquoise piece the size of a silver dollar. He reeked of cologne so strong, Laredo's eyes watered.

"You're lookin' right pretty," Laredo teased the foreman.

Wiley laughed. "I'm off to visit the Widow Johnson in Brewster. Grady can work himself into an early grave if he wants, but I've got places to go, people to see. Don't be concerned if I'm a bit late this evening." He winked and all but danced out the door.

If Laredo remembered correctly, Brewster was at least a hundred miles east of Promise. Wiley's cheer was contagious, though, and he couldn't keep from smiling at the older man's pleasure. His task finished, Laredo carried the saddle back into the barn and returned his tools. He'd watched Savannah walk out to the car this morning, a Bible in her hand, and knew she was headed for church.

He couldn't remember the last time he'd darkened the door of a house of worship.

As twelve-thirty approached he found himself listening and watching for Savannah. He would have enjoyed spending more time with her, but her watchdog of a brother made that difficult. Every time they were alone for more than a few minutes, Grady showed up. Rather than place Savannah in the awkward position of having to defend her actions, widening the rift that already existed between brother and sister, Laredo made his excuses and left. He'd dined with them only once, the night of his arrival, preferring to eat with Wiley in the bunkhouse ever since.

When he left the barn, Laredo saw the car, which meant Savannah was back. He must have stood in the same spot for five minutes trying to decide what to do. Grady was out checking the herd, so he'd probably be away for several hours. This was the perfect opportunity to seek out Savannah's company. A tempting thought.

On the other hand he wasn't doing her any favors by leading her on. He had nothing to offer her other than a few stolen kisses. Besides, he'd already decided that, once he'd earned enough to pay for the truck repairs, he'd be on his way. And yet . . .

He shook his head. He barely knew the woman, and even if a relationship developed between them, it would do no good. He'd be living in a small secondhand trailer while he built his business from the ground up. It'd be years of blood and sweat before he had anything to show for his efforts. One day in the distant future his stock would be legendary; he was certain of it. But until then . . .

When he left Promise, he wanted to go without regrets. Savannah was sweet and gentle, and he'd rather cut off his right arm than hurt her. He wasn't stupid; he saw the look in her eyes. Even though she tried to hide it, she was interested. Damn it all, so was he!

She was the type of woman a man introduced to his mother. Savannah deserved more than a flirtation. He should go back to the bunkhouse now before he started something he couldn't stop. Something he had no *right* to start.

The decision was taken from him when Savannah stepped onto the back porch. When she saw him standing there, staring at the house like . . . like a stunned steer, she paused. A look of pure joy lit up her face.

"I was just about to ask you to join me for lunch," she said.

He knew he should politely decline, but he hadn't the heart to disappoint her—or deny himself the pleasure of her company. "I'll wash up and be inside in a minute."

On his way toward the house he started whistling; when he realized what he was doing, he stopped. He shouldn't be this happy. Damn it all, he was looking at trouble with his eyes wide open and grinning like a schoolboy.

The scent of roast beef greeted him as soon as he entered the kitchen. Savannah was bent over the stove, pulling a tray of biscuits from the oven. The scene was a homey one. After years of meals on the run, it was a rare treat to sit down at a real table, to have lunch with a woman, to eat in a civilized and leisurely fashion.

"When did you have time to make those?" he asked. She couldn't have been home more than ten minutes.

"Early this morning," she said, scooping the biscuits from the tray and placing them in a breadbasket. Everything else was already on the table.

He seated her and bowed his head while she said grace, then reached for a biscuit. It was too hot to hold, and he tossed it between his hands, making Savannah laugh. A man could get used to hearing this woman's laugh, he mused. Warning signs flashed in every direction, and again Laredo ignored them.

"They're buttermilk biscuits," she said. "The recipe was my mother's." She waited for him to take his first bite.

The biscuit was incredible. The best he'd ever tasted. He told her so and watched her eyes light up at the compliment.

"It'll just be the two of us. Grady's busy just now." She didn't meet his eyes.

Laredo already knew as much. "Would you rather I ate in the bunkhouse?" he asked.

"Oh, no! I like being with you."

"Me, too." He supposed he shouldn't tell her that but found it impossible to keep to himself.

Savannah started passing him serving dishes. "How was your morning?" she asked, handing him the platter of sliced roast beef.

He wanted to tell her he'd missed her; instead, he helped himself to the carrots and potatoes. "I wrote a couple of letters," he said as he set the bowl aside.

Their conversation felt stilted and awkward in the beginning, as if they were unsure of each other, afraid of saying too much or too little. But gradually he grew comfortable speaking with her again. There was a naturalness about Savannah. When she asked him questions, her interest was so obviously sincere that he couldn't help responding with equal sincerity.

Following the meal, they sat and lingered over coffee. Savannah asked about his family and perhaps because he'd written to his mother earlier, he described his early years in Texas before his father had gone off to war.

She was such a good listener that Laredo continued, recounting his father's death and the move to Oklahoma to live with his mother's parents, both dead now. He told it all as casually as if he was discussing the weather. In an unemotional voice, he talked about the painful details of those early unhappy years, things he'd rarely shared with anyone.

He sensed that Savannah intuitively understood the significance of the memories he confided in her. She understood and appreciated that he was sharing a piece of his soul, although he made light of it, even joked. But he suspected that the pain revealed itself in the pauses, the unspoken words, and that she was attuned to it.

Her questions were thoughtful and perceptive. After a time he thought he should reciprocate. "What about you, Savannah?" he asked. "Tell me about your family."

She left the table so fast he wondered if his question had offended her. She stood with her back to him, supporting herself on the kitchen counter. He longed to place his hand on her shoulders. Apologize.

He of all people should know enough to respect the privacy of another's pain. After talking about himself nonstop for more than an hour, with her constant encouragement, he'd felt a certain right to ask. It was a right he didn't have. Savannah owed him nothing. Nothing. He was the one in her debt.

"Savannah, I'm sorry," he whispered. He raised his hands to touch her and dropped them just as quickly.

She was still turned away from him, her head still lowered. "Did you know I have two brothers? Grady and Richard."

"No, I didn't know that."

"Richard's younger than me. He's twenty-nine." She turned then, to face him.

"Does he live close by?" he asked gently.

She shook her head. "I don't know where he is. Neither Grady nor I have seen Richard in six years—since the day we buried Mom and Dad."

Laredo didn't know how to respond. He continued to fight the urge to put his arms around her and found it more and more difficult to resist. Speaking of her younger brother clearly upset her.

"He . . . disappeared." Her voice was shaking with emotion.

"Savannah, listen, you don't need to say any more. I shouldn't have asked." Her pain was right there, and so real it was agony to see. He felt helpless, unable to console her.

"No . . . please, I want to tell you."

He nodded.

She took a moment to compose herself. "Apparently Dad told Grady that if anything were ever to happen to him, Grady should go to the safe-deposit box at the bank in Brewster." She paused and bit her lower lip. "The day before the funeral Grady and Richard visited the bank together. You can imagine how shocked they were to discover that the safe-deposit box was full of cash. Grady estimated there must have been close to forty thousand dollars there, along with a letter.

"Dad wrote that he'd seen what had happened to people who put their faith in life-insurance companies and after the savings-and-loan fiasco, he didn't trust banks much, either. He didn't want Mom and us three kids to worry about finances, so he'd been putting the money aside little by little for years. His plan was that there'd be enough money to pay the inheritance taxes on the ranch, plus keep the place going. I don't even think my mother knew.

"The next day we buried my parents," Savannah whispered, and her voice quavered with remembered pain. "I recall almost nothing about that day. Again and again I've gone over the details in my mind and it's all a blank. I remember the people—so many friends and family came. I remember how kind and generous everyone was. That part I have no problem with. What I can't recall is the last time I saw Richard. He vanished without a word to anyone. At . . . at first we assumed that something terrible had happened to him. That in his pain and grief he'd done something crazy. I was worried sick. Grady, too."

Slowly Savannah raised her eyes and Laredo could see that they'd filled with tears. When she spoke again, her voice was small and weak. "He took the money—every dime. As best as we can figure, he left the funeral and went straight to the bank, forged Grady's signature and cleaned out the safe-deposit box. He took what belonged to all three of us. He left us with nothing. We'd just lost Mom and Dad. Our grief was unbearable, and he made it worse with his betrayal. Neither Grady nor I have heard from him since." Some of her tears spilled over. "Grady's never been the same. He's practically killed himself trying to hold on to the ranch, and I think he hates Richard.

"I can't hate him—he's my brother. You see, Laredo, in one day I lost my parents, and I lost both my brothers, too."

Nothing could have kept Laredo from reaching for her then. When he did, she came to him as though he'd held her a thousand times. It felt so . . . *right* to press her against his heart. Her body was warm and pliant, molding to his as naturally as if they'd been designed for each other.

Laredo had no idea how long they stood there. Not nearly long enough, of that he was sure. Savannah's arms were around his middle, her face buried in his chest. His hands were in her hair, his eyes closed, savoring the wonder of being close to someone this beautiful and this good.

He didn't hear the door open, but he should have realized it was bound to happen.

The screen door slammed and Laredo's eyes shot open. Instinctively his arms tightened around Savannah before he reluctantly released her and faced her brother. Eye to eye. Man to man.

"What the hell do you think you're doing with my sister?" Grady Weston shouted.

GRADY MULLED OVER what he had to say before he confronted Savannah. Pacing the living room floor, he carefully weighed each word.

Okay, so maybe he'd been out of line earlier when he found her and Smith clinging to each other like lovers. The sight had distressed him and before he could stop himself he'd exploded.

He didn't want to fight with Savannah. She was his sister, but damn it all! Her infatuation with Laredo Smith—or whatever his name might be—had deprived her of all reason. It was more than he could bear, watching her make a fool of herself over this useless drifter.

Unfortunately his methods of convincing her hadn't worked so far, and Grady realized he needed to change his tactics. To this point, all that his anger and frustration had netted him was the silent treatment. He'd never known a woman who could say more without uttering a word.

Okay, okay, he was willing to admit he'd made mistakes, too. Earlier in the week Savannah had cooked him his favorite dinner as a peace offering, but he'd been so angry he'd chosen to overlook the gesture. He'd been wrong to ignore her outstretched hand, but he was man enough to admit it. He hoped to make peace with her now—hoped he could persuade her to see reason.

Savannah had given him the cold shoulder since he'd walked in on her and Smith in the kitchen. For the rest of the day she'd conveniently disappeared and had retired to her room as soon as it was dark. She wasn't asleep; he could hear her moving about upstairs, as restless as he was here below.

He continued pacing, then decided to talk to her now, before the opportunity was lost. Before he changed his mind. He headed up the stairs, taking them two at a time, paused outside her bedroom, inhaled deeply and knocked. Loudly.

"Yes?" his sister said through the door. Her voice was anything but warm, and the door stayed closed.

"Savannah, I'd appreciate the opportunity to discuss the matter of

Laredo Smith with you," he said. It'd taken him ten minutes to come up with those words, to strike the proper tone. He thought he sounded formal, calm, even lawyerly.

The door opened and she stood stiffly in the doorway, blocking the entrance. "Downstairs might be more comfortable," he suggested, gesturing down the narrow staircase.

She hesitated, then reluctantly nodded.

Grady relaxed slightly, and wondered how much this peace was going to cost him. Being on the outs with his only sister distressed him more than he cared to reveal.

Savannah followed him down the stairs and took a seat on the sofa. "You owe me an apology, Grady."

"All right, all right," he said, raising both arms in surrender. "I apologize."

"How about apologizing to Laredo?"

That was going too far, but Grady was smart enough to see that arguing the point wouldn't serve his purpose. "I want to discuss Laredo," he said again, and because it was impossible to hold still, he stood up and resumed his pacing. This next part was the most difficult. "I'm worried about you," he said.

"I'm thirty-one years old and I don't need my brother treating me like a child. You're not my guardian. I was mortified today, Grady. Simply mortified."

His behavior had embarrassed him, too, but he hadn't been able to prevent it. Walking into the house and finding Savannah in a man's arms had been a shock.

"I apologize," he muttered again. He walked the full length of the room and turned back.

"Then why did you act like . . . like a bull on the rampage?"

Grady didn't know what to tell her other than the truth. "I'm afraid you're going to be hurt."

"My life is none of your concern."

On the contrary, he thought, what happened to her was very much his concern. He was her brother. She was naive about men—especially con artists like Laredo Smith—and whether she realized it or not, she needed him. At least he could be counted on to keep a level head. "Savannah, you're setting yourself up for heartache, getting involved with a drifter."

She sighed as if to say he clearly had no concept of how she felt. Perhaps he didn't, but that didn't change the facts.

"Laredo's been the perfect gentleman," she explained calmly. "I was crying and he comforted me."

"He made you cry?"

"No." The word was filled with exasperation. "I told him about Richard, and I always cry when I talk about Richard."

Grady's jaw tightened at the mention of his younger brother, but he didn't want to discuss him now. He crossed to Savannah and squatted down in front of her. "Savannah, look at me."

"I like Laredo."

"I know you do, and that's what troubles me."

"But why? Haven't you seen how hard he's worked in my garden? He's done nothing but show me kindness."

Grady ground his teeth in frustration. "There are things about him you don't know," he said as gently as he could.

"Grady, look at me, really look. My youth is slipping through my fingers and I've been given this . . . this precious gift, this blessing, a chance to love and be loved. I'm not going to let you or anyone else ruin it for me."

"Love." The word felt like acid on his tongue. "You *love* him? You hardly know him!"

She lowered her gaze to her clenched hands. "I *could* love him, I know I could, and he could love me, too. He understands me and I understand him."

"You've known him what? Three days? Four? Savannah, for crying out loud, what's happened to you?"

She looked at him then, and to his amazement she smiled. "Something wonderful, Grady, something really wonderful." She touched his arm and nearly blinded him with the brilliance of her smile. "I feel alive, truly alive for the first time in years. I'd forgotten how good it felt."

"Savannah, Savannah," he moaned. She made this so damned difficult.

"Grady, please be happy for me."

"I can't."

"Then don't ruin it for me, please. That's all I ask."

He stood, feeling the pain of what he had to tell her until the words felt like bricks loaded on his back. "You can't trust him."

"How can you say that?" Her face wore a look of pure puzzlement. "Laredo's been nothing but trustworthy."

"You can't trust him," Grady repeated.

"I'd trust him with my life. Do you honestly think I'm such a bad judge of character? He's patient and generous, and for you to say otherwise proves you don't really know him."

"You're naive. He'll use you, and when he's finished, he'll leave you to face the consequences alone."

His words were followed by a shocked angry silence. Then she said, "That comment was unworthy of you."

Well, she'd wait a long time before he'd apologize. He hated what he had to tell her next. Hated to be the one to destroy the fairy tale she'd built around this cast-off cowboy. "Ask me where I was this afternoon," he demanded.

Savannah blinked. "Where were you?"

"I stopped off at Cal Patterson's to make a phone call."

"You couldn't do it here?"

"No. Cal's got the names and phone numbers of all the district members in the cattlemen's association." He waited until the information sank in.

"You tried to find out about Laredo," she said, and her voice dropped to a whisper.

"Savannah, listen to me. It gives me no joy to tell you this, but your precious Laredo Smith was fired from his last job."

She remained outwardly calm, but Grady noticed her clenched hands in her lap. "I talked to Earl Chesterton myself," he continued. "Smith was fired and for a damn good reason." If that didn't convince her of the truth about this man, nothing would.

A moment of shocked silence followed, or what he mistook for shock. To his amazement, Savannah slowly smiled. "Oh, Grady, how worried you must have been, but there was no need. I already knew all about that."

Four

Grady wasn't looking forward to talking to Frank Hennessey, but he'd delayed his visit to the sheriff long enough. His fingers tightened on the steering wheel as he drove toward town, and his thoughts darkened with his fears. It bothered him that his sensible, intelligent sister had been taken in by a lowlife like Smith.

One thing Grady couldn't tolerate was a thief. As far as he was concerned, stealing what belonged to another was about as low as a man could go. His feelings, no doubt, were influenced by what Richard had done. From the time his younger brother was an infant, he'd been spoiled and coddled by their parents. Savannah was guilty of catering to him, as well—along with everyone else. Even in high school, when Richard should have been maturing and accepting adult responsibilities, he'd made it an art form to pawn off his obligations on others. From early childhood Richard had charmed his way through life. How that boy could talk, Grady recalled cynically. He'd often watched in astonishment as Richard, so glib and smooth, managed to get out of one scrape after another. Nothing had been his fault. Someone else was always to blame. His brother had continually found ways to shift the responsibility for his failures and problems onto other people.

Richard was a charmer, a ladies' man and a smooth talker, but Grady had never suspected his brother was a thief. Then he'd learned the truth. After the shock of the theft had worn off, Grady had been left to face the reality of their dire financial circumstances. He'd even blamed himself. He should never have taken Richard to the Brewster bank or let him know where he kept the key to the safe-deposit box. But Grady had trusted him. And learned the hard way that it had been a mistake.

He wasn't willing to make a second mistake, especially not where his sister was concerned. Savannah was all the family he had left, and he wasn't going to lose her.

In the beginning Grady's opinion of this outsider had been tainted by Savannah's attitude. For the first time in more years than he could remember, she'd challenged his judgment. So Grady's natural inclination was to dislike the man she'd favored, against his advice. But he *had* tolerated Laredo Smith's presence. He'd even taken some good-natured ribbing from Wiley and Caroline Daniels about being unreasonable. Given time, he might have put the drifter on the payroll himself. As Wiley and Savannah had reminded him often enough, they needed extra help.

He wouldn't hire Smith now, though. Not after what he'd learned. No way in hell would he offer a job to a known thief.

Grady had discovered everything he needed to know about Laredo Smith in his short conversation with Earl Chesterton. He wanted Smith off his land as soon as possible and as far away from Savannah as could be arranged. Frank would understand, and because the sheriff was fond of Savannah, he'd be eager to help Grady send him packing.

His sister's words—*Don't ruin this for me*—echoed in Grady's head, and although he believed he was making the right choice, he felt a sense of guilt. The last thing he wanted was to see Savannah hurt. He wanted to get rid of this drifter, but he had to manage it in such a way that Savannah would agree it was the only prudent course of action.

For that he needed Frank Hennessey's help.

Grady considered it his duty to protect his sister. She claimed she knew everything necessary about Laredo; Grady doubted that. A thief was a thief, and if Smith had stolen once, he'd steal again. Grady strongly suspected this cowboy had tangled with the authorities on more than one occasion. That was what he intended to find out from Frank Hennessey. Faced with the raw truth, Savannah would have no qualms about sending Smith on his way.

Grady found Frank Hennessey relaxing at his oak desk, feet propped on the edge and hat lowered over his eyes as he enjoyed a midafternoon snooze. Frank had represented the law in Promise for as long as Grady could remember, and while an able lawman, he took business in his stride.

Grady closed the door a little harder than necessary and Frank used his index finger to lift his Stetson off his forehead just enough to let him take a peek at his visitor.

"Howdy." Frank greeted him lazily with the familiarity that years of friendship allowed. "What can I do for you, Grady?"

Grady hesitated, unsure how to begin. At last he blurted, "I've got trouble."

The older man's smile faded and he slowly straightened. "What kind of trouble?"

Grady removed his hat and rubbed a hand across his brow. "I need to ask a favor of you, Frank. Now, I know you wouldn't normally do this sort of thing, but it's the only way I can think of to save Savannah."

"What's wrong with Savannah?" Frank asked abruptly, gesturing toward the hard wooden chair that sat alongside his desk.

It gave Grady no pleasure to drag family business into the open; however, he had no choice but to involve Frank. "You've heard about Savannah hiring a drifter to work in her rose garden?"

Frank's mouth angled into a half smile. "The story's been all around town twice by now, and Dovie was full of the news." He paused to chuckle appreciatively. "Apparently Dovie didn't think Savannah had it in her to stand up to you."

Grady hated the thought of folks talking about Savannah behind her back and let Frank know his feelings on the matter with a dark scowl.

Apparently Frank got the message because he cleared his throat and looked apologetic. "You know how women love to gossip," he said with a disapproving frown—although it was well-known that the sheriff wasn't opposed to indulging in the habit himself.

The fact that the news had spread all over town complicated things. Grady figured all he could do now was get to the point and leave the problem in Frank's capable hands.

"I don't trust him. First off, I've got to think Smith's a phony name."

"He might have picked something more original than Smith if that's the case, don't you think?" Frank asked, rubbing his chin thoughtfully.

"Why he chose that name isn't the point," Grady argued. " 'Laredo Smith' sounds about as real as a three-dollar bill."

"Other than not liking his name, have you got a reason not to trust him?" Frank asked next.

"Plenty." Surely Frank didn't think he'd come to him over something trivial! "Smith mentioned that he last worked for Earl Chesterton on the Triple C over in Williamsburg, so I called Earl and talked to him myself. Found out Earl fired Laredo Smith for stealing." He spit out the last word. Even saying it left a bad taste in his mouth.

Frank's eyebrows lifted. "Why didn't Earl press charges?"

"I asked him that myself." The other rancher would have saved Grady a great deal of trouble if he had. "Apparently it was one man's word against another's and no way to prove who was telling the truth and who wasn't. Earl fired them both."

"I see," Frank murmured. "Seems to me that if Smith had something to hide, he wouldn't have mentioned working on the Triple C."

Grady sighed and wondered why no one else viewed the situation with the same concern he did. "I'm asking you to do a background check on Smith," he said, and realized he was expecting a great deal of their friendship. Frank had every right to deny his request, but Grady hoped he wouldn't.

The sheriff frowned and his chair creaked noisily as he leaned back and considered Grady's request. "I understand you're worried about Savannah and I can't say I blame you. Your sister is one of the most kind-hearted people I know, and if this saddle bum hurts her, he'll have me and half the town to deal with."

"You'll do it, then?" Grady said with relief.

"I'll check him out," Frank said reluctantly.

The two exchanged handshakes and Grady left. On his way out of town, he decided to stop off at the post office and talk to Caroline. If he couldn't get through to his sister, maybe her best friend could. Reversing direction, he headed down Maple, then sat in the parking lot, debating the wisdom of his decision. In the past year or so he'd begun to notice Caroline Daniels. She was younger than Savannah, and while they'd been friends for several years, he'd always thought of her as a kid. For some time now it'd become difficult to view Caroline as anything but an attractive woman.

However, Caroline was also opinionated and headstrong. More often than not, her views clashed with his own, and as a result, they argued frequently. Another problem existed, as well.

Maggie.

Grady enjoyed the five-year-old, but for reasons he didn't understand, the little girl was terrified of him. Savannah baby-sat her on Monday nights while Caroline did volunteer work, and it had reached the point that Grady stayed out of sight rather than intimidate the little girl.

Things being what they were, it was a risk to ask for Caroline's help, but one he was willing to take. More than anything, asking Caroline to join forces with him proved how desperate he'd grown to get Savannah to see reason.

Thankfully Caroline was alone when he approached the front counter.

"Hello, Grady," she said, glancing up from the mail she was sorting.

"Have you had lunch yet?" he asked.

Her eyes widened—but she was no more surprised by his invitation than he was himself.

"It's three-thirty."

"Coffee, then," he suggested gruffly, feeling gauche for not looking at the time. No wonder his stomach growled; he'd missed lunch entirely. Which also went to show how desperate he'd become.

"I don't suppose it'd hurt if I took a few minutes off," she said, and set the mail aside.

Definitely curious, Caroline invited him behind the counter. She located a clean mug for him in the back room and filled his cup and her own. "What's on your mind?" she asked.

"Savannah." Grady couldn't see any need to beat around the bush. "I'm worried about her and that drifter."

"He has a name," Caroline said, stirring a spoonful of sugar into her coffee.

"Sure. *Smith.*"

"Laredo Smith."

"All right, Laredo Smith," he said impatiently. Grady didn't know what it was about Caroline that attracted and irritated him at the same time. Lately he found it difficult to carry on a decent conversation with the woman, although he did actually like her.

"What's the problem?" Caroline asked, her eyes meeting his above the rim of her mug.

"I'm afraid he's going to abuse her generosity." In Grady's opinion, the wrangler was already guilty of that and more.

"Don't you trust your sister's judgment?"

"Of course," he flared. "It's just that she's naive and vulnerable. Savannah doesn't have a lot of experience with men, especially smooth talkers like Laredo Smith."

"Laredo's a smooth talker?" Caroline echoed. "I hadn't noticed." The mug was at her lips again, and it seemed to him she purposely held it there to hide a smile. Apparently his concern for Savannah amused her.

"Is something funny?" he challenged, disliking the way she made him the target of her humor.

"Of course not." The amusement left her eyes, replaced by a mock seriousness that infuriated him even more.

"I can see coming here was a mistake," he said, putting the mug down with a clatter. "I should have known you'd find this all a joke." He turned away, but she stopped him.

"Grady."

He hesitated.

"Listen, I doubt there's as much to worry about as you think. Savannah's the most levelheaded person I know."

Grady used to believe the same thing. "She's not herself. He's changed her."

"Yes, he has," Caroline admitted.

At last they could agree on something. "Then you know what I'm saying?"

"Grady," she said, her look gentle, "Laredo *has* changed Savannah, but he's changed her for the better. Don't you see how happy she is? You can't be around her and not feel it. I might not be the best judge of character, but I don't think Laredo is evil incarnate the way you seem to. Maggie was full of stories about him Monday night after I picked her up. She thought he was great. It isn't every man who'd sit and read to a five-year-old until she fell asleep. Savannah said the three of them spent an hour in the calving barn, showing Maggie the newborn calves."

"In other words she likes Smith," Grady muttered. Maggie liked Smith but not him. Caroline apparently didn't realize the insult she'd delivered.

"It's much more than that."

"Really?" He didn't even try to hide his sarcasm.

"What is it you're really afraid of?" she asked.

For the first time Caroline sounded concerned. He held her gaze a long time, then finally said, "I don't want anyone to take advantage of her."

"She's old enough to know her own mind."

"She's too damn trusting."

"Is that bad?"

"Yes," he stormed. "I'm afraid he's going to take advantage of her. I'm afraid Savannah's going to end up alone and pregnant."

The eyes that had just a moment ago revealed the first shred of understanding and compassion flickered with a jolt of unanticipated pain. It took Grady only an instant to realize what he'd said.

"In other words you're afraid your sister will end up like me?"

Grady struggled for the words to apologize. They didn't come easy to a man like him. "I didn't mean that the way it sounded," he said.

"Of course you did."

He probably should have left well enough alone, but he was desperate and he knew Savannah would listen to Caroline before she would him. "Will you talk to her?" he asked hopefully. At her absent look he continued, "About getting rid of Smith before he can hurt her."

"No," she said flat out.

"No?"

"You heard me. If I was going to talk to anyone about this, it'd be you." Caroline's voice gained strength. "And what I'd say, Grady, is leave Savannah to live her own life."

"And make a fool of herself?"

"Yes, if that's what it takes. She's not a child to be chastised and ridiculed; she's a woman with a woman's heart. Grady, I swear if you do anything to spoil her chance of finding happiness, I'll never forgive you."

"Happiness with a saddle bum like Smith?" He might have laughed if there'd been any humor in the suggestion.

"Yes," Caroline responded without hesitation.

Furious, more with himself than with Caroline, Grady stalked out of the office. He should have known better than try to reason with Savannah's best friend. She was as stubborn as his sister. And less tactful about it, too.

"GOOD AFTERNOON, Laredo," Savannah said shyly as she joined him in her rose garden. She carried out a tray and two tall glasses of iced tea. Rocket was at her side, so old now that he found it difficult to move. Generally he stayed in the house, but he appeared to be a little more energetic than usual just now and had followed her outside and into the warm sunshine.

Laredo's efforts were in evidence in every corner of her small paradise. Never had her garden looked more beautiful. The beds were meticulously groomed. Even the roses themselves had responded to his care. They'd burst into flower days earlier than anticipated. Some would claim it was due to the unusually warm spring, but Savannah chose to believe it was because of the love and care she and Laredo had given them.

"Afternoon," he said, leaning on the hoe.

It never failed. Her heart—like her beautiful roses—bloomed with excitement and joy whenever she saw him. He was tall and strong and lovely. She realized that "lovely" wasn't a word often associated with men, but she could find none more appropriate. Beyond everything else Laredo had given her, the most precious was the way she felt around him. Savannah had never considered herself beautiful, but that was how he made her feel. Beautiful. Feminine. Desirable.

"Would you like some iced tea?" she asked.

"That'd be great." He set the hoe aside, removed the tray from her hands and led the way to the small wrought-iron table in the farthest corner of the garden. She'd purposely placed it there amidst the old roses in order to enjoy their fragrance and special beauty. Rocket followed them there and with a groan sank down in the table's shade.

"I'm about finished with the hoeing," Laredo said, bending down to stroke the dog's ears.

This was a problem. He completed each task with speed, skill and determination. She longed to urge him to slow down, to linger over each small assignment so that the work would last, but he never did. From the first he'd set out to prove his worth and he'd done so, many times over.

Another day, two at the most, and he'd have completed her list. Everything thereafter would be a make-work project. Not that she couldn't come up with some.

"Wiley stopped by earlier," he said, and downed half the tea in a series of deep swallows. He wiped the back of his hand across his mouth, then leaned forward and stroked Rocket's ears again. Savannah's gaze rested on the dog who'd once belonged to her father and she smiled as he snored softly, already asleep.

"He told me about Roanie's sore leg and he asked me to look at it. You don't mind, do you?"

If anything, Savannah was relieved. All three realized it'd be best if Grady didn't know about Laredo doctoring one of the horses. Nevertheless it'd be a shame to let the old roan suffer. Especially when Laredo could help—save them the expense of calling the vet.

"Of course I don't mind," she assured him.

"I'll probably need to rub in some ointment and wrap up the leg."

She nodded. "I'm grateful." If Grady wouldn't say it, she would, but her appreciation extended far beyond any expertise Laredo offered in the area of horses. He'd blessed her life in the week since his arrival. One week. Seven fleeting days, and yet it felt as though he'd always been part of her life. People would say it was fanciful or ridiculous, but in an odd way, Savannah felt as if her life had been on hold while she waited for Laredo to find her.

She smiled to herself, amused that Grady was making such a fool of himself, all the while calling *her* the fool. Considering the fuss her older brother had made, anyone would think she'd become Laredo's lover when in reality he hadn't so much as kissed her.

But she wished he would. . . . She'd dreamed of it endlessly, hungering for his touch. Grady had chastised her for claiming to love Laredo on such short acquaintance, and for the first time in recent memory she'd lied to her brother. She'd told him she didn't love Laredo but that she could.

The truth was she *did* love him. She loved him for the gentle care he gave her roses. For his loving way with animals. For his honesty. For his tender patience with Maggie and, most important, for the joy he'd brought into her life. Each day she awoke happy and excited, knowing he'd be in the kitchen to greet her. Each night she laid her head on her pillow, her mind full of dreams she'd never dared to believe possible, never believed were meant for a woman like her.

So, while it was true he hadn't touched her except for that one time he'd held her in the kitchen, she knew instinctively that he shared her feelings. She felt his love in a thousand ways. Unspoken, but real. As intense as her own for him.

Yes, Grady had called her a fool, and perhaps she was. But if being considered a fool meant she was this happy, then he could call her whatever name he liked.

"Is there anything more I can do for you this afternoon?" Laredo asked.

She shook her head. "I'll be leaving soon."

"If you're going into town, would you mind checking on my truck at Powell's Garage?"

"I . . . I can do that for you later in the week, if you want, but I wasn't planning on going into town." Savannah had hoped to avoid any questions about her destination. She'd hoped to slip quietly away and return to the ghost town. It had taken her a full week to gather the courage to go back, but despite her reservations, she'd decided to do it. She was sure there were more old roses to be found.

"Savannah," Laredo said, touching her hand. "You're headed back to Bitter End, aren't you?"

She lowered her eyes and nodded, knowing that, like Grady, he'd disapprove. "I want to look for more roses. If the plants in the cemetery survived, there're bound to be others." In the days since her last visit Savannah had managed to convince herself that the darkness, the sense of oppression, had come from her own imagination. It'd been nerves and excitement, that was all. Grady had warned her about the ghost town so often that her head had been filled with nonsense. After a while she'd come to believe it. And even if what she'd experienced was real, she'd managed the first time and would again.

"Your brother—"

"Grady disapproves of a great deal in my life just now. I'm going back to Bitter End, Laredo, with or without Grady's approval."

The strength of her objection appeared to catch him unawares. "Surely your brother has a reason for not wanting you there?"

"You know Grady," she answered. "He's overprotective."

"I don't know your brother," Laredo told her quietly, "but everything he says and does is because he loves you and is concerned about you. It might be best to heed his advice."

If Savannah hadn't fallen in love with Laredo already, she would have lost her heart right then and there. He'd defended Grady, when Grady had done nothing but cause him problems.

"He doesn't understand," she murmured.

"Where is this place?" Laredo asked. "I haven't heard anyone else talk about a ghost town in this area."

"I don't think many people know about it." Grady had located the town as a teenager and promised he'd take her there himself. It was the only time she could remember her brother breaking his word. "Grady was there once, but he refused to talk about it afterward. No matter how much I pleaded, he refused to give in. All he'd say was that he was never going back and he certainly wasn't going to take his little sister there."

"Then how'd you find the place?"

She laughed lightly. "It wasn't easy. It took me weeks."

"Why now? Because of the old roses?"

Savannah smiled. "I read an article in one of my gardening magazines about a man who found a huge number of old roses in a ghost-town cemetery. I'd nearly forgotten about Bitter End, but once I remembered, I couldn't stop thinking about it. I asked Grady as much as I could without arousing his suspicions, but eventually he caught on and wouldn't give me any more information."

Laredo frowned. "Savannah," he pleaded, "if your brother's that worried about it, then so am I. Don't go."

Her heart sank. Not Laredo, too. "Please don't ask that of me," she whispered.

He got up and walked around the table to stand in front of her. "Then don't do it alone," he said urgently.

"But there isn't anyone—"

"There's me."

Savannah leaned back to see him more clearly. "You'd do that for me?"

He nodded and knelt in front of her, his expression earnest. "Promise me, Savannah."

"I promise." She needed to touch him. She couldn't have explained why, but the yearning inside her was too strong to ignore. Hesitantly she pressed one hand to his cheek, her palm curving around his jaw. The skin was stubbled with his beard, and yet she'd never felt anything more sensual.

Laredo closed his eyes and gripped her wrist with a strength she hadn't expected. "You make it damn near impossible," he said from between clenched teeth.

"Impossible?" she whispered. She found it difficult to breathe or swallow. Her heart beat at an alarming rate, and she feared he would guess how his closeness unnerved her.

"Don't you know?" His words were half groan, half speech, as if her touching him, even in the most innocent way, caused him pain. She felt the urgency in him and the restraint. She honored him for that restraint—but she didn't need it anymore.

"I want you to kiss me, Laredo. I've dreamed about you every night." Her raspy voice was barely audible.

"Savannah, please."

"Please what? Ignore my heart? I can't! I tried, Laredo, I really did."

He cradled her face, and their eyes met. In his she read determination and a kind of desperation. "Grady's made it difficult enough for you," he said. "I can't, I won't make it—"

"I don't care what my brother thinks," she choked out, stopping him by placing her fingertips to his lips. "I know my heart, Laredo, and my heart wants you very much."

His hands slid from the sides of her face and into her hair. Then slowly, inch by thrilling inch, he brought her mouth to his.

The instant their lips touched, Savannah felt her heart leap with a burst of joy. It overtook her, drove everything else from her mind.

His mouth was warm and moist, and he tasted of iced tea and fresh mint. He moved his lips hungrily against hers, molding her mouth to his with a heat that seared her senses. Although her experience with lovemaking had been limited, she'd had her share of kisses. But never like this. Never with this kind of heat, this degree of passion. Had it happened with anyone else, it would have frightened her.

Soon their arms were wrapped completely around each other in a struggle to get closer. She realized the fierceness with which they clung must be hurting his ribs. She tried to say something, to shift her hands, but he wouldn't allow it, his movements urging her to hold him closer, hold him tighter.

The kiss grew hotter and hotter as they each sought to give more, take more, be more. Laredo's breath came hard and fast. Her own echoed his.

With a moan, Laredo finally broke away, his shoulders heaving. "That shouldn't have happened," he said in a tortured voice. "I don't want to hurt you."

"You could never hurt me," she assured him, her face against his chest. In all her days she'd never been more brazen with a man, asking him outright to kiss her, to hold her. But hard as she tried, Savannah couldn't make herself regret what she'd done. If anything she wondered why it had taken her so long. She'd had no idea kissing could be this . . . incredible. Her friends should have told her!

"Say something," she pleaded. "I need to know you're feeling it, too."

"I think I knew the minute you stopped to offer me a ride." He got to his feet and walked away from her.

"Laredo?"

"I promised Wiley I'd check on Roanie. Remember?"

In other words their discussion was over; he had nothing more to say. Nor did he wish to hear what *she* might say. "All right," she said, hanging her head in defeat.

He got as far as the garden gate, then turned back. "You won't go to the ghost town without me?"

"No," she promised.

He nodded. He seemed about to speak again but hesitated. If he dared apologize for kissing her, she didn't know what she'd do. Probably scream in frustration. That would be an unprecedented event—Savannah Weston screaming! She gave an involuntary giggle.

Savannah watched him leave, then carried the tray of empty glasses back into the house. Despite his withdrawal, his abrupt departure, she felt like dancing around her kitchen. He'd kissed her! And it had been wonderful.

Not only had Laredo kissed her, he'd said he'd been thinking about it for days. The same as she had. That was enough to make her heart wild with joy. But there was more. He'd as much as said he loved her.

"Oh, please," she prayed, closing her eyes and clasping her hands, "let it be true. Don't let this be a cruel joke." But she knew otherwise; she'd felt it in the wonder of his kiss.

With the afternoon free, Savannah baked chocolate-chip cookies, one of her many specialties. She tucked a dozen inside the freezer to save for Maggie's visits and filled the cookie jar with the rest.

Because the kitchen door was open, she heard Grady's truck pull into the yard, followed by his near-frantic shout.

"Savannah!"

It wasn't her name that shook her, but the way he yelled it. Rushing to the door, she found him stalking toward the house.

"Grady, for heaven's sake, what's wrong?"

"You're not to talk to him!"

"Grady," she said, her patience gone. "We've already had this discussion. Laredo—"

"Not *Laredo*," he barked as if she were slow-witted or being purposely obtuse.

"*Who?*"

"Richard."

"Richard?" She saw him then, her younger brother. Her "big boy," the baby she'd loved and cared for and spoiled. He walked slowly down the long driveway, hefting his suitcase, eyes focused on the house as if the sight of it was the only thing that kept him on his feet.

"Richard," she cried, and pressed her hands to her mouth. "Grady, how could you drive past him like that?"

"He's not welcome here, Savannah."

"Grady, he's our *brother*." Not caring what he thought, she flew out the door and raced down the stairs. Richard. He was here at last. Now they'd learn the truth, the real truth, and everything would be right with their world again.

Richard had come home.

Five

Richard had changed, Savannah mused. Although dusty from the road and weary to the bone, he'd acquired a look of sophistication she hadn't seen six years ago. This was Richard, her brother, but at the same time he was someone she no longer knew. None of that mattered, however, the instant he wrapped his arms around her and joyously hugged her close. Her tears mingled with laughter and pleas that he put her down.

"Savannah, oh, it's so good to see you." His face brightened with excitement. "You're even more beautiful than I remembered."

Wiping the tears from her cheek, she smiled up at him. "I can't believe it's you."

"I'm home. You have no idea how good this old place looks." He gazed longingly toward the house.

Her heart warmed in that moment, and she was almost willing to forgive him the agony his betrayal had cost them.

"Don't get comfortable, little brother." Grady's eyes were savage. He stood on the top step, feet apart, arms akimbo, barring the door.

Slowly Richard set Savannah away from him and faced his brother.

"Grady," she said in warning. Despite his faults, Richard *was* their brother and the least they could do was hear him out. "Give him a chance to explain."

Richard looked from brother to sister. He advanced slowly toward Grady, then paused. "I don't blame you, Grady. You have every right to be angry."

"You've got that straight."

"What I did was despicable." Richard stretched out his arm to Savannah, as if he needed her to stand with him. She stepped to his side, wanting to right the past and thrust all the ugliness behind them. They were a family, and if they couldn't forgive one another, then they'd be hypocrites to sit in church every Sunday. The Good Book was full of the power of forgiveness. Only this wasn't what Grady wanted to hear. Not now. Not yet. He demanded his pound of flesh first, and while Savannah understood his anger, she wanted him to give Richard the opportunity to set things straight.

"Despicable is only one in a long list of words that come to mind when I think of you." Grady's face was hard and unyielding. He'd braced his feet apart in a way that said it would take the strength of ten men to budge him from that porch. Nothing Richard could say would change his mind. Savannah had bumped against that pride of his often enough to know. Unless something drastic happened, Grady wouldn't let Richard set foot in the home where he was born and raised.

Her younger brother hung his head in shame. "I don't blame you for hating me."

"Oh, Richard, you don't know how difficult it was for us," Savannah said, despite her determination to hold her tongue.

Richard's face crumpled with regret. "I'm so sorry. I was young and stupid, and then once I owned up to what I'd done . . . I couldn't face you and Grady. I was too ashamed."

"You stole that money from your own flesh and blood!" Grady spit out.

"I was crazy with grief," Richard pleaded, sounding the same way he had as a child when he knew he'd done something wrong. "I didn't think. All I knew was that Mom and Dad were gone."

"And Dad had stored away a hunk of cash," Grady said.

Richard gestured weakly. "I was never cut out to be a cowboy, even you have to admit that," he said, and glanced up at Grady for confirmation. "I could read the writing on the wall. With Dad gone you'd expect me to help around the place, and it just wasn't in me. Still isn't. Cows and me never saw eye to eye. You said it more than once yourself." He gave a crooked half smile, enticing Grady to agree with him.

Grady remained cold and silent, his eyes as hard as flint.

"I know it was wrong to take that money. A thousand times since, I've cursed myself for being so stupid, so greedy."

"You should have phoned," Savannah chastised. "You could have let us know where you were. Grady and I were worried sick." She looked to her brother to continue, to explain what they'd endured because of Richard.

Once again Grady's cool silence was answer enough.

"I thought about coming home," Richard said in a small pleading voice. "You don't know how many times I've thought of it. You're right, Savannah," he said, rushing his words. "I should've called. I know that now, but I was afraid of what you'd say. I didn't have the courage to face you."

"What happened to the money?" Grady threw the question at his brother with a vengeance.

"The money," Richard repeated, and the sigh that followed said it all.

"You blew it," Grady said with disgust.

"I put it up as capital in a business venture. My plan," he said, glancing desperately to Savannah and then Grady, "was to triple it and share the profits with you two. I thought if I did that, you'd forgive me and let me come home. Then we could go on the way we always have. But—" he paused and looked away "—the venture went sour."

"In other words you lost everything."

Richard nodded slowly. "The investment wasn't as solid as I was led to believe. It was a bitter lesson. But you have to understand," he added, motioning toward Grady, "I was desperate to come home." His voice shook as though the memory was as painful to him as it was to Savannah and Grady. "By this time I missed you both so much I would have done anything to find a way home."

"You could have written," Savannah said. "Even if you weren't ready to talk to us . . ." For months she'd prayed for a letter, a phone call, anything that would explain what had happened. She'd refused to give up hope, refused to believe Richard would steal from them and then just disappear. After six months she stopped making excuses, and when they hadn't heard from him after a year, his name was dropped from their conversations.

"I *wanted* to write," Richard said, leaping on her words. "I tried. As God is my witness, I tried, but I was never good with words. How could I possibly explain everything in a letter?"

Grady snickered loudly. "Seems to me you're about as slick with words as a snake-oil salesman."

A flash of pain appeared in Richard's eyes. "You really hate me, don't you, Grady?"

"How could we hate you?" Savannah answered in Grady's stead, fearing his response. "You're our brother."

At her words Richard rallied somewhat and gazed around the yard. "You've obviously done all right by yourselves. The ranch looks great."

"No thanks to you."

"Think about it, Grady," Richard challenged. "What good would I have been to you if I'd stuck around? As far as I'm concerned, cows smell bad, have a negative disposition and are always needing something done to them. If I'd stayed, I wouldn't have been any help. Okay, I admit taking the money was pretty underhand, but all I really did was lay claim to part of my inheritance a little early."

"We almost lost the ranch," Savannah felt obliged to tell him. Surely he must have realized that? "Richard, I don't think you have a clue how hard it's been for Grady and me," she said.

"I'm sorry," he repeated with what sounded like genuine regret. "How many times do I need to say it?"

"Sorry?" Grady said the word as though it were the foulest obscenity.

Richard ignored the outburst. "I'll admit that what I did was rotten, but would it really have been such a bad thing if you'd been forced to sell the land?"

"What do you *mean?*" Savannah asked, certain she wasn't hearing him correctly. This land had been in the Weston family for generations. Their ancestors had settled here, worked the land, raised cattle. Generations of Westons had been buried here in a small cemetery plot overlooking the main pasture. This land was their heritage, their birthright. Their future. That Richard could suggest selling it revealed how little he understood or appreciated the legacy.

"These days everyone knows its not a good idea to eat a lot of red meat," he explained when it became apparent that his words had upset her. "The beef industry's been declining steadily for some time, or so I hear. Actually I'm surprised you've held on to the old place this long."

Savannah's heart sank. It seemed impossible that Richard shared the same blood that flowed through Grady's veins and hers. But he was her brother and she refused to turn her back on him, despite his shortcomings. Despite his betrayal.

"You think because you say you're sorry it makes everything right?" Grady asked, his voice shaking with such rage Savannah feared he was near exploding. "Do you honestly believe you can walk back into our lives as if you'd done nothing wrong? I'm here to tell you it's not going to happen."

Confused and uncertain, Richard looked to his sister for support. "But I'm willing to do whatever's necessary to make it up to you."

"Give me back six years of constant hard work," Grady shouted. "Days that stretched fifteen hours without rest. Days in which I did the work of two men. Backbreaking work. Can you do *that,* little brother?"

Richard stood still and silent.

"For six long years I fought off the wolf at the door. For six years I dealt with grief and stress and worry so bad I couldn't sleep." He climbed down the steps, one step for each statement. Anger seethed below the surface unlike anything she'd ever seen in Grady. Not the explosive kind common with him, but the deep bitter anger that gnawed at a man's soul.

"I can't change the past," Richard muttered, his shoulders hunched, "but I'd hoped we could put all this behind us and start fresh."

"Not on your life," Grady said. He stood face-to-face with Richard now, glaring at him. "You haven't shown any true regret. Not once have you asked Savannah and me to forgive you. As far as I'm concerned, you got your inheritance, and you wasted it. Now get off *our* land."

"You want me to leave?" Richard sounded incredulous. He looked at Savannah but she turned away. "You're my family!" he cried. "The only family I've got. You don't mean this. Okay, okay, you're right, I should have asked you to forgive me. I meant to—that was the real reason I returned. Like I said, I want to make it up to both of you."

Savannah wavered, ambivalent.

"You should have thought of that sooner," Grady replied, his voice clipped.

She'd hoped they could resolve their differences and make Richard a part of their lives again, but Grady was right. Richard hadn't revealed any sincere sorrow for the agony he'd caused them. But then he'd always been weak and easily influenced. Nevertheless he was their brother; it came down to that. If for no other reason than to honor the memory of their parents, she wanted there to be no ill will between them.

"You're serious?" Richard's face clouded with disbelief. "You want me off the ranch?"

"I've never been more serious in my life."

Brother stared down brother.

"I . . . I'm without a job. I was working at . . . at a sales job, and they downsized. I don't have anywhere to go. I left instructions for the check from my severance package to be mailed here." He glanced hopefully at Savannah and then at Grady.

Savannah silently pleaded with Grady, but he refused to look in her direction. It was hell staying quiet, especially when Richard begged for her help.

"You, too, Savannah?" he whispered in the hurt voice that tugged at her heart. "Do you want me to leave, too?"

Savannah was in torment, not knowing how to respond. Of course she wanted him to stay, wanted their lives to return to the way they'd been before. But she didn't know if that was possible.

"I'm ruined," he whispered brokenly. "The money's gone. I lost my job and I have no savings. All I could think about was getting back to you and Grady. Making things right again."

Tears filled her eyes and she bit her lip, trapped as she was between the strong wills of her two brothers.

Not waiting for her reply, Richard leaned down and reached for his suitcase. Apparently he was weaker than they realized because he staggered, but caught himself in time to keep from collapsing.

Savannah could hold her tongue no longer. "Grady, please! He's about to faint. One night," she begged, sliding her arm around Richard's waist. "Let him stay one night."

For a moment she didn't think Grady would relent. "All right," he gave in, his reluctance clear, "but he sleeps in the bunkhouse. First thing in the morning he's out of here. Understand?"

"Thank you, brother," Richard said softly. "You won't be sorry, I promise you that. I'll find a way to make it up to you and Savannah. I didn't know, didn't realize . . . I'll do whatever you want if you'll just let me stay. You're the only family I've got."

LAREDO HADN'T MEANT to listen in on the scene outside the house. But he'd been in the garden at the time, and it had been impossible to ignore. He wasn't sure what had finally occurred between Savannah and her two brothers, but the three had apparently come to some kind of understanding. He didn't see Savannah again until dinnertime, and when he entered the house, she was all aflutter. He smelled biscuits baking, their aroma more enticing to him than the world's most expensive perfume. An apple pie cooled on the kitchen counter beside a standing rib roast, recently taken from the oven.

When she saw him, her beautiful face brightened with a shy smile of welcome. "Richard's here."

"So I understand." Laredo had tried to put the events of the early afternoon behind him and hoped she had, as well. Kissing her had been a mistake, one he regretted. His weakness for her complicated an already difficult situation.

The last thing he wanted was to let her believe in something that could never be. His property—three hundred acres in Oklahoma—was waiting for him. That and his horse. They were all he had. And they were almost nothing compared to the Westons' huge spread. Compared to what Savannah had now. It would be cruel to mislead her into thinking she could be part of his future. But if the kissing continued, it'd be as hard for him to walk away as it would be for her to let him go.

"He hasn't eaten in two days," she said, explaining the frenzy of cooking that had taken place that afternoon. "I baked his favorites just the way Mom would have."

"How's Grady dealing with this?"

A sadness came over her and some of the excitement drained from her voice. "Not very well, unfortunately. He won't let Richard stay more than the night. He's forcing him to sleep in the bunkhouse. Richard said he was willing to work for his keep, and I think if I reason with him, Grady might let him stay on until his severance check arrives. I'm hoping he will, but it's hard to tell with Grady."

"Savannah!" Footsteps echoed as Richard Weston bounded down the stairs from the upstairs bedroom and burst into the kitchen. "I found my old guitar." He slid the strap over his shoulder and ran the pick over the tight strings, laughing with childish delight.

"I couldn't make myself throw away your things," Savannah admitted.

Walking about in his stocking feet, Richard circled the kitchen playing a mellow country hit Laredo recognized from the early nineties. A song of Reba's, if memory served him.

The family resemblance was strong, Laredo noticed. Richard was a younger, slimmer, blonder version of Grady, good-looking and suave. Apparently he'd inherited a double portion of charm, as well. He serenaded his sister, causing Savannah to blush unmercifully. Laredo knew he should leave, but he found himself enjoying the scene.

When Richard finished the song, he set the guitar aside and glanced in Laredo's direction, his eyes questioning.

Savannah's gaze followed her brother's. "This is Laredo Smith," she said. She reached for Laredo's hand, tucking it in both of hers. "He works for me."

"Really, Savannah," Richard joked. "I never suspected my older sister would have her own boy-toy." He laughed then, as if he found the comment hilarious.

Any goodwill Laredo had felt toward the other man vanished with the ugly suggestiveness of his remark. Savannah's face turned a deep shade of scarlet, and it was all Laredo could do to keep his mouth shut.

"It's n-not that way with us," she stammered.

"Whatever you say, big sister," Richard responded. "Hey, when's dinner? I could eat the entire roast myself." He gripped Savannah by the shoulder and noisily kissed her cheek. "I can't tell you how good it is to be home. I've missed you, Savannah, almost as much as I've missed your melt-in-the-mouth buttermilk biscuits."

"I need to be getting back," Laredo said, eager to check on Roanie. "I just stopped by to tell you I won't be here for dinner."

"You won't?" Savannah's eyes pleaded with him, and he realized she'd been counting on his support at the dinner table. She appeared to have forgotten that Grady had no particular fondness for him, either. He wished he could help her, but feared he'd do her cause more harm than good.

"Wiley invited me to play poker with him and his friends tonight," he explained to justify his absence. "The game's over at the Double Z bunkhouse."

She forgave him with a brave smile. "Have fun."

"Will everything be all right here?" He watched Richard walk past Rocket and give the old dog a vicious shove with his foot. His anger flared again, but he said nothing.

"Everything's going to be just fine," Richard answered on her behalf. "Grady can be downright stubborn at times, but he'll come around. Don't worry, I'll make sure big brother doesn't hassle her." He placed his arm around his sister's shoulders and squeezed hard. Savannah winced and Laredo battled the urge to grab the man by the shirtfront and jerk him away.

ALTHOUGH LAREDO didn't see Savannah again that evening, it didn't mean she wasn't on his mind. He worried about her dinner with her brothers, which burdened his concentration to the point that he lost at poker. Twenty bucks was more than he could afford to throw away in a poker game. By the end of the evening he regretted accepting Wiley's invitation.

He and Wiley returned to find Richard in the bunkhouse, sitting on the edge of his bed, strumming his guitar and singing drunkenly at the top of his lungs. Wiley snorted in contempt and headed immediately for his small room. Richard didn't seem to notice. He interrupted his song every so often to reach for a whiskey bottle and gulp down a swig. He held it up in silent invitation when he saw Laredo.

"Care to join me?" he asked. "I broke into Grady's private stock. By the time he misses it, we'll both be long gone." He laughed as if stealing liquor from his brother was some kind of triumph.

"No, thanks," Laredo muttered in disgust.

"I should've been a country singer," Richard announced at the end of a barely recognizable Garth Brooks tune. Not that his singing voice was all that unpleasant, but the words were badly slurred.

"I've got talent, you know?" He lifted the bottle to his mouth, gulped down another swallow and threw back his head. "Ahh." He gave an exaggerated shudder. "Powerful stuff. My big brother only buys the best." He set the guitar down on the floor, holding it carelessly by the neck.

Laredo was tired; he'd put in a full day and his thoughts were heavy. In addition, he was worried about Savannah and how the animosity between the two brothers would affect her. She was the one stuck in the middle between two angry men, struggling to maintain the peace. One brother was stubborn and unyielding, the other manipulative and demanding.

He wished there was some way he could protect her.

Twice Laredo had to ask Richard to turn out the light. "Give me five minutes," was the response both times. The light Laredo could handle; it was a small matter to turn on his side and put his back to the harsh glare. But the drunken singing and guitar strumming weren't as easily ignored.

By midnight he'd had enough. He threw back the covers, walked over to the wall and flicked off the switch himself. "You got a problem with that?" he challenged. His day had started at five that morning and he desperately needed to sleep.

A tense silence followed. "Whatever," Richard muttered. He dropped or shoved something onto the floor, and the crash echoed through the room. Frankly, Laredo didn't care. He was through with the niceties as far as Richard Weston was concerned.

Laredo awoke at dawn, showered, shaved and was preparing for his day when he happened to notice Richard. He stopped, squinting as he took a closer look. He'd heard movie stars and the like used such devices, but he'd never personally seen one.

Richard Weston lay sprawled across the bed, his arms and legs dangling over the edge of the small mattress. He wore silk pajamas and, of all things, a black satin sleep mask to protect his eyes against the sunlight. Never in all his life had Laredo seen a more incongruous sight in a bunkhouse.

Shaking his head, he stopped in the barn to check on Roanie before he made his way to the kitchen for coffee. Squatting down, he gently tested the roan's leg, working with practiced hands, exploring the damage to the delicate muscle. The swelling was down and the pain had apparently lessened.

After coffee and a solitary breakfast, Laredo worked in the rose garden; he installed the trellises he'd built earlier in the week and transplanted some shrubs Savannah wanted him to move. She hadn't come outside and he guessed she was still busy in the house. Actually he hoped she'd treat herself and sleep in. She must have been exhausted yesterday, cooking for her ungrateful brother. He gritted his teeth just thinking about the other man.

Shortly after noon Richard wandered out of the bunkhouse, looking as if he hadn't been awake more than a few minutes. His hair was mussed and he yawned as he strolled across the yard, his shirt unbuttoned. He wore canvas shoes without socks.

Before going to the house for lunch, Laredo decided to rewrap Roanie's leg and apply the ointment again. He was half-finished when he felt someone's presence. He turned around and found Grady standing outside the stall watching him.

"I understand I'm in your debt," he said with the pride of a man who preferred to owe no one. He looked tired and drawn, as if he hadn't slept much. For the first time since making Grady's acquaintance, Laredo felt sorry for him.

"No problem," he said, straightening. He rubbed his hand down Roanie's back, reassuring the gelding that all was well.

Grady lingered. Apparently there was something else on his mind. "Savannah told you about the ghost town, didn't she?"

"She mentioned it," Laredo said stiffly.

"I thought she might have." Grady leaned against the stall door. "Listen, I haven't made my feelings any secret. I don't like you, Smith. Nor do I trust you. A man who steals gets no respect from me."

"For what it's worth, I didn't do it," Laredo said, although he doubted Grady would believe him.

"I have even less respect for a liar."

Laredo tensed. If it wasn't for Savannah, he'd have had his fist down the other man's throat. He'd worked hard to prove himself, but apparently a good day's labor wasn't enough for Grady Weston.

"You should know I've asked Sheriff Hennessey to do a background check on you, although I suspect Smith is probably an alias."

Laredo's hackles were already raised, but defending himself again would be a useless waste of breath. He exhaled sharply. "Fine. To be fair, if Savannah was my sister, I'd do the same thing. You're looking to protect her. I can't blame a man for that."

If Grady was surprised, he didn't show it.

"I'm pleased to hear you say that, because she needs protecting."

Savannah's brother had Laredo's attention now. "What do you mean?"

"Unfortunately she mentioned finding Bitter End to Richard and he seemed far too interested. I heard the bastard when I was washing up for dinner. He was hinting that she should take him there." He paused. "I don't want it to happen."

Laredo agreed with Grady. "She's already promised me she wouldn't return alone. I hope she doesn't go with Richard, either."

Surprise flickered in Grady's intensely blue eyes. "So she did plan to go back." He scratched the side of his head. "Why on earth would she do such a thing?" He looked to Laredo for the answer.

"The roses," he said, amazed Grady hadn't figured it out.

"She's already got more roses than she knows what to do with. How could she possibly want more? What's wrong with that woman? Why would she risk her fool neck over a few flowers?"

"She's after old roses," Laredo explained.

"Old roses." The two words were part of a deep sigh. Grady seemed lost in thought for a minute and then his gaze found Laredo's again. "I don't want her going there with Richard or anyone else, for that matter. It's not safe. Regardless of my feelings toward you, I care about my sister and I'd appreciate your help."

"You might find this hard to believe, Grady, but I care about Savannah's well-being, too."

"Then keep her away from Bitter End."

Laredo wasn't sure he could do that. "I'm not making any promises, but I'll do what I can."

Grady nodded wearily. "That's all I ask." He hesitated, glanced over at Roanie's leg and then back to Laredo. "We could use a wrangler this time of year. Are you interested in the job?"

"I'd need to square it with Savannah."

"That isn't what I asked," Grady said, his words sharp.

"I'm interested," Laredo answered.

"Fine," he said. "You can start after lunch."

Damn, but the old town looked good. It was midafternoon as Richard slowly drove Grady's battered pickup down Main Street. He'd barely been back twenty-four hours, and it felt as if he'd never left. Well, not quite, but close enough. He'd thought about returning to Promise more than once—but not driving his brother's clunky truck.

Despite the town's familiarity, a lot had changed over the years. The savings-and-loan had a sign that alternately flashed the time and the temperature. Damn if that didn't beat all. Next thing he knew the town would have its own Dairy Queen.

Luck was with him. Slowly but surely he'd manage to wriggle his way back into Grady's good graces—enough, at any rate, to convince his big brother to let him stay for a while. It wouldn't take long to win Savannah back, but then his sister had always been a soft touch. Grady, however, wasn't nearly as easy. So far, it was Richard two, Grady zilch.

Because not only was Richard staying at the ranch, he had the truck. Okay, Savannah had been the one to give him the keys, but what Grady didn't know wasn't going to hurt him.

His brother was a fool. Grady could have sold that ranch ten times over and lived off the profits for years. Instead he'd half killed himself holding on to twenty thousand smelly cattle-filled acres. Richard had listened to the spiel about their forefathers struggling against impossible odds and all that garbage. So what? He wasn't about to let the ranch or anything else tie him down. He had better ideas than following a bunch of senseless cattle around all that godforsaken land.

Richard pulled into the first available parking spot and hopped out of the cab. Six years away, and he still knew this town inside out, recognized every street and practically every building. On the other hand, no one was going to recognize *him,* dressed as he was. What he needed, Richard decided, was new clothes.

His first stop was Jordan's Town and Country. Max Jordan who owned the place would be close to retirement by now.

"Max," Richard said as he walked into the Western-wear store. He greeted Max as if they'd been the best of friends, slapping the older man jovially on the back. "Don't you know me?" he asked. "Richard. Richard Weston."

"Richard." The other man's eyes brightened with recognition. "When did you get back?"

"Yesterday. Listen, does Grady still have an open account with you?" He fingered the pearl buttons on a polished-cotton shirt and checked the cost, raising his brows at the price.

"That's one of our designer shirts," Max said, and steered him toward another less pricy rack of clothes.

Richard returned to the original shirt. "Do you have it in a forty-two?"

"I think I just might," Max said with some surprise. He shifted hangers as he searched out sizes. "Yup, got one right here."

"Great. Grady said I should buy what I need."

"Not a problem," Max assured him, grinning at the prospect of a big sale. "How's Grady doing these days? I don't see much of him."

"He works too hard," Richard said. And it was true. His brother needed to relax and not take everything so seriously.

"It's good to see you, my boy," Max said, watching Richard try on a pair of three-hundred-dollar snakeskin boots. They fit perfectly, as if they were just waiting for him. "I'll take these, as well."

"Good choice."

Grady wouldn't think so, but Richard would pay him back. Eventually.

"I've got to say I still miss your parents," Max continued. "They were good people. My, but your mother knew how to cook, and your pa, why, he was the life of the party."

The word "party" struck a pleasant chord with Richard. He didn't imagine there'd been much celebrating around the Yellow Rose since he'd been away. Not with Grady being such a tightwad. He doubted his brother even knew how to laugh anymore, and Savannah ran and hid from her own shadow.

"Funny you should mention a party," Richard said as the owner tallied the bill. "Grady's throwing a bash to welcome me home on Sunday. You're welcome to come. Bring the missus too."

"Who else'll be there?"

"The whole town's invited. Spread the word, will you?"

"Sure. It'll be great for everyone to get together. Haven't had a real party all spring, and it's weeks yet until the big summer dance."

Richard left soon after signing his name to the yellow slip. On the sidewalk outside Jordan's he ran into Ellie Frasier. "Ellie," he said, and did a double take. "Little Ellie?" Only she wasn't so little anymore. She'd been in junior high when he was a high school senior, and he remembered thinking then that she was going to be a looker. He'd been right.

She stared at him blankly.

"Richard!" he cried, and spread his arms wide. He was surprised she didn't recognize him in his new shirt, hat and boots. His gaze lowered to her full breasts. He always had been partial to a well-endowed woman. Yup, he could see he'd come home in the nick of time. No ring on her finger, either. Not that it mattered. Often, forbidden fruit was all the sweeter.

"Richard Weston?"

"The one and only."

She asked the same questions as Max—when he'd arrived, what he'd been doing, how long he planned to stay and so on. He was vague until he mentioned the party.

"Bring whoever you want, but be sure to save me a dance, all right?" He winked, letting her know he was interested.

"I don't know . . . My dad's been sick and—"

"Come, anyway," he urged. "You need the break, and what better way to put your troubles behind you than to kick up your heels and party?"

Dancing. That meant music. They were going to need a band, and on short notice. That'd cost a few extra bucks, but hey, no problem. Grady was tight with a penny, but he probably had plenty of cash stored away. His older brother was too much like their father to cut it close to the bone.

"Who's playing at the Chili Pepper these days?" he asked, referring to the best barbecue pit in town.

Ellie named a band he hadn't heard of. He nodded and headed in that direction. While he was there, he'd arrange to have Adam Braunfels set up a barbecue. They were going to need lots of food. Naturally Savannah would want to cook up most of it herself, make salads and such; she'd insist on that the same way Mom would if she were alive.

He remembered his parents with fondness. Their deaths had put an unexpected crimp in his life, but Richard was a survivor. The years had proved that. He'd weathered his current troubles, hadn't he? He was home and as safe as a babe in arms.

By the time Richard drove back to the ranch, he'd made a number of arrangements for the party. He'd ordered a dozen cases of beer and he'd made sure there was going to be plenty of soda pop for the youngsters. Millie over at the flower shop had suggested Chinese lanterns and agreed to set them up early in the afternoon. For a price, naturally, but she'd been reasonable about it.

Savannah was working in her garden when he arrived. She wore one of those long dresses of hers with an oversize straw hat and looked more like a nun than the big sister he remembered. Briefly he wondered what was up between her and that prickly hired hand.

"My, don't you look beautiful this afternoon," Richard said as he waltzed through the gate. "As pretty as one of your roses."

She blushed and Richard was struck by how truly pretty she was. It surprised him.

"Listen, sis, I probably shouldn't have done this, but I ran into some friends in town."

Savannah straightened and dabbed the sweat from her brow. "I imagine everyone was glad to see you."

"They were, but there just wasn't enough time to visit with everyone the way I wanted. I hope you don't mind, but I invited a few people over for dinner Sunday evening. You wouldn't mind cooking up some of your prize-winning potato salad, now, would you?"

"For how many?"

Richard laughed and hugged her close. "Enough for about 150."

Six

Grady swore Richard must have invited the entire population of Promise to this so-called party. Neighbors and friends whirled around the makeshift dance floor, while others sat in the sunshine and exchanged gossip. Grady didn't want anything to do with it.

The first he'd heard of Richard's party was when he found Savannah in the kitchen this morning cooking her heart out. The next thing he knew, Millie Greenville from the local flower shop was stringing Chinese lanterns around the backyard and asking him when he intended to set up the tables. According to Millie, he was going to need at least twenty to accommodate everyone.

Before he fully comprehended what was happening, people started to arrive. The lead singer of the Hoss Cartrights asked him questions he couldn't answer. Apparently they didn't need his help because the next time he stepped out of the barn, they'd set up a stage, plugged in their sound equipment and spread a bale of straw across the lawn for a dance floor.

Richard, dressed in his fancy new duds, was in his element. Grady didn't know what had possessed him to give in to Savannah's pleadings to let their worthless brother stay on until his severance check showed up. Grady wasn't entirely convinced there *was* a check. Furthermore he wondered where the hell Richard was getting the money to pay for his new clothes, not to mention this party. The guy was supposed to be broke. Well, maybe he had a chargecard he hadn't told them about.

As for Richard's staying on, Savannah insisted it'd only be a few days. Richard needed to recuperate, rest up. To hear her tell it, you'd think he'd been working on a chain gang for the past six years and was practically at death's door. Judging by the energy his kid brother displayed on the dance floor, he'd recovered quickly, Grady thought.

The beer flowed free and easy. Grady was on his second bottle himself: The Chili Pepper's spicy barbecue sauce sizzled on the large tin-drum grills, filling the air with a spicy smoky aroma. The dinner line extended halfway around the house.

Those who weren't eating or dancing mingled in the yard, making themselves at home. Grady had originally decided not to participate in Richard's party, but his standoffishness hadn't lasted long.

Cal and Glen Patterson, neighboring ranchers and friends, arrived then. They sat with him on the porch steps. Grady couldn't remember the last time he'd shot the breeze with the brothers. The three of them had grown up together and remained close to this day. As close as Grady allowed anyone to get.

"I didn't think you'd ever welcome Richard back," Cal said, leaning back, a beer in one hand. Cal and the sheriff were the only two who knew about Richard's theft. It wasn't the kind of information you shared about family.

"I didn't welcome him back." Grady wanted that understood right then and there. This party wasn't his idea.

Grady noticed Sheriff Hennessey twirling Dovie Boyd around the dance floor. His opinion of the lawman had fallen several degrees when he'd failed to turn up anything on Smith. If the man was doing his job, he grumbled to himself, Frank would be down at the office right this minute, instead of partying.

"If you aren't responsible for this welcoming, then whose idea was it?" Cal asked. "Savannah's?"

"Nope. Richard organized it himself." Grady took another swallow of beer. The cold brew helped relieve his growing sense of frustration. Again he wondered how Richard intended to pay for all this. Surely he wasn't expecting *him* to foot the bill. That would be too brazen even for Richard.

His mistake, Grady realized, was giving in and allowing Richard to stay that first night. Now his younger brother had manipulated him once again—made it look as if Grady had welcomed him back with open arms. As far as he was concerned, Richard couldn't leave soon enough.

Savannah had been slaving in the kitchen since before dawn. Neighbors he hadn't seen in months had brought over pies, cakes and an assortment of side dishes; they'd delivered picnic tables and dozens of lawn chairs. And now Grady was indebted to each and every one of them. His neighbors would be looking for return favors, too. Especially of the social kind. It wouldn't take long for the invites to arrive, and he'd be expected to accept. Damn it all. He'd never been a party goer and didn't intend to start now.

"What I'd like to know," Grady muttered to his friends, "is how the hell he's paying for all this."

"Did you ask him?" Glen, the younger of the Patterson brothers, inquired.

"I didn't have a chance." The party was happening before Grady even knew there was going to be one. If he'd had a clue what his brother was up to, he would have put a stop to it. The last time he'd seen this many people had been the day he buried his parents. Leave it to Richard to dredge up the most pain-filled memory of his life.

"Who's that?" Glen asked, directing their attention to a blond woman walking in from the driveway. The row of cars stretched all the way to the road. Fifty at last count.

Grady didn't recognize the newcomer, either. She was young and pretty, if such attributes mattered to him, which they didn't. She didn't seem to know many people because she stood at the edge of the crowd, looking self-conscious in a pin-striped power suit. Whoever she was, she'd completely overdressed for the party.

Cal sat up and gave her a long stare. "Isn't that the new doc? Jane something-or-other."

"She's a doctor?" Glen asked with disbelief. "Promise has a lady doctor? When did all this happen?"

"Last week." Cal nudged his brother with an elbow. "Don't you two read the paper?"

"Who has time?" Grady wanted to know.

"Cal keeps the weekly edition by the john, don't you, big brother?" Glen teased.

"Well, it gets read, doesn't it?" Cal chided. "Her picture was on the front page. She's here on one of those government programs."

"What government program?"

"I don't know the name of it, but the paper said she agreed to work off her medical-school loans by volunteering her skill in a deprived area."

"Promise is a deprived area?" This was news to Grady.

"Must be," Cal muttered, sounding as surprised as Grady.

"Hey, we got a doctor who didn't fight in the battle for the Alamo?"

Doc Cummings had retired at the first of the year at the age of seventy. At least he admitted to being seventy, but in Grady's opinion, he was on the shady side of that figure. He'd delivered Grady and just about everyone else in town under forty. Rumor had it that Doc Cummings was lazing his days away on the Gulf coast now, eating shrimp and soaking up the sunshine. Grady wished the old coot well.

Caroline Daniels strolled past, carrying a bowl of potato salad. She returned a minute or so later with an empty one. Straining, Grady glanced into the kitchen and caught a glimpse of Savannah feverishly making another batch of salad. Smith was there with her, sitting at the table and dutifully peeling potatoes. Those two were as thick as thieves, despite all his warnings. His talk with Laredo Smith hadn't made any difference; he suspected Savannah was still planning a return visit to Bitter End. It hadn't been easy swallowing his pride and asking for Smith's help. The wrangler appeared to have gotten the wrong message, too, because he spent every available minute with Savannah, just as if Grady had given the pair his blessing. He hadn't. Despite his job offer, he wanted the other man off the ranch and the sooner the better.

"Are you going to dance with me or not?" Breathlessly Ellie Frasier plopped herself down next to Glen. They were good friends and had been for years. Grady had never understood how a man could be friends with a woman and not get romantically involved. But that seemed to be the way it was with Glen and Ellie. They were friends and nothing more.

Ellie needed a confidant these days, according to Cal. Her father was terminally ill and had been transferred to a hospital in San Antonio. Her mother was spending all her time there while Ellie ran the family store. Grady sympathized; he knew all too well the pain of losing a parent. Ellie was young to be taking on such heavy responsibility, but from what he heard, she was up to the task. She spent as much time as possible visiting her father, and between driving to San Antonio and managing the business, she was running herself ragged. It surprised him a little that Ellie was at the party, and he guessed Glen had something to do with that. Getting away from all the emotional pressures was probably the best thing for her.

"So what about that dance, Patterson?"

"Seems to me you've already got yourself a dance partner," Glen said. He stared pointedly in Richard's direction. Grady's brother was at his most charming, teasing and laughing with the women, exchanging jokes with the men. Outgoing, personable, the life of the party—and self-appointed guest of honor, to boot.

"I gotta say," Ellie said, speaking to Grady, "your brother's mighty light on his feet."

Yeah, in more ways than one. Grady was tempted to say it but didn't. He frowned, instead. Richard had been on the dance floor for hours without revealing any signs of slowing down. Grady suspected his brother had danced with every woman in town at least once, and the pretty ones twice. He'd taken a liking to Ellie, that was for sure. Grady had seen the two of them dancing three or four times already. He wanted to issue a word of caution, seeing how vulnerable Ellie must be feeling, but he bit his tongue. She'd find out soon enough what kind of man his brother was.

"I'd forgotten how much fun Richard could be," Ellie said.

"He's a regular laugh fest," Grady agreed sarcastically; he couldn't help it. Ellie studied him for a moment and he hoped she'd gotten the message.

"Don't mind Grady," Glen said, looping his arm around Ellie's shoulders. "He's just sore because he doesn't have anyone to dance with."

Grady's frown deepened. He wasn't about to make a fool of himself in front of the entire town. While Richard might know his way around a dance floor, Grady had been cursed with two left feet. The last time he'd attempted to dance he'd been in his teens and forced to wear a suit and boutonniere.

"I haven't seen this many people since the Willie Nelson Fourth of July picnic," Cal said. Like Grady, his friend wasn't much of a social animal. Glen was by far the most outgoing of the three men. He'd tried to drag Grady off to the town's biggest function—next to the cattlemen's dance and the rodeo—for the past six years. Every Fourth of July Promise threw a Willie Nelson picnic, hoping the popular entertainer would agree to visit. Willie had politely declined each year, but the town councillors hadn't let that deter them from holding the affair in the singer's honor.

"Come on," Ellie urged, tugging at Glen's hand. "I want to dance." With a show of reluctance, Glen untangled his feet and stood.

The pair were out of earshot when Cal spoke. "We won't see him the rest of the night. Once he's out on the floor, he won't quit."

"Go ahead if you feel like it," Grady told his friend. "No need to keep me company."

"No thanks. I'm happy to sit here for a while."

Cal lingered an hour or so, not that they said much. This was what Grady enjoyed most about his friend. They didn't have to fill every silence with idle chatter. A couple of times he was on the verge of mentioning Savannah's recent trek to the ghost town, but he held his tongue. The last time either one of them had talked about Bitter End, they'd been in their teens. Anyway, there wasn't anything Cal could tell him he didn't already know. Besides, Savannah was his concern, not his neighbor's. After a time Cal drifted away to get himself some barbecue.

Laughter and music abounded. It disgusted Grady to watch his brother. Richard continued to be sociable and entertaining, the focus of the party. It certainly hadn't taken him long to put the good people of Promise under his spell. Once again Grady wondered how his brother intended to pay for all this, but it wasn't his concern, and he wasn't going to worry about it.

The kitchen door opened and Caroline stepped outside. Her gaze caught Grady's; she waved, then walked over to where Adam Braunfels was handing out beer. She collected two.

Grady was somewhat surprised when she brought the extra bottle over to him. "You look like you could use this," she said, and sat down on the step beside him. She tucked one knee under her chin while her foot tapped to the beat of the music.

Grady saluted her with the bottle and took a long swallow of beer. Neither spoke for a few minutes; both of them just stared at the dance floor. Finally Caroline said, "He's really something, isn't he?"

"If you came over here to sing Richard's praises, I don't want to hear them."

"This might surprise you, Grady, but I'm not a fan of your brother's."

It *was* news to Grady, and he found himself grateful that at least one other person hadn't been blinded by Richard's charm. "I get the impression you aren't particularly fond of me, either," he said wryly.

She grinned. "I don't dislike you. I don't always agree with you, but you're not half-bad."

It wasn't much of a compliment, but Grady would take what he could get. "Hey, careful. Sweet talk just might turn my head."

Caroline burst into laughter.

Grady smiled for probably the first time that day. "So you're not one of Richard's adoring fans." Funny how that one bit of information encouraged him.

"If it was up to me, I'd string Richard up by his thumbs. Savannah's been stuck in the kitchen for hours. I don't think she had any idea what to expect. Richard had told her to plan for about 150 people—she assumed he was joking."

Right then and there Grady decided that, come morning, Richard was off the Yellow Rose. He didn't care how many arguments Savannah made in their brother's defense. They should've run him off the property the minute he set foot on their land. Grady shook his head. Surely Savannah would agree with him now.

"Maggie certainly seems to be taken with him," he noted, frowning as he brought the beer bottle to his lips. His younger brother danced with the five-year-old, twirling her about the floor. The youngster's shrieks of delight could be heard over the music. Richard's success with Maggie rankled, especially since the child ran away in terror whenever she laid eyes on Grady. Somehow or other, without realizing what he'd done, Grady had frightened the kid. For the life of him, he didn't know how it'd happened, and despite his efforts, he hadn't been able to repair the damage.

Caroline kept a close watch on her daughter. "She's easily swayed by charm, it seems."

"She isn't the only one."

"Are you jealous, Grady?"

"Hell, no," he protested before he had a chance to fully consider the question. On second thought, he had to admit there was a grain of truth in Caroline's words.

It was bad enough that Richard had implied—or outright said—that Grady and Savannah were throwing him this party. The fact that he had just about every woman in town fawning over him and almost every man eager for his company only added insult to injury.

"I don't suppose I could convince you to take a spin," Caroline said, motioning with her head toward the dance floor.

"Not on your life."

Caroline sighed as though disappointed. "That's what I thought."

"Hey, you don't need me." He gestured toward a group of single men standing under a live oak tree. "Any one of them would be happy to dance with you."

"I suppose." But she didn't budge and, truth be known, he was glad she didn't. He thought of inviting her to go bowling with him—that would be more to his liking—but hesitated. It'd been so damn long since he'd gone out on a date he wasn't sure how to go about asking.

Then it dawned on Grady that maybe Caroline was interested in him. "Are you saying you want to dance with *me?*" In other circumstances he probably wouldn't have asked, but he'd downed three beers on an almost empty stomach and his inhibitions were definitely lowered.

"I might be," she responded.

He mulled over her answer. He liked Caroline, admired her for the good friend she was to Savannah, and while he'd certainly noticed her, found her attractive, he'd never thought to make anything of it.

"You should get married," he said, and for the life of him, Grady didn't know what had prompted him to suggest such a thing. Horrified, he stared down at his empty beer bottle.

"Do you have anyone in mind?" Caroline asked.

"Not me." He wanted that understood.

"Don't worry, Grady, you aren't in the running."

He'd asked for that, but he didn't like hearing it. Then, thinking he should resolve this before things got out of hand, he decided to explain. "Maggie needs a father."

Caroline was on her feet so fast it made his head spin. "Don't tell me what my daughter needs or doesn't need, Grady."

"Fine, I won't."

"Good," she declared, and stomped away.

Women! They had to have the last word. But after Caroline left, Grady regretted the conversation. Worse, he knew he was one hundred percent at fault. He should never have said the things he had. It wasn't his place to suggest Maggie needed a father. It had made him sound judgmental or disapproving when that wasn't his intent at all. He respected Caroline; he just thought her life as a working single mother was too hard. And he hated the way little Maggie seemed so susceptible to any man's charm. Any *con* man's charm. Well, nothing he could do about it now.

The sun set and after a while someone lit the Chinese lanterns. The lights swayed in a soft breeze, casting shadows that danced about the yard. The band switched from lively melodies and line dances to slower, more mellow songs. Couples, wrapped in each other's arms, slowly circled the floor.

Families with young children packed up their youngsters and started home, prompted by thoughts of work and school in the morning. Playing the role of gracious host to a T, Richard escorted them to their cars, then stood in the driveway and waved them off.

"Nice party," Adam Braunfels said as Grady headed toward the house, around nine o'clock.

"Not *my* party," he was quick to tell the owner of Chili Pepper.

"I hope everything was satisfactory," Adam said next.

Grady tucked his hands in his back pockets. "Great. I certainly didn't hear any complaints."

"Good. I want you to know I was as fair as I could be with the tally."

Grady didn't know what Adam was talking about or, rather, why Adam was telling *him*, but he nodded his head, which had started to pound. He hadn't eaten since breakfast and his mind continued to dwell on his disastrous conversation with Caroline.

Adam pulled a slip of paper from his hip pocket and handed it to

Grady. "I'd appreciate if you could write me a check now, Grady, before I go back to town."

"What?" He was sure there'd been some mistake.

"For the barbecue," Adam explained as if he were dense. Grady knew why he wanted to be paid; what he didn't understand was why Adam expected *him* to do it.

"I already said this wasn't my party."

Adam's mouth thinned. "I don't care whose party it is, I need my money."

"And you expect me to pay?"

"Yes."

"This is Richard's business." Grady was about to walk off when Richard raced to their side.

"I need my money," Adam repeated, looking from one brother to the other.

Richard's feet shifted nervously. "Would you mind paying him, Grady?" he asked. "I honestly thought my check would be here before now." He looked down at his boots. "I . . . I feel horrible about this."

Arms folded, Adam stared at Grady, ignoring Richard completely.

Grady felt as though the top of his head was about to explode. He had no choice but to pay up. His brother had done it to him again. Either he wrote Adam a check now or he came off looking like the bad guy.

LAREDO WAS ELBOW DEEP in the kitchen sink when Frank Hennessey walked into the room. The sheriff nodded politely at Savannah, who sat with her feet propped up on a chair. It was the first time all day Laredo could get her to take a break. He knew she was exhausted. Hell, he was himself, and he hadn't worked near as hard as she had.

While he hadn't been particularly fond of Richard before, Laredo actively disliked him now. He'd been around men like the younger Weston in his time. Fast talkers. Users. Selfish and thoughtless. Richard certainly knew which buttons to push when it came to his sister, Laredo had noticed. All he had to do was mention their mother, and Savannah crumbled. It infuriated him to watch the jerk take advantage of her that way.

Laredo knew Grady was on to Richard, but he suspected Savannah wasn't. Even if she did find out what kind of man her brother was, she was perfectly capable of overlooking it, and that worried Laredo.

"If you don't mind, Mr. Smith, I've got a few questions I'd like to ask you," the sheriff said.

A little confused, Laredo lifted his hands from the dishwater and reached for a towel. He didn't like the idea of the sheriff singling him out, but he didn't want to make a fuss in front of Savannah, either.

"Is there a problem, Sheriff?" Savannah asked, looking concerned.

"No, no." Hennessey caught Laredo's glance. "Perhaps you'd like to step outside, Mr. Smith."

"Sure." Laredo dried his hands and squelched his growing sense of irritation. Grady had put the lawman up to this; he'd admitted it earlier himself. Not that Laredo had anything to hide, but he hated the way it made him look to Savannah.

He waited until they were in the cool night air before he spoke. "I don't have any kind of record."

"Wrong," the lawman was quick to correct him. "You ran a red light back in 1995."

Stuffing his hands in his back hip pockets, Laredo glared at the sheriff. "I stand corrected."

Hennessey ignored the sarcasm. "I got a couple of questions for you."

"Fire away." Laredo clamped his teeth together, anger simmering.

"How long do you plan to stay in Promise?"

"As long as I damn well please." His tolerance for this kind of treatment was gone.

"Listen, Smith, it won't do you any good to get smart-mouthed with me. If you want trouble, you don't need to look any farther than right here. I can make enough trouble to last you a lifetime. Now I suggest you check your attitude." He gave him a moment to let the warning take hold, then repeated the question.

"I plan on heading out as soon as I can pay for the repairs to my truck." Laredo kept his voice a monotone and trained his gaze on the barn door.

The lawman's crisp voice mellowed when he next spoke. "Miss Savannah's a mighty fine woman."

Laredo's eyes clashed with the sheriff's. "You think I don't know that?"

"No one wants to see her hurt."

"I don't, either," Laredo said. He didn't understand why everyone assumed he'd purposely do anything to hurt Savannah.

"For reasons I can't quite grasp, she seems to have taken a liking to you. But if you're leaving soon, I figure you'll be gone before there's any real damage done."

Laredo kept his mouth shut, knowing the lawman would use anything he said against him.

"Look, I know I'm speaking out of turn here, Smith. It's none of my affair when you come or go. All I'm saying is that a lot of folks around here think highly of Savannah. No one wants to see her used, especially by a drifter who'll desert her without a second thought. You get what I'm saying?"

Laredo pressed his lips tightly closed in order to hold his tongue.

"Good. Like I said, Savannah's the sweetest gentlest soul in these parts, and if you or anyone else decides to take advantage of her, you'll answer directly to me. You got that, boy?"

Laredo's shoulders ached because of the stiff way he held his back. It'd been a lot of years since anyone had called him "boy." Laredo hadn't liked it then and liked it even less now.

"You heard me?" Sheriff Hennessey asked, more forcefully this time.

"Loud and clear."

The lawman nodded and slapped Laredo amiably on the shoulder. "I'm glad we had this little talk. Now you go back to whatever you were doing, and I'll give Miss Dovie one last spin around the dance floor."

Laredo didn't comment. He stood rigid and angry while the sheriff strolled away.

"Laredo?" Savannah said his name softly as she joined him. "Is there a problem?" The distress in her voice melted away his anger. Hennessey was only speaking his mind, prompted, of course, by Grady. The long hours he'd spent working with Roanie hadn't been enough to prove himself to Savannah's brother. But Laredo didn't imagine Grady was ever going to accept him, no matter what he did. Not that it was necessary, other than to ease Savannah's mind. The situation weighed heavily on her, and for that reason alone, it bothered Laredo.

"Everything's fine," he told her.

"You sure?"

"Positive." He took her hand and led her to the porch swing, then sat down beside her. After a few moments he slipped his arm around her shoulders and she rested her head against his chest. To hell with Grady Weston, Laredo decided. He was holding Savannah and he didn't give a damn *what* her older brother thought.

Despite his defiant attitude, Laredo had taken the sheriff at his word. Hennessey could easily make trouble for him. He wasn't looking to cause problems, but he wasn't going to run off with his tail dragging between his legs, either.

Savannah was quiet, and after a moment he assumed she'd gone to sleep. Content to hold her, Laredo entertained himself by watching the party, which was still in progress, although the numbers had dwindled considerably. He figured things must be winding down.

When the band took a break before their final set, Richard brought out his guitar. Taking advantage of the more or less captive audience, he started playing. A dozen people gathered around him. A few children, including Maggie, camped at his feet. A sing-along ensued, and Richard performed several of the songs he'd massacred a few nights earlier in the bunkhouse. Only this time he managed to do a respectable job of carrying a tune, and the words were recognizable.

Twenty minutes later the band returned, and the lead singer encouraged all the men to bring their sweethearts onto the floor. Laredo watched as Richard chose Ellie Frasier—and even managed to steal a kiss when he thought no one was looking. He didn't dance with Ellie long, though, changing partners and dancing with several elderly ladies and then with Maggie and a few of the other children still at the party. The little girls' delight at having the guest of honor pay them such attention sounded in their excited shrieks. The guy was smooth, Laredo gave him that.

"Is this the sweetheart dance?" Savannah asked him, lifting her head from his shoulder.

"That's what he said."

She sighed deeply. Laredo had never been much of a ladies' man, but he knew what that sigh meant. Savannah wanted to dance the sweetheart dance with him, but she wouldn't ask. He had to be the one to invite her.

Damn, he wasn't any good at this romance stuff, but he hated to disappoint Savannah. Nor was he good at dancing. It always made him feel awkward and uncomfortable. Especially in front of an audience. And especially when it was this slow music.

Rather than disillusion her, though, Laredo stood and extended his hand in a courtly fashion. "May I have the honor of this dance?"

Her responding smile was worth any embarrassment he might bring on himself, Laredo decided. Savannah's beautiful blue eyes filled with happiness. "Does this mean I'm your sweetheart, Laredo Smith?" she asked softly.

Hennessey's words of warning echoed in his ears. But hell, the man could arrest him for all he cared just then. "It must."

Savannah placed her hand in his and stood.

"Be warned, I might step on your foot," he muttered under his breath as they approached the dance floor.

"I suggest you watch your own feet. It's been a long time since I did anything like this."

Laredo should have known Savannah would find a way to put him at ease. Being with her always made him feel . . . special. As though he alone, of all men, was worthy of this good and beautiful woman. Right this minute he could almost believe it. . . .

Several couples swayed to the romantic music, holding each other close. One couple was deeply involved in a kiss.

Laredo drew her into his arms and concentrated on moving his feet in a box step, mentally counting to four. One step back, one step to the right, one step forward and then to the left.

"Laredo," she whispered in his ear, wrapping her arms around his neck. "Relax, okay?"

"But—"

"All I really wanted was for you to hold me."

That was all he wanted, too. He shut his eyes and pulled her into the shadows. He kissed her ear, smiling when he felt her shiver.

"Like that, do you?"

"Oh, yes."

He rubbed her back.

"I like that, too."

Laredo was just beginning to feel that he had the hang of this when she captured his earlobe between her lips and gently sucked on it. His eyes flew open and his blood went hot. He slowly let the breath drain from his lungs, then locked his hands at the small of her back. Soon she was flush against him. With her softness touching him like that, in the most intimate places, Laredo lost count of the steps. Not long afterward, he discontinued dancing altogether, other than to shuffle his feet a little.

"Laredo," she whispered. "I'm glad Grady asked you to stay. I'm glad for a lot of reasons."

"Me, too," he whispered. "So glad . . ."

The song continued and he closed his eyes again, wanting to savor these moments. His heart felt so full it actually hurt. Until now, with Savannah in his embrace, Laredo hadn't thought such a possibility existed. But his heart ached. Not with grief or pain but with love.

Of all the memories that could have come to him at a time like this, the one that did was of his father. The last memory he had of his father still alive.

Laredo had been a young boy when his father left for Vietnam. He didn't understand about war; all he knew was that the man he adored was going away. He'd hidden in the barn, thinking if no one could find him, maybe his father wouldn't have to leave. Naturally his childish plan hadn't worked, and he'd been found in short order.

Then his dad had taken him on his lap and held him for a long time without saying a word. When he did speak, he'd promised Laredo that, no matter what happened while he was away, nothing—not distance, not time, not even death—would separate Laredo from his father's love.

Months later, when Laredo had stood in front of a cold casket and watched his father's body lowered into the ground, he'd recalled those words. At the memorial service he'd stood proud and tall. His mother and grandparents had wept, overcome with grief, but Laredo's eyes had remained dry.

Emotion welled up inside him now and he understood, perhaps for the first time, the intensity of the love his parents had shared. The depth of it. With this revelation came the knowledge that he felt the same way about Savannah. His mother had never remarried, and Laredo finally understood why.

A gruff voice broke into his thoughts and he lifted his head from Savannah's to see her older brother standing by the side of the dance floor.

"I don't like the way you're holding my sister."

Laredo released Savannah. Grady Weston's face was flushed and angry.

"Grady, please!" Savannah reluctantly moved away from Laredo. "You're making a scene and embarrassing me."

"Leave us alone," Laredo warned. Their eyes met, challenged, clashed. His willingness to make peace with Grady had vanished after that talk with the sheriff.

Before he realized exactly how it had happened, he and Grady were facing off, their fists raised.

"Grady, stop!" Savannah cried, and when it did no good, she turned to Laredo. "If you care for me, you won't do this."

Laredo did care, so damn much it terrified him. But this was one fight he wasn't walking away from.

"Please," Savannah said, stepping directly in front of him.

Laredo felt himself weakening.

Caroline Daniels arrived then and slid her arm through Grady's. "It seems to me that what you need is a nice hot cup of coffee," she announced, steering him toward the kitchen.

Laredo watched the two of them walk toward the house.

Savannah slipped her arms back around Laredo's neck. "I believe this dance was mine," she said, nestling close to him once more.

A lot more than this dance belonged to Savannah Weston, Laredo realized. She also owned his heart.

Seven

The early-morning sun shone cheerfully on the Yellow Rose. Savannah had been much too tired the night before to worry about cleanup, but in the revealing light of day, the entire front yard was a disaster. The Chinese lanterns sagged. Paper plates and napkins littered the once-flawless grass amid a welter of abandoned tables and chairs. The straw from the dance area stretched like a spider web from one end of the lawn to the other.

While the coffee brewed, Savannah dragged a garbage can into the yard. She'd only been working ten or fifteen minutes when Grady joined her. Wiley and Laredo followed, yawning. Savannah quickly distributed plastic garbage bags, since there was far too much trash for one container.

"Where's Richard?" Grady demanded.

"Sleeping," Wiley said with a chuckle. "What did you expect?" He began picking up litter and stuffing it into a bag.

"Then drag his sorry ass out here. It was his party. The least he can do is clean up the mess he created."

"Why should he start now?" Again the question came from Wiley.

"I got better things to do than this," Grady grumbled, stuffing his own armload of garbage into a bag.

"I didn't hire on to do housekeeping, either," the foreman put in.

Savannah had heard enough. "Stop it—both of you!" she shouted, unable to bear the bickering. It was rare for her to raise her voice, let alone yell, and she immediately got everyone's attention. Grady and Wiley stopped and stared at her; even Rocket lifted his head, as if shocked by her outburst.

A frown creasing his brow, Laredo paused in his raking and waited.

"I didn't ask for your help," she said. "If you're going to complain, then leave. I'd rather tend to the cleanup myself than be subjected to your foul moods." The comment was directed at Grady. Her good feeling about her brother—the fact that he'd hired Laredo—was rapidly fading.

"I'm in one hell of a fine mood," Grady barked, grimacing in a parody of a smile. "I'm as happy as can be." Savannah thought he looked like he was posing for the cover of *Mad* magazine, but restrained herself from saying so.

"You're happy?" Wiley asked, his words drenched with sarcasm. "You look about as happy as when you wrote out that check to Adam Braunfels for the barbecue."

This was the first Savannah had heard about it. "Why'd you pay Adam?"

"I didn't have any choice," Grady snapped. "He wanted his money and Sleeping Beauty in there—" he gestured at the bunkhouse "—didn't have it. What the hell else could I do?"

Savannah wished she hadn't asked, since the money was obviously a sore spot with Grady. Not that she blamed him, but surely Richard expected his check soon, otherwise he wouldn't have thrown himself this party.

"It was good of you to pay Adam," she said, wanting Grady to know she appreciated his dilemma. "Money's tight just now."

"My money got even tighter with the party," Grady muttered. "I hope to hell he doesn't expect me to pay for everything, because I won't do it." He sounded as though he wasn't sure who he was trying to convince, her or himself.

"Richard will make good on it," Savannah felt obliged to say. Her younger brother had made plenty of mistakes, but he'd learned his lesson. At least that was what he claimed—and what she desperately wanted to believe.

Although the party had drained her physically and emotionally, she'd enjoyed watching Richard with their neighbors. He'd been a gracious host, warm and welcoming, and it gave her a sense of pride. He was like their father in that way—although admittedly not in others.

Mel Weston had always been the life of the party. Friendly, charming, universally loved. Her world had gone dark without him there—to call her his princess, to give her encouragement and approval and unconditional love. Having Richard home again produced a flood of happy memories and she didn't want those destroyed. Not if she could help it. So she was willing to give him the benefit of the doubt.

Everyone had mentioned what fun Richard was and how the children had adored him, especially Maggie. Seeing them together had done

Savannah's heart good. The five-year-old tended to shy away from men, but she'd taken to Richard at first meeting, and he'd been wonderful with her, paying her lots of attention.

"I kissed that money goodbye the minute I signed the check," Grady grumbled, telling her in no uncertain terms that he continued to distrust Richard.

"He'll pay you back," Savannah insisted.

Grady stared at her long enough to make her uncomfortable. "When are you going to learn, Savannah? What's it going to take? Richard's a user. He'll never amount to anything because he's never been made accountable. I want him off this ranch, understand?"

"You're wrong, Grady. Richard might have a few bad habits—we all do—but he has a good heart. I refuse to believe otherwise."

"Don't kid yourself. As soon as he's awake, I want him to pack up and leave. I've paid his debts for the last time."

"You don't mean that!" Savannah couldn't believe her brother could be so hard.

"I want him gone by noon."

"Grady . . . please." Her voice cracked with emotion. "Don't do this."

"I'm not giving in to you this time," Grady said, stuffing more garbage deep into the plastic bag.

Savannah jumped at the fierce anger she heard in him.

"Don't talk to her like that," Laredo demanded, walking over to Savannah. The animosity between him and Grady was worse than ever, Savannah knew. She had no idea what had possessed her brother to cause a scene on the dance floor.

In a replay of last night Laredo and Grady glared at each other with mutual dislike.

"What do you suggest we do?" Wiley asked her, apparently finding the men's behavior amusing. "Get a hose and cool 'em both down?"

"That doesn't sound like a bad idea," Savannah responded, grateful for his sense of humor in this tense situation.

"Okay." Wiley took charge. "We're done here," he said, stepping directly in front of Laredo.

Savannah thought Laredo might challenge the foreman, but after a short hesitation he nodded and set aside the rake. As he turned to head for the barn, he caught her watching him and winked.

Savannah blushed with pleasure, remembering the dance they'd shared. After spending all day and most of the evening in the kitchen, her hair damp with sweat and her clothes spattered with mustard and mayonnaise, she must have looked a sight. Yet he'd called her his sweet-heart and looked at her as if she were beautiful. Savannah had always known she was no beauty. She'd never been one to turn men's heads, and being shy had made it worse.

Over time she'd given up hope she'd ever find love. She'd never felt real attraction for a man, and as far as she knew, had never inspired it, either. All these years she'd been certain that a husband and family were for others and not for her. Her roses and her pets had become like her children. Grady constantly complained about the way she spoiled Rocket, but the dog was old, and if he was more comfortable in the house, she had no objection to letting him inside. And although Grady complained, she noticed that he was as guilty as she was about sneaking him leftovers.

Her musings returned to Laredo, and her heart softened at the thought of him. In less than two weeks, he'd changed her life, given her reason to dream, given her the most precious of human emotions—hope.

She loved him. It was that simple. That profound.

"I suppose you're waiting for me to apologize for making an ass of myself last night," Grady said, breaking into her thoughts. She'd almost forgotten he was there.

"You owe Laredo and me an apology."

He paused, then to her amazement, agreed with her. "I suppose I do. My only excuse is that I was furious with Richard and took it out on Laredo. I realize I acted like an idiot. I don't have any excuse other than I'd been drinking on an empty stomach."

The irony of it, Savannah mused, was that Grady had ended up paying for a dinner he hadn't bothered to taste.

"I'd be obliged if we could put the incident behind us," he said stiffly.

"On one condition."

He held up his hand to stop her. "I already know. You want me to apologize to Laredo."

"You didn't start this morning any better than you left off last night."

"I know." He wiped a hand down his face and she noticed that his eyes were tired and sad, and she wondered if he'd gotten any sleep whatsoever. "I'll talk to him later."

"What do you have against him?" she asked, genuinely curious. "Laredo isn't anything like you think. He's thoughtful and hardworking and—"

"Do you mind if I listen to you sing his praises some other time?" Grady asked from between clenched teeth.

"Oh, Grady." It was then she realized her brother was suffering from a hangover. After his confrontation with Laredo, he'd apparently continued drinking—and probably not beer, either. The first moment she could Savannah had escaped to her room, taken a quick shower and fallen into bed. She'd fallen asleep immediately but woke periodically throughout the night. At least tired was all she felt—not hung over, like Grady.

"Yeah," he groaned. "I had a few drinks after everyone went home. Figured it'd calm me down. It didn't. But guess what? I found there was booze missing—my good single-malt Scotch. Where do you think it went?"

Savannah shook her head.

"Starts with 'R.' "

"Oh, no. Are you *sure?*"

Grady gave her a cynical look and returned to his garbage collecting.

When the cleanup was finished, Grady grabbed a cup of coffee and headed about his day; Savannah went back to the house. It was almost eleven before Richard bothered to make an appearance.

"Good morning, my beautiful Savannah!" He kissed her noisily on the cheek, then hopped onto the kitchen counter, bare feet dangling while he nursed a mug of coffee. "What's for breakfast?"

"It's almost time for lunch."

He didn't react. "I was looking forward to sampling some of those fluffy scrambled eggs of yours. I woke up dreaming about eggs all gooey with melted cheese and toasted homemade bread."

"Richard," she said, angry with him and needing to let him know, "how could you have left Grady to pay Mr. Braunfels for the barbecue?"

"I feel really bad about that. I explained the situation to Adam earlier, and he seemed okay with me paying when I could. I wonder what happened to make him change his mind."

She wanted so much to believe Richard, but it was becoming more and more difficult.

He must have realized that, because he leaped down off the counter, crossed the room and reached for her hand. "Savannah," he said, holding her gaze, "I promise you by everything I hold dear that I'll reimburse Grady the minute my check arrives. You've got to trust me."

She wanted to, but the doubts refused to go away.

"You're the only one who believes in me," Richard said in obvious distress. "If it wasn't for you, Grady would have kicked me off the ranch that first day. Give me this opportunity to prove myself, that's all I'm asking."

Savannah studied her brother, hoping against hope that he'd fulfill his promises.

The beginnings of a smile lit up his eyes. "I can hardly wait to see the look on Grady's face when I give him the money. Won't he be shocked?" He laughed as if viewing the scene that very moment.

Savannah relaxed. Richard was her brother. He'd made mistakes, painful ones, but he was older now, mature. He couldn't help his impulsive sociable nature—couldn't resist throwing that party. However, he wouldn't take advantage of her and Grady a second time, she was sure of it.

"Do you believe me?" The color of his eyes intensified as his gaze implored her to give him the benefit of the doubt.

Savannah couldn't refuse him. "I believe you," she whispered, and silently prayed he wouldn't let her down.

Richard squeezed her hand. "You won't be sorry, Savannah, I promise you. I'm going to prove Grady all wrong, just you wait and see. Then you can say 'I told you so' to our high-and-mighty brother. You trusted me when no one else would, and someday you'll be able to laugh in Grady's face."

"I'd never do that." Her older brother might be strong-willed and opinionated, but his intentions were good.

"Are you going to scramble me up some of my favorite cheese eggs?" he asked in a cajoling voice.

She'd finished washing the breakfast dishes fifteen minutes earlier. "All right," she conceded. Richard gave her a hug, then climbed back onto the counter while she took the eggs, cheese and milk from the refrigerator.

"I was looking around your garden and noticed some of those roses you were telling me about. Where'd you find those pretty white ones?"

"Oh, this place and that," she said, and while she was pleased by his interest, the less he knew about her venture into Bitter End the better.

"You went there, didn't you?" he asked, lowering his voice.

"There?"

"Don't play games with me, Savannah. You're no good at it."

Her cheeks flushed hot pink. Richard was right, she'd never been any good at games. He was curious about the ghost town and this wasn't the first time he'd bombarded her with questions. Some about roses, others about the town itself.

"Did you go inside any of the buildings?" Richard asked. "They're still standing, right? Imagine that after all these years. What stories those walls could tell! It amazes me, you know, that Bitter End could be sleeping in those hills with only a handful of people even knowing about its existence."

"It is rather remarkable," Savannah agreed.

"I bet the buildings were in sad shape?"

"I didn't investigate the town itself," she said. The cemetery was as far as she got. Whatever was there had driven her back before she'd set foot in the actual town. But she'd know the answer to her brother's questions soon enough. Today was it, she'd decided. She was going back for a second visit, despite all Grady's efforts to keep her away.

"So where exactly is it?" Richard asked.

"Oh, sort of east of here," she said vaguely. "I had a hard time finding it." That was all she planned to say on the matter.

"Weren't you afraid?" he teased.

She wasn't sure how to describe her wariness. "Not really," she said, downplaying the eerie sensation she'd experienced on her first visit. She added the beaten eggs to the small skillet as the butter sizzled.

"I really don't think visiting the place again is a good idea," Richard surprised her by saying. Not that *she* wanted him there, but a few days ago, he'd certainly been dropping hints to that effect. He buttered the toast when it popped up and sat down at the table, awaiting his breakfast.

"I *have* to go back," she said, surprised she had to fight Richard on this, too. Grady and Laredo had formed an uneasy partnership in their efforts to keep her from returning. "There're bound to be other roses," she explained, although it wasn't necessary. All three men knew her reasons. "I might find an even rarer form. I can't tell you how thrilled I was with my original discovery."

"Think carefully before you go back," Richard said, smiling gratefully when she set the plate of steaming eggs in front of him. "You'd be wise to heed Grady's advice, Savannah. A ghost town isn't any place for you to go exploring alone."

"Earlier you said you wanted to come along. You—"

"I said that?" He flattened his hand against his chest. "Not me. I'm as chicken as they come. You won't catch me anywhere close to Bitter End. I have a healthy respect for the supernatural."

Savannah refused to be dissuaded, but she didn't intend to discuss it further. She'd do what she did the last time—steal away before anyone knew she was gone.

GRADY SAT IN HIS OFFICE and pinched the bridge of his nose, hoping that would help him focus on the long row of ledger numbers. He hadn't slept more than a couple of hours the entire night. Instead, he'd been leaning over the toilet, examining parts of it that were never meant to be viewed from this perspective.

Hard liquor had never agreed with him. Especially in quantity. After he'd embarrassed himself and Savannah, he'd holed up in his office with a bottle of cheap whiskey. The good stuff had disappeared, as he'd told his sister—but he hadn't been in any mood to appreciate the difference.

This morning his head throbbed with a vengeance. He couldn't think, couldn't work. Richard had been back less than a week, and already Grady was reduced to a useless piece of . . . He didn't finish the thought.

The phone pealed and he slammed his eyes closed as the sound pierced his brain, shattering what little serenity he'd managed to recover. He waited for Savannah to answer.

No one knew he was in his office, and that was the way he wanted it.

The phone rang a second time and then a third. Where the hell was Savannah? If not her, Richard? Rather than suffer the agony of a fourth ring, Grady grabbed the receiver.

"Who the hell is it?" he snarled.

A shocked silence greeted him, followed by a sob, then tears and "Mommy, Mommy."

Damn. It'd been Maggie for Savannah, and he'd frightened the poor kid half out of her wits.

"Maggie," he shouted, wanting to apologize for his outburst. Apologize was all he seemed to do these days. He felt faint stirrings of hope when he heard someone pick up the receiver.

"Maggie, listen—"

"It's Caroline," she interrupted coolly. "And this must be Grady." She didn't give him a chance to respond before she added, "What exactly did you say to Maggie to upset her like this?"

"I didn't know. I thought . . ." Even his tongue refused to work properly.

"Obviously you *didn't* think."

He could hear Maggie softly weeping in the background.

"I'm sorry, Caroline," he said. "Hell, I didn't know it was Maggie. I certainly didn't mean to frighten her."

"What's gotten into you, Grady?"

He braced his forehead against his hand. If the answer was that simple, he would've saved himself a great deal of embarrassment. The truth was he didn't know any longer.

"You made an ass of yourself last night."

"Nice of you to remind me." Leave it to a woman to kick a man when he was down.

"You had too much to drink."

"You brought me one of those beers," he felt obliged to remind her.

"So this is all *my* fault?"

Grady closed his eyes at her outrage. "No," he admitted, feeling about as low as a man could get. "I accept full responsibility."

The silence stretched between them until Caroline slowly released a deep breath and asked, "Where's Savannah?"

"I don't know. I expected her to pick up the phone." Clearly so had Maggie, who continued to weep noisily in the background.

"Is she all right?" Caroline asked.

"She was this morning." And not afraid to set him down a peg or two, although he knew he'd asked for it.

Maggie's cries subsided into soft muffled sounds.

"What are you doing home?" he asked Caroline. She should be at the post office, but then, he wasn't one to talk, seeing as he should be out on the range with Wiley. Or working in the barn with Laredo Smith.

"Maggie wasn't feeling well this morning, so I took the day off."

"How's she doing?"

"She's feeling better—or she was," Caroline said pointedly.

"I'd like to talk to her if you'd let me, so I can apologize." He wasn't sure he knew *how* to talk to a five-year-old, but he didn't want her cringing in terror every time she was out at the ranch. She was a sweet little girl and Savannah was deeply attached to her.

"I don't know if she'll talk to you."

"Ask her, will you?" His hand tightened around the receiver while he waited. In the background he could hear Caroline reasoning with the child. He was somewhat amused when he heard her compare him to the beast in *Beauty and the Beast*. He made a lot of loud noises and sounded mean, Caroline said, but deep down he was really a prince who'd been put under a spell.

Caroline returned to the phone a couple of minutes later. "I'm sorry, Grady, but I can't convince her to give you a second chance."

"I can't say I blame her," Grady said with a sigh. "I was pretty rough when I answered."

"She called to tell Savannah she had a tummy ache."

"My kind of sympathy wasn't what she was looking for, was it."

The sound of Caroline's half chuckle did more to lift his spirits than anything had that day.

"I guess you could say that," she said softly.

"I have been a beast, haven't I."

"You could say that, too."

"Since she won't let me talk to her, will you tell Maggie I'm sorry? I promise I won't shout at her again." He didn't know if it would do any good, but it was the best he could manage. The next time Maggie visited the ranch, he'd try to square things with her.

"I'll let Savannah know you phoned," he said, reaching for a pen. If he didn't write it down, he'd forget, and he didn't think Caroline would be willing to forgive him that on top of everything else.

They exchanged goodbyes and he replaced the receiver.

With an effort he glanced down at the ledger and reached for the calculator, determined to make good use of his time. He couldn't laze in bed until noon like his worthless brother.

LAREDO ASSUMED he'd find Savannah in the rose garden, but she was nowhere in sight. Nor was she in the house. He'd done everything short of knocking on her bedroom door.

Grady had disappeared, as well, but that was more a blessing than a matter of concern.

Unsure where to search next, Laredo headed back to the barn. It was one of the last places he expected to find Savannah. A niggling sense of fear refused to leave him. She'd looked pale that morning, and although he hadn't been eager to clash with Grady so soon after their last confrontation, he wasn't about to let him harass Savannah.

The barn door creaked as he pushed it open. Light spilled into the interior and Savannah spun around. Her eyes instantly widened with guilt.

Laredo had no idea what she'd been doing, but clearly it was something she didn't want anyone knowing.

"Savannah?"

"Hi." Her smile was a bit sheepish.

"What are you doing in here?"

"Nothing. I was—"

"Savannah," he said, and held out his arms, needing to reassure her. She didn't hesitate, not so much as a second. He brought her into his embrace and hugged her. "Don't ever play poker, sweetheart. Your expression's a dead giveaway."

Her arms circled his waist and she pressed her face to his shoulder. "I'm so sorry about what happened last night," she said.

This was the first chance they'd had to discuss the incident, but Laredo preferred to drop the entire thing. He'd been at fault, too, eager to put her brother in his place for embarrassing Savannah. And he'd been angry after his chat with Hennessey, knowing Grady had instigated the sheriff's questioning.

"Let's put it behind us, okay?"

He felt her deep sigh. "Is that what you want?" she asked in a solemn voice.

"Yeah."

"I'm willing to forget it—except for one thing." She tilted her head back and gazed at him with wide adoring eyes.

"What's that?" Laredo didn't know what he'd done to deserve having such a beautiful woman look at him that way.

"I could put the . . . incident behind me if Grady hadn't cheated me out of my sweetheart dance."

"Not all of it."

"I begrudge every second he stole from me."

Laredo kissed the top of her head and reached behind him to take hold of her hands. "Don't you hear the music?" he asked.

"Music?" Her eyes narrowed as if she was straining to hear before she realized what he was doing. She smiled then, and it was all he could do not to cover her mouth with his.

"I believe there *is* music in here," she said, her face alight with happiness.

"There must be."

Laredo danced her about the barn floor, making turns so wide that her skirt flared straight out as they whirled around. Savannah threw back her head and laughed with such pure joy Laredo was soon smiling himself.

They whirled faster and faster until they were both winded and ready to collapse with laughter. Savannah pressed her hand to her throat as she drew in a deep breath.

"Okay, confess," he said once he'd caught his own breath. He leaned against the wall and watched as the amusement left her.

"Confess?"

"What were you up to earlier?"

He watched as she shifted her feet a couple of times before she lowered her head. "You'll be angry with me."

Laredo didn't think that was possible. "Why?"

"I was about to break the promise I made you. I—I'm sorry. . . ."

Then it dawned on him. She'd been gathering equipment to sneak away to that damned ghost town. He exhaled sharply, grateful he'd found her when he had. He was disappointed, too. He'd expected Savannah to be a woman of her word.

"I'm sorry," she said again, with such genuine regret that he couldn't help forgiving her. "Richard and I were talking about Bitter End this morning, and I felt this urge to go there again. Now. Today. I have to, Laredo. Because of the roses." She glanced down at her feet. "And I didn't want Richard to know. Or Grady. I wasn't sure where you were . . . and I've got to leave quickly." She raised her head to look at him. "Can you come with me?" she asked, her expressive eyes filled with hope. "It won't take much time. I'll leave Grady a note and explain."

Grady might owe him a favor, but Laredo didn't feel ready to collect it quite this soon. Then he changed his mind.

"All right," he said, "we'll do it."

She clapped her hands, then forgetting herself, leaped forward and kissed him on the mouth. "I'll pack up a lunch and afterward we can have a picnic."

He hadn't the heart to disappoint her, but his idea of how he wanted to spend the day wasn't sitting in some field full of bluebonnets, lingering over sandwiches. Not even with Savannah . . . He thought of all the chores that awaited him. Chores Grady counted on him to do.

"How long will we be?"

"Not too long," she promised. "All I want to do is walk around and see if there are any other roses. We won't stay."

He nodded.

"There's a lovely spot a few miles down the road where the river bends. We can have lunch there." She wasn't about to drop this picnic idea of hers, and really, he supposed, it was a small thing to ask.

With their plans set, Laredo loaded the shovels and other tools into the back of the pickup. As he did, an uneasiness settled over him. Apparently what Grady had told him about the place had made a stronger impact than he'd realized. His uneasiness grew into dread and refused to leave him.

They weren't even off the ranch yet, and already he was convinced they shouldn't go.

Eight

The truck pitched and heaved, first left and then right, as they neared Bitter End. Savannah hung on as best she could, but her shoulders continued to slam against Laredo's, jarring them both. Thankfully they were able to follow the tire tracks from her last visit, otherwise she wasn't sure she could have located it a second time.

"I can't believe you found this place on your own," Laredo said, his hands gripping the steering wheel tightly.

"It wasn't easy—took me weeks of searching."

More than once she'd been tempted to forsake the idea, but the thought of finding old roses had spurred her onward. Her patience had been richly rewarded. Not only had she discovered the White Lady Banks, her most valuable find to date, but on that same day she'd come across Laredo.

The truck pitched sharply and Laredo cursed under his breath.

"We're pretty close now," she assured him. His face was tense with concentration, and although he drove cautiously, he couldn't avoid jolting the truck on the rough ground. There was barely even a track.

Savannah was grateful Laredo had agreed to escort her back to the ghost town, but what she looked forward to even more was their picnic. They were rarely alone. This stolen time was bound to be special.

Laredo eased the truck to a stop when they could go no farther.

"It's only a short walk from here," she promised.

The trek was difficult, through brush and dense cedars, and they were both breathless before the town came into view.

"So this is Bitter End," Laredo muttered as he climbed over rocks to a limestone ledge that overlooked the town. He offered Savannah his hand.

She took it and stepped up. From the outskirts Bitter End resembled any other ghost town. A row of forsaken buildings lined the main street, four or five on each side, in various states of disrepair, various stages of dying. Paintless shutters hung crookedly by empty windows. The stillness and lack of sound gave it an eerie unreal feeling. Wind-tossed tumble-weeds had wedged in the corners and along the boardwalk. A quick inspection didn't reveal any visible plant life, but there had to be some roses. The ones in the cemetery had survived. Others would've, too.

The largest building in town was the church, which sat on a hill at the far end of town, next to the cemetery. Time had left it remarkably un-touched. It'd remained white and unblemished except for the charred steeple, which had apparently been struck by lightning. At the other end of town was a corral.

They clambered down a rocky embankment into the town itself. Then it happened just as it had on her first visit. The feeling of sadness and pain. Whatever possessed Bitter End wasn't ghosts or spirits, of that she was fairly certain, but a sorrow so strong even the years hadn't dimmed it.

She looked at Laredo, who faced the town squarely, feet slightly apart, ready, it seemed, for anything. He stood there silently, as if he was listening and yet heard nothing.

"Do you feel it?" she whispered. Normal tones didn't seem right. On her previous visit she hadn't murmured a word. She'd been in and out of the town within ten minutes. Just long enough to dig up the roses and replace them with a bush from her own garden.

"Are you sure you want to go ahead with this?" Laredo asked. He, too, spoke in a whisper, unwilling to disturb whatever it was that awaited them.

Savannah slipped her arm through his. "I'm positive."

"Then let's get it over with and get the hell out."

"There aren't any ghosts here," she told him, still in a whisper.

"Whatever you say." He smiled for the first time since their arrival.

"It won't take long to look for more roses," she said. The presence of another person—someone she trusted—made the town seem a little less frightening.

If Laredo wasn't in such an all-fired hurry to leave, it might have been fun to explore the interior of some of the buildings. But then again, Savannah had the distinct impression they were trespassing as it was.

"Where do you want to start?" Laredo asked as they neared the main street.

"Anyplace is fine. I was in the cemetery earlier." She motioned toward the church and the graveyard behind it. They walked side by side, holding hands. His warm grasp lent her reassurance.

The farther they went into town, the stronger the sense of sorrow became. With each step down the narrow street, the feeling grew darker. During her last visit she'd hurried through Bitter End as quickly as possible on her way to the cemetery, trying to shake off the sense of misery and unease.

She'd actually enjoyed visiting the graveyard. The sensation hadn't been nearly as powerful there, and she'd been fascinated by the headstones. Most of the names and dates on the simple markers were no longer legible, but that hadn't stopped her from picturing the kind of life the people of Bitter End had lived. It would have been a harsh existence, battling hunger, disease and the elements.

Savannah recalled the stories she'd read about the frontier days when Texas had been wild and unforgiving. Stories she would one day read to her own children.

Her own children.

The thought caught her unprepared. All these years Savannah had assumed she'd never marry. Since meeting Laredo she'd begun to believe that all things were possible for her. A husband and a family of her own. Despite the eeriness of the place, Savannah's heart gladdened.

After a few minutes exploring the town's streets, Savannah realized that the trip had been a waste of time and energy. Whatever flowers, roses or otherwise, once bloomed in Bitter End had long since died. Nothing grew inside the town. Nothing. Everything was dead, including the land itself.

The lone tree, an oak with gnarled limbs, was hollow and lifeless. It stood in silent testimony to a time and place long forgotten.

"Don't you think it's a bit bizarre that there's nothing alive here? Not even a weed?" Laredo commented.

She nodded. The only plants that had survived one-hundred-plus years were the roses she'd discovered at the cemetery. "I want to go back," she said.

"I couldn't agree with you more," Laredo murmured.

"I mean, to the cemetery," she said.

He hesitated. "Are you sure that's wise?"

"I don't know, but I'm curious about the grave site where I found the roses." It didn't add up in Savannah's mind. If those roses had survived, then it made sense that other plants would have, too.

"In my humble opinion," Laredo said, his words barely audible, "we shouldn't tempt fate. Let's leave while the leaving's good. All right?"

His hand gripped Savannah's with such force that her fingers throbbed. He wasn't intentionally hurting her, she knew, but reacting to the tension inside him.

"All right," she agreed. "We'll go. I'll look some other time."

"No." The force behind the single word brought her up short.

"I don't want you coming back here," he said with an urgency that baffled her. "Not for anything. Understand? This place gives me the creeps."

Despite her love for him, she couldn't make that kind of promise. "No. Someday there might be a very good reason for me to return."

Clearly, he wanted to argue the point, but right then, leaving appeared to be a higher priority. Frequently looking over his shoulder, Laredo led her back toward the faint path that would take them to the truck.

As they walked, the sensation gradually lifted from her shoulders. Savannah could feel it slipping away. Like a silk scarf dragged across a palm, the sensation faded until it was completely gone.

Once they reached the pickup, Laredo helped Savannah inside, then climbed in himself. He couldn't seem to start the engine fast enough. His anxiety, even greater than her own, was contagious.

Savannah didn't want to know what had created the feeling that pervaded Bitter End. There was nothing good in that town and maybe there never had been.

LIFE WAS FILLED with mysteries, Laredo told himself. The answers weren't always meant to be known. That was the way he felt about this ghost town. Grady hadn't said much about it, only that it wasn't a safe place for Savannah. Her brother couldn't trust her not to return on her own, so he'd put aside his dislike and distrust of Laredo and sought his help.

For the first time Laredo appreciated Grady's fears. He didn't know what the hell had happened in that town. But he didn't need to know. As far as he was concerned, Bitter End could continue as it had for more than a hundred years without interruption from him.

He leaned against the tree trunk and watched Savannah unpack the picnic basket. He still wasn't keen on lazing away the afternoon under a flowering pecan, but his objection to the wasted time felt much less urgent now.

The spot she'd chosen for their picnic was as lovely as she'd promised. The river flowed swiftly nearby, the clean sound of water a sharp contrast to what he'd experienced a short time before.

Savannah finished unloading the wicker basket and quickly assembled them each a plate—roast-beef sandwiches, yesterday's potato salad, homemade pickles. They ate in companionable silence for a while, then both spoke at once.

"You felt it, too, didn't you?" she asked.

"Was it the same as before?" he asked.

They paused and grinned, then Laredo took the lead. "I'll tell you what," he said. "Let's not talk about the town."

"Why not?"

He wasn't sure if she was disappointed or relieved. "I want to talk about you."

"Me?" She shook her head. "You already know everything."

"No, I'm sure I don't. For instance, who taught you to cook like this?" He couldn't remember a time he'd eaten better. Not in years. Not since he was a child, when he'd been too young to appreciate a home-cooked meal.

"My mother loved cooking. Baking, too. Mealtime was a matter of pride to her. I guess we're more alike than I realized." Her eyes grew wide. "You would have liked her, Laredo—she was a wonderful woman."

He didn't doubt that, not with the way he felt about Savannah. Relaxed as he was, the sun behind him, the sound of the river singing nearby, Laredo yawned, lulled by the serenity of the spot. "You'd like my mother, too."

He hadn't meant to talk about himself, but once he'd mentioned his mother, she wouldn't let the subject drop. Before long he was answering her questions, talking about his mother in Tulsa. About her being widowed in 1972. And how she'd moved back to the same house where she'd been born and raised, the house where she still lived. How she'd been dating the same man for twenty years without any plan to marry him.

"I know I'd like her," Savannah said wistfully. Then she lowered her gaze until her long lashes grazed the high arch of her cheek. "Would you . . . Never mind." Savannah reached for a blade of grass and nervously twisted it around her finger.

"Would I what?" he prodded, enjoying her discomfort. Little did she realize that he'd do just about anything for her. All she had to do was ask.

Her eyes fleetingly held his before she glanced away. "Would you like to put your head in my lap?" she asked.

This was what dreams were made of, he decided as he rested his neck against her thigh. It didn't take long for her fingers to weave their way into his hair, her touch soft and gentle. A memory rushed forward, one of his father and mother. His mother cutting his father's hair in the kitchen. Laredo couldn't have been more than four at the time, but he recalled the loving way his mother's hands had smoothed back the hair from his father's brow. His father had reached for her hand and kissed her palm.

Without realizing it, Laredo caught Savannah's fingers and brought them to his lips. His heart constricted with the strength of emotion that coursed through him.

He didn't intend to kiss her, but that was a natural progression. As natural as drawing his next breath. He lifted his head from the sanctuary of her lap and gently met her mouth with his. The hunger that surged to fire in his blood stunned him. The strength of his desire would have frightened her had he acted on it, Laredo thought. Instead, he involved himself in the kiss, his lips lingering on hers.

One kiss, he promised himself. But it soon became obvious that a single kiss wasn't enough for either of them. They exchanged one after another, each more intense than the last. Laredo had to call on every ounce of willpower he possessed to stop.

"I like it when you kiss me," Savannah whispered. She kept her eyes closed as she spoke.

"I like it, too," he confessed.

"Don't stop," she pleaded.

Once again Laredo found himself in the position of being unable to refuse her.

The kiss was even better than the others; he'd assumed that was impossible. Savannah lay on the blanket, smiling up at him and he leaned over her.

"You taste so good I don't want you to ever stop," she whispered when he hesitated.

"Sweetheart, you don't know what you're asking."

"I do," she murmured, her mouth moist and slightly swollen from his kisses. "I want you to kiss me forever."

That didn't sound like a bad plan to Laredo, but sooner or later, kissing wouldn't be enough to satisfy either one of them. They were fast approaching that point now.

"Savannah," he whispered, wondering how he could explain why it wasn't a good idea to continue.

He didn't get a chance. She locked her arms around his neck and drew his mouth down to hers again. He tried to show her without words what she did to him. This kiss was fierce, as fierce as his growing need.

He urged her lips apart and swept her mouth with his tongue, fully expecting— Hell, he didn't know *what* he was expecting. Certainly not this acceptance, this welcoming. His breath jammed in his lungs as the kiss deepened. While he waged war with his needs, she returned his lovemaking with an eagerness that destroyed his restraint. Her nails dug into his shoulders as if to bring him closer, become part of him. Laredo was convinced she didn't really grasp the overwhelming physical intensity of his reaction, didn't realize what she was doing to him.

Above all, he didn't want her ending up in a sexual situation she wasn't ready for.

When he could endure no more, he abruptly broke off the kiss and rolled away. His shoulders heaved with the strength of will it had taken to leave her.

"Did I do something wrong?" she asked after a moment.

He waited until he'd caught his breath before he answered. "I wouldn't say that."

"Then why did you stop?"

He closed his eyes. "I don't think you understand—"

"Don't treat me like a child, Laredo. I know exactly what was happening."

He felt depleted; he hadn't the energy to argue with her. She made him vulnerable. Much more of this kissing would have sent him over the edge. He knew his limits and they'd been reached.

He sat up and smiled. Or at least made the effort to smile. In an attempt to clear his head, he took several deep breaths.

"I called about the repairs to the truck," he said, not looking at her. He focused on the tree limbs overhead, hoping she realized why he'd abruptly changed the subject.

His announcement was greeted with silence.

"Paul said the parts were in and all he needed was the go-ahead from me." Laredo paused and waited for a response.

More silence.

Finally she said, "I know what you're doing, Laredo."

"Do you?" He doubted it.

"You're telling me that you're leaving Promise as soon as you can."

So she did know, and if she was that smart, she'd probably figure out the rest. "I don't want to hurt you, Savannah."

"You couldn't," she said, her voice small. "You've already brought me such incredible happiness. When you do . . . leave—" she appeared to have trouble saying the word "—don't worry that I'll do anything to stop you. I'm grateful for each day we can be together. Grateful for each moment . . . each kiss."

He didn't see it that way. After all, he was the one in *her* debt. "I think we should get back before anyone misses us." He was strongly tempted to resume their lovemaking, and he couldn't be sure he possessed the determination to resist.

"Not yet," she pleaded softly. "I left a note in the kitchen so no one'll worry."

He didn't know what would happen if they kissed again—and didn't think he could afford to find out. He stood, removing himself from temptation.

"Just a few more moments." She regarded him with such longing he found it impossible to refuse her.

"All right," he said, and sat back down on the blanket. "But only a few minutes longer. Okay? And no kissing."

She nodded and thanked him with the sweetest of smiles.

A few minutes soon became two hours. Savannah closed her eyes and was immediately asleep. Laredo wondered if she'd gotten much rest the night before. He knew *he* hadn't. He suspected that the only one who'd enjoyed the luxury of a night's uninterrupted sleep was Richard.

He knew how Savannah felt about her brother and feared it was only a matter of time before Richard disappointed her. Laredo didn't want to see that happen, but he was helpless to protect her.

Uncomfortable with his thoughts, Laredo sat against the tree and watched Savannah, appreciating her gentle beauty. Each minute was a gift; she'd been the one to express that thought, and he, too, had discovered the truth of it.

The world, his mother once told him, had a way of making all things equal. A divine order. *We receive back what we give,* or something along those lines. He hadn't paid close attention at the time and now wished he had. But it seemed to him that meeting Savannah made up for everything that had ever gone wrong in his life. Every broken promise. Every unmet expectation, every unfair act.

But why did he have to meet her *now?* He snapped off a blade of grass and chewed on the end. Why would he meet this woman—and fall in love with her—when he had nothing to offer but hardship?

Laredo loved Savannah; he'd admitted that early on. He loved her enough to leave her, rather than ask her to scrimp and sacrifice with him. She deserved far better. He refused to cheat her of the comfort and certitude that were her right.

ELLIE FRASIER was busy in the back room dealing with a shipment from one of her main suppliers when Richard Weston strolled in. He wore a crisp pair of jeans, his fancy boots and brand-new Stetson, and looked more like a country singer than a rancher.

"So this is where you've been hiding yourself," he said. He gazed at her boldly, eyes roaming from her hair to her booted feet, letting her know without words that he liked what he saw. Ellie wasn't opposed to a bit of flattery now and again. Lord knew Glen and the other men in her life were damned stingy with their appreciation.

It had come as a shock to see Richard again after all these years. At first she hadn't recognized him. As a schoolgirl she'd had a crush on him. Richard Weston had been an "older" man, both handsome and charming. That much hadn't changed.

"I thought I'd let you take me to lunch," he said, glancing over her shoulder to read the clipboard.

"I don't have time today." She wouldn't have minded spending her lunch break with him, but she was simply too busy. She'd taken on her father's responsibilities, as well as handling her own. Glen had suggested she hire someone to look after the books, and while she knew he was right, she'd delayed.

"You could use some time off," Richard said, evidently disappointed she'd refused him. "And I'd love the company."

"I wish I could."

"Come on," he said. "It'll do you good." He sent her an appealing boyish grin. "I can be a fun guy, you know."

"I noticed." Ellie didn't bother to disguise her smile. The welcome-home party had been just the tonic her sinking spirits needed. The pressures of holding down the feed store and the worries over her father's health had exhausted her.

Glen stopped off a couple of times a week to offer moral support. He was her best friend, and his down-to-earth humor had gone a long way to bolster her courage and resolve. At Richard's party she'd relaxed and enjoyed herself for the first time in weeks. She'd danced with Glen and with Richard—and Richard had even kissed her. It was the closest thing to a date she'd had in months.

"Maybe I will escape for an hour or so," she said, surprising herself. "The world won't come to an end without me."

"Great." A smile lit up his handsome face.

Not too often was a woman given the opportunity to realize her schoolgirl dreams, Ellie mused. Okay, so she'd been fifteen and impressionable, but Richard Weston had been by far the most attractive boy in Promise. There hadn't been a girl in school who wouldn't have given . . . whatever for the chance to go out with him. Richard had played it cool, though. He'd never dated one girl for any length of time. In that sense he hadn't changed; he must be close to thirty now and had yet to settle down.

"Where do you want to go?" he asked.

Seeing as there were very few restaurants in town, Ellie didn't figure there were many options. "You choose."

"How about your house?" He leaned close enough for her to catch a whiff of his musk-scented aftershave.

"My house?"

"Sure, we can rustle up something for lunch and then snuggle on the sofa for a while and talk about old times."

He had a smile that would charm a snake. "What old times?" Ellie asked.

"We can make that part up as we go along." His voice fell, heavy with suggestion.

"Richard!" The man was a blatant flirt.

"Why not?"

"First, I'm the world's worst cook. Trust me, you wouldn't want to eat anything I've made myself. Second, snuggling up on the sofa, tempting as it sounds, is the last thing I have time for."

"I bet I could convince you otherwise."

"Really?" This guy was too much. She shook her head and tossed the clipboard on a shelf facedown. "And just how do you intend to do that?"

He grinned that boyish grin again and reached for her hand, tugging her after him.

"Hey, where are we going?"

"Someplace private—where I can show you what I mean." He looked furtively around, then pulled her inside the office and closed the door.

"Richard?"

The next thing she knew he had her pinned against the wall. He'd kissed her at the party; she'd enjoyed the attention—and the kiss hadn't been bad, either. Maybe it was just what she'd needed to revive her energy and enthusiasm. All work and no play had dulled her senses, but Richard Weston had brought them back to life.

His kiss now was deep and sultry. By the time he lifted his head from hers, Ellie's knees felt weak.

"How was that?" he asked.

"Not bad." Her reply was breathless, despite her effort to sound casual. Her hands were flattened against the wall behind her, as if to prop her up. She took a deep breath. Her emotions must be in a sorry state, indeed. In fact, everything in her life seemed to be in a constant state of upheaval.

"There's a lot more where that came from," he promised. He ran the tip of his index finger down the V of her shirt, trailing it lower, close to the curve of her breast.

"Unfortunately," she said, slapping his hand away, "I can't squeeze an affair into my busy schedule."

"Where there's a will there's a way."

"Richard, please, I'm flattered but—"

He interrupted her with a second kiss. This one wet and seductive and a little too rough.

Ellie couldn't believe she was allowing this to continue. What she'd said was true—she was flattered, but she wasn't one to indulge in casual sex. Or casual anything.

"I've got responsibilities."

"Don't we all?"

"Richard!"

"That's my name and I certainly like to hear you say it, but not quite like that." His hands massaged her tired shoulders. Against every dictate of her will, Ellie closed her eyes.

"I want you to whisper my name when we're in bed . . ."

She gasped. "I can't believe you're actually serious!"

"I've never been more serious. I thought about you when I was away . . . and I wondered if you were married. I'm glad you're not."

"You didn't even know who I was!"

"Are you kidding? Believe me, I knew, but a guy can get arrested for thinking the way I did about you back then."

Ellie recognized a lie when she heard one. "I appreciate the offer, I truly do, and if I have a vacancy anytime soon, I'll give you a call."

"Hey, don't be hasty here. We were going to lunch, remember?"

A loud knock sounded on the office door. "Ellie, are you in there?"

Glen Patterson. Arriving like the cavalry the minute she needed rescuing. His timing couldn't have been better.

"Come on in," she called, moving toward the door.

Glen let himself inside and frowned when he saw Richard.

"I was trying to talk Ellie into getting away for an hour or so. To have lunch," Richard explained, his smile as friendly as if they'd been involved in harmless conversation instead of a kiss.

It might have helped if Glen had displayed a shred of jealousy, but he didn't. "Good idea," he said, glancing at Ellie. "You need to get out more."

"I can't today. Maybe some other time," she said, and scampered past the two men.

Ten minutes later Glen found her in the storeroom going through the order. "Richard's gone?" she asked.

"Yeah. He hasn't changed much, has he?"

"How do you mean?"

Glen didn't answer until she glanced up from the clipboard.

"He's a wheeler-dealer."

"So I noticed," she said with a chuckle. She fanned her face and deliberately expelled a breath.

"Hey, what does that mean?"

"What do you *think* it means?"

Glen thought about that for a moment, and either didn't get it or wasn't willing to say it out loud.

"Let's put it like this," Ellie said. "Richard Weston was interested in a whole lot more than lunch."

Glen's eyes widened considerably.

"Why does that shock you? Does it surprise you to realize other men might look on me as more than one of the guys?"

Again he took his time responding. "Not really. You're about the best damn friend I've ever had. And you're game for just about anything."

"Within limits," she said, thinking of Richard's proposal.

"Within limits," Glen agreed, then laughed. "Hell, maybe it isn't such a bad idea, after all."

"You and me?"

He looked stunned. "Hell, no. You and Richard."

Nine

Sunday morning Maggie slipped into Savannah's pew and leaned against her just as Wade McMillen approached the pulpit. Slipping an arm around the child, Savannah pulled her close, acknowledging just how much she'd come to love her friend's daughter. They'd formed a special bond, and it wasn't unusual for Maggie to sit with Savannah during church services.

A talented speaker, Wade often used humor in his sermons. The theme of this morning's talk revolved around the opportunities God presented. Savannah found herself laughing along with the rest of the congregation as Wade relayed the story of a man stuck on a rooftop in a flash flood.

Three times a rescue team had come for him, and each time the man insisted that God would provide. The man died and went to heaven and confronted the Lord, demanding to know why his faith had gone unanswered.

"I sent the Red Cross, a boat and a helicopter," God told him. "What more could I have done?"

Wade had a way of communicating truth without being obtrusive, dogmatic or self-righteous. Savannah often wondered why he remained unmarried when any number of eligible young women in Promise would have been thrilled to be his wife. It was a frequent source of interest, gossip and speculation at any gathering of church members.

Maggie squirmed as the sermon drew to a close. She smiled up at Savannah and silently turned the pages of her hymnal, waiting until the choir stood to sing and she could see her mother.

The love she felt for this child poured through Savannah's heart, and with it a desire so deep and so long denied that it bordered on pain. Until she'd met Laredo, she'd relinquished the dream of ever becoming a bride—and, of course, along with that, a mother.

The yearning to bear a child of her own burned in her heart now. She closed her eyes and her mind instantly filled with the image of a young boy of five or six. He was dressed in jeans, a shirt, hat and boots, a miniature version of Laredo. The child trailed after him as they headed toward the corral. Father and son. Their child, hers and Laredo's. The thought moved her so strongly, she battled back a sudden urge to weep. Savannah felt a thrill of pure happiness at the sheer wonder of having found Laredo.

What a wonderful husband and father he'd be. Laredo had been patient and gentle with Maggie from the first, while Grady groped clumsily in his effort to make friends with the little girl. Laredo was a natural with children, and it was easy to imagine him surrounded by a whole brood of them.

Most important of all Laredo loved her. She was confident of that. Not that he openly confessed his feelings. But Savannah didn't need a formal declaration or flowery words to know how he felt. A hundred times, more, he'd shown her his feelings.

Laredo was protective of her, his manner traditional in the very best way. He was thoughtful and considerate, sensitive to her moods and needs. As far as Savannah was concerned, his actions spoke far more eloquently than anything he could ever say. Last week, for instance, while she was working on the design for her catalog, he'd brought in a cup of coffee, set it on the desk beside her, kissed her cheek and silently left the room. Another day he'd seen her carrying a heavy load of laundry outside to hang on the clothesline, and he'd rushed to her side and carried it for her.

Wiley had teased Laredo unmercifully that day, pretending he was in dire need of assistance, mincing around and flapping his hands in a ridiculous imitation of a woman in distress. Laredo had paid no attention to his antics.

After the Sunday service was dismissed, Caroline met Savannah in the front of the church. "I thought you said Richard was coming with you this morning," her friend said.

"I thought he would." Savannah was deeply disappointed in her younger brother. Grady was barely speaking to her, which was nothing new, and all because she continued to champion her brother's cause. Despite Richard's reprehensible actions, he *was* their brother. No matter what he'd done, she wouldn't allow Grady to throw him off the ranch. He had nowhere else to go. He'd told her he was still waiting for the money that was supposed to be in the mail; he seemed so sure it would be arriving any day. Because she believed him—*had* to believe him—she'd lent him money herself, although she didn't let Grady or Laredo know that.

"Do you think he's ever going to change?" Caroline asked. "I'm just so afraid that if you trust him, you might be setting yourself up for heartache."

"He's my brother," Savannah said simply. She was convinced that their mother, had she been alive, wouldn't have allowed Grady to kick Richard out, either.

"There's something different about you," Caroline said when she reached her car.

"Different?" Although she formed the word as a question, Savannah knew what Caroline meant. And it was true. She wasn't the same woman she'd been as little as a month ago. "I'm happy," she said, blushing profusely. "Really truly happy."

"Laredo?" Caroline asked.

Savannah lowered her eyes and nodded.

"I like Laredo," Maggie announced. "And Richard."

"What about Grady?" Caroline coaxed her daughter.

Maggie pinched her lips together tightly. "Grady's . . . okay, I guess, but he yells too much."

"I don't think she's forgiven him for shouting at her over the phone. I've tried to explain that he's—"

"A beast like from *Beauty and the Beast,*" Maggie supplied. "I don't care if he *is* a handsome prince. When he yells I have to cover my ears."

"Oh, Maggie," Savannah whispered, feeling wretched. "Grady likes you very much and wants to be your friend, too."

"Then he shouldn't shout at me on the phone," she said in an eminently reasonable tone.

Savannah wanted to shake Grady. She didn't know what had possessed him to explode at Maggie. His only excuse, weak as it was, had something to do with not knowing who was on the other end of the line.

It was getting to the point that she barely knew what to think of her own brother. She wasn't sure who'd changed the most in the past few weeks, Grady or her. She knew having Richard around troubled him, and while Grady talked about throwing Richard out, she sensed that he struggled with what was right the same way she did. Richard was a charmer, but of the two men, Grady was the one with heart.

"Would you like to join us for dinner?" Savannah asked her friends, thinking it might help Maggie feel more comfortable with Grady. "I've got a huge roast in the oven, and fresh-strawberry shortcake."

"Mmm." Maggie licked her lips. "Strawberries are my favorite." Wide-eyed, she looked up at her mother.

"Not today, Savannah. I'll take a rain check."

"But Mommy . . ."

Maggie's disappointment was a soothing balm to Savannah's own. Since the phone incident Caroline hadn't been out to the ranch. Whenever Savannah suggested she visit, her friend came up with a convenient excuse, or in this instance, just a polite refusal. It bothered Savannah and she hoped the uneasiness between Grady and Maggie would soon resolve itself.

When Savannah arrived back at the ranch, she discovered Richard sitting on the porch, strumming his guitar and singing softly. He stopped and waved when she pulled into the yard, then strolled over to the truck.

"Where were you all morning?" he asked as if her disappearance had worried him.

"Church. I thought you said you were coming with me."

"I would've if you'd woken me up."

"You're an adult, Richard."

His fingers stilled, the pick poised above the guitar strings. "You're not angry with me, are you?"

She sighed. "No."

He grinned boyishly and continued his song while Savannah went into the house. She set her Bible aside and checked the oven. The noonday meal was the primary one on Sundays. In the evening they all fended for themselves, giving Savannah time to pursue her own interests.

An hour later Savannah served the roast, and dished up hot-from-the-oven buttermilk biscuits, mashed potatoes and gravy, corn, a large green salad and strawberry shortcake for dessert. The meal vanished in minutes with lavish compliments from Richard and quiet appreciation from Laredo, Wiley and Grady.

Everyone disappeared afterward, leaving Savannah to herself. The afternoon was lovely, the sky blue and bright, the sun warm without the intense heat of summer. Spring was Savannah's favorite time of year. After spending an hour in her garden, she arranged a vase of roses and set them in the kitchen, allowing their fragrance to fill the room.

When she'd finished, she picked up her knitting and sat on the porch, Rocket stretched out beside her. There was silence all around her, except for the soughing of wind in the greening trees and the occasional distant sound of traffic from the highway. Without informing anyone of his plans, Richard had disappeared. Grady had vanished into his office to catch up on some reading and Wiley was visiting his widow friend in Brewster. She didn't know where Laredo had gone, but she hoped he'd join her, as he often did.

Enjoying the Sunday-afternoon tranquility, Savannah lazily worked the yarn and needles. It didn't take long for Wade McMillen's message to make its way into her thoughts. *God-given opportunities.* She mulled over the opportunities that had recently come her way. Quickly, inevitably, Laredo sprang to her mind.

Deeply absorbed in her thoughts, she wasn't aware of his approach until he stepped onto the porch.

"It's a lovely afternoon, isn't it?" she said, delighted when he claimed the empty rocker beside hers. For as long as she could remember, her parents had sat in these very chairs, side by side, lifelong companions, lovers and friends.

Laredo watched her hands moving the needles and the yarn. "My mother knits, too," he said.

"My grandmother was the one who taught me." She reached for the pattern book and showed him the cardigan she was making for Maggie. The needles clicked gently as she returned to her task.

"Church this morning was great," she went on. "I enjoy Wade's sermons." She told him about the man in the flood, and Laredo laughed at the punch line, just as she knew he would. Someday she hoped Laredo would attend services with her, but she hadn't had the courage to ask him. Not yet.

Courage. She'd missed opportunity after opportunity in her life because she was afraid. Afraid of what, exactly, she didn't know. No more, she decided then and there.

"Wade got me to thinking," she said. If she didn't tell Laredo what was in her heart now, she'd always regret letting this opportunity slip by. She used her knitting as an excuse to avoid eye contact.

"Thinking?"

"About the opportunities that have come into my life . . . lately."

Laredo leaned back in the rocker and relaxed, closing his eyes.

"I've never dated much," she said. "I suppose it shows, doesn't it?"

He lifted his hat brim enough to look at her. "It's not a disadvantage, if that's what you're asking."

She *felt* at a disadvantage, though, talking to him about such things, but forged ahead anyway. "It's a bit of a detriment," she said, trying to disguise the trembling in her voice. Her heart beat so fast she felt nearly breathless.

"I wouldn't want to change anything about you, Savannah."

"Thank you," she whispered, encouraged by his response.

He apparently thought their conversation was over, because he sat back in the chair once more, stretched out his legs and lowered the brim of his hat.

"There's something I need to say and I'm not sure how to go about it." Her fingers felt clammy and stiff, and she let the knitting lie idle in her lap as she composed her thoughts.

"You can tell me anything, you know that."

Despite the turbulent pounding of her heart, Savannah felt a sense of calm. "Since I don't have much experience in this kind of situation, I hope you'll forgive me for speaking frankly."

She had his attention now, and he lifted the brim of his Stetson with one finger. "Situation?"

Gripping the knitting needles tightly, she continued, "I need to know if there's a proper way for a lady to speak of certain . . . matters with a gentleman. Matters of the heart," she added nervously.

Laredo's position didn't alter, but she thought she saw him stiffen. "That part I wouldn't know."

"I see." Her mouth grew dry with anxiety.

An awkward silence followed while she carefully weighed her words. "Considering that you seem to be as much at a loss as I am, perhaps the best way to discuss this would be in a straightforward manner. My mother used to say, 'Nothing works better than the truth.' "

"Savannah . . ."

He tried to stop her, but she wouldn't let him, not while she had the courage to go on. Inhaling deeply, she began to speak. "I love you, Laredo. My heart's so full, some days I don't think I can contain all this joy. I want to thank you, to let you know how grateful I am to have met you."

Her words appeared to stun him. Slowly Laredo sat upright and stared straight ahead, not responding to her words at all. If they'd brought him any pleasure, he wasn't letting it show.

She waited, her hands trembling now at the bold thing she'd said. "Perhaps I've spoken out of turn, but it seems that when a woman loves a man she—"

"Savannah," he interrupted quietly. "Don't say any more. Please."

The color of acute embarrassment erupted in her cheeks. "Is saying I love you improper?"

"There's nothing improper about you. It's me."

"You?" She was utterly confused, completely on edge. She feared what would happen next.

"I'm not the right man for you."

The relief was so great she nearly laughed aloud. "Oh, Laredo, how can you say such a thing? Nobody's ever been more right for me in my entire life."

"Savannah, I have nothing . . ."

"Do you think that matters?"

"Yes," he said quietly. Intensely. "It does."

She waited a moment, then told him with gentle insistence, "For most of my life my parents and then Grady were sure they knew what was right for me. The amazing part of all this is that no one ever bothered to ask my opinion. I'm thirty-one years old, and believe it or not, I know what I want. I want you. I love you."

He leaned forward and pressed his elbows to his knees as though her words had brought him pain, instead of joy.

Her back went rigid. "I apologize if I've embarrassed you."

"It's not that. Savannah, listen to me. I'm truly honored that you love me, but it won't work. It just won't work." His voice sagged with regret, with defeat.

"Is it— Don't you care for me?" It seemed impossible he didn't share her feelings. She'd been so sure. And she'd hoped that revealing *her* love would free him to acknowledge his.

He hesitated. "I . . ."

"If you tell me you don't return my affection, then I'll apologize and never mention it again." Although she made the offer, Savannah had no doubts. Laredo couldn't have held her or kissed her with such gentle passion if he didn't care for her.

He waited so long to answer she feared he was about to lie. "You already know what I feel."

She closed her eyes in gratitude. "I do know." Now that he'd admitted the truth, she felt confident enough to continue. "Once we're married—"

"Married?" He half rose from his seat, his voice harsh with shock.

His reaction jolted her. When two people loved each other, marriage seemed to be the next step. And really, given she was already over thirty, there was no reason to wait. Especially if they intended to start a family, which she sincerely hoped they would. The sooner the better.

"I assumed . . . I hoped," she faltered, then blushed when she realized he might not consider marriage necessary. "I'm afraid that if we don't legally marry, my brother will object. I . . . I would, however, defy him, if that were . . . necessary." But she prayed with all her heart it wouldn't be.

Laredo stood up and walked over to the railing, holding on to it, his back ramrod-straight with tension. "I won't marry you, Savannah."

Her heart sank as she absorbed the firm conviction in his statement. "I see," she said, struggling to hide her disappointment. "As I said earlier, while marriage would offer certain advantages, I'm willing to forgo the . . . legalities."

He whirled around. "Savannah, dear God in heaven, don't you understand what I'm saying?" He knelt in front of her, his eyes wide with pain. "It isn't that I *won't* marry you. I can't."

"Can't?" The awful possibility dawned. "Are you . . . do you already have a wife?"

"No."

She brought both hands to her heart in a gesture of relief.

"Look at me!" he demanded. "I don't have a pot to piss in. I don't have one damn thing to give you. Do you honestly think I'd take you away from your home, your family and friends, your roses and everything else to live in a *trailer*? Because that's all I've got—a lousy trailer."

Feeling his pain, his inadequacy, she touched his cheek lovingly. "Do you think it matters to me where we live? As for my garden, I can start another. You're all I need, all I'll ever need."

He closed his eyes. "Savannah, I can't. I'm sorry, but I can't." His hands squeezed hers with enough strength to make her fingers ache.

"I'm offering you my heart, my love, my life," she said, her voice barely audible.

He claimed both her hands with his own, then turned them over and pressed his lips to her palms. When he raised his head, his eyes held hers. "You'd give all this up for me?"

"I wouldn't be giving up anything, Laredo. I'd be gaining so much more."

THAT NIGHT Laredo sat up in his bunk, his back against the wall, his mind whirling. Savannah had almost made him believe it was possible for the two of them. He was well aware that she'd be the one to make all the sacrifices; while that didn't seem right or fair, she'd assured him of her willingness to do it. To do whatever was necessary for them to be together.

Laredo rested his head between his hands and dreamed with his eyes open. A growing sense of excitement, of possibility, grew within him. *He loved her.*

Richard strolled into the bunkhouse and threw himself down on the cot where he'd slept that first time. Some nights he slept in the house; Laredo wished this was one of them. He supposed it depended on whether or not Grady was in the house and likely to notice. Despite her older brother's insistence, Laredo knew Savannah would never make Richard leave. She'd even let him stay in his boyhood room, perhaps allowing herself to believe that everything was all right again. Other nights, Richard slept in the bunkhouse. Grady must be around this evening.

"Hey, what're ya doing?" Richard asked.

"Thinking," Laredo answered shortly, hoping Weston would take the hint.

"So you're trying to steal Savannah away from us."

How did Richard know? "Do you have a problem with that?" Laredo demanded, suspicious of the other man's intentions.

"None whatsoever." Richard's hands flew up and he grinned broadly. "As long as you love her," he added in melodramatic tones.

"I do." Not until the words escaped his lips did Laredo realize he had no problem telling Richard how he felt, although he'd never once told Savannah he loved her, not in so many words, at least.

"Ain't love grand," Richard said with an exaggerated sigh. He flopped back on the cot and gazed up at the ceiling. "At least in the beginning."

Laredo let the comment slide, although it hit its mark. Bull's-eye. What started out beautiful could often end up a disaster.

"Savannah's a real sweetheart," Richard continued. "Did you notice how hard she worked cooking for the party? Actually, if I know my sister, she was grateful to stay in the kitchen. It's always been difficult for her to deal with crowds, even people she's familiar with and known most of her life. I don't know why she's so damn shy. Take her out of her element and she wilts like a flower without water."

Laredo frowned, wondering if Richard was actually delivering a subtle message, one he would deny if asked, but would gleefully recount as an I-told-you-so if it came to pass.

"If you have something to say, then just say it," Laredo muttered.

"Me?" Richard's voice echoed his surprise. "I'm not saying anything other than how pleased I am for the two of you."

"Nothing's been decided." Laredo wanted to correct that impression right off.

Richard rolled his head to one side to get a better look at Laredo. "Really?"

"Really."

"Well, if everything goes as planned, it'll be wonderful. I know she'll make you happy, and once the kids start coming . . ."

"Kids?" The word exploded from Laredo's lips before he thought to censor it. They wouldn't be able to afford kids for years, although he knew Savannah was eager for a family. He was, too, but it just wasn't going to be possible, not until he'd established himself, had some income he could count on.

"I wouldn't advise you to wait too long," Richard was saying. "Savannah's already over thirty. Apparently the older the woman the more likely the chance of complications." He shook his head wisely and sounded as if he knew what he was talking about.

"I hope you've got good health insurance," he added. "From what I've heard, having a baby costs thousands of bucks these days."

Health insurance? Laredo could barely afford to put food on the table, let alone worry about extras. He knew Savannah, too. If there were problems, she wouldn't let him know because she wouldn't want him to worry.

"What about her rose garden?" Richard asked next. "We both know how important that is to her."

"She's talked about moving part of it," Laredo responded, but his mind was still stuck on the possibility of something happening to Savannah, miles from town, with few friends or neighbors. The reality of what he was asking hit him hard. It sounded romantic and exciting—the two of them building a home together, breeding quarter horses—until he thought about the risks.

"Moving part of the garden," Richard repeated. "Great idea." He sat up, tapping one foot on the floor. "You be real good to my big sister now, you hear?" Clapping his hands together, Richard laughed. "Hey! I'll bet you want me to keep my mouth shut about this in front of Grady. Right?"

Laredo didn't answer. The next time he looked up Richard was gone, which was just as well. Savannah's brother had opened his eyes to a few home truths. While it was fine to dream about making Savannah his bride, a dream was all it would ever be. He couldn't take her away from everything she knew and loved, couldn't put her health and happiness at risk. One of them had to keep a level head, and it looked like the responsibility had fallen to him.

He loved her, but he couldn't marry her. *Wouldn't* marry her. As soon as it could be arranged, he'd get out of her life. For her own good, as well as his own.

*   *   *

A WEEK LATER, as Grady sat on Starlight and watched over the grazing herd, his thoughts grew dark and oppressive. Sometimes he could cast off these moods when they threatened. More often, like now, he couldn't. He worried more and more about Savannah; he wasn't sure what had happened to his sister, but she hadn't been herself. Not for days. Outwardly nothing seemed wrong; she was as pleasant and cordial as always. Still, the difference was there. It seemed as if the light had gone out of her eyes somehow. The joy he'd seen in her of late had vanished.

He was no expert when it came to romance, but the answer was obvious. Something had happened between her and Laredo, who seemed equally miserable. Clearly they'd suffered some sort of falling-out. It was bound to happen, Grady realized.

He hated to see his sister hurt, and it made him feel helpless. He had no idea what to do, what to say. He'd even considered talking to Caroline, this being a woman thing and all. Savannah's best friend might be able to see her through this disappointment.

If only he could talk to someone about Richard. He supposed Cal Patterson, as his closest friend, would be that person. And yet he felt embarrassed. Ashamed. He hardly knew how it had happened, but Richard had managed to sweet-talk his way back into the family. It hadn't taken long for Savannah to pick up where their parents had left off, Grady thought with some bitterness. She spoiled him, indulged his every whim, pandered to his wishes as if he deserved a hero's welcome.

Grady still wanted Richard off the ranch, but every time he got to the point of ordering him to leave, he found he couldn't. Either because of Savannah's pleading or his own sense of . . . what? Obligation? Family loyalty? Pity? The one thing Grady had insisted on was that Richard sleep in the bunkhouse, but his worthless brother had found a way to thwart even that.

It had started innocently enough, with Richard cleaning out his old bedroom, sorting through his things. Before long he'd started sleeping up there. Some nights, anyway; Grady never knew for sure. It was another way Richard kept him off balance.

Grady shifted his weight in the saddle, tired after a long day. Just when he was about to head back to the ranch, he noticed another rider approaching at a gallop.

Laredo Smith. He waited for the man to join him.

"Problems?" Grady inquired.

"Not really."

From the way he'd ridden out here Grady wondered if the house was on fire. "There's a reason you came to see me, isn't there?"

"There is."

Apparently Smith was having a difficult time spitting out the words. He looked even worse than Savannah, pale and lifeless.

"You were right, Grady," he said without emotion. "Have been from the first."

Grady liked the way this conversation had started. With Richard pulling the wool over everyone's eyes, it felt good to be told he was right about something. "How do you mean?"

"About me."

Grady's smile faded. This wasn't what he wanted to hear, wasn't what he'd expected, either. "In other words, you're the thief Earl Chesterton suspected?"

"No." His denial was quick. "Not that."

Grady would have been disappointed had it been the truth. Smith had proved himself a hardworking and talented horseman, probably the best he'd ever hired. He still didn't trust him, though, especially where his sister was concerned, and because of that, Grady had made a point of being difficult, demanding, even unreasonable. Laredo hadn't responded in kind, not once, and in the process had earned Grady's respect.

"You claimed I wasn't good enough for Savannah," Laredo said bluntly.

Grady frowned. He really didn't like the turn this conversation had taken. "What's going on between you two?" he asked, eyes narrowed.

Laredo ignored the question. "I need a favor."

"You got it."

His immediate response appeared to surprise Smith. "You might not be so fast to agree once you hear it involves money."

Grady sobered; the wrangler was right. "How much?"

"I need a loan. Enough to pay for the repairs on my truck and get me to Oklahoma."

"Any particular reason you're anxious to be on your way now?"

Smith rested his hands on the saddle horn and averted his face. "I've got my reasons."

"I don't suppose those reasons have anything to do with my sister?"

"They might."

"You hurt her, Smith, and you'll regret it." Grady was torn. On the one hand, Savannah's happiness seemed to depend on this man; on the other, he'd prefer to see Smith leave, get clear away from her. Grady suspected Smith's departure would come too late, that Savannah was already in too deep, emotionally committed to a drifter.

"Why the hell do you think I need that money so damned bad?" Laredo asked savagely. "The sooner I'm out of her life the better. Listen, I don't expect you to give me that loan without collateral. I'll leave the title to my truck with you until I can pay you back. Agreed?"

Grady mulled it over, not the decision to lend Laredo money—he had no problem with that—but why, exactly, Laredo seemed so anxious to leave. He sighed. He wasn't sure if he should interfere in the man's private affairs; he certainly wouldn't have appreciated anyone meddling in his.

"Agreed?" Laredo said again.

"There's another way," Grady said thoughtfully. Laredo stared at him long and hard before Grady continued. "You could stay here. I'll make you an offer that'll make it worth your while. A partnership—you and me and Savannah. I understand you're interested in breeding quarter horses. You could do that here on the Yellow Rose just as well as in Oklahoma."

Either Laredo was speechless at the offer or he was shocked that Grady knew this much about him and his plans. Grady credited Wiley for the information. His foreman had a loose tongue.

"If you're trying to bribe me into staying, all I can say is you've insulted the finest woman I know."

"It isn't a bribe," Grady insisted, damning himself for his inability to say things the way he wanted. "All I'm trying to do is give you another option." He stopped and boldly met the other man's eyes. "You love my sister, don't you?"

"Loving Savannah doesn't have anything to do with the loan," Laredo said stiffly. "Look, I have almost nothing to bring to a marriage. Nothing that's *mine,* that I worked for. I can't give her the things she's used to and deserves to have. I won't ask her to give up what she's got here. And a partnership . . . well, there's no way I could buy into the Yellow Rose, so a partnership is charity, pure and simple. I work for what I get—I don't accept charity."

Laredo's anger seemed to burn itself out and he said, "That loan. Are you willing to give it to me or not?"

"It's yours if you want it, but—"

"I want it."

"All right," Grady said, and thrust out his hand. For the very first time he believed in Laredo's sincerity. For the first time he fully accepted that his sister had chosen a man who deserved her love. A man he respected. A man he'd misjudged.

Laredo gripped his hand, and not for the first time Grady noted the intense sadness in his eyes. Grady refused to let go, demanding Laredo's full attention. "Are you sure this is what you want?"

Laredo nodded. "I'm sure."

He rode off with the same urgency with which he'd approached.

Grady frowned, wishing there was something he could do. But he knew that neither Savannah nor Laredo would appreciate his intrusion in their lives. This was between them; they had to work it out themselves— or not.

Bad as he felt for both of them, he could do nothing.

LAREDO NOTED the number on the small single-story dwelling in a quiet neighborhood and glanced down at the address on the slip of paper. He was about to commit perhaps the most cowardly act of his life. But what else could he do?

He stepped out of the truck and walked down the narrow path to the front door, a long narrow box tucked under his arm. He hesitated briefly, then rang the doorbell. It didn't take long for someone to answer. Maggie Daniels's eyes lit up in delight when she saw who it was.

"Hi, Laredo!"

Caroline revealed no such pleasure. "What are you doing here?"

He removed his hat. "I need you to do something for me if you would."

Savannah's friend didn't invite him inside, and it was just as well. He wanted to leave now, immediately. As he'd told Grady, the sooner he was able to put some distance between Savannah and him, the better.

"Come in," Caroline finally said, unlocking the screen door.

Laredo declined. "Thanks, but this should only take a moment." He handed her the box. "Would you mind giving this to Savannah for me?"

"You can't do it yourself?"

"No, ma'am."

She didn't accept the box. "Why not?"

"I don't plan on seeing her again." Saying the words created a terrible sense of loss. He might be convinced that leaving was for the best, but that didn't make it any easier. He'd gotten the loan from Grady, and after supper Wiley had driven him into town to pick up his truck. He'd said his goodbyes to everyone.

Everyone except Savannah.

Although he called himself every name in the book, he couldn't make himself do it. He couldn't look her in the eye and pretend he didn't love her, and that was the price she'd demand before he left. She'd insist he say it to her face and he wouldn't be able to.

It occurred to him as he drove away from Powell's Garage that this feeling of grief and fear and loss must be similar to what his father had experienced when he left for Vietnam all those years ago.

"Well, if you won't come in, I'll join you on the porch." Caroline opened the screen door and stepped outside. Maggie, dressed in purple pajamas, followed her mother.

"I'd be much obliged if you'd give this to Savannah for me." He repeated his request.

Caroline's smile was knowing. "You love her, don't you?"

Laredo couldn't have denied it if he'd tried. "Sometimes love isn't enough."

"Really." She crossed her arms and walked to the porch railing and stared into the night sky. "Don't you think Savannah deserves to have you give her that gift yourself?"

"She deserves a great deal more than I can ever give her."

Caroline turned and faced him, leaning against the railing.

"What's in the package, Mommy?" Maggie asked.

"A gift for Savannah," her mother answered.

"Can I see?"

Laredo opened the box. As a parting gift and a token of love, it wasn't much, but it was all he could afford. "It's a shawl." He brought it out to show the little girl.

When Caroline saw the antique white silk threaded with gold strands, she sighed in appreciation. "It's perfect for her."

He was tempted to smile. He'd realized the same thing when he noticed it in the window of Dovie's shop. Instantly, he'd pictured Savannah sitting on the porch, the shawl wrapped around her shoulders. He'd never thought of himself as romantic, but in some small way he hoped that when she wore it, she'd feel his love. He hoped she'd understand that even though he'd left her, he would always love her.

"I know I'm asking a lot of you," Laredo said to Caroline.

"No," she replied. "The one you're asking a lot of is Savannah."

He recognized the truth of that immediately.

"Like I said," Caroline went on, "she deserves to have you give her this gift."

He shook his head. "I can't. Either you do it or I'll mail it."

Caroline hesitated. "Is there any message to go with it?"

He shook his head. He'd already said more than he'd intended.

"Nothing, Laredo?" Her eyes begged him not to be so cruel.

"Tell her . . ." His throat felt thick.

"Yes?"

"Tell her thank-you." He set his hat back on his head and hurried down the walkway.

Maggie tugged at her mother's sleeve. "Where's Laredo going?"

"I don't know, sweetheart. Laredo!" Caroline called to him.

He looked back.

"How'd you manage to pay for the repairs to your truck?"

He stood silent, refusing to answer her.

It didn't take Caroline long to figure it out. "Grady. He lent you the money, didn't he?" She leaped down the porch steps and planted her hands on her hips. "That son of a—" She bit off the last word.

Laredo climbed into his truck and started the engine, desperate to leave before he found an excuse to stay.

Ten

‘‘What do you mean Laredo's gone?'' Savannah didn't understand what Caroline was telling her. He'd been on the ranch earlier that day; she'd seen him herself. They'd both made an effort in the past week to pretend their discussion had never taken place. But it had, and her declaration of love stood between them. It was something they could neither forget nor ignore.

Every time Savannah thought about the foolish way she'd exposed her heart, she grew weary with self-recriminations and regret. Her rash behavior had embarrassed them both, yet she realized she probably couldn't have kept silent any longer. She loved Laredo, and hiding her feelings had become increasingly more difficult.

"He asked me to give you this," Caroline said with a regretful sigh, handing her a rectangular box.

"It's really pretty!" Maggie added enthusiastically.

"You've talked to him?" Savannah said. The pain was immediate. Laredo had left, and instead of coming to her, he'd gone to Caroline. He'd talked to Caroline, but not to her. He'd left without even a good-bye.

"He was on his way out of town when he stopped by and asked if I'd give you this."

Savannah felt an overwhelming need to sit down. Slowly sinking onto a kitchen chair, she brought her fingers to her mouth to suppress a cry. *Laredo isn't coming back.*

"Do you want me to open the box for you, Savannah?" Maggie volunteered, eagerly lifting a corner of the box as she spoke. "It's so pretty and you're going to like it. Mommy did and so did I."

Caroline restrained her daughter by placing her hand on Maggie's shoulder. "Let Savannah open it when she's ready, okay, sweetheart?"

The child looked disappointed, but she nodded.

Savannah slid her fingers over the top of the box, but lacked the courage to look inside. All her strength went into holding back the tears that burned her eyes.

Laredo was gone. Without a word of farewell, without a note. Nothing. The pain of his leaving had devastated her. But in some odd inexplicable way she understood why he'd left so abruptly.

Laredo Smith *couldn't* say goodbye. He loved her too much to hurt her more. Loved her too much to refuse if she'd asked him to stay. And so he'd done the only thing he could. He'd slipped away like a thief in the night; he'd stolen her heart and taken it with him.

"Savannah, are you all right?"

She nodded even as she felt swallowed up in the emptiness.

Caroline's fingers gripped hers tightly. "I'm so sorry," she whispered.

Somehow Savannah managed to look at her friend. She could lie and offer reassurances, but she hadn't the strength to maintain a facade. It would be easy enough to fool Grady and Richard, but not Caroline.

"It's a shawl," Maggie blurted, unable to hold back any longer. "A pretty white one with gold—"

"Maggie," Caroline snapped.

The little girl lowered her head and bit her lip.

"A shawl . . . How nice," Savannah said, struggling. Knowing Maggie was impatient for her to open the gift, she pulled off the lid. The child was right; the shawl was quite possibly the loveliest one she'd ever seen. Lifting it from the tissue paper, she let the delicate fabric slide across her fingers. "Was there . . . did he give you any message for me?"

Caroline hesitated, then said gently, "He wanted me to thank you."

Her heart was breaking, the pain raw and real, and yet—despite the emotional intensity of the moment—Savannah smiled.

"Thank you." She repeated his message. This, too, she understood. The simple words held a wealth of meaning and in some ways were more valuable to her than the gift he'd asked Caroline to deliver.

Despite his desertion, Laredo had thanked her for loving him. Even though he'd walked out of her life with the same suddenness with which he'd entered it, he'd wanted Savannah to know her love had touched him. He couldn't say it himself, so he let someone else say it for him.

Caroline's eyes flashed with anger. "I don't understand why he'd do such a thing! He admitted he loved you—he said as much."

"I know."

"But when I asked why he was leaving, all he'd say was that sometimes love wasn't enough—whatever the hell that means." Caroline sat down, then got to her feet again and started pacing.

Savannah didn't try to explain. What Laredo apparently didn't grasp, and what she'd been unable to make him believe, was that his love was the one thing she'd ever need.

He seemed to think a prosperous ranch would make her happy, or a million head of cattle. A luxurious ranch house. A rose garden. Those things gave her security and contentment, true. But Laredo's love gave her happiness, and it gave meaning to everything else in her life. She'd tried to convince him that she'd happily work at his side, that their love would allow them to create a new security and contentment of their own. Why couldn't he believe her?

"Can I go sit on the swing outside?" Maggie asked.

Caroline nodded. "Stay on the porch."

Maggie assured Caroline she would, and the screen door slammed behind her. Caroline brewed Savannah a cup of strong coffee, then brought it over to the table. "Drink this," she ordered. "You look pale as a sheet."

Savannah raised the cup to her lips. Surprisingly the coffee revived her.

Caroline poured herself a cup and sat down next to Savannah. "I know you probably don't want to hear this at the moment, but I'm going to say it, anyway." She paused long enough to inhale deeply. "Right now, you're hurting too much to believe that everything happens for a reason. I don't know why, but that's the way it seems to work.

"When I discovered I was pregnant with Maggie, I felt as if the world had caved in on me. I was young and stupid and determined not to let a mistake ruin my life. First I thought the father would marry me, but . . . well, that was impossible. I'd already decided I wanted to have this baby, so I was left to deal with the pregnancy alone."

In all the years they'd been friends, this was the first time Caroline had discussed anything to do with Maggie's birth. Or Maggie's father.

"When I couldn't hide that I was pregnant any longer, I had to tell my mother. I expected her to be furious, to call me all the names I'd called myself. Instead, Mom asked me a few questions and then held me. We both cried.

"It was what I'd needed most—her love. She talked about how difficult it must have been for me to keep this pain bottled up inside me all those weeks. I didn't want to tell her about Maggie's father, but I did, and how stupid I'd been to think he actually loved me . . ." Her voice wavered and it was a moment before she could continue. "You see,

Savannah," she whispered with emotion shining in her eyes, "this mistake was really a gift. I made a mistake, but *Maggie's* not a mistake. She's my heart and my joy. I can't imagine life without her."

The screen door opened just then, and Maggie flew into the room and raced across the kitchen. Breathless, she wrapped her arms around Caroline's leg, hiding her face against her mother's jeans.

Grady followed her inside, looking frustrated and confused.

"What'd you do this time?" Caroline demanded.

"Not a damn thing," Grady said. "I saw Maggie outside and thought it was time the two of us talked, but it seems she's not ready."

Maggie clung to her mother's leg all the harder.

"It'd help if you hadn't yelled at her on the phone," Caroline suggested calmly.

"How was I supposed to know it was Maggie?" he shouted in return.

"He's yelling again," Maggie surfaced long enough to announce.

"Explain to her that it was all a mistake, would you?" Grady said in a strained voice, gesturing at Maggie. "She's right, I was a beast. But I'm willing to be a prince, too, if she'll give me the chance."

"You're too mean to be a prince," Maggie said next. Breaking away from her mother, she climbed into Savannah's lap and locked both arms around her neck. "I don't like Grady 'cause he yells."

"He's not one of my favorite people, either," Caroline said, glaring at Savannah's brother.

"What'd I do *now?*" he groaned. "Damn, but it's hard to understand women. I haven't talked to you in days—what could I possibly have done to offend you?"

"You know very well what you've done."

Clearly perplexed, he shrugged. "I'm afraid you're going to have to tell me, because I haven't got a clue."

"You're lower than a . . . a worm," Caroline said.

"So what else is new?" Grady sounded bored.

"Caroline?" Savannah said her friend's name softly, confused by the display of anger. "What did Grady do?"

Still glaring at him, Caroline crossed her long legs. Her foot swung with a furious rhythm. "I wasn't going to tell you," Caroline said, speaking to Savannah, "but you'll figure it out soon enough. Grady gave Laredo the money so he could pay off the repairs on his truck."

Savannah felt as if she'd been punched, as if the air had been forced from her lungs. She looked at her brother in shock and pain and disbelief. The abruptness of Laredo's leaving was almost more than she could bear, but knowing that her own *brother,* her own flesh and blood, had made it possible—had no doubt *encouraged* it—was like a knife in the back. She gasped. "Grady?"

"I didn't *give* him the money," Grady said, and his gaze darted between her and Caroline as if he didn't understand what he'd done that was so wrong. "I *lent* him the money."

He'd betrayed her.

There was nothing more to say.

Barely aware of what she was doing, Savannah stood and slowly placed one foot in front of the other. Hardly knowing how she'd managed it, she climbed the stairs to her room, dragging herself one step at a time.

"What'd I do that was so terrible?" her brother shouted after her. "Tell me, Savannah! I want to know!"

"Leave her alone," Caroline said angrily, her voice drifting toward Savannah as she climbed the stairs. "If you can't figure it out, trust me, I'll be happy to fill in the blanks. And you know what? I'll use small words so you'll be sure to understand."

GRADY DELAYED speaking to Caroline about Laredo for ten days. He knew he needed to say something—to explain, to talk about Savannah, to ask her advice. He saw her enter the Winn-Dixie one evening and followed her inside. He didn't want Caroline to assume he'd sought her out; he intended her to believe their meeting was accidental.

Taking a cart and maintaining a safe distance behind her, he trailed her into the produce section. Savannah was the one who did all the grocery shopping, and other than picking up a necessary item now and again, he was rarely in the supermarket.

He paused in front of a pyramid display of bright juicy-looking oranges, and with one eye on Caroline and the other on the task at hand, he reached for an orange. To his horror, the entire display collapsed.

Grady saw it happen as if in slow motion. He attempted to catch as many as possible before they tumbled to the floor, his arms moving frantically in every which direction. In the end he abandoned the effort, kneeling on the linoleum floor surrounded by fruit.

Everyone in the produce department stopped and stared at him. Even small children pointed and snickered. Grady smiled weakly and searched for a witty remark, but like everything else these past few weeks, his wit failed him.

He was about to turn tail and run when Caroline squatted down beside him. "This is another fine mess you've created, Grady Weston."

He didn't need Caroline to tell him that. If he wanted to make a fool of himself, he wouldn't choose to do it in front of half the store. Nope, he preferred to manage that with just one or two onlookers. Like Caroline. And his sister.

Together they gathered the spilled oranges and set them back on the display case. "Is there a reason you followed me in here?" she asked bluntly.

"Was I that obvious?"

"Don't apply to the Secret Service, all right?"

Since it was entirely obvious that running into her hadn't been an accident, he got straight to the point.

"Do you have time for coffee?" he asked, and then because he was afraid she might think he was asking her out, he added, "I'm worried about Savannah. I'd feel better if I talked about this with someone."

She checked her watch, and Grady had the feeling time wasn't her major concern. "Talked about this with just anyone?" she asked.

"With you," he amended, burying his pride. He owed Caroline this much.

"Let me phone the day care," she said, "and then I'll meet you at the bowling alley."

"Okay. See you there in a few minutes." He was eager to make his escape before he toppled a display of something *really* embarrassing— like feminine hygiene products.

The café in the bowling alley served some of the best food in town. It was certainly the most reasonably priced, with coffee only a quarter a cup. They served decent coffee, too. There was always a special; according to the reader board outside, today's was T-bone steak and a baked potato. And the place stayed open all night on weekends. In Grady's opinion, it was a damn good deal. Although he wasn't interested in a steak at the moment. . . . Even if he'd been hungry, he couldn't have choked it down.

Arriving first, he found an empty booth and turned over two mugs. The waitress brought him a couple of menus and smiled. "Haven't seen you in a while, Grady."

"Hello, Denise. How're Art and the kids?" Grady had attended high school with Denise a hundred years ago. While he was out chasing cattle, his classmate had married, had three kids and started working here part-time.

"I can't complain. Billy's in junior high this year."

Hard to believe, Grady thought. Art and Denise's oldest boy was reaching his teens and *he* wasn't even married yet.

Denise filled his mug with coffee. "Are you going to order something to eat?"

"Not me, but Caroline might."

"Caroline Daniels?" Denise filled the second mug.

He nodded, disliking the flicker of interest in her eyes.

"Are you two seeing each other now?" she asked, her interest far too avid.

Grady opened his mouth to deny everything. He didn't have to.

"No way," Caroline answered for him as she slipped into the booth. She handed Denise the menu, effectively dismissing her, and reached for the sugar dispenser. "You had something you wanted to say about Savannah."

"Yeah." This was more difficult than he'd imagined.

"Is she all right?" Caroline leaned back against the patched red vinyl upholstery, and he noted for the first time how pale she was. He didn't comment because sure as hell she'd make something of it—something he'd never intended. His only chance to have a peaceful conversation was to stick to the matter at hand and ignore everything else. Still, he wondered.

"How come you haven't been out to the ranch?" he blurted. His sister needed a friend, and he'd expected Caroline to be there for her, especially now.

"I stopped by a couple of times when you weren't around."

"On purpose?" he asked, thinking she'd taken to avoiding him because of Maggie.

"No, it just happened to work out that way. I haven't gone anywhere in a couple of days. I've been dealing with postal inspectors all week. I had my own crisis to handle, but fortunately that's behind me now." She cradled the mug between her hands. "I've phoned Savannah every day." Her eyes held his. "Is something going on with her that I don't know about?"

"Not with Savannah, exactly," he said, then looked away, finding her scrutiny uncomfortable. "First off, I was wrong about Laredo Smith."

That captured her attention, he could tell. She raised her eyebrows but said nothing. Not yet, anyway. Naturally she'd delight in hearing how wrong he'd been.

"I should have accepted Savannah's assessment of his character," Grady said, embarrassed that he'd allowed his fears to get in the way. Admitting he'd made a mistake had never come easy. "I . . . came to some, well, erroneous conclusions about Smith. The result was that he and I got started on the wrong foot."

"You should tell Savannah this, not me."

"I have!" he snapped, then took a deep breath in an effort to control his impatience. When he spoke again, he lowered his voice. "I did tell her, but I wanted you to know, as well."

"Should I be grateful?"

Grady decided to ignore the sarcasm. "Laredo came to me and asked for a loan. Despite what you think, I'm not blind. I knew something wasn't right. I didn't want him to leave and I told him so."

This appeared to surprise Caroline. Her eyebrows rose again. "You did?"

"Yes—not that it did any good. In the end I agreed to lend him the money and he insisted on giving me the title to his truck. The day he left I apologized for the scene at Richard's party and we shook hands." He stared into the steaming mug. "I took my aggravation with Richard out on Laredo and made a complete ass of myself."

Caroline didn't disagree with him. Not that he expected she would.

"Although it's none of my business," he said, "Laredo as much as admitted he loved Savannah."

"He told me that, too." Caroline shook her head in dismay. "What I can't fathom is why he felt he had to leave. What is it about men? I don't understand it. Laredo Smith is loved by the sweetest, kindest, most wonderful woman he's likely to meet in ten lifetimes and what does he do? He walks out on her without a word. It doesn't make sense." She tossed her hands in the air as if to say she'd never understand the male of the species.

"A man has his pride, especially a man like Smith, but my guess is Richard had something to do with it." It was the first time he'd suggested this to anyone, and he was curious to see how Caroline would react. He half expected her to jump all over him and insist he quit trying to blame Richard for everything, including the national debt. She said nothing for several moments.

"I wouldn't put it past him," she murmured at last.

Grady was so damn grateful that she agreed with him it was all he could do not to hug her right then and there. If Denise was going to spread rumors about him and Caroline, *that* would give her something to talk about.

"Did you ask Laredo if Richard said anything to him?"

"No," he told her reluctantly.

"Why the hell not?"

"Well, because . . . I was trying to get him to stay." Grady didn't know what Caroline had thought he could do. It wasn't like he could hogtie the wrangler until he agreed to marry his sister. Grady hadn't intended to tell Caroline this, but suddenly he wanted her to know. "I offered Laredo a partnership in the ranch. I realize now it must have come as quite a surprise to him. Hell, I surprised myself."

He'd already known Savannah was in love with Laredo; that day he'd learned about Smith's love for Savannah, too. This man was important to her happiness; if it was in Grady's power to make her happy, he was willing to do whatever it took.

He noticed how Caroline's face tightened as she considered this information. "What'd he say to that?"

Glancing away, Grady relived the terse conversation. "That he didn't accept charity and I'd insulted Savannah and him. Hell, everything I do these days is wrong. I was only trying to help." He reached for his coffee. "At first I thought Laredo didn't love Savannah, but now I think he loves her too much."

Caroline gave a hard shake of her head. "As far as I'm concerned, he'd better not show his face around here, because I swear I'll wring his neck if he does."

Grady was a little taken aback by the vehemence of her response.

"All this crap about pride and honor—it's asinine, that's what it is." Her lips thinned. "Never mind him. How's Savannah doing?"

"You said you haven't seen her in the past couple of days, didn't you?"

Caroline nodded. "Why? What's up?"

"Something's happened—she's changed."

"Of course she's changed! She's hurt and angry. And I can't blame her."

"It's more than that."

Caroline leaned closer. "What do you mean?"

"Like you said, she's hurt—but I can't imagine how that would lead to . . . this." He didn't know how to say it without sounding demented, so he just plunged in. "Hell, I don't know what's happened to her, but two days ago she cut her hair."

"Savannah?"

"It's been long for so many years I didn't recognize her. It's shoulder-length now and in a—" he made a circular motion with his finger "—pageboy, I think is what you call it. The ends tuck under sort of nice and neat."

This left Caroline speechless.

"Then yesterday I found her in jeans."

"Savannah?"

"Yeah. I didn't know she even owned any."

"But why?" Caroline asked, clearly puzzled. "Why'd she do these things?"

"I have my suspicions and I'll tell you right now, it makes my blood run cold."

"Really," Caroline said thoughtfully, "when you think about it, what's so terrible about Savannah cutting her hair and updating her wardrobe?"

"I'm worried." Grady didn't mind admitting it, either. "This morning I saw her standing on the porch looking down the driveway as if she expected Laredo to come back. Personally I wish to hell he would, but I don't think it's going to happen."

"I hope you didn't tell her that!"

"Of course not!" What kind of idiot did Caroline think he was, anyway? "Then she told me Laredo Smith was a fool," he added.

"I couldn't agree with her more," Caroline muttered.

"You know what I think? I think Savannah's decided to look for a husband." He spoke quickly, finding the subject of marriage an uncomfortable one with Caroline.

Caroline gave an elaborate shrug. "There's nothing wrong with marriage, although neither of *us* seems interested in it."

"I agree—nothing wrong with it. But I'm afraid that in Savannah's current frame of mind any man will do."

"Did she have someone in mind?"

"Not that I'm aware of." But Grady knew his sister, and while he wasn't an expert, he recognized the look. Savannah was on the prowl. And when a woman set her mind on marriage, he believed, there was damn little a man could do but run for shelter.

"You're sure about this?" Caroline frowned.

"Not a hundred percent, but it's fairly obvious."

Then to his consternation, Caroline burst out laughing.

Grady didn't take kindly to being the butt of a joke. "What's so damned funny?" he demanded.

"You! I don't think Savannah's on the prowl, as you put it, but if she does find a decent man to marry, more power to her. There's too much love in her heart to waste. If Laredo doesn't want to marry her, then so be it. Eventually she'll find a man who does."

"In some tavern?"

"Savannah's not into that scene."

"That's what I thought, but then Richard . . ." Grady hesitated, uncertain he should tell her this, but if Caroline could help . . .

"What about Richard?" she asked, her laughter draining away quickly.

It helped that his no-good brother hadn't fooled Caroline, that she recognized the kind of man he was. "Richard offered to take her barhopping and introduce her around."

"Terrific," Caroline said sarcastically. "All the best men hang around bars. Is she going to do it?"

"I don't know," Grady said. "I just don't know."

GLEN PATTERSON sat down in front of the television with a cold can of soda. He was supposed to meet Ellie for dinner, but she'd phoned and said she'd be hung up until after seven. This was a difficult time for his friend. Twice this week he'd made excuses to drive into town and check up on her. The last report he'd heard on her father wasn't good. The doctors seemed to think John Frasier wouldn't last more than another week or two.

"You're frowning," Cal said as he stepped into the living room. It wasn't as neat and orderly as when their mother had done the housekeeping, but it wasn't as bad as it might've been, either. The two brothers had hired a woman to come in once a week to clean ever since their parents had retired and moved into town to open a bed-and-breakfast.

"I was just thinking," Glen said.

"Worried about Ellie?"

"Not really." He downplayed his concern rather than admit it to his brother.

"Maybe you *should* be worried," Cal said as he claimed the recliner. He sat down and stretched out his long legs.

"Do you know something I don't?"

Cal didn't look at him when he spoke. "I hear Richard Weston's got his eye on her."

"Richard? He's harmless. Okay, so he likes to flirt, but Ellie knows that."

"You jealous?"

If anyone understood his relationship with Ellie, it should be his own brother. "Why would I be jealous? Ellie and I are friends. Nothing more. Nothing less."

Friends. It shouldn't be a difficult concept to understand. Cal and Grady Weston had been good friends for years. It just so happened that *his* best friend was a member of the opposite sex. People had been trying to make something of it for years.

Cal regarded him skeptically.

"What?" Glen asked in annoyance.

"Men and women can't be friends."

Glen had his older brother on that one. "Wrong. Ellie's like one of the guys. She always has been—you know that."

Cal folded his hands over his trim stomach. "In other words, it doesn't bother you she's been seeing Richard."

"Not in the least." It did a little, but not enough to really concern him—and not for the reasons Cal might suggest. Glen was afraid that Ellie was especially vulnerable just then, and he didn't want Richard Weston to take advantage of her.

"You know how Grady feels about him," Cal said.

"Yeah, so what? Richard wasn't cut out to be a rancher—we both know that. He has a right to come home now and then, don't you think?"

Cal was silent for a moment. Then he said, "If I were you, I'd keep my eye on Ellie."

Glen found himself frowning again. Cal had a suspicious nature but he hadn't always been this cynical or distrusting. Glen traced it back to Jennifer Healy—Cal had been engaged to her a couple of years ago, and Jennifer had dumped him. Afterward Cal's disposition had soured, particularly toward women. It bothered Glen and he'd tried a number of times to steer his older brother into a new relationship, but Cal didn't seem interested.

"Well, I know for a fact that Richard can be a real bastard," Cal added. "If you're Ellie's friend, like you say, you'd better warn her."

"Warn?" Obviously Cal hadn't been around her often enough. Ellie had a mind of her own and wouldn't take kindly to his interference.

Anyway, he just couldn't take Richard seriously as a threat. An annoyance, yes, but not a threat.

Eleven

As Savannah drove toward Bitter End, she considered the unmistakable fact that her family was worried about her. She'd shocked everyone by cutting her hair, no one more than herself. The decision had come on the spur of the moment, without warning or forethought.

She'd been washing her face as she did each morning and happened to catch her reflection in the bathroom mirror. For a long moment, she'd stood there staring.

How plain she looked. How ordinary. Carefully, critically, she examined her image and didn't like what she saw. That was when she decided something had to be done. Anything. Not until she reached for the brush did she consider cutting her waist-length blond hair. One minute she was staring in the mirror, the next she had a pair of scissors in her hands.

Savannah knew she'd shocked Grady and Wiley that first morning. They'd come into the kitchen for breakfast and stopped cold, unable to keep their mouths from sagging open. Her brother squinted and looked at her as if she were a stranger. Not that Savannah blamed him. She *felt* like a stranger.

Naturally Grady, being Grady, had simply ignored the change after that and didn't say a word. Frowning, he sat down at the table and dished up his breakfast as though there was nothing out of the ordinary. And Wiley, being Wiley, couldn't resist commenting. He approved of the change and said so, forcing Grady to agree with him.

Savannah began to like her new look. Everything that followed after she'd cut her hair was a natural progression of this first action. She'd worn the ankle-length dresses for comfort and out of habit. The jeans were leftovers from her high school days and, surprisingly, still fit.

Of the three men Richard had been the most complimentary about the new Savannah. Her younger brother had done his best to flatter and charm her. To his credit his efforts had made her laugh, something she hadn't done in quite a while. She worried about Richard and his finances, but again and again he assured her the check would be coming soon. The one who surprised her most was Grady. It was as if he'd forgotten about Richard, but her younger brother was smart enough to avoid him. He spent his evenings in town, and while Grady was out working, Richard practiced his guitar or serenaded her. The past few afternoons he'd joined her on the porch to keep her company. It helped distract her from thoughts of Laredo, and Savannah was grateful. A couple of times he'd attempted to talk her into going to town with him to, as he put it, live it up a little. He seemed to believe that all she needed was a new love interest. Another man, who'd take her mind off Laredo.

What Richard didn't understand was that she couldn't turn her feelings on and off at will. He prodded her, claiming it would lift her spirits to get out and circulate. While she appreciated his efforts, she wasn't ready. In truth she didn't know if she would ever be. Not that she intended to mourn the loss of her one and only love for the remainder of her days. She'd given herself time to accept that Laredo was out of her life; after that, she was determined to continue on as she had before.

Easier said than done.

Savannah's hands clenched the steering wheel as she came to a particularly bumpy stretch of road. Although she knew Grady highly disapproved of her going back to the ghost town, she'd decided to do it, anyway.

Not because of the roses, either, She'd already discovered, the day Laredo had come with her, that no other flowers were to be found there, old roses or otherwise. The land was completely barren. Nevertheless, she felt compelled to return for one last visit.

Her reason was nebulous, hard to analyze or explain. But Savannah didn't care. The why of it no longer concerned her. She felt drawn in some indefinable way to this lifeless empty town.

She was pitched and jolted around as she drove slowly toward Bitter End. Oddly, the truck seemed to remember each turn, and she followed without question, parking in the same spot and hiking the rest of the way.

As she neared the place, the memories of her last visit with Laredo immediately came to mind. For weeks now she'd managed to curtail her thoughts of him, telling herself it did no good to brood on might-have-beens; he was gone and nothing she said or did would bring him back. She had no choice but to accept his decision.

At least that was the sane and sensible approach. In reality it just hurt too damned much to linger over the memories.

Every time she stepped into her garden the first thing she saw were the trellises he'd built for her. The roses he'd fertilized and cared for had exploded with fresh blooms. She would cut and arrange them, knowing that his hands had touched these very stems.

It hadn't been easy. None of it.

Caroline worried about her, too, and phoned frequently to check on her. Rather than come right out and tell her she was concerned, her friend manufactured excuses for her calls. She still wasn't coming out to the ranch very often, but Savannah blamed Grady and his talent for frightening Maggie.

As she climbed onto the rocky ledge, Bitter End came into view. She stared at the church at the outskirts of town. The whole place looked peaceful and serene from here, and she wondered about the sadness and oppression she'd experienced on her last visit. Maybe it was her imagination, after all. Laredo's, too. He'd shared her uneasiness and hadn't been able to get her away fast enough.

But as she walked past the church and down the main street, the sensation returned. The feeling seemed to wrap itself around her, but Savannah refused to be intimidated. She wasn't going to run away.

Not this time.

She moved forward carefully and deliberately. The sidewalks had been built a good two to three feet off the ground and were lined with railings. A water trough, baked for a hundred years in the unyielding sun, sat by the hitching post. Savannah advanced toward it, thinking that, instead of walking down the center of the street as she had with Laredo, she'd take the sidewalk and explore a couple of buildings along the way.

Just then she heard a bird's mournful cry reverberating in the stillness. The wind whistled, a keening sound, as though someone was grieving some great loss. Sagebrush tumbled down the hard dirt street. She stopped, looking around, and realized there was something different.

"The rocking chair," she said aloud. She was certain no chair had been there before. But now one stood outside the mercantile store, creaking in the wind, and her heart lodged in her throat.

Determined not to give in to the fear that sent goose bumps skittering up her arms, she strolled fearlessly ahead. Her bravado didn't help. The feeling of dread persisted.

In that instant she understood. It was an emotional understanding and it told her why she'd come, what had driven her back to the ghost town. Standing in the middle of town, she looked up and down the barren street and saw nothing but tumbleweeds and dust.

The street was stark. Empty. Bare. Even the land refused to nurture growth.

This town, this lifeless unproductive street, was like her life. She lived holed up on the ranch with her unmarried brothers. Her entire life revolved around their needs, their wants, their demands.

Her roses and her mail-order business were tolerated, but no one had offered her one word of encouragement. Except Laredo. Grady cared about her; she didn't mean to belittle his concern. But he hadn't the time or energy to invest in understanding her or her needs. As for Richard, although she loved him, she knew he'd never been able to look past his own interests.

Until Laredo, her existence had been empty. Outwardly focused, with no regard for her own happiness, her own growth. *Before Laredo. After Laredo.* Savannah smiled to herself. It seemed her entire life would now be divided into two parts. Before he'd come and after he'd left.

How odd that she'd find herself smiling like that. Just when she'd recognized her life for what it was. Shallow. Without a center.

The restlessness she'd held at bay all this time felt as though it would crush her. Ignoring the unhappiness had done no good. Repressing it hadn't worked. For weeks she'd been fighting headaches and listlessness. For weeks her body had tried to tell her what standing alone in the ghost town had finally made her understand.

She saw a small corral across from the hotel, a large rock beside it. Savannah walked over and sat there, trying to assimilate what she'd learned about herself.

A memory came to her. One she'd long forgotten. She'd been barely ten when her father had been tossed from his horse. He'd badly broken his leg but had somehow managed to crawl to safety and avoid further injury.

Savannah remembered how her mother, frightened and ashen-faced, had run to his side and held his hand while she drove him to the clinic. Mel Weston had smiled and, between deep breaths, assured his wife that the pain told him he was still alive.

That was what this pain told Savannah. She was alive. She could still feel and love and be. Laredo had taught her that, and so much more. For the first time in her adult life, she recognized how much love her heart could hold.

No matter how much it hurt, she'd do it all again.

She bowed her head against the wind as it blew sagebrush about her feet. Tears filled her eyes, but they weren't the same tears that had burned her face in weeks past.

Savannah had made peace with herself.

GRADY NOTICED a difference in Savannah the minute she got out of the truck. Her face radiated a serenity, an acceptance, one that had clearly been hard-won.

His sister hadn't told him where she was going, but Grady could guess and he hadn't liked it. Not one damn bit. How she'd come away from Bitter End with any kind of tranquillity was beyond him. Half a dozen times he'd considered going after her and talked himself out of it, knowing Savannah wouldn't appreciate his interference.

She joined him in the kitchen and put on water for a pot of tea. "I'm going to be all right now," she told him.

Grady wasn't sure what to say. He'd wanted to talk to her about the last conversation he'd had with Laredo, wanted to comfort her, but he feared he'd do more harm than good.

"I won't be going back," she said next as she took the china teapot from the shelf above the stove. She didn't say where and he didn't ask.

"Good," was all Grady said, at a loss for words.

"Would you care for a cup of tea?" she asked, sounding almost like her old self.

Grady preferred dark strong coffee and Savannah knew it. The offer was more a gesture of reconciliation, an outstretched hand. "Tea sounds wonderful," he said.

Savannah smiled and brought down an extra cup and saucer.

In the days that followed, the transformation in his sister became more apparent. Color returned to her pale cheeks and a radiance to her face. She started to sing and hum once again and baked his favorite chocolate-chip cookies. Savannah was back, and yet it wasn't quite the same Savannah as before. These changes were very subtle.

His sister had always been a fearless advocate for people she believed in. Now she believed in herself, too. Her fledgling mail-order business took off like gangbusters once she finished her catalog. Orders poured in from across the country—surprising even Savannah, who'd barely got her catalog mailed out when the responses started to arrive, at a fast and furious pace. The fax machine was in constant use. She soon became known as an expert on old roses and two awards came in quick succession. First she was honored with the grand prize by the Texas Rose Society for one of her premiere roses, which she'd named Laredo's Legacy. The following day, she was asked to speak at next year's Rose Festival in Tyler, Texas, known as the rose capital of the world. Public speaking terrified Savannah, and Grady suspected she'd politely decline. To his amazement she accepted.

Grady wasn't the only one who noticed the changes in Savannah. Caroline did, too. Even Richard, self-centered as he was, commented on her new attitude. Grady was proud of her, exceptionally proud, and he wanted to let her know. He could think of only one way. He ordered her prize-winning rose, Laredo's Legacy, and together with Savannah, planted it at their parents' grave. Savannah had thanked him with tears shining in her eyes.

His sister, Grady realized, was quite possibly the most incredible woman he'd ever known. How odd that it had taken him so long to realize it.

Twelve

Humming softly to herself, Savannah checked the living room one last time to be sure everything was in place. Laredo had been gone more than six weeks now, and she'd stopped waiting for him, stopped dreaming he'd return. Her life had settled back into a comfortable groove, and the happiness she'd found with him would forever be part of her. That happiness, that sense of possibility, was what she chose to remember, rather than the emptiness she'd felt at his leaving.

It was Savannah's turn to host the women's group from church, and her nerves were fluttering. Within a couple of hours twenty women would crowd into the living room to plan a church dinner.

Earlier in the day she'd baked apple pies, and because Grady had been such a good sport about everything lately, she'd made a lemon meringue pie for him, too. The scent that lingered in the house was an enticing mixture of cinnamon, nutmeg and lemon.

"Is Caroline coming?" Grady asked, walking into the kitchen. Just as he was about to stick his finger into the lemon pie, she slapped his hand.

"You can have a piece later," she told him. "And, yes, Caroline's coming."

"What about Maggie?"

Savannah carried the pie to safety. "She'll be with Dovie Boyd."

"Dovie?" He sounded almost disappointed. "She's old enough to be Maggie's . . ."

"Grandmother," Savannah supplied. "Caroline's mother and Dovie were good friends, and Dovie likes to fill in as Grandma every now and again. Why are you so curious?"

He shrugged and strolled out of the kitchen. Savannah didn't have time to wonder about it. As soon as she finished the last of the dishes, she needed to shower and change clothes.

Two hours later the living room was filled with the chatter and laughter of women. Savannah handed out copies of her apple-pie recipe and refilled coffee cups from her mother's silver pot. She was joking with Millie Greenville from the flower shop when the room went strangely quiet. Everyone had turned to look behind Savannah. Certain Richard was up to one of his tricks, she turned around, too, ready to chastise him. She froze.

Laredo stood in the doorway, his Stetson in his hand. He looked about as uncomfortable as a man could get—as though it was all he could do not to turn tail and run.

"Hello, Savannah," he said.

She couldn't have responded had her life depended on it. He looked travel-weary. His jacket was dusty and his face pale beneath his tan, but Savannah had never seen anyone more beautiful.

He seemed to be thinking the same thing about her because for that long, unbroken moment he didn't take his eyes off her.

"I can see I've come at a bad time," he said, glancing away from Savannah long enough to scan the room. All the women were openly curious about him; Savannah had never heard anything louder than this silence.

"You couldn't have come at a better time," Caroline insisted, leaping to her feet. "It looks to me like you'd appreciate a slice of Savannah's apple pie. Sit down and make yourself at home while I dish it up for you. Savannah'll see to your coffee."

A space magically appeared between two women sitting on the sofa. Savannah remained frozen, unable to breathe or think. This was unfair. Just when she'd forged a new path for herself, accepted his absence, he was back.

Unable to hide his discomfort, Laredo settled down between Nell Bishop and Ellie Frasier, looking as out of place as a junkyard dog sitting between toy poodles.

Caroline served him a huge slice of apple pie. "Perhaps you'd like to tell Savannah why you're here?" the postmistress asked pointedly.

The room fell silent again, awaiting Laredo's response. Every eye was on him. Including Savannah's. His gaze darted about the room, and he swallowed noticeably. "I've come to ask Savannah to be my wife."

The silver coffeepot in Savannah's hands suddenly weighed a hundred pounds, and she set it down on the silver platter with a clank. The buzz of voices surrounded her. Her heart raced and everything felt unreal.

At that precise moment Grady burst into the room. "Is that Laredo's truck parked in the yard with the horse trail—?" He came to an abrupt halt when he realized he'd walked into the middle of the church group.

"I believe it is," Caroline answered, gesturing toward Laredo.

The wrangler sprang to his feet, looking at Grady with unmistakable relief.

"What are you doing here?" Grady demanded.

Savannah wanted to stop him, to explain that Laredo had already been through one inquisition and that was enough, but she wasn't given the chance.

"I've come to ask your sister to marry me." Laredo answered as he had earlier, only this time there was a hint of challenge in his voice, as though he expected Grady to argue with him.

Again a murmur arose.

Edwina Moorhouse's old bones creaked as she stood and motioned at Laredo. "All right, young man, tell me what makes you think Savannah should marry you."

Color surged into Laredo's neck and crept upward. "I love her," he answered simply.

"So does everyone else in this room," Lily put in, following her sister's lead and standing up.

"And we're not about to let some stranger steal her away." This from Millie Greenville.

"That . . . that was one of the reasons I left," Laredo explained haltingly. "I didn't want to take Savannah from her home and family."

"How has that changed?"

Laredo motioned with his head toward Grady. "I decided to take her brother up on his offer."

"What offer?" Savannah asked, turning to regard her brother.

Grady had started to ease his way toward the kitchen. "Ah, perhaps we should talk about all this later. In private," he added pointedly.

"It's time for us to go," Caroline suggested. The ladies began to gather their purses, but Edwina called a stop to it.

"Now just a minute. I'm seventy-five and too old to go without my sleep. I can tell I'm not going to rest until I hear Savannah's answer. Do you love this man?" she asked, pointing at Laredo.

Savannah nodded.

"You're willing to marry him?"

Again she nodded, more forcefully this time.

"It's been a while since Wade performed a wedding ceremony," Nell Bishop piped up. Her mother-in-law agreed, trying to remember whose wedding that was.

"I always did love a summer wedding," Lily Moorhouse said, glancing from Laredo to Savannah.

"A wedding's just what this town needs," Louise Powell declared, as though that should be the last word on the subject.

But it wasn't. The group of delighted women became engaged in the conversation, exchanging ideas, offering suggestions. The level of noise and excitement rose perceptibly and wedding plans flew in all directions. Millie suggested white and pink roses for the bridal bouquet, but white calla lilies for the arrangement on the altar. Louise had strong opinions on the meal that should be served. Edwina recommended some musical selection.

Through all this Laredo's eyes remained locked with Savannah's, and it seemed to them that only the two of them were present. She felt his love; it warmed her, even from halfway across the room. His expression told her how miserable he'd been without her, how lonely. She knew that, like her, he'd struggled with the pain. He'd also struggled with pride. But in the end his love, *their* love, was stronger. Laredo Smith needed her as badly as she needed him.

"I do think we should leave now, don't you, ladies?" Caroline tried again, gathering up empty plates and cups.

A chorus of agreement followed this time, and everyone stood.

"Well, that's that," said Edwina. "Come on, Lily, if we hurry home we'll be in time for a game of cribbage before 'Jeopardy' comes on."

The room emptied more quickly than Savannah would have thought possible. She happily forgave Caroline for abandoning the stack of dishes. In less than a minute the crowd was out the door, and the sound of cars starting replaced the chatter of twenty women.

"You cut your hair," Laredo said now that they were alone. He stood half a room away from her, his hat in his hands.

Savannah raised her fingers to touch it.

"It looks wonderful." His voice dipped. "*You* look wonderful. You're more beautiful now than ever. I didn't think that was possible."

"You look wonderful, too." She smiled. "What happened?" she asked suddenly, the words rushing from her lips. "Why'd you go?"

"For all the wrong reasons. My pride, mainly, and my fear."

"Fear?"

"My mother told me I was a fool to have listened to . . . my doubts. I sold my land in Oklahoma," he said, "and brought Renegade with me. If you're agreeable, I'll accept Grady's offer to become a partner in the ranch. Renegade will be my stake, and in time the Yellow Rose will have the finest quarter horses in the country. I promise you that. I don't have a lot to offer you, not nearly as much as you deserve, but I love you, Savannah." He took a step closer. "I didn't realize how much until I reached Oklahoma. My land was there, my dream, and it meant nothing if you couldn't share it with me."

"I thought my life was over when you left," she whispered. "You didn't even say goodbye."

"I couldn't—but I swear I won't leave you again. Mom's right—I'm too much like her. I'll only love once in my life, and if I let you go, there won't be a second chance. I couldn't ask you to wait, but I realize now that I couldn't wait, either. I love you too much."

"I love you, too, so much . . . Why are you standing way over there when I'm right here?"

Laredo covered the space between them in three strides. None too soon she was in his arms. It was heaven to feel his lips on hers, warm, moist, hungry. His kiss told her everything. How much he wanted her, needed her. How much he loved her.

Savannah felt the steady beat of his heart beneath her palm and returned his kiss in full measure, clinging to him. Her heart was full enough to burst.

"Children?" she managed the question between kisses.

"As many as you want. Oh, Savannah, I can't wait for you to meet my mother. She loves you already." His arms tightened about her.

From behind them Grady cleared his throat loudly. "I take it everything's been decided?"

Laredo tucked his arm around Savannah's waist and held her close. "We're getting married as soon as it can be arranged."

"Good. I assume that's Renegade in the trailer?"

Laredo nodded. "I'm taking you up on your offer, Grady, but I want it understood right now that I'll pay my own way. I'm here because of Savannah, not because of anything you offered. Understand?"

Grady held up both his hands and grinned widely. "Understood."

"HOT DAMN," Richard said as he sauntered into the room, guitar slung over his shoulder. "You mean there's going to be a wedding in the family? Well, all I can say is better late than never!"

TEXAS
TWO-STEP

One

A month ago this had been her family home.

Ellie Frasier stood on the tree-lined sidewalk in Promise, Texas, staring up at the traditional two-story house with its white picket fence. The Sold sign stared back at her, telling her that nothing would ever be the same again. Her father was dead, and her mother gone.

This was the house where she'd been born and raised. Where she'd raced across the front lawn, climbed the pecan tree and hung upside down from its branches. On that very porch she'd been kissed for the first time.

Oh, how she'd miss that porch. Countless pictures had been taken of her on these steps. Her mother holding an infant Ellie in her arms the day she brought her home from the hospital in Brewster. Every Easter in a frilly new dress and every Halloween in a costume her mother had sewn for her.

The day Ellie turned thirteen and wore panty hose for the first time, her dad had insisted she have her picture taken on the porch. Then at eighteen, when she was a rodeo princess for the Brewster Labor Day Festival, her father had posed her on the front steps again. At the time he'd told her he'd be taking her picture there in her wedding dress before she left for the church.

Only, her father would never escort her down the aisle.

The rush of pain came as no surprise. She'd been dealing with it for weeks now. And before that, too, while he was in the hospital, desperately ill. But Ellie couldn't believe he would actually die; death was something that happened to other people's fathers, not her own. Not yet. He was too young, too vital, too *special,* and because she'd refused to accept the inevitable, his passing had hit her hard, throwing her emotionally off balance.

Even then, she'd been forced to hold her grief inside. Her mother had needed her to be strong. Ellie's personality was like her father's—forceful, independent and stubborn. Her mother, on the other hand, was fragile and rather impractical, relying on her husband to look after things. She'd been unable to deal with the funeral arrangements or any of the other tasks that accompany death, so they'd fallen on Ellie's shoulders.

The weeks that followed were like an earthquake, and the aftershocks continued to jolt Ellie, often when she least expected it.

Her mother had given her the worst shock. Within a week of the burial service, Pam Frasier announced she was moving to Chicago to live with her sister. Almost immediately the only home Ellie had ever known was put up for sale. By the end of the first week they'd had an offer.

Once the deal was finalized, her mother packed up all her belongings, hired a moving company, and before Ellie could fully appreciate what was happening, she was gone. Whatever she'd left behind, Pam told her daughter, was Ellie's to keep. The family business, too. Pam wanted nothing from the feed store. John had always intended it to go to Ellie.

Squaring her shoulders, Ellie realized there was no use delaying the inevitable. The key seemed to burn her hand as she approached the house for the last time and walked slowly up the five wooden steps. She stood there for a moment, then forced herself to unlock the front door.

A large stack of boxes awaited her. Ellie had a fair idea of what was inside. Memories. Years and years of memories.

No point in worrying about it now. Once she'd loaded everything up and carted it to her rented house, she had to get to the feed store. While her customers had been understanding, she couldn't expect unlimited patience. George Tucker, her assistant—he'd been her father's assistant, too—was trustworthy and reliable. But responsibility for Frasier Feed was Ellie's, and she couldn't forget that.

Which meant she couldn't take the time to grieve properly. Not when she was short-staffed during the busiest season of the year. June brought with it a flurry of activity on the neighboring cattle ranches, and many of those ranchers would be looking to her for their feed and supplies.

By the third trip out to her truck Ellie regretted turning down Glen's offer of help. Glen Patterson was quite possibly the best friend she'd ever had. Although she'd always known who Glen was—in a town the size of Promise, everyone knew everyone else, at least by sight—there was just enough difference in their ages to keep them in separate social circles during their school years.

The Pattersons had been buying their feed from Frasier's for years. Her father and Glen's dad had played high school football together. For the past few years Glen had been the one coming to town for supplies. When Ellie began to work full-time with her dad, she'd quickly developed a chatty teasing relationship with Glen.

She was lighthearted and quick-witted, and Glen shared her sense of humor. Before long she'd found herself looking forward to their verbal exchanges. These days whenever he stopped by, Ellie joined him for a cup of coffee. They usually sat on the bench in front of her store, idling away fifteen or twenty minutes, depending on how busy she was. When the weather discouraged outdoor breaks, they sat in her office to enjoy a few minutes' respite.

It got to be that they could talk about anything. She appreciated his wry good sense, his down-to-earth approach to life. Ellie tended to obsess about problems, but Glen took them in stride. While she ranted and raved, he'd lean his chair against the building wall and tuck his hands behind his head, quietly listening. Then he'd point out some error in her thinking, some incorrect assumption or faulty conclusion. Generally he was right. His favorite expression was, "Don't confuse activity with progress." She could almost hear him saying it now.

It'd been a week or more since his last visit, and Ellie missed him. She could count on Glen to distract her, make her smile. Perhaps even ease this gnawing pain. But when he'd offered to help her sort through the boxes, she'd declined, moving everything on her own. Knowing she'd have to face these memories sooner or later and preferring to do it alone.

Within minutes of her arrival at the feed store, the place was bustling. Naturally she was grateful for the business, but she would have liked a few moments to herself. Then again, perhaps it was best to be hurled into the thick of things, with no chance to dwell on her grief and all the changes taking place in her life.

It was almost two before Ellie could dash into her office for ten minutes, to collect her thoughts and have lunch. Although her appetite was nonexistent, she forced herself to eat half a sandwich and an apple. At her desk, she sifted through the phone messages and found one from Glen. It was unusual for him to call during the day, especially in early summer when he spent most of his time working with the herd. Just knowing she'd been in his thoughts buoyed her spirits.

Since his parents had moved into town and opened the local bed-and-breakfast, Glen and his older brother, Cal, had taken over management of the ranch. Thus far they'd kept the spread operating in the black, doing whatever work they could themselves and hiring seasonal help when necessary. In the last few years, they'd begun cross-breeding their cattle with Grady Weston's stock.

The phone rang and, thinking it might be Glen, Ellie reached eagerly for the receiver. "Frasier Feed."

"Ellie, I'm glad you answered. It's Richard Weston."

If it couldn't be Glen, then Ellie felt pleased it was Richard. He'd recently returned to Promise after a six-year absence, and they'd gone out on a couple of dates before her father's condition worsened.

"How are you?" Richard asked in a concerned voice.

"Fine," she responded automatically, which was easier than confessing the truth. She just couldn't talk about her grief, her deep sense of loss. Maybe Glen was the only person she could share that with, Ellie reflected. But not yet. It was too soon. For now, she needed to forge ahead and do what was necessary to get through the day.

"You've been on my mind a lot the last couple of weeks."

"I appreciate your thoughtfulness, Richard, I really do." Ellie was sincere about that. She'd been a schoolgirl when he left Promise, and like every other female in her class she'd had a major crush on him. Richard was still the best-looking man in town. The years away had refined his features, and he was suave in ways ranchers could never be. City-suave. She liked him well enough but didn't expect anything from their friendship. To be frank, she was flattered that he sought her out. The huge flower arrangement he'd sent for her father's funeral had touched her, it was the largest one there and stood out among the other smaller arrangements. A number of the townsfolk had commented on it.

"I received the thank-you card," he said. "The flowers were the least I could do."

"I wanted you to know how much Mom and I appreciated it." She paused. "It was nice of you to do that for us."

"I'd like to do more, if you'd let me," he said, softly. "If there's anything you need, make sure you phone."

"I will." But it was unlikely she'd take him up on his offer. Not even Glen, her best friend, knew how emotionally shaky she was. The pain was still so new, so raw, that she had to deal with it herself before she could lean on anyone else. Her father had been like that, too, and she was, after all, her father's daughter.

"You know, Ellie," Richard said next, "I think it'd do you a world of good to get out."

A date? Now? No way. Ellie wasn't ready, and besides, she had a million things to do before she gave a thought to her social life. She was about to tell him that when he spoke again.

"Nell Bishop called to tell us she's having a birthday bash for Ruth this Friday night. Sounds like she's going all out. How would you feel about tagging along with me?"

Ellie hesitated.

"You need to relax a little. Have a few laughs," he added with the same empathy he'd shown earlier. "Let me help you through this."

Ellie had received an invitation herself. Attending a party was the last thing she felt like doing, but Nell was a good friend and a good customer. She needed to make at least a token appearance.

"I probably won't stay long," she qualified, thinking it would be best if Richard went without her. They could meet there.

"No problem," Richard quickly assured her. "I'm not much into this birthday thing myself. The only reason I told Nell I'd come was so I could ask you."

"Oh, Richard, that's so sweet."

"Hey, that's just the kind of guy I am."

"If you're sure you don't mind leaving early, I'd be happy to go with you." Ellie had always been fond of Ruth Bishop. She knew that Ruth and Nell had supported each other through the trauma of Jake's death. Nell had lost the love of her life; Ruth had lost her son. Nell had struggled to hold on to the ranch despite numerous hardships, financial and otherwise. Ruth had been a wonderful help, and Ellie was sure Nell had planned this party as a means of thanking her mother-in-law.

"I'll swing by your place around six," Richard suggested.

"Six would be perfect." They chatted a couple of minutes longer, and as she hung up the phone, Ellie realized she was actually looking forward to an evening out. It would feel good to laugh again, and Richard was always entertaining.

THE SUN BEAT DOWN on Glen Patterson. He and his brother were on horseback, driving almost four hundred head of cattle to one of the far pastures. With two hired hands, seasonal help, they'd shuffled all the cattle through narrow chutes, vaccinating them.

Removing his Stetson, he wiped his brow, then glanced quickly at his watch. Ellie had been in his thoughts most of the day. He shouldn't have listened to her protests; he should've stopped at her parents' house that morning despite everything. Ellie could use a helping hand, whether she was willing to admit it or not. The woman was just too damn stubborn.

In his view she'd declined his offer mostly out of pride. He wondered if she felt mourning should be done in private, and he wanted to tell her she didn't have to hide her grief, that it was okay to accept an offer of help. She didn't have to do everything herself. He knew it had all been a brave front, but he didn't have much choice other than to accept her decision.

Vaccinating the herd was not Glen's favorite task. Still, it was better than checking the cows and heifers for signs of pregnancy, although he strongly suspected the animals weren't any keener on the practice than he was himself. Glen wished to hell someone would invent a urine test for cows.

"I think I'll head on back," Glen told his brother. They'd reached the pasture, and the cattle began to spread out.

Cal's attention didn't waver from the last stragglers. "Going into town?" he asked.

Glen raised his hat a bit. "I was thinking about it," he said with some reluctance. His brother's ability to read his mind was uncanny at times. And damned irritating.

A telltale quiver at the edges of Cal's mouth signaled the beginnings of a smile. "You're going off to see Ellie, right?"

"So what?" Glen didn't care for that tone of voice. His brother never had understood how he and Ellie could be friends and nothing else. But then, Cal had an attitude when it came to women, no matter who they were. Not that Glen blamed him. If a woman had publically humiliated *him* the way Jennifer Healy had humiliated his brother, Glen supposed his own feelings toward the opposite sex would be tainted, too. At times, however, Cal's lack of perspective annoyed him.

"You two should own up to a few truths," Cal announced, as though being two years older gave him some kind of wisdom—or authority.

"Truths?"

"You and Ellie have something going."

"You're right," Glen admitted, and he could see that agreeing with Cal had taken his brother aback. "We're friends. Is that so difficult to understand?" Glen couldn't figure out what it was with his brother, and a few others, too. Even Grady Weston, his lifelong friend and fellow rancher, obviously believed there was more between him and Ellie than friendship.

The fact was that in four years they'd never so much as held hands— which should say something. He simply enjoyed Ellie's company, and she enjoyed his. Anything romantic would ruin one of the best damn friendships he'd ever had. Ellie felt the same way. Okay, so they'd never openly discussed it, but then there was no reason they should. They understood each other. An unspoken agreement.

Yes, that was it; he felt better for having analyzed the situation.

"Ellie and I have an understanding," he explained with a sense of satisfaction. Cal wouldn't argue with that. "It's like the way you and I never talk about Bitter End."

Cal's eyes narrowed. Only a small number of families in Promise knew about the ghost town hidden in the Texas hills. Few ever mentioned it. Once, as teenagers, Grady, Cal and Glen had decided to look for the town themselves. It was supposed to be a summertime adventure. Something they could brag about to their friends. It'd taken them weeks to find the place, but eventually they'd stumbled on it. The town, with its abandoned buildings and eerie silence, had terrified them so much they'd never gone back. Not only hadn't they returned, they rarely spoke of their experience.

"What's Bitter End got to do with Ellie?" Cal demanded.

"Nothing. What I mean is, you and I don't discuss Bitter End, and Ellie and I don't talk about our relationship because it's understood that neither of us is interested in a romance. Why's that so hard to accept?"

"Fine," Cal said with a snort of disbelief. "You believe what you want and I'll pretend not to notice the truth."

Glen was fast losing patience. "You do that, big brother." He didn't know what made Cal think he was such an expert on women. He was tempted to say so, but restrained himself. "I'll see you tonight sometime," he said, eager to set off. Ellie might act as if clearing out her childhood home was no big deal; Glen knew otherwise.

"Whenever," Cal said without apparent interest.

Glen eased Moonshine into an easy canter and headed toward the ranch house. One of these days Cal would find the right woman and that would shut him up. Glen had never been too impressed with Jennifer Healy; as far as he was concerned, Cal had made a lucky escape. Unfortunately his older brother didn't see it that way. Being ditched by his fiancée had made him cynical about women.

Switching his thoughts to Ellie, Glen smiled. He could almost see the quizzical smile she sometimes wore, could almost hear the sound of her laughter. That was what Ellie needed now—a reason to laugh. Laughter was a great emotional release, and she'd kept her feelings hidden inside for far too long.

He'd shower first, Glen decided, make himself something to eat and be on his way. Cal could sit in front of the tube if he wanted, but Glen had other plans. Much better ones.

GRADY WESTON's throat felt parched as a dried-up creek bed. He walked into the ranch house and straight to the refrigerator. His sister, Savannah, made a tall pitcher of iced tea for him and Laredo every afternoon. Not bothering with the niceties, he reached for the glass pitcher and drank directly from that.

"Grady!" Savannah admonished him, coming into the room. Grady's old dog, Rocket, followed her, his movements slow and awkward. She carried an armful of fresh-cut old roses, their pungent scent filling the kitchen.

He finished one last swallow and set the pitcher down on the counter, then wiped his mouth with the back of his hand. "Where's Richard?" he demanded, not wanting to hear about his lack of manners.

Okay, he should've taken the time to grab a glass, but damn it all, he was tired and thirsty. He added *irritated* to the list the moment he glanced out at the drive and saw that his pickup was missing. If it turned out that his no-good brother had absconded with his truck, his irritation would quickly turn to fury.

"I . . . don't know where Richard is," Savannah answered, and lowered her gaze. The way she avoided meeting his eyes was a sure sign that she had her suspicions but wasn't willing to share them.

"He took the truck, didn't he?"

Savannah shrugged, then nodded.

"I figured as much," Grady growled, his anger mounting. Six years earlier Richard had stolen all the family's money and promptly disappeared. Savannah and Grady had been left to deal with the aftermath of their parents' deaths, the inheritance taxes and all the legal problems, while Richard was busy squandering every dime on God only knew what. Then, this past spring, he'd shown up, down on his luck and needing a place to live until the severance check from his last job arrived. Or so he'd told them. Savannah chose to believe Richard's story, but Grady wasn't going to trust him again. Not by a long shot.

Should've kicked him off the ranch the first day. He would have, in fact, if it hadn't been for his softhearted sister. In the weeks since, Grady had called himself every kind of fool. Opportunity after opportunity had presented itself to send Richard packing, but he hadn't taken advantage of a single one.

Grady had tried to reason it out in his own mind, especially after Richard had thrown himself a welcome-home party and stuck Grady with the bill. Deep down, Grady recognized that he *wanted* to believe Richard had changed. Even when every bit of evidence claimed otherwise. As the oldest he felt a responsibility to make everything right. He looked for ways to honor the memory of his parents. Ways to hold on to the ranch.

Their mother had spoiled Richard; her youngest son had been her favorite. She might be partly to blame for his self-centered behavior, but regardless of what he'd done, she'd have expected Grady to give him shelter. Even now, six years after her death, Grady found himself seeking her approval.

"Where'd he go this time?" Grady asked, disgusted more with himself than with his brother. Richard was a master when it came to manipulating people. He was charming and a clever conversationalist, unlike Grady who was often loud and brusque. He wished he'd inherited some of Richard's success with the ladies, but he was too old and too stubborn to change now.

Savannah slowly shook her head.

"Does that mean you don't know where Richard went or you don't want to tell me?"

"A little of both," she confessed.

Despite his anger, Grady smiled and sat down at the table. "I probably would've given him the keys if he'd asked," he admitted with a certain reluctance.

"I . . . didn't actually give him the keys, but I told him where they were."

Savannah sat down across from him. It struck Grady how beautiful his sister was. As little as six months ago he would never have thought of her that way. She was just Savannah, his kindhearted younger sister. A woman who rarely raised her voice, rarely disagreed. A picture of calm serenity, while he struggled to contain his explosive temper. A woman who'd always been happy with her quiet low-key life.

Then one day, out of the blue, his sister had changed. No, he corrected himself, she'd always been strong in ways that made others seem weak, but he'd failed to recognize or appreciate those qualities in her. It had been quite a lesson she'd given him. She'd begun to assert her own needs; she'd made him aware that she wanted more from life than he'd realized or been willing to acknowledge. These changes came about because of Laredo Smith, a drifter who'd stumbled into their lives. A cowboy. A godsend. Grady and Laredo were partners now. The wedding had taken place a few weeks earlier in her rose garden, with only a few close friends as guests. In time the newlyweds would be building their own home and starting a family. Grady looked forward to having children on the ranch.

Falling in love had transformed his sister into a woman of true beauty. It was as if all the goodness inside her had become outwardly visible. He wasn't the only one who'd noticed, either. A couple of months ago she'd cut her hair—formerly waist-length—and begun wearing jeans instead of those long loose dresses. All at once other men had started to take heed. Too late, however, because her heart belonged to Laredo.

"What time did he leave?" Grady asked, rubbing his face tiredly. The problems with Richard just seemed to multiply. The money he'd claimed was coming had yet to arrive, although he'd managed to reimburse Grady five hundred dollars.

Grady had serious doubts about any so-called severance pay owed to Richard. He suspected the money was just the beginning of a long list of lies his brother had been feeding them.

To Grady's relief, Savannah no longer actively championed Richard's cause, and he knew she felt as troubled as he did about their younger brother. Neither was comfortable at the thought of kicking him off the ranch entirely. Besides, Richard occasionally made himself useful, running errands in town and making token efforts to help around the ranch.

"He left about three this afternoon."

"He didn't go into town, did he?"

Savannah hesitated. "I don't think so, but then, he didn't tell me where he was headed."

"I could have used an extra hand this afternoon," Grady murmured.

But they both knew Richard's answer to that. He was never cut out to be a rancher, which was the reason he'd given for fleeing with the family money—his share of the inheritance he called it, since he wanted no part of the ranch. The excuse stuck in Grady's craw every time he thought about it.

"He's been keeping himself busy," Savannah said, and held his gaze a moment longer than usual. Neither one of them was entirely sure what he did with his time. He disappeared for hours at a stretch without telling anyone where he went or who he was with. Normally Grady wouldn't care, but considering Richard's history, it was worrisome.

"I heard him talking to Ellie on the phone earlier," Savannah told him. "He invited her to Ruth's birthday party."

This didn't give Grady any cause for celebration. He'd noticed his younger brother's growing interest in Ellie Frasier. The fact that she'd recently inherited the family business hadn't escaped Richard's notice, and Grady worried that his brother's interest might be leaning more toward that feed store than to Ellie. She'd dealt with enough grief to have anyone exploit her now.

"She doesn't know, does she?" Savannah asked.

Grady shook his head. Few people in Promise were aware of Richard's crime. It was something Grady preferred not to share. No one wanted his friends and neighbors to learn that his only brother had robbed him blind. Only a handful of folks knew Richard had run off with every penny in the family coffers the day they buried their parents. Vanished for six years until he'd needed help himself.

Grady cursed under his breath and waited for Savannah to chastise him.

She didn't, and Grady soon realized why. The screen door opened and Laredo walked into the kitchen. The wrangler's gaze immediately met Savannah's and they exchanged a tender look.

They fascinated Grady. His sister and her husband were so deeply in love he doubted either one remembered he was in the room. Savannah stood and poured Laredo a glass of iced tea, which the man accepted gratefully. After downing the contents in four or five gulps, Laredo set the glass aside and hugged her close.

Grady watched his brother-in-law's eyes drift shut as he savored holding Savannah. In all his thirty-five years, Grady had never seen any two people more in love. Watching them lost in each other's embrace was almost painful, reminding him how alone he was. He realized he wasn't an easy man to love—he knew that—and he doubted any woman would put up with him for long. Yet he couldn't watch Savannah and Laredo and not wish for that kind of contentment himself.

Grady had never felt lonely before, never given much thought to marriage. *Someday* was about as close as he'd gotten to thinking about any future romance and then only if he could find a woman willing to look past his very noticeable flaws.

There hadn't been *time* to give any consideration to his marital status and romantic hopes—such as they were. It'd taken him six years of backbreaking labor to dig the ranch out of debt. If all went well with this year's herd, they'd be completely in the black once again.

"Caroline's coming over later," Savannah murmured.

Grady wasn't sure who the comment was meant for. Probably him. Nor was he sure whether she intended this as a warning or as . . . something else. Caroline Daniels was Savannah's best friend and the town's postmistress; he couldn't seem to get along with her, but he was afraid Savannah still had matchmaking ambitions concerning them. A completely hopeless and wrongheaded idea. Lately his sister and Caroline had spent a lot of time discussing and designing house plans, and while that didn't affect Grady one way or another, he often found himself in the company of Caroline's five-year-old daughter, Maggie. He'd been gruff and impatient with the girl not long ago, and she would barely look at him now. Grady felt bad about that.

And it irritated him no end that Maggie had taken to Richard, and

being the smooth-talking charmer he was, his younger brother soon had
the kid eating out of his hand.

Grady considered his squabbles with Caroline more her fault than
his. He admired people who spoke their minds, but Caroline did it a little
too often for his liking.

"Are you going to Ruth's birthday party?" Savannah asked.

Grady hesitated, but only for a moment. "Probably not."

His sister's eyes flared briefly and he knew that wasn't the response
she'd wanted.

"Why not?"

He wasn't accustomed to explaining his decisions, but Savannah had
that look about her, and he knew it was better to deal with the subject
now than postpone it.

"Do I need a reason?"

"Laredo and I are going," she said, wrapping her arm around her
husband's waist. "Ruth's a sweetheart, and it means a great deal to Nell
that there be a nice turnout."

"Cal's not going." Grady couldn't resist pointing this out, although
he didn't feel he should have to.

"That's exactly my point," Savannah returned. "If you're not careful,
you're going to end up just like Cal."

"And what's wrong with Cal?" Although he asked the question,
Grady knew what she meant. Ever since Jennifer had more or less left
him at the altar, Cal Patterson had little that was good to say about
women. His cynical attitude got to be a bit much, even for Grady, but
now wasn't the time to admit it.

"There's nothing wrong with Cal that a good woman wouldn't cure."

"Savannah would like you to ask Caroline to the party," Laredo
inserted. He wasn't much of a talker, but when he did speak, he cut to
the chase. No beating around the bush with Savannah's husband.

"What? You want me to *what?*" Grady pretended his hearing was
impaired and stuck his finger in his ear. He thought he was pretty comical.

Savannah didn't. "Is there a problem with Caroline?" she demanded. Her eyes flashed with spirit and Grady could see it wasn't going
to be easy to mollify her.

"Nope."

"You'd be fortunate if she accepted!"

"Of course I would," he agreed with more than a touch of sarcasm.

"Grady!"

Chuckling, he held up his hands in surrender. "Caroline's all right," he said. "It's just that we don't see eye to eye about a lot of things. You know that, Savannah. I like her, don't get me wrong, but I can't see the two of us dating."

"Because of Maggie?" Savannah asked.

"Not at all," Grady assured her, knowing how close Savannah and the little girl were.

"Savannah thought it'd be a good idea if the four of us went to Ruth's party together." Again it was Laredo who spelled out Savannah's intentions.

"Me and Caroline?" Grady burst out. He bent forward and slapped his hands on his knees in exaggerated hilarity. "Me and Caroline with you two?" Even more amusing. The lovebirds and him . . . with the postmistress. Yeah, good idea, all right. Great idea. He and Caroline could barely manage a civil word to each other. "You've got to be kidding. Tell me this is a joke."

"Apparently not." The cool voice came from the back door.

Grady's blood turned cold. Caroline Daniels and Maggie stood just inside the kitchen, and a single glance told him she'd seen his whole performance, heard every derogatory word.

TWO

The boxes awaited Ellie as she unlocked her front door and stepped inside the small rented house. Stacked against the far living-room wall, they represented what felt like an insurmountable task. She paused, her eyes drawn to the piled-up cartons. If she was smart, she'd move them out of sight and deal with the emotional nightmare of sorting through her father's things when she was better able to handle it.

But she wouldn't put this off. Again she was her father's daughter, and he'd taught her never to procrastinate. The thought of those boxes would hound her until she'd gone through every last one of them.

A number of delaying tactics occurred to her. There were letters to write, phone calls to make, people to thank; nevertheless, she recognized them for the excuses they were. The remains of her father's life would still be there, demanding her attention. Occupying her mind.

It would be easy to focus her anger on her mother, but Ellie was mature enough to recognize and accept that Pam Frasier had been pampered all her life. She'd been indulged and shielded from all unpleasantness from the time she was a child. First by her family and then by her husband. John Frasier had treated his wife like a delicate Southern blossom and protected her like the gentle knight he was.

His lengthy illness had taken a toll on Ellie's mother. To her credit Pam had done the best she could, sitting by his side for long periods at the hospital. But unfortunately she had required almost as much care and attention as her husband; she had trouble dealing with any form of illness and was horrified by the thought of death. And so, comforting John had mostly fallen to Ellie.

Dealing with John's effects, coping with the memories, was just one more obligation her mother couldn't manage. Heaving a sigh, Ellie rolled up her sleeves and tackled the first box.

Clothes. Work clothes the movers had packed. Ellie lovingly ran her hand over his favorite sweater, the elbows patched with leather. Pam had wanted him to throw it out—too old and shabby, she'd said. It astonished Ellie that her parents had ever married, as different as they were. They'd met while her father was in the service, and although no one had said as much, Ellie was convinced her mother had fallen in love with the uniform. Their courtship was far too short, and all too soon they were married and John was out of the army. He'd returned to Promise with his bride and joined his father at the family feed store. Ellie had been born two years later, after a difficult pregnancy. John had assured his wife he was perfectly content with one child and there was no need for more. Even as a young girl Ellie had realized her father intended to groom her to take over the store. Not once had she thought of doing anything else. She'd majored in business at the University of Texas at Austin, and although she'd dated several young men, she'd never allowed any relationship to grow serious. She couldn't, not when it was understood she'd be returning to Promise and the feed store. After graduation, she'd found a small house to rent a few blocks from her parents and started working with her dad.

Ellie kept the sweater, but rather than unpack the rest of the clothes, she set the box aside, along with the next two, all of which contained items from his closet. The local charities were always in need of good clothes, and it would be an easy matter to drop them off.

When she opened the fourth box, Ellie paused. The old family Bible rested on top of a photo album. Carefully, using both hands, she lifted the fragile book from its cardboard shelter. The Bible had been in her father's family for a hundred-plus years, handed down from one generation to the next. Ellie had known about it; she'd read the names listed in the front for a high-school report years before, but hadn't opened it since. In fact, she wasn't sure where her mother had stored it.

Curious, she sat down on the sofa and set the book on the coffee table. Leaning forward, she opened it. Once again she read the names listed, reacquainting herself with each one, recalling what her father had told her about her ancestors.

Her great-great grandparents, Jeremiah and Esther Frasier—good Biblical names, Ellie mused—together with their three sons, whose births were also noted, had placed all their worldly possessions in a covered wagon. Then with courage and faith they'd ventured west, risking all for the promise of land in Texas.

Ellie ran her index finger down the names of the three children, pausing over the youngest, Edward Abraham. His birthday was recorded and then the date of his death only five years later. No reason was listed, only a tear-smudged Bible reference. *Matthew 28:46.* Not recognizing it, Ellie flipped the pages until she located the verse. *"My God, my God, why have you forsaken me."*

The agony of Esther's loss seemed to vibrate from the page. With her own heart still fragile from the pain of her father's death, Ellie was keenly aware of this young mother's anguish over the loss of her son. Unable to read more, she closed the Bible and put it aside.

As she did, a single piece of cloth slipped from between the pages and drifted onto the coffee table. Ellie reached for it and frowned. The muslin square had yellowed with age; each side was no bigger than six inches. In the middle of the block was an embroidered bug that resembled a giant grasshopper. The detail was exquisite, each infinitesimally small stitch perfectly positioned. Nevertheless, it was an odd thing to place inside a Bible. What could possibly have been important enough about an embroidered grasshopper to save it all these years, tucked between the pages of a family Bible? But these were questions for another time, another day.

Her stomach growled and, glancing at her watch, Ellie realized it'd been almost six hours since she'd last eaten. She carried the Bible into her bedroom and placed it on her dresser top, then rummaged around her kitchen until she found the ingredients for a tuna salad.

An hour later a half-eaten salad and an empty milk glass on the carpet beside her, Ellie happened upon the box of John Wayne videos. Her father had loved the Duke. In the worst days of his illness, it was the one thing that was sure to calm him. These movies were as much a part of his heritage as the family Bible. She placed them in the cabinet below her television and on impulse inserted one into the VCR.

McLintock! with Maureen O'Hara was one of Ellie's favorites. Soon she found herself involved in the movie, the boxes forgotten. She didn't have to unpack *every* box that night, she decided.

With the lights dimmed she sat cross-legged on the sofa, watching the television screen. This particular John Wayne classic had been a favorite of her father's as well. Only a few months earlier, he'd suggested that when Ellie decided to look for a husband, she wouldn't go wrong if she found a man like the kind John Wayne usually portrayed.

Where the tears came from, Ellie didn't know. One moment she was laughing at the very place she laughed every time she saw the movie, and the next her cheeks were wet with tears.

Chastising herself for being too sentimental, she dried her eyes with a napkin. A minute later, the tears started again. Soon they flowed with such vigor she required a box of tissues.

It didn't take Ellie long to realize that the movie had triggered the release she'd needed all these weeks. Stopping the flow of tears was impossible, so she gave up trying, sobbing openly now. With a tissue pressed to each eye, she sniffed, then paused, holding her breath, thinking she'd heard a noise unrelated to the movie.

The sound was repeated and Ellie groaned.

The doorbell.

She yearned to ignore it, but anyone who knew her would recognize her car parked out front.

With a reluctant sigh, she walked slowly toward the door. She glanced through the peephole, but whoever was there had moved out of her range of vision.

"Who's there?" she demanded.

"The big bad wolf."

Glen.

"Damn," she muttered under her breath, frantically rubbing at the tears on her face. "Go away," she called out. "I'm not decent." Which wasn't far from the truth. He was her friend and a good one but she didn't want him or anyone else to see her like this.

"Come on, Ellie, open up."

"Not by the hair of your chinny, chin, chin," she called back.

"Then I'll huff and I'll puff and I'll blow your house down."

She hesitated, unsure what to do.

"Ellie, for heaven's sake, grab a towel or whatever and let me in."

He twisted the knob and she realized he was going to enter with or without her permission. This was what she got for not keeping her front door locked, but it was a habit she'd never developed. No need to in a town like Promise.

"Come on in," she said, finally opening the door.

"You're dressed," he said with some surprise. "I thought you said—" Apparently he noticed her tear-blotched face, because he stopped short.

She squared her shoulders, not knowing what he'd do or say. They'd laughed together, disagreed, teased and joked, but she'd never allowed Glen or anyone else to see her cry.

His hand rested gently on her shoulder. "I thought as much," he whispered.

It would have been better if he'd made a joke of it, Ellie mused. She might have been able to laugh off her embarrassment if he had.

"It's the movie," she said, pointing to the television set behind her.

"I . . . started watching it and . . ." To her utter humiliation, the tears came back in force.

"Ellie?"

She turned her back to him. "I'm not fit company just now," she managed.

"Do you want me to leave?" he asked from behind.

Did she? Ellie didn't know. Wrapping her arms around her middle, she couldn't remember a time she'd felt more alone. Her beloved father was gone and her mother had all but abandoned her. It wasn't supposed to happen like this. Her father had been everything to her.

"Ellie?" Glen questioned again.

"You'd better go."

A long moment passed. Anyone else would have left by now, but Glen hesitated, as though he couldn't make himself do it. That was when Ellie knew she wanted him to stay.

"Would . . . would you mind sticking around for a while?" she choked out.

"Of course." With his arm loosely about her shoulders, he steered her back to the sofa. "Sit here and I'll get you something to drink."

She nodded, grateful once again that Glen Patterson was her friend. A good stiff drink was exactly what she needed. Something strong enough to dull the pain.

Within a couple of minutes Glen returned with a tall glass. Ice clinked against the sides when he handed it to her.

She appreciated his tact and understanding and accepted the glass. Tentatively tasting the drink, she tried to remember what she had stored in the liquor cabinet above the refrigerator. Vodka? Gin?

Almost immediately she started to cough and choke.

Glen slapped her hard on the back.

She needed a moment to catch her breath. When she did she glared at him with narrowed eyes. "You brought me *ice water?*" she cried. The man had no sense of what she was suffering. None whatsoever, or he'd realize that a time like this required liquor.

"What's wrong with water?" he asked with a look of such genuine innocence that Ellie knew it would do no good to explain.

She dismissed his question with a wave of her hand and gestured for him to sit down.

Glen claimed the empty space next to her on the sofa. "Do you want to talk about it?" he asked.

"No," she said, and for emphasis shook her head. "Just watch the movie."

"All right." He leaned back and stretched his arms along the back of the couch. With one foot resting on the other knee, he seemed perfectly at ease.

Ellie did her best to focus on the movie, but it was pointless. So was any attempt to hold back the tears that pooled in her eyes, then leaked from the corners, making wet tracks down the sides of her face. At first she tried to blink them away. That didn't help. Neither did holding her breath or staring up at the ceiling. She drank the glass of water and, when she could disguise the need no longer, made a frantic grab for the box of tissue.

"I thought as much," Glen said for the second time. He placed his arm around her shoulders and pulled her against him. "It isn't the movie, is it?"

"What makes you ask that?" she sobbed.

"Because I know you."

Men always assumed they knew a woman when they didn't have a clue. And Glen Patterson was as clueless as any man she'd ever known, friend or not.

"As I said earlier, I'm not very good company at the moment." She blotted her eyes with a fresh tissue. In an effort to distract her thoughts, she showed him the old Bible with the names of family who'd lived and died over a hundred years ago. When she talked about Edward Abraham's death, the tears began again.

"Hey, if I'd been looking for scintillating company, I would've stayed home with Cal," Glen said, then laughed at his little joke.

They both knew Cal was about as much fun as a rampaging bull these days.

"Come on," he urged with real tenderness. "Let it all out."

She swallowed a sob. It would have been better, she thought now, if he hadn't stayed, after all. But it felt good to lean on someone. So good. Ellie feared that once she lowered her guard and gave way to her emotions, it would be like a river overflowing its banks. All semblance of control would vanish. As close a friend as Glen was, she preferred to shed her tears alone.

"Relax," he instructed, sounding like the older brother she'd never had. He squeezed her shoulder and rested his chin against her hair. "It's okay to cry. You have the right."

"I couldn't make myself believe it," she sobbed into his chest. The doctors had explained soon after he was diagnosed that his condition was terminal. No hope.

"Believe what?" Glen asked softly.

"That he was dying. I should have been prepared for it, but I wasn't."

"He was your father, Ellie. How could you prepare to lose your father? How could anyone?"

"I—I don't know." Her whole body shook; she couldn't control the tremors.

"Quit being so hard on yourself, okay?"

"I wanted to celebrate his life," she added. "Not . . . not act like this." She felt as though she were walking around with a giant hole inside her. Grief overwhelmed her. She missed him in a thousand different ways. Every minute, every hour, she found reasons to think of him. Everything she said and did reminded her of how close they'd always been. She couldn't walk into the store without confronting evidence of him— his work, his personality, his plans for the future. If that wasn't bad enough, every time she looked in the mirror it was his deep blue eyes that stared back.

"You *are* celebrating his life," Glen murmured, and his lips brushed the top of her head.

"I am?" Easing herself from his embrace, she raised her face to look up at him.

"You were the apple of your father's eye," Glen reminded her. "He couldn't keep the buttons of his shirt fastened, he was so proud of you."

While Ellie knew that was true, it felt good to hear Glen say it. "He was a wonderful father." She bit her lower lip to keep it from trembling.

"The best." Glen gazed down at her and with his thumb caught a tear as it rolled from her bottom lashes and onto her cheek.

He paused with his finger halfway across her face and when her vision cleared, Ellie noted Glen's look of surprise. Their eyes met, widened. They couldn't seem to stop gazing at each other's faces. Ellie suddenly felt herself frowning, but before she had a chance to analyze what was happening, she realized something else.

Glen was going to kiss her.

She could have moved, avoided his kiss and the embarrassment that was sure to follow, but curiosity got the better of her. As his mouth slowly lowered toward hers, her eyes drifted shut. She half expected him to draw back at the last second, but he didn't—and she was glad.

His lips were moist and warm as they settled gently on hers. The gentleness lasted only a moment, and then he thrust his fingers into her short hair and increased the pressure of his mouth. Ellie felt the heat in him, the unaccustomed desire. And she felt his tension. She understood it, because she was feeling the same thing. A sense of discomfort, even guilt. This was Glen, her friend. And they were kissing like lovers, like a couple well beyond the range of friendship.

Ellie slipped her hands up his chest and anchored her fingers at his shoulders. The kiss took on another dimension. The hunger that had been held in check was replaced by heady excitement. Ellie opened to Glen without restraint, reserving nothing. He deepened the kiss until they both trembled. When he abruptly broke it off, his breathing was heavy and labored. So was hers.

Slowly Ellie opened her eyes. Glen was staring at her, his forehead creased in a deep frown.

"What was that?" she asked, her voice barely above a whisper.

"A kiss," he said, sounding almost angry.

"I know that. What I'm asking is . . . why?"

"Why?" he repeated, sounding as uncertain as she was. "Because . . . because you were crying."

"So?"

"It was shock therapy," he said, easing himself away from her, gently at first and then as if he couldn't move fast enough. He scooted unceremoniously to the side of the sofa.

Not knowing what to think, much less say, she blinked.

"It worked," he said, as if this entire incident had been carefully planned. "You're not crying, are you?"

Ellie raised her fingertips to her face. He was right.

"I had to do *something*," he said, sounding more like himself now—confident, amused, down-to-earth.

"Something," she repeated, trying not to press her fingers against her slightly swollen lips.

"Anything," he added. "I was getting desperate. You feel better, don't you?"

She had to consider that for a moment. But it was true.

"Hey, I didn't mean . . ." He hesitated as if not sure how to continue.

Ellie wasn't sure she wanted him to. "Me neither," she told him quickly, far more comfortable dropping the matter than exploring it further. Glen was a damn good friend and she didn't want one stupid kiss to ruin this friendship.

He relaxed visibly. "Good."

She smiled and nodded. "I gotta admit, though," she said, eagerly falling back on the comfortable banter they'd always enjoyed. "You're one fine kisser."

"Damn fine," he agreed, and puffed out his chest in a parody of male pride. "You aren't the first one to tell me that."

Ellie rolled her eyes toward the ceiling.

"You aren't so bad yourself."

"Don't I know it." Standing, she hooked her thumbs in the belt loops of her jeans and rocked on her heels. "Plenty of other guys have told me I'm hot stuff."

"I can see why."

They laughed then, both of them, but Ellie noticed that their laughter had a decidedly shaky sound to it.

"SHAKY" PRETTY WELL described how Glen felt. An hour later he pulled into the long driveway that led from the highway to the Lonesome Coyote Ranch. He trembled every time he thought about kissing Ellie.

Fool that he was, he'd given in to a crazy impulse and damn near made the biggest mistake of his life.

Glen blamed Cal for this. His brother was the one who'd planted the idea, claiming Glen's relationship with Ellie was far more than friendship. Cal had just said it a few too many times and hell—Glen shook his head—one minute he was looking down at Ellie and the next thing he knew they were kissing. What scared the living daylights out of him was how incredibly good the kiss had been. It wasn't *supposed* to be that good, but it had shot straight off the Richter scale.

Oh, yeah, Ellie had shaken him up plenty.

Thank goodness he'd been able to make light of the incident, brush it off. Ellie had seemed just as eager to put it behind them. For the first time in years he'd been uncomfortable with his best friend. With Ellie. All because of an impulsive kiss, something that never should've happened.

He parked the truck and sat in the stillness of the night to gather his wits about him. He recalled how the kiss had ended and she'd looked up at him, her striking blue eyes wide with shock. Damn if it hadn't taken every ounce of willpower he possessed not to kiss her again.

Thank God he hadn't. Gratitude welled up inside him. Had they continued much longer they would've ruined everything. Knowing he was being less than subtle about it, he'd gotten the hell out of that house. Again Ellie had obviously felt relieved to be rid of him. With any luck they'd both forget the entire incident. For his part he never intended to mention it again, and he sincerely hoped Ellie didn't, either.

Once he felt sufficiently calm, he climbed out of the truck and walked into the house. Cal sat in the kitchen with ledgers spread out across the table. He glanced up when Glen entered the room and did a double take.

"You okay?"

"Why shouldn't I be?" Glen demanded sharply.

"No need to bite my head off," his brother snapped back. "What happened? You have a spat with Ellie?"

"No."

"I see," Cal returned, not bothering to suppress a smile.

"I'm going to bed," Glen announced.

"Good idea," Cal called after him. "Sleep might improve your disposition."

Glen stomped up the stairs and was breathless by the time he entered his bedroom. He closed the door and sagged onto the edge of the mattress. With his elbows resting on his knees, he inhaled deeply several times. No wonder he was shaking. He'd had a narrow escape.

THE NIGHT WAS ALIVE with sound. The intoxicating aroma of old roses filled the air. Katydids chirped and the porch swing creaked as Savannah and Laredo swayed back and forth, back and forth. The stars were generous with their glittering bounty that night. It all said *romance*, the romance of song and story, and it suited Savannah's mood perfectly.

She leaned her head against Laredo's shoulder and his arm held her close. Even now, resting in her husband's strong embrace, she found it difficult to believe this wonderful man loved her.

"What's on your mind?" he whispered.

Savannah's lips eased into a ready smile. "I was just thinking how fortunate I am that you love me."

Laredo went still, and she knew his thoughts; he didn't need to voice them. It was that way sometimes when people were deeply in love. Their marriage was like a miracle, an unexpected gift—and it had come when they were least prepared for it. Because of that, they'd come close to losing it all.

"I loved you when I left you," Laredo said, his voice hoarse with the intensity of his feelings. "I worry sometimes that you don't know how difficult it was to walk away from you."

"I did know, and that's what made it so hard," she confided. She would never fully comprehend it, but Laredo had believed that she deserved someone who could give her more than he could. It was one of life's cruel ironies—without him, money, land and possessions meant very little. But with his love she was rich beyond measure. It was the most precious thing she'd ever had.

The kitchen door creaked open and Savannah's older brother stepped onto the porch. She wasn't too pleased with Grady's poor timing, but decided to overlook it. Not for the first time, either. Look what he'd done just the other day, when he'd made those comments about Caroline at the worst possible moment.

Grady walked to the porch steps and stared into the night sky. "I decided to attend the birthday bash for Ruth," he said without glancing in their direction.

Savannah heard the reluctance in his voice and realized the decision hadn't been an easy one.

"With Caroline?" she asked, trying not to sound eager.

He hesitated before answering. "I thought about asking her, then decided against it."

Savannah knew that if he let himself Grady would enjoy Caroline's company. Unfortunately he bungled all her efforts at playing matchmaker. What she'd hoped was that he'd become comfortable enough with Caroline at the birthday party to invite her to the Cattlemen's Association dance later in the month. The dance marked the beginning of summer and was the most anticipated event of the year.

"Why *don't* you ask Caroline?" She was losing patience with him.

"Because I didn't think she'd want to after the way . . . Hell, you should know the answer to that. I made a fool of myself."

"Caroline was more amused than angry," Savannah assured her brother.

"Yeah, well, that's not how I saw it. I thought I'd invite someone else."

"Like who?"

"I don't know . . ."

"How about the new doctor?" Savannah suggested. Dr. Jane Dickinson had replaced Doc Cummings at the Health Clinic when he retired. She'd read in the local newspaper that Dr. Dickinson had agreed to stay on for three years as a means of repaying her medical-school loans. If Grady wasn't going to ask Caroline, then this new doctor was a good choice.

"No, thanks."

"What's wrong with *her?*"

"Nothing . . . everything." Grady didn't elaborate.

The problem with her brother, Savannah realized, was a complete lack of confidence in himself when it came to women. Grady failed to recognize his own masculine appeal. His *considerable* appeal. She suspected that Richard's presence made it worse. Richard was handsome and sociable, a smooth talker who had no difficulty attracting female companionship. Grady, on the other hand, was awkward around women and constantly seemed to say the wrong thing.

Savannah edged closer to her husband. "Um, Grady, I don't think it's a good idea to wait until the last minute."

"You don't?"

Both Savannah and Laredo shook their heads.

Grady rubbed the back of his neck. "The hell with it," he muttered. "Nell didn't say anything about bringing a date. If Cal shows up you can bet he'll be without a woman. Nothing says I need one, either."

Savannah resisted the urge to box his ears. "Do you intend to live the rest of your life alone, Grady?"

Her brother didn't answer her for a moment. "I don't know anymore. It just seems to be the way things are headed." With that, he went back inside.

"I almost feel sorry for him," Laredo said.

"It's his own fault." Savannah didn't mean to sound unkind, but her brother was too stubborn for his own good. "If he'd open his eyes, he'd realize Caroline's perfect for him."

"You can't push him into a relationship with your friend, love."

Savannah realized that. "But . . ."

"It'll happen for Grady when the time is right."

"How can you be so sure?"

"It did with us."

Sighing, Savannah dropped her head against his shoulder once again. This was her favorite time of day, sitting in the moonlight with Laredo, feeling his love enclose her.

They kissed then, and the sweetness of it was enough to bring tears to Savannah's eyes. She savored the contentment of being in his arms, wishing everyone could experience this kind of love. Grady and the embittered Cal Patterson and Caroline and . . .

"Ellie Frasier needs someone, too," she said wistfully.

"Are you the resident matchmaker now?" Laredo teased.

"Yes—even if it *is* self-appointed." She nudged him with her elbow. "Now—a man for Ellie."

"Not Richard."

"Not Richard," Savannah agreed. "Glen Patterson."

Laredo laughed lightly. "You're way off base with that one, Savannah. I can't see it. They make much better friends than they ever would lovers."

The evening was much too fine to argue. She didn't need Laredo to agree with her to know she was right.

Three

Nell Bishop flipped the braid off her shoulder and surveyed the yard. Everything was ready for Ruth's surprise party. The Moorhouse sisters, both retired schoolteachers, were keeping her mother-in-law occupied in town. Knowing Edwina and Lily, they'd take their assignment seriously. The last Nell heard, they'd planned a visit to the library, followed by a little birthday celebration at Dovie Boyd's antique shop. Dovie had recently added the Victorian Tea Room, and each afternoon at three, she served tea and scones. Sometimes she added cucumber sandwiches and a small glass—or two—of the Moorhouse sisters' special cordial, which she made from a recipe handed down by their maternal grandfather.

Nell gathered that the sandwiches tended to be dry but the cordial was well worth the price of admission. The Moorhouse sisters would bring her back at the start of the festivities. All three would probably be a little tipsy and in a fine party mood.

It was time the Bishop family did a bit of celebrating. Jake wouldn't have wanted them to spend the rest of their lives grieving. Things had been difficult for Nell since her husband's death, but with Ruth's help she'd managed to hold on to the ranch.

"Mom, where do you want me to put the potato chips?" Jeremy called from the back porch steps. Her eleven-year-old son stood with a huge bowl in his hands, awaiting her instructions.

"Set it on the first picnic table," she answered, pointing at the line of five covered tables that stretched across the freshly groomed yard. She'd spent half the day spiffing up the flower beds and mowing the grass and the other half cooking. Fried chicken, her special recipe for chili, a smorgasbord of salads, plus a huge homemade birthday cake.

Jeremy carried the bowl to the table, then promptly helped himself to a handful. Nell bit her tongue to keep from admonishing him not to spoil his dinner. This was a celebration and she wasn't going to ruin it by scolding her children. Both Jeremy and nine-year-old Emma had been helpful and cooperative, as excited about the party as she was herself.

Jeremy's hand stopped midway to his mouth and he cast a guilty look at his mother.

"All I ask is that you save some for the guests."

He nodded, smiling hugely. "We got plenty."

How like Jake her son was. She couldn't look at him and not be reminded of the only man she'd ever loved. They'd grown up together, she and Jake, and Nell knew from the time she'd first started thinking about boys that one day she'd marry Jake Bishop. It had taken him several years to reach the same conclusion, but men were often slower when it came to figuring out these things.

Both Nell and Jake were tall and big-boned. Nell was nearly six feet by the time she stopped growing. She had the kind of looks that were usually described as handsome, not pretty. And certainly not cute. The only man she'd ever known who hadn't been intimidated by her size—or treated her like one of the boys—had been Jake, and that was because he was six feet four inches himself.

Jake had taught her the wonders of being feminine. They'd had almost ten years together, and she'd treasured every one of them. Some folks expected her to remarry, but she'd yet to meet the man who could match the husband she'd lost. Nell wasn't willing to accept second best, not after loving Jake.

For the first year after Jake's death in a tractor accident she'd felt cheated and angry. It had taken her another year to accept his death and to reshape her life now that her husband was gone. With his mother's love and support she'd been able to keep the ranch, raise her kids, plan for the future.

She was a good cook, an able manager and, thanks to Jake, knew a great deal about ranching. More than she'd ever wanted to learn, in fact. The time had come to put all that knowledge to good use.

The party was to serve a dual purpose. To celebrate Ruth's birthday of course. And also to announce that she was opening her doors and turning Twin Canyon into a dude ranch. By the end of next year she hoped to be giving a group of greenhorns a taste of the real Texas.

Her research had shown that the cowboy era was alive and well in the minds of adventurous Americans. The travel agents she'd spoken with had assured her they could fill the bunkhouse with tourists eager to spend their vacation dollars learning about life in the Old West.

And Nell was just the one to teach them. She'd feed them her chili, get them on the back of a horse and demonstrate how to herd a few head of cattle. Take them on a trail drive—like in the movie *City Slickers*. And after all that, she'd gladly accept their credit cards.

"Mom!" Emma called, her freckled face smeared with frosting from the birthday cake. "Should I put the candles in now?"

"Not yet."

"Hey!" Jeremy hollered. "*I* was supposed to lick the beaters!" He grabbed a fresh supply of potato chips, apparently to compensate for the frosting he'd missed.

"Wash your face," Nell instructed her daughter. "I need your help out here."

"Yeah," Jeremy said with an air of superiority. "Help Mom."

"I am," Emma insisted. "I tasted the frosting to make sure it was good."

Despite herself, Nell laughed. "Come on, you two. The party's going to start soon and I want all the food on the tables, ready for the buffet." She headed for the house to collect paper plates and napkins.

"Will Grandma be surprised?" Emma asked.

Nell knew how hard it had been for her daughter to keep the birthday party a secret. "Very," she promised. "And Grandma's going to have a wonderful time. We all are."

She was sure of it.

THE BIRTHDAY PARTY was already in full swing when Ellie and Richard arrived. People clustered about the yard, talking in small groups. There was an air of joy and festivity that Ellie found infectious. Party sounds—laughter, animated conversation and music—were everywhere. Ellie began to hope she might actually enjoy herself the way she used to.

She glanced around and realized she was looking for Glen. Although she'd agreed to attend the party with Richard Weston, she wished now that she'd turned him down.

She hadn't seen Glen in three days. Not since he'd kissed her. Hadn't heard from him, either. While it wasn't unusual for them to go a week or longer without talking to each other, for some reason this three-day stretch felt more like three months.

She had no intention of mentioning the kiss, but that didn't mean she hadn't been thinking about it. As a matter of fact, she'd thought of little else, and she wondered if the incident weighed as heavy on Glen's mind as it did hers.

Probably not.

"I should have brought my guitar," Richard said, pressing his hand against her back as he steered her into the yard.

Richard had a fairly good singing voice and he'd entertained a crowd at his welcome-home party a few months earlier. He seemed quite impressed with his musical talent—excessively so, in Ellie's opinion. Although his voice was pleasant, it would assure him a position in the church choir but nowhere else.

"Did I tell you how beautiful you look this evening?" he asked.

"Twice," she murmured. One thing about Richard, he was a charmer. His remarks were nice to hear, but she didn't take them seriously.

"I'm pleased to see you're keeping track of how often I say it," he muttered with a tinge of sarcasm.

Ellie gave him a sharp look. She was well aware of the kind of man Richard Weston was. She'd seen him in action and had to admire his skill. He issued his compliments with just enough wonder in his voice to sound sincere. Some women might believe him, but she wouldn't allow herself to be deluded. She also suspected that Richard didn't like her perceptiveness.

Ellie was delighted to see that Nell had gotten the big turnout she'd wanted. No one ever came right out and said it, but the town was proud of Nell Bishop. They were attending this party as much for her as for Ruth. Folks wanted Nell to know they respected the way she'd managed to keep the ranch in operation. The way she'd stood against popular opinion and refused to sell. At the first sign of financial difficulty, a lot of well-meaning friends had suggested she get rid of the ranch. Ellie wasn't sure she would have advised otherwise, but Nell had insisted on keeping the small spread. It had been her husband's heritage; now it was her children's. More than that, Ellie realized, the ranch was part of Jake, and Nell had deeply loved her husband.

"Help yourself to a plate," Richard urged as they neared the picnic tables. Ellie surveyed the wide assortment of hot dishes and salads. From the look of it, Nell had cooked everything herself.

A card table was stacked with brightly wrapped birthday presents, and Ellie added hers to the pile. Busy seeing to some other guests, Nell waved a hand in greeting and Ellie waved back. Ruth sat in the seat of honor, a rocking chair, with her friends circled around her. The older woman, who was normally quiet and reserved, appeared to relish being the center of attention. Jeremy and Emma raced about the yard with several other children in hot pursuit.

"You ready to eat?" Richard asked, sounding as if it'd been at least a year since he'd last sat down to a decent meal.

"Sure." Ellie reached for a paper plate and suddenly, out of the corner of her eye, caught sight of Glen. She turned slightly and noticed that he sat under the shade of an oak tree chatting with Grady Weston. He seemed to see her at the same time, and their eyes locked and held for an embarrassingly long moment. Any other time she would've waved and gestured for him to save her a place. But not now. Instead, she pretended she hadn't seen him and proceeded down the buffet line.

Apparently Richard was aware of the moment and staked his claim by sliding his arm about her waist and nuzzling her neck. Ellie didn't dare look in Glen's direction for fear of what he'd think.

"Richard," she murmured under her breath. "Stop it."

"Stop what?" he asked. "I can't help it if I find you irresistible."

"Yeah, right." What he found her, Ellie surmised, was a trophy. The victor's spoils, to wave beneath Glen's nose. Although close in age, Richard and Glen had never been friendly, and while they weren't openly hostile to each other, there was no love lost, either.

Ellie filled her plate and tried to ignore Richard as he added a spoonful of this and that, insisting she sample every dish. Considering all the attention he paid her, anyone might have assumed they were a long-time couple. All this solicitude embarrassed her.

"Would you kindly stop?" she said, and despite her displeasure, she laughed at the woebegone look he wore.

"I can't help myself," he said. "You're the most beautiful woman here." Ellie just shook her head.

They found an empty space on the grass, shaded by the house. The scent of freshly mowed lawn and a row of blooming roses mingled with the sights and sounds of the party.

Far more aware of Glen than she wanted to be, Ellie talked nervously, telling Richard about her week. He didn't pay much attention until she mentioned the old family Bible she'd found among her father's things.

"How old did you say it was?"

"More than a hundred years," Ellie answered. Although there were a number of dates entered in the Bible, she wasn't sure when it had first been purchased.

"Your ancestors were part of the original group that settled in Bitter End?"

"From what I understand they were."

"Have you ever been there?" Richard surprised her by asking next.

The question was ridiculous. No one had, no one she knew, anyway. Bitter End was a mysterious almost mythical town people whispered about. Its location remained a secret, and despite her childhood curiosity, her father had told her very little. But as far as she could figure, there simply wasn't that much to tell. The town had been settled shortly after the Civil War and for unknown reasons was later abandoned. A scattering of the original settlers—Ellie's ancestors among them—then founded Promise.

Richard's eyes darted around as if to gauge whether anyone was listening in on their conversation. "I've been to Bitter End," he whispered dramatically. "Not that long ago, either."

"Get out of here!" It was all a joke and she wasn't going to fall for it. If she did, he'd laugh at her for believing him, and she didn't want to be the brunt of his teasing remarks.

His eyes narrowed and he bent toward her. "I'm serious, Ellie."

If Bitter End was anywhere in the vicinity, people would be flocking to it—ghost towns were fascinating, this one particularly so because of the mystery surrounding the original settlers' departure.

"Have you noticed that people don't talk about it much?" he asked, lowering his voice again. He made it sound as though the residents of Promise had conspired to keep the town a secret—to which *he* held the key.

Ellie frowned, unwilling to play his nonsensical game.

"It isn't called a ghost town for nothing." Richard shivered as if a sudden chill had raced up his spine.

"Richard," she snapped, "if this is a joke, I'm not amused."

His expression was earnest as he shook his head. "I swear to you on my parents' grave I'm serious."

"You've seen Bitter End yourself?" Even now she wasn't sure she should believe him.

"Yes," he insisted. "So have others."

"Who?" She didn't know anyone who'd been to the ghost town, and she'd spent her entire life in Promise.

"Glen Patterson for one."

Now she *knew* he was joking. Glen was her best friend, and he would certainly have mentioned this if it was true.

Richard must have read the doubt in her eyes because he added, "He found it, along with my brother and Cal, when he was a kid. If you don't believe me, ask him yourself."

Ellie intended on doing exactly that.

"When were you last there?" she asked, still feeling suspicious.

"Recently."

"How recently?"

"This week."

Ellie's curiosity went into overdrive. "You'd better not be razzing me, Richard."

"I swear it's the truth."

"Will you take me there?"

He hesitated.

"Richard, you can't tell me about Bitter End and then refuse to show it to me! What's it like? Where is it? Are any of the old buildings still standing? And how in heaven's name did you find it?"

Chuckling, he held up his hand to stop her. "Whoa! One question at a time."

"All right," she said, her heart pounding with excitement. She wanted to see this place. Her father's great-grandparents had settled there. It was in Bitter End that they'd buried their five-year-old son, the child whose name was in the old Bible.

"How'd you ever find it?" she asked again.

"It wasn't easy," he said, licking his fingertips and seeming to savor her attention as much as he did Nell's fried chicken. "I knew it was real because I'd heard . . . the others talk about it years ago, but they refused to tell me where it was. So I started looking on my own a few weeks ago—and I found it."

"Why wouldn't they tell you?"

"For the same reason I'm not telling you."

"Oh, no, you don't!" She wasn't going to let him pull that on her.

"Ellie," he murmured, his gaze pinning hers, "it's haunted."

"I ain't afraid of no ghosts," she teased, quoting the popular movie *Ghostbusters*.

Always quick with a laugh or a smile, Richard revealed neither. "I'm not joking."

"I'm not, either. I want you to take me there."

He shook his head, obviously regretting that he'd ever brought up the subject. "That's not a good idea."

"Then I'll have Glen take me."

Richard's face hardened. "It's dangerous there, Ellie. Anything can happen. I wouldn't feel right about taking you to someplace like Bitter End."

"I don't care. I want to see it. Just once," she pleaded.

Again he hesitated.

"Please?" she asked softly.

Richard sighed, and Ellie's gaze drifted to Glen, partly because she was curious about what he was doing, but also as a subtle message. If Richard wouldn't take her, odds were she could convince Glen to.

"All right, all right," he muttered irritably.

"When?"

"Soon."

"Tomorrow?"

Richard looked decidedly uncomfortable. "I . . . I don't know."

"We'll make a day of it," she coaxed, eager to explore the old town. Besides, Richard might change his mind if she didn't act quickly.

"You can't tell *anyone*."

"Why not?"

"Ellie, you don't seem to understand how serious this is. It was a mistake to mention it in the first place."

"Okay," she said, knowing that if she didn't agree he'd never take her there. "I won't tell anyone else."

"I want your word of honor," Richard insisted. "I'm not kidding, Ellie. The place is dangerous, and I don't want some fool kid to break his neck because you let word out. The minute kids around here know about it, you can bet someone's going to get hurt. I don't want that on my conscience."

Ellie didn't want it on hers, either. "You have my word, Richard."

He nodded, apparently accepting her promise. "I'll take you tomorrow afternoon, then. Be ready by two."

DESPITE HIS BEST intentions, Glen couldn't keep his eyes off Ellie and Richard. They sat huddled together, their heads close, deep in conversation. He would've sworn Ellie was too smart to be taken in by a charlatan like Richard Weston. Okay, so maybe Richard was on the level—Glen didn't really know, for Grady was as reluctant to talk about his brother as he was about everything else.

"Looks like Ellie and Richard might have more in common than I realized," Glen muttered. He noted the concerned expression on Grady's face.

"I'd say she's pretty vulnerable right now," Grady commented. He seemed to be asking Glen to keep an eye on Ellie. "Someone needs to watch out for her."

Glen's own concerns mounted. He didn't like the way those two were gazing at each other—as though nobody else was around. In fact, it bothered him. *Really* bothered him.

"How good a friend are you?" Grady asked.

"Good." Good enough for him to kiss her, Glen mused. Not just any kiss, either, but one that had damn near knocked his socks off. He'd thought of little else for three days and three sleepless nights. Every time he closed his eyes she was there in his mind, and damn it all, he found himself wanting to kiss her again.

He worried that he'd ruined their friendship, and from her reaction when she arrived at the party, that looked all too likely. As for the way things were developing between her and Richard—well, he didn't trust Grady's younger brother, not one bit. The guy was too glib, too smooth. And that was only the half of it.

Glen had heard from Cal how Grady got stuck with the bill for Richard's welcome-home party. It was all a misunderstanding, Richard claimed, but Glen would bet his last dollar Grady'd never see that money again.

Some time later, when the opportunity presented itself, Glen made his way over to Ellie. Richard was preoccupied singing a jazzed-up version of "Happy Birthday" to Ruth. Glen never did trust a man who craved being the center of attention. Anyone else would have asked Ruth to stand up, would have made *her* the focus. Not Richard. He had everyone gather around him, and it seemed to Glen he treated Ruth's birthday like an afterthought, like a mere pretext for his own performance. Typical. Richard sure hadn't changed.

"Nice party," he said, strolling casually to Ellie's side.

She stood at the edge of the group and Glen was grateful she hadn't taken a front-row seat to Richard's antics. Grady's brother had plenty of other admirers at the moment and seemed to have forgotten his date. Glen, however, resisted pointing this out to Ellie. "Good news about Nell and her dude ranch," he said, instead.

"Sure is," Ellie responded. "I really think she can make it work."

"Yeah. Nell can do it if anyone can."

Ellie nodded. "I haven't seen you in a few days."

"I've been busy."

"Me, too."

"I noticed," he said, thinking about the way she'd cozied up to Richard.

Ellie laughed. "You sound jealous."

"Not me." He raised both hands in a dismissive gesture, then realized she was making an effort to put their relationship back on its previous footing. "But I could be," he said, falling into the easy banter they'd so often exchanged.

"I'm glad to hear it." Her smile was like a splash of sunshine, and

Glen felt a rush of relief. She was as determined as he was to forget that stupid kiss. "You're a good friend, Ellie."

"Not as good as I'd hoped."

His heart went still. "What do you mean?"

"You didn't tell me about Bitter End," she accused him, turning to meet his eyes.

"*What?*" He hadn't been to the ghost town since he was a teenager, and once was enough. There was something dangerous about that place—and he wasn't thinking about the abandoned wells, either.

"Who told you?" he demanded, although the answer was obvious.

"Richard."

"Listen, Ellie," he said, gripping her elbow. He longed to take her by the shoulders and shake some sense into her, but he knew she wouldn't listen and he'd hurt his cause more than help it. "I'd forget about Bitter End if I were you."

"Why should I? This is the most exciting thing I've heard in ages. My father's great-grandparents belonged to the first group of settlers, you know." She paused and studied him. "Glen, what's so bad about this town? Why doesn't anyone talk about it? If you know where it is and other people do, too, why is it a deep dark secret?"

Glen wasn't sure how to explain it to her, especially since he didn't fully understand it himself. All he could remember was the eerie sense of danger and oppressiveness he'd experienced the one and only time he'd been there. He couldn't have been more than fourteen at the time. Cal, Grady and he had inadvertently overheard their parents discussing the old town and decided to locate it on their own. It'd taken them weeks to find it, but instead of feeling a sense of triumph and elation after their first visit, they'd been terrified. They'd hardly spoken of it since.

"I don't want you going there," he ordered, rather than answer her questions. The second those words left his lips, Glen recognized his mistake. Ellie wasn't going to take kindly to anyone telling her what she could or couldn't do.

"Too late. Richard's driving me there tomorrow afternoon."

"No, he's not." Even knowing he was digging himself in deeper didn't prevent Glen from blurting it out.

"You don't have any right to tell me that."

"Ellie, listen to me—"

"I've heard everything I care to hear. I thought we were friends."

"We are," he said, his mind spinning. He realized that the thought of Ellie in that deserted town frightened him. All his protective instincts snapped into place—instincts he'd never associated with Ellie. "I don't want you going there."

"You're being ridiculous. You found it, and now I want to see it, too. It was okay for you, but not for me? I don't accept that, Glen."

"If you value our friendship, you won't go."

Ellie looked at him as though she'd never seen him before, and once again Glen realized he'd said it all wrong. "If you value my opinion . . ." he altered hurriedly, but he could see it was already too late.

"I don't think I know you any longer," she whispered. It wasn't her words as much as the way she said them, in a hurt voice that vibrated with doubts.

He'd known it was going to happen, had worried about it for days. He just hadn't thought it'd be so soon. That kiss really had ruined everything. Every shred of closeness they'd once shared was gone. They seemed incapable of even the most basic communication.

"Fine," he said, furious with himself and taking it out on her. "Go ahead and do as you like. Just don't say I didn't warn you." Having botched the entire conversation, he whirled around and walked away. Ellie would discover everything she needed to know about Bitter End soon enough. But she wouldn't have him standing guard over her when she did.

"YOU READY?" Richard asked, entering the feed store fifteen minutes past the time they'd agreed to meet.

"As ready as I'll ever be." The argument with Glen weighed heavily on her mind. She'd considered phoning Richard to beg off, but she refused to allow Glen to tell her what to do. She had as much right as anyone else to visit Bitter End.

Richard laughed. "Just remember you're the one who insisted on going." He sang a few bars of the theme song from *Ghostbusters,* and Ellie laughed, too. He certainly seemed to be in high spirits, which helped to reassure her.

Glen, on the other hand, had made it sound as if going to Bitter End meant risking life and limb. While she might have been willing to listen to reason, she'd deeply resented the way he'd spoken to her. He'd given her *orders,* for heaven's sake.

Everything about their short exchange rankled. Ellie felt bad about it herself, wanting their relationship to return to the way it had been before the kiss. She should have stopped him, should have known anything physical between them would lead to problems. The only reason she'd let it happen was that she'd been so upset. Glen had regretted it, too; he'd as much as told her.

Richard helped her into the truck, which Ellie realized was Grady's. His spirits remained high as he drove out of town, down the two-lane highway.

Suddenly he veered off the road into a rocky meadow with cedar shrubs and knee-high weeds.

"So this is the way?"

"No," he said. "I just want you to think it is." The pickup pitched sharply right, one of the front tires slamming against a rock. Ellie was shoved into the door, hitting her shoulder hard. She yelped in pain.

"Sorry," Richard said, slowing the vehicle. "You okay?"

"Fine. What about the truck?" She assumed he was stopping to survey any damage to the wheels, but she was wrong.

He leaned toward her and opened the glove compartment, removing a black handkerchief.

"What's that?" she asked.

"A blindfold."

"A what?" she exploded.

"Blindfold," he repeated calmly. "I thought about this carefully and it's the only way I'll agree to take you to Bitter End."

"You're joking, right?"

"I'm taking you against my better judgment. If Grady ever found out, he'd have my hide."

"Glen wasn't too pleased about it, either."

"You told him?" Richard's eyes flared with anger.

"Yes, we . . . we exchanged a few words and left it at that."

"Tell him you changed your mind."

Ellie stared at Richard in shock. "You want me to lie?"

"Well, not lie . . . exactly. Just let him assume you followed his advice. Understand?"

"A lie by omission is still a lie."

"Whatever. Just do it." He held up the blindfold.

"I'm not wearing that."

"Then I'm not taking you to Bitter End." The way he said it made her realize he wasn't kidding. The facade vanished, and she viewed a side of Richard she'd never seen before. A side that wasn't cordial or friendly but, rather, dark and menacing.

"I have to wear the blindfold?"

He nodded, then his face relaxed into a boyish grin. "Think of it as a game."

"All right." But she didn't like it, and her dislike intensified when he placed the handkerchief around her eyes, tying it securely at the back of her head.

"Can you see anything?"

"No."

"You're sure?"

"Positive." His repeated questions irritated her.

He started the truck again and pulled back onto the highway. He seemed to be driving around in circles. When he finally did leave the road, she was completely confused and had no idea what direction he'd taken. On the rough off-road terrain, the truck bounced and heaved in every direction.

Ellie lost track of time. It might have been fifteen minutes or an hour, she didn't know. All she knew was that they'd stopped.

"Richard?"

He didn't answer. But she knew immediately that they were close to Bitter End. She *felt* it. A heavy uncomfortable sensation descended on her, a feeling that was completely at odds with the sun's warmth pouring through the windows.

"We're here, aren't we?" she asked.

Silence.

"Richard?"

Silence again.

She heard a soft eerie sound, a creaking that could have been the truck door opening. Or was it something else? Something sinister.

"This is ridiculous," she said, and lifted the blindfold from her eyes. Richard wasn't beside her, nor was he visible from where she sat. Squinting into the sunlight, she climbed out of the truck.

The first thing she saw was a faint footpath leading away from the truck. Not knowing what else to do, she followed it, clambering over rocks and forcing her way through the undergrowth. Soon the town came into sight; she could see it clearly from a limestone outcropping just above. She stopped and stared.

Bitter End was surprisingly intact. A number of buildings, some of them stone, some wood, stood along a main street, which was bordered by a plank walk. A church steeple showed in the distance, charred by fire. She saw a hotel and livery stable with a small corral. Even a building that had apparently been a saloon.

She still couldn't see Richard anywhere.

"Richard!" she called again. "Where are you? If this is a joke I'm not laughing."

She half-slid, half-ran down the incline to the town.

She felt a sudden chill on her bare arms. Although the day was warm and windless, the town was decidedly cold.

"Richard!" she shouted again.

Nothing.

Cautiously she ventured onto the street, but her companion was nowhere to be seen. Panic clawed at her stomach as she spun around. "Richard! For the love of God, where are you?"

Four

Caroline was busy sorting mail when she heard a customer at the front counter. Because the post office was open only two hours on Saturdays, she often did a brisk business then.

Setting aside the stack of letters, she stepped out to the customer-service area. When she recognized Grady Weston, her posture immediately became defensive; she could feel it. Generally Savannah—and now occasionally Richard—collected the mail for the Yellow Rose Ranch. Grady hadn't been into the post office since last May and he'd come only because he was seeking her help. But then, he'd been worried about Savannah's relationship with Laredo Smith. A relationship he'd tried to destroy. He hadn't trusted Laredo, and he hadn't understood Savannah. In fact, Grady had seriously underestimated both of them.

"Morning, Grady," she said warily. The last time she'd seen him, he'd been laughing hysterically at the prospect of attending Ruth's birthday party with her.

"Caroline." He nodded, looking about uncomfortably. He removed his Stetson and held the brim with both hands.

"Can I help you?" she asked.

He blinked as though someone had lifted him off his horse and hurled him straight into the middle of town. He shook his head in a puzzled way, apparently wondering how he happened to be there in the post office, talking to her.

"Do you need stamps?" she asked.

"No." He shifted his weight from left to right. "I, uh, came for another reason."

She waited impatiently for him to continue. Grady had never been a smooth talker like his brother, but Caroline suspected his hesitation had something to do with their last unfortunate meeting.

"It's about what I said the other day—or what I said that you heard. What I mean to say . . ." He snapped his jaw closed and she noticed the color creeping up his neck. "Savannah said you weren't really offended, but I can't help feeling that—"

"Don't worry about it," she said, rather than have him endure this embarrassment any longer. "Let's put it behind us."

He relaxed visibly. "That's kind of you. I didn't mean anything by it."

"I know. Savannah shouldn't play matchmaker—she has no talent for it." Caroline was all too aware that her best friend was in love with love. Savannah wanted Caroline to know the same happiness herself but unfortunately was convinced Grady was the man she'd find it with.

Caroline knew she was at fault, too. She should have discouraged Savannah from the first, but deep down part of her had *wanted* Grady to notice her. She liked Grady, perhaps more than she should, seeing that they couldn't even carry on a conversation without arguing about *something*.

"I wouldn't have minded going to Ruth's party with you. I realize I must have sounded like I'd rather pluck chickens, but that isn't so."

Despite his apology, his attitude tweaked her pride.

"You have to admit it was a crazy idea," he said, holding her gaze. "You and me going out together." He seemed to expect some response from her.

"Let's drop it, all right?" She slapped the mail down on the counter and glared at him, not completely understanding her own anger.

He flinched at the sound. "Now what'd I say?" he demanded.

"Nothing."

"Then why are you looking at me like you're madder than hops?"

Caroline shook her head. "You're the only man I know who can apologize with an insult."

"I insulted you?" His jaw went slack with astonishment.

Caroline drew a deep calming breath and held up her right hand. "Let's just say we'll agree to disagree."

He frowned and twisted the rim of his Stetson. "I need to know what we're agreeing to disagree about."

She gave an impatient sigh. The man was completely and utterly obtuse. "You and I both love Savannah," she said with exaggerated slowness. "But when it comes to each other, we don't see eye to eye, which is fine. We don't really need to. I have my life and you have yours. You don't want to go out with me and that's fine, too. Because frankly I'm not all that interested in you, either."

His eyes narrowed. "In other words you're turning me down before I even get a chance to ask you to the Cattlemen's Association dance."

He was asking her to the dance? So *that* was what this was all about.

Now he was the one who was agitated. He gestured with his hand as if he wasn't sure how to continue. "I take the better part of the morning driving into town," he finally managed. "I've got an entire herd of cattle that need tending, but instead, I waste a good part of my day just so I can invite you to a stupid dance. Then before I can even get the words out, you're telling me you'd rather go out with a polecat than with me. Well, if that doesn't beat all." He slammed his hat back on his head with enough force to make her recoil.

"You wanted to ask me to the dance?" she asked, recovering in record time, "and I'm supposed to be grateful?"

"No . . . yes," he faltered, then ignored the question. "Why else would I drive into town on a Saturday?" Not giving her time to respond, he added, "Cal's right. A woman's nothing but trouble."

Caroline's heart sank. She would have enjoyed attending the biggest dance of the year with him. Instead, she'd ruined any chance she had of stepping onto the dance floor with Grady Weston.

"I told Savannah this wouldn't work," he said with the self-righteous attitude of a man who thinks he's been right all along. "As far as I'm concerned, this is the last time I'm inviting you to any social function in this town. If you want a date you're going to have to ask *me*."

The insinuation that he was the only man who'd ask her out infuriated Caroline. "I don't need you in order to get a date."

"Oh sure, I suppose you're interested in Richard, too."

"Richard? What's he got to do with anything?"

Grady opened and closed his jaw, but apparently decided against explaining. "Never mind. I'm out of here."

Caroline stretched out her hand to stop him, but it was too late. Grady had already turned and was storming out of the post office, leaving the door to slam in his wake.

"My, oh my, what's gotten into that young man?"

For the first time Caroline noticed Edwina and Lily Moorhouse standing in the post-office foyer. Both women continued to dress as if they still spent their days at the front of a classroom. Caroline couldn't remember ever seeing either one in anything but well-pressed shirtwaist dresses. On Sunday mornings and at important social functions, they wore dainty hats with matching purses and spotless white gloves.

Lily, the younger and less talkative of the two, clutched her mail to her breast as if in mortal fear of having Grady rip it from her.

Edwina, who'd never had a problem sharing what was on her mind, was sputtering about "that young man."

"I apologize, ladies," Caroline said. "Grady and I were having a . . . difference of opinion."

"So it seems." Edwina pinched her lips together, clenching her purse tightly with both hands.

"Are you all right?" Lily asked.

Caroline shook her head, dismissing the older woman's concern. But the encounter had left her more shaken than she cared to admit.

"You like him, don't you?" Lily asked in a soft voice, and reached across the counter to pat Caroline's hand.

Caroline nodded. Yes, she did like Grady—even if they didn't get along—and it was well past time she admitted it. But then, her judgment in men wouldn't exactly earn her any awards. Maggie's father had left her pregnant, and every other romantic relationship in her adult life had ended badly. "I guess some women are better judges of character than me," she said.

"Grady's a fine young man," Lily insisted, apparently over her shock.

"He's got a heart of gold," Edwina agreed. "But if you want my opinion, I think that young man's constipated."

"You think so, sister?" Lily frowned thoughtfully.

"Indeed I do. You be patient with him, Caroline, and he'll come around. Mark my words."

"I couldn't agree with Edwina more," Lily said, brightening somewhat. "There's nothing wrong with that young man that a large bowl of stewed prunes wouldn't cure."

"Or Grandpa's cordial."

"Indeed!"

ELLIE'S HEART hammered in her ears as she stepped backward, slowly edging her way onto the path toward the truck. Richard was still nowhere to be seen.

Glen's warnings about the ghost town echoed in her mind. Even Richard had advised her not to come. She'd been the one to insist on making the trip, certain that Glen, at least, was being overprotective.

What was worse—far worse—was this . . . sensation, this feeling. It was as though she was being watched. And judged. And . . . disliked. Her pulse still thundered in her head, gaining volume and intensity. Her feet dragged heavily as she walked. It almost felt as if someone had bound her arms and legs and was slowly tightening the rope, binding her.

All she could think about was escape. But she couldn't leave, couldn't just turn and run. Somehow, someway she had to find out what had happened to Richard. Although every dictate of her heart and mind urged her to get out of there, she couldn't abandon him.

Besides, she hadn't a clue how to find her way back to Promise. She'd have to search this place and—

"Boo!"

Ellie screamed and leaped a good three feet off the ground. Richard threw back his head and laughed hilariously, as if her terror was the funniest thing he'd seen in years.

Furious, Ellie clenched her hands into fists and glared at him.

"Hey," he said, continuing to chuckle, "you're the one who claimed not to be afraid of ghosts."

"Where'd you go?" she demanded, gripping his arm and clinging tightly. She was too frightened to stay angry for long.

"Hey," he repeated softly, "you're really scared, aren't you?"

"You know I am!"

"Sweetheart, it was a joke."

"A stupid one."

"Okay, okay, it probably wasn't the best thing to do, but you were so sure nothing was going to frighten you. Sorry," he said with a casual shrug. "The real danger is letting your imagination run away with you."

Her fingers tensed on his arms. "I don't like this place."

"I told you." He sounded cool and unaffected.

"Don't you feel it?" she asked, studying him.

"Feel what?"

"The . . . sense of oppression."

He looked at her as if she needed a psychiatrist. "I don't feel anything. Come on, let me show you around. Old as it is, there's still lots to see."

Even though she was curious, Ellie shook her head. "I think we should head back."

"We just got here. Don't you want to check out the mercantile? I actually found some bloated canned goods left on the shelf. Can you believe it? The cash register is there, too. I looked, but there wasn't any money inside."

Did he actually expect there to be cash for his taking? Ellie wondered.

"What happened to the church?" she asked, gesturing toward the small hill at the far end of the main street.

"I didn't go in. Doesn't interest me. Outside looks like it got hit by lightning."

Ellie stared, fascinated despite her fears.

"Come on," Richard urged again, "let's explore."

Ellie realized it wasn't likely she'd come back for a second visit. "Okay, show me the mercantile," she said, uncertain even now that it was a wise thing to do.

"Sure." He took her hand and led her up the two steps to the raised wooden sidewalk. The old boards creaked with their weight, making an eerie inhuman sound. It looked as though the town had been fairly prosperous at one time. A hotel and saloon, a livery stable, a small corral. The sun-bleached planks of the boardwalk were bleached and splintered with age, and several sections had rotted through.

"Watch your step," Richard said, and slipped his arm around her waist, holding her unnecessarily close.

"Maybe we should go to the hotel," he whispered suggestively. "Find a room with a bed."

"No, thanks," she murmured.

"Hey, don't be so quick to turn down a good thing. We could have a lot of fun together."

"No, thanks," she said again, her tone reinforcing the message.

"Pity. We could be good together."

Ellie sincerely doubted that.

As Richard opened the door to the mercantile, the hinges squeaked loudly and Ellie shivered. The sensation persisted, the feeling that she was being watched.

The inside of the old store was like something out of a museum. The counter stretched the length of the room, with shelves built behind it. What Richard had said was true; there were several tin cans scattered about. The cans themselves were swollen, their labels faded.

"What happened to make people move fast enough to leave goods behind?" Life was hard in the Old West, and food was often in short supply.

"Who knows?" Apparently Richard didn't find her question of any interest.

The cash register was there, too, the till open. Bramble weeds littered the floor. Ellie saw a couple of old barrels and a table, but no chairs.

"Okay, we've seen it," she said. "I'm ready to go back."

"You don't want to see anything else?"

"No." Her curiosity was gone and all she wanted now was to escape. Even knowing that her father's great-grandparents had walked these very streets and stepped inside this store wasn't enough to keep her.

"Come on, let's go look at the hotel," Richard urged again. "There's quite a fancy staircase—if you ignore the occasional broken step."

"Richard!" The hotel had to be riddled with danger. If the staircase collapsed or they fell through a damaged floor, heaven only knew how long it'd be before someone found them.

Glen would come. Ellie was genuinely relieved that she'd told at least one other person where she was headed, even if he disapproved. If she did turn up missing, Glen would leave no stone unturned. He'd look for the town until he located it again. Then he'd mount a search-and-rescue effort, enlist everyone's help. He wouldn't rest until he knew exactly what had happened and why. He was that kind of man. That kind of friend.

"I want to check the cemetery," she decided as they left the mercantile.

"The cemetery? As jittery as you are?" Richard said. "Why?"

"I want to look for a grave. A little boy by the name of Edward Abraham Frasier." Since the Bible had given no information about what had caused his death, perhaps a grave marker would.

"All right," Richard agreed, but she could see he wasn't enthusiastic.

The sensation of someone following them grew less intense as they walked toward the outskirts of town. The gate to the cemetery hung by one hinge.

"Someone's been here recently," Ellie said, stopping just inside the fenced area. The dirt had been churned recently to plant a rosebush.

"Savannah," Richard said. "She was after some old roses and replaced the ones she took."

"Savannah's been here?" Ellie wasn't completely surprised. Savannah scoured the highways and byways for old roses, hoping to find unfamiliar and unusual species. And replacing the roses she'd removed? Savannah never took without giving; it was her nature.

"What was the name again?" Richard asked.

"Edward Abraham Frasier." Some of the graves were marked with wooden crosses that had badly deteriorated with age. And only a few names were legible on the stone markers. After a couple of minutes she gave up the effort.

"You done yet?" Richard asked, sounding bored.

"Yeah." While she wished she'd found the grave, she didn't want to linger in town any longer.

Richard held her hand as they scrambled up the incline, then followed the rocky path that led to the truck. He helped her into the cab— obviously charm died hard—and climbed inside himself. "Put on the blindfold," he instructed her, turning the ignition key.

Ellie complained under her breath. He had nothing to worry about; she had no intention of returning to Bitter End. She didn't know what had made her ancestors leave the town; all she could say was that she didn't blame them.

Once the blindfold was securely in place, Richard put the truck into gear.

The ride back to Promise was accomplished in half the time it had taken to drive out. Once again the truck pitched and bucked over the uneven terrain, leaving Ellie to wonder how he'd found Bitter End on his own. Of one thing she was sure—neither Glen nor Cal would have taken him there. Nor would Grady or Savannah. No one she knew would purposely return to Bitter End. She wouldn't. Never again. Glen was right; once was more than enough.

Richard dropped her at the feed store. "Thanks," she said, and was about to open the door and climb out when he stopped her.

"Hey, there's no need to rush, is there?"

She did have work to do. "Well—"

"Don't you want to thank me?" he asked.

"I thought I already had."

"A kiss wouldn't hurt." Without giving her a chance to respond he reached for her shoulders and brought his mouth to hers. Technically it was a kiss, but Ellie experienced none of the warmth or gentleness she had with Glen. None of the surging passion. What Richard classified as a kiss was little more than the touching of lips.

Apparently he wasn't satisfied, either, because he opened his mouth and twisted it over hers. Ellie still felt nothing. Which surprised her, considering how attractive the man was.

Richard released her and smiled. "I'll give you a call soon," he said as though nothing was amiss. "We could have something good together, Ellie. Think about it, all right?"

She stared at him, at a total loss for anything to say. The kiss that had left her cold had somehow convinced him they could become romantically involved.

"You're coming to the Cattlemen's dance with me, right?" he asked, when she finally climbed down from the truck.

"Ah . . ." She stood with one hand on the door, ready to close it. "I'll let you know for sure, but I don't think so."

Richard's eyes widened with surprise. "But I'll see you there?"

"I . . . I don't know." She wasn't in the mood for much partying. "Perhaps," she said vaguely.

"In any case I'll see you soon," Richard said cheerfully, and with a jaunty wave drove off.

Ellie walked into the store and George Tucker handed her a pile of pink slips. "Glen Patterson called three times," he muttered in a way that told her he wasn't keen on being her secretary. George's expertise didn't extend to the office.

"Glen phoned?" Her heart reacted immediately.

"Would you kindly put that young man out of his misery?" George asked. "I've got better things to do than answer his questions about you."

Smiling to herself, Ellie headed for her office in the back of the store. Maybe, just maybe, there was some hope that she and Glen could resurrect their friendship, after all.

GLEN HADN'T BEEN worth a plugged nickel all day. Glen and Cal had been out at Cayuse Pasture, which was approximately twelve miles square in size. They were grazing about 400 cows and yearlings there. Even the dogs didn't want anything to do with him, and Glen saw their point. His mood had been murderous all day. Three times he'd left Cal and the other hands to race back to the house so he could call Ellie. His frustration rose each time he was forced to leave a message with George. Now that he was back at the ranch house, he discovered his disposition hadn't improved. The answering machine showed that Ellie hadn't tried to call him back, which meant she was still with Richard in Bitter End. He didn't like it, not one damn bit.

"If you're so concerned about Ellie," Cal said, "why don't you drive into town and find out what happened to her?" Cal himself would be driving into town later for his weekly visit to Billy D's, the local watering hole. Most single ranchers met at Billy D's for a cold beer on Friday and Saturday nights. Then some of them would wander over to the café in the bowling alley or the Chili Pepper for a barbecued steak. Adam Braunfels served up one of the best T-bones in the state. Glen would probably join his brother and friends—after he'd talked to Ellie.

"You're letting a woman mess with your mind, little brother," Cal said with the voice of one who'd been disillusioned by love. He opened the refrigerator and reached for a can of soda. "Take my advice or leave it—that's up to you. But the way I see it, Ellie's already got a ring through your nose."

"The hell she does," Glen argued. Sure, she'd been on his mind, but *only* because he was worried about her and Richard visiting Bitter End.

"I was thinking about moseying into town early," Glen admitted, making light of it.

"Yeah, fine," Cal said with a decided lack of interest. "Why don't you just marry Ellie and be done with it?"

Glen frowned at his brother, but rather than become involved in a pointless argument he tore up the stairs to shower and change.

By the time Glen reached the outskirts of Promise, anger simmered just below the surface. He intended to check in with his friends at Billy D's in a while, but he wouldn't rest easy until he'd spoken to Ellie. He needed to see for himself that she was all right.

When he arrived at the feed store, George Tucker took one look at him and pointed him toward the business office. So Ellie was back, but she hadn't bothered to return his calls.

The door was half-open and Glen saw Ellie sitting at the desk, her fingers flying over calculator buttons. She glanced up when he walked into the room. Under normal circumstances he would have poured himself some coffee. Not this afternoon. At least not yet. He wanted to find out what her mood was like first.

"You went to Bitter End, didn't you," he said quietly. Although he wished she'd taken his advice, his relief that she was safely home overrode any real anger.

"Did you honestly expect me not to?"

"No," he said, knowing his actions the night of Ruth's party had made that impossible.

"I . . . I wasn't overly impressed with the town," she admitted.

Well, he thought, that was a start in the right direction.

"Why didn't you ever mention it before?" she asked, and he noticed a hurt tone in her voice.

"I never talked about it with anyone." He walked across the room and reached for the coffeepot. "If I'd told you, you would've wanted to see it for yourself—which you did."

"To tell you the truth, I understand why you didn't want me there."

That was what he'd figured. "I was worried about you," he said.

"I know. I talked to Cal a few minutes ago."

Glen frowned. He could just imagine what his brother had said. On second thought he didn't want to know.

"You plan on making a return visit?" he asked, instead, keeping the question light.

"Go back? Not on your life."

"Good." He raised the mug to his lips and took a sip of coffee.

"I think we should talk," Ellie surprised him by saying.

"Talk?" He froze, not sure he liked the sound of this.

She laughed softly, and Glen realized how much he'd missed hearing that. She had a deep rich laugh, unlike a lot of women he knew who had delicate laughs. Ellie's was robust and confident, as if she didn't need to prove her femininity by being reserved. He found her unique in any number of other ways.

"We can try to ignore it, pretend we've forgotten it, but the best way to deal with . . . what happened is to discuss it."

His eyes held hers. "Are you talking about . . ." He was having as much trouble saying the word as she was.

"The . . . kiss." There, she'd said it.

"The kiss," he repeated in low tones, as though this were something dark and dangerous. He was beginning to think it was.

Ellie laughed, and soon he did, too.

"We should acknowledge that we were caught up in a momentary impulse," she suggested primly. "And . . . Oh, hell, let's just forget it."

Leaning against the edge of her desk, Glen cradled his coffee mug in both hands. "I don't think that'll work."

"Why not?" Ellie stood and replenished her own coffee.

Because they'd been friends all these years, Glen knew exactly what she was doing. What had prompted her sudden burst of activity wasn't a craving for more coffee but an effort not to let him see what was in her eyes.

He set his mug aside and touched her shoulder. She jerked around as though he'd burned her.

"I don't want to forget the kiss," he said with blinding honesty. He didn't recognize it as the truth until the words left his lips.

"You don't?" She sounded startled.

"Do you?" He was a fool to ask, but he couldn't have held back the question for anything.

"I . . . I don't know."

"Yes, you do." If he could hang out his pride to dry, then she'd damn well better be prepared to do the same thing.

She blinked twice. "All I want is for us to be friends."

"We are. That hasn't changed."

"But it *has!*" she cried, gesturing wildly with her hands. "That kiss changed everything. I used to be able to talk to you."

"You still can."

"No, I can't."

"Try me," he challenged.

She threw back her head and laughed, but this time her amusement lacked sincerity. "We can talk about anything, can we?" she flung at him.

"Fine, then we'll talk about how Richard's kisses leave me cold and how all I could do was compare the way I felt when I was in your arms."

Glen didn't hear anything beyond the first few words. "So you're kissing Richard now. Is there anyone else I don't know about?"

"See?" she cried, tossing her arms in the air. "My point exactly."

"What point?"

"We can't talk."

"We're already talking! What do you mean?" This was the kind of convoluted conversation women suckered a man into—giving him just enough rope to hang himself. Glen had seen it happen often enough and had always managed to avoid it with Ellie. Until now.

"You said there wasn't anything I couldn't discuss with you, and already we're at each other's throats."

"I am not at your throat!" he shouted, his patience gone. The entire day had been a waste. First he'd fretted about her with Richard in Bitter End. Then he'd attempted to revive their friendship, only to learn she'd been locking lips with Richard Weston.

"You're welcome to him," he said, setting the mug down forcibly enough to send coffee sloshing over the sides. "As far as I'm concerned, you and Richard deserve each other."

"Oh, please, now you're acting like a jealous fool."

He was out the office door before he realized he'd had more than one reason for seeing Ellie. He walked back and leaned against the doorjamb, crossing his arms.

Ellie glanced up and waited.

"You going to the dance?" he asked finally, as if her answer didn't really matter.

"I . . . haven't decided yet. Are you going?"

"Yeah."

"Then I probably will, too."

"See you there?" he asked, his mood brightening.

She nodded. "Will you wait for me?"

He nodded, grinning.

She smiled back.

Five

As the evening wore on, Glen's feelings toward Richard Weston grew even less friendly. He resented the other man's putting Ellie at risk by escorting her to Bitter End. The more he thought about it, the more irritated he got. Richard's dating Ellie had never set right with him, either. Especially now, when she was at a low point in her life following her father's death and her mother's move to Chicago. Although Ellie generally had a level head, Glen didn't want Pretty Boy taking advantage of her.

And then there was his own unresolved—and unexpected—attraction to her. . . . But no, the real concern was Ellie's vulnerability to a superficial charmer like Richard.

The only thing to do, Glen decided, was speak to Richard personally. Clear the air. Set him straight. He'd wait for the right opportunity. He was well aware that Ellie wouldn't appreciate his having a chat with Richard on her behalf, but she didn't need to know about it, either. Someone had to look after her interests. Glen liked to think of himself as her guardian. Okay, *guardian* was probably the wrong word, seeing as they were close to the same age. What she could use was a sort of . . . advocate. A concerned friend. Yes, that was it. An advocate. Someone who had her best interests at heart. Stepping in where needed.

With his role clear in his mind, he held off until late Wednesday afternoon before driving out to the Yellow Rose Ranch and confronting the youngest Weston. This was between him and Richard. Man to man.

He turned into the drive and parked in the yard beside Grady's truck, then slowly climbed out of the cab. Savannah was in her rose garden wearing a wide-brimmed straw hat to shield her face from the sun. Richard sat on the front porch, strumming a guitar, apparently so involved in his music that he didn't see or hear Glen's approach. Rocket,

Grady's old black Lab, slept on the porch, sprawled out on a small braided rug.

Carrying a wicker basket filed with fragrant pink roses, Savannah waved and walked toward Glen.

"Howdy, neighbor," she said, smiling her welcome.

"Savannah." He touched the tip of his Stetson. "Beautiful day, isn't it?"

"Lovely," she agreed.

"I'm here to see Richard," Glen announced, narrowing his gaze on the man who still lounged on the porch.

"He's practicing his guitar." She gestured unnecessarily toward Richard. He'd leaned the chair against the side of the house and propped one foot on the porch railing.

"Would you care for a glass of iced tea?" Savannah offered.

His throat was dry; something cold and wet would be appreciated. "That's mighty kind of you."

Richard's sister moved toward the house, then paused at the bottom step and turned. With a slight frown she said, "Is there trouble, Glen? Between you and Richard?"

"Not at all," he was quick to assure her. He was determined that this would look like nothing more than a friendly conversation between neighbors. And if he just happened to mention Ellie . . .

Obviously relieved, Savannah disappeared into the house, and Glen approached Richard. The younger man ignored him until Glen pulled at the chair beside his and plunked himself down.

Richard's fingers paused over the strings. "Howdy, Glen."

"Howdy." Although Glen had mulled over what he intended to say, he found that actually speaking his mind was surprisingly difficult. "Do you have a few minutes?"

"Sure." Richard set the guitar down on the porch, holding it by the neck. "I've always got time for a friend."

Friend. Glen hesitated, since he didn't exactly view Richard that way.

"What can I do for you?" Richard asked companionably.

"Well . . ." Nope, he wasn't very good at expressing himself, Glen thought. "I've been concerned about Ellie."

"Really?" Richard asked. "Why?"

"Her father dying and then her mother leaving so soon afterward."

Richard nodded. "I see what you mean. She seems to be handling it pretty well, though, don't you think?" He picked up the guitar, laid it across his lap and played a couple of chords.

"That's the thing about Ellie," Glen explained, speaking with authority. After all, he knew Ellie far better than Richard did. "She can put on a good front, but there's a lot of emotion churning beneath the surface."

Richard chuckled. "You're right about that! She's a little fireball just waiting to explode. I've always been attracted to passionate women." His tone insinuated that he'd been close to getting scorched by Ellie a few times—as if he knew her in ways Glen never would.

Glen shifted uncomfortably, angered by the insinuation, but was saved from responding by Savannah, who carried out a tray with two tall glasses of iced tea and a plate of homemade oatmeal cookies.

"Thanks," Glen said, accepting a glass.

Richard had reached for his, plus a cookie, before Savannah could even put the plate down. "I can never resist my sister's cookies," he said, and kissed her on the cheek. "No one bakes better cookies than Savannah."

His sister smiled at his praise, then quietly returned to the kitchen. Glen watched her go, and realized that with very little effort, Richard had won over Savannah, too—despite all the grief he'd brought the family. No doubt about it, the guy was an expert when it came to manipulating women. Glen felt all the more uneasy, wondering how to handle the situation. He wanted Richard to keep his distance from Ellie, but he didn't want to be obvious about it. If he made a point of warning Richard off, the bum would be sure to tell her what he'd said. Probably snicker at him, too.

The best way, he decided, was to state his concerns in a natural straightforward manner. "Ellie told me you took her to Bitter End," he began, struggling to disguise his anger.

Richard threw back his head and laughed boisterously. "I scared the living daylights out of her, too."

Glen hadn't heard about that and was forced to listen to Richard's story of how he'd blindfolded her, then slipped out of the truck and hidden.

By the time he finished, Glen's jaw hurt from the effort it took not to yell at the man. "I don't think it's a good idea to be taking anyone up to that ghost town," he said as calmly as he could, realizing anew that he actively disliked Richard Weston. He hadn't cared for him as a teenager and liked him even less as an adult.

"I couldn't agree with you more," Richard said, once his amusement had faded. "It was a mistake to even mention Bitter End. Once I did, she was all over me, wanting to see the place. When I finally said I'd take her, she wasn't in the town five minutes before she wanted to leave.

"Surprising how much of that town's still standing," Richard said next, helping himself to a second cookie.

Glen figured if he didn't take one soon, Richard would devour the entire plateful before he'd even had a taste. Deliberately he reached for a cookie, then another. He took a bite; they *were* as good as Richard claimed.

"How'd you find the town?" Glen asked.

"Since you, Cal and Grady didn't see fit to include me when we were kids, I didn't have any choice but to seek it out on my own."

"But why now?"

"Why not?" He shrugged as if it was of little consequence. "I've got plenty of time to kill while I wait to hear on my next job. I work for an investment company."

"I didn't realize that."

"I don't tell a lot of people," he said. "Most recently I was working with a smaller institution, specializing in loans and investments. Unfortunately, as you're probably aware, the larger institutions are swallowing up the smaller ones, and I was forced to take a short vacation while the company reorganizes. It seemed as good a time as any to visit my family."

"Investments? Really?" Richard certainly possessed the polished look of a professional. And he knew how to talk the talk. Glen was a bit confused, though; he'd been under the impression that Richard had a different sort of job—sales or something. Oh, well, he supposed it didn't matter.

"Yup." Richard ran the guitar pick over the strings and laughed easily. "I bet you didn't know I'd made quite a name for myself, did you?"

Glen sobered when he realized how smoothly Richard had diverted him from the subject of Bitter End, but he wasn't going to allow the other man to get away with it for long.

"You won't be taking Ellie back to the ghost town, will you?" Glen asked in a tone that told Richard he was in for a fight if he did.

"Not likely!"

"Good." Then, in case he might consider showing the town to others, Glen added, "Or anyone else?"

"Hardly." Richard's response was immediate; but Glen noted the way his hand stilled momentarily over the guitar. "I wouldn't have taken Ellie, but like I said, once I mentioned it she was all over me, wanting to see the place. It was either drive her there myself or let her go looking for it on her own."

That much was true, Glen conceded.

"Do you and Ellie have something going . . . romantically?" Richard surprised him with the directness of the question.

Glen hesitated, unsure how to respond. Before he allowed himself to confess what he'd denied to everyone, including himself, he shook his head. "We're just friends."

"That's what I thought." Richard sounded smug and satisfied.

"Any particular reason you're asking?"

"Yeah. I'm interested in her myself, and I don't want to step on your toes if I can help it."

Glen frowned. "Like I said earlier, this is a bad time for Ellie."

"She needs someone like me," Richard said, bending over the guitar and tightening a couple of strings. "What I'd like to see her do is sell that business and get on with her life. Her daddy stuck her with that feed store, but there's no need for her to hold on to it."

Glen shook his head. Ellie loved the store with the same intensity her father had. She recognized her contribution to the community and took pride in meeting the needs of the local ranchers. The feed store had become the unofficial gathering place in town, and that was because Ellie, like her father, made folks feel welcome.

Everyone dropped in at Frasier Feed, to visit, catch up on local news and gossip, swap stories. The large bulletin board out front offered free advertising space for anyone with something to trade or sell. The pop machine was there, too, with a couple of chairs for those who wanted to take a load off their feet.

Ellie sell out? Never. Apparently Richard didn't know her as well as he thought.

"She's interested in me, too, you know," Richard added.

This definitely came as surprise to Glen. She'd admitted the two of them had kissed, but in the same breath had told him she preferred his kiss over Richard's. At least, that was what he *thought* she'd said. The last part of their conversation had been lost on him. They'd snapped at each other, gotten annoyed with each other and instantly regretted it. Glen had come to mend fences with her, not destroy them, and he'd turned back to ask her about the dance. He'd made it clear that he looked forward to spending the evening with her.

She'd told him basically the same thing. They'd meet there. He'd wait for her.

"She's attending the dance with me," Richard stated nonchalantly.

"With you?" Glen couldn't believe what he'd just heard. "The Cattlemen's Association dance?"

"Yeah. She had some concern about the two of us being there together, though. Neither of us wants to start any talk."

"Talk?"

"About seeing one another exclusively."

"I see." Glen's hand tensed around the cold glass.

"You going?" Richard asked pointedly. "If I remember correctly, this dance is one of the biggest social events of the summer."

"I'll probably be there," Glen said. And he'd make damn sure Richard kept his paws where they belonged, because the first time he saw Mr. Investment Manager touching Ellie, Glen would be dragging him outside and rearranging his dental work. Even if Ellie *did* prefer Weston, as it now appeared.

"Who are you taking?" Richard probed.

"I . . . don't know yet," Glen confessed, and then because he didn't want it to look like he couldn't get a date, he added, "I was thinking of asking Nell Bishop."

"Sure," Richard said with an approving nod. "Ask Nell. I bet she'd be happy to go with you."

Glen gulped down the rest of his tea and stood. "Glad we had this conversation," he said, when in reality he was anything but. Only this time his anger was directed at Ellie. She'd played him for a fool. A fool! She'd led him to believe she didn't have a date. Moreover she'd indicted in no uncertain terms that she'd welcome his company there. *Wait for me,* she'd said.

What she intended, he now realized, was that he'd arrive and then stand there twiddling his thumbs while she danced her way across the room in Richard Weston's arms. Well, if that didn't beat all. The why of it wasn't too clear, but he figured Ellie was still mad at him and this was her revenge.

"Don't be a stranger," Richard said as Glen started toward his truck. "And don't worry about me taking Ellie up to Bitter End again, either."

"I won't." He wouldn't worry about a lot of things concerning Ellie, he mused, his anger festering. If it wasn't for Richard letting slip that she'd agreed to be his date, Glen would have arrived at the dance completely unawares.

Maybe Cal was right. Maybe women *couldn't* be trusted.

FRANK HENNESSY had been the duly elected sheriff of Promise for near twenty years. He knew everyone in town and they knew him. Because he'd been in office for so long, folks were comfortable coming to him with their problems. Minor ones and ones that weren't so minor. Sometimes he suggested they talk to Wade McMillen, the local preacher, and other times he just listened. Mostly folks felt better after they'd talked. More often than not a solution would present itself, although he'd barely say a word. Then folks would credit him when the answer had been there all along buried deep within themselves.

These days Frank had been hearing a lot about Richard Weston. Not that it surprised him. He knew Richard had absconded with the family inheritance the day Grady and Savannah had lowered their parents into the ground. Many a night he'd sat with Grady while the young man grappled with what to do—whether to press charges or not. In the end he'd decided not to pursue a case against Richard, but it had taken Grady damn near six years of constant struggle to work his way out of the red.

Now Richard was back, and Frank had heard from two or three of the local merchants that he was running up charges and not paying his bills. Frank didn't like the sound of this. What to do about it had weighed heavily on his mind for a couple of days.

He'd urged Max Jordan from Jordan's Town and Country outfitters to mention the bill to Grady, but Max didn't want to carry tales to Richard's big brother. Besides, he'd sold two vests like the one Richard had bought after he'd worn his about town. Frank would say one thing about the youngest Weston: he was a real clotheshorse. Max said he'd moved some other high-end clothing items because of Richard and was therefore willing to cut the young Weston a little slack.

For the moment, Millie Greenville was amenable about the money Richard owed her, as well. Grady had ended up paying for the flowers Richard had bought for his party; Frank knew that and had his doubts as to whether Grady would ever be repaid. Although Richard was already two months past due in paying her for the flowers he'd ordered since, she'd decided not to press the issue. He'd sent a huge arrangement for John Frasier's funeral and a number of other small bouquets to women around town. According to Milly, Richard had apologized and given her a plausible excuse; she'd chosen to believe him. But it was a little worrisome having four hundred dollars outstanding at the end of the month, all owed by the same customer.

Then there was the matter of the tab Richard was running at Billy D's. Apparently Richard had been more than generous about buying other people's drinks. It wasn't unusual for him to order a round for his friends and their friends, too, and then tell Billy just to add it to his tab. When Billy mentioned it to Frank, the money owed was close to five hundred dollars. Richard had fed the tavern owner some cockeyed story about being an investment broker, expecting a commission check that was due any day. Again Billy was willing to wait, seeing as Richard always drew a crowd. He was clever and amusing and people seemed to enjoy themselves when he was around.

Frank looked at his watch and eagerly shoved back his chair. "I'll be over at Dovie's," he said to his deputy on his way out the door. Ever since Dovie had opened her Victorian Tea Room, he stopped by each afternoon around four-thirty, after she'd finished serving tea and scones. The store was generally quiet then, and she'd usually offer him something to satisfy his sweet tooth.

Dovie was his friend. His *special* friend. If it was up to her, they'd be married, but Frank wasn't the marrying kind. He had no interest in giving up his freedom, although if any woman could tempt him to relinquish his bachelor status, it'd be Dovie. They'd been dating more than ten years now, and about once a year she got uppity about the absence of an engagement ring. Frankly he liked their arrangement just the way it was, and if pressed, Dovie, he suspected, would admit she did, too. Twice a week he spent the night at her house—the two best nights of the week. No, he figured, this marriage business was a token protest on her part. The situation was ideal for both of them as it stood; Dovie liked her freedom as much as Frank liked his, and this way they enjoyed the benefits of a steady relationship. Best of both worlds.

Frank entered the antique shop and once again admired how Dovie had artfully arranged five tables in the corner of her compact store. To his relief, the tea room was empty, and he hoped she'd take a few minutes to sit down and chat with him.

"Afternoon, Dovie," he said, pulling out a chair at his favorite table. She'd done the shop up all fancy. Real elegant. The tea room, too. All the tablecloths and matching napkins were good linen, and tea was served on a china service with sterling silver.

Frank was impressed by Dovie's creative style. She'd taken several bulky pieces of heavy antique furniture—dressers and wardrobes and the like—and used them to display her goods. She positioned things attractively: fringed silk scarves dangled from open drawers, as did long jet necklaces of 1920s vintage. Linens and lace doilies, and large hats with feather plumes and nets sat on shelves. Mismatched antique china, porcelain oil lamps, silver candelabra—she had knickknacks everywhere. Pricey ones, too. Dovie didn't sell junk; she sold *treasures*. She made sure he understood that. Far be it from him to question such matters.

Frank had never seen a woman more in love with things. Every square inch of the shop was used for display. The ladies in town loved to browse there. Most men were afraid to move a foot inside for fear they'd knock something down and end up paying for it.

Dovie looked up from tallying her receipts to send Frank a welcoming smile. As always, it made his heart beat a little faster. He returned the smile and settled back to wait.

When she was finished, Dovie poured him a cup of coffee and brought it, with a slice of warm apple crisp, to the table. Actually he'd been looking forward to her bread pudding with brandy sauce, but since he never paid for these treats, he could hardly complain.

"You look like you've been busy," he said.

"I have." She took the chair across from him, removed her shoes and rubbed her tired feet. "Ellie Frasier was in and bought the Gibson-girl dress for the dance. My, she looked lovely. I know it was more than she wanted to spend, but once she tried it on, she was sold. I don't think I appreciated what a pretty young woman she is," Dovie said absently.

Frank sneaked a peek at Dovie's ankle. She had a fine pair of legs. He'd always been taken with her trim ankles, and never had understood why she insisted on wearing long dresses. It was criminal the way she hid those shapely legs of hers.

One bite of the apple crisp and Frank closed his eyes, savoring the combination of tart and sweet flavors.

"Good?" she asked, even though Frank was sure she already knew it was.

"Excellent."

He ate the rest of it in record time.

"You've got something on your mind, Frank," Dovie said. "I can always tell. Are you going to say what it is?"

"Someone's going around charging a lot of money with local merchants," he told her reluctantly. "I'm not convinced he's planning to pay off his debts."

"Someone?" Dovie repeated. "You don't need to say who. I can guess."

He'd already said more than he should have, so he left it at that. He trusted Dovie. She wasn't like some women who just couldn't keep anything to themselves. He'd never known her to break confidences or spread rumors. It was one of the many things he valued about her.

"What are you going to do about it?"

"I don't know that I *can* do anything. He hasn't broken any laws."

"True," she said, looking thoughtful. "But you might have a chat with him. Man to man—or rather, sheriff to miscreant. I recall you had plenty to say to Laredo Smith not long ago."

Frank ignored the comment about his talk with Laredo, especially since he regretted having said a word. He'd made one mistake in judging character recently and didn't want to make another. He couldn't be one-hundred percent sure, after all, that Richard *didn't* have money coming in.

"I don't know what I could say to this guy." Frank didn't have any right to question Richard about his financial affairs.

"Frank, a lot of small businesses can't afford to take losses. Some months it's all we can do to pay the rent, let alone make a living wage. Let him know you're on to him."

"But he hasn't done anything that warrants my speaking to him."

"He doesn't know that. Let him think you have plenty of reasons. Put the fear of God into him before he robs the entire community blind," she urged. "Before he puts one of us out of business."

Frank knew how close to the edge some businesses operated. Dovie herself wasn't going to get rich with her antique shop, although it was one of the most popular stores in town.

"If nothing else," Dovie added, "it might make him think twice before charging something again."

"True." Frank rubbed his chin. It wasn't his place to tell shop owners who they should extend credit to and who they should avoid, but he hated the thought of Richard's taking advantage of good honest folk.

Dovie drank a little more of her coffee, then carried the china cup to the small kitchen in the back room. Frank followed her with his empty cup and plate.

"You need someone to help you out here now you've got the tea room," he said. It was clear to him she was working far too many hours, and while he'd encouraged her to add the Victorian Tea Room, he was concerned about the toll these extra hours took. The fatigue, the lack of private time.

"You're right, I could use another pair of hands," she said. "But I can't afford to put anyone on the payroll just yet."

Frank slipped his arms around her waist. "I guess you've picked out something special to wear to the dance," he said, nuzzling her neck. "I'm going to be the envy of every man there."

"You've been kissing the Blarney stone again, haven't you?" Dovie teased.

"The only thing I'm interested in kissing is the widow Boyd." Not giving her time to object, he turned her in his arms and brought her mouth to his. She was soft and warm and her gentle kisses fired his blood to life.

"Frank," she whispered, breaking off the kiss. She looked flustered, her face red and her hands flying around her head checking that her hair was still tucked in place. "For the love of Ireland, it's the middle of the afternoon! Anyone could walk in."

"Let them."

"You're getting mighty bold, Mr. Sheriff." Her eyes narrowed slightly. "Are you ready to take the leap yet?"

Marriage. She hadn't mentioned it in nearly a year. Her question had the effect of a bucket of cold water dumped on his head. His discomfiture must have shown in his face, because Dovie giggled and quickly kissed his jaw.

"You'd better go now," she said good-spiritedly.

"I've got to talk to a certain young man," he said. But he stole another kiss on his way out the door.

THE ANTIQUE WHITE cotton-lawn dress, lavishly trimmed in lace, was quite possibly the most beautiful dress Ellie had ever owned. She hadn't intended to buy it. But every time she walked past the window of Dovie's store, she'd stopped and admired it. On impulse she'd decided to examine it up close. It was fate, she told herself. Fate. First of all the dress was her size, and when she tried it on, it fit like a dream. The moment she saw her reflection in Dovie's mirror, she knew she had to have it for the dance.

Perhaps she was putting too much stock in what Glen had said. He hadn't formally asked her to the dance, but he'd told her he'd be there. He'd also let her know he'd be waiting for her to arrive.

It was *almost* a date. She and Glen. Every time she thought about it, a warm feeling came over her. She and Glen together. Dancing. Kissing. A couple.

Her stomach fluttered and she pressed her hand over it, closing her eyes. So much had happened in the past few weeks. For a while, after her father's funeral and her mother's move to Chicago, Ellie had felt alone. Abandoned and unloved. She didn't feel that way now.

She realized that a lot of her new optimism was because of her changing relationship with Glen. If he'd stayed a little longer the last time he was in the store, they would've kissed again. All her instincts told her that. What surprised her was that she wouldn't have minded. In fact, just the opposite.

Maybe friends did make the best lovers, which she'd heard and read for years. She'd never thought of Glen in those terms before, but now she was ready to move on to a different kind of relationship with him—a romantic one. She thought he was, too. And if he had any doubts about his feelings, the moment he saw her in that dress his mind would be made up.

She grinned when she thought how smart a saleswoman Dovie was. If the woman had gushed all over her when she tried on the dress, she might not have purchased it. Instead, all Dovie had done was smile and escort Ellie to the full-length mirror.

Dovie didn't need to sell the dress; the dress had sold itself.

Ellie ran her hand down the sleeve one last time, then shut the office door. Tonight she'd take it home, hang it in her closet and look forward to Saturday the way a high-school junior anticipates her first prom. She could hardly wait to see Glen's reaction.

Near closing time Nell Bishop showed up with a list of needed supplies.

"I had a wonderful time at Ruth's party," Ellie told her as she looked over the list.

"Ruth's still talking about it," Nell said.

"And I think it's great you're going to start a dude ranch."

"Well, I don't have any takers yet."

"But you will." Ellie was sure of that.

"Are you going to the dance?" Nell asked suddenly.

Ellie smiled; the Cattlemen's Association summer dance appeared to be on everyone's mind. "I didn't think I would at first but . . . I had a change of heart. So I'll be there. What about you?"

Nell shook her head. "I don't know . . ."

Ellie understood Nell's indecision. While almost everyone came with a date, it wasn't necessary. Technically she herself was attending the function dateless.

"You don't need to worry if you don't have an escort," Ellie assured her, and was about to explain her own situation when Nell continued.

"It's not that." She wore a puzzled frown. "I'm just wondering if there's something in the air, because I received two invitations in one hour."

It was time the men in this town woke up and realized what a wonderful woman Nell Bishop was. "That's great!"

"First Grady Weston phoned. Now, I like Grady, don't get me wrong, but I've always thought of him as . . ." Again she hesitated, as if unsure what to say next. "I just don't see Grady and me as a couple. If he's going to ask anyone, it should be Caroline Daniels. Those two are perfect for each other."

So Ellie wasn't the only one who'd noticed. "I've always wondered what's kept them apart."

Nell shook her head. "I can't figure it out."

"Do you think it's Maggie?" Ellie asked, referring to Caroline's five-year-old daughter.

"I can't imagine why."

"I don't think Grady's comfortable with kids," Ellie said. She tried to remember seeing Grady with children and couldn't recall a time she had.

"Maybe, but I've got kids, too. In fact, he chatted with Jeremy for a couple of minutes first. Then when I got on the phone . . . he invited me."

"What did you tell him?"

Nell shrugged. "I didn't know what to say. No one's asked me out since Jake died, and I got so flustered I don't know if I made sense. I think I asked him to give me some time to think about it. He agreed."

"I like Grady," Ellie murmured. He wasn't an easy man to know, but he was fair and honest and hardworking.

"I'd no sooner recovered from that when I got another call," Nell said. "It was Glen Patterson."

Glen's name came out of the blue like a flash of lightning. "Glen?" Ellie repeated, the name buzzing in her ear. "Did you say Glen Patterson?"

"Yes. If Grady's invitation surprised me, Glen's knocked me for a loop." She laughed softly. "I think I must have done a fairly good imitation of a guppie. All I could do was open and close my mouth."

The fluttery sensation was back in the pit of Ellie's stomach, only this time it resembled nausea rather than happy anticipation. Ellie had assumed—*believed*—that Glen had wanted her to be his date.

"So you're going to the dance with Glen," Ellie said bluntly, struggling to hide her feelings.

"No. I told him the same thing I told Grady."

"Maybe you should go with both of them. Dangle one on each arm," Ellie suggested, trying for a lighthearted response.

Nell laughed. "Maybe I should. That'd really turn some heads, wouldn't it?"

Somehow Ellie managed a smile. The dress was going back to Dovie's that very afternoon. She'd been an idiot to spend that much money trying to impress a man who'd already approached another woman. Perhaps he thought he'd walk into the Grange Hall with a woman on each of *his* arms. Well, in that case, Glen Patterson had another think coming.

"There's a problem with Glen, though," Nell said, studying Ellie.

"What's that?" she asked, feigning interest.

"It's similar to the one I have with Grady. I always thought you and Glen would make a wonderful couple."

"Glen and me?" Ellie laughed as though it was the funniest thing she'd heard in weeks. "Nah, we're nothing more than friends. If you want to go to the dance with him, don't let me stand in your way. He asked *you*, didn't he?"

"Yes, but—"

"Don't worry about it," Ellie said, surprised how convincing she sounded. "It's no big deal."

"You're sure?"

"Absolutely."

On second thought, Ellie mused, as she rang up Nell's purchases, she was keeping the dress. Not only that, she'd be dancing every dance.

And she hoped Glen got a really good look at her, wearing her beautiful dress and dancing with every attractive single man who asked.

He could eat his heart out!

Six

This was bound to be an interesting evening, Cal Patterson thought. He climbed into his truck wearing fresh-washed Wrangler's, a string tie and polished boots. The big dance. Which meant there should be lots of entertaining activity as men and women of all ages flirted outrageously; making fools of themselves and each other. A few romances were always made at this kind of event, and a few broken. Yup, it was fascinating to watch, all right, especially if you were a disinterested observer. Like him.

But not like Glen.

Cal wasn't sure where Glen had gone Wednesday afternoon, but his brother had returned in one hell of a mood. While he might not know the particulars, Cal would wager a case of beer that his brother's rotten mood involved Ellie Frasier.

When Cal had made the mistake of mentioning Ellie in connection with the big dance, Glen had all but exploded. Even before Cal could ask any questions, Glen had slammed out the door, but not without dropping a couple of hints first. If Cal guessed right, Ellie had decided to accept Richard Weston's invitation over Glen's.

While her choice surprised him, Cal was the first to admit that women were inconstant creatures who rarely knew their own minds. Best to keep your distance. Next thing Cal knew, his little brother had asked Nell Bishop; it hadn't done Glen's ego any good when she'd turned him down, too.

Cal himself had been fool enough to let one woman kick him in the gut and had found the experience as painful as anything he'd ever known. By God, he wasn't about to let it happen a second time. Glen, however, seemed destined to learn this particular lesson on his own.

Apparently his younger brother was a slow learner, because tonight he'd come downstairs in a new denim blazer and a pair of blue jeans so crisp they squeaked. His boots were polished to a gloss. One look dared Cal to comment.

He didn't, but he could tell it wasn't dancing that interested Glen. His brother intended to prove to Ellie, and quite possibly himself, that he didn't need her to have a good time. In other words, he was determined to act like a world-class idiot in front of the entire town.

Cal could almost guarantee that before the end of this night, Glen was going to do something really stupid. Now, that would have some entertainment value, but more important, Cal considered it his brotherly duty to be there to pick up the pieces afterward. He felt for Glen; he'd been through this, too. Heartbroken and humiliated.

Oh, yeah, *definitely* best to keep your distance from women.

Cal heard the band playing when he parked his truck in a long line of vehicles outside the Grange Hall. Cars and trucks were crammed bumper to bumper on both sides of the two-lane highway; obviously the parking lot had filled early in the evening. From the look of things everyone in town had shown up for the dance that traditionally kicked off summer.

The piercing strains of a fiddle cut into the night, followed by a banjo and Pete Hadley's melodic voice. Light spilled out of the open doorway and Cal could see a number of the married men clustered outside for a breath of fresh air. That, and a swallow or two of the hard stuff. Cal wasn't much of a drinking man himself. A cold beer now and again was more to his liking.

Someone shouted a greeting and Cal raised his arm in silent salute, but didn't stop to chat. He'd given his brother two hours—two hours during which he'd have his pride booted to hell and gone. If all went according to his calculations, Glen would be drunk soon or wish he was. Give him another hour. At that point Cal would step forward and haul him home.

The poor guy was in love, and while that alone guaranteed disaster, the worst of it was that Glen refused to admit it. Seeing his brother in such sad shape was akin to looking back two years and remembering the way he'd been with Jennifer. It amazed him now he hadn't seen her for what she was. He'd been so deeply infatuated with her he would have done anything to make her happy. Anything to prove how much he cared.

He'd asked her to be his wife, and six months later she'd humiliated him by canceling their wedding at the last minute. All because he wouldn't give up ranching and move to San Antonio or Houston. Jennifer, who'd transferred from Phoenix, Arizona, to take a short-lived job as an assistant bank manager, had wanted out of small-town America.

She'd wanted to move him to a city so crowded he'd never be able to breathe.

Cal had loved Jennifer, but he couldn't change who he was, not even for her. When he wouldn't dance to her tune, she pulled out of the wedding only two days before the event. Then she'd skipped town, leaving him to deal with the explanations and the embarrassment. Last he'd heard, Jennifer was living in Houston with some salesman.

He should have realized from the first she was a city girl at heart. But, like Glen, he'd been in love and hadn't recognized what was right there in front of him. Pushing thoughts of his ex-fiancée from his mind, he headed toward the hall.

The huge room was packed, forcing Cal to twist and turn as he made his way through the crowd. Men and women stretched across the hardwood floor in long rows, line dancing to the "Boot-scootin' Boogie." He remembered a few steps himself; Jennifer had insisted he learn the basics, despite the fact that he'd been born with two left feet.

When that song was over, the couples dancing started. Cal peered around, looking for Glen, and finally spotted him. His brother stood on the opposite side of the room, leaning against the bar, his narrowed gaze trained on the dancers. It didn't take a genius to figure out who held his attention.

Ellie.

Cal's eyebrows arched when he saw the object of his brother's affection. He'd never seen Ellie look prettier. The dress wasn't one with a Western flavor, which appeared to be the popular choice, but more old-fashioned. Elegant. She looked *damn* pretty, and Glen wasn't the only one who'd noticed, either.

Richard Weston had his arm tightly wrapped around Ellie's waist. From all appearances they were deeply involved with each other. This was worse than Cal had expected. He knew the type of man Richard Weston was, and he'd figured Ellie would've caught on fast enough herself. Apparently he'd overestimated her ability to judge character. It was a shame, too, because Richard was a user.

This protective feeling toward Ellie surprised Cal. He didn't want to have *any* feelings toward women. Whatever you did, you got your teeth kicked in. Wasn't worth it. Nosiree, he'd learned his lesson the hard way.

As he looked back at his brother, his eyes strayed to the woman standing directly to Glen's left. It took him a moment to remember who she was. The new doc. The first time he'd noticed her she'd worn a power business suit to a barbecue; now she was dressed in jeans and a snap-button Western shirt. Not exactly appropriate attire for the year's most formal event. Cal couldn't help feeling sorry for her, even if she *was* a city girl, but suspected she found this hick-town dance highly amusing. He could picture her phoning her city friends and making fun of the way people dressed and talked in Texas.

The doc must have sensed his scrutiny because she glanced across the room and looked squarely back at him. He glared in her direction, wanting her to know that he didn't like her attitude—or what he assumed her attitude to be.

The music ended just then, and before Cal could stop him, Glen marched onto the dance floor and headed straight for Ellie.

THIS WAS WORKING OUT even better than Ellie had hoped. Glen hadn't been able to take his eyes off her all evening. Richard viewed Glen as competition. She was well aware that his attentions had more to do with one-upmanship than any real interest in her; nevertheless she found flattery a balm to her wounded pride. She knew it was a superficial and childish reaction, but she couldn't help it. Glen had really hurt her by asking Nell to the dance. Temporarily, at least, being with Richard was a way of assuaging that pain.

The one bad side effect was that Glen's presence had brought out a possessiveness in Richard she wasn't sure she liked.

The only man she wanted to dance with hadn't even approached her. He'd followed her every move but hadn't made one of his own. Glen must've been reading her thoughts, though, because as soon as the music ended, he squeezed through the maze of people and stopped directly in front of her.

"The next dance is mine," he announced, his grim eyes challenging her to contradict him.

She stared at him, astonished. This was a side of her friend she'd never seen. Demanding, intense. Generally he took everything in his stride, live and let live, that sort of thing. But this . . . Ellie didn't know what to think.

"You've danced with Richard three times now. It's my turn."

"You're counting?"

"Yes," he snapped. He grasped her about the waist, dragged her close and clenched her hands as if expecting Pete to break into the "Beer Barrel Polka."

"Isn't this dance mine?" Richard asked with a look of sardonic surprise.

"She's dancing with me," Glen responded before she had a chance to answer.

"Ellie?" Richard turned to her with lifted brows.

Glen's arms tightened around her defiantly.

"It's all right," she assured the other man. "I'll dance with Glen." She waited until Richard had left the dance floor, then burst out, "What's gotten into you?" She had to raise her chin to look him in the eye.

"Plenty," he responded gruffly.

The music started again and Glen whirled her to the opposite side of the room and as far away as possible from Richard. The dance number was a mournful ballad about love gone wrong. Ellie found it a fitting choice. Couples flocked onto the dance floor, their arms around each other like clinging blackberry vines.

Glen didn't say anything, but he held her close, arms tight, jaw tense. But gradually he relaxed and so did she. They'd just found their rhythm when Richard approached and tapped Glen on the shoulder.

"My turn," he said with the smug certainty of a man who knew he'd eventually get what he wanted.

Ellie saw Glen's eyes flare in annoyance before he slowly released her. With his high sense of drama Richard grabbed her about the waist and dipped her backward until Ellie gasped, thinking her feet were about to go out from under her. Then Richard pulled her upright and danced her to the other side of the room, away from Glen.

Just when she'd adjusted her steps comfortably to Richard's, Glen was back. Without a word he tapped Richard on the shoulder. Richard gave Glen a flinty-eyed glare, then unwillingly released her.

Glen gathered her back in his arms, but they hadn't taken more than a couple of steps before Richard interrupted a second time. The two men scowled at each other.

"This is ridiculous!" Ellie cried. "What's the matter with you, Glen?"

"Me?" he exploded.

"You heard the lady," Richard said with a mocking smile that suggested Glen was making a nuisance of himself.

"You're no better," she snapped, hands aggressively on her hips.

The music faded and the couples closest to them stopped dancing to stare at the unfolding scene. Ellie had never been so embarrassed in her life. Before another minute had passed, Frank Hennessey was standing between the two men. Although he wasn't at the dance in his capacity as sheriff, he was the law in town and no one questioned his right to intervene. Dovie Boyd, who was with him, cast Ellie a sympathetic look.

"Is there a problem here, boys?" Frank asked, placing emphasis on the last word. It was a not-so-subtle reminder that this sort of skirmish was generally reserved for adolescents.

"Nothing Richard and I can't settle *outside*," Glen said.

"Glen!" Ellie couldn't believe her ears.

"That's fine with me," Richard answered quickly, raising his fists.

"Just one minute." Frank put a hand on each man's shoulder. "No one's going outside. If there's anything to settle, we'll do it right here and now." He nodded at Glen. "What's the problem?"

"I'd like to finish the dance with Ellie without Richard cutting in."

"Hey, it's a free country," Richard said, his tone cocky.

"Richard and I can settle this between us, man to man." Glen flexed his hands a number of times, letting Richard know he welcomed the opportunity to shove a fist down his throat.

"Neither of you is leaving this hall," Frank stated in a friendly but unmistakably firm tone. "At least not in your present frame of mine."

"I asked Ellie to dance first," Richard insisted.

"The hell you did!" Glen shouted.

"Ellie?" Frank turned his attention to her. "Which one of them yahoos you want to dance with?"

She glanced from one man to the other. Richard wore a smug contemptuous look and Glen's dark brooding expression didn't make her feel much better. It was as if he thought he had squatter's rights or something.

"Neither one," she announced coolly.

Glen's mouth sagged open. "Fine," he muttered.

"But, sweetheart . . ." Richard objected.

Unwilling to listen to either one of them, Ellie turned abruptly and muttered to Dovie and Frank, "I'm going to get a glass of punch." Glen and Richard were insufferable fools, she told herself, both of them plagued with oversize egos. She refused to allow them to make an idiot out of her, too.

Every eye in the room was focused on Ellie as she marched off the dance floor. She could feel the heat building in her face; she could hear the curious whispers all over the room.

Savannah and Caroline met her at the edge of the dance floor and gathered close around her. "Are you all right?" Savannah asked.

Ellie didn't know how to answer. Glen and Richard had made spectacles of themselves and a laughingstock of her. "I'm so furious I could scream."

Savannah nodded. "I know exactly what you mean. Sit down and I'll get you a glass of punch. It'll calm your nerves."

In her present mood it would take a whole lot more than a cold drink to calm her. Thankfully the music had started again, and as people resumed dancing, they seemed to have forgotten the incident. To Ellie's annoyance, Savannah wasn't the one who returned with the punch; Glen brought it to her, instead. She glared up at him before accepting the glass.

He stood beside her for a couple of moments, then wordlessly claimed the empty chair next to hers.

Ellie crossed her legs and turned slightly, granting him a partial view of her back.

"You might have let me know," he said after several tense minutes.

"Know what?"

"That you'd accepted Richard's invitation to the dance."

"Oh, that's rich." She twisted around to face him, struggling to keep her voice under control. "You make a point of asking if I was going to be at the dance and I thought—I *assumed* . . . I spent a fortune on the dress, and the next thing I hear, you invited Nell."

"You bought that dress for me?" His face brightened and the beginnings of a smile edged up the corners of his mouth.

"You'd look pretty silly in a dress, Glen Patterson. No, I bought it for me."

He grinned roguishly at that, but his amusement faded when it became clear that Ellie was about to end the conversation.

"You'll note I'm not here with Nell," he said softly.

"Nell came with Grady, then."

"Grady asked her, too?" Glen's mouth snapped shut and he leaned hard against the back of the chair. He focused his attention on the dance floor. "I'd never have invited her if you hadn't agreed to go with Richard. I thought you and I were going to meet here."

"That's what I thought, too."

"But you said yes to Richard, anyway."

Ellie bristled. "I didn't until I'd heard you'd asked Nell."

Glen's face went blank, then his eyes narrowed suspiciously. "Why, that slimy . . ." he muttered. "Richard told me—" Glen stopped abruptly as if he'd already said more than he intended.

"Told you what?" Ellie pressed.

"Nothing. It doesn't matter," he muttered.

"There's no need to get short-tempered with me." Ellie crossed her arms and glared straight ahead.

Beside her, Glen crossed his arms, too, and scowled darkly at the other side of the room.

* * *

IT WAS NOW OR NEVER, Caroline decided. Pete Hadley had just announced that the next dance was ladies' choice. Heart pounding, Caroline slowly approached Grady. He sat next to Cal Patterson, and they were deeply involved in conversation. Her guess was that it had something to do with Glen and Ellie. The pair were the subject of a great deal of comment tonight. Little wonder, considering the scene they'd created earlier. Both of them now sat at the end of a row of seats, arms crossed and looking about as miserable as any two people could get.

About as miserable as *she'd* been the past few days—since her most recent encounter with Grady.

Couples were already heading toward the dance floor, and if she waited any longer, she'd miss the opportunity entirely. Savannah, on Laredo's arm, cast her an encouraging smile and nodded in Grady's direction. Savannah had actually been the one to persuade her to clear the air with Grady.

Grady and Cal's conversation halted as she reached them. Grady looked up at her as if he couldn't imagine why she was standing in front of him, blocking his view.

"Would you care to dance?" she asked, gesturing weakly toward the couples already circling the polished floor. Her pulse increased by fifty beats a minute, and she was sure he was going to humiliate her by refusing.

Grady frowned.

"It's ladies' choice," she elaborated, her voice growing small.

Grady glanced to either side. "You're asking *me?*"

"No," she snapped, her anger saving her. "I thought I'd start at the front of the row and work my way down. If you refuse, I'll ask Cal next. Come on, Grady, it shouldn't be such a difficult decision."

It seemed for a moment as if he was about to decline, then, to her enormous relief, he got to his feet. "I'm not much good at this," he muttered.

He walked stiffly at her side to the dance floor. Then he put his arm around her waist, but maintained a space between them as if he feared she carried something contagious.

"I don't generally bite," she said, amused more than insulted.

"Promise?" he asked, and drew her somewhat closer.

The music was soft and mellow, and they shuffled their feet a bit, not really dancing, which was fine with Caroline. Her skill was limited, too. She looked out over the dance floor and recognized quite a few couples. Savannah and Laredo were lost in each other's arms. How she envied the happiness her friend had found. Caroline's heart ached with a sudden loneliness for that kind of love and contentment.

"Why'd you ask me to dance?" Grady asked gruffly.

"I figured I'd have to," she said. "The last time we spoke, you said *I'd* have to ask *you.*"

She felt some of the stiffness leave his body. "In other words the ball's in my court now."

Caroline grinned. "Something like that."

Grady's hold on her tightened and he gave a deep sigh as he eased her closer. For several moments, neither one spoke.

Caroline knew she'd have to bring up the subject of their last argument. This was her opportunity to mend fences with Grady, and she didn't want to waste it. "I felt bad after our conversation the other day."

"I did, too," he said. "I'm a bit of a hothead."

"And I'm too impatient."

They didn't seem to have much more to say after that, and before long the dance was over.

"I didn't step on your toes, did I?" he said as they walked off the floor.

"I seem to have survived."

He grinned, and she smiled back. Caroline held her breath, hoping maybe now he'd ask her to dance. He didn't.

"Thanks," he said when they returned to the sitting area.

"You're welcome." Caroline turned away, swallowing her disappointment.

GLEN COULDN'T SIT STILL. He'd been home from the dance for an hour and hadn't stayed in any one position for longer than five minutes. He sat down in front of the television, then bolted upright and stalked to the kitchen, thinking feverishly.

He brewed himself a cup of instant coffee and carried it into the living room. Cal was watching the late-night newscast and glanced curiously in his direction.

Glen sat back down, but was squirming a few minutes later.

"What in tarnation is the matter with you?" Cal demanded when Glen bounded out of the recliner for the sixth time in as many minutes.

"Nothing's wrong," Glen lied.

"You're thinking about Ellie again, aren't you?"

He was, but Glen had no intention of admitting it. "What makes you say that?"

Cal gave a bark of laughter. "Because, little brother, you've got it written all over you."

"Got what?"

"You've fallen for Ellie."

Glen opened his mouth to deny it, but changed his mind. After the spectacle he'd made of himself in front of the entire community, he'd look like an even bigger fool claiming otherwise. He did have feelings for Ellie, but he hadn't decided what they were. He was protective of her, like a brother, but his reactions to Richard and his behavior that evening had proved it was more than that. He wasn't sure anymore what he felt.

"Richard drove her home," he muttered, stating for the first time what had been on his mind since leaving the dance.

"You don't trust him to be a gentleman?"

"Damn right, I don't." The more Glen thought about Richard alone with Ellie, the more agitated he got. It would be just like that scumbag to try something with her. Ellie knew how to handle herself, but she was vulnerable, and Richard was just the kind of man who'd try to take advantage of that.

"I'm driving into town," he announced. He wanted to reassure himself that Richard had gone—and he wanted to talk to Ellie.

"Now?" Cal glanced at his watch. "It's nearly midnight."

"I don't care what time it is." Decision made, Glen reached for his jacket and hurried to the door. He should have followed Ellie home, that was what he should've done, but they'd barely spoken after their big scene.

"You might phone her first," Cal suggested.

Glen paused and considered his brother's idea, then shook his head. "I have things to say, and that's best done face-to-face."

"What are you going to say to her this time of night?" Cal wanted to know.

"I'm not sure yet," Glen admitted, letting the screen door bang shut. He hadn't worked anything out; maybe the moment would bring some inspiration.

The drive into town was accomplished in record time. He parked on her street, drew a couple of shaky breaths and headed for her house. He rang the bell, and when she didn't immediately appear, he pounded on the door.

The porch light went on and then he heard Ellie moving about on the other side. "Who's there?"

"Glen!" he shouted loud enough to wake half the neighborhood. "Open up, Ellie. I need to talk to you."

"It's the middle of the night," she protested, but he heard the lock turn.

She was wearing a flannel robe cinched at the waist. Her hair was mussed and he could see he'd roused her from bed. She didn't invite him inside, which was just as well.

"I'm warning you," she muttered. "This had better be important."

"It is." Then to his acute embarrassment, his mind went blank. Not only that, he couldn't keep his eyes off her. Even without makeup, her hair flattened on one side, she was beautiful. It astonished him that he'd spent all that time with her week after week, year after year, and never really seen her.

"Would you kindly stop staring at me!"

Glen hadn't realized he was. "Is Richard with you?" he asked, and knew immediately that this was the worst possible thing he could have said.

In response Ellie slammed the door in his face.

Glen clutched the frame, knocked his forehead against the door and gritted his teeth. Hoping she'd give him the opportunity to redeem himself, he pressed the doorbell again.

"Ellie, I'm sorry, I didn't mean that," he shouted, praying she could hear him.

His apology was met with silence. Then finally, "Go away."

"I can't," he said, utterly miserable.

The porch light went out. Feeling completely dejected and the biggest fool who'd ever roamed the earth, he sat on the top step. He propped his elbows on his knees and dangled his hands between his legs, lacking even the energy to get up and walk to his truck.

He must have sat there a good ten minutes before he heard the door open softly behind him. If he hadn't been so thoroughly depressed, he would have leaped to his feet and begged Ellie to forgive him. But in his current frame of mind, he was convinced she'd phoned Sheriff Hennessey. He wouldn't have blamed her.

To his surprise she sat down next to him.

"I'm sorry, Ellie," he whispered, still not looking at her. "I can't believe I asked you something so stupid."

"I can't believe you did, either."

"I kept thinking about him driving you home, and I don't know, something crazy came over me." Even knowing he'd probably infuriate her further, Glen asked, "Did he kiss you?"

She groaned and, leaning forward, buried her face in her hands.

"Is that a yes or a no?"

"It means it's none of your business."

So Richard *had* kissed her. Glen would bet just about anything on that. It was obvious; otherwise she'd have been quick to deny it. His heart sank. At one time it wouldn't have bothered him, but now it did. A hell of a lot.

"What's happened to us?" she asked. "We used to be such good friends."

"We were," he agreed. "Good friends."

"And then you kissed me."

Talk about mistakes—but Glen really couldn't make himself regret that kiss. He'd relived it for days, remembering how it felt to hold Ellie in his arms, taste her lips, touch her hair. How it felt to be so *close*.

"Damn me if you want, but I'd give anything to kiss you right now," he whispered.

He was aware of her scrutiny and half turned to meet her gaze. "Because you think Richard kissed me earlier?" she asked.

"No," he said softly. "Because I need to." He reached for her, and his heart swelled with joy when she met his lips with an eagerness that matched his own. This was what he'd wanted, what he'd needed all along. Ellie in his arms. Ellie at his side.

"This is what I want, too," she whispered, her lips moving over his.

Glen kissed her again. For the first time that evening—that entire week—he was at peace.

Seven

Ellie slipped into the pew Sunday morning five minutes after the service had started. Organ music surged through the church as she took the last seat, reached for the hymnal and joined the congregation in song. At first she suspected the attention she'd generated was due to her tardiness. It wasn't that she'd overslept. Far from it. The night had been her most restless since before her father's death.

She'd tossed and turned and fretted, and when sleep finally claimed her, it was fitful. She blamed Glen for that—and for a whole lot more. It was because of him she was late, but at the moment she'd have been willing to blame him for global warming.

Even after the song had ended and Pastor Wade McMillen started his sermon, Ellie felt the scrutiny of friends and neighbors. That, too, could be directly attributed to Glen. The man had single-handedly made her the object of speculation and gossip. Wringing his neck would be too good for him. First he'd embarrassed her in front of the entire town by making a spectacle of himself fighting over her. If that wasn't enough, he'd woken her out of a dead sleep, insulted her—then kissed her senseless. Ellie couldn't recall a time anyone had confused her more.

Not that she was Richard's champion. No way! He'd intentionally provoked Glen, leading him to believe the two of them were involved when it simply wasn't true. Besides, Richard was selfish and untrustworthy, and Glen was . . . Glen. Her friend.

Naturally Glen had skipped church. Richard, too. No doubt the effort of carting around their massive egos had worn them out, she thought irritably. It might have helped had they shown up to divide the attention now directed solely at her.

By concentrating on Wade's sermon, she managed to pretend she didn't notice her newfound celebrity status. At the end of the service following the benediction, she hoped to slip away unnoticed; it soon became apparent that this wasn't going to happen. The organ music filled the church as the congregation started to flow outside and Ellie was surrounded.

"I saw everything," Louise Powell purred, sidling up to Ellie as though they were long-standing friends. "It isn't every woman who has two men virtually at each other's throats."

"I think you misunderstood what happened," Ellie said desperately.

"I've known Glen Patterson all my life," Ruth Bishop was saying behind Louise, "and when he wants something, he gets it."

"I wouldn't underestimate Richard Weston," Louise said. "He's a man of the world. Ellie could do worse."

Ellie hated it when people spoke as if they knew more about her life than she did.

"Stay close to me," Edwina Moorhouse whispered, suddenly slipping next to Ellie and taking her arm. "Lily," she instructed her younger sister, "go on the other side." Again for Ellie's ears only, she added, "Just keep walking. We'll have you out of here in no time."

Ellie found herself grateful for the Moorhouse sister's protection. Especially from Louise Powell, the town gossip, a woman who enjoyed meddling in the affairs of others, often under the guise of concern.

"Ladies, ladies," Louise said in a sharp voice, tagging behind Ellie and the Moorhouse sisters. "*I* was chatting with Ellie."

"You aren't any longer," Edwina declared, stepping in front of Ellie.

If it hadn't been so ridiculous, and if she hadn't felt so tired and worn-out, Ellie would have laughed. Each sister positioned herself in a way that told Louise she'd have a fight on her hands before they'd willingly abandon Ellie. The two unlikely guardians were dressed in their Sunday best, with crisp white gloves and pillbox hats.

"All I wanted to do—"

"We know very well what you were doing, Louise," Edwina said in a voice that reminded Ellie of her schooldays.

"Louise," Lily said, not unkindly, "do you remember in sixth grade when Larry Marino . . ."

Louise's face turned beet red. "I remember," she whispered.

"It would be embarrassing if news of you and Larry somehow got around town, wouldn't it?"

"That was nearly forty years ago!" Louise protested.

"And just as scandalous today as it was back then," Lily said primly. "Now, as Edwina was saying, Ellie's with *us*."

"Oh, all right." The other woman flounced off with her rumpled dignity and returned to where her husband stood impatiently waiting.

"Lily!" Edwina gasped. "What happened between Louise and Larry in the sixth grade?"

Lily covered her mouth with her hand. "God's honest truth, sister, I don't know."

"Sister, you amaze me."

"You!" Ellie giggled. She could certainly have dealt with a busybody like Louise Powell on her own, but this was much more fun.

Edwina waited until Louise was out of earshot, then she turned around and regarded Ellie with deep affection. "Are you all right, Ellie?"

"Of course."

"I'd like to box a few ears," Lily said. "We didn't teach our students to stare, did we, sister?"

"Positively not."

"I hope you're willing to forgive everyone's curiosity?"

"It's only natural, I suppose," Ellie said agreeably. "Especially in light of what happened at the dance."

"Yes, we did hear about that." Lily patted Ellie's hand. "I realize you didn't ask Edwina's or my advice, but I feel compelled to offer you a few words of wisdom."

"Since your mother isn't here," Edwina inserted.

"Please do." Ellie had always loved the Moorhouse sisters and wouldn't even consider turning down anything they offered.

"We may never have married, but Edwina and I do know a thing or two about love."

"I'm sure that's true."

Edwina caught Ellie's hand in her own. "Follow your heart, child."

"Yes, indeed, follow your heart," Lily echoed.

"I will," Ellie promised, and she would, just as soon as her heart had sorted everything out.

Still thinking about their advice, Ellie drove home, stopping first at the grocery store to pick up a few essentials. When she turned onto her street, she noticed the pickup outside her house. She groaned when she found Richard sitting on her porch, waiting for her return.

He was the last person she wanted to see. Not that she was ready to see Glen anytime soon, either. She refused to think about the kisses they'd shared or the reasons he'd come by her house after the disastrous dance. Her fear was that he saw Richard and himself as rivals for her. And that this had influenced his actions and his declarations.

What he didn't know was that Richard hadn't kissed her. Not for lack of trying, mind you, but because she was in no mood for him or his games.

Realizing she had no escape, Ellie pulled into her driveway and climbed out of the car. Richard glanced up, apparently surprised to see her loaded down with groceries.

"Ellie," he said, smiling brightly. He leaped to his feet and raced down the steps to take the bags out of her arms. "You should have said something," he chastised as if he'd waited all day for the honor of carrying her groceries.

Ellie tried to refuse his help, but he'd have none of it. "Hey, it's the least I can do." It also gave him the perfect excuse to follow her into the house, Ellie noted despondently.

He set the bags on the kitchen counter and immediately started unpacking them. "Look at this," he said as if finding a dozen eggs was akin to discovering gold. "I swear I was thinking just five minutes ago how much I'd enjoy a mushroom-and-Swiss-cheese omelet." Gesturing like a magician, he pulled a paper sack of mushrooms free of the bag, along with a slab of Swiss cheese. "It's fate," he said, his eyes twinkling.

"Richard, I don't think—"

"I'll cook," he said. He clasped her shoulders and backed her into a kitchen chair. "Sit down and make yourself at home."

"I am home," she interrupted, amused despite herself at his audacity.

He stopped a moment and smiled, then said, "So you are."

She started to stand, but he wouldn't allow it.

"I'm cooking," he said cheerfully, pushing her into the chair again.

"Richard—"

"I won't take no for an answer." He opened the cupboard door and took out a small bowl. Before Ellie could stop him, he was whirling about her kitchen as if he'd been cooking there his entire life.

To his credit he seemed to know what he was doing.

"You look especially lovely this morning," he said, pouring the eggs into the skillet.

"Yeah, yeah." Ellie was in no mood for empty flattery. "I've heard that before."

"Only because it's true." He whistled something jaunty as he edged a spatula under the omelet.

The doorbell rang and with a wave of his hand Richard motioned for her to answer it.

Ellie was too concerned with how to expel Richard from her home to be affronted by his peremptory manner—or to worry about who'd come calling unannounced. Hindsight being what it was, she wished later she'd given the matter some thought before she opened the door.

Glen Patterson stood on the other side.

Ellie's mouth fell open. She hadn't expected to see him.

"Glen!"

"Who is it, sweetheart?" Richard asked, stepping out of the kitchen, a dish towel tucked at his waist. He carried the frying pan and spatula in his hands and didn't miss a beat when he saw Glen.

"Howdy, neighbor," he called. "I'm stirring up a little brunch here. You're welcome to join us if you want."

Glen's eyes hardened as he looked at Ellie. She tried to tell him without words that it wasn't how it seemed; that she hadn't *asked* Richard to join her, he'd come uninvited. But Glen had already formed his own opinion, and nothing she did now was likely to change it.

"I'll be back another time," he muttered.

"Stay," Richard urged like a gracious host. "Cooking is one of my talents. Ask Ellie."

It was all she could manage not to wheel around and kick Richard in the shin.

THREE DAYS HAD PASSED since Glen had stumbled on Richard cooking Ellie's breakfast. Three miserable days. He still couldn't think about it and not get mad.

He hadn't seen Ellie, hadn't talked to her in those three days. Generally he dropped in the feed store for supplies on Tuesday afternoons. Almost always they'd spend a few minutes together, joking, teasing, laughing. There'd been damn little of that lately. He didn't drive into town on Tuesday, and he wasn't eager to make the trip on Wednesday, either. It would do Ellie good to miss his company, not that he'd received any indication that she had.

Ellie preyed on his mind, making him next to useless around the ranch. Disgusted, Cal sent him out to check fence lines. If that was meant to distract him, it hadn't worked. Grandpa Patterson used to say: never approach a bull from the front, a horse from the rear or a fool from any direction. Well, Glen couldn't help feeling like a fool, and his mind seemed to be spinning in *every* direction.

His thinking was clouded with thoughts of Ellie as he trotted back toward the ranch. When he wasn't thinking about her, he was brooding about Richard Weston. Glen feared Richard was using the time he stayed away from Ellie to further his own cause.

If that was true, then so be it. If Ellie wanted Richard, fine, she was welcome to him but he'd figured she had more sense.

A man had his pride, too. Glen had kissed Ellie on two occasions now, and if he could recognize that they had something pretty special, why couldn't she? Okay, so they hadn't talked about their feelings, but Glen had been hoping to do that on Sunday. Only he couldn't, because Richard was there, playing Julia Child.

The way he saw it, Ellie owed him an apology. She'd misled him, kissing him like she had, then cozying up to Richard. He'd never have taken Ellie for the type of woman who'd play one man against another, but he'd seen the evidence with his own eyes.

Cal was waiting for him when he led Moonshine into the barn.

"Are you picking up supplies this week or not?" Cal demanded.

"I'll get them," Glen replied without enthusiasm.

"If it's a problem, I'll drive into town myself."

"It's no problem," Glen said. Damn it, he couldn't stay away a minute longer, and he knew it.

By the time Glen cleaned up and drove into town, his throat was parched. More to fortify his courage than to cure his thirst, he decided to stop at Billy D's for a cold beer.

Billy D himself was behind the bar when Glen sauntered in. The ranchers tended to congregate here when they came to town, and there was usually someone he knew. Billy was the friendly sort and something of an institution in Promise. He baked a decent pizza, and his fried chicken was as good as any colonel's; but few people came to Billy D's for the food. It was the one place in town, other than the bowlng alley and the feed store, where ranchers could shoot the breeze and unwind. And at Billy's they could do it over a beer.

"Well if it ain't Glen Patterson himself," Billy called out when Glen walked in.

A couple of ranchers lounging against the bar raised their hands in greeting.

Glen tipped his Stetson a little farther back on his head.

"You want a cold one?" Billy asked.

"Sounds good." Glen stepped up to the bar and set some money down on the counter.

With practiced ease Billy slid the thick mug down the polished bar and Glen grabbed it before it flew past.

"Keep your money. It's on the house," Billy said, smiling broadly.

Glen arched his brows and lifted the mug to his lips. Nothing tasted better than a cold beer on a hot day, especially when it was free. It slid down the back of his throat, easing away the taste of several hours of eating dust.

"Any reason you're giving away beer this afternoon?" he asked when he'd downed half the mug.

"Only to you," Billy informed him.

"What's so special about me?"

Billy gave him a look that suggested he open his eyes. "I figure you're gonna set Richard Weston on his ear. In fact, I'm waitin' to see it."

Glen frowned. "I don't have any fight with Weston." Ellie would probably love it if he acted like an idiot—yet again—but he was finished with that game. Those two were welcome to each other. Glen had decided to wash his hands of the whole thing. If Ellie wanted to marry Richard, then he wasn't going to stand in her way.

"You don't care?" Billy looked as if he wanted his beer back. "Richard's been by, and to hear him talk, he's done everything but put an engagement ring on Ellie's finger. You aren't going to let that happen, are you?"

"What am I supposed to do about it?" Glen asked, hardening his heart in order to avoid showing his feelings.

Billy frowned. He braced both hands on the bar and leaned forward as though to get a better look at Glen. "You're serious about this?"

"Damn right, I'm serious."

"That's not the impression I got Saturday night. The three of you are the hot topic of conversation this week, dancing that Texas two-step of yours. Some folks've started placing bets on which of you is gonna marry Ellie."

"As far as I'm concerned Richard can have her." It was a bold-faced lie, but Glen considered it damage control. For his ego *and* his reputation.

"Personally I think you're the better man," Lyle Whitehouse said. His back was to the bar and he'd rested his elbows behind him. Lyle worked at a ranch closer to Brewster than to Promise, but he'd worn out his welcome at more than a few places. He had a reputation as a hothead, although he hadn't started any fights at Billy D's. Yet.

Jimmy Morris stood beside him, his stomach pressed to the bar and one boot on the brass foot rail. "When you're talkin' marriage, it isn't a matter of bein' better," he said ponderously. "Ladies choose who they choose."

"True enough," Lyle agreed. "But it doesn't hurt to try a bit of persuasion . . ." He winked. "You know what I mean."

"Richard seems to think he's got an edge on you," Billy informed Glen, "and no one likes a man who's too confident."

"Even if he does buy the drinks," Jimmy added.

"Richard's celebrating already?" Glen asked, wondering if Richard knew something no one else did. Maybe he'd already asked Ellie and maybe she'd given him an encouraging response. The thought twisted his gut. To this point he'd trusted Ellie's judgment. More or less. He was miserable and uncertain about her and Richard, but he'd always supposed that in the end Ellie would turn to him. Because of their friendship and everything they had in common . . . and their kisses.

Those kisses in the wee hours of Saturday night had been wonderful, the best of his life. He found it hard to believe they'd meant so little to her.

"Weston's so sure of himself he's taking odds."

"Making himself the favorite," Billy said, his mouth thinning with disapproval.

"Naturally," Jimmy muttered, and took a swallow of beer.

"We were kinda hopin' you'd set him down a peg or two," Lyle said in a tone that suggested more than one rancher had pinned his hopes on Glen.

Glen didn't know what it was about Richard Weston. He'd never met anyone so likable, yet so universally disliked. He could be charming, witty and fun, and at the same time he was the biggest jackass in the state of Texas.

"What do you think?" Billy pressed.

"You're not gonna take this sittin' down, are you?" Lyle asked.

"You gotta do something," Jimmy added. "We got money on you!"

All three men looked to Glen. Unfortunately he didn't know *what* the hell to do.

ONE OF THE MOST DIFFICULT things Richard Weston had ever done was return to Promise—broke, his tail between his legs, seeking a handout from his family. Once he was home again, he figured he'd die of sheer boredom inside a month. Promise was about as Hicktown, U.S.A., as it could get. He stared at the walls of his old bedroom and sighed. Never in a million years did he guess he'd end up back here.

What intrigued him was how gullible folks in Promise were. Everyone—well, except for the sheriff and he couldn't *prove* anything—accepted his lies without pause or question. In fact, he'd gotten a little careless, but it didn't seem to matter. He'd certainly been right in assuming that he'd be safe here, at the ranch—safe from his troubles back east.

The boredom, though. He sighed. And the cows . . .

It'd taken him the better part of six years to get the stench of cattle from his skin. He'd never understood the attraction of following a bunch of pathetic-looking beasts from pasture to pasture. As far as he was concerned, cattle were headaches on the hoof. Yet his father and his brother had always acted as though there was nothing more wonderful in life than ranching. But it sure wasn't for him; never had been, never would be. The mere thought of sitting in a saddle all day made him want to puke, although God knew Grady had done his best to get him to do some work around the place. Thus far, he'd managed to avoid doing anything of consequence. He'd volunteered to run errands, which gave him free use of the pickup—something that had come in handy for other reasons. The tradespeople around Promise trusted him, assumed he was taking care of ranch business. And he was. But he was seeing to his own needs, as well.

To his surprise he'd discovered some pleasant distractions in Promise. Ellie Frasier, for one. She was a sweet thing, pretty, too, if a guy didn't mind small breasts and skinny legs. Personally he preferred a more voluptuous woman, but Ellie came with certain monetary compensations. A prosperous business, plus a healthy inheritance from her daddy, who'd doted on his only child.

It wouldn't hurt him any to get his hands on old-man Frasier's money. He could use it. He was in trouble, but all it took was money in the right places and his problem would vanish.

For now he was safe enough in Promise. No one knew about his family, and even if they managed to track him to Texas, they'd never find his hiding place.

He had Savannah to thank for that. He'd always been lucky—at least until his present difficulties. But then, everything had a way of working out. This latest episode was a good example.

No, he decided, lying on top of his quilt, hands folded behind his head, there could be worse things in this world than marrying Ellie Frasier. He'd ask her soon, and if she was opposed to selling the business, then he'd take it over. He could do well with it, too—aside from the fact that it would provide collateral for raising quick cash.

Actually Richard liked the idea of becoming a local businessman. He could remember one of his teachers, Lily Moorhouse, telling him he should be a politician. The old biddy just could be right. In a year or two he might even consider running for mayor. Promise could use his kind of leadership. This hayseed town needed someone to bring it into the twenty-first century.

The town had real possibilities, if he could convince people to listen to his ideas. For starters they needed to close down the bowling alley; in his view it gave the place a white-trash image. He'd buy up land outside town and get some investors to build a shopping complex. If not that, he'd bet he could get one of the big discount stores interested in the area. It was time the local shop owners found out about competitive pricing.

Everything hinged on Ellie. They'd kissed a couple of times, and although she didn't exactly set him ablaze, she wasn't bad. He knew she was sweet on Glen Patterson. That might be cause for concern if Patterson wasn't so intent on putting his foot in his mouth, which he seemed to do with increasing regularity. Fortunately for Richard.

Poor guy was out of his league with women, unlike Richard who had the whole mating ritual down to an art. The way he figured it, Ellie would agree to marry him before the end of the month. Maybe sooner. When he turned on the charm, there wasn't a female within six states who could refuse him. Little Ellie Frasier didn't have a snowball's chance in hell.

And over at Billy D's Richard stood to pick up a few extra bucks betting on his own chances in the Texas two-step.

Altogether a sweet deal.

FOR MOST OF HIS ADULT life Glen had been confident and self-assured. He'd taken over the family ranch with his brother, worked hard, kept his nose clean. Romantic involvements had been light and ultimately insignificant, causing no pain when they ended. Until now there'd been little to disrupt his calm existence.

Any problems he either solved himself or sought advice from Cal. This was the first time since he was thirteen years old that he felt the need to speak to his father about girls. Women. What his grandfather used to call "personal matters."

His parents had moved into town a few years ago. His father had suffered a heart attack, and although the doctors had said he was good as new following his bypass surgery, his mother wasn't taking any chances. For years they'd talked about moving into Promise one day. His father had insisted he wasn't ready to retire, so they'd bought the Howe Mansion, which wasn't really a mansion, just the largest house in town. Before another year was up it'd been renovated and turned into a bed-and-breakfast.

Glen had had his doubts about this venture. Cal, too. But their parents had proved them both wrong. The bed-and-breakfast was thriving, and so were Phil and Mary Patterson.

His mother complained that she didn't see near enough of her sons. That being the case, she certainly looked surprised to see Glen when he walked into her kitchen.

"Hi, Mom," he said, slipping up behind her and kissing her cheek.

Mary Patterson hugged him as though it'd been a week of Sundays since his last visit. "Taste this," she said, sticking a spoon in his face.

"What is it?" Glen asked, jerking his head back. He preferred not to be part of a culinary experiment.

"Chili. I'm practicing for the cook-off."

"Mom, that's not for months yet."

"I know. This is a new recipe I've been playing around with. What do you think?"

Despite his better judgment, Glen tried the chili and tried to hide his response. It tasted . . . well, not like food. Not like something you'd seriously consider eating.

"It needs work, right?" she asked, studying him.

He nodded. For her guests his mother generally stayed with plain basic food. Good thing. "This recipe needs a rethink, Mom."

She sighed and tossed the spoon into the sink. "I was afraid of that."

"Where's Dad?" Glen asked, hoping to make the inquiry sound casual.

"Upstairs. The sink in the bathroom's plugged again." Her gaze didn't waver from his. "Something on your mind?"

He nodded. He could never hide anything from his mother.

"Does it involve Ellie Frasier?"

"Yeah."

She grinned and pointed toward the stairway off the kitchen. "Talk to your father, but if you want advice about how to romance her, talk to me. Your father doesn't know a damn thing about romance."

Hiding a smile, Glen headed for the stairs. Just as his mother had said, he found his dad lying on the tile floor staring up at the sink, wrench in hand.

"Hi, Dad."

"I thought I heard you downstairs talking to your mother." Phil Patterson slid out from beneath the sink and reached for a rag to dry his hands. "And to think she was worried about me working too hard on the ranch. If anything's going to kill me, it'll be this sink."

Glen sat down on the edge of the tub.

"Did you have something you wanted to ask me, son?"

Leaning forward, Glen removed his Stetson, slowly turning it in his hands. "How many years have you and Mom been married?"

"Well, your brother's thirty-six, so this year we had our thirty-seventh anniversary. Thirty-seven years! Damn, it doesn't seem that long. Hell if I can figure out when I got old."

"You're not."

Phil smiled. "That's my boy. Buttering me up, are you? So what do you need?"

"Just some advice."

"Be glad to help if I can." With an exaggerated groan, he stood up, lowered the toilet seat and sat there.

Glen wasn't sure where to start. "When did you know you loved Mom?"

Phil considered the question for a moment. "When she told me I did." He chuckled and Glen joined in. "Don't laugh too hard, boy, it's the truth. We'd dated in high school some, but she was two years younger. After I graduated, I enlisted. Joined the Navy. We wrote back and forth and I saw a little of the world. Eventually your mother graduated and went away to college in Dallas. We didn't see each other for three years, but we kept in touch. I must say she wrote a lot more letters than me.

"Then one Christmas, we both happened to be home at the same time. It was a shock to see her again. We'd been friends, stayed in touch, but somehow I'd never noticed how pretty she was."

Glen nodded; his mother was still a pretty woman.

"I wasn't the only one who noticed, either," his father continued. "She got more attention than a prize heifer at the state fair. Until that Christmas I'd always thought of her as a friend. We'd dated from time to time, but it was nothing serious. That Christmas my eyes were opened."

"Did you ask her to marry you then?"

"Hell, no. I wasn't happy about other men paying attention to her, but I figured if she wanted to date someone else, I didn't have the right to stand in her way."

"You were sweet on her, though?"

"Yeah, but I didn't realize how much until we'd kissed a few times."

Now that was something Glen could understand. "Did you try to talk to her?"

Phil chuckled again. "I sure did, but all we seemed to do was argue. Nothing I said was right. I told her I thought she was pretty, and even that came out like an insult."

This story was sounding more familiar by the minute. "So what happened?"

His father grew thoughtful. "It was time to head back to the base, and I knew if I didn't try to explain myself one last time, I might not get another chance. I called her all evening, but she was out—you can imagine how *that* made me feel, especially since I couldn't very well ring her doorbell in the middle of the night." He smiled at the memory. "So I stood outside her bedroom and threw stones at the window until she woke up.

"It's not a good idea to wake your mother out of a sound sleep, even now. It took me a while to convince her to hear me out. Luckily she agreed and sat with me on the porch. By that time I was so confused I didn't know what to say."

Glen edged closer to his father, keenly interested in the details of his parents' courtship.

"I stammered and stuttered and told her how much I valued her friendship and hated the idea of returning to Maine with this bad feeling between us. That was when she looked me full in the eye and asked if I loved her."

His mother had always been a gutsy woman and Glen admired her for it. "What did you tell her?"

"I didn't know what to say. It was the first time I'd ever thought about it. We were friends, hung around with the same crowd, exchanged letters, that sort of thing. She wanted to know if I loved her, and for the life of me I didn't have an answer."

It went without saying that wasn't what his mother had wanted to hear.

"When I hesitated, Mary leaped to her feet and announced I was the biggest fool who'd ever lived if I hadn't figured out how I felt about her after three years. My, was she mad." Shaking his head, he rubbed the side of his jaw. "Her eyes had fire in them. In all the years we've been married, I've only seen her get that riled a handful of times. She told me if I married some Yankee girl I'd regret it the rest of my life."

He paused a moment, lost in his memories. "Then before I could stop her, she raced into the house. By the time I'd gathered my wits and followed her, she was already running up the stairs. Her father and her mother both stood on the landing, looking down at me as though they wanted to string me up from the nearest tree."

"What'd you do?"

"What I should have done a hell of a lot sooner. I shouted up at her father for permission to marry his daughter."

That scene filled Glen's mind. His father a young sailor, standing at the bottom of the stairs, watching the love of his life racing away. "What'd Mom do?"

"She stopped, halfway between her parents and me. I'll never forget the look of shock on her face as she turned around and stared at me."

"She burst into tears, right?"

"No. She stood here, calm as could be and asked me when I wanted the wedding to take place. Hell if I knew, so I said that was up to her, and she suggested six months."

"I thought your anniversary was Valentine's Day."

"It is. Once we decided to get married, I wasn't willing to wait six months. By summer she was pregnant with your brother." He looked at Glen. "Why all these questions?"

"Just curious."

"You going to ask Ellie to marry you?"

"I've been thinking about it."

His father's grin widened. "Did she tell you you're in love with her yet?"

"Nope. I don't think she realizes it herself."

Phil stood and slapped him on the back. "Then start a new family tradition and tell her yourself, boy. It's about time the men in this family took the initiative."

Eight

Richard rolled out of bed and reached for his jeans. Savannah was making breakfast, and if his nose didn't deceive him, it smelled like one of his favorites. French toast.

Yawning, he grabbed a shirt on his way out the door and bounded down the stairs and into the kitchen.

"Mornin'," he said, yawning again. He glanced at the wall clock and was surprised to see it was after nine. A midmorning breakfast cooked specially for him meant his sister was planning on a little heart-to-heart. Damn.

"Morning," Savannah returned in that gentle way of hers. At times it was all he could do not to leap behind her, waving his arms and screaming at the top of his lungs. He wondered if he'd get a reaction from her even then. Somehow he doubted it.

"Grady needs you to drive into town this morning."

"No problem." Actually Richard liked running errands. They suited his purpose. Every time Grady sent him into town, he managed to pick up an item or two for himself and put it on his brother's tab without Grady's knowing a thing about it.

Savannah delivered a plate to the table where Richard sat waiting. He dug into the meal after slathering his hot toast with plenty of butter and syrup. Savannah didn't disappear, which meant the errand for Grady wasn't the only thing on her mind.

"There's been plenty of talk around town about you and Ellie," she said, clutching the back of the chair opposite his.

The tension in her fingers told him she felt awkward addressing the subject. Lord, his sister was easy to read!

"That so?" He stuffed another forkful of French toast in his mouth.

"Ellie's a real sweetheart."

He shrugged.

Savannah pulled out the chair and sat down.

Damn it, he'd asked for that. Knowing his sister was fond of the other woman, he should have talked her up, fabricated a few things, let his sister think he'd fallen in love with Ellie. He hadn't, but his interest in her was definitely high at the moment. A lot was riding on this, and if he managed to manipulate the situation to his liking, it meant staying in the community. After fixing his current problems of course. Yeah, he could see a future here. Become one of the leading lights in Promise. Turn this place around. And it all hinged on little Ellie Frasier.

"I don't want you to hurt her, Richard."

This was quite a statement from Savannah. "Hurt Ellie?" He tried to look shocked that she'd even suggest such a thing.

"Ellie's . . . fragile just now."

"I wouldn't dream of doing anything to hurt Ellie." He set his fork down as if to say the mere idea had robbed him of his appetite.

"Then your intentions are honorable?"

Leave it to Savannah to sound like she was living in the nineteenth century. She could've set up camp at Bitter End and fit right in.

"Of course my intentions are honorable. In fact, I intend to ask Ellie to be my wife." Richard assumed this was what Savannah wanted to hear, but she didn't react the way he'd expected. He'd hoped that when he mentioned words like "wife" and "marreiage," she'd go all feminine on him and start nattering about wedding plans.

"It's a big step for me," he added, thinking she'd be quick to praise his decision.

Savannah frowned. "I heard about this little lottery thing you've got going."

"Oh, that." He dismissed her concern with an airy gesture. Word traveled fast in small towns and he'd forgotten that.

"I don't think placing bets on . . . on love, on whether Ellie's going to marry you or Glen, is such a good idea."

"It was a joke," he said. What Savannah didn't understand and what he couldn't tell her was that the whole thing had gotten started when he'd had one too many beers. Naturally he'd taken a lot of ribbing about the fiasco at the dance.

The whole thing was Glen Patterson's fault. In Richard's opinion, the rancher owed him an apology. Ellie had been *his* date and Glen had been way out of line butting in at the dance.

"Joking with another person's affections—"

"I'm not joking with Ellie," Richard interrupted. "I love her, Savannah," he said, doing his best to look and sound sincere. What he really loved about Ellie Frasier was the store and her inheritance. That Ellie wasn't hard on the eyes was a bonus. Marriage wasn't such a bad idea either. He could grow accustomed to bedded bliss, not to mention regular meals. Savannah had spoiled him, preparing elaborate dinners and baking his favorite goodies, although she tended to do less of that these days.

"It isn't only Ellie I want to talk to you about."

"You mean there's more?" He tried not to sound perturbed, but really, this was getting ridiculous. He didn't need his big sister prying into his private life, nor did he appreciate this need she had to lecture him. He'd been out of the schoolroom too many years to sit still for much more of this.

His sister pursed her lips in exactly the way their mother used to. "I got a phone call from Millie about an unpaid flower bill."

"Millie?"

"You know Millie." Her tone left no room for argument.

"Oh, that Millie." He was walking a tightrope when it came to a number of charges he'd made in town during the past few months. He'd hoped to have moved on by now, but this romance with Ellie had fallen into his lap and he couldn't let the opportunity just slip through his fingers. He'd also made contingency plans—no fool he. He'd found the perfect hiding place when and if he needed it. But he couldn't leave Promise yet and perhaps not for some time. Keeping Grady and Savannah in the dark until he'd secured his future was proving to be something of a challenge.

"Millie said you owed her four hundred dollars. I realize your . . . check hasn't arrived yet—" she didn't meet his eyes "—but you *have* to make some kind of arrangement with Millie."

He toyed with the idea of being shocked to hear it was that much money, but thought better of it. "Well, I have just a little money left." He hoped that was vague enough so she wouldn't question it. "In fact, I was in just yesterday and made a payment," he said.

"I talked to Millie yesterday and she claimed she hadn't seen you in weeks." Savannah's eyes had never been that cool before.

"I didn't see Millie, just one of her employees."

"I didn't know Millie had anyone working for her."

Savannah pinned him with her gaze.

"Summer help, I assume," he murmured. "I've got the receipt up in my room if you want to see it." He put the right amount of indignation into his voice to make sure she understood he found her lack of trust insulting.

"If you say you made a payment, then I don't have any choice but to believe you."

Richard shoved his chair away from the table. "I'm getting the distinct impression I'm no longer welcome around here." He stopped short of reminding her he'd been born and raised in this very house, fearing that might be overkill, even with a softhearted woman like his sister.

"It isn't that."

"I've come home," he said, tilting his chin at a proud angle. "It wasn't easy to arrive on your doorstep with nothing. Now that I'm here, I've realized that I made a mistake ever leaving. Promise is my home. I've fallen in love and I want to make a new life for myself with friends and neighbors I grew up with. People I've known all my life. If you want to kick me out, then all you or Grady need to do is say the word and I'll be gone." He drew the line and dared her to cross it. Basically it was a gamble, but one he was willing to take. He'd been a gambler most of his life, after all—one who usually had an ace up his sleeve.

"I won't ask you to move," she said after a moment.

He hadn't really thought she would.

"But I'm giving you fair warning—tread lightly when it comes to Ellie."

He widened his eyes, disliking her brisk tone.

"And pay your bills. Once Grady gets wind of this, there'll be trouble. His nature isn't nearly as generous as mine."

"You haven't got a thing to worry about," Richard said, and as a conciliatory gesture, he carried his plate to the sink.

IT HAD SOUNDED so simple when Glen talked to his father nearly a week earlier. Asking Ellie to marry him had seemed the right thing to do. But Richard's interest in her had muddied an already complicated issue. From the gossip circulating around town, Weston had definitely taken advantage of the time Glen stayed away.

Fine. Great. Wonderful. If Ellie was so impressed with Richard, she could have him. At least that was what Glen told himself a dozen times a day, but no matter how often he said it, he couldn't quite make himself believe it.

"I don't know what the hell I'm going to do," he muttered. He sometimes did his thinking out loud, and talking to a horse was safer than talking to certain people. As he cleaned the gelding's hooves, Moonshine perked up his ears in apparent sympathy.

"You talking to me?" Cal shouted from the other side of the barn.

Glen didn't realize his brother was anywhere nearby. "No," he hollered, hoping to discourage further conversation.

It didn't work.

"Who you talking to, then?"

"No one!" he snapped. Glen was the first to admit he hadn't been great company lately. That was one reason he'd kept to himself as much as possible and avoided Cal.

"You still down in the mouth about Ellie?" Cal asked, sounding much closer this time.

It was on the tip of Glen's tongue to tell his brother to mind his own damn business. Lord, but he was tired of it all. Tired of being so confused by this woman he could no longer think. Tired of worrying she'd actually marry Richard. Tired of feeling miserable.

"How'd I get into this mess?" Glen asked hopelessly.

"Women specialize in wearing a man down," Cal said, peering into the stall.

"Ellie isn't Jennifer," Glen felt obliged to remind him. That was the problem with discussing things with Cal. His brother refused to look past the pain and embarrassment his ex-fiancée had caused him. Everything was tainted by their ruined relationship.

"I know."

Glen lowered Moonshine's foot to the ground and slowly straightened. The small of his back ached. He pressed his hand to the area and massaged the sore muscles before he opened the stall door.

Glen watched Cal carry a bucket of oats to his own gelding. Suddenly it was all too much. He couldn't stand it any more. Damn it all, he *loved* Ellie and if she wasn't willing to come to him, then by God he'd go to her. The rush of relief he experienced was overwhelming.

"I'm asking Ellie to marry me," he said boldly, bracing himself for the backlash of Cal's reaction.

Cal went very still. Finally he asked, "Is that what you want?"

"Damn straight it is."

"Then . . . great."

Glen blinked, wondering if he was hearing things. The one person he'd expected to talk him out of proposing was Cal.

"You love her?"

"Of course I do," Glen said. "I wouldn't ask a woman to share my life if I didn't."

Cal laughed and slapped Glen on the shoulder. "So I guess congratulations are in order."

Glen rubbed his hand across the back of his neck. He didn't feel like throwing a party just yet.

"When are you going to ask her?"

"I . . . I don't know yet," Glen confessed. He'd only decided this five seconds ago.

He glanced at his watch. If he showered quickly he could make the drive into town and talk to Ellie before she left the shop. It seemed fitting that he ask her to marry him at the feed store, considering that most of their courtship had taken place there. At the time, however, he hadn't *realized* he'd been courting her.

"I think I'll do it tonight," he said. Feeling euphoric, he'd dashed halfway out of the barn when Cal stopped him.

"Have you got her an engagement ring?"

A ring? Damn, he hadn't thought of that. "Do I need one?"

"It doesn't hurt."

Glen could feel the panic rising up inside him. Cal must have seen it, too, because he offered Glen the ring he had in his bottom drawer.

"I've still got the one I bought for Jennifer."

"But that belongs to you."

"Go ahead and take it. It's a beautiful diamond. After Ellie agrees, then the two of you can go shopping and pick out a new one if she wants. Although this one's perfectly good."

Things were beginning to fall nicely into place. "Thanks." As Glen recalled, Cal had gone for broke buying Jennifer's diamond. Damn shame to keep it buried in a drawer. If Ellie liked that ring, he'd buy it from his brother; she need never know the ring was slightly used.

A quick shower revitalized him. He sang as he lathered up, then raised his face to the spray, laughing as the water rushed over him. When he'd finished, he shook his head like a long-haired dog fresh from a dip in the pond. Still smiling, he dressed in a clean shirt and jeans.

He felt drunk with happiness.

Glen didn't sober up until he reached town. Then and only then did the seriousness of his mission strike him. Not once had he given any thought to how he would word his proposal.

This was quite possibly the most important conversation of his life and he hadn't even rehearsed it! His father had spoken to his potential father-in-law and not the bride. But even if Ellie's father were alive, that approach didn't really work anymore. Too old-fashioned.

He thought about getting down on one knee and spilling out his heart, but immediately dismissed the idea. No one did that sort of thing these days. Much too formal. By the same token, he didn't want to make an offer of marriage sound like an invitation to go bowling, either. All he could do was hope the right approach presented itself when the moment arrived.

It was nearly closing time when he got to the store. Ellie was on the loading dock at the far end of the building, giving instructions to a delivery-truck driver as Glen parked his own truck in front of the store and turned off the engine. She damn near fell off the dock in surprise when she saw him.

That was promising, Glen thought. She must've missed him. He'd missed *her* like hell, and telling her so was probably as good a place to start as any. Having decided that much, he climbed out of the cab and walked up the steps.

"Hello, Glen," Ellie's assistant greeted.

"Hi, George."

"Good to see you," George Tucker said, then added in a low voice, "Damn good."

"Glad to hear it." Glen sat down in one of the lawn chairs by the front door near the soda machine, and waited until Ellie was free. It took almost ten minutes to supervise the unloading of a truckload of hay, but he was a patient man.

Ellie signed the necessary papers, then stood there for a moment, blinking into the sun. Her face was pink, and the hair at the back of her head was damp and clinging to her neck. It'd obviously been a long hot day.

"Do you have a few minutes?" he asked when she'd finished. "I'd like to talk to you—*privately.*" He added this last bit in case Richard was anywhere around.

"Privately," Ellie repeated. Small vertical frown lines appeared between her brows.

"There's, uh, something I'd like to discuss with you. Privately," he said again.

"Do you want a cold drink?"

It was almost like old times, he told himself. Casual, relaxed, two friends talking.

"Something cold'd hit the spot," he said, answering Ellie's question.

She retrieved change from her pocket and slipped the coins into the pop machine. She handed him one of the cold damp cans and pressed the other to her forehead, then claimed the chair beside his.

Glen opened his drink, pulling back the tab with a small hissing sound, and took a long swallow.

George appeared. "Do you need me to do anything else?" he asked.

Ellie shook her head. "You're free to go, thanks, George."

"I'll see you in the morning, then," he said, turning the Open sign to Closed on his way past.

It might have been Glen's imagination, but Ellie's assistant seemed eager to be on his way.

Ellie answered his question before he could even ask it. "It's his bowling night," she explained.

His parents were like that, Glen mused. Often, his dad didn't need to voice his thoughts for his mother to know what he was thinking. Sometimes that was true of close friends, as well. With Ellie, he could have love *and* friendship, and surely that was the best way to enter a marriage.

The late-afternoon sun blazed, but the heat didn't seem nearly as bad, now that he was sitting in the shade with Ellie. A slight breeze stirred, cooling his skin, ruffling her hair.

"You wanted to talk to me," Ellie began.

"Yeah." Glen had hoped to make this as natural as possible.

"You haven't been in for a while," she said, staring straight ahead.

Ten days, not that Glen was keeping track or anything. Cal had taken care of the errands these past two weeks while Glen stayed close to the ranch.

"I've been busy," Glen said, deciding it probably wasn't a good idea to mention he'd been waiting to hear from her.

"So have I."

Glen could just imagine who she'd been busy with, but he didn't dare say that. Richard Weston wasn't a name he wanted to introduce into their conversation—although he did wonder how much she'd been seeing of the guy.

"I wanted to talk to you about the dance first," he said, and although he tried, he couldn't keep his voice from sounding stiff. The events of that night still rankled him.

"I don't think it's necessary, seeing how—"

"I'd like to apologize," he interrupted. If she wasn't willing to admit her part in the disaster, then he'd be man enough to seek her forgiveness for his own role.

"Oh."

"I didn't mean to make us both fodder for gossip."

"I know you didn't," she said, her voice softening perceptibly.

"You and I've been friends for quite a while now."

She nodded. "Very good friends."

Glen stuck his hand in his pocket and felt for the diamond ring. Holding on to it lent him the courage to continue. This was harder than he'd thought it would be, but too important to ruin with nerves. All he had to do was remind himself that this was Ellie, his longtime friend. In the years to come he wanted to be able to tell his children and his grandchildren about this day with the same sense of wonder and excitement he'd heard in his father's voice when he'd relayed the tale of proposing to their mother.

"Since your dad's gone, I feel a certain duty to protect you."

"A duty?" A chill edged her voice.

"Well, not a duty exactly. More of . . . an obligation to see that no harm befalls you." He knew he must sound stilted, kind of old-fashioned, but he couldn't seem to help it.

"What do you mean by harm?"

The hell if he knew. "Perhaps 'harm' isn't the best word, either. I want to look after you."

"I'm not a child, Glen."

"No, no, I don't mean to imply that you are." He could feel the sweat starting to break out across his forehead. Working his way up to this marriage proposal was harder than freeing a stuck calf from a mud hole. He swallowed painfully as he prepared to continue.

Ellie eyed him in consternation.

"What I'm trying to say," he started again, gulping down some air, "is— Oh, damn." He catapulted to his feet, finding it impossible to stay seated any longer. "Listen, Ellie, I'm not good at this. I'm the one responsible for embarrassing you and—"

"What the hell are you talking about?" she demanded.

Glen paced the porch, walking past the soda machine several times. "It hasn't been easy deciding what to do, I want you to know that."

"I'm not asking you to *do* anything."

"I know, but I feel responsible."

"Then I absolve you of all responsibility." She waved one arm as if holding a magic wand.

"It isn't that easy," he muttered.

"What's this all about?" she asked again.

Glen tilted his head back and expelled a long breath. This wasn't going well. He should have practiced on Cal first, at least gone over what he intended to say, sought his brother's advice.

Ellie had stood up, too.

It was now or never. Taking the plunge, he squared his shoulders and met her look head-on. "I think we should get married."

"Married!" The word exploded out of her mouth. Almost as if she'd been struck, Ellie sat back down, gripping the sides of her chair with both hands. Then . . . she began to laugh. A deep robust laugh.

Glen was deflated. This woman had a great deal to learn about a man's pride, he reflected sadly.

"You're serious?" she asked when her laughter had dwindled to a low chuckle.

"I have a ring," he said, pulling it out to prove his point. He held it between index finger and thumb.

Ellie's eyes widened.

Dismissing his earlier plan, he decided she should know the truth about this particular ring. "Actually I borrowed it from Cal. This is the diamond Jennifer returned when she broke the engagement."

She stared at him as if she hadn't heard a word he said.

"I couldn't very well propose without a ring," he explained. "If you don't like it, you can choose another one later, although I've got to tell you I think Cal would give us a good deal on it. But I'll leave that decision up to you."

Ellie blinked back tears and Glen relaxed. He knew once he got the word out, everything would be better.

"Why now?" she asked, her voice cracking. "What made you propose today?"

"We're friends," he said. "That's one reason. I enjoy being with you more than any woman I've ever known. You've got a lot of excellent qualities and . . ." He was running out of things to say. "Basically it's time."

"Time?"

"To get married. I've been thinking along those lines recently—"

"Because of Richard?"

Glen had hoped to get through this conversation without any mention of the other man. He cleared his throat. "Not entirely."

Her responding smile was slight. "At least you're honest enough to admit he has something to do with this."

"Hey, it wasn't me who sat on a porch kissing one man and then having brunch with another the next morning." He wondered how *she'd* have felt if he'd shown up at her house with another woman on his arm. She wouldn't have liked it any better than he'd liked seeing her with Richard. He wanted to tell her that, but figured he'd come off sounding jealous. Hell, he *was* jealous.

"You didn't stick around long enough for me to explain."

"What was there to say?" It was obvious enough to Glen what had happened, and frankly he wasn't interested in hearing the details. Anyway, that was all in the past. What mattered now was the future.

"I'm flattered, Glen, that you'd ask me to marry you."

"What do you think about the ring?" He held it up so she could get a better view. Cal had spared no expense with this beauty, but Glen realized he'd prefer to have Ellie choose her own ring. Something unique to her. To them.

Ellie's hand closed over his. "Give the ring back to Cal."

"I'm glad, because I'd rather the two of us shopped for one together."

She shook her head. "I'm sorry."

"I *said* I'd rather the two of us picked out a diamond together," he told her again, only louder.

"I heard you the first time," she said impatiently. "What I meant was that I'm sorry, but no. I can't marry you."

It took him a moment to realize what she was saying. "You're turning me down?" Each one of those words seared a hole through his heart. When he recovered from the shock, he asked, "Do you mind telling me why?" He had to know. Maybe he should have left things as they were, collected his shattered pride and gone home—but he couldn't. "I . . . I thought we had something special."

"We do. Friendship. You said it yourself, remember?"

He nodded.

"I don't want a husband who proposes marriage to me because it's an obligation."

"I didn't mean it like that." His voice sounded odd to his own ears. A little ragged and faraway.

"When and if I agree to marry anyone, I want it to be for specific reasons."

"Okay, that sounds fair." Weren't *his* reasons specific? Glen's ego came to the rescue, and the anger and pain in his voice were less evident now. More controlled.

"Reasons other than *it's time* and *you have excellent qualities.* Reasons other than *I should get married now and you'll do.*"

"I didn't say that!"

"No, but you might as well have. Oh, and I almost forgot, you said you *owed* me."

"Owed you what?"

"I might not get the words right so bear with me." He could tell she was being sarcastic but wasn't sure why. "Something about duty because you'd embarrassed me in front of the whole town."

"I . . . I didn't mean it to sound like that. Damn it, Ellie, you're putting words in my mouth."

"I don't need any favors, Glen."

He looked at her, afraid she was about to cry, but he was mistaken. Her face was strong and confident. She could give him all the excuses in the book, but he knew what was going on here and wasn't shy about saying it, either.

"It's Richard, isn't it? You're in love with him."

"That's it!" she cried.

"I thought as much." He shoved the ring back into his pocket. He'd tell his brother to bury it—the diamond must be hexed.

"The thing is, Glen, you're too late."

"Too late?" He didn't know what the hell she meant by that, but he wasn't sticking around to find out.

Ellie, however, insisted he hear her out. "Richard came by earlier and he proposed. Sorry, Glen, he beat you to the punch."

Nine

Not for a single moment would Cal describe himself as a romantic. Despite that, he felt good about encouraging his little brother to go and propose to Ellie Frasier. He'd even given him the ring!

Good enough to tell his neighbor. It wasn't often that Cal had reason to shoot the bull over a telephone; usually a beer at Billy D's served the same purpose, but even better. However, this news was too good to keep to himself.

Grady answered on the second ring.

"It's Cal," he announced.

"Something wrong?" Grady asked right off.

They'd been best friends since first grade, and Grady knew him about as well as anyone ever would. Over the years they'd been through a lot together. As kids, they'd explored Bitter End. Later Grady had talked to him about his parents' deaths, his problems with Richard, his concerns about Laredo. And it was Grady Cal had gone to when Jennifer canceled their wedding, Grady who'd gotten him home safely when he'd fallen down drunk. Grady who'd talked some sense into him when he badly needed to hear it.

"Glen's driving into town to ask Ellie to marry him," Cal said without preamble. He wasn't a man who wasted words.

"You're kidding!" Grady sounded shocked.

"No. He's been acting like a wounded bear for damn near two weeks and then I found him mumbling to himself in the barn, about as miserable as I've ever seen him. Tried to talk to him, but he damn near bit my head off. I'd had enough. I figured he should either fix what was wrong or forget Ellie."

"And Glen listened?"

"No, I didn't get the chance to give him my advice. He decided to marry her all on his own."

"That's great." Cal heard the relief in Grady's voice and knew his neighbor harbored his own set of fears when it came to Ellie Frasier. "At least she won't be marrying Richard, then."

"Not if Glen has anything to say about it." Cal knew Grady didn't trust his younger brother, and with damn good reason.

"I was thinking of celebrating," Cal continued. "You're welcome to join me if you want. There's cold beer in the fridge, plus a bottle of the hard stuff if you're interested." An invitation from Cal was about as rare as a phone call.

"I might just do that."

A couple of minutes later Cal hung up the receiver, feeling more like his old self than at any time since his broken engagement. Grinning from ear to ear, he reached for a beer and walked outside, where he leaned comfortably against the porch railing. In years past he'd spent many an evening in this very spot, looking out over the land, knowing that cattle grazed peacefully in the distance. In certain moods, wistful moods, he liked to imagine a wife standing at his side and the sound of their children's laughter echoing in the house.

Glen married.

Cal had known it would probably happen one day, and he'd always wondered how'd he react, seeing that, despite his imaginings, he'd likely remain a bachelor himself. In fact, he felt surprisingly good about having played a small role in his brother's romance. He'd known Glen was in love with Ellie months before it even occurred to Glen.

Glen's feelings for her had been apparent for a long time. He'd drive into town and return a couple of hours later and talk of little else. Ellie amused him, challenged him, comforted him. She fired his senses. And all that time Glen had insisted it was "just" friendship.

Right! Cal nearly laughed out loud. It was friendship and a whole lot more.

The sound of an engine broke into Cal's musings, and he looked toward the driveway as Grady's truck pulled into view. Good, his neighbor was going to take him up on his offer.

Grady leaped down from the pickup and raised a bottle of whiskey high above his head. "Glen getting married. Hot damn, this calls for a party," he shouted.

Cal lifted his beer in salute and let out a cheer.

"So Glen's really dong it," Grady said, taking the porch steps two at a time. "He's marrying Ellie."

"Unless the woman's a fool and turns him down."

"Ellie Frasier's no fool," Grady said with confidence.

"He took the diamond I bought Jennifer," Cal explained as he headed into the house for a couple of tumblers and some ice.

"Glen asked Ellie to marry him with Jennifer's ring?" Grady followed him, sounding worried.

"It's just a loan. I figure Ellie'll want to choose her own diamond later." He dumped the ice cubes into two mismatched glasses.

"You think that was wise?"

"Well, yeah. This way Glen wasn't proposing to her empty-handed."

The two men returned to the porch and Cal poured two generous measures of the honey-colored liquor over the ice, but he noted that his friend's worried frown didn't go away. "What harm could it do?" he asked.

"Probably none." Grady sat down with Cal in the white wicker chairs and relaxed. Leaning back, he stretched out his long legs and crossed his ankles, then with a deep contented sigh, raised the tumbler to his lips.

Cal tasted his own drink. His eyes watered as the whiskey burned its way down his throat.

"I have to tell you," Grady admitted, "it does my heart good to know Richard's out of the picture with Ellie."

"Mine, too." Cal wasn't fond of the youngest Weston. Richard was a difficult person to understand. Witty, amiable, a natural leader—and yet he'd squandered his talents, in Cal's opinion, anyway. Richard had taken a wrong turn and he'd never gotten steered back on course. It was unfortunate, too, because he could have been a success at just about anything he chose.

"I told Savannah," Grady mentioned casually, "and she's delighted for Glen." Then, looking as though he might have done something wrong, he glanced at Cal. "You don't mind, do you?"

"She won't tell anyone else, will she?" Not that it mattered; word would be out soon enough.

"I doubt it." Grady didn't seem to know for sure.

Cal wasn't really worried, though. Savannah—sensitive and kind, the complete opposite of Richard—would never say anything to ruin another person's happiness. She'd never cheat Ellie out of the pleasure of spreading the news herself.

"Which one of us is gong to be next?" Cal asked, although he already had his suspicions. Grady. He'd seen the way his friend's eyes followed Caroline Daniels at the Cattleman's dance. Later, when she'd asked him to dance during the ladies' choice, Grady had been so thrilled he'd nearly stumbled all over himself. Not that he'd let on, but Cal knew. Yup, it'd be Grady for sure.

First Glen and then Grady. Soon all his friends would be married, and he'd be living on the ranch alone. The picture that formed in his mind was a desolate one but preferable to the thought of letting another Jennifer Healy into his life.

The sound of a vehicle barreling up the driveway caught Cal's attention.

"Glen?" Grady asked.

"I didn't expect him back so soon." Cal set his tumbler aside.

"You think everything went all right, don't you?"

"Don't know why it wouldn't." But Cal was beginning to feel some doubts, considering the speed at which Glen had been driving.

The slam of the truck door echoed through the quiet evening.

"I don't like the look of this," Grady said in a low voice.

Cal didn't, either. He dashed down the porch when he saw Glen moving toward the barn. "I wonder what happened," he said. "I'd better find out. Be back in a couple of minutes."

Cal didn't want to think about what might have gone wrong, but clearly something had. He opened the barn door and searched the dim interior. It took his eyes a moment to adjust, and when he did finally see Glen, his uneasiness intensified. His brother was pitching hay like a man possessed.

"I take it things didn't go so well between you and Ellie," Cal said, hoping he sounded casual.

"You could say that." Glen's shoulders heaved with exertion. "What's Grady doing here?"

"We're . . ." He almost slipped and said they were celebrating Glen's engagement. "We're just shootin' the breeze."

Silence.

"You *did* talk to Ellie?"

Glen stopped midmotion, the pitch fork full of hay. "We talked."

Cal wondered how to proceed. "Did she like the ring?" he asked, and realized immediately it was probably a tactless question.

"She didn't say."

"I see."

"I doubt it." Glen stabbed the fork into the ground, breathing hard, his face red from exertion.

"Do you want to tell me about it or would you rather work this out on your own?"

Glen took a couple of moments to think it over. "I . . . I don't know," he mumbled.

Another silence. Cal knew it was up to Glen to talk or not.

"I owe you an apology," Glen surprised him by saying next.

"Me? What for?"

Glen looked him full in the eye. "When Jennifer walked out on you, I was secretly glad. As far as I was concerned, you got a lucky break. I thought she wasn't the right woman for you. I didn't stop to consider how you must have felt, how damn hard her leaving was on you."

Cal didn't quite understand how all this talk about Jennifer applied to the current situation, but he didn't want to interrupt Glen.

"Hurt like hell, didn't it?"

Cal wasn't going to deny it. "At the time it did. I don't think about it much anymore."

Glen reached into his pocket for the diamond that had once belonged to Cal's ex-fiancée. He stared at it for several seconds. "I wonder how long it'll take me to forget Ellie," he said, sounding as if he was speaking to himself. He raised his head as he handed Cal back the ring, and the look in his eyes spoke of blinding pain.

"Ellie's decided to marry Richard Weston."

NOT ONCE HAD ELLIE SAID she'd *accepted* Richard Weston's proposal, but that was what Glen had immediately assumed. It hurt that he'd actually believe she would marry anyone else when it should be clear as creek water that she was in love with him!

She let herself into her house and slumped down on the sofa, discouraged and depressed. She'd always known that Glen wasn't much of a romantic, but she'd hoped he could at least propose marriage without making it sound like an insult. He'd said all the wrong things. He'd talked about an obligation to "take care" of her; well, no thanks, she could take care of herself. He'd said it was "time" he got married—so what did that have to do with her? He'd referred to her "excellent qualities" as though he was interviewing her for a job! Perhaps worst of all, he'd half admitted that his sudden desire to propose had been prompted by his effort to out do Richard Weston.

The one thing he'd never said was that he loved her.

Crossing her arms, she leaned her head back and closed her eyes. It was at times like this that she missed her father most. He always seemed to know what to do, and Ellie feared that in her anger she'd badly bungled her relationship with Glen. She feared that nothing would ever be the same again.

She knew about the lottery at Billy D's and all the Texas two-step jokes. She hated the idea of being in the middle of some stupid male rivalry, and everything Glen said only reinforced that. It bothered her, too, that he'd come to her with a used engagement ring, a leftover from his brother's failed romance. She'd drawn the only sensible conclusion, which was that he'd been in such a rush to get to her before Richard proposed, he hadn't taken the time to buy his own ring.

Now she didn't know what to do. She loved Glen and wanted more than anything to be his wife, but at the same time she needed to feel that she was more to him than a trophy, a way of triumphing over Richard. Deciding to marry someone wasn't like switching dance partners—even in the Texas two-step!

She needed Glen to acknowledge that he loved her, and she needed to understand that his feelings for her had nothing to do with Richard. She wanted Glen to look into his heart.

But she worried he wouldn't be able to see beyond his own disappointments.

GLEN SAT AT THE BREAKFAST table and stared glumly at the kitchen wall, sipping his coffee. It was barely five and he was already on his third cup.

Cal ambled down the stairs, yawning loudly. "You're up early," he muttered as he headed for the coffeepot.

Glen didn't tell his brother that he hadn't been to sleep yet. He'd gone to bed and closed his eyes, but it'd done no good. He'd finally gotten up at three-thirty and sat waiting for the tightness in his chest to go away so he could breathe without this pain.

"You feeling all right?" Cal asked.

His brother was more awake than Glen had given him credit for. "I'm fine."

Cal leaned against the kitchen counter, holding his coffee mug with both hands, and studied Glen.

"I said I was fine," Glen said a bit more gruffly than he intended. He wasn't up to talking. In time the details would come out, the same way they had when Jennifer canceled the wedding. Cal had been tight-lipped for weeks, then gradually, bit by bit, Glen had pieced it all together until he had a fairly accurate picture of the events that led up to the final scene.

Cal's face seemed to darken. "It doesn't seem either one of us is the marrying kind," he said, then pushed away from the counter and left the house.

His eyes burning from lack of sleep, Glen toyed with the idea of taking the day off, but instinctively realized that would be his worst choice. He needed to stay busy. Otherwise thoughts of Ellie and Richard would drive him crazy.

Downing the last of his coffee, he followed Cal.

The day dragged. Glen had never felt wearier in body and spirit. By late afternoon he knew the only way to find peace was to seek out Richard Weston and congratulate him. Then he'd talk to Ellie and wish her and Richard every happiness. He was sincere about that; he loved her enough to want her to have a good life.

He didn't tell Cal where he was going when he was finished for the day. Nor did he bother to shower or shave.

Cal had just ridden in when Glen was ready to leave.

"Did Ellie mention anything about the wire cutters I ordered?" Cal asked, stopping him.

Glen froze at the mention of her name. He might as well get used to it. She was as much a part of his everyday life as this ranch.

"I'll ask her if you want," Glen said.

Cal looked as if he wanted to say something, but hesitated. Then, "I didn't mean . . . I forgot."

"Don't worry about it. Frasier's has been our supplier for a lot of years and I don't think we should change things now." He was man enough to accept being rejected, or he'd like to believe he was, anyway.

Ellie, ever sensitive and thoughtful, was probably worried about him. That would be just like her. Glen didn't want her to think her decision had ruined their relationship. They could still be friends. Sort of. Not the way they'd been in the past but . . . friendly.

Glen headed for the Weston place. He found Richard loading supplies into the back of Grady's pickup when he arrived. The other man looked mildly surprised when Glen sought him out. He stood there with a case of canned goods balanced on his shoulder, his stance defensive.

"You wanted to talk to me?" Richard asked.

"I came to congratulate you." No need to hedge. This wasn't a conversation he relished having, and the sooner he'd finished the better.

"Congratulate me?" Richard echoed. "Did I win the lottery and someone forgot to tell me?"

Glen didn't appreciate the joke. "In a manner of speaking."

Richard leaned forward and dumped the box onto the open tailgate. "What's up, Patterson?"

"It's about you and Ellie."

Richard scowled. "What about us?"

"I understand you asked her to marry you."

"What of it?"

"I also understand that she's accepted."

Richard had started to remove his gloves, one finger at a time. His head snapped up at Glen's statement. "Ellie's a hell of a woman, isn't she? I didn't realize she'd decided to let the word out." He nudged Glen with his elbow. "But then, that's just like my Ellie."

My Ellie. The words hurt like alcohol on a cut, and Glen flinched before he could hide his reaction. Recovering quickly, he forced a smile. "I couldn't agree with you more," he said. "Ellie's one of a kind."

Richard slapped him hard on the back. "I guess you could say the best man won."

"Yeah, I guess you could say that," Glen answered, clenching his teeth.

"I don't suppose she happened to mention a wedding date, did she?" He laughed. "Seems the groom's always the last to know."

"Can't say as she did."

"It'll be soon, if I have anything to say about it." Richard hopped onto the tailgate, his legs dangling. "The wedding will be a small intimate affair right here in Savannah's rose garden. Family and a few friends. You're invited of course."

"Thank you."

"Hey, no problem." Richard began whistling; Glen might not have much of an ear for music; but he recognized the "Wedding March."

He tried not to let it distract him. "I want to wish you both every happiness," he said formally.

"That's good of you, Glen, and I appreciate it. I'm sure Ellie will, too." Richard thrust out his hand. "I realize it was difficult for you to lose her, but I want you to know, I plan to make Ellie happy. The two of us would like to consider you a friend."

"I hope you will." This was what made Richard so damn difficult to understand, Glen mused. One minute he was a jackass; the next, he was a regular joe. "If you need anything, give me a call," he offered.

"I will."

Glen climbed back into his pickup. Despite his dislike of Richard, he felt better for having cleared the air between them. Although he'd dreaded talking to the guy, he was glad now that he had.

He hoped everything would go as well with Ellie.

The ache in his gut intensified as he drove into town. When he entered the feed store, she was ringing up a sale for Lyle Whitehouse. She didn't notice Glen until she handed Lyle his package. Her hand froze in midair and she gaped at him as if she couldn't believe her eyes. Recovering quickly, she released the bag.

Lyle turned around, and when he saw Glen, he grinned broadly. Then he winked and gave him a thumbs-up as he walked out of the store.

"Hello, Glen," Ellie said tentatively.

"Ellie." He nodded once. "Cal wanted me to ask you about those wire cutters he ordered."

"They won't be in until Monday," she said, sounding oddly breathless.

"I'll tell him." He felt awkward and tongue-tied again, the way he had when he proposed. He waited a moment, just staring at her. "I have a few things to say. Is now a good time?"

"As good as any," she said stiffly. She remained on her side of the counter while he stayed on the other.

Damn she was beautiful. That wasn't the kind of thing he should be thinking, he told himself, and glanced away. "First, all I really want is for you to be happy."

"I am happy," she said a little too loudly.

"Good."

Ellie moved out from behind the cash register and started restacking blocks of salt.

"I was hoping we could remain friendly," he said, moving up behind her.

"I was hoping that, too."

Glen raised his hands to place them on her shoulders, the need to touch her almost impossible to resist. He paused, then with unprecedented determination dropped his arms to his sides. He had no right to touch Ellie anymore. She was engaged to another man.

"You've been my closest and dearest friend," she whispered, and turned to face him. "I don't know what I would've done without you when Dad was so terribly ill . . . and since."

Glen wasn't sure if she'd come toward him or if he'd stepped toward her, but all at once they were standing mere inches apart. Their eyes avoided meeting, but their slow labored breathing seemed to keep pace.

"I needed you," she whispered, "and you were there for me."

Again he reminded himself that she was engaged to Richard, and yet all he could think about was kissing her one last time. Just one kiss, to tell her goodbye, to wish her well.

Everything within him yearned for her. It seemed natural to stand this close; it seemed even more natural to hold her, but he managed to resist. He mustn't feel these things any longer, mustn't allow himself to look at her this way. Mustn't kiss her again.

His heart went wild when Ellie stepped into his arms. When she raised her lips to his. Her kiss nearly buckled his knees. It began as a simple, almost chaste touch, her warm mouth on his. Unfortunately it didn't stay chaste long. Glen slipped his arm around her waist and against every dictate of common sense, urged her closer. If this was to be their last kiss, then he'd make sure it was one they'd both remember.

The kiss spoke far more eloquently of his need and love for her than any words he'd ever uttered. Ellie moaned and he cradled her face with both hands. The kiss grew molten-hot and would have grown hotter had they continued. Abruptly Glen released her, trembling with the restraint it demanded to pull away.

She stared at him, wide-eyed, then pressed the back of her hand against her mouth.

"I suppose you're waiting for an apology," he said, knowing that kiss should never have happened. "I'll give you one if you insist, but it'd be a bold-faced lie. This is only the third time we've kissed, and it's the last. It has to be." He reached out to stroke her hair and whispered, "Be happy, Ellie. Be very happy."

Looking as if she'd been struck dumb, she continued to stand there, staring up at him.

"Richard doesn't deserve you," he said, his voice gruff with pain, "but I don't, either." He touched her cheek, loving the feel of her skin beneath his fingertips. Then he turned and walked out of the store.

ELLIE DIDN'T MOVE for five solid minutes after he left. Her hand remained poised at her lips, the taste and feel of him still clinging to her mouth.

Little of what he'd said made any sense—but they hadn't been able to communicate effectively in weeks. Except when they kissed. . . . They'd been best friends for years, able to talk about anything, and then overnight it had all changed.

The big oaf. He'd screwed up his marriage proposal and now he was back, kissing her senseless and saying the most beautiful words she'd ever heard. He hadn't actually said he loved her, although his kiss was pretty persuasive. What he'd said was, "Be happy." And if he didn't love her, he wouldn't have told her that. Because Glen Patterson was an honest man.

Glen's kiss still lingered on her lips when Richard casually sauntered into the store.

"Darling," he said, flashing her an easy smile. He grabbed her in a bear hug and soundly kissed her cheek.

Furious, Ellie wiped away his kiss, not wanting his touch to taint what she'd shared with Glen. "Let go of me," she ordered. One thing she detested was being manhandled. When Richard didn't immediately comply, she elbowed him hard in the ribs.

"Ouch," he muttered, holding her at arm's length. "Why didn't you tell me yourself?"

"Tell you what?"

"That you'd decided to accept my proposal." He glared at her as if suddenly aware that something wasn't right.

"Who told you that?" Although she could almost predict his answer.

"Glen Patterson," he murmured. "It's all a joke, isn't it?" His lip curled into a snarl.

She *was* going to kill Glen, no doubt about it. "Not a joke," she said feeling genuinely sorry, "but a misunderstanding."

"Well, that's just fine," Richard spit. "I just went and bought myself a new suit for the wedding."

"Oh, Richard." She brought one hand to her mouth. "Glen didn't understand—"

"What the hell am I supposed to do about the suit?" He actually made it sound as though they should get married because of a new set of clothes.

"Can you return it?"

"I don't think so," he said, his voice tight with anger.

"I am sorry, Richard."

He looked as if he wanted to plow his fist through something. "It wouldn't have worked, anyway," he said. "You're too uptight. Making love to you would have been like warming up an ice cube."

Ellie had heard all she cared to. "I think you should go. And take your insults with you."

"Fine. Whatever. Patterson really had me fooled—he must've enjoyed playing me for an idiot. Tell him I'm not going to forget his sick joke." That said, he bolted out the door.

If Glen's actions earlier had confused her, Richard's outraged her. She hadn't missed the threat, but as far as she knew, Glen had nothing to fear from Richard Weston. He should worry about what *she* planned to do to him, instead.

George, who'd gone on an errand, was back fifteen minutes later. The minute he walked into the store, Ellie reached for her truck keys. "I have to go," she said. "Can you close up shop for me?"

"I . . . I guess."

It wasn't like her to walk out before five, but it couldn't be helped.

She was in her truck and headed out of town in five minutes flat. She managed the forty-minute drive in thirty; half an hour was not long enough to cool her anger even slightly.

Glen and Cal must have heard her coming because both men stepped onto the porch when she arrived. She glared at Glen with undisguised fury.

"Ellie, is something wrong?" he asked, walking down the steps toward her.

With her hands planted on her hips, she yelled, "Did you actually believe for one minute I was going to marry Richard Weston?"

He hesitated, fifteen or so feet away. "That's what you said."

"I said," she returned from between clenched teeth, "that Richard had proposed. I did *not*, I repeat, *not* at any time state that I'd accepted his proposal of marriage."

Glen's face was stricken. "You didn't?"

"I most certainly did not. Furthermore, anyone with eyes in his head would know it's *you* I love."

"You love me?"

"Don't pretend you didn't know, Glen Patterson. I've loved you forever." But at the moment she wasn't particularly happy about it.

"Then you'll marry me, right?" Glen looked like he was about to fly across the yard and haul her into his arms.

Ellie stopped him cold in his tracks. "Give me one good reason why I'd want to marry a man who's got the brains of a tumbleweed."

"She loves you, all right," Cal shouted from the porch steps.

"You stay out of this," Ellie shouted back, pointing an accusing finger at Glen's brother. "You encouraged him to do it, didn't you?"

"Yup." Cal seemed downright proud of himself.

"The next time Glen asks you for advice, ignore him." Then she threw open the truck door and climbed inside.

"Ellie!" Glen started toward her. But when she revved the engine, he apparently knew better than to press his luck. He stayed where he was. Good thing, because in her current frame of mind she was liable to run him over.

When the dust had died down, Ellie glanced in her rearview mirror and groaned. Cal and Glen Patterson were leaping about, hugging each other wildly.

Ten

Glen Patterson had never been happier. Ellie loved him. *Him.* Not Richard Weston. And by golly, she was going to marry him, too!

"I knew it," Cal announced cheerfully, as though he was personally responsible for the unexpected turn of events.

"Did you ever see such a woman?" Glen asked, watching Ellie drive away. Damn, but she had spunk. It wasn't every woman who would've come out here to confront him the way she had.

Cal chuckled. "Don't think I've ever seen a female that mad." He glanced at his brother. "How're you going to get her to marry you?"

That was a question Glen hadn't considered. Of course Ellie would marry him. She loved him. He loved her. Marriage was the natural result of such feelings. Sure, she was mad at him right now, but she'd cool off and they'd sit down and talk this out and plan for their future together. "Any suggestions?"

"From me?" Cal adamantly shook his head. "Didn't you hear? Ellie wasn't too impressed with the advice I gave you earlier, although I don't know what I said that was so wrong. Do you?"

"Nope." Women baffled him just as much as they did Cal. "So, who should I ask for advice?"

Cal thought it over a moment. "Mom?"

"Not Mom," Glen said. He loved his mother, but she was sure to meddle. All mothers did. Once she heard about this, she'd want to fix it; she'd want to talk to Ellie and act as a go-between and generally get involved. Glen shuddered. He preferred to handle the situation himself.

Cal shrugged. "Dovie, then. She's got a good head on her shoulders."

"Dovie," Glen repeated slowly. Yes. She was a good choice.

After a night without sleep, followed by one of the most emotionally

draining days of his life, Glen nearly nodded off during dinner. As soon
as the evening chores were done, he showered and went to bed. He'd
figure out what he should say to Ellie. Tomorrow . . . He'd figure it out
tomorrow. As he drifted into sleep, he actually felt happy for the first
time in weeks.

The next afternoon Glen opened the door to Dovie's Antiques.
Glancing around, he immediately removed his hat. Little wonder the
women in town loved this place. It was full to the rafters with pretty
things, and smelled a little like Savannah's garden. If his nose didn't
mislead him, he caught the scent of some mighty fine brandy, too. Must
be what she used to make that famous cordial of hers.

"Hello, Glen." Dovie was her usual lighthearted self. "What can I do
for you this fine day?"

"Ah . . ." For the life of him, Glen couldn't think of a single way to
start the conversation.

Dovie regarded him expectantly. "I'll have you know, young man, I
have my money riding on you."

"I beg your pardon?"

"Do you think only the men are in on Billy D's lottery?"

"Oh, that." Glen had forgotten all about that silly lottery. He stood
just inside the door, arms tight against his sides, for fear one wrong move
would send hundreds of fragile little things tumbling to the floor.

"Come on inside, Glen," Dovie encouraged. "You aren't going to
break anything."

He took a few cautious steps, then glanced anxiously around the
store and back at Dovie.

"Is there a problem?" she asked with concern.

Glen had always liked his mother's friend. It was Dovie who'd suggested the bed-and-breakfast idea and who'd helped his mother decorate
the old Howe Mansion.

"I need some advice," he finally said. The last time he'd been this
unsure of himself—not counting the day he proposed to Ellie—was when
he'd roped his first calf in the Brewster rodeo at the age of ten.

"The advice is free, but the tea will cost you a dollar."

"Tea?"

"I think best when I'm sitting down." Smiling, Dovie motioned
toward the assembled tables and chairs in one corner of the shop.

"All right," he agreed.

"I take it this all has to do with Ellie?" Dovie asked, leading him to a
small table covered by a pretty floral cloth.

"You know, then."

"I know you and Richard made first-class fools of yourselves at the dance."

Glen wished folks would forget about that. "It's gotten worse since."

Dovie carried a blue-and-white china teapot and two cups to the table. "I was afraid of that."

"Cal suggested I talk to you about Ellie. You see, I want us to get married. I tried asking her and it didn't turn out the way I'd hoped. Can you help me?"

"I can try." Dovie poured him some tea, then served herself. "Milk? Sugar? Lemon?"

Glen shook his head mutely. He generally sweetened his tea, but he wasn't willing to do it with one of those miniature silver spoons. He already felt like an oversize buffoon in this dainty little shop.

"How would you like me to advise you?" Dovie asked.

"Can you tell me what I can say to convince Ellie to marry me?"

Dovie frowned slightly. "Perhaps you should tell me how you proposed the first time."

Glen recalled what he could of their conversation. "Best I can remember, she started getting hostile when I mentioned I felt responsible for embarrassing her at the dance."

Dovie nodded, and Glen continued, "I told her I admired her and I wanted to marry her. That was when I brought out the diamond ring I borrowed from Cal."

"You *borrowed* an engagement ring?"

"Just so I'd have something to offer. I wanted Ellie to know I was serious, and a man doesn't get more serious than diamonds."

Dovie was frowning again.

"Was that so terrible?" Glen demanded. "All I want is for Ellie to know how much I love her."

"Why don't we start with telling her that this time?" Dovie suggested.

"Ellie already knows how I feel about her." It was incomprehensible to him that she wouldn't. He'd made himself the laughingstock of the entire town over her. When she'd rejected his marriage proposal, he'd swallowed his pride and wished her happiness, even at the cost of his own. A man didn't say those kinds of things to a woman he didn't love. "She's *got* to know," he added.

"A woman likes to hear the words, Glen."

It was that simple? Of course he loved Ellie, and if all he had to do was tell her how much . . . He reached for his hat and got eagerly to his feet. "Great. I'll let her know right now."

Dovie grabbed his shirtsleeve. "I'm not finished yet."

"Oh." He sat back down.

"Is there anything else you plan to tell Ellie?"

Glen wasn't sure he understood the question. Perplexed, he gave it a moment's thought. "Just that I can't get married next Tuesday because the farrier's coming."

"Oh, dear." Dovie briefly closed her eyes.

"That's the wrong thing to say?"

"Well . . . yes."

"Thursday's not good, either. I play poker at Billy D's on Thursdays, but I'd be willing to give that up if Ellie decided she wanted to get married then."

"Have you considered that Ellie might want a church wedding?"

He hadn't, and the mere suggestion made his blood run cold. All this time he'd been thinking they'd fly off to Vegas and get married the same night. A quickie wedding, because now that the decision had been made, he was ready. Strike while the iron's hot, as the farrier might say.

"Besides, I think you might be getting ahead of yourself," Dovie murmured. "First you've got to convince Ellie to be your bride."

"Right." If the truth be known, he'd given more thought to the honeymoon than the wedding. He was in love, and damn it all, he wanted to make love to Ellie. "Why does this have to be so complicated?" he wanted to know. "I love her, and she's already confessed she loves me."

Sighing, he took a careful sip of his cooling tea. "When she was going through her father's things, she found this old Bible passed down from his family," Glen said, thinking out loud. "She showed it to me and turned to the page where her family's names and dates are listed. Weddings, deaths, births—you know. All day, I've been thinking about Ellie and me entering our names in that Bible, and someday, God willing, writing down the names of our children. I love Ellie, and it's a love that'll last all our lives. Maybe a hundred years from now one of our great-great grandchildren will come upon that Bible and wonder about us. I'd want them to know—just from the way we lived—that despite everything life threw at us, our love survived."

"Oh, Glen, that's beautiful," Dovie said softly, and squeezed his hand.

"It was?"

"Tell Ellie that."

"About putting our names in her family Bible?"

"Yes. Speak from your heart and don't mention the farrier, all right?"

"I'll do it." Glen felt immeasurably better.

GRADY RELAXED against the back of a molded plastic bench in the bowling alley. Lloyd Bonney had asked if he'd substitute for him the next two weeks while he was on vacation. It'd been ages since Grady had last bowled, but Lloyd was a likeable guy and he hated to turn him down. That wasn't the only reason, either; for the first time in six years, he was able to indulge himself with a few leisure activities. He used to enjoy bowling and had been fairly good at it.

He was a bit rusty, but he'd bowled a decent series tonight. It felt good to be with friends, to laugh again. Finally he had the financial security and the extra time to make it possible. This evening had whetted his appetite for more.

He was on his way to Billy D's afterward when Max Jordan followed him outside.

"Grady, you got a moment?"

"Sure."

Max shifted his gaze away from Grady. "Listen, I realize this is a bad time and all, but I need to talk to you about Richard."

"Yeah?" Grady didn't like the sound of this.

"He charged a few things at my store—clothes and boots—when he first came back to town and he hasn't paid me and . . . well, it's been almost three months now."

Grady's grip tightened on his bowling bag. "How much does he owe you?"

Max stated an amount that made Grady's stomach clench. His brother must have picked out the most expensive clothes in the store.

"Earlier this week he charged a new suit," Max continued. "It's a pricey one, and—"

"You let him do that even when he hadn't paid you for the other things?" Grady was furious with his brother, and with Max, too.

Max lowered his eyes to the pavement. "I feel like an old fool now. Richard stopped in the store and told me he was getting married. I was pleased for him and Ellie. It wasn't until later that I learned they weren't engaged, at all."

"It isn't your fault." Grady blamed himself as much as anyone. It'd been a mistake to let Richard stay at the ranch for even one night. He knew the kind of man his brother was, and still he'd allowed Richard to take advantage of him. Well, no more. He was sending that bastard packing.

"I'll take the suit back," Max said.

"I'll personally see that he returns it," Grady told him. "I can't tell you how bad I feel about all this."

"And the other money he owes? Richard had me put it on the family account, but so far I've mailed all the bills to him."

"I'll make sure he takes care of it right away," Grady pledged. Richard would pay one way or another, he decided. He should have realized sooner what was happening. His no-good brother arrives in town, throws himself a party and buys some fancy duds to go along with everything else.

Max Jordan wasn't the old fool; Grady was. Why hadn't he guessed where Richard's clothes had come from? Why hadn't he known Richard would pull something like this?

The evening that had started out with such promise was ruined. Grady changed his mind about meeting his friends for a beer and headed directly back to the ranch, instead. He was having this out with Richard once and for all.

The lights in the house were off when Grady got home. He attacked the stairs with a vengeance and didn't bother to knock on his brother's door. It shouldn't have surprised him to find the bed empty, but for some reason it did. Although it was about midnight, Richard wasn't anywhere to be found. Why the hell shouldn't he party half the night, seeing as he hadn't done a lick of work all day, or any day since he arrived? Grady resisted the temptation to slam the door shut.

He lay awake half the night, listening for his brother's return. Eventually he'd fallen asleep and never did hear him come home. But then, Richard seemed to have a sixth sense about such things; even as a child, he'd been able to smell trouble and avoid it.

In the morning another check of his brother's room showed that Richard hadn't been home that night.

"Have you seen Richard lately?" he asked his sister when he went downstairs for breakfast.

Savannah shook her head. "He's probably still sleeping."

"His bed is empty." Grady used his fork to grab a pancake from the stack in the middle of the table. "When you see him, tell him I need to talk to him, all right?"

"Problems?"

Grady didn't want to involve Savannah in this, but she knew him too well not to realize something was wrong. He tried distancing her with another question. "Did Laredo leave the house already?"

"What's Richard done?" Savannah asked, ignoring the question.

Grady sighed and set down the jar of maple syrup. "Max Jordan talked to me last night about some money Richard owes him. Apparently our dear little brother has charged a few things at Max's he hasn't bothered to pay for."

Savannah didn't comment, but he saw sadness on her face.

"It makes me wonder if he's been doing the same thing with anyone else in town." Grady grabbed another pancake and picked up the syrup again.

"He has," Savannah confessed in a small voice.

"And you knew about it?"

"I . . ." She bit her lip. "I just found out about it myself. Millie Greenville talked to me last week. She suggested that perhaps we could trade something for the money Richard owes her. My roses, for example."

Grady slammed the syrup jar down. "You didn't agree to this, did you?"

"No."

"Good."

"But—"

"I won't hear of it, Savannah, and neither will Laredo. Richard's the one who owes that money, not you and not me. He's going to repay it, too, if it's the last thing he ever does. Every penny."

"I know," she said. "Laredo and I've already discussed what to do, and he's as adamant as you are."

Grady's fork sliced viciously across the pancake. He forced himself to relax, knowing his anger would ultimately hurt him far more than it would Richard.

Laredo had saddled the horses and was waiting for him outside when he finished his meal. Savannah walked out, too, and with an agility Grady envied, her husband leaned over his horse's neck and kissed her.

"If Richard shows up, tell him . . ." Grady paused, then shook his head. "Don't tell him anything. Let me do the talking this time."

Savannah nodded. "He's been making himself scarce lately."

"Now we know why, don't we?"

The sadness was back in his sister's eyes before she turned away and hurried into the house.

* * *

RICHARD DOMINATED Grady's thoughts for the rest of the day. By the time he got home, he was ready to read his brother the riot act. To his surprise Richard was there waiting for him.

"I understand you want to talk to me," his brother said.

Grady was so angry he needed every bit of self-control not to explode with it. "Damn right I want to talk to you."

"It's about the stuff I charged in town, isn't it?"

"Yes. I can't believe you'd take advantage of our good name to—"

"Listen, Grady, you've got every right to be mad, but I don't need a lecture."

"That's too bad because—"

"Before you get all bent out of shape, let me say something. I've been sick with worry about those charges. Ask Savannah if you don't believe me. I have some money owed to me, quite a bit as it happens—you know that. It was supposed to have been mailed to me long before this." He frowned thoughtfully. "It must have been misdirected. I've spent weeks trying to track it down."

If anyone knew what it was like to be low on cash, it was Grady, but he wasn't falling for his brother's lies again. He opened his mouth to tell him so when Richard continued.

"I figured I'd have those bills paid off before now. I haven't charged anything in weeks."

"What about the suit?" Grady flared.

His brother's expression became pained. "That was a . . . mistake. I was tricked into thinking Ellie had agreed to marry me and didn't learn until later it wasn't true." He inhaled sharply. "In my excitement I went down and bought myself a decent suit for the wedding."

"Max said he'd let you return it."

Richard smiled slightly. "As it happens the money was at the post office when I picked up the mail this afternoon. The first thing I did was pay off all the bills." He slid his hands into his jeans pockets. "I realize it was a mistake not to discuss this with you earlier."

"Yes, it was." Grady's relief was tremendous. The problem was solved and the family's good name redeemed. And none of the business owners was losing any money.

"I'm sorry you had to find out about it the way you did."

While reassured that the money matters had been properly dealt with, Grady wasn't willing to make any further allowances for his brother. Richard had worn out his welcome. "Now that your money's here, you'll be reimbursing me—and then moving on, right?"

"Yes. I appreciate you letting me stay this long. I know it's been an inconvenience, but I didn't have anywhere else to go. We've had our problems over the years, and I'm hoping we can put those behind us now." He held out his hand for Grady to shake.

Grady accepted it, glad to see that his brother had revealed the maturity to confront him man to man.

Perhaps there was hope for Richard, after all.

ELLIE HAD BEEN RESTLESS all day. With the big Fourth of July weekend coming up, business was slower than it had been in weeks. She found herself waiting, watching, hoping to see Glen—and was furious with herself for caring.

She was finished with men, Ellie told herself. She'd rather herd goats than be married, but even as she entertained the thought, she realized it was a lie. Although she was fond of Savannah's goats, she was more than fond of Glen Patterson. Not that he deserved her affections!

Once the store had closed for the day, she returned home. The afternoon heat was intense, so she made herself some iced tea. She tugged her shirt free of her waistband, propped her bare feet on the coffee table and let the fan cool her. But it was going to take more than a fan and a glass of iced tea to revive her sagging spirits.

Because of the fan's drone she didn't hear her doorbell. When she finally realized someone was at her door, she got to her feet and hurried across the room. She threw open the door and on the other side of the screen was the largest bouquet of flowers she'd laid eyes on. While she couldn't see the man behind it, she could easily identify him by his boots.

Glen.

He waited a moment, then peeked behind the flowers and beamed her a smile. That slow sexy smile of his, capable of melting the hardest hearts, the strongest wills.

"Hello, sweetheart," he said, his smile growing wider. "Aren't you going to let me in?"

Wordlessly she unlatched the screen door and opened it for him.

He carried in the flowers and set them in the middle of her coffee table. They towered over it, filling the room with a profusion of glorious scents. Then he kissed her cheek and said, "I'll be right back."

When he returned, his arms were laden with gifts. She noted the chocolates, the basket of exotic fruit, the bottle of champagne. He set everything down next to the flowers and added three wrapped gifts.

"What's all this?" she asked, glancing at the table and then at him.

"Bribes," he said, looking very pleased with himself.

"For what?"

"I'll get to that in a moment." Taking her by the shoulders, he guided her back to the sofa. "Sit," he instructed.

She complied before she realized she should have made at least a token protest about being ordered around, but curiosity won her over.

"Here," he said, handing her the smallest of the wrapped gifts. "Open this one first."

Christmas didn't yield this many presents. "Don't think you can buy my love, Mr. Patterson."

"I don't need to, Ms. Frasier," he said confidently. "You already admitted you love me."

For the fleetest of seconds Ellie wanted to argue, tell him she'd been emotionally distraught at the time, but it was the truth—she did love him.

Inside the package she found a pen. An attractive looking ballpoint pen. Puzzled, she raised questioning eyes to him.

"Do you like it?" he asked.

"It's very nice," she said, puzzled but nevertheless excited. Before she had time to say anything more, he thrust another package at her. "This one is next." He knelt on the floor beside the sofa while she unwrapped a shoe-size box.

"Are you going to tell me what this is all about?" she asked. She tore away the paper and stared in utter amazement at the mismatched items inside.

The first thing she pulled out was a Cal Ripkin baseball card. Next she removed a shoelace, followed by rose-scented bath salts from Dovie's store, and, last, an ordinary key. Ellie examined each thing again, wondering what she was missing. As far as she could tell, the items weren't linked in any way.

"Is there a reason you're giving me one shoelace?"

He grinned. "It's blue."

She would have described it as a dark navy, closer to black—but that was beside the point. "The key?" she asked, holding that up next.

"That's to Bob Little's vacation home on the Gulf."

"Why do you have it?"

"I borrowed it," he replied, as though that answered the question.

"I see." But she didn't. Changing tactics, she reached for the pen. "What about this?"

He gazed into her eyes. "The pen is for something special. I was hoping we'd use it to write our names in that old family Bible of yours. Maybe Wade should do it for us after the wedding ceremony, but then—" He stopped abruptly and leaned back on his heels. "I'm doing this all wrong again, aren't I?" Not giving her time to answer, he continued, "I spoke with Dovie earlier and she advised me how to go about this, but now I've forgotten almost everything."

"You spoke to Dovie?"

He ignored her question. "Honest to goodness, Ellie, I don't know what I said that was so terrible when I asked you to marry me before, but whatever it was I couldn't be sorrier. I love you. I mean that."

"I know." She felt tears brimming in her eyes. She'd waited a long time for Glen to tell her how he felt.

"You do?" His relief was evident. "Dovie said I needed to tell you that, but I was sure you already knew. And I want it understood that my proposal doesn't have anything to do with the bets Billy D's taking over who you're going to marry."

"I'd forgotten about that."

"I had, too, until Dovie reminded me. I love you, Ellie," he said again.

"I know, but it doesn't hurt to say the words every now and then. Or to hear them."

"Dovie said the same thing." He brightened at that, then clasped both her hands in his and got back on his knees. "Will you marry me, Ellie?" he asked solemnly.

When she didn't immediately respond, he reached for the box she'd just opened. "I wanted to be kind of traditional about this," he said. "The baseball card is something old. I've had it since I was in junior high. The scented bath salts is something new. The key's something borrowed, since Bob said we could use his house on the Gulf for our honeymoon. And the shoelace is something blue."

"Oh, Glen."

"I'm miserable without you. Nothing seems right."

It hadn't been right for her, either.

"I know Dovie said I shouldn't mention this, but I want you to know that even though we've waited two months for the farrier's appointment, I'd cancel it if you decided Tuesday was the day you wanted to get married. I'm that crazy about you."

"You're sure this isn't because of Richard."

"Yes," he said firmly. "Very sure. Although I'm grateful to him, otherwise I don't know how long it would've taken me to realize I love you."

"Then I'm grateful to Richard, too."

"We'll buy an engagement ring together, anything you want. Only please don't make me wait much longer." His eyes filled with such hopeful expectation she couldn't have denied him anything. "Ellie, you're my friend, the best friend I've ever had. I want you to be my lover, too. My wife. The mother of my kids. I want us to grow old together."

Rather than respond with words, Ellie wrapped her arms about his neck and lowered her mouth to his. She'd yearned for this from the moment he first kissed her. She understood now, with all her heart, what poets meant when they wrote about being completed by a lover, a spouse. She felt that. He completed her life.

Glen placed his arms around her waist and pulled her from the sofa so that she was kneeling on the floor with him. They kissed again and again, each kiss more fervent than the last.

"I hope," he said, drawing back from her a fraction, "that this means yes."

"Mmm. Kiss me."

"I have every intention of kissing you for the rest of our lives."

"That sounds nice." And it did. She tightened her arms around his neck. "What's in the other box?"

"It's for the honeymoon," he mumbled.

"You were sure of yourself, weren't you?"

"No," he countered, nibbling her neck. "I was a nervous wreck. We *are* getting married, aren't we?"

"Oh, yes." She sighed as his hands closed over her breasts. "Married," she repeated, liking the sound of it.

"We're going to have a good life together," Glen whispered. He kissed her. "I promise." Another small kiss. "I'm crazy about you, Ellie."

Ellie grinned. "You already said that. But for the record, I'm crazy about you, too."

She pressed her lips to his.

Eleven

Time was running out and Richard knew it. He had to leave Promise and soon. It wouldn't take Grady more than a few days to discover there *was* no money. The check Richard had given him was written on a closed account; it was going to bounce like a rubber ball, and when Grady found out . . . Nor would he be able to hold off paying his creditors much longer. All he needed was a week or so to get everything ready. No one would think to look for him in that old ghost town. He'd just quietly disappear.

Until then, he had to keep the wool pulled over his brother's eyes. Even if it meant doing work he'd sworn he'd never do again. That morning Grady had insisted Richard fill in for one of his summer hands who'd suddenly taken ill. This time Grady wouldn't listen to any excuses, and Richard was forced into what he considered slave labor.

"I don't know how much good I'm going to be," he told Laredo as he saddled Roanie.

"A little extra help is all Grady is looking for," Laredo said.

Savannah's husband hadn't made any effort to disguise his dislike of him. It hadn't bothered Richard to this point. He wasn't a big fan of Laredo's, either, although he had to admire the way the wrangler had finessed himself a partnership with Grady. Smith had apparently sold some land in Oklahoma and was investing it in stock for their quarter-horse operation. There'd been a celebration the day Laredo discovered his newly purchased mare was pregnant with Renegade's foal. From all the fuss, anyone might assume it was Savannah who was pregnant, not some horse.

"Grady wants us to weigh calves and get them into the holding pens," Laredo said as they rode toward the pasture.

"What for?" Richard demanded, bouncing in the saddle. He'd never been able to get comfortable on a horse. If he was going to be working his butt off, quite literally, then he wanted an explanation of his duties.

"They need to be weighed."

"Is he selling them?"

"Eventually. He wants to be sure they're healthy and gaining weight the way they should before we send them to market."

Richard stifled a groan. Anyone looking at those smelly animals could see they were doing fine. Better than he was, Richard thought bitterly. Already his backside hurt. By the end of the day he was bound to have blisters in places people didn't normally talk about—but then that was exactly what Grady had planned.

His brother was punishing him, Richard knew, for Grady was vindictive and a sore loser. He'd been jealous of Richard's skills and talents for years. The only reason he'd insisted Richard mount up this morning was to get back at him for the embarrassment of being confronted by Max Jordan a few nights earlier.

It would do no good to complain about it now. He didn't want to give Grady the satisfaction of knowing he'd succeeded in making him miserable.

After they'd ridden for several minutes, they came to the holding-pen area. Laredo told him to dismount, then had him sort through the calves. It was his duty to separate the steers from the heifers. No easy task, and it irked Richard that his son-of-a-bitch brother-in-law took such delight in the trouble he had. Even the dog seemed to be working against him, instead of with him. Laredo was at the gate while Richard herded the cattle one way or the other. All too frequently, Laredo had to correct him, but then, Richard had never been any good with animals. He hated ranch life, and Grady knew it. His brother was unfairly trying to make him pay for circumstances beyond his control.

When they'd finished sorting the calves, they broke the steers into twenty-head lots and weighed them. Nothing hurt Richard's ears more than the sound of ill-tempered cattle thundering onto the scale. They weren't any more interested in being weighed than Richard was in finishing the task.

"Are they loaded?" Laredo shouted.

"Isn't it lunchtime yet?"

"No. Answer the question."

"They're on the scale," he shouted back, waving his hand in front of his face. Not only were cattle stupid and nasty, their stench gave him a headache.

Laredo did whatever he did with the controls of the scale and checked the balance. Richard watched it bob back and forth until the correct weight was found. Then the steers were moved into the holding pen.

Laredo seemed pleased with the results. "They've gained an average of fifty pounds in the past twenty days," he said.

"Whoopee."

Laredo ignored him. "At this rate they'll weigh around six hundred pounds by the sale date."

"Great," Richard muttered, seeing that his sarcasm was lost on the wrangler. He stared at his watch. "Isn't it lunchtime yet?"

"Soon." Laredo shoved back his hat with the heel of one hand. "When we're finished here, Grady wants us to vaccinate the steers."

"*What?* You mean my brother actually expects me to give them shots? With a needle?"

"So it seems."

"I hate needles." Damn it, Laredo hadn't mentioned this earlier, and Richard just knew the omission had been on purpose. Probably figured he was saving the best for last, the bastard.

"I don't suppose the calves are fond of being vaccinated, either."

"Fine, then let's skip the entire procedure."

Laredo didn't bother to respond, and Richard accepted that there was no help for it. But down the line, his big brother was going to pay for the trouble and humiliation he'd caused. Oh, yes. Grady had learned about the bill with Max, but he didn't know about the others. Not yet. And by the time he *did* discover the amount of money Richard had charged . . . well, Richard would be long gone. Bye-bye Yellow Rose.

Who'd be smiling then? Who'd be feeling smug and superior? It was enough to carry Richard through the rest of the day.

ELLIE SPENT as much time as she could with Glen, but not nearly enough to satisfy either one of them. A September wedding date had been set, and she was busy making plans. At the moment Glen and his brother needed to get the herd to market; that was their immediate priority and not something Ellie could help with.

"I thought I'd find you in here," Glen said.

Ellie, who was in the sick pen with a couple of calves, smiled up at her fiancé. He wore his Stetson and cowhide chaps. His approach warmed her heart.

"Are these two going to make it?" she asked. Most calves had slick hair, bright eyes and big bellies, but the calves in the pen looked dull-eyed and thin.

"They don't have anything a little bit of medicine and some tender loving care won't cure."

"Good."

Glen joined her in the pen. "When did you get here?"

"Fifteen minutes ago. George is closing up this afternoon."

He kissed her briefly. "Thank him for me."

"He's going to have to get used to it. When we're married, I'll be leaving early sometimes."

Glen wrapped his arm around her waist. "I like the sound of that word."

"Married?"

He nodded, and opening the gate, ushered her out of the barn and toward the house. "I like the sound of it more and more every day."

"So do I," she admitted softly. And she thought to herself that her father would have liked the idea of his Ellie married. To her friend, who was his friend, too. She imagined him smiling, telling her she'd chosen well. John Frasier had liked Glen and respected him. Her only regret was that her father wouldn't be there to walk her down the aisle or dance at his daughter's wedding.

"Give me time to shower," Glen said as they entered the house. "I'll be back before you know it." He smiled down at her and then, as if he couldn't restrain himself, kissed her once again.

While Glen cleaned up, Ellie went into the kitchen to start dinner. Since they'd made their engagement official, she'd stopped by the ranch two or three nights a week. It only made sense for them to eat together. She'd taken a few cooking lessons from Dovie on preparing basic meals. Meat and potatoes, mostly. Next thing, she'd tackle pies. She enjoyed practicing in the big ranch-house kitchen, especially with Glen there to cheer her on. Ellie found she begrudged every minute she couldn't spend with him, and she knew he felt the same way.

She had a roast in the oven and was peeling potatoes when Cal walked into the kitchen. "Hey, Ellie, how's it going?" he asked.

"Great," she said, dropping a freshly peeled potato into a kettle of water.

"You don't have to do this, you know. But let me tell you I appreciate every morsel."

Ellie grinned up at him. She was discovering that she liked Cal. Actually she always had, but he could be a difficult man to understand because he often seemed so remote, and sometimes even gruff. She'd been spending more time with him lately, and they'd developed a comfortable rapport. Ellie had even talked him into attending the Fourth of

July celebration with her and Glen. To all appearances, he'd enjoyed himself, although he hadn't asked anyone to dance at the evening festivities. It was a well-known fact that he didn't trust women, although he was obviously pleased for her and Glen.

"You're welcome to join Glen and me for dinner any time after we're married," she told him. They'd already decided it would be most beneficial, considering her business, for Glen to move into town after the wedding and commute to the ranch every day. Soon they'd be setting up an appointment with a Realtor and looking at houses. Glen hoped to have the deal closed by August so that once they were married, they could move right in. Ellie hoped that was possible, too.

As soon as Glen reappeared, his hair wet and glistening from the shower, Cal quickly left the room. Glen's arms circled hers from behind and he kissed her neck. "Damn, but I love you."

Now that he was comfortable with the words, he said them often; he seemed to delight in sharing his feelings.

"I love you, too." The words had no sooner left her lips when she turned in his arms to face him. "I'm worried about Cal."

"Cal? What's wrong with my brother?"

"Nothing love wouldn't cure."

Glen frowned and took Ellie by the shoulders. "You've got that look in your eye. I've seen it in my mother's and Dovie Boyd's."

"What look?"

Glen kissed the tip of her nose. "I don't know what it's called, but it's what comes over a woman when she thinks she knows what's best for a man."

"I'm not trying to be a . . . a matchmaker, Glen!"

"But you think Cal needs a woman."

"He needs to fall in love."

"He did once," Glen reminded her.

"Next time it needs to be with a woman who'll love him just as much in return. Who'll appreciate him for who he is without trying to change him."

"And where do you intend to find such a woman?" Glen asked, his gaze holding hers.

"I don't know, but she's out there and just waiting for someone like Cal."

Glen eased Ellie back into his embrace and kissed her with a thoroughness that left no question about his own love for her. "You're a terrible romantic, Ellie Frasier-soon-to-be-Patterson."

"I'm a woman in love and I want my almost-brother-in-law to find happiness, too."

"He'll have to look for his own partner if he wants to do a Texas two-step."

Glen drew her closer still.

She smiled up at him. "Well," she said, "that's the thing about the two-step. There's no changing partners if you do it right." She raised her mouth to his in a teasing kiss.

"You can bet on that." And he kissed her back.

CAROLINE'S CHILD

One

Clutching the mail in one hand, Grady Weston paced the narrow corridor inside the post office. He glanced distractedly at the row of mailboxes, gathering his courage before he approached Caroline Daniels, the postmistress.

His tongue felt as if it'd wrapped itself around his front teeth, and he was beginning to doubt he'd be able to utter a single sensible word. It shouldn't be so damned difficult to let a woman know he found her attractive!

"Grady?" Caroline's voice reached out to him.

He spun around, not seeing her. Great. Not only was he dreaming about her, now he was hearing her voice.

"Open your box," she instructed.

He fumbled for the key and twisted open the small rectangular door, then peered in. Sure enough, Caroline was there. Not all of her, just her brown eyes, her pert little nose and lovely mouth.

If he'd possessed his brother's gift for flattery, Grady would have said something clever. Made some flowery remark. Unfortunately all he managed was a gruff unfriendly-sounding "Hello."

"Hi."

Caroline had beautiful eyes, dark and rich like freshly brewed coffee, which was about as poetic as Grady got. Large and limpid, they reminded him of a calf's, but he figured that might not be something a woman wanted to hear, even if *he* considered it a compliment. This was the problem, Grady decided. He didn't know how to talk to a woman. In fact, it'd been more than six years since he'd gone out on an actual date.

"Can I help you with anything?" she asked.

He wanted to invite her to lunch, and although that seemed a simple enough request, he couldn't make himself ask her. Probably because their relationship so far hadn't been too promising. Calling it a "relationship" wasn't really accurate, since they'd barely exchanged a civil word and had never so much as held hands. Mostly they snapped at each other, disagreed and argued—if they were speaking at all. True, they'd danced once; it'd been nice, but only when he could stop worrying about stepping on her toes.

Who was he kidding? Holding Caroline in his arms had been more than nice, it had been *wonderful.* In the month since, he hadn't been able to stop thinking about that one dance. Every night when he climbed into bed and closed his eyes, Caroline was there to greet him. He could still feel her softness against him, could almost smell the faint scent of her cologne. The dance had been ladies' choice, and that was enough to let him believe—hope—she might actually hold some regard for him, too. Despite their disagreements, *he'd* been the one she'd chosen to ask.

"You had lunch yet?" Grady asked, his voice brusque. He didn't mean to sound angry or unfriendly. The timbre of his voice and his abrupt way of speaking had caused him plenty of problems with Maggie, Caroline's five-year-old daughter. He'd been trying to get in the kid's good graces for months now, with only limited success. But he'd tried. He hoped Caroline and Maggie gave him credit for that.

Caroline's mouth broke into a wide grin. "Lunch? Not yet, and I'm starved."

Grady spirits lifted considerably. "Well, then, I was thinking, seeing as I haven't eaten myself . . ." The words stumbled all over themselves in his eagerness to get them out. "You want to join me?"

"Sure, but let me get this straight. Is this an invitation, as in a date?"

"No." His response was instinctive, given without thought. He'd been denying his feelings for her so long that his answer had come automatically. He feared, too, that she might misread his intentions. He was attracted to Caroline and he wanted to know her better, but beyond that— he wasn't sure. Hell, what he knew about love and marriage wouldn't fill a one-inch column of the *Promise Gazette.*

Some of the happiness faded from her smile. "Understood. Give me a few minutes and I'll meet you out front." She moved out of his range of vision.

Grady closed the box, but left his hand on the key. How could anyone with the skills to run a thriving cattle ranch in the Texas Hill Country be such a fool when it came to women?

He rapped on the post-office box hard enough to hurt his knuckles. "Caroline!" Then he realized he had to open the box. He did that, then stared through it and shouted for her a second time. "Caroline!"

Her face appeared, eyes snapping with impatience. "What's the rush?" she demanded. "I said it'd take me a few minutes."

The edges of the post box cut into his forehead and chin and knocked his Stetson askew. "This *is* a date, all right?"

She stared back at him from the other side, and either she was overwhelmed by his offer to buy her lunch or surprised into speechlessness.

"All right?" he repeated. "This is a date."

She continued to look at him. "I shouldn't have asked," she finally said.

"I'm glad you did." And he was. He could think of no better way to set things straight. He hadn't invited her to lunch because he needed someone to pass the time with; if that was what he'd wanted, he could have asked his sister, Savannah, or her husband or Cal Patterson—or any number of people. No, he'd asked Caroline because he wanted to be with *her*. For once he longed to talk to her without interference or advice from his matchmaking sister. It didn't help to have Maggie there hiding her face in her mother's lap every time he walked into the room, either. This afternoon it'd be just the two of them. Caroline and him.

Grady respectfully removed his hat when she joined him in the lobby.

"This is a pleasant surprise," Caroline said.

"I was in town, anyway." He didn't mention that he'd rearranged his entire day for this opportunity. It was hard enough admitting that to himself, let alone Caroline.

"Where would you like to eat?" he asked. The town had three good restaurants: the café in the bowling alley; the Chili Pepper, a Texas barbecue place; and a Mexican restaurant run by the Chavez family.

"How about Mexican Lindo?" Caroline suggested.

It was the one he would have chosen himself. "Great."

Since the restaurant was on Fourth Avenue, only two blocks from the post office, they walked there, chatting as they went. Or rather, Caroline chatted and he responded with grunts and murmurs.

Grady had long ago realized he lacked the ability to make small talk. Unlike his younger brother, Richard, who could charm his way into—or out of—anything. Grady tried not to feel inadequate, but he was distinctly relieved when they got to the restaurant.

In a few minutes they were seated at a table, served water and a bowl of tortilla chips along with a dish of extra-hot salsa. He reached for a chip, scooped up as much salsa as it would hold and popped it in his mouth. He ate another and then another before he noticed that Caroline hadn't touched a single chip.

He raised his eyes to hers and stopped chewing, his mouth full.

Caroline apparently read the question in his eyes. "I don't eat corn chips," she explained. "I fill up on them and then I don't have room for anything else."

He swallowed and nodded. "Oh."

A moment of silence passed, and Grady wondered if her comment was a subtle hint that she was watching her weight. From what he understood, weight was a major preoccupation with women. Maybe she was waiting for him to tell her she shouldn't worry about it; maybe he was supposed to say she looked great. She did. She was slender and well proportioned, and she wore her dark brown hair straight and loose, falling to her shoulders. In his opinion she looked about as perfect as a woman could get. Someday he'd tell her that, but not just yet. Besides, he didn't want her to think he was only interested in her body, although it intrigued him plenty. He admired a great deal about her, especially the way she was raising Maggie on her own. She understood the meaning of the words responsibility and sacrifice, just like he did.

She was staring at him as if she expected a comment, and Grady realized he needed to say something. "You could be fat and I'd still have asked you to lunch."

Her smooth brow crumpled in a puzzled frown.

"I meant that as a compliment," he sputtered, and decided then and there it was better to keep his trap shut. Thankfully the waitress came to take their order. Grady decided on chicken enchiladas; Caroline echoed his choice.

"This is really very nice," she said, and reached for the tall glass of iced tea.

"I wanted us to have some time alone," he told her.

"Any particular reason?"

Grady rested his spine against the back of his chair and boldly met her look. "I like you, Caroline." He didn't know any way to be other than direct. This had gotten him into difficulties over the years. Earlier that spring he'd taken a dislike to Laredo Smith and hadn't been shy about letting his sister and everyone else know his feelings. But he'd been wrong in his assessment of the man's character. Smith's truck had broken down and Savannah had brought him home to the ranch. Over Grady's objections she'd hired him herself, and before long they'd fallen in love. It came as a shock to watch his sane, sensible sister give her heart to a perfect stranger. Still, Grady wasn't proud of the way he'd behaved. By the time Laredo decided it'd be better for everyone concerned if he moved on, Grady had wanted him to stay. He'd gone so far as to offer the man a partnership in the ranch in an effort to change his mind. Not that it'd done any good. To Grady's eternal gratitude, Laredo had experienced a change of heart and returned a couple of months later. Love had driven him away, but it had also brought him back.

Savannah and Laredo had married in short order and were now involved in designing plans for their own home, plus raising quarter horses. Savannah, with her husband's active support, continued to grow the antique roses that were making her a name across the state.

In the weeks since becoming his brother-in-law, Laredo Smith had proved himself a damn good friend and Grady's right-hand man.

"I like you, too," Caroline said, but she lowered her gaze as she spoke, breaking eye contact. This seemed to be something of an admission for them both.

"You do?" Grady felt light-headed with joy. It was all he could do not to leap in the air and click his heels.

"We've known each other a lot of years."

"I've known you most of my life," he agreed, but as he said the words, he realized he didn't *really* know Caroline. Not the way he wanted, not the way he hoped he would one day. It wasn't just that he had no idea who'd fathered Maggie; apparently no one else in town did, either. He wondered what had attracted her to this man, why she hadn't married him. Or why he'd left her to deal with the pregnancy and birth alone. It all remained a mystery. Another thing Grady didn't understand about Caroline were the changes in her since her daughter's birth. In time Grady believed she'd trust him enough to answer his questions, and he prayed he'd say and do the right thing when she did.

Their lunches arrived and they ate, stopping to chat now and then. The conversation didn't pall, but again he had to credit Caroline with the skill to keep it going. Half an hour later, as he escorted her back to the post office, Grady was walking on air.

"I'll give you a call tomorrow," he said, watching her for some sign of encouragement. "If you want," he added, needing her reassurance.

"Sure."

Her response was neither encouraging nor discouraging.

"I'd like to talk to Maggie again, if she'll let me."

"You might try this afternoon, since she's spending the day with Savannah."

This was news to Grady, but he'd been busy that morning and had left the house early. He hadn't spoken to Savannah other than a few words over breakfast, and even if he'd known Maggie was staying with his sister, he wouldn't have had time to chat with the girl that morning.

"I'll make a point of saying hello," he said. His heart lifted when it suddenly struck him that he'd be seeing Caroline again later in the day, when she came to pick up Maggie.

They parted. Whistling, Grady sauntered across the asphalt parking lot toward his truck. He felt damn good. The afternoon had gone better than he'd hoped.

He was about to open the cab door when Max Jordan stopped him.

"Grady, have you got a moment?" The older man, owner of the local Western-wear store, quickened his pace.

"Howdy, Max." Grady grinned from ear to ear and didn't let the somber expression on Max's face get him down. "What can I do for you?"

Max shuffled his feet a couple of times, looking uncomfortable. "You know I hate to mention this a second time, but Richard still hasn't paid me for the clothes he bought three months ago."

The happy excitement Grady had experienced only moments earlier died a quick death. "It was my understanding Richard mailed you a check."

"He told me the same thing, but it's been more than two weeks now and nothing's come. I don't feel I should have to wait any longer."

"I don't think you should, either. I'll speak to him myself," Grady promised.

"I hate to drag you into this," Max muttered, and it was clear from his shaky voice how much the subject distressed him.

"Don't worry about it, Max. I understand."

The older man nodded and turned away. Grady climbed into his truck and clenched the steering wheel with both hands as the anger flooded through him. Leave it to his brother to lie and cheat and steal!

What infuriated Grady was that he had no one to blame but himself. He'd allowed Richard to continue living on the Yellow Rose. Allowed him to tarnish the family name. Allowed himself to believe, to hope, that the years away had changed his brother.

All his illusions had been shattered. They were destroyed like so much else Richard had touched. He'd done his damnedest to ruin Grady, and he'd come close. But Richard had succeeded in ruining his own life—his potential to be a different person, a worthwhile human being.

Charming and personable, a born leader, Richard could have accomplished great things. Instead, he'd used his charisma and personality to swindle others, never understanding that the person he'd cheated most had been himself.

Six years earlier Richard had forged Grady's signature and absconded with the cash their parents had left—cash that would have paid the inheritance taxes on the ranch and covered the burial expenses. Grady and

Savannah had found themselves penniless following the tragedy that had claimed their parents' lives. It'd taken six long backbreaking frustration-filled years to crawl out of debt. Grady had sacrificed those years to hold on to the ranch while Richard had squandered the money. When it had run out, he'd returned home with his tail between his legs, looking for a place to stay until he received a severance check from his last job—or so he'd said.

Deep down Grady had wanted to believe in Richard. His sister had begged him to let their younger brother stay. But she didn't need to beg very hard or very long for him to relent. Unfortunately it had become apparent that a liar and a cheat didn't change overnight—or in six years. Grady's brother was the same now as the day he'd stolen from his family.

Despite the air conditioner, the heat inside the truck cab sucked away Grady's energy. It should have come as no surprise to discover that Richard had lied to him again. This time would be the last, Grady vowed.

Oh, yes, this episode was the proverbial last straw.

HIS DAYS IN PROMISE were numbered, Richard Weston thought as he sat on his bed in the bunkhouse. It wouldn't be long before Grady learned the truth. The whole uncomfortable truth. Actually he was surprised he'd managed to hold out this long; he credited that to his ability to lie effectively. But then, small-town folks were embarrassingly easy to dupe. They readily accepted his lies because they wanted to believe him. The years had finely honed his powers of persuasion, but he hadn't needed to work very hard convincing the business owners in Promise to trust him. Being born and raised in this very town had certainly helped. He nearly laughed out loud at how smoothly everything had gone.

Actually Richard did feel kind of bad about leaving a huge debt behind. Max Jordan was decent enough, even if he was an old fool. Billy from Billy D's was okay, too. One day—maybe—when he had money to spare, he'd consider paying everyone back. Grady and Savannah, too. That would shock his uptight brother.

It might all have worked if Richard could've persuaded Ellie Frasier to marry him. He experienced a twinge of regret. He must be losing his knack with women. Nothing could have shocked him more than Ellie's informing him she'd chosen Glen Patterson, instead.

Damn shame. Glen was a real hick, not all that different from Grady. Why Ellie would marry Glen when she could have had *him* was something he'd never understand. Women were fickle creatures, but until recently he'd been able to sway them to his way of thinking.

Not Ellie. How he would've loved to get his hands on her inheritance.

That money would have gone a long way toward solving his problems. Well, it didn't do any good to cry over might-have-beens. He was a survivor and he'd prove it—not for the first time. Nothing kept Richard Weston down for long.

Calculating quickly, Richard figured he had only a few days before everything went all to hell. He was ready. Grady seemed to think he idled away his days, but Richard had been working hard, preparing what he'd need. He'd been planning for this day almost from the moment he'd gotten back to Promise. Grady needn't worry; before long Richard would be out of his brother's hair.

Sure he had regrets. He'd thought about returning to Promise lots of times over the years, but he'd never suspected it would be for the reasons that had driven him here now.

When he'd first arrived on the ranch, he'd felt a faint stirring of emotion. It'd been a little less than six years since he'd set foot on the old homestead. Those feelings, however, hadn't lasted long and were completely dead now, especially since Grady had tossed him out of the house and forced him to sleep in the bunkhouse.

Richard couldn't grasp what it was that had kept his father and now his brother tied to a herd of four-footed headaches. He hated cattle, hated the way they smelled and bawled, the way they constantly needed care. Hated everything about them. This kind of life was never meant for him. Sadly no one appreciated that he was different. Better, if he did say so himself. Not even his mother had fully recognized it. Unfortunately neither did Savannah. Now that she'd married Laredo, she was even less inclined to side with him.

Sad to say, his time on the Yellow Rose was drawing to a close.

"Richard?"

Maggie Daniels peeked into the bunkhouse. The kid had become something of a pest lately, but he'd always been popular with children. They weren't all that different from women, most of them, eager for his attention.

"Howdy, cupcake," he said, forcing enthusiasm into his voice. "Whatcha doin'?"

"Nothing. You want to play cards?"

"I can't now. How about later?" He leaned against the wall, clasping his hands behind his head.

"You said that last time." Her lower lip shot out.

Yup, kids were just like women; they pouted when they didn't get their way.

"Where's Savannah?" Richard asked, hoping to divert the kid's attention.

"In her garden."

"Didn't I hear her say something about baking cookies this afternoon?" He hadn't heard any such thing, but it'd get rid of the kid.

"She did?" Excitement tinged Maggie's voice.

"She told me so herself. Chocolate chip, my favorite. Why don't you ask her, and when you're finished you can bring me a sample. How does that sound?"

Maggie's eyes lit up and Richard laughed. He loved the fact that she preferred him over Grady. His big lug of a brother didn't know a damn thing about kids. It was comical watching him try to make friends with Maggie. She wouldn't have anything to do with him, and for once in his life Richard outshone his big brother.

"Come on, I'll go with you," he said, changing his mind. "We'll go talk to Savannah about those cookies."

"She's busy in her rose garden."

"But not too busy for us." Richard felt certain that was true. Savannah had a soft spot in her heart for the child and could refuse Maggie nothing. If he'd asked her on his own, chances were he wouldn't get to first base, but with Maggie holding his hand, Savannah was sure to capitulate.

For some reason Richard wanted one of those cookies. And he wanted it now.

He wasn't sure why—maybe just to pull Savannah's strings a bit. But Richard prided himself on getting what he wanted. Whenever he wanted it.

"You're full of surprises, Grady Weston," Caroline muttered to herself as she drove down the highway toward the Yellow Rose. The afternoon had dragged even though she'd been busy. Despite the heavy flow of traffic in and out of the post office, Caroline had frequently glanced at her watch, counting down the hours and then the minutes until closing time. And until she saw Grady again. . . .

His invitation to lunch had caught her by surprise. She'd all but given up hope that he'd ever figure it out. In the past six months she'd done everything short of sending him a fax to let him know she was interested. When it came to romance, Grady Weston was as blind as they come. Not that she was any better; it'd taken her years to work up enough courage to give love a second chance.

She'd dated occasionally but never found that combination of mutual attraction and respect with anyone except Grady. Unfortunately she wasn't sure he recognized his own feelings, let alone hers. Twice now she'd decided to forget about him, and both times he'd given her reasons to believe it might work for them. Like showing up this afternoon and taking her to lunch.

She sped up, hoping their lunch date really *was* a beginning. She wanted a relationship with Grady, a romance—maybe even marriage eventually. Oh, my, but she did like him. He was honest, loyal, hardworking. She admired the way he'd struggled to hold on to the ranch despite grief and crippling sacrifices. Year after year she'd watched him do whatever it took to keep the Yellow Rose, to keep what was important to him and Savannah.

Caroline and Savannah had always been close, but never more so than now. Caroline's mother had died the year before, and it was Savannah who'd stood by her side and cried with her. Having buried her own mother, Savannah understood the grief that suffocated Caroline those first few months. It was also during that time that Maggie had grown so attached to Savannah, who'd become like a second mother to her. It pleased Caroline that her daughter loved Savannah as much as she did herself.

However, the five-year-old felt no such tenderness for Grady. Caroline sighed as her thoughts drifted to their rocky relationship. Grady's loud voice had made the child skittish from the first, and then one afternoon when Maggie was feeling ill, she'd phoned Savannah. Grady had answered the phone with a brusque demand, and from that moment forward Maggie would have nothing to do with him.

It was a problem, and one that continued to bother Caroline. If a romantic relationship developed between her and Grady the way she wanted, the way she dreamed, then Maggie and Grady would need to make their peace. True, Grady regretted the incident and had tried to undo the damage, but the child was unrelenting in her dislike of him.

As she reached the long gravel driveway leading to the Yellow Rose, Caroline decreased her speed to make the turn. A few moments later the large two-storey ranch house came into view. Rocket, Grady's old dog, lumbered stiffly down the porch steps to greet her, tail wagging.

Laredo was working in the corral while Savannah stood at the fence watching him put their prize stallion through his paces. Maggie was with Savannah, her feet braced against the bottom rail and her arms resting on top. When she heard the car, she leaped down and dashed toward her mother.

Maggie hurled herself into her arms as soon as Caroline stepped out of the car. "Me and Savannah baked cookies!" Her young voice rang with glee. "And Richard said he never tasted better. He ate five cookies before he could stop himself." She slapped both hands over her mouth as though she'd blurted out a secret.

"How many did you eat?" Caroline wanted to know. It would be just like Richard to let the child spoil her dinner with cookies.

"Too many," Savannah answered for her, giving Caroline an apologetic half smile.

"We'll have a late dinner," Caroline said, dismissing her friend's worries. "I had a big lunch." She was about to tell Savannah about her lunch date when Grady burst out of the barn.

"Have you seen Richard? Has he shown up yet? He's got to be around here somewhere." Grady's face was distorted with rage.

Maggie edged closer to Caroline and wrapped her arm around her mother's waist.

"Grady," Savannah said in that low calming way of hers.

If Grady noticed Caroline, he gave no indication.

"Did I hear someone call for me?" Richard said, strolling out of the house as though he hadn't a care in the world. He was a handsome man, lean and muscular, probably the most attractive man Caroline had ever known. But, in Richard's case the good looks were superficial. She'd watched as he skillfully manipulated and used others to his own advantage. Even Grady and Savannah. She was amazed that Grady had allowed him to continue living on the ranch—yet at the same time, she understood. Like Savannah, Grady wanted to believe that Richard had changed.

Grady whirled around at the sound of Richard's voice. "We need to talk." His voice boomed and Maggie hid her face against Caroline's stomach.

"Max Jordan said he hasn't been paid," Grady shouted.

A shocked look stole over Richard. "You're joking! He didn't get the check? I put it in the mail two weeks ago."

"He never got it because you didn't mail it."

"What do you mean?" Richard demanded.

The two men faced off, Grady's anger spilling over in every word and Richard looking stunned and hard done by.

"Grady, please," Savannah said, hurrying toward her older brother and gently placing a hand on his arm. "Now isn't the time to be discussing this. Leave it until later."

"She's right," Richard said. "In case you hadn't noticed, we have company."

It was obvious that Grady had been so consumed by his anger, he'd barely realized they weren't alone. "Caroline," he murmured, and his face revealed both regret and delight. He seemed uncertain about what to say next. "Hello."

"How's my cupcake?" Richard asked, smiling at Maggie.

The little girl loosened her grip on Caroline's waist, turning to Richard as he spoke. He threw his arms open and she raced eagerly toward him.

"That's my girl," Richard said, catching Maggie and sweeping her high into the air. He whirled her around, the pair of them laughing as if it'd been days since they'd seen each other.

Savannah sidled closer to Caroline. "Grady's been looking for Richard all afternoon," she said in a quiet voice, "and he's been conveniently missing until now."

Caroline understood what her friend was saying. Richard had played his cards perfectly, appearing at the precise moment it'd be impossible for Grady to get a straight answer from him. Then he'd used Maggie's childish adoration to make Grady look even more foolish.

"Maggie," Caroline called.

Richard set the child back on her feet. Together the two of them joined Caroline and Savannah.

"I do believe Maggie has stolen my heart," he said, his eyes bright with laughter.

"Does that mean you'll marry me?" Maggie asked, grinning up at him.

"Sure thing."

"Really?"

"He won't marry you," Caroline said, reaching for her daughter's hand.

"Don't be so certain," Richard countered. He crouched down beside Maggie, but he was looking at Caroline.

"Hi, Maggie," Grady said, choosing that moment to try again. The anger had faded from his face, but he still held himself rigid.

Caroline gave him credit for making the effort to win Maggie over.

Her daughter wasn't easily swayed, however. She buried her face in Richard's shoulder.

"There's no need to be afraid of Grady," Richard whispered to Maggie—a stage whisper that carried easily. Then he smiled in a way that suggested Grady was wasting his time. In other words, Grady didn't have a snowball's chance in hell of convincing Maggie he wasn't an ogre. Richard's meaning couldn't have been clearer.

"I don't like Grady," Maggie announced, pursing her lips.

"Maggie!" Caroline admonished her.

"She's right, you know," Richard said, teeth flashing in a wide grin. "Grady just doesn't get along with kids, not like I do."

Caroline clamped her mouth shut rather than reveal her thoughts. She didn't trust Richard, *couldn't* trust him, not after the way he'd used his family. Used anyone who'd let him.

"I'm thinking Maggie needs someone like me in her life," Richard said. "Which means there's only one solution."

"What's that?" Caroline knew she was a fool to ask.

"You could always marry me," he said, and leaned over far enough to touch his lips to Caroline's cheek. "Put me out of my misery, Caroline Daniels, and marry me."

"Oh, Mommy, let's do it!" Maggie shouted, clapping her hands. "Let's marry Richard."

TWO

Grady was pleased that his sister had convinced Caroline and Maggie to stay for dinner. Now all he had to do was behave. It never seemed to fail—whenever he had a chance to make some headway with Maggie, he'd do something stupid. He wanted to blame Richard, but as usual he'd done it to himself.

His brother brought out the very worst in him. As Grady washed up for dinner, he hoped this evening would give him an opportunity to redeem himself in both Caroline and Maggie's eyes.

The table was already set and the food dished up in heaping portions. A platter of sliced roast beef rested in the middle, along with a huge bowl of mashed potatoes, a pitcher of gravy, fresh corn on the cob and a crisp green salad. There was also a basket filled with Savannah's mouthwatering buttermilk biscuits. His sister was one fine cook. He'd miss her when she moved into her own house with Laredo. But it was time, well past time, that she had a home and a life of her own. He knew from his talks with Laredo that they'd already started to think about adding to the family.

"Dinner looks wonderful," he said. Grady made an effort these days to let Savannah know how much he appreciated her. Over the years he'd taken her contributions for granted, discounting her efforts with her roses and her fledgling mail-order business—a business that now brought a significant income. He'd even made fun of her goats, which he considered pets rather than livestock. Now that she was married and about to establish her own home, Grady recognized just how much he was going to miss her.

Savannah flushed with pleasure at his praise.

The compliment had apparently earned him points with Caroline, too; she cast him an approving smile. Grady held in a sigh. He needed all the points he could get when it came to Caroline and Maggie. If everything went well, this evening might help him recapture lost ground with the child.

Everyone began to arrive for dinner. With the scent of the meal wafting through the house, it wasn't long before all the chairs were occupied—except for one. Richard's. It was just like his spoiled younger brother to keep everyone waiting.

"Where's Richard?" Maggie asked, glancing up at her mother.

Grady was asking himself the same question.

"He's coming, isn't he?" Maggie whined.

Even from where he stood Grady could sense the little girl's disappointment.

"I don't know, sweetheart," Caroline answered.

"There's no need to let our meal get cold," Grady said. If Richard chose to go without dinner, that was fine by him. If anything, he was grateful not to have his brother monopolizing the conversation, distracting both Caroline and Maggie. Grady pulled out his chair and sat down. Laredo, Savannah and Caroline did so, as well. The only one who remained standing was Maggie.

"What about Richard?" she asked in a small stubborn voice.

"I guess he isn't hungry," Caroline said, and pulled out the chair next to her own for Maggie.

"He promised he'd sit next to me at dinner."

"It isn't a good idea to believe in the things Richard promises," Grady said as much for Caroline's ears as for her daughter's. He hated to disappoint the five-year-old, but it was God's own truth. Richard was about as stable as beef prices. His loyalties constantly shifted toward whatever was most advantageous to him, with little concern for anyone else.

His playful marriage proposal to Caroline worried Grady. She'd laughed it off, but Grady found no humor in it. Apparently his brother knew Grady was interested in Caroline and thus considered her fair game. It would be typical of Richard to do what he could to thwart any romance between Caroline and Grady by making a play for her himself. Grady knew that made him sound paranoid, but he thought his fears were justified. Experience had been an excellent teacher.

He reached for the meat and forked a thick slice of roast beef onto his plate, then passed the platter to Caroline.

Maggie folded her arms and stared defiantly at Grady. "I'm not eating until Richard's here."

"Maggie, please," Caroline cajoled. She glanced at Grady, her eyes apologetic.

"Grady yelled at Richard."

Once again Grady was the culprit. "I shouldn't have yelled, should I?" He was careful to speak in a low quiet voice. "I do that sometimes without thinking, but I wasn't angry at you."

"You were mad at Richard."

No use lying about it. "Yes, I was."

"And now he won't come to dinner."

"I think Richard has other reasons for not showing up," Caroline explained as she placed a scoop of mashed potatoes on her daughter's plate. "Do you want one of Savannah's yummy buttermilk biscuits?"

Maggie hesitated for a long moment before she shook her head. "I won't eat without Richard."

"Did I hear someone call my name?" Richard asked cheerfully as he stepped into the kitchen. "Sorry I'm late," he said, not sounding the least apologetic. He pulled out his chair, sat down beside Maggie and reached for the meat platter all in a single graceful movement.

Caroline's child shot Grady a triumphant look as if to say she'd known all along that Richard hadn't lied to her.

Grady's appetite vanished. For every step he advanced in his effort to make friends with Maggie, he seemed to retreat two. Once more Richard had made him look like a fool in front of the little girl. And once more he'd allowed it to happen.

"Is it true you want to marry my mom?" Maggie asked Richard with such hopefulness that the question silenced all other conversation.

"Of course it's true." Richard chuckled, then winked at Caroline.

"I think you should," Maggie said, hanging on Richard's every word.

Grady didn't speak again during the entire meal. Not that anyone noticed. Adored by Maggie, Richard was in his element, and he became the center of attention, joking and teasing, complimenting Savannah, even exchanging a brief joke with Laredo.

Caroline was quiet for a time, but soon, Grady noted, Richard had won her over just as he had everyone else. Despite his disappointment, Grady marveled at his brother's talent. Richard had always savored attention, whereas Grady avoided the limelight. It had never bothered him before, but now he felt a growing resentment, certain Caroline was about to be caught by the force of Richard's spell. Other than Ellie Fraiser, Grady had never known any woman to resist his brother's charms. Ellie was the exception, and only because she was already in love with Glen Patterson, although neither of them had recognized the strength of their feelings for each other—until Richard interfered. Indirectly, and definitely without intending it, Richard had brought about something good.

Still, if it hadn't been for Glen in Ellie's life, Grady wondered what would have happened. That, at least, was one worry he'd escaped.

As soon as he could, Grady excused himself from the table and headed toward the barn. He would have liked to linger over dinner, perhaps enjoy a cup of coffee with Caroline on the porch, but he could see that was a lost cause.

Not until he'd stalked across the yard did he recognize the symptoms. Damn it all, he was *jealous*. The only woman he'd ever cared about, and Richard was going to steal her away. The problem was, Grady had no idea how to keep him from Caroline.

To his surprise Laredo followed him outside. Like Grady, his brother-in-law was a man of few words.

"Don't let him get to you," Laredo said, leading the way into the barn.

"I'm not," Grady told him, which wasn't entirely a lie. He knew the kind of man Richard was; he knew the insecurity of Richard's charm. He didn't like the fact that his brother was working on Caroline, but he wasn't willing to make a fool of himself, either. Other men had made that mistake before him. Glen Patterson, for one. The poor guy had come off looking like an idiot at the Cattlemen's Association dance. Richard and Glen had nearly come to blows over Ellie, with half the town looking on. They might have, too, if Sheriff Hennessey hadn't stepped in when he did.

"Good." Laredo slapped him on the back and the two went their separate ways.

Grady didn't stay in the barn long. He gave himself ample time to control his resentment, then decided that, while he wasn't going to accept the role of fool, he didn't intend to just give up, either. He'd tried to make sure Caroline understood that their lunch today was more than a meal between friends. Hell—despite what she'd said—he didn't know if she ever considered him a friend.

Grady found her sitting on the porch with Savannah sipping hot tea. Maggie sat on the steps cradling her doll. He strolled toward the women, without a clue what to say once he joined them. He supposed he'd better learn a few conversational rules, he thought grimly, if that meant he'd have a chance with Caroline.

The two women stopped talking as he approached, which led him to surmise that he'd been the topic of conversation. He felt as awkward as a schoolboy and, not sure what else to do, touched the rim of his hat.

Savannah, bless her heart, winked conspiratorially at him and stood. "Maggie," she said, holding out her hand to the little girl, "I found one of my old dolls this afternoon. Would you like to play with her?"

Maggie leaped to her feet. "Could I?"

"You bet."

As Savannah and Maggie disappeared into the house, Grady lowered himself onto the rocker his sister had vacated. He felt as tongue-tied and unsure as he had that afternoon. Taking a deep breath, he forced himself to remember that he'd been talking to Caroline all her life. It shouldn't be any different now.

"Beautiful night, isn't it?" he commented, thinking the weather was a safe subject with which to start.

"Those look like storm clouds to the east."

Grady hadn't noticed. He gazed up at the sky, feeling abashed, until Caroline leaned back in her rocker and laughed. He grinned, loving the sound of her amusement. It was difficult not to stare. All these years, and he hadn't seen how damn beautiful she was. While he could speculate why it'd taken him this long, he didn't want to waste another minute. It was all he could do to keep his tongue from lolling out the side of his mouth whenever he caught sight of her. He longed to find the words to tell her how attractive she was, how much he liked and respected her. It wasn't the first time he'd wished he could issue compliments with Richard's finesse.

"Come on, Grady, loosen up."

"I'm loose," he growled, and noted how relaxed she was, rocking back and forth as if they often sat side by side in the evening. His parents had done that. Every night. They'd shared the events of their day, talked over plans for the future, exchanged feelings and opinions.

The memory of his mother and father filled his mind. Six years, and the pain of their absence was as strong now as it had been in the beginning. Some nights Grady would sit on the porch, the old dog beside him, and silently discuss business matters with his father, seeking his advice. Not that he actually expected his father to provide answers, of course; Grady was no believer in ghosts or paranormal influences. But those one-sided discussions had helped see Grady through the rough years. It was during those times, burdened with worries, that he'd been forced to search deep inside himself for the answers. And on rare occasions, he'd experienced moments when he'd felt his father's presence more intensely than his absence.

"You've gotten quiet all of a sudden," Caroline said.

"I want to talk to you about Richard." His words were as much a surprise to him as to Caroline.

"Oh?" Her eyebrows rose.

"I realize you must find his attention flattering, but like I said earlier it isn't wise to believe anything Richard says." The lazy sway of her rocking stopped. "I know you probably don't want to hear this," he added. It wasn't pleasant for him, either. Regardless of anything between them, though, Grady's one concern was that Richard not hurt Caroline.

"I appreciate what you're doing, but I'm a big girl."

"I didn't mean to suggest you weren't. It's just that, well, Richard has a way with women."

"And you assume he's going to sweep me off my feet, is that it?" The teasing warmth in her voice was gone, replaced by something less friendly.

"You think I want to say these things?" he asked, inhaling sharply. "It isn't really you he's interested in, anyway.'

"I beg your pardon?"

Grady wished he'd never introduced the subject. Clearly Caroline wasn't going to appreciate his insight, but once he'd started he couldn't stop. "Richard knows how I feel about you and—" He snapped his mouth closed before he embarrassed himself further. "I'm only telling you this because I don't want you to get hurt again." He didn't know what madness possessed him to add the *again.* He realized the moment he did that Caroline had taken his advice the wrong way.

Grady had never asked her about Maggie's father, didn't intend to do so now. Heaven knew she was touchy enough about the subject. The only other time he'd said something, months earlier, she'd been ready to bite his head off.

"This discussion is over," she said, jumping to her feet.

"Caroline, I didn't mean— Oh, hell, be angry if you want." With an abrupt movement, he got out of the chair, leaving it to rock wildly. Once again he'd botched their conversation. "It appears you don't need any advice from me."

"No, Grady, I don't."

It damaged his pride that she'd so casually disregard his warning. "Fine, then, for all I care, you can marry Richard." Not giving her a chance to respond, he stalked away, absolutely certain that any hope of a relationship was forever ruined.

His fears were confirmed less than an hour later when he left the barn and saw her again. She was in her car with the driver's window rolled down. Richard was leaning against the side of the vehicle, and the sound of their laughter rang in the twilight.

The unexpected twist of disappointment and pain caught Grady off guard. Well, that certainly answered that.

Caroline must have noticed him because Richard suddenly looked over his shoulder. Grady didn't stick around. It was too hard to pretend he didn't care when he damn well did. His stride was full of purpose as he crossed the yard and stormed into the house, sequestering himself in the office.

His emotions had covered the full range in a single day. He'd taken Caroline to lunch and afterward felt . . . ecstatic; there was no other word for it. Before dinner he'd been like a kid, thrilled to see her again so soon. Now, just a few hours later, he'd been thrown into despair, convinced beyond doubt that he'd lost whatever chance he might have had with her.

It was enough to drive a man to drink. He sat in the worn leather desk chair and pulled open the bottom file drawer. His father had kept a bottle of bourbon there for times when nothing else would do, and Grady had followed the same practice. The bottle was gone—which had happened before. Grady suspected Richard, with good reason, but at the moment he didn't really care. He wasn't much of a drinking man. A cold beer now and then suited him just fine, but he'd never enjoyed the hard stuff.

The knock on the office door surprised him. "Who is it?" he barked, not in the mood for company.

"Richard." His brother didn't wait for an invitation but opened the door and sauntered in. He immediately made himself at home, claiming the only other chair in the room. He leaned back, locked his fingers behind his head and grinned like a silly schoolboy.

"So what's up with you and Caroline?" he asked.

Grady scowled. The last person he wanted to discuss with his brother was Caroline. "Nothing."

His denial only served to fuel Richard's amusement. "Come on, Grady, I've got eyes in my head. It's obvious you've got the hots for her. Not that I blame you, man. She's one nice-looking woman."

Grady didn't like Richard's tone of voice, but prolonging this conversation by arguing with him would serve no useful purpose. "Listen, Richard, I've got better things to do than sit around discussing Caroline Daniels with you."

"I don't imagine it would take much to talk her into the sack, either. She's already been to bed with at least one man—what's a few more? Right?"

Grady ground his teeth in an effort to control his irritation. "I don't think it's a good idea for us to discuss Caroline." He stood and walked over to the door and pointedly opened it.

"I wouldn't mind getting into her bed myself one of these days," Richard went on.

Despite everything he'd promised himself, Grady saw red. He flew across the room and dragged his brother out of the chair, grabbing him by the front of his shirt.

Richard held up both hands. "Hey, hey, don't get so riled! I was only teasing."

Grady's fingers ached with the strength of his grip. It took a moment to clear his head enough to release his brother.

"You don't want to talk about Caroline, fine," Richard said, backing toward the door. "But you can't blame a guy for asking, can you?"

DRIVING HOME, Caroline realized she not only distrusted Richard Weston, but thoroughly disliked him. Before she'd left the Yellow Rose, he'd gone out of his way to let her know that Grady had asked Nell Bishop, a local widow, to the Cattlemen's dance earlier in the summer. What was particularly meaningful about the information was that Caroline knew how hard Savannah had tried to convince Grady to invite *her*. He almost had. She remembered he'd come into the post office a few days before the dance, but within minutes they'd ended up trading insults. That was unfortunate. He *had* mentioned the dance, though, leaving her to wonder.

Their verbal exchanges were legendary. Only in the past couple of weeks had they grown comfortable enough with each other to manage a civil conversation.

Now this.

Caroline didn't believe Richard. She strongly suspected that almost everything out of his mouth was a lie. If the story about Nell *was* true, she would've heard about it. To the best of her knowledge Nell hadn't even attended the dance. Not that it was unusual for her to avoid social functions—it was widely known that Nell continued to grieve for Jake, the only man she'd ever loved. He'd been her high-school sweetheart, and their affection for each other had been evident throughout the years. Caroline had often wondered if Nell would remarry.

"Ask her." Caroline spoke the words aloud without realizing it.

"Ask who, Mommy?" Maggie looked at her mother.

"A friend." She left it at that.

"About what?"

"Nothing." She smiled at her daughter and changed the subject.

As it turned out she had the opportunity to chat with Nell sooner than she'd expected. The following afternoon on her way home from work Caroline stopped at the local Winn-Dixie for a few groceries.

She collected what she needed and pushed her cart up to the checkout stand—behind Nell.

"Howdy, friend," Nell said cheerfully. "Haven't seen you in awhile."

"Nell!" Caroline didn't disguise her pleasure. "How are you?"

"Great. I've been working hard on getting the word out that I'm turning Twin Canyons into a dude ranch. The brochures were mailed to travel agents last week."

Caroline admired her ingenuity. "That's terrific."

The grocery clerk slid Nell's purchases over the scanner, coming up with the total. She paid in cash, then glanced around. "Jeremy!" she called. "Emma." She reached for the plastic bags, giving a good-natured shrug. "I warned those two not to wander off. I know exactly where to find them, too—the book section. They're both crazy about books, especially the Babysitters' Club books and that new series of kids' Westerns by T. R. Grant. I can't buy them fast enough."

Caroline recognized both series. T. R. Grant was the current rage; even Maggie had wanted Caroline to read her his books. Maggie was still a bit young for them, but it wouldn't be long before she devoured Grant's books and the Babysitters' Club by herself.

"Have you got a moment?" Caroline asked, opening her purse to pay for her own groceries.

"Sure." Nell waited while Caroline finished her transaction. "What can I do for you?"

As they walked toward the book display at the far end of the Winn-Dixie, Caroline mulled over the best way to approach the subject of Nell and Grady. She wasn't sure why she'd allowed Richard to upset her, especially when she believed it'd all been a lie. Not that she'd blame Grady for being attracted to Nell. In fact, at one time she'd believed they might eventually marry. They seemed right together somehow; both were ranchers and both had struggled against what seemed impossible odds.

In the back of her mind Caroline had always suspected that when the time was right, they'd discover each other. Grady and Jake had been good friends, and Grady had been a pall bearer at Jake's funeral. Grady and Nell were close in age and would make a handsome couple. Grady was an inch or two over six feet, with a broad muscular physique not unlike Jake's. There weren't many men who'd suit Nell physically, since she was nearly six feet herself.

"I hope you don't think I'm being nosy, but I heard a rumor . . ." Caroline blurted before she lost her nerve. This was even more embarrassing than she'd feared.

"About what?" Nell frowned.

Caroline drew a breath and held it until her lungs ached. "About you and Grady Weston."

Nell frowned again. "Me and Grady?"

Caroline nodded.

"Grady's a friend," Nell said. "I've always liked him and if I were ever to consider remarrying, I'd certainly think about Grady."

Caroline broke eye contact. This wasn't what she'd wanted to hear.

"He's a good man and he'd make an excellent husband and father," Nell continued, then asked a probing question of her own. "Is there any reason you're asking?"

"Not really."

"He asked me to the dance last month," Nell added, as if she'd suddenly remembered.

So it was true. Caroline's spirits sank.

"In fact, I received two invitations to the dance within a few hours." This was said with a note of amusement.

"Two? Grady and who else?"

Nell's mouth widened in a smile. "You aren't going to believe this, but both Grady Weston and Glen Patterson asked me to the dance."

"Glen?" That was a kicker, considering he was now engaged to Ellie Frasier. Those two were so deeply in love it was difficult to imagine that little more than a month ago Glen had invited Nell and not Ellie to the biggest dance of the year. In the end he'd gone by himself and then he'd practically come to blows with Richard over Ellie. Richard—always the spoiler.

"I don't know what was in the air that day," Nell murmured. "Grady and Glen calling me up like that."

"Did you go to the dance?"

"Briefly," Nell said, "but Emma had an upset stomach that day. I made an appearance, said hello to some friends I don't see often and left shortly after the music started."

"Grady was there," Caroline said, fondly recalling their one dance. Ladies' choice, and she'd been the one to approach him. Those few short minutes in Grady's arms had been wonderful. Afterward she'd hoped he'd ask her to dance himself, but he'd wandered back to where he'd been sitting with Cal Patterson and hadn't spoken to her again. Caroline had felt bitterly disappointed.

". . . any reason?" Nell asked.

Caroline caught only the last part of the question. "Reason?" she repeated.

"That you're asking about me and Grady?"

"Not really," she said, then figured she owed her friend the truth. "He asked me to lunch the other day."

"And you went?"

Caroline nodded.

"And you had a good time?"

"A great time," Caroline admitted.

Nell shifted the weight of the groceries in her hands. "Listen, Caroline, if you're worried about there being anything romantic between me and Grady, don't give it another thought. Grady's one of the most honorable men I know, but—" her voice dipped with emotion "—I'm still in love with Jake."

"Oh, Nell." Caroline hugged her friend.

"Oh, damn it all," Nell said, blinking furiously. "I've got to scoot. I'll see you soon, okay?"

"Sure." It would be good to sit down and talk with her friend. Both their lives were so busy it was difficult to find the time.

"Jeremy. Emma." Nell called her children again, and the two came running.

Caroline waved them off and headed toward the parking lot, deep in thought. So, what Richard had told her was true. This was what made him dangerous. He tossed in a truth now and then just to keep everyone guessing. But for once, she wished he'd been lying.

GRADY HAD BEEN PENSIVE ever since the night Caroline stayed for dinner, Savannah observed. He sat at the kitchen table, supposedly writing out an order for Richard to pick up at the feed store later that afternoon. But for the last five minutes, all he'd done was stare blankly into space.

Savannah had to bite her tongue. Laredo had repeatedly warned her against any further matchmaking efforts between her brother and Caroline, but he might as well have asked her to stop breathing. Grady was miserable and Caroline hadn't been any happier. If it was within her power to bring them together—these two people who were so obviously meant for each other—what possible harm could it do?

Considering that thought, Savannah poured her brother a fresh cup of coffee.

Grady glanced up and thanked her with an off-center smile.

"Something on your mind?" she asked. If he voluntarily brought up the subject, all the better.

"Nothing important," he murmured, and reached for the steaming mug. He raised it tentatively to his lips, then glanced at her as if tempted to seek her advice.

Savannah held her breath, hoping Grady would ask her about Caroline. He didn't.

"The church dinner's this weekend," she said, speaking quickly.

Grady responded with what sounded like a grunt, the translation of which she already knew. He wasn't interested.

Savannah glared at him. If she wrung his neck, she wondered, would he have any idea why? "Caroline's bringing her applesauce cake," she added casually. "Her mother's recipe."

At the mention of her friend's name, Grady raised his head. "Caroline's going to the church dinner?"

"Of course." At last, a reaction. Her brother might be one of the most intelligent men she knew, but when it came to women he was the class dunce. "I'm bringing my chicken teriyaki salad," she added, as if this was significant.

"Is Laredo going?"

"Yes, and Ellie and Glen and just about everyone else in town."

"Oh."

Savannah figured she was due a large heavenly reward for her patience. *Oh.* Was that all he could say? Poor Caroline.

"It isn't a date thing, is it?"

Savannah didn't know how to answer. If she let him assume everyone was bringing a date, it might scare him off. On the other hand, if she said nothing, someone else might ask Caroline.

"This shouldn't be such a difficult question," Grady said, glaring at her.

"Yes and no. Some people will come with dates and some won't."

He mulled that over. "Does Caroline have a date?"

Savannah had to restrain herself from hugging Grady's neck and crying out for joy. He wasn't as dense as she'd thought. "Not that I know of." This, too, was said casually, as though she hadn't the least bit of interest in Caroline's social life.

"Oh."

Grady was back to testing her patience again. She waited an entire minute before she ventured another question.

"Are you thinking of inviting her and Maggie?"

"Me?" Grady's eyes widened as if this were a new thought.

"Yes, you," she returned pointedly.

"I'm . . . thinking about it," he finally said.

Her face broke out in a smile and she clapped her hands. "That's wonderful."

"What's wonderful?" Richard asked, wandering into the kitchen. He reached for a banana, peeled it and leaned expectantly against the kitchen counter.

Grady and Savannah exchanged looks. "The church dinner," she answered for them both.

"Yeah, I heard about that," he said with his mouth full. "Either of you going?"

"I think so." Again Savannah took the initiative.

"Then I'll give some thought to attending, too."

Both Grady and Savannah remained silent.

"I should probably have a date, though, don't you think?" He pondered his own question. "Caroline. I'll ask Caroline," he said triumphantly. "She'll jump at the chance to go with me."

Three

"**Y**ou're a damn fool, that's what you are," Grady muttered as he barreled down the highway toward Promise, driving twenty miles over the speed limit.

The reason for this hasty trip had to do with Caroline Daniels. By dinnertime he'd recognized that either he made his move now and invited her to the church dinner or let Richard beat him to the punch. Of course he could have just phoned and been done with it, but that didn't seem right, not when anyone on the ranch could pick up a telephone receiver and listen in on the conversation. By anyone, he meant Richard. Besides, Grady preferred to talk to Caroline in person; it seemed more . . . meaningful.

He'd never been good at this courtship thing, but damn it all, he wasn't going to let his brother cheat him out of taking Caroline and Maggie to that church dinner. Richard wasn't interested in Caroline—Grady was sure of it—any more than he'd fallen head over heels in love with Ellie Frasier. His brother was far more concerned with cheating him out of the pleasure of Caroline's company. Except that he had no intention of standing idly by and letting it happen.

Once he'd made his decision, Grady knew he should act on it. Naturally there was always the risk that he'd arrive at Caroline's with his heart dangling from his sleeve only to learn that Richard had already asked her out for Saturday night.

Even knowing he might be too late didn't stop him. He wanted to attend the dinner with Caroline and Maggie more than he'd wanted anything in a long while. It surprised him how much.

The drive into town, during which he thought about the approach he'd take with Caroline, seemed to take no time at all. His goal was to ask her to be his date before Richard did, and at the same time keep his pride intact if she refused. No small task, considering past experience.

He parked in front of Caroline's small house and leaped out of the truck cab. Eager to get this settled, he took the steps up to her front door two at a time and leaned on the buzzer.

Caroline opened the door, her face registering surprise.

"Grady, hello." She recovered quickly and held the screen door wide.

"Would you like to sit outside for a spell?" he asked, instead gesturing toward the porch swing. Since he was nervous about this entire thing, staying outside in the semidarkness felt more inviting than her well-lit living room.

"Sure."

She glanced over her shoulder, and Grady noticed Maggie playing by herself in the background. She had her dolls sitting around a small table and was chatting amicably as she stood in front of her play kitchen cooking up a storm. He grinned at the sight.

Caroline sat down, but Grady found it impossible to keep still.

"Did Savannah phone?" he asked. It would be just like his sister to give Caroline a heads-up. He hadn't announced where he was going when he left the ranch, but Savannah knew. After all, she was the one who'd steered him in this direction in that less-than-subtle way of hers. Grady tolerated Savannah's matchmaking only because he wasn't opposed to her efforts to promote a romance between him and Caroline. Frankly he could use the help. He wasn't keen, however, on letting her know that.

"Savannah phone me?" Caroline repeated. "No, she hasn't."

Grady released a sigh, and some of the tension eased from between his shoulder blades. "What about Richard?"

"What about him?"

"Have you spoken to him recently—say, in the last four or five hours?"

"No," she answered curtly. "Is there a reason for all these questions?"

Grady could see that Caroline was growing impatient but he needed the answers to both questions before he could proceed. "Of course there's a reason," he snapped, annoyed with his lack of finesse when it came to romance. "I don't want to end up looking ridiculous, thanks to Richard."

"What's Richard got to do with anything?" Caroline demanded.

"If he's been here first, just say so and I'll be on my way." The thought of Richard and Caroline together did funny things to his stomach. He'd never been a jealous man; it was an unfamiliar—and unpleasant—sensation. But he wasn't about to let Richard walk all over him.

"It seems to me, Grady, that you don't need Richard in order to look ridiculous. You do a damn good job all by yourself!"

Her words took him by surprise. He exhaled, counting to ten, in an effort to calm his racing heart, then leaned against the porch railing and faced her. "All I want to know is if Richard already asked you to the church dinner."

Her eyes briefly widened when she understood the reason for his unexpected visit. Caroline smiled slowly and sweetly. It was a smile he'd seen all too rarely from her. He found it difficult to look away.

"Why do you want to know?" she asked.

"I told you already," he blurted out. "If Richard's already asked you, then I'll save my breath."

"What if I said he hasn't asked me? Does that mean you will?"

His pride was a fierce thing and had gotten him into trouble with her in the past. He tucked his hands in his back pockets, shrugging as if it was of little concern. "I might."

Caroline set the swing in motion and relaxed enough to cross her legs. She was wearing shorts, and the movement granted him the opportunity to admire those legs.

"Let me put it like this," Caroline said after a moment. "If Richard *had* asked me, and I'm not saying he has, I'd turn him down."

"You would?" This gave Grady second thoughts. If she'd turn down his brother, there was nothing to say she wouldn't do the same with him. "What about me?" he asked before considering the question.

"But you haven't asked me," she reminded him.

If she was leading him on a merry chase, he swore he'd never forgive her. "Will you . . . would you and Maggie be my date for the church dinner Saturday night?"

The joy that lit her eyes was all the answer Grady needed. His heart felt as if it might fly straight out of his chest.

"We'd love to go with you," Caroline answered without hesitation.

"That'd be great. Great!" He started to leave, but caught the toe of his boot on a toy Maggie had left on the porch and damn near fell on his face. Not that it would have mattered. He was too damn happy to let a minor humiliation detract from his pleasure.

He was halfway to his truck when Caroline stopped him. "Do you want me to meet you at the church?" she called out.

"No." What kind of date did she think this was, anyway? "I'll pick you both up." Just so there was no room for misunderstanding, he added, "This is a date, Caroline."

"Any particular time?"

Details. Leave it to a woman to be concerned about something like that. "When do you want me?"

"Six-forty-five sounds about right."

"Then that's when I'll be here."

She walked to the porch steps and wrapped her arm around the white column. "I'll look forward to seeing you Saturday."

It would have been the most natural thing in the world to jump up and shout, he was that happy. Happy enough to feel almost drunk with it. Damn it all, he hadn't even kissed Caroline yet. If he got giddy from a little thing like this, he could only begin to imagine what it would be like the first time they made love.

REVEREND WADE MCMILLEN liked nothing better than social gatherings at the church, and this one was special, celebrating the one hundred and twentieth anniversary of the date Promise Christian Church had been established. He'd been ministering to this small but growing flock for five years now. It was his first assignment, and friends in the ministry had told him there was something special about a minister's first church. This had certainly proved to be the case with Wade. The parishioners who crowded the church hall were as much his family as the people he'd left behind.

Raised in Houston, Wade had been around cattle ranchers and oil men from the time he was old enough to pull on a pair of cowboy boots. No one was more surprised when he was called to the ministry than Wade himself. His experience in Promise had shown him that he loved his work more than any other occupation he might have chosen.

Long tables at the far end of the hall were heaped with a variety of some of the best home cooking in Texas. Main courses, salads, desserts. Once the food had been readied, Wade led the assembled families in grace, then stayed out of the way while the women's group got the buffet lines going. His role in all this was to make sure dinner went smoothly and everyone had what he or she needed.

"In my opinion," Louise Powell said, pulling Wade aside, "Savannah Smith's teriyaki salad with *chicken* should be considered a main course and not a salad. It's misleading for those of us who're watching our weight to be tempted with salads that under normal circumstances would be considered a main course."

Louise and her friend Tammy Lee Kollenborn had been a trial to Wade from the start, but he wasn't alone in his struggles with these two women. Heaven help him if he inadvertently crossed either of them.

"I'm afraid I'm the one to blame for that," Wade explained, attempting to sound apologetic. "Savannah put it on the table with the main courses, and I suggested that since it was technically a salad, it belonged there."

"I see," Louise said, and tightly pinched her lips together, letting him know she disapproved.

"I'll make sure I don't make that mistake again," he said. "Perhaps next year you'd volunteer to help the women's group set up the hall. I'm sure they'd appreciate your advice on such important matters as what should and shouldn't be considered a salad."

"I'll do that," she said with a tinge of self-righteousness. She patted his hand and excused herself to return to her husband.

The buffet line had dwindled down to only a few stragglers, and rather than become embroiled in any more culinary controversies, Wade reached for a plate and a set of silverware, then stepped to the end of the line.

He scanned the group, looking for an empty seat. The circular tables seated eight, perfect for accommodating four couples. The Royal Heirs, the seniors' social group, occupied four of those tables. No space there.

Ellie Frasier and Glen Patterson sat in a corner of the large bustling hall with their friends. There were a few empty spaces, but their table would fill up soon. He enjoyed Ellie and Glen and was counseling them before their wedding. They'd been in for three sessions now, and he had a strong feeling they were well suited. Their marriage would be a good one, built on a foundation of friendship.

Savannah and Laredo Smith were sitting next to Ellie and Glen. Now, there were two he'd never suspected would be right for each other. Savannah was a gentle soul, a special woman who'd touched his heart. Laredo had drifted into town; somehow he and Savannah had been drawn together. Love had changed them both, Savannah especially. Looking at them now, just a short time after their wedding, it was difficult to remember that they'd been together only months rather than years.

Frank Hennessey, the town sheriff, got in line behind Wade. "This is a great spread, isn't it, Rev?"

"As I've said more than once," Wade reminded the other man, "Promise Christian has some of the best cooks in the state of Texas."

"Amen to that." Frank handed Dovie Boyd a plate before reaching for one himself. Both close to retirement age, the two had been seeing each other for as long as Wade had served the community, but apparently didn't have plans to marry. Wade had never questioned them about their relationship. That was their business, not his. He was fond of Frank and

Dovie. He found their company delightful and was happy to let Dovie spoil him with a home-cooked meal every now and then. The woman was a wonder with apple pie.

One of Nell Bishop's children raced across the room, and Wade's spirits lifted. He'd sit with Nell, he decided. The widow might feel like odd man out, being there without a date, and since he was alone himself, well, it would work nicely. Nell was a safe dinner companion; everyone knew she wasn't interested in remarriage. If Wade chose to dine with one of the single ladies, some women in the congregation, Louise Powell and Tammy Lee Kollenborn in particular, were sure to read it as a sign of incipient romance.

So Nell was the perfect choice. No pressures there. Not only that, he had a great deal of respect and affection for her family. He'd enjoy spending the evening with them.

But Nell was sitting with her mother-in-law and their table was full.

Wade had to admit he felt lonely. Everyone present seemed to be part of a couple, and those who were single had found partners. Even Grady Weston had a date, and frankly, Wade was pleased with his choice. He'd long admired Caroline Daniels; she and Grady seemed right together, a thought that had occurred to him more than once since Savannah's wedding.

Not until Wade was at the end of the dessert table did he spot the ideal location. He smiled, amused that the vacant seat was at the very table he'd considered moments earlier. The empty spot was next to Cal Patterson. Wade got along just fine with the rancher, although the man had a reputation for being prickly. Cal sat with his brother Glen, but Glen wasn't paying him any heed. The younger Patterson's concentration was held by Ellie, and rightly so.

"Mind if I join you?" Wade asked Cal.

"Mind?" Cal muttered, sliding his chair over to give Wade ample room. "I'd be grateful."

"This is a great way to celebrate the church's birthday, isn't it?" Wade asked, digging into his food with gusto. He never ate better than at church dinners.

"Growing up, I can remember looking forward to the third Saturday in July," Cal said. "My mom made her special baked beans every year. Still does. Apparently the recipe's been handed down from one generation to the next for at least a hundred years. If I remember right, it originally came from back East."

Wade took a forkful of the baked beans and nodded approvingly.

"Mmm." He chewed slowly, savoring every morsel. "There's a lot to be said for tradition, especially when it tastes this good."

"She only bakes 'em once a year and it's always for the church." Having cleaned his own plate, Cal pushed back his chair and folded his arms. Wade's gaze followed Cal's. Grady and Caroline stood in the dessert line with Savannah and Laredo. The four were engaged in conversation and appeared to be enjoying themselves.

"Grady and Caroline make a handsome couple, don't they?" Wade asked, testing the waters with the older Patterson brother. This couldn't be easy on him, especially after Cal's own unfortunate experience a few years earlier. His wedding had been canceled just two days before the ceremony. Cal had taken the brunt of the embarrassment when his fiancée abruptly left town.

Wade and Cal had shared some serious discussions afterward and bonded as friends. But Cal hadn't mentioned Jennifer's name, not in all the time since. The subject of marriage appeared to be taboo, as well. More than once Wade had been tempted to remind Cal not to judge all women by Jennifer's actions. It might be a cliché, but time really was a great healer. When Cal was ready, Wade believed he'd date again.

"It's about time Grady opened his eyes," Cal said, grinning.

"About Caroline?"

"Yeah. Those two have been circling each other for a year, maybe more. If one of 'em didn't make a move soon, I was going to rope 'em together myself."

Wade chuckled, enjoying the image.

"Seems that every time Grady gets close to making a move, something happens and he takes off like a jackrabbit."

Little Maggie Daniels raced past at that moment, and Wade caught her about the waist to keep her from colliding with Nell Bishop's son. "Whoa there," he said, laughing. "What's the big hurry?"

Maggie covered her mouth and giggled. "Petey was chasing me."

"Be careful, understand?"

Maggie bobbed her head, and Wade pointed to the corsage on her wrist. "Who gave you flowers?"

"Grady," Maggie answered with such pride her entire face lit up. Her eyes fell to the pink and white carnations on her wrist. "He yells sometimes."

"Does it bother you?"

Maggie had to think about that a moment before she shrugged. "He bought Mommy flowers, too. She was surprised and so was I, and when Mommy asked him why, he said it was 'cause we're special."

"You are very special." Wade smiled.

Maggie's return smile revealed two missing front teeth. "Mommy likes him," she said, and Wade had the feeling that she'd decided perhaps Grady wasn't such a bad guy, after all.

Petey Bush approached. "Wanna hold hands?" the six-year-old boy asked.

Maggie looked to Wade for permission. "I think it'll be all right," he advised.

She nodded solemnly and the two children strolled off hand in hand.

"It's a sorry day when five- and six-year-olds have an easier time getting a date than we do, don't you think?" Cal asked him.

A sorry day indeed, Wade mused.

CAROLINE HAD a wonderful time at the dinner. A *perfectly* wonderful time, she reflected as they walked out to Grady's truck. Everything about the evening had been like a dream. Not once had she exchanged a cross word with Grady. Not once had they disagreed. Not once had he yelled at Maggie. There just might be hope for them.

Maggie, worn-out from the evening's activities, fell asleep between them in the truck. She slumped against Caroline, her head in her mother's lap. When Grady pulled up in front of the house, she was still asleep. It seemed a shame to disturb her.

Grady must have thought the same thing, because he turned off the engine and made no move to get out of the truck. The only light available was from a quarter moon set crookedly in the dark Texas sky.

Night settled about them. Neither one of them spoke. For her own part, Caroline wanted the evening to last as long as possible. If it never ended, that was fine with her.

"I had a lovely time," she finally whispered.

"Me, too."

She assumed he'd open the truck door then and was pleased when he didn't.

"It was sweet of you to bring Maggie and me flowers."

"It was the only way I could tell you how much—" He halted mid-sentence.

"How much . . . ?" she prodded.

"I like you both," he finished.

"Do you, Grady?" she asked, her voice low.

"Very much." He brought his hand to the side of her face, and Caroline closed her eyes, delighting in the feel of his callused palm against her cheek. Smiling to herself at how far they'd come, she leaned into his hand.

"Do you think it'd wake Maggie if I kissed you?" he asked, whispering.

Caroline didn't know, but she was prepared to risk it. "I'm game if you are."

Still Grady hesitated. "This is the first time Maggie's been willing to have anything to do with me. I don't want to ruin that."

"If you don't kiss me *now*, Grady, I swear I'll never forgive you!"

He laughed softly and without further delay took her face between his hands. Once again Caroline shut her eyes, just for a moment, treasuring these rare moments of intimacy.

Slowly Grady bent toward her and she angled her head to accommodate his movement. His mouth was so close to hers. So close she could feel his breath against her skin. So close she could sense his longing— and admit her own. Yet he hesitated, as did she.

Caroline realized—and she suspected that Grady did, too—that everything between them would be forever changed if they proceeded with this kiss. It was more than an ordinary kiss. It was a meeting of two hearts, an admission of vulnerability and openness.

Caroline wasn't sure who moved first, but chose to think of what followed as a mutual decision. An inexorable drawing together.

The kiss was gentle, almost tentative. His hand drifted to the back of her neck, urging her forward.

Grady kissed her again, and this time his mouth was more demanding, more insistent. Within only a few seconds, Caroline felt as though she'd experienced every possible emotion. When he released her, his breath was ragged.

"I'm sorry, I—"

Rather than let him ruin everything with an apology, she kissed the corner of his mouth.

Maggie stirred and they both froze. Caroline prayed her daughter wouldn't awake, wouldn't unconsciously end these precious moments with Grady.

"Is she asleep?" he asked, speaking so quietly she had to strain to hear. His voice was more breath than sound.

"Yes . . ."

They waited breathlessly. When it seemed he wasn't going to kiss her again, Caroline took the initiative and leaned toward him. The strength of their attraction stunned her. It was as though they couldn't get close enough. Their mouths twisted and strained in a passionate desperate kiss, but that lasted only a moment.

Then sanity returned. Reluctantly they eased away from each other. Grady rested his shoulders against the seat cushion, tilted back his head and sighed deeply.

Caroline swallowed. "I'd better get Maggie inside," she whispered.

"Right." When he opened his door, the light blinded Caroline and she was grateful when he immediately closed it, making the least noise possible.

Coming around to her side, he opened the door, helped her out and then reached for Maggie, carrying her toward the house. Caroline had expected to carry Maggie herself. She'd always done so; she was accustomed to it. Grady's action brought to life a complexity of feelings—gratitude, relief, even a slight sense of loss.

"You get the door," Grady said.

Caroline unlocked the door. With only a night-light to guide them, she led him to Maggie's bedroom at the rear of the house. She folded back the covers on the bed and Grady carefully set the little girl down. Caroline removed her daughter's shoes and put them aside.

Grady smoothed the hair from Maggie's brow, touched his fingertips to his lips and pressed his hand to the little girl's brow. The gesture was so loving, so *fatherly,* that Caroline had to turn away.

Grady followed her into the darkened hallway. She continued to the front door. She didn't want him to leave but dared not ask him to stay.

"Thank you again," she whispered. "For everything." The front door remained open and light spilled in from the porch.

Grady didn't move.

Slowly she raised her eyes to his. The invitation was there, and it was simply beyond her to refuse him. He held his arms open. Less than four steps separated them, but she literally ran into his embrace. He caught her about the waist, and she wrapped her arms around his neck. They kissed again with an urgency that left her weak, an urgency that drained her of all thoughts save one—the unexpected wonder and joy she'd discovered in his arms.

Until that night, Caroline hadn't realized how lonely she'd been, how long the nights could be. In Grady's arms she felt whole and needed and beautiful.

When the kiss ended, she buried her face in his neck.

"I could hold you forever," he whispered.

"I could let you." She felt his smile.

"Don't tempt me more than I already am," he warned.

It was heaven knowing he found her attractive. He held her close while she struggled to regain her composure. Caroline was grateful for those few quiet moments before he slowly released her.

He placed his hands lightly on her shoulders. "I want to see you again."

"Yes." It didn't matter when or where.

"Soon."

She was almost giddy with the wonder of what was happening. "Please."

He smiled, and as though he couldn't help himself, he kissed her again. Their kissing only seemed to get better and better. "Why did it take you so long?" she asked when she'd recovered enough to speak.

"Because I'm a pigheaded fool."

"I am, too." No need denying it. She was as much at fault as Grady.

"No more."

"No more," she echoed.

"Tomorrow," he suggested. "I can't wait any longer than that to see you again."

"Okay. When? Where?"

"Can you come out to the ranch?"

"Yes, of course. I'll come after church."

"Wonderful," he whispered, and kissed the tip of her nose. "Perfect."

She slipped her arms around his middle. "Oh, Grady, is this really happening or am I dreaming?"

"Nothing gets more real than the way you make me feel."

She smiled. Never would she have believed that Grady Weston was a romantic.

"About Maggie . . ."

He stiffened, and she stopped him by pressing her index finger against his lips. "Don't worry about her. Everything will work out."

"I don't mean to frighten her."

"I know."

"Did she like the flowers?"

Caroline kissed the underside of his jaw. "Very much."

"Did you?"

"More than I can say." She trailed kisses toward his ear and reveled in the way his body shuddered against hers when she tugged on his earlobe with her teeth.

"Caroline," he breathed. "You're making this impossible."

"Do I really tempt you?"

"Yes." His voice was low but harsh. "You don't have a clue."

Actually she did. "Kiss me one more time and then you can leave."

He hesitated, then gently captured her face between his hands and angled his mouth toward hers. The kiss, while one of need, was also one of elation, of shared joy. All this time they'd wasted, all the time they'd let pride and fear and doubt stand between them.

Caroline needed him and he needed her. Savannah, a woman with real insight into people, had tried to tell her that. And Caroline knew she'd tried to convince Grady, too. She was aware of Savannah's matchmaking efforts because her friend had told her; she was also aware that Savannah had been frustrated by one setback after another.

Caroline supposed she was as responsible for those setbacks as Grady. She'd always been attracted to him, but felt confused, unprepared. She'd been hurt terribly once and with that pain had come fear. For years she'd been afraid to love again. To trust again.

Deep within her, she recognized that Grady would never abandon her. Not Grady. He was as solid as a rock.

His final kiss was deep and long.

It took a moment for Maggie's voice to break through the fog of her desire.

"Mommy! Mommy!"

Grady groaned and reluctantly let Caroline go.

She turned to find Maggie standing in the dim light, rubbing the sleep from her eyes. "What is it, sweetheart?"

Maggie ignored the question and, instead, glared at Grady. "What are you doing to my mommy?" she demanded.

Four

Sunday morning was the one day of the week Jane Dickinson—*Dr.* Jane Dickinson, she reminded herself—could sleep in. Yet it was barely six and she was wide awake. Tossing aside the sheet, she threw on her robe and wandered barefoot into the kitchen.

"Texas," she muttered. Who would've believed when she signed up for this that she'd end up in the great state of Texas? The Hill Country was about as far as anyone could get from the bustling activity of Los Angeles.

Jane had *tried* to make a go of life in small-town America, but she was completely and utterly miserable. In three months she hadn't managed to make a single friend. Sure, there were lots of acquaintances, but no real friends. Never in her life had she missed her friends and family more, and all because of money. She'd entered into this agreement with the federal government in order to reduce her debts—three years in Promise, Texas, and her medical-school loans would be paid off.

Maybe she should just admit she'd made a mistake, pack her bags and hightail it out of this godforsaken town. But even as the thought entered her mind, Jane realized that wasn't what she wanted. What she wanted was to find some way to connect with these people, to become part of this tight-knit community.

The residents of Promise seemed willing enough to acknowledge that she was a competent physician specializing in family practice. But they came to see her only when they absolutely had to—for prescription renewals, a bad cough or sprain that couldn't be treated at home. Jane's one major fault was that she wasn't Dr. Cummings. The man had retired in his seventies after serving the community for nearly fifty years. The people of Promise knew and trusted him. She, on the other hand, was considered an outsider, and worse, some kind of Valley Girl or frivolous surfer type.

Despite her up-to-the-moment expertise, she had yet to gain the community's confidence. Everything she'd done to prove herself to the people of Promise had been a miserable failure.

Rejection wasn't something Jane was accustomed to dealing with. It left her feeling frustrated and helpless. In medical school, whenever she felt overwhelmed and emotionally confused, she'd gone jogging. It had always helped clear her thoughts, helped her gain perspective. But she hadn't hit the streets even once since she'd come here. With a new sense of resolve, she began to search for her running shoes, reminding herself that *she* was the one who'd agreed to work in a small community. She was determined to stick it out, even if it killed her.

Dressed in bright yellow nylon running shorts and a matching tank top, she started out at an easy nine-minute-mile pace. She jogged from her living quarters next to the health clinic down the tree-lined streets of Promise. The community itself wasn't so bad. Actually it was a pretty little town with traditional values and interesting people. Ranchers mostly. Down-to-earth folk, hardworking, family-oriented. That was what made her situation so difficult to understand. The people were friendly and welcoming, it seemed, to everyone but her.

Jane turned the corner onto Maple Street. At the post office she took another turn and headed up Main. A couple of cars were parked in front of the bowling alley, which kept the longest hours in town; it was open twenty-four hours on Saturdays and Sundays. It wasn't the bowling that lured folks at all hours, but the café, which served good solid meals and great coffee at 1970s prices.

Jane's feet pounded the pavement and sweat rolled down the sides of her face. She'd barely gone a mile and already her body was suggesting that she hadn't been exercising enough. She knew she'd ache later but didn't care; she was already feeling more optimistic.

She rounded the corner off Main and onto Baxter, running past the antique store owned and operated by Dovie Boyd. Dovie lived in a brick home just around the corner. Despite the early hour, she was standing in the middle of her huge vegetable garden with her watering can in hand.

Jane had often admired the older woman's lush garden. The pole beans were six feet high, the tomatoes bursting with ripeness and the zucchini abundant. Jane marveled at how one woman could possibly coax this much produce from a few plants.

"Morning," Jane called.

Dovie smiled and raised her hand in response.

Jane continued down the street, full steam ahead. She'd gone perhaps twenty yards when she realized it'd happened to her again. She'd never been a quitter in her life and she wasn't going to start now. She did an abrupt about-face and headed back.

Dovie looked surprised to see her.

Jane stopped and, breathing heavily, leaned forward and braced her hands on her knees. "Hello again," she said when she'd caught her breath.

Without a pause Dovie continued watering. "Lovely morning, isn't it?"

"Beautiful," Jane agreed. Slowly she straightened and watched Dovie expertly weave her way through the garden, pausing now and again to finger a plant or pull a weed.

"Do you have a minute, Mrs. Boyd?" she asked, gathering her nerve. She rested her hands against the white picket fence.

Widening her eyes, Dovie turned. "What can I do for you, Dr. Dickinson?"

"First, I'd like it if you called me Jane."

"Then Jane it is."

The older woman's tone was friendly, but Jane sensed the same reserve in her she'd felt in others.

"What am I doing wrong?" She hadn't intended to blurt out the question like that, but couldn't help herself.

"Wrong?" Dovie set the watering can aside.

"What's wrong with *me*?" she amended.

"I don't think anything's wrong with you." The other woman was clearly puzzled by the question. "What makes you assume such a thing?"

Attitudes were so difficult to describe. How could she explain how she felt without sounding snobbish or self-pitying? But she had to try.

"Why am I standing on this side of the fence while you're on that side?" Jane asked as she paced the cement walkway. "Why do I have to be the one to greet others first? People don't like me, and I want to know why."

Dovie lifted one finger to her lips and frowned, apparently deep in thought. "You did greet me first, didn't you?"

"Yes, but it isn't only you. It's everyone." Jane paused, struggling with her composure. "I want to know why."

"My goodness, I'm not sure. I never realized." Dovie walked toward the short white gate and unlatched it, swinging it open. "Come inside, dear, and we'll sit down and reason this out."

Now that Jane had made her point, it would have been rude and unfair to refuse, but to her embarrassment she discovered she was close to tears.

"Sit down and make yourself comfortable," Dovie said, and gestured toward the white wrought-iron patio set. "I'll get a pot of tea brewing. I don't know about you, but I tend to think more clearly if I have something hot to drink."

"I . . . Thank you," Jane said, feeling humble and grateful at once. The few moments Dovie was in the kitchen gave her time to collect herself.

Soon Dovie reappeared carrying a tray with a pot of steaming tea and two delicate china cups, as well as a plate of scones. She set it down on the table and poured the tea, handing Jane the first cup.

Jane felt a bit conspicuous in her tank top, sipping tea from a Spode cup, but she was too thankful for Dovie's kindness to worry about it.

"All right now," Dovie said when she'd finished pouring. "Let's talk." She sat down and leaned back in her chair, pursing her lips. "Tell me some other things that have bothered you about Promise."

Jane wasn't sure where to start. "I have this . . . this sense that people don't like me."

"Nonsense," Dovie countered. "We don't know you well enough to like or dislike you."

"You're right. No one knows me," Jane murmured. "I need a friend," she said with a shrug, offering the one solution that had come to her.

"We all need friends, but perhaps you need to make more of an effort to give people a chance to know you."

"But I *have* tried to meet people," she said in her own defense.

Dovie frowned. "Give me an example."

Jane had a list of those. An inventory of failures cataloged from the day she'd first arrived. "The party for Richard Weston," she said. It was the first social event she'd attended in the area. Richard had been warm and friendly, stopping her on the street and issuing a personal invitation. Jane had been excited about it, had even told her family she was attending the party. But when she got there, she'd ended up standing around by herself. The evening had been uncomfortable from the start.

As the new doctor in town Jane appeared to be a topic of speculation and curiosity. The short newspaper article published about her earlier in the week had added to the attention she'd garnered. People stared at her, a few had greeted her, asked her a question or two, then drifted away. Richard had been the star of his own party, and the one time he'd noticed her, she was sure he'd forgotten who she was. For a while she'd wandered around, feeling awkward and out of place. Mostly she'd felt like a party crasher and left soon after she'd arrived.

"You *were* there, weren't you?" Dovie murmured with a thoughtful look.

"Yes." Not that it'd done Jane any good.

"You came in a suit and high heels, as I recall," Dovie added.

"I realized as soon as I arrived the suit was a mistake," Jane said. At the time she'd felt it was important to maintain a professional image. She was new in town and attempting to make a good impression.

"And then jeans and a cotton top to the Grange dance."

"I didn't realize it was a more formal affair." She hadn't lasted long there, either. "I wasn't sure what to wear," Jane confessed. She'd come overdressed for one event and underdressed for the other. "But," she said hopelessly, "I had no way of knowing."

Dovie nodded, silently encouraging her to continue.

"I showed up for the Willie Nelson Fourth of July picnic, too, but no one bothered to tell me Willie Nelson wouldn't be there." That had been a major disappointment, as well.

Dovie giggled and shook her head. "The town council's invited him nine years running, and he's politely declined every year, but we've never let a little thing like that stand in our way. This is Willie Nelson country!"

"Someone might have said something." Jane didn't take kindly to being the only one not in on the joke.

"That's something you can only learn by living here. Next year, you'll know."

If I'm here that long, Jane thought.

"Another thing," she said. "What's all this about a ghost town?" Jane asked next.

Dovie's expressive eyes narrowed. "Who told you there was a ghost town?"

Jane wondered at the swift change in her newfound friend. "I overheard two children talking. One of them mentioned it."

"Don't pay any attention to those rumors, understand?"

"Is there one?"

"That's neither here nor there," Dovie said, but not unkindly. "We have other more important matters to discuss."

"Such as?"

Dovie's head came back. "You." Her face was set, her voice firm. "You're right, you do need a friend."

"Are you volunteering to take me under your wing?" Jane asked, and hoped Dovie understood how very grateful she'd be.

"I'm too old." Dovie's response was fast. "I'm thinking of someone more your age." She tapped her index finger against her chin. "You and Ellie Frasier would get along like gangbusters. Unfortunately Ellie's busy getting ready for her wedding just now, so you'll need to be patient."

"Oh." Jane's voice was small.

"Until then, you and I have our work cut out for us."

Jane frowned, not sure she understood. "What work?"

Dovie's expression told Jane she'd overlooked the obvious. "We need to find out what's wrong with everyone in this town. I've decided there's nothing wrong with *you,* Dr. Jane. It's everyone else, and I'm determined to find out what."

"ALL THE COMFORTS of home," Richard Weston said out loud. He stood in the middle of the dirt road that ran through the ghost town. "Bitter End, Texas," he continued, "population one." He laughed then, the sound echoing down the long dusty street littered with sagebrush and rock.

Hitching his thumbs in the waistband of his jeans, he sauntered down the dirt road as if he owned it, and for all intents and purposes, he did.

For the time being Bitter End was his home. He was proud of the good job he'd done carving out a comfortable place for himself. He figured he'd be stuck here for a while. How long wasn't clear yet. A man on the run didn't have a lot of alternatives.

Everything was about to catch up with him. His brother already knew he hadn't paid that old coot Max Jordan, and he wasn't going to be able to hide all the other charges he'd made, either. Although Grady's business account had sure come in handy. But he'd stretched his luck to the max in Promise.

Time to move on. Hide again, only no one would ever think to look for him here. He was as safe as a babe cuddled in his mother's loving arms. Richard had a sixth sense about when to walk away. He'd come to trust his instincts; they were what had kept him out of prison this long.

Richard kicked the toe of his snakeskin boot into the hard dry ground. He'd arrived in Promise penniless, miserable and afraid to glance over his shoulder for fear the law—or worse—was hot on his tail. He'd decided to head back to Promise on the spur of the moment, when he awoke one morning and found himself outside El Paso without money or transportation. Hitchhiking, he made his way to the central part of the state.

Luck had blessed him all his life. He hadn't been back long before he discovered Savannah had visited Bitter End. As soon as his older sister mentioned the ghost town, he'd known what to do.

Little by little Richard had managed to squirrel away supplies, making the trek so often he no longer lost his way. Each day he managed to take something from the ranch or buy supplies on ranch credit. In the beginning it was little things, items not easily missed. Seldom-used equipment no one would notice was gone. Gradually he'd worked in the larger pricier necessities. He'd been clever about it, too.

Still congratulating himself, Richard walked up the old wooden steps to the boardwalk. He sat down in the rocking chair he'd discovered in one of the buildings and surveyed the town. His domain.

He'd been born under a lucky star, Richard told himself, and its shine hadn't faded. He marveled anew at the crafty way he'd charged much of what he needed. Grady didn't have a clue, either. Richard would charge something nonsensical like tractor parts to Grady's account, knowing no one would think to question that. Later, making sure it wasn't the same salesclerk, he'd return the part and use the credit to purchase what he really needed. In the weeks since his return he'd accumulated all the comforts of home, and the best part was that it had been at his brother's expense.

"Oh, yes, I'm going to be real comfortable now," he said, grinning broadly. Tucking his hands behind his head, he leaned back. "Thanks, Grady," he said with a snicker.

Slowly his smile faded. None of this hiding out would be necessary if the situation with Ellie Frasier had worked out differently. It would have been easy to let that sweet young thing soothe away his worries, but his hopes had died a humiliating death, thanks to Glen Patterson.

Why any woman would choose some cowboy over him was beyond Richard. Clearly Ellie had no taste. In the beginning he'd been drawn to the inheritance her daddy had left her, figuring he'd talk her into marrying him, get his hands on the money and then skip town.

As time progressed and he came to know Ellie, he'd actually found himself thinking about sticking around and making a go of life in Promise. Money in the right places would put an end to his current troubles. For a while he'd toyed with the idea of getting involved in local politics. Promise could use a mayor like him, not some hick but a man with an eye to the future. Then maybe for once he'd be able to stay out of trouble, make a new life for himself. Start over. But unfortunately it hadn't panned out.

Standing, Richard glanced at his watch. He hadn't moved here yet, so he had to be conscious of the time. Although his sister and brother hadn't said much, they were aware of his absences, and he didn't want to arouse their suspicions.

Richard headed to where he'd parked the pickup. After several failed attempts, he'd found a new way into the town, one that didn't necessitate a long walk.

The wind whistled behind him, a low plaintive cry that sent shivers down his spine.

"Oh, no, you don't," he said. Naturally there'd been talk about ghosts in Bitter End. The one time he'd brought Ellie with him, she'd been squirming out of her skin in her eagerness to leave. She claimed it was a feeling she had, a sense of oppression. His sister had said she, too, could feel something weird in the old town.

Yeah, right.

Not Richard, at least not until that very moment. The wind increased in velocity, whistling as he walked away, his back to the main street.

"I don't hear anything, I don't feel anything," he said aloud, more in an effort to hear the words than to convince himself.

The sensation, or whatever the hell it was, didn't dissipate until he was safe inside his brother's dilapidated truck. With the doors locked Richard relaxed, suspecting he'd viewed one too many episodes of "Tales from the Crypt."

As he drove off, another thought entered his mind.

Caroline Daniels.

He had no real interest in her himself, but he could have her and he knew it. His brother was sweet on Caroline; that was easy to guess, just from the way Grady looked at her. It might be rotten of him, Richard thought with a grin, but he sure did love to play the spoilsport.

His brother had as much charisma as an overripe tomato, yet Grady was the one sitting pretty on a prosperous ranch, living high, while Richard had to worry about where his next meal was coming from. Some things in life just weren't fair, and if he wanted to even them out a little, he could see no harm in it. Besides, he subscribed to the idea that, regardless of the star he was born under, a man made his own luck. Or, at least, enhanced it.

"You don't know how good you've got it, big brother," Richard said. It shouldn't be hard to lure Caroline away from Grady—and it didn't hurt any that her kid was crazy about him. Kids had always liked him, and Richard had encouraged them. For some reason a lot of people put stock in their kids' opinions and preferences. As far as he was concerned, it didn't matter a damn what some kid thought, although he didn't mind using a child to manipulate the parent.

Maggie was a great example. She preferred him over Grady, which made him the leading man when it came to winning her mother's affections. He found Caroline kind of irritating, though; he didn't care for the way she looked at him.

What he enjoyed most of all was playing himself off against his brother. He loved it when he could frustrate Grady, but his older brother made it much too easy; he took all the fun out of it. Well, not *all* the fun. Poor old Grady—would he never learn? Richard smirked. When he was around, Grady didn't stand a chance with the ladies.

GRADY FELT LIKE A KID waiting for prom night—a kid who had a date with the prom queen. The chance to see Caroline again was worth cutting short his sleep. It meant getting up earlier than usual to deal with morning chores. But he'd managed, surprising Wade as much as he did Savannah and Laredo when he slipped into the pew two minutes before services were due to start.

He hadn't come to hear the sermon, but he figured God would forgive that. He'd come for Caroline. She sang with the choir, and the possibility of seeing her again so soon after the church dinner was irresistible.

Grady still walked on air after last night's kisses. Even Maggie's interruption hadn't ruined the evening. He'd been at a loss for words when she'd stumbled upon Caroline and him with their arms locked around each other. Rather than try to explain, he'd left the matter in Caroline's capable hands and departed soon afterward.

The last thing she'd said before he walked out the door was that she'd stop by the ranch Sunday afternoon.

Mere hours away.

The service was upbeat, and Wade's message caused him to nod his head in agreement a number of times. The minister used humor and lots of anecdotes, which made for an interesting sermon. Before he realized it, the hour was over and the congregation dismissed with a benediction.

Pastor Wade McMillen stood in the doorway as people left. "Good to see you, Grady," he said, giving Grady's hand a hearty shake. "But somehow I don't think it was my sermon that interested you."

Grady grumbled some noncommittal reply. Damned little escaped Wade's attention. As if to prove him right, Wade caught Jeremy Bishop by the shoulder, stopping him on his way out the door.

"That must have been an interesting book you were reading in church," he said with an encouraging smile.

Jeremy squirmed uncomfortably before he reached inside his shirt. With obvious reluctance he withdrew a slim paperback novel.

"T. R. Grant?" Wade said, and cocked one eyebrow at the title.

Jeremy's eyes grew round. "You've never heard of T. R. Grant?"

"Can't say I have," Wade admitted.

"He's great!"

Wade chuckled. "I'm sure he is. Maybe I should read him, too."

"I've read everything he's ever written. I can lend you one of his books if you want."

"I'll take you up on that offer." Wade ruffled the boy's hair and returned his attention to Grady. "I see that things are developing nicely between you and Caroline Daniels."

Grady tensed. He had no desire to discuss his private life.

As if he knew that, too, Wade slapped him lightly on the back. "It took you long enough," he said with a laugh. Before Grady could respond, Wade had begun talking to someone else.

Grady met Caroline on the front lawn. He saw her speak to Wade, then glance at him, smiling shyly. The yard was crowded with people visiting and chatting, but everyone appeared to fade from sight as Caroline approached.

"Hello again," he said, which was probably the stupidest thing he'd ever uttered. Not that he cared.

"Hello." Her voice had a deep breathless quality.

"Were you able to reassure Maggie?" He'd felt bad about leaving her to make the explanations, but feared any effort on his part wouldn't have come out right.

"She understands."

"But does she approve?"

Caroline's eyes avoided his, which was answer enough in itself. "It isn't up to Maggie to approve or disapprove of whom I kiss."

He exhaled slowly and would have said more except that he couldn't stop looking at Caroline. She was so damn pretty, any coherent thought didn't stand a chance of lasting more than a second or two. It was her eyes, he concluded, a deep rich shade of chocolate. No, he decided after a moment, it was her soft brown hair. He remembered the silky feel of it bunched in his hands when he'd kissed her. He remembered a whole lot more than the feel of her hair. . . .

"So you're coming to see Savannah this afternoon?" he asked, trying to redirect his thoughts. If he continued in this vein much longer, he'd end up kissing her right then and there just to prove how real last night had been.

"No."

Grady's disappointment was sharp. "You're not? But I thought—"

"I'm coming to see you."

His heart, which had gone sluggish with discouragement, sped up, and he could feel his pulse hammering in his neck.

"Hi, Grady," Maggie said, joining her mother. She clung to her mother's arm and looked up at him with a slight frown.

"Hi, Maggie. I hear you're coming out to the ranch this afternoon."

The child continued to stare at him, and although she made no comment, Grady saw the way she moved protectively close to her mother.

"Did Savannah tell you about the new colt we have?"

She nodded.

"He's only a few days old, but he's already handsome. I bet you'd like to see him."

Again she nodded.

Grady glanced at Caroline. "Do you think Maggie's old enough to visit the colt?"

"I can, can't I, Mommy?" Maggie twisted around and gazed up at her mother with imploring eyes.

"I think it should be all right, as long as you stay with Grady."

"I will, I will," she promised.

"That new colt needs a name," Grady added. "Maybe you could help us decide what to call him."

Her eyes got huge. "Could I really?"

"If you can think of a decent name for such a handsome boy. We'll let you take a gander at him first, pet him a few times and then give you the opportunity to think up a name."

"That's kind of you, Grady," Caroline said.

They walked toward the parking lot, in no particular hurry. "What time will you be by, do you think?" he asked, restraining himself from suggesting she should come right that minute.

"Maggie needs lunch and a nap first."

"She can eat with us—you both could—and then Maggie could nap. Savannah'll be more than happy to watch her." After she finished wringing his neck for inviting company without consulting her first. "While Maggie's resting, perhaps you and I could . . ." For the life of him, he couldn't think of a single respectable thing for the two of them to do.

"Go riding," Caroline inserted. "I'll borrow some jeans from Savannah."

She could have suggested mud wrestling and he would've agreed.

"Well . . . I suppose we can alter our plans just a little," Caroline said, smiling softly.

It took a moment for the words to sink into his consciousness. "You could? Great."

"Are we going to Savannah's?" Maggie asked, tugging at the sleeve of her mother's dress. "Are we leaving now?"

"It looks that way," Caroline answered.

Maggie clapped her hands, celebrating the good news.

"I'll see you there, then," she said to Grady, opening the passenger door for Maggie. Her daughter leaped inside, eager to be on their way.

Grady opened the driver's side for Maggie. "Drive carefully."

She got in and assured him she would.

Grady stepped away from the car when she started the engine; he watched her back out of the parking space and turn out of the driveway before he realized that he'd attracted a number of curious stares. In particular, he noticed Edwina and Lily Moorhouse studying him.

The two sisters were retired teachers, as prim and proper as the spinster schoolmarms of nineteenth-century Promise. They smiled approvingly in his direction before they leaned toward one another, heads close enough to touch, talking up a storm. He'd been in their classes as a boy and could well recall the speed with which those two could chatter. Two hundred words a minute, he guessed, with gusts up to four fifty.

Their tongues were wagging now, but frankly, Grady didn't care. He was about to spend the afternoon with the woman who'd dominated his thoughts for months. The woman who dominated his dreams.

Grady arrived back at the Yellow Rose less than five minutes behind Caroline. He found her in the kitchen with Savannah, preparing Sunday dinner. She paused when he entered, then glanced around her.

"Did you see Maggie?"

"Maggie?" He shook his head.

"She wasn't on the porch?"

"Not that I noticed." He stuck his head out the door and couldn't see her.

"I told her not to leave the porch." Caroline sighed with impatience. She set aside the tomato she was slicing and reached for a towel.

"She came to me for a carrot not more than a minute ago," Savannah said.

"She probably went into the barn to see the new colt." Grady blamed himself for that.

"She knows better," Caroline murmured. "It's not safe there."

"Don't worry, she's only been gone a minute," Savannah said reassuringly.

"I'll get her," Grady offered, eager to prove to Maggie that he could be as charming and wonderful as Richard.

"Are you sure you don't mind?" Caroline asked.

"Not in the least." Grady headed toward the barn, whistling as he went. The interior was dark after the bright sunlight, and he squinted until his eyes adjusted to the change in lighting.

"Maggie," he called out.

No answer.

"Maggie," he called again.

A soft almost mewing sound followed. Grady whirled around. The noise came from Widowmaker's stall. When he looked inside, Grady's heart froze. Maggie was huddled against the wall, her face white with terror.

Just then, the ill-tempered stallion thrashed out with his hooves, narrowly missing the child.

Five

Grady knew that he had to make his move fast or Maggie could be seriously hurt. Widowmaker snorted and began to paw the floor. Unwilling to give the stallion an opportunity to get any closer to the child, Grady threw open the stall door, grabbed Maggie and literally swung her out of harm's way.

Maggie let out a scream. With his heart pounding, Grady firmly held the squirming child against him, trying to comfort her and at the same time calm his own fears. Unfortunately he failed on both counts.

The barn door flew open and Savannah and Caroline rushed breathlessly inside.

"Mommy! Mommy!"

Grady released Maggie, who raced toward her mother, nearly stumbling in her eagerness to escape his clutches. Caroline held her arms open and the child sobbed hysterically as she fell into her mother's embrace.

"What happened?" Savannah asked.

"Somehow Maggie got into Widowmaker's stall," Grady explained. His knees shook so badly he sank onto a bale of hay.

"Dear God," Savannah whispered, and lowered herself onto the bale beside him. "Is she hurt?"

Grady didn't think so.

Caroline's eyes were filled with questions, but it was impossible to talk over the sound of Maggie's crying.

"What about you?" Savannah asked. "You didn't get kicked, did you?"

"I'm fine." Which wasn't entirely true. Grady figured just seeing Maggie in that stall cost him five years of his life. God only knew what would have happened if he hadn't gotten there when he had. The thought wasn't one he wished to entertain.

Gathering the child in her arms, Caroline made her way out of the barn. Savannah and Grady followed. His sister returned to the house, but Grady lingered outside, not knowing how to help although he wanted to do *something*. He waited for a clue from Caroline, who sat on one of the porch steps as she cradled her daughter. Maggie continued to sob almost uncontrollably, hiding her face in her mother's shoulder. Caroline stopped whispering to the child and started to sing in a low soothing voice gently swaying back and forth.

Grady pulled out the rocking chair and Caroline's eyes revealed her gratitude as she sat down in it. When the song was finished, she talked softly to Maggie, reassuring the little girl once more that everything was fine and there was nothing to be afraid of.

Grady paced the area in front of the porch, waiting, wondering what he should do next. If anything. Gradually Maggie quieted. Then she straightened and glanced around.

"Hello, princess," he said, remembering that was what his father had called Savannah. It seemed to suit Maggie. "Are you okay?"

Maggie took one look at him and burst into tears. Within seconds she'd buried her face in her mother's shoulder again.

"What'd I say?" he asked, unable to understand what he'd done now. He'd hoped the child would view him as her hero since he'd saved her from certain harm. Apparently that wasn't the case.

"She's embarrassed," Caroline explained.

"Embarrassed?" he shouted, forgetting how his booming voice terrified the little girl. Maggie burrowed deeper into her mother's embrace.

Savannah opened the screen door and stepped onto the porch. "Dinner's ready if anyone's interested," she announced.

Grady wasn't. His appetite was gone. Conflicting emotions churned in him—he felt angry and relieved, frustrated and pleased, confused and happy. He wanted to hug Maggie and thank God she was safe, and at the same time chastise her for giving him the fright of his life.

"I think it might be best if I took Maggie home," Caroline said.

"No." Grady's protest was instantaneous. "I mean, you need to do what you think is best but . . ." He didn't know what he wanted other than to spend time with her, but now it seemed that wasn't going to happen.

"I'll see if I can settle her down," Caroline offered. She held Maggie in her arms and continued to rock, humming softly.

Grady sat on the top step and marveled at her gentle manner with the child. The way she calmed Maggie helped quiet his own heart. No one seemed to realize it, but he'd suffered quite a jolt himself. Rocket sat next to him, his head nestled on Grady's lap. The old dog had belonged to his father, and in the years since his parents' deaths, Grady had spent many a late-night sitting quietly with Rocket. Talking a bit, mostly just thinking. The dog had often comforted him.

When he was sure he wouldn't disturb the child's slumber, Grady dragged the vacant rocker next to Caroline.

"Thank you," she whispered. Reaching out, she squeezed his hand. "I hate to think what could have happened if you hadn't arrived when you did. Maggie knows better. I'll have a talk with her later, but I don't think you need to worry about anything like this again. I don't believe I've ever seen her so frightened."

"I was terrified myself." He wasn't ashamed to admit it.

Caroline closed her eyes as though to shake the image of her daughter in the stallion's stall from her mind.

It was difficult for Grady not to stare at her.

"Go and have your dinner," she said a moment later. "I'm only going to stay a few more minutes."

"I'm not hungry," he said, wishing he could convince her to stay.

"I'm sorry, Grady, for everything."

He gestured with one hand, dismissing her apology.

"I was looking forward to riding with you this afternoon," she said.

He'd forgotten the ostensible reason for her visit. He shrugged as if it was no big thing. "We'll do it some other time."

She brushed the hair away from Maggie's sweet face. "I'd better go."

The screen door opened and Savannah poked her head out. "Do you want to put Maggie down on my bed?" she asked. "I'll watch her so you two can . . ." She didn't finish the statement, but Grady knew his sister. She'd been about to say, "so you two can have some time alone together."

Caroline shook her head. "Maggie's had a terrible fright and she's embarrassed because she knows she did wrong. I need to talk to her and it'd be best if I did that at home."

"I'll walk you to your car," Grady offered. He stuffed his hands in his back pockets as he stood up.

"I'm so sorry, Savannah," Caroline whispered.

"I'll see you again soon, won't I?"

"Of course."

Savannah and Grady walked down the porch steps with Caroline holding the sleeping Maggie. "Laredo and I are driving into Fredericksburg to talk to our builder next Wednesday. If everything goes according to plan, we'll be in our own home by October."

The house would be empty without Savannah, but Grady refused to think about it. At least her new home wouldn't be far from the ranch house, no more than a five-minute walk.

"The house plans are ready?"

Savannah looked inordinately proud. "Laredo and I finished going over everything Friday afternoon and gave our approval to the builder. You can't imagine how much time and effort went into that."

They reached the car, and Grady opened the passenger door so Caroline could set Maggie down. The child didn't so much as stir when Caroline placed the seat belt around her.

"Seeing as Laredo and I will be gone most of Wednesday, perhaps that would be a good day for you two to get together." Savannah made the suggestion casually, as though she often arranged her brother's schedule.

"Ah . . ." Grady was a little embarrassed by her obviousness.

"I can come over after work," Caroline said, smiling at him. "But I don't know if the sitter can keep Maggie."

"Bring her with you," Savannah said. "That'll give the three of you time together. It's important for Maggie to feel comfortable around Grady."

He was warming to the idea. "Perhaps we could all go riding," he said. "I've got a nice, gentle horse I'll put you and Maggie on." He thought it would be fun to show them the herd and stop at a few special spots along the way. He was proud of the Yellow Rose.

"That would be wonderful!" Caroline sounded enthusiastic; her voice and movements seemed animated, even excited.

"Then it's a date," Grady said.

"I'll see you soon." Savannah turned to leave, hurrying back to the house.

Grady and Caroline stood in the yard, and Maggie slept on contentedly as a cool breeze passed through the open door.

"I'd better get going," Caroline said.

Grady noticed the reluctance in her words, felt it himself.

"I'm glad we had a little time together, anyway."

"Me, too."

There was a moment's silence, then Caroline did something completely out of character, something that stunned him. Without warning, she stepped forward and kissed him.

Caught by surprise, Grady was slow to react. A second later he clasped her in his arms, so deeply involved in the kiss that he didn't care *who* saw them. Even Richard.

Neither one of them was able to breathe properly when the kiss ended.

Their balance seemed to be affected, too. Grady gripped her elbows and she held on to his waist.

Their eyes met and she smiled the softest, sweetest, sexiest smile he'd ever seen.

"What was that for?" he asked, his voice thick with passion.

"For saving Maggie."

"Oh." He cleared his throat. "I once saved a wounded falcon."

She kissed his cheek.

"It was hurt real bad."

Her lips inched closer to his.

"Richard broke his arm when he was eight and I carried him home. Will you reward me with a kiss for that, as well?"

"Grady!" she protested with a laugh. "Enough."

He loved the sound of her laughter. Because he wanted to hold her one last time, he scooped her into his arms and swung her around. Throwing back her head, she continued to laugh with such sheer joy it infected his very soul. They hugged for a long time afterward, content simply to be in each other's arms.

This was heaven, Grady told himself. Heaven in its purest form.

GLEN WAS AT FRASIER FEED early Tuesday evening just as he'd promised. Ellie'd had a long grueling day; not only was the store exceptionally busy, their wedding was less than a month away and there was an endless list of things that needed to be done.

"I'm glad you're on time," she said, smiling at him, loving him. She marveled again at how they'd both been so incredibly blind to their feelings. Obtuse was the word for the pair of them.

"Hey, when was I ever late?" Glen teased.

Ellie rolled her eyes and hung the Closed sign in the shop window. She started toward the office where she kept her purse, but hadn't gone far when Glen caught her hand and stopped her.

"Not so soon. Aren't you going to let me know how pleased you are to see me?"

"I see you every day," she reminded him.

"We aren't even married and already you're treating me like an old hat." He wore a woebegone look.

Laughing, Ellie locked her arms around his neck and gave him a kiss he wouldn't soon forget. Neither would she.

"Oh, baby," he whispered, his eyes closed. "How much longer until the wedding?"

"Less than a month." Her head buzzed with everything they still needed to do, to decide and plan. "Sometimes I wish we could just run away and get married."

"That idea appeals to me more and more," he murmured.

Ellie was tempted herself, but reason soon took over. "Your mother and mine would never forgive us."

"In that case, let's live in sin and give them something to really be upset about."

Despite herself, Ellie giggled. "You always make me laugh."

"I'm glad to know you find me a source of entertainment."

"Always," she joked, kissing him again, lightly this time.

He released her with a reluctance that warmed her heart. Ellie retrieved her purse from the office and tucked in her to-do list.

"When are we scheduled to meet with the Realtor?" Glen asked.

"Not until seven." Where they would live had been a major decision. If she moved out to the ranch with Glen and Cal, she'd be commuting to Promise each day. If Glen moved into town, then he'd be the one commuting. In the end they'd decided to buy a house in town. Glen would continue working with his brother for a number of years, but hoped someday to start his own spread. When the time came, they'd buy a ranch closer to town, but that was years in the future.

Glen checked his watch. "Do we have time for a quick bite to eat?"

"If you want."

He growled. "I'm starving."

"All right, cowboy, let's stop at the Chili Pepper for a quick sandwich."

Only a few months ago Ellie's life had been empty enough to swallow her whole. Her father had died, and then her mother had unexpectedly sold the family home and moved to Chicago. For the first time in her life Ellie had been utterly alone. That was when she realized how much she'd come to rely on her best friend—and eventually know how much she loved him.

They walked to the restaurant and managed to get a booth. Both were familiar enough with the menu not to need one. Ellie ordered the barbecue sandwich and a side of potato salad, and Glen chose a slab of the baby back ribs. He also asked for a pitcher of ice-cold beer.

"Dovie took me to lunch this afternoon," Ellie said when the beer arrived.

"Anything going on with her these days?"

"She wanted to know how the wedding plans were coming along, and . . ." Ellie hesitated.

"And?" he prodded, pouring them each a beer.

"Have you met Dr. Dickinson yet?"

"Doc Cumming's replacement? Not officially. Why?"

"Dovie asked if I'd, you know, take her under my wing."

"The doctor?" Glen set his mug down on the table.

"Apparently she's not adjusting to life in Promise."

Glen relaxed against the red vinyl upholstery. "How do you mean?"

"She doesn't fit in, and Dovie seems to think what she really needs is a friend, someone to introduce her to people, show her the ropes."

"Do you have time for this?" Glen asked, zeroing in on Ellie's own concern.

"Not just now."

"Don't think you're going to have a lot of spare time once we're married, either," he said with a twinkle in his eyes. "I plan on keeping you occupied myself."

"Oh, really?" Although she enjoyed bantering with him, Ellie could feel the heat rise in her cheeks.

"What that doctor really needs is something or someone to occupy her time."

"I suppose you're going to suggest a man," Ellie said.

"You got something against men?"

"Just a minute." Ellie put down her mug too quickly, then used her napkin to wipe up the spilled beer. "You just might be on to something here."

Glen frowned. "What do you mean?"

"Why don't we introduce the new doc to Cal?" An idea was beginning to take shape in her mind, and fast gaining momentum.

"My brother?" Glen sounded incredulous.

"Yes, your brother!" She snorted. "Do you know any other Cal?"

Glen stared at her as if seeing her for the first time. "You're not serious, are you?"

"Yes, I am. They're perfect for each other."

Glen slapped the side of his head, pretending there was something wrong with his hearing. "Let me get this straight. The woman I love, the very one who couldn't see the forest for the trees, is about to take on the role of matchmaker."

"It only makes sense."

"You haven't even *met* the woman."

"I most certainly have," Ellie protested.

"When?"

"The Cattlemen's Association dance," she informed him primly, neglecting to mention that it had been a ten-second conversation and they'd done nothing more than exchange first names.

"Okay, Ms. Romance Expert, explain to me why you think my brother should meet this Mary."

"Her name is Jane."

"Jane," he corrected. "What's so special about her?"

"I don't know," Ellie was forced to admit. "But I do know one thing. . . ."

"What's that?"

"Cal needs someone."

Their meal arrived and Glen reached for a blackened rib and dipped it in the pungent smoky barbecue sauce that was Adam Braunfels's speciality. "Does Cal know his life is lacking?" he asked.

"Not yet."

"Are you going to tell him, or are you volunteering me for the job?"

Glen appeared to find her idea highly entertaining, but she ignored his unwarranted amusement. "Neither of us will need to tell him," she said.

Glen made a show of wiping the sweat from his brow. "Boy, am I relieved."

"Cal will discover this all on his own."

"Listen, honey, I hate to burst your bubble, but Cal's a confirmed bachelor. I don't even remember the last time he went out on a date. He's sworn off women for good."

"You sure about that?"

"Well, it's been more than two years now, and he still isn't over Jennifer."

"Then it's about time he *got* over her." She sounded more confident than she felt, but she wasn't going to let a little thing like male pride stand in her way. Cal needed someone in his life, but he was too stubborn to realize it. Like most of the male sex he simply needed a little help. She'd aim him in the right direction and leave matters to progress as they would.

Eventually Cal *would* see the light; he'd figure it out on his own. As soon as she and Glen were married, Cal would be in that ranch house all by himself. It wouldn't take him long to discover how large and lonely a house could be with just one person living there.

"You look thoughtful," Glen said.

"It's going to be up to us." She nodded firmly.

"Us?" He raised both hands. "Not me! Forget it. If you want to play matchmaker with my big brother, you go right ahead, but don't include me."

A little respect for the validity of her idea—bringing two lonely people together—would have gone a long way, but Glen was having none of it.

"Good luck, sweetheart," he said, reaching for a French fry. "I have to admire your spirit.'

"I don't believe in luck," she told him with the confidence of one who knows. "I believe we shape our own destinies." *And occasionally someone else's.*

LATE WEDNESDAY AFTERNOON Caroline drove into the yard of the Yellow Rose Ranch. She'd been looking forward to this all week.

As she parked, the screen door opened off the back porch and Grady stepped outside.

Caroline climbed out of the car, and Maggie slipped her small hand into Caroline's as he approached.

"Will Grady yell at me?" Maggie whispered.

"Of course not," Caroline assured her.

Grady smiled at them and it was difficult for Caroline to look away. His face was alight with such pleasure she had to catch her breath. They'd known each other for years, she and Grady; they had a history, most of it unpleasant. Both were opinionated, strong willed. But she'd always admired Grady, always thought him honorable and decent. She'd carefully guarded her heart for a lot of years, and he was the first man, the only man, to get close enough to make her dream again.

"Hi," she said, feeling self-conscious.

"Hello." His gaze left her and traveled to Maggie. He bent down on one knee to be eye to eye with Caroline's daughter. "How are you, princess?"

"Fine." Maggie kicked at the dirt with the toe of her shoe and lowered her head to stare at the ground. "I'm sorry I went into the big horse's stall."

"You were looking for the colt, weren't you?"

Maggie nodded and kept her head lowered. When she spoke, even Caroline had trouble understanding her. "I won't do it again."

"Good for you," Grady said. "It's a wise woman who learns from her mistakes."

"And man," Caroline added.

Grady threw back his head and laughed loudly. At the sound Maggie leaped two feet off the ground and flew into her mother's arms, her own small arms tight around Caroline's neck.

"What'd you say to her this time?" Richard asked as he sauntered out of the bunkhouse.

"Richard!" Maggie twisted around, her face wreathed in smiles.

"How's my cupcake?" Richard asked, holding out his arms to the youngster.

Maggie squirmed free of Caroline's embrace and hurried toward the other man. Richard cheerfully caught her, lifted her high above his head and swung her around. Maggie shouted with glee.

"What are you doing here?" Grady asked, frowning.

The smile on Richard's face faded. "This is my home."

"Not anymore. Nothing here belongs to you."

The message was clear. Grady was telling his younger brother to keep away from Caroline and Maggie.

Richard laughed as if to say the mere suggestion was ludicrous. "How can you bar me from something that was never yours?" he asked. He switched his attention to Maggie.

"Maggie, I think—" Caroline started, but was interrupted.

"I like Richard!" her daughter cried. "Not Grady, *Richard.*"

Richard tossed a triumphant gaze at Grady.

"Richard shows me magic tricks and dances with me."

"Grady saved your life," Caroline reminded Maggie. After looking forward to this time with Grady all week, she wasn't about to let Richard ruin it.

Maggie's head drooped against Richard's chin and her arms circled his neck. "I still like Richard best."

"Of course you do," Richard cooed. "All the women in this town do."

"Except Ellie Frasier," Grady said in low tones.

The air between the two men crackled. Richard raised his eyebrows. "Well, well, so my brother knows how to score a point."

"Caroline and Maggie came here to visit me."

"If that's the way you want it," Richard said, and slowly set Maggie down. "I didn't realize they were your exclusive property. It's a shame because Caroline and I might have renewed an old acquaintance. We used to be good friends, remember?"

"We were never friends, Richard," she said, intensely disliking him.

"So that's the lay of the land, is it?" Richard said, with a half smile that implied her words had wounded him. As though his heart was capable of entertaining anything other than selfish pursuits, she thought in disgust.

He walked away then, and despite everything, Caroline experienced a twinge of sadness. She regretted the waste of his skills, his potential. She'd known him all her life, but she didn't really *know* him. She didn't think anyone was capable of fully understanding Richard.

Grady reached for her hand. "I'm sorry, Caroline."

"It's fine. Don't worry about it."

Maggie didn't share her opinion, but Caroline wasn't concerned.

"Would you like some lemonade?" Grady asked her daughter. "I made it specially for you." He sounded downright pleased with himself.

"That sounds yummy, doesn't it?" Caroline said.

Maggie didn't answer.

"We'll take a glass," Caroline responded for both of them.

Grady led the way to the kitchen and got out three glasses. "It dawned on me the other day that I'm going to be living the bachelor life in a few months. I never spent much time in the kitchen, not with Mom around and then Savannah doing all the cooking." A sadness came over him at the mention of his mother. Grady wasn't one to openly display his emotions, but Caroline knew that the deaths of his parents had forever marked him. He never talked about the accident—they'd drowned in a flash flood—or the horrible weeks that followed with the discovery of Richard's theft and disappearance.

"I suspect Wiley and I'll starve to death before the end of the first month," he said, making a lighthearted shift of subject. Wiley had been foreman on the Yellow Rose for as long as Caroline could remember.

"I don't think Savannah will let that happen."

"Can I play with Savannah's dolls?" Maggie asked, tugging at her mother's arm.

"Don't you want to go riding?" Grady asked, sounding disappointed.

Maggie shook her head; Caroline supposed she'd been scared off by the incident on Sunday. It might be a while before she was interested in horses again. In any event, dolls had always been her first choice.

"You be careful with Savannah's things, you hear?" Caroline warned.

"I will," Maggie promised, and skipped off, her lemonade untouched.

"She enjoys playing with dolls, doesn't she?" Grady said.

"More than anything."

Grady carried their lemonade into the living room and set both glasses down on the coffee table.

"I imagine you're wondering why we're sitting in here rather than outside," he said.

As a matter of fact she was.

"It's too damned difficult to find a way to hold you if you're sitting in that rocking chair," he confessed. "Damn it, woman, I haven't thought about anything but kissing you again from the moment you left last Sunday."

It was heaven to hear him say it, and hell to confess it herself. "Oh, Grady, me, too!"

Neither made a pretense of drinking the lemonade. The minute they were on the sofa, they were in each other's arms. Their first kiss was urgent, like a thirsty traveler drinking in cool water, not taking time to savor the taste or feel of it. Their second kiss was more serene.

Caroline wanted this, needed this, and Grady hadn't disappointed her. His own display of eagerness warmed her heart. A delightful excitement filled her, allowing her to hope, to dream.

"Is this really happening to us?" she asked. She shifted around and rested her back against his chest. He spread light kisses down the side of her neck.

"If it's not, don't wake me."

"When did this come about?" She closed her eyes and moaned softly when his teeth nipped her ear, sending shivers up her spine. "Grady," she groaned, half in protest, half in encouragement.

"Kiss me," he pleaded.

He didn't need to ask twice. She twisted around and offered him her mouth. The havoc his touch created within her was much too powerful to resist.

Caroline was too involved in their exchange to hear the door open.

Grady abruptly broke off the kiss. Stunned by the sudden change in him, she didn't notice Savannah for several seconds.

"Oops." Her best friend sounded infinitely cheerful. "I think we came back a little too soon, Laredo."

Six

"This is incredible!" Caroline cried, galloping after Grady. The wind blew in her face as her pinto followed Grady's horse across the wide open range. She hadn't gone horseback riding in ages, and it felt wonderful, exhilarating. Caroline couldn't remember a time she'd experienced such a sense of freedom. Not in years and years. This lighthearted feeling could only be attributed to one thing—the fact that she was falling in love with Grady.

"Come on, slowpoke," Grady shouted over his shoulder, leading her farther from the ranch house. He hadn't said where they were headed, but he seemed to have a destination in mind.

"Where are you taking me?" she called, but either he didn't hear or chose to ignore the question.

Bless Savannah's matchmaking heart. When she'd returned early, she insisted they go riding, saying she'd look after Maggie. Grady and Caroline had both made token protests, but it didn't take long for Savannah to convince them to sneak away.

The day was lovely, not excessively hot for an August afternoon. Surprisingly it was several degrees cooler than it had been earlier in the week. The grass was lush and green because of the early-summer rains, and the air smelled fresh.

During the last few days Caroline had been giving a lot of thought to her relationship with Grady. Both were mature adults. He'd recently turned thirty-six and she was almost twenty-eight. She knew what she wanted in life, and he seemed to have set his own course, too. She liked him and deeply respected him. Recently, very recently, she'd admitted she was fast falling in love with him. Already she was beginning to believe they could make a decent life together.

Grady crested a hill and stopped to wait for her. His eyes were bright, alive with happiness, and Caroline wondered if the joy she read in them was a reflection of her own.

"Are you ready for a break yet?" he asked.

"I'll rest when you do," she told him, not wanting to hold him up.

"In other words you're willing to follow me to the ends of the earth."

She laughed rather than confess the truth of it. "Something like that."

"Seriously, Caroline, my backside is far more accustomed to a saddle than yours. I don't want to overtax that part of your anatomy."

"I didn't know you were so concerned about the care and comfort of my butt," she teased.

Grady threw back his head and laughed boisterously.

She urged the pinto into an easy trot, and Grady caught up with her in short order. They rode in companionable silence for several minutes. Gradually he led her toward some willow trees growing along the edge of a winding creek. The scene was postcard picturesque.

"There's a nice shady spot here." Grady pointed to a huge weeping willow whose branches dipped lazily into the water.

They paused there. Grady dismounted first, then helped her down. Caroline had been around horses most of her life and certainly didn't need any assistance. But she didn't stop him; she knew he wanted to hold her, and she wanted it, too. She could find no reason to deny either of them what they desired.

He held her a moment longer than necessary and she pretended not to notice. Bracing her hands against his shoulders, she slowly eased her body toward the ground. Even then he didn't release his firm grasp on her waist.

His eyes were intense, focused only on her. Time seemed to stop. Everything around her had an unreal dreamlike quality. Sound filtered lazily into her mind—the whisper of a breeze through the delicate branches of the willow, the creek's cheerful gurgle, the bird song of early evening.

"I used to come here when I was a boy," Grady said. He still held her, but more loosely now. "I used to think it was a magic place."

"Magic?"

"Bandits hid in the tree, waiting to ambush me, but I was too smart for them." Laugh lines crinkled at his eyes as he spoke.

"When I was a little girl, I used to hide in an oak tree in our backyard. I was sure no one could see me."

He removed his glove and brushed a strand of hair from her temple, his callused fingers gentle against her face. "Once I'd rid the place of the bandits, I'd sit and think . . . and pretend."

"I'd dream," she told him, realizing as she did that this was the first time she'd ever told anyone about the oak tree.

"Any particular dream?" he asked.

"Oh, what most girls dream," she said. "Girls who've read *Cinderella* and *Rapunzel* and *Snow White*—I adored those stories. I'd dream about being a princess in disguise. A handsome prince would fight insurmountable odds to come to me and declare his love."

He grinned. "At your service."

"Oh, Grady, are you my prince?" She felt foolish when she'd said the words, but he looked at her so seriously, all joking gone.

"There's nothing I'd like more," he said in a quiet voice.

The air between them seemed electric, charged with tension, and Caroline was convinced she'd die if he didn't kiss her soon. Judging by the glitter in his eyes, Grady must have felt the same way. He muttered something unintelligible, then unhurriedly lowered his mouth to hers.

He tightened his arms around her waist, almost lifting her from the ground. Caroline ran her fingers through his hair. His Stetson tumbled from his head, but he didn't seem to notice. The kiss went on and on.

Abruptly he broke it off and shook his head. "I shouldn't have done that. I'm sorry. I'm moving too fast. It's just that—"

"No, that's not it."

His hands were in her hair, too, and he held her against him. With her ear pressed to his heart, she could hear its desperate pounding.

"I can't seem to keep my hands off you," he whispered.

"You don't hear me complaining, do you?"

"No, but . . ." His chest expanded with a deep sigh. "Oh, hell, Caroline, I haven't made any secret of the way I feel about you."

"It's how I feel, too," she confessed.

Holding her hand firmly in his, he guided her toward the creek, stopping long enough to retrieve a spare blanket from his saddlebag. He pulled back the dangling willow branches and bowed, gesturing her in. "Welcome to my castle."

"Castle?" she repeated. "I thought it was a bandits' hideout."

"Not anymore," he murmured. "I'm your handsome prince, remember?"

All Caroline could do was smile. And if her smile was a little tremulous . . . she couldn't help it.

He spread the blanket on the ground, and once she was seated, he returned to his saddlebag. To her surprise, he produced a bottle of cool white wine, two stemmed plastic glasses and a piece of cheddar cheese.

"You shock me, Grady," Caroline told him as he opened the bottle with his Swiss Army knife.

"I do?" He glanced up, a look of amusement on his face as he cut the cheese and handed her a slice.

"This is so *romantic.*"

"If you think this is something, just wait."

Caroline raised her head. "You mean there's more?" She savoured a bite of the sharp cheddar.

"Much more." He leaped to his feet and returned to the horses. Again opening a saddlebag, he drew out a small gold-foil box.

"Chocolates?" Caroline squealed with delight.

"I figured these were the kind of thing a man gives a woman when he comes courting." He didn't look at her; instead, he busied himself carefully pouring the wine.

Caroline loved the way he used the old-fashioned term. *"Are* you courting me, Grady?" She'd meant to sound demure, but her question had an urgency about it. "Are you being serious?" She had to know.

"This is about as serious as a man gets," he said, and handed her a plastic cup of wine. "Shall we make a toast?" he asked, holding up his glass.

She nodded and touched her glass to his.

"To the future," he said, then amended, "Our future."

Caroline sipped the wine. The chardonnay was delicate, smooth, refreshing. One sip and her heart started to pound, the force of it growing with every beat. It took her a moment to realize what was happening.

She was in love, really in love. It both terrified and excited her. And with that realization came another. She needed to tell Grady about Maggie's father. He had a right to know the truth, although the thought of telling him brought a dull ache to the pit of her stomach.

"You're quiet all of a sudden," Grady said.

"I was just thinking." She shrugged off his concern.

"That could be dangerous to your mental health," he teased. He leaned forward, his lips moist with wine, and gently kissed her. His mouth lingered in a series of short nibbling kisses far more potent than the wine.

"I can't make myself stop kissing you," he said, leaning his forehead against hers.

"I can't stop wanting you to kiss me," she told him. She moved her hands along his neck, loving the feel of his skin. "I . . . I want to talk to you about Maggie." She closed her eyes, fighting back the tension that gripped her. The sooner she got this over with, the better.

"I'm trying, Caroline, I honestly am."

"I know . . . but what I want to say doesn't have anything to do with how she feels about you."

Grady went very still.

The heavy pounding of her heart echoed in her ears, drowning out her thoughts. She couldn't look at him while she spoke of that pain-filled time. Before she could stop herself, she was on her feet.

"It's about Maggie's father." She clenched her hands until the knuckles were white. Her stomach tightened. The only one who knew the full truth had been her mother. Caroline was well aware that other family members and certainly her friends had speculated for years about who'd fathered Maggie, but she'd never told them. Never told anyone. Never felt the need until now.

"Caroline, you're very pale. Is this really so difficult for you?"

She bowed her head and exhaled slowly. "It's much harder than I'd thought it would be."

He stood up and moved behind her, placing his hands on her shoulders. "Then forget it. My knowing isn't necessary, not if it upsets you like this."

"But it *is* necessary." He had no idea how much.

"Then you can tell me some other time," he insisted. He bent to kiss the side of her neck. His mouth lingered and her head fell forward. "I want our afternoon to be special. I don't want anything to interfere with that."

"But you have a right to know." She paused and swallowed. What he didn't seem to understand was that telling him wouldn't get any easier. In fact, the longer she waited . . .

His hands gently stroked the length of her arms. "Let's not spoil our afternoon with memories best forgotten. There'll be plenty of time for you to tell me everything—but not today."

"Aren't you curious? Don't you want to know?"

He released a long sigh. "Yeah, I am," he said after a moment. "Perhaps I'm a little afraid, too. I don't want anything to ruin what we have."

"Oh, Grady." He made it so easy to delay telling him the truth. Easy to thrust it into the future with excuses she was far too willing to accept and he was just as eager to suggest.

"I'm your prince, remember?"

"I remember," she replied dutifully.

"Good." He kissed her then, his mouth touching hers in a quick caress. "Now let's get back to our wine."

He waited until she'd settled herself on the blanket before he handed her the glass he'd refilled. Positioning himself behind her, he eased her against him. Caroline closed her eyes as he gently fingered the fine strands of her hair.

"I told you this is a magic place."

"Mmm."

"Reality will find us soon enough, so let's enjoy the magic while we can."

Caroline had to admit she was willing to do just that.

MAGGIE PUT Savannah's dolls back on the bedroom-window seat and looked out again, hoping to see her mommy. She'd gone horseback riding with Grady and they'd been away a long time. Longer than she wanted them to be. She was ready to go home now.

Bored, she put on her backpack and wandered into the kitchen where Savannah was kneading bread dough.

"When's Mommy coming back?" she asked.

"I don't know, sweetheart, but I imagine they'll be here soon."

"Where's Richard?" Maggie asked next.

"I don't know."

"Can I watch television?"

"Of course, but get Laredo to turn it on for you, okay?"

"I can do it," Maggie insisted. She turned on the television at home and it wasn't hard.

"Grady got a new satellite dish and it has three remote controls."

There was his name again. Not only did Grady shout, but he made it so she couldn't prove to Savannah how smart she was.

"Laredo's in the barn, but he'll be finished any minute."

Maggie glanced wistfully toward the barn, but she wouldn't go in there alone, not anymore. The last time, she'd gotten into trouble, and Grady had yelled at her again and grabbed her. He'd been scared, too; she could tell when he pulled her away from the horse and held her.

"I'd do it for you, sweetheart, but I've got my hands buried in bread dough." Savannah explained.

"That's all right." Not wanting to wait inside, Maggie walked onto the porch. She sat on the top step, and Rocket ambled over to lie down beside her. She rubbed his ears for a few minutes because Savannah had told her he liked that. Then she rested her chin on her folded hands, looking out over the ranch yard, hoping she'd find something to do. Something that wouldn't get her in trouble.

She caught a flash of color and saw Richard coming out of the bunk house. Her spirits lifted immediately. Leaping off the steps, she raced to his side. "Richard!"

He jerked around, then smiled when he saw her. Maggie liked Richard's smile, but what she enjoyed most were his magic tricks. Once he pulled a coin out of her ear. Another time he had her draw a card out of the middle of a deck and then told her what card it was. He was right.

"Howdy, kiddo," Richard said.

"Wanna play?" she asked, skipping after him.

"Not now."

"Nobody wants to play with me," she said, hoping he'd feel sorry for her and offer a game or a few tricks.

"Sorry, kiddo, I've got things to do."

Maggie's face fell. Everyone was too busy for her. "Can I help?" she asked, thinking if he finished early, he might take time to play.

No," he said sharply. He sounded almost like Grady when he was mad, and Maggie gasped.

Richard squatted down. "Maybe we can play, after all. How about a game of hide-and-seek?" he suggested. "You go hide and I'll come and find you."

This was great, better than she'd expected. "Okay." Maggie glanced around, looking for a place to hide, somewhere Richard wouldn't find her.

"Are you closing your eyes?" she asked.

"You bet I am, kid."

Maggie didn't like the way he said it, but she was so pleased to have someone willing to play with her that she didn't care.

"Don't peek," she warned, and raced around the corner.

"I wouldn't dream of it," he called after her.

He said that in a way she didn't like, either. Almost as if he was mad but without raising his voice. Maggie tore across the yard, her pack slapping against her back, and hid in Savannah's garden. She liked the smell of the roses. She crouched down under the table on the patio . . . but Richard didn't come and he didn't come. She got tired of waiting.

He was probably looking in places near the barn, she decided. Sneaking out of the rose garden, she crept on tiptoe closer to where she'd last seen him. Circling around to the other side of the barn, she saw Grady's truck that Richard sometimes drove. He didn't usually keep his truck there. The truck bed was covered with a sort of blanket but bigger.

Richard would never think of looking for her there. The tailgate was down, and by standing on a box she was able to climb inside. The floor hurt her knees and it was dark and warm inside, almost like a cave under the heavy cloth. There was lots of other stuff, too. She found a rolled-up sleeping bag and leaned against it.

"Richard!" she called, thinking he might need help finding her.

Nothing.

It was getting so hot under the blanket that she took off the backpack. Soon her eyes grew heavy with sleep. She decided to put her head down on the sleeping bag, but just for a few minutes until Richard found her.

Just until then.

THIS WAS SO EASY it was embarrassing, Richard Weston told himself. The pickup, formerly owned by Grady—as he liked to think of it—sped down the road toward Bitter End. No one would think of looking for him there. No one would even guess.

Luckily his brother's head was in the clouds these days. Grady Weston in love—if it wasn't so damn funny, it'd be sad. Grady had fallen in love—for the first time, Richard was sure—at the age of thirty-six—and it wasn't a pretty sight. For a couple of weeks now he'd been walking around the house with his tongue hanging out of his mouth and his eyes glazed over. It was a wonder he hadn't tripped down the stairs and broken his damn neck.

Actually Richard wouldn't have minded doing the dirty deed with Miss Caroline himself. He'd bet that woman was some hot number in the sack. Still, he felt grateful to her for keeping Grady distracted. His blockhead of a brother didn't have a clue what he, Richard, was up to. Before Grady figured it out, he'd be long gone. Yup, it was that easy.

Richard laughed aloud. "Idiots." He hated to say this about his own flesh and blood, but both Grady and Savannah were dolts. It was kind of sad that they'd be gullible enough to let him drive off with several months' worth of supplies. He'd even managed to acquire a small gasoline-powered generator—one he'd put onto his brother's business account, naturally. Of course Grady wouldn't know anything about it for a couple of weeks.

Richard almost wished he could be a fly on the wall when the bills started coming in. Grady would have a conniption. Richard felt a mild twinge of guilt about that, but hell, he didn't have any choice. Not really. He had to eat, and while the portable television might seem an extravagance, it wasn't. How would he know what was going on in the world without watching the evening news? It wasn't like he was going to get cable in the old ghost town, either. All he had were rabbit ears. He'd be lucky to receive one station, possibly two, but that was probably just as well. Otherwise he'd be tempted to laze around and waste his whole supply of gasoline on running the TV.

By the time he reached the turnoff to the dirt road that wound up the far side of the valley, he was lost in his thoughts.

He knew himself well enough to realize he'd find it difficult to stay cooped up in Bitter End, with no companionship and few diversions. There were sure to be times when he'd welcome an excuse to venture into Promise, or any one of the other small towns that dotted the Texas hill country.

He couldn't do that, however. Grady was bound to report the truck as stolen, and sure as shootin', Richard would have a lawman on his tail five minutes after he hit the highway. But a stolen vehicle was only a small part of Richard's worries—just one more complication in his already complicated life.

Hell, all the lawmen in three states would give their eyeteeth to get their hands on him. So the last thing he needed was to be pulled in for driving a stolen truck.

A shiver raced down his spine. He didn't want to think about that.

The road grew bumpy and he slowed. For a moment he thought he heard a sound, a cry of some kind, but he strained his ears and didn't hear it again.

Imagination was a funny thing, he mused. Could be dangerous, too. On a recent visit to Bitter End, he'd had the impression that someone was watching him. Someone or something. A vague feeling, mildly uncomfortable.

He blamed Ellie Frasier for that. She'd given him the willies the time he'd brought her to Bitter End. The minute they left the truck, she'd started making noises about this "feeling." He hadn't felt a damn thing, while she was practically crawling out of her skin. Naturally that was for the best, since he certainly didn't want her coming back and bringing her friends along.

Ellie hadn't been able to get out fast enough. Whatever the feeling was, it had never bothered Richard—until that last visit. He'd probably just heard too much about this so-called sensation. He didn't understand it, but he was counting it as a plus. The town's reputation for eeriness meant that people would stay away. He'd have to control his own imagination, not let ghost stories and strange noises spook him.

As he neared Bitter End, he reduced the truck's speed. He'd found a spot in the ghost town where he could hide the pickup, so if anyone did happen to stumble in, they wouldn't see it.

He stopped in front of the wooden stable, which leaned heavily to one side. He'd say one thing for the folks who'd originally built this place. They'd been great craftsmen. Most of the buildings still stood, despite their age.

He drove the truck into the decrepit stable and jumped down from the cab. He was about to close the door when he caught a movement under the canvas tarp.

He froze. Sure enough, he saw it move again. Believing in the element of surprise, he moved quietly to the back of the truck and firmly gripped the edge of the blanket. With no warning, he jerked it away from the bed.

Maggie Daniels screamed and cowered in a corner. It took them both a moment to recover, but she was faster.

"Richard!"

"What the hell are you doing here?" he demanded.

The smile on her face disappeared. "We were playing hide-and-seek, remember? I fell asleep. . . ."

Richard swore.

Maggie's eyes grew round. "If my mommy was here, she'd wash your mouth out with soap."

As far as he could see, Richard had few choices. He could dump the kid on the highway—but would she shut up about where she'd been? He could keep her in Bitter End. Or he could do away with her entirely. Kidnap and murder charges wouldn't look good on his rap sheet. But he might not have any other options.

Damn it, what was he going to do now?

GRADY HAD NEVER been one to idle away time, nor had he been known to sit under a willow tree and soak in the beauty of a summer evening. Not for the past six years, at any rate. It'd taken him that long to get the ranch into the black. He'd earned a decent profit last year and would again this year, God willing. He finally felt good about his life and he didn't want his happiness compromised now with talk of Maggie's father. He tried to tell himself it didn't matter—but it did. Caroline had wanted to tell him, and curious though he was, he'd persuaded her to wait. Grady recognized that his behavior was uncharacteristic; generally he faced problems head-on. But he knew why he didn't want to hear what she had to say. Admitting it didn't come easy, not by a long shot. Intuitively he feared that once she told him about Maggie's father, nothing would be the same between them. Sitting with her in the shade of the willow tree, holding her close, loving her—these moments were far too special to invade with difficult truths. So he'd delayed the inevitable, hurled it into the future until he felt more ready to deal with it.

Caroline lay down on the blanket beside him, her head resting against his thigh. Lazily he brushed the hair from her face. She was so damned beautiful he could barely manage not to stare at her. Barely manage not to kiss her again. They'd done plenty of that this afternoon. She'd tasted of wine and chocolate, and Grady thought he'd never sampled a more intoxicating combination. Sweet and potent at the same time.

He'd as good as told her he was interested in marrying her. A man didn't go courting otherwise. It was time for him to settle down. Glen was about to make the leap into marriage, and with Savannah married and she and Laredo building their own home, he'd soon be alone. But it wasn't just the events in other people's lives that had convinced him.

It was Caroline and Maggie. Whenever he was with them, he didn't want their time together to end. His life felt empty when they weren't around.

He tried to tell Caroline that, but he couldn't manage the words. He discovered it was damned hard to admit how much he needed someone else. He'd never felt this way before, and it frightened him.

"I could almost go to sleep," Caroline murmured. Her eyes remained closed and he ran his index finger down the side of her jaw. Her skin was soft and smooth. Lovely. *She* was lovely.

Her lips eased into a smile. "You're right."

"Well, I don't know what I'm right about, but I like the sound of those words."

"Every man does," she teased.

"Flatter my ego and tell me why I'm right."

"This place," she whispered. "I don't think I've ever felt so . . . content. So relaxed."

"Me neither." Today was the first time he'd spent more than ten minutes here in years, and already they'd been gone at least two hours.

"I wonder . . ." she began wistfully.

"What?" He bent forward to graze his lips across her brow.

"If you have any other magic tricks up your sleeve."

"That's Richard's specialty, not mine."

Caroline frowned. "You provided a magical afternoon for me," she said. "Wine and chocolates and this beautiful place."

"The kissing wasn't half-bad, either."

Her eyes fluttered open and she gazed up at him with such longing he couldn't possibly have resisted her.

Caroline wrapped herself in his embrace the moment he reached for her. Grady was shocked by the intensity of his own craving. It felt as though he'd waited his entire life for this afternoon and this woman.

His tongue danced with hers and he worked his fingers into her hair, loving the feel of it, clean and silky smooth. Fifty years of this, and he swore he'd never tire of her taste.

"I suppose we'd better think about getting back," he said reluctantly, feeling cheated that their magical time had come to an end.

"How long have we been gone?" Caroline asked. Not waiting for a response, she glanced at her watch. She gasped and jumped to her feet. "Oh, my goodness, we've been away for over two hours!"

"I know."

"But Maggie . . ."

"She's with Savannah."

"I had no idea we'd been gone this long." She started cleaning up the area, her movements fast and jerky.

"Caroline, you don't have anything to worry about."

She turned slowly to face him, obviously comforted. "Thank you Grady. I do know that. I'm just not used to . . . any of *this*." She made a gesture that took in their surroundings, the remains of their picnic and Grady himself.

He helped her mount—because he wanted to, not because she needed any assistance. They rode back to the ranch, joking and laughing, teasing each other the way lovers do.

As the house came into view, his eyes were drawn to its silhouette against the darkening sky. Solid, secure, welcoming. His home had always seemed a natural part of the landscape to him. It belonged there. And for the first time in years, he felt that his life was what he wanted it to be.

It wasn't until they neared the corral that Grady noticed something was amiss. He saw Laredo, and the minute the other man caught sight of Grady and Caroline, he ran into the house, calling for Savannah. She rushed out onto the back porch.

His sister's face was red, her eyes puffy as though she'd been weeping. That wasn't like her.

"What is it?" he asked as he dismounted.

"Oh, Caroline, I'm so sorry." Savannah's voice trembled and she covered her mouth.

Confused, Caroline looked to Grady. "What's wrong?"

Grady walked around his gelding and helped Caroline down from her horse. Her hands trembled as she held his arms.

"Where's Maggie?" she asked, her voice oddly calm.

"That's the problem," Laredo said, moving to stand next to his wife. He slid his arm around Savannah's shoulders.

"You don't know where Maggie is?" Caroline asked, and again Grady heard that strange calm in her voice.

"I . . . She went outside, and the last time I checked she was sitting on the porch," Savannah cried. "I've looked everywhere, called for her until my voice was hoarse. I don't know where she could have gone."

"Apparently she'd come out to look for me," Laredo said.

"Did you see her?" Grady demanded.

"No." Laredo shook his head.

"Oh, Caroline," Savannah wept, "I'm so sorry! I should never have let her leave the house."

Caroline's fingers dug into Grady's arm. Her eyes were wide and filled with terror when she looked at him, seeking reassurance.

Grady's heart felt like a lead weight in his chest. "We'll find her," he promised.

Seven

The calls lawmen dreaded most were domestic violence and missing children. Frank Hennessey was no exception. The report of a missing child made his blood run cold. He preferred dealing with a drunken belligerent husband any day of the week if it meant he didn't have to see the face of a parent whose child couldn't be found. Frank had never married, never had children, but he'd been a firsthand witness to the agony parents endure when their child disappears. All his years of law enforcement had convinced him there was no deeper pain than the loss of a child.

The call that Maggie Daniels had gone missing came minutes before Frank was due to go off duty. Grady Weston phoned it in. There'd only been one other time Frank had heard Grady sound the way he did this evening, and that was the day his parents had drowned in a flash flood.

"Are you sure she hasn't fallen asleep somewhere in the house?" Frank felt obliged to ask.

"We're sure, Frank." Grady's impatience crackled over the telephone line.

"Was she upset about anything?"

"No, she was excited about visiting the ranch," Caroline answered, apparently from one of the extensions.

"Maggie didn't run away, if that's what you're thinking," Grady told him angrily.

In fact, Frank's questions had been leading to that assumption. It was the most common scenario, even with kids this young. He sighed heavily. He hadn't been around children much, but he'd taken a real liking to Caroline's fatherless child. She was a sweetheart, and the thought of anything happening to her made his insides twist.

"Are you coming out to take a report or not?" Grady demanded.

"I'm on my way." Frank replaced the receiver. Grady sounded as worried and frustrated as he would if he were the child's father. In situations such as this the families were often impatient and angry, lashing out at authority because of their own helplessness. Frank had seen it before. Some of the cases he'd worked on came with happy endings. The lost child was found safe and promptly returned to the parents.

The other cases, two in his career, would forever haunt him. *Missing.* He'd come to think of it as the ugliest word in the English language. The first child had turned up dead; the second was never seen again.

Although the highway was deserted, Frank ran the lights on his patrol car as he sped toward the Yellow Rose Ranch. The entire forty minutes it took him to drive from town, he kept hoping against hope that by the time he arrived, Maggie would've been found. He wasn't a superstitious man, nor did he believe in intuition, but his gut told him that wouldn't be the case.

He was right.

No sooner had he pulled into the yard than the door opened and Grady hurried onto the porch. Caroline was with him, looking paler than he'd ever seen her. Grady's eyes were dark with anxiety.

"Thank you for coming," Caroline said, her voice determined. She was a strong woman and Frank deeply admired her grit.

Grady held the door open for him. "Savannah's got coffee brewing," he said, leading the way into the kitchen.

Frank looked around at the small group assembled there. Laredo had his arm around Savannah, who seemed on the verge of collapse. Her eyes were red and swollen, testifying to the tears she'd already shed.

"It's my fault," she said.

"No one's laying blame," Grady told her, his eyes softening. He brought the coffeepot over to the table where a number of mugs had been set, and he filled each one.

"But I was supposed to be watching her," Savannah explained as Frank doctored his coffee with milk.

"It doesn't matter who was watching her," Caroline said, her voice shaking slightly. "What matters is that we don't know where Maggie is now."

"We'll find her," Wiley Rogers, the foreman, insisted. "Don't you worry about that. Not a one of us will rest until Maggie's found."

Frank had heard words like that before, and he'd watched as families invested every penny of their life's savings in the effort. He'd watched them invest the very heart and soul of their existence in tracing a missing child, sometimes to the point that the entire family was destroyed. He'd assumed when he moved to Promise fifteen years ago that he'd never have to deal with this sort of agony again, but he'd been wrong. It was staring him in the face this very minute.

"Savannah, since you were the last person to see Maggie, why don't we start with you." He withdrew a small notebook from his shirt pocket. "You *were* the last one to see her, right?"

Savannah nodded and Laredo moved closer to his wife's side as if to protect her. Frank pitied her, understood the grief and guilt she must feel. He glanced away and surveyed everyone else in the room.

It was then that he noticed one family member was missing. "Where's Richard?" he asked, interrupting Savannah.

"In town, I suspect," Grady said.

"Driving what?"

"My pickup's missing, so I guess he has that."

Frank walked over to the telephone. "I want him here."

"Of course," Savannah said.

"You don't think he'd take Maggie with him, do you?" Caroline asked, looking to Grady and Savannah for the answer. "I mean, we assumed he left earlier, before Maggie turned up missing, but . . ." She let the rest fade.

"It isn't a good idea to assume anything." Frank walked over to the wall phone and lifted the receiver. He barked out a few orders, then instructed his deputy to drive through town and find Richard Weston. If Richard wasn't there, Al was to find out the last time anyone saw him and report back to Frank as soon as possible.

While he waited for Al to return the call, Frank finished the interview with Savannah and Laredo. An hour passed before the phone rang. Caroline leaped from her chair and her eyes grew wide and hopeful when Grady reached for the receiver. Without a word he handed the telephone to Frank.

Richard Weston was nowhere to be found. Neither was Grady's truck. No one had seen him, not that day or the day before. Al reported that he wasn't the only one looking for Richard, either, but Frank decided these people had enough trouble on their hands. He didn't intend to add to it.

"You don't honestly think Richard took the child, do you?" Savannah asked after he'd relayed the details of Al's findings.

"At this point I won't discount any coincidence. Maggie's missing and so is Richard."

"But I'm sure he left long before Maggie disappeared," Savannah said.

"I'm not." This came from Laredo. "I saw the truck. And I saw it while Maggie was in the house with you."

* * *

UNABLE TO SLEEP, Caroline sat on the dark porch, her arms wrapped protectively around her middle. Frank had left several hours earlier. There was nothing more he could do; he'd already alerted law-enforcement officers across Texas and in the adjoining states to keep their eyes open for Maggie. Savannah had given the sheriff Maggie's school photograph and he'd taken it into town with him. Soon Maggie's likeness would be seen in every law office in the Southwest. The search was on for Richard, too, with an all points bulletin issued for his arrest. Caroline knew that had something to do with information the sheriff had received, information about a crime Richard had committed back East. She didn't know what it was, and right now she didn't care. Finding Maggie was the only thing that mattered.

With nothing further to be done at the moment, everyone had turned in for the night. Frank had offered to follow her home, but Caroline refused to leave. If Maggie—she paused and rephrased the thought—*when* Maggie came back, Caroline wanted to be right here at the ranch waiting for her.

Although everyone had gone to bed, she knew no one would sleep well. She accepted one of Savannah's nightgowns and made the pretense of going to bed, too, but the room felt suffocating. Within minutes she'd dressed again and made her way through the house and outside. She sat on the porch steps and stared into the bleak darkness.

It wasn't long before Grady joined her. Wordlessly, with barely a sound, he sat down on the step next to her and clasped her hand. Her fingers tightened around his.

"I'm so afraid." It was the first time she'd verbalized her fears.

"I am, too."

She pressed her head against his shoulder and he placed his arm around her, drawing her close.

"Do you think she's with Richard?" Caroline couldn't shake the thought. They'd both disappeared around the same time, but that made no sense. Richard might be a lot of things, but a child-snatcher wasn't one of them. Caroline could think of no plausible reason for him to take Maggie.

"I can't imagine that even Richard would do anything like this," Grady said, his voice little more than a whisper.

Caroline reminded herself that Frank believed there might be a connection between Maggie's disappearance and Richard's. She just couldn't understand what it might be.

"You should try to sleep," Grady urged.

"I can't." Every time she closed her eyes her imagination tormented her. She couldn't bear the thought of her daughter hurt and crying out for her. But that was what filled her mind and heart and made sleep impossible.

"I can't, either."

"Oh, Grady," she whispered, her voice breaking. "Where can she be?"

He waited a moment before he answered, and she knew he was experiencing the same frustration she was. "I wish I knew."

As the night wore on, it became more and more difficult for Caroline to hope. When she couldn't stand the silence any longer, she buried her face in her hands and cried, "I want my daughter!"

She tried to be strong, but she didn't think she could hold back the tears. Hysteria was edging in on her. She could feel it pushing her closer to the brink.

All at once she was completely wrapped in Grady's arms. She clung to him, shaking almost uncontrollably as she muffled her sobs against his chest. His hold on her was firm, solid, and she needed him as she'd rarely needed anyone in her life. She wept until there were no tears left.

"This might be the worst possible time to tell you this," Grady whispered, his mouth close to her ear. "I love you, Caroline."

"Oh, Grady," she sobbed.

"I know it's new, and it might take some getting used to, but let my love be your strength for now. Lean on me if you can. Let me help you bear this. I'll do everything in my power to get Maggie back."

She was holding him, clutching his shoulders, like a lifeline. "I love you, too," she whimpered, but didn't know if he'd heard her.

"We'll get through this," he promised. "We'll find Maggie."

He sounded confident and sure, and she clung to the promise of his words.

"It's going to be all right, understand?"

She nodded, desperately wanting to believe him.

Oh, God, she prayed, *please bring my little girl home.*

But God seemed far away just then.

MAGGIE'S EYES were sore from crying, but she didn't want Richard to hear her because he'd already gotten mad and yelled at her. She huddled in the corner of the old stone building that used to be a store. It was getting dark, but there was still some light coming in through the open door. Richard had told her not to leave the room and then he'd disappeared. Maggie didn't like Richard anymore, even if he *could* do magic tricks.

He was mean and he said bad words and he threw things, too. After he found her hiding in the back of Grady's pickup, he started acting like Billy Parsons when he had a temper tantrum at his brother's birthday party. The only thing Richard didn't do was throw himself down on the ground and start kicking.

Her stomach growled, but Maggie had already looked around for something to eat and hadn't found anything. She wished she'd gone horseback riding with her mommy and Grady. She was afraid of horses after last Sunday—but not nearly as afraid as she was now.

"Richard," Maggie said, risking his wrath by walking out of the store. "I want to go home now, okay?"

"Yeah, well, you can't have everything you want." He was sitting outside and he had a big bottle in his hand. Every now and then, he'd take a drink. Her mother had told Maggie it wasn't good manners to drink out of a bottle, but she didn't tell Richard that because he'd only yell at her again.

"Can we go back to the ranch?" she asked.

"No." He growled the word at her and laughed when she leaped back, frightened by the harsh sound of his voice. "I've got an idea," he said, leaning toward her. "Why don't you go fall in an empty well and save me a lot of trouble?"

Maggie hurried back into the old store and sat down on the lone chair. When it grew dark, she ventured over to the stable where he'd parked the truck. There was enough moonlight to find her way, but she walked very carefully, afraid of holes in the road and snakes . . . and Richard. Climbing into the bed of the pickup, she curled up with the sleeping bag she'd found earlier. She was cold and hungry and more afraid than she'd ever been in her whole life.

Every once in a while she could hear Richard singing. He played his guitar and sang, but his voice didn't sound right. It was like he'd mashed all the words together. She used to think he had a good voice; she didn't think so anymore.

Soon she fell asleep and didn't awake till light peeked through a crack in the stable door. She was so hungry her stomach hurt.

She clambered out of the truck and walked back to the main street. The early morning was very still.

Richard was asleep in the rocker. His guitar lay on the wooden sidewalk beside him, and he'd slouched down in the chair with his feet stretched out. His arms dangled over the edges of the rocker until his fingertips touched the ground close to the empty bottle. His head lolled to one side.

"Richard," she whispered. "I'm hungry."

He opened his eyes and blinked a couple of times.

"I'm hungry," she repeated, louder this time.

"Get out of here, kid."

"I want my mommy," she said, and her lower lip wobbled. "I don't like it here. I want to go home."

Richard slowly sat up and rubbed his face. "Get lost, will ya?"

Maggie didn't mean to, but she started to cry. She'd always thought Richard was her friend, and now she knew he wasn't.

"Stop it!" he shouted, and scowled at her.

Sobbing, Maggie ran away from him.

"Maggie," he called after her, but she didn't stop, running between two of the buildings.

"Damn it."

Maggie pretended not to hear him and, thinking he might try to follow her, she crept down the side of a building, then slipped inside another store.

The town was old. Really, really old. Older than any place she'd ever been. It smelled old. None of the buildings had paint, either. It sure seemed like no one had lived here for a long time. Some of the places had stuff inside. The store had a table and chair and shelves. But there were only a few cans sitting around—they looked kind of strange, like they might burst. Plus a cash register. She'd tried to get it to work, but it wouldn't open for her.

Maggie wasn't sure what kind of shop this had been, but it had a big cupboard. Maybe she could hide from Richard there. She opened the door and saw that it had shelves. On one of the shelves was a doll. A really old one, with a cotton dress and apron and bonnet. The doll's face had been stitched on. It wasn't like any doll she'd ever seen. The only one she owned with cloth arms and legs was Raggedy Ann, but her clothes were bright and pretty. This doll's clothes were all faded.

"Are you scared, too?" she asked the doll.

The stitched red mouth seemed to quaver a bit.

Suddenly she heard Richard's footsteps outside.

"Maggie, damn it! You could get hurt racing around this old town."

Maggie didn't care what Richard said—she didn't like him. She crouched down inside the cupboard and shut the door, leaving it open just a crack so she could see out.

"Are you hungry?" he called. She watched him stop in the doorway, staring into the building. Maggie's heart pounded hard and she bit her lower lip, afraid he might see her.

"Come on, kid," he growled.

Maggie clutched the old doll to her chest and closed her eyes. She wanted Richard to go away.

"I'm going to cook breakfast now," he said, moving away. He continued down the sidewalk with heavy footsteps. "When you're ready, you can come and eat, too."

Maggie waited a long time and didn't move until she smelled bacon frying. Her stomach growled again. The bacon smelled so good. It'd been hours and hours since she'd eaten.

Her grip on the doll loosened and she looked into its face again. It was a sad face, Maggie realized, as if the doll was about to cry. Maggie felt like crying, too. She missed her mommy.

Slipping her backpack off her shoulders, Maggie opened it and carefully tucked the sad doll inside.

"I cooked you some bacon and eggs," Richard called.

This time Maggie couldn't resist. She pushed open the cupboard door and slowly walked out of the old building.

"There you are," Richard said, holding out a plate to her.

Maggie didn't trust Richard anymore and moved cautiously toward him. If he said something mean, she was prepared to run.

"I'm sorry I yelled at you," Richard told her.

"What about the bad words?"

"I'm sorry about those, too."

"Will you take me home now?" she asked, standing in the middle of the dirt street.

Richard stood by the post where people used to hitch their horses. He didn't look like he was sorry, even if he said he was.

Maggie's stomach was empty and making funny noises.

"You really want to go home now?" Richard asked. He sounded surprised that she'd want to leave. He made it seem like she was supposed to be having fun.

"I want to see my mommy."

"Okay, okay, but we need to talk about it first." He set the plate of food aside and sat down on the steps leading to the raised sidewalk.

"Why?"

He scratched his head. "Do you remember Grady getting mad at Savannah about coming to the ghost town?" he asked.

Maggie nodded. Grady had been real upset with Savannah when he found out she'd been to the town. Savannah had come to look for special roses, and Grady had stomped around the house for days. Even Laredo wasn't happy when Savannah wanted to come back and look for more roses.

"Now, this is very important," Richard said, his voice low and serious. "You mustn't let anyone know where you've been, understand?"

Her chin came up a little. "Why not?"

"You love your mommy, don't you?"

Maggie nodded.

"If anyone finds out you've been here . . ." He stopped and glanced in both directions as if he was afraid someone might be listening. "If anyone finds out, then something really bad will happen to your mother."

Maggie's eyes grew big.

"Do you know what ghosts are?" Richard asked.

"Melissa Washington dressed up in a sheet and said she was a ghost last Halloween," Maggie told him.

"There are good ghosts and bad ghosts."

"Which kind live here?" Maggie whispered.

"Bad ones," he whispered back. His voice was spooky. She wondered if he was trying to scare her on purpose.

"Bad ones?" she repeated, faintly.

"Very bad ones, and if you tell anyone, even your best friend, then the bad ghosts will find out and hurt your mother."

"How . . . how will they hurt Mommy?"

"You don't want to know, kid." He squeezed his eyes shut and made an ugly face, as if just telling her about it would upset him.

Maggie blinked, not sure she should believe him.

"Remember when Wiley cut his hand and Savannah had to wrap it up for him?"

"Yes . . ."

"That's what bad ghosts will do to your mommy, only it wouldn't just be her hand."

Maggie forgot all about the smell of bacon. Wiley's hand had bled and bled. Blood had gotten everywhere, and she could remember being surprised that one hand had so much blood in it. Just looking at it had made her feel sick to her stomach.

"You wouldn't want anything bad like that to happen to your mommy, would you?"

Maggie shook her head.

"I didn't think so."

"Can I go home now?"

He studied her for a long time. "You won't tell anyone?"

"No."

"Cross your heart?"

"Cross my heart." She made a big X over her heart.

"I'd hate to see your Mommy hurt, wouldn't you?"

Maggie nodded.

"Then maybe it'd be all right if I took you home."

Maggie sighed with relief. She was tired and hungry, and all she wanted was to see her mother again.

Richard helped her into the cab of Grady's truck. He made her curl up on the seat and keep her head down so she couldn't see as they drove away. Every time she closed her eyes she thought about a bad ghost and what might happen to her mother if she told anyone where she'd been. She still wasn't sure if Richard was lying, but she couldn't take any chances. She remembered how angry Grady had been with Savannah. When she asked her mother about it, Caroline had explained that Savannah had gone to a dangerous place. Now Maggie understood why Grady was so upset. That town was really creepy, and the more she thought about it, the more she believed there were bad things in those buildings.

The ride was bumpy and she was tossed about, but Richard wouldn't let her sit up and look out the window until they were on the real road.

"Remember, kid, you never saw me. Got that?"

"I never saw you," she repeated solemnly.

"Your mother's life depends on you keeping your trap shut. You wouldn't want your mother dead, would you?"

"No."

"Good. Just remember that the first time you're tempted to tell someone where you were."

"I'll remember. I won't tell." Maggie didn't want her mommy to die. Not like her grandmother. Or Savannah's parents. Or Emma Bishop's daddy.

Richard didn't drive her all the way back to the Yellow Rose. He stopped at the top of the driveway, leaned across her and opened the truck door.

"Remember what I said," he told her again. His eyes were mean.

"I'll remember," she promised, and before he could change his mind, she climbed out of the truck. She stumbled as she jumped down and fell, scraping her elbows. She began to cry, hardly noticing that Richard had driven off, tires squealing.

With her backpack hitting her shoulder blades, Maggie raced toward the ranch house. The driveway was long and her legs felt like they were on fire before the house finally came into view.

Grady stood on the porch with a cup of coffee, but the moment he saw her, he gave a loud shout and flung the cup away. Then he leaped off the porch without using any of the steps and ran toward her.

Almost immediately afterward, her mother threw open the screen door and placed both hands over her mouth. Then she started running, too. Maggie had never been so happy to see her mother. She was even glad to see Grady. He waited for Caroline and let her go to Maggie first. Maggie liked that.

Her mother caught her in her arms and held her tight, then started to cry. She was worried about the bad ghosts, Maggie reasoned. She didn't need to be afraid, because Maggie wouldn't tell. Not anyone. Not ever.

Grady wrapped his arms around them both. He closed his eyes the way people did in church when they prayed. When he opened them again, he smiled at her. Maggie liked the way he smiled. It was a nice smile, not mean.

"Boy, we're glad to see you," he said.

SAVANNAH WIPED the tears from her face as she strolled along the pathway in her rose garden. But this morning she didn't appreciate the beauty of the roses. Nor did she find the solace she normally did here. If she lived to be a hundred years old, she didn't want to go through another day like the past one.

Although Caroline had repeatedly told her it wasn't her fault that Maggie had turned up missing, Savannah blamed herself. She'd been preoccupied with baking bread, her head full of the romance developing between her brother and her best friend. What she *should* have been doing was keeping careful watch over her best friend's child.

"I thought I'd find you here." Laredo walked up from behind her.

She didn't want him to know she'd been crying, but wasn't sure she could hide it.

"Sweetheart, why are you still upset? Maggie's home safe and sound."

"I know."

"Then what's bothering you?"

Her chest tightened, and she waited until the ache eased before she answered. "My brother."

Laredo clasped her shoulders. "Richard?"

She nodded. "He was involved in Maggie's disappearance. I know it."

"I have to admit it's mighty suspicious."

"Maggie won't say a word. Everyone's tried to get her to say where she was, but she refuses. Even Frank Hennessey can't get her to budge."

"It doesn't matter. She's home now."

"But it *does* matter," Savannah said passionately. "Laredo, tell me, where did Grady and I go wrong?"

"Sweetheart, your brother's an adult who makes his own decisions.

You didn't do anything wrong. You're his sister, not his mother, and even if you were, I'd say the same thing. Richard is his own person, responsible for himself."

"In my head I agree with everything you're saying, but that doesn't take away the pain."

Laredo guided her to the patio set and made her sit down in one of the white wrought-iron chairs.

"I was the one who convinced Grady to let him stay."

"Yes, but that's because Richard's your brother."

"If I'd listened to Grady that first night, none of this would have happened."

"Oh, my love, that's the risk of having a gentle heart. Someone's bound to take advantage of it. I'm sorry it had to be your own brother."

"He's hurt so many people." That was what troubled Savannah most. It wasn't just she and Grady who'd been hurt, but others. Who knew how many? Wherever he'd spent the past six years, she had no doubt he'd left victims behind. People like the shopkeepers in Promise. He'd defrauded them, humiliated them, and ultimately *she* was the one to blame. Savannah didn't know if she could forgive herself. "I should've let Grady kick him out that first day," she muttered fiercely.

"You don't think he's coming back?"

She shook her head. "All his things are gone."

"Everything?"

She nodded and swallowed tightly. "Including Grady's truck."

Laredo swore under his breath. "Did Grady talk to Sheriff Hennessey?" he asked.

Savannah looked down at her clenched hands. "Yes," she said, her voice small. "That was when he learned . . ."

"Learned what?"

She sighed. "There's more, Laredo. Richard's charged thousands of dollars' worth of goods in Promise. He owes money to everyone in town. There was never any check. He didn't intend to pay for any of the things he charged and now he's gone." She squeezed her eyes shut in an effort to keep the tears at bay. "You should have seen the look on Grady's face when Frank told him. It was the same look he had six years ago—when he found out what Richard did then. After Mom and Dad died . . ."

Savannah hadn't thought herself capable of such intense anger. She looked her husband in the eye and said, "I think I hate my own brother."

Eight

Richard had been gone a week. To Grady, his brother's disappearance was both a blessing and a curse. Only now was Grady getting a complete picture of the damage Richard's extended visit had wrought. Every day since his brother had vanished, a fistful of new bills arrived, charges Richard had made using the family's accounts.

The bills were stacked on Grady's desk, and whenever he looked at them, his anger mounted. He'd made a list of money owed and checked it three or four times before he could grasp the full extent of what Richard had done.

While a majority of businesses in town accepted credit cards, ranchers tended to avoid them. Grady carried only one, and it was tucked in the back of his wallet for emergencies. All his purchases were paid for with cash or put on account, then paid in full at the end of each month.

In the weeks since his return, Richard had taken it upon himself to run into town to pick up supplies, and Grady had let him. Sending his worthless brother on errands had seemed innocent enough, and it freed up Laredo, Wiley and him for the more serious ranching chores. What Grady didn't know was that every time Richard had driven into town, he'd charged clothing, expensive liquor, all kinds of things, on the family accounts. It added up to nearly eight thousand dollars, not including the money still owed on some of his earlier purchases. Richard had masterfully hidden what he'd done, robbing Peter to pay Paul, returning goods and buying other things with the credits. He'd managed to disguise his actions using a number of clever cons. Merchants had trusted him. Trusted the Weston name.

Now Richard was gone, and just like six years earlier, Grady was stuck with the mess he'd left behind.

Unable to tolerate looking at the stack of past due notices, Grady grabbed his hat and abandoned his office. The day was hot, although it was only nine in the morning, and he was supposed to meet Wiley and the hired hands near Gully Creek.

He was halfway to the barn when he saw Frank Hennessey's patrol car coming down the driveway, kicking up a plume of dust in its wake. Grady paused and waited for the lawman. With any luck Frank would have some word about Richard and the stolen truck. Whereas Grady hadn't filed charges against his brother six years ago, he felt no such compulsion now. He wanted Richard found and prosecuted to the full extent of the law.

Richard deserved a jail term, if for nothing more than the agony he'd caused Caroline by kidnapping Maggie. Until the day he died, Grady wouldn't understand what had prompted his brother to steal away with the child.

For her part Maggie seemed to have made a full recovery. Thank God. She clung to Caroline, but that was understandable. She refused to talk about where she'd gone or who she'd been with, but anyone with half a brain knew it'd been Richard. If Grady had anything for which to thank his useless brother, it was that he'd had had the common decency to bring Maggie back to her mother.

Frank parked the patrol car in the yard and slowly climbed out of the driver's seat. "Morning, Grady." He touched the brim of his hat.

"Frank." Grady nodded in greeting. "I hope you've come with good news."

"Good and bad, I'm afraid," Frank said. By tacit agreement the two men headed toward the house for coffee. Savannah was busy in her office, updating her rose catalog on the computer, but she'd recently put on a fresh pot.

Grady poured them each a cup but didn't sit down. When it was a question of receiving news about Richard, he preferred to do it standing up.

"What have you learned?" Grady asked, after giving Frank a moment to taste the coffee. He leaned against the kitchen counter and crossed his ankles. Frank remained standing, as well.

"First, your truck's been found."

This was an unexpected and pleasant surprise. Grady had driven the old Ford pickup for ten years now, and he'd grown attached to it. The thought of being forced to buy a new one had rankled, especially in light of the mounting bills.

"Richard abandoned it in Brewster," Frank said, "and stole another."

While he wasn't surprised, Grady would almost rather lose his truck permanently than have his own brother steal some other rancher's vehicle.

"It was a newer model," Frank said with a soft snicker. "Apparently yours was a bit too old to suit his image."

Grady didn't miss the sheriff's well-placed sarcasm.

"Only this truck had an additional advantage," Frank muttered.

"What's that?"

"The owner kept a rifle mounted in the back window."

Grady took a moment to mull over the information. "You don't think Richard would actually use it, do you?"

The lawman shrugged. "Given the right set of circumstances, I wouldn't put it past him."

Grady had never thought of Richard as violent. He'd proved himself to be a weasel and a lowlife, but the fact that he might be brutal enough to use a weapon against another human being surprised even Grady. "What makes you think that?" Grady asked, afraid of what Frank was going to say. Last night he'd alluded briefly to something Richard had done back East, but at the time they were all too concerned about Maggie to give it much thought. "What do you know about Richard?"

The sheriff had never been one to hedge, and he didn't do so now. "It gives me no pleasure to tell you this, but there's been an arrest warrant issued for him from New York City."

"New York? On what charge?"

"The list is as long as my arm," Frank said with real regret. "Extortion for one. Richard's been involved in a number of scams, most of them bilking immigrants from Central and South America. Apparently he fed them a pack of lies, luring them into the country with promises of housing and jobs. Promises he had no intention of keeping. He set them up in warehouses in horrible conditions, forced them into menial jobs from which he collected most of their pay. It made big news on the East Coast when his activities were uncovered. Somehow he managed to scrape together the bail, then hit the road the minute he was freed."

Grady had been angry at his brother and furious at himself, too, for allowing Richard to worm his way back into their lives with his hard-luck story. Richard had taken advantage of his family; that was bad enough. But to learn he'd made a profession of stealing from others made Grady sick. How was it that his own brother—born of the same two parents, raised in the same household—could have lowered himself to such depths? If he lived to be an old man, Grady would never understand what had turned Richard into the type of person who purposely hurt others.

"I'm sorry to be the one to tell you this, Grady," Frank said again.

"I realize that." His voice sounded strange even to his own ears.

"When and if we find Richard, I won't have any choice but to arrest him."

"I understand." Grady wouldn't expect anything less. It was what his brother deserved.

"I talked to the New York district attorney this morning. The state wants him bad. Apparently there's been quite a bit of press regarding his arrest and the charges brought against him. He's hurt a lot of people, Grady."

"What happened to him? What made Richard the way he is?" The questions were rhetorical; Grady didn't actually expect the sheriff to supply an answer.

Frank shook his head. "Hell if I know. I liked Richard. He was always charming and clever—but somehow that turned into conniving and untrustworthy. Why he's like that, I couldn't say. Over the years I've met other people who were just as rotten, and I don't believe environment or bad circumstances is always the explanation. Your parents were God-fearing folk, and they raised him right. The fault lies within Richard himself."

Although Grady already knew as much, it helped to have a lawman as experienced as Frank confirm it.

"Eventually Richard will be caught," Frank said, as if he felt the necessity to prepare Grady for the inevitable. "And when he is, he'll be headed straight for prison."

It hurt to think of his brother doing jail time, but Grady's sympathies went out to all the people Richard had cheated, himself included.

Grady walked Frank out to his patrol car, then made his way to the barn. He whistled for Rocket and stopped abruptly when the dog didn't come. Rocket's hearing was getting bad, and he'd grown arthritic; these days, he mostly enjoyed lazing about on the front porch. But he still liked to accompany Grady to the barn. Just to reassure himself, Grady decided to check on his dog. Rocket had belonged to his father and was already middle-aged—seven years old—at the time of the accident. In the hard, financially crippling years that followed, the dog had become Grady's constant sidekick and friend. He'd shared his woes, frustrations, joys and sorrows with Rocket, and the old dog always gave him comfort.

A smile came to him when he saw the dog lying on his usual braided rug. He whistled again. "Come on, boy, we've got work to do."

Rocket remained still.

As Grady approached, the front porch, his steps slowed. He wasn't sure when he realized his faithful companion was gone, but by the time he reached the porch steps, his heart was full of dread.

"Rocket," he whispered, and hunkered down beside the dog.

One touch confirmed the worst. Rocket had died, apparently in his sleep.

An intense sadness settled over Grady. On a ranch dogs came and went, and he'd learned the downfall of becoming too attached to any one animal. But Rocket was special. Different. Rocket was a loyal, intelligent dog—the best dog he'd ever had; Rocket was also the last tangible piece of his father.

His throat ached and he bowed his head for several minutes, not even trying to fight back the tears.

Once he'd composed himself, he sought out his sister. He found her working in her garden. "I need a shovel," he announced without emotion, as if he didn't know where one was kept.

As he knew she would, Savannah guessed immediately that something wasn't right. "What happened?"

He steeled himself and told her. "Rocket's gone. It looks like he died in his sleep."

He watched as the sadness transformed her face. Tears filled her eyes. "Oh, Grady, I'm so sorry. I now how much you loved him."

"He was just a dog," he said with a stoicism he didn't feel.

"Not an ordinary dog," she added gently.

"No, not ordinary," he agreed, the pain of loss tightening his chest. "If you agree, I'd like to bury him in your garden by the rosebush you named after Mom."

She nodded mutely.

They worked side by side, brother and sister. Grady dug the grave, grateful for the physical effort that helped vent his pain. Again and again he was forced to remind himself that Rocket was just a dog, like a dozen or more who'd lived and died through the years. But he couldn't make himself believe it.

When he finished, he placed a rock as a marker. Savannah stood beside him.

"Goodbye, Rocket," she whispered.

"Goodbye, old friend," Grady said.

Savannah sobbed and turned into his arms. Grady held her, battling back emotion himself. An image came to mind, a memory—his father crouched down and Rocket running toward him, leaping into his arms, joyfully licking his face. Their reunion would be a happy one, but Grady knew there'd be a hole in his heart for a long time to come.

* * *

"I'M GLAD we could finally meet for lunch," Ellie Frasier said, sliding into the booth at the bowling alley café.

Jane Dickinson smiled in welcome. She'd been waiting ten minutes, but she tended to be early, a habit her family had instilled in her. This lunch date was something she'd really looked forward to, although it had been difficult to arrange with both their schedules so busy. But Dovie had encouraged Jane to meet Ellie, mentioning her in almost every conversation.

Jane had come to think of Dovie as a mentor and friend. Stopping to talk with her that first morning she'd gone for a jog had been one of the smartest things she'd done since moving to Promise. Unfortunately Dovie was still the only person in town she knew on a first-name basis. Despite her efforts to become part of the community, friendly gestures from the other residents of Promise were few and far between.

"So . . . Dovie thought it would be a good idea for the two of us to get to know each other," Ellie said, reaching for the menu.

"I realize you're getting married soon," Jane said as a means of starting the conversation. "You must be terribly busy. . . ."

Ellie nodded. "The wedding's only a couple of weeks away." A wistful look stole over her face.

Jane recognized that look—it was the look of a woman in love. Jane envied her happiness. After medical school and then working as an intern, followed by her residency at a huge public-health hospital in Los Angeles, there hadn't been time in her life for anything other than medicine. Now she was trapped in Texas with only one friend and zero prospects for romance.

Ellie did little more than glance at the menu before she set it aside.

Jane had spent several minutes reading over the selections, but had failed to make a choice. "You know what you're going to have?"

"I almost always order the chicken-fried steak."

The thought of all those fat grams was enough to make Jane feel queasy. Even the salads listed on the menu were ones she normally avoided—coleslaw with mayonnaise dressing, for instance. Most of the food was battered and fried. Even the vegetables. Okra coated in cornmeal and cooked in a deep fryer. The same with tomatoes. It was a wonder anyone lived beyond twenty-five in this town. The eating habits here were probably the unhealthiest she'd seen in years. It was time the people of Promise caught up with the latest information on health and diet.

"The chicken-fried steak is great," Ellie coaxed when Jane continued to study the menu.

The waitress arrived with her pad and pen. Ellie gave the woman her order, then chatted briefly while Jane reviewed her choices one last time.

"I'll have a green salad with avocado if you've got it."

The waitress—Denise, according to her name tag—wrote it down on her pad.

"With dressing on the side."

Denise exchanged a scornful glance with Ellie before she called the order in to the kitchen. The woman's reaction was typical of what Jane had encountered the past few weeks.

"What did I do that was so wrong?" Jane asked, leaning forward.

"First off, we Texans pride ourselves on our food."

"The diet around here is appalling," Jane blurted without thinking. "Everything is loaded with fat. Chicken-fried steak, barbecued meat, chili without beans—doesn't anyone appreciate the high fiber content of kidney beans?"

"It's exactly this attitude that's causing your problems, Doc."

"What attitude? All I'm trying to do is set better health standards for the community! It's a wonder you aren't all dead or dying."

"And a wonder you haven't been tarred and feathered," Ellie snapped.

Jane's mouth sagged open. She might have laughed if Ellie hadn't looked so serious.

"You want to know why people are unfriendly?" Ellie asked. "Perhaps you should look at how *you* come across. Rude, superior and know-it-all! The only reason I agreed to talk to you is because of Dovie, who for reasons I don't understand has taken a liking to you."

The woman was spitting mad, and other than pointing out a few basic truths, Jane still didn't know what she'd done that was so offensive.

"As far as everyone in this town is concerned, you can take your salad-eating wine-sipping butt and go back to California. We don't need some surfer chick telling us what's good for us, understand?"

Jane noted that the other customers had gone quiet. Several heads nodded in agreement. "I see," she said, struggling to hold on to her composure. "But unfortunately I've signed a contract and I'm stuck here for three years. So if I'm going to live in this community—"

"Then I suggest you change your high-and-mighty ways."

Swallowing her pride, Jane nodded. "I'm probably going to need a little help."

"You need a lot of help."

Jane decided to let that comment slide. "I'd appreciate a few words of advice."

Ellie didn't answer right away. "You sure you're up to this?"

Jane smiled. As far as she could see, she didn't have any choice. "Be gentle, all right?"

A smile cracked Ellie's lips. "I'll try."

Jane sighed. They'd started off on the wrong foot, but she sensed Ellie could be an important ally, and she badly needed a friend her own age. Dovie was kind, but it would take more than the assistance of one woman to help her fit in.

"Denise." Ellie waved her arm and called for the waitress. "Doc wants to change her order."

"I do?"

"You said you're willing to learn. Now's your chance. Your initiation, if you like. First, I'll teach you how to eat like a Texan. We can both diet tomorrow."

Jane swallowed, then nodded. "What is it I want to order?"

Ellie motioned to the waitress. "The doc here will have the chicken-fried steak, fried okra and an extra scoop of gravy on her mashed potatoes."

"All *right*," Denise said with smiling approval, writing it on her pad. "Do you want a side salad with that?" she asked.

It would probably be the only healthy part of the entire meal. "Sure." Jane was about to remind her to leave off the dressing, when Ellie added, "Put the dressing right on top of it, too, will you, Denise?"

The waitress grinned from ear to ear. "Not a problem."

Jane decided then and there that either she'd adjust to life in Texas . . . or die trying.

MAGGIE GASPED and bolted upright in bed, unsure for a moment where she was. Her skin felt clammy, and she was breathing fast. A moment later she realized it had only been a dream. She'd been in the town again, the one with the bad ghosts. Richard was in her dream, too. He was looking at her and his face kept getting wider and longer as if he were staring at her through a wavy mirror.

His voice boomed loud, too, and he kept telling her what would happen to her mother if Maggie told anyone where she'd been. Again and again she promised him she wouldn't tell, and she hadn't. Not anyone. Not even her dolls.

Kicking aside her blankets, Maggie stole out of the bedroom and sneaked down the hallway, guided by the night-light, to her mother's bedroom. She stood and watched her mother sleeping, checking to make sure she was safe and no bad ghosts had gotten her.

"Maggie?" Her mother's eyes fluttered open.

"I had a bad dream," Maggie whispered.

Her mother tossed back the sheet, silently inviting Maggie into bed with her. Maggie was glad; it was a rare treat to sleep with her mommy. She climbed onto the bed and her mother wrapped an arm around her, then gently brushed the hair from her brow.

"Was it a very bad dream?" she asked.

"A scary one," Maggie told her.

"Do you want to tell me about it?"

Maggie shook her head. She didn't want to think about Richard ever again. She remembered that he didn't know she'd taken the doll, and if he found out, he might send the bad ghosts after her. As soon as she could, Maggie had removed the doll from her backpack and hidden it inside a big tin in her closet. No one knew it was there. Not Mommy. Not Richard. Not anyone.

Safe in her mother's arms, Maggie closed her eyes.

"You're not frightened now, are you?"

Maggie shook her head, but it wasn't true. "A little," she confessed.

"Did I tell you Grady's coming over tomorrow after church, and we're going to the park for a picnic?"

Maggie's spirits buoyed. "We are?" Usually they went out to the ranch and visited with Savannah and Laredo, too.

"Does that sound like fun?"

Maggie nodded eagerly. "Will Grady push me on the swing?"

"If you ask him."

Maggie closed her eyes again and sighed deeply. "Grady's not so bad. I'm sorry his dog died." She'd liked Rocket.

She felt her mommy nod. "He's going to miss him."

"I'm going to miss him, too," Maggie said. "Maybe we can make Grady feel better."

"He doesn't frighten you anymore?"

Maggie shook her head. "He does a little when he yells, but if I plug my ears I don't really hear it."

"He doesn't mean to yell, it's just . . . part of his nature."

Maggie wasn't entirely sure what that meant. But she knew that ever since the morning Grady found her running down the driveway and she saw his face light up with a smile, she'd liked him better. Until then, she'd never seen Grady smile, not a real smile, anyway. He'd hugged her again and again that day, and her mommy, too. Later he'd taken her into the barn and held her hand so she wouldn't be afraid of Widowmaker and let her see the new colt.

Grady had reminded her that she had yet to choose a name for him. She'd chosen "Moonbeam," and Grady said it was a pretty name. Wiley had teased him about it and said it sounded like one of those hippie names from the sixties—whatever that meant—but Grady had insisted Moonbeam was it. She'd chosen well.

"I think Grady's special," Maggie announced suddenly. She no longer felt any doubt. Richard had been fun at first, but he wasn't a real friend.

"I do, too," her mommy said softly.

CAROLINE HAD READIED the picnic basket and cooler before church, packing everything that didn't need to be refrigerated. It had been Grady's idea to go on a picnic in Pioneer Park and she suspected she knew why. Ever since she'd brought up the subject of Maggie's father, he'd been waiting for her to tell him. She wished now that she'd ignored his advice the day they'd gone horseback riding. The day Maggie disappeared. It would make everything far less complicated now. She pushed the worry to the back of her mind, determined to have a good time. If the subject arose, she'd deal with it then.

The park sat in the very center of town and took up four square blocks. It had a wading pool for toddlers, as well as Promise's one and only swimming pool, complete with diving board. The grass was lush and green and meticulously groomed. A statue of a pioneer family stood proudly in the middle, along with a plaque that described the pioneers' role in Texan history. The paved walkways all led directly toward the statue.

Maggie loved the playground, and Caroline appreciated Grady's willingness to indulge her child. Ever since that terrible night, Grady had given special attention to her daughter.

Caroline didn't know what she would have done without Grady. That night had been a turning point for all of them. For her and Grady, and for Grady and Maggie.

The doorbell rang and Maggie screamed from inside her bedroom, "I'll get it!" Caroline heard her race for the door.

The only person it could be was Grady. He'd followed them home from church, driving the old Ford pickup, which had been returned to him a few days before. Maggie had already changed out of her Sunday-school dress and into shorts. Caroline wore a sleeveless yellow cotton dress, with a wide straw hat and sandals, the same clothes she'd worn to the service. Grady sent her a purely masculine look of approval as Maggie dragged him by the hand into the kitchen.

"It's Grady," Maggie announced unnecessarily. "Can we go now?"

"Soon. I've got to load up the potato salad and fried chicken first."

"Mommy makes the best potato salad in the world," Maggie said. "She lets me peel the hard-boiled eggs and help her stir."

"No wonder it's so good," he said, and glanced from Maggie to Caroline.

The look, however brief, made Caroline wonder if he was speculating about who had fathered her child. Then again, she might be imagining it. Every time they were together, she became obsessed with her secret, with the need to tell Grady. She loved this man and she feared what would happen once he learned the truth.

"Go put on your running shoes," Caroline instructed her daughter. Maggie dashed out of the room, eager to comply.

Grady watched Maggie go before turning his attention to her. "I didn't embarrass you in church this morning, did I?"

"No," she answered, wondering what he was talking about.

"I couldn't keep my eyes off you."

"I didn't really notice . . ." She hated this tension, this constant fear that any look he gave her, any silence, meant he was wondering about Maggie's father. Soon, she promised herself. She'd tell him soon. Perhaps even today.

Grady gripped her about the waist and they kissed, sweetly and unhurriedly. "I didn't hear a word of Wade's sermon," he whispered into her hair, holding her close.

"Me, neither." But not for the reasons he assumed.

"Wade stopped me on the way out the door," Grady said, grinning, "and told me there'd be a test on the sermon next week. Not to worry, though, he was willing to share his notes."

Caroline managed a smile. "I think Wade's the best thing that's happened to Promise Christian in a long time."

"You're the best thing that's happened to me," Grady whispered. "Ever." He reluctantly let her go when Maggie tore into the kitchen.

The five-year-old was breathless with excitement. "I'm ready!" she cried.

Caroline added the potato salad and fried chicken to the cooler, and Grady carried it to his pickup. The three of them piled into the front and drove to the park.

Caroline noticed that Maggie was especially quiet on the short drive. She was concerned the child might be reacting to her tension. But Mag-

gie's spirits lifted the instant they arrived at the park. Grady lugged the
picnic supplies to a vacant table, and while Caroline covered it with a
plastic-coated tablecloth, Maggie insisted on showing Grady her favorite
swing.

"Go on, you two," Caroline said, waving them away. Once again she
noticed—or thought she did—the way Grady studied Maggie. Briefly she
wondered if he'd guessed.

Determined to ignore her worries, at least for the moment, Caroline
spread a blanket on the grass in a shady area. When she'd finished, she
slid the cooler beneath the table and out of the sun.

The sound of Maggie's laughter drifted toward her, and Caroline
looked up to discover her daughter on the swing set with Grady standing
behind her.

"Higher!" Maggie shouted. "Push me higher!"

Grady did, until Caroline held her breath at the heights the swing
reached. She pressed her hand to her mouth to keep from calling out a
warning, knowing she could trust Grady with her daughter. She gasped
once when the swing buckled, but Grady swiftly caught it and brought it
back under control.

Eventually he stopped the swing and Maggie returned to earth.
Squealing with delight, she still had energy left to run back to their picnic
table.

"Did you see, Mommy?" Maggie cried. "Did you see how high Grady
pushed me?"

Caroline nodded. "I saw."

"I could touch the sky with my feet. Did you see? Did you see?"

"Yes, baby, I saw."

The afternoon was lovely. After they ate, Maggie curled up on the
blanket and quickly fell asleep.

Now, Caroline commanded herself. *Tell him now.* But she couldn't
make herself do it, couldn't bear to see the look in his eyes when he
learned the truth. Avoiding his gaze, she brushed the soft curls from her
daughter's brow.

"Any effects from her night away from home?" Grady asked. "Has she
told you anything of what happened?"

"Not a word, but she woke up last night with a nightmare and wouldn't
tell me about it."

"Poor thing."

Caroline gazed down at her slumbering child, loving her with an intensity that went beyond anything she'd ever known, even the strong love

she felt for Grady. "She's back, safe and sound, and for that I'm grateful."

"I am, too."

Caroline leaned against Grady, letting him support her weight, his hands resting on her shoulders.

"Savannah reminded me that it's Maggie's birthday next week. I'd like to give her something special, but I need to ask you about it first. She seems quite taken with Moonbeam, so—"

"You're giving her the colt?" Caroline could barely believe her ears. At the same time she realized that the mention of Maggie's birthday created a natural opening to talk about her child's father. To reveal his name.

No! she couldn't tell him, Caroline thought in sudden panic.

"Of course we'll keep Moonbeam at the ranch."

While the offer was tempting, horses weren't cheap to maintain.

"The gift includes room and board." Grady answered her question even before she could ask it.

"That's generous of you."

"She's going to be six, right?"

"Yes."

His gaze softened as he studied the little girl. "You said once that you'd dated Cal."

Caroline felt as though her lungs had frozen. This was as close as Grady had come to asking her outright about Maggie's father.

"I did," she said, and looked away. He reached for her hand. "Now that Richard's gone—"

"Do you mind if we don't talk about my brother?" Grady said, interrupting her. "I want to escape him for a few hours if I can."

"Of course, but—"

"I'd much rather concentrate on other things just now, like how good you feel in my arms."

Caroline closed her eyes.

"It doesn't matter, Caroline," he whispered close to her ear.

"What doesn't matter?"

"About Maggie. I already love her."

"I know. It's just that . . ." Caroline liked to think she would have continued if Maggie hadn't chosen that precise moment to awake.

"Can we go swing again?" she asked Grady.

He grinned. "This time let's bring your mother, too. All right?"

Maggie took Caroline's hand and the three of them headed toward the swing set, the subject she was about to broach shelved once again.

The day ended far sooner than Caroline and Maggie would have wished. Grady dropped them off at seven and went to check in with Frank Hennessey. Caroline assumed it had to do with Richard, but she didn't ask and he didn't volunteer.

The light on her answering machine was flashing, and while she unpacked the picnic basket, she played it back.

"It's Savannah. Give me a call when you get home."

Tucking the phone to her ear, Caroline punched out her friend's number. As she waited for Savannah to answer, she set the leftovers in the refrigerator.

"Hi, it's me, Caroline. You called?" she asked when Savannah picked up the receiver.

"I did." Savannah sounded pleased about something, but didn't elaborate. In fact, she appeared to be waiting for Caroline to speak first.

"Um, Savannah, was there a particular reason you called?" Caroline finally ventured.

"Aren't you going to tell me, or is it a big secret?"

"Savannah, *what* are you talking about?"

The line went silent. "He didn't ask you?"

"Ask me what?"

"Oh, dear," Savannah said with an exaggerated sigh. "When he left this morning, Grady was as fidgety as a drop of cold water on a hot skillet."

"Maybe he's got heat rash," Caroline teased. "Now tell me what this is all about."

"Grady," Savannah said, as if that much should be obvious. "And then in church, the poor man couldn't keep his eyes off you."

"This isn't making a lot of sense, Savannah Smith."

"And I was so sure, too."

"Sure about what?" Caroline demanded.

"That Grady was going to ask you to marry him."

Nine

Every pew in Promise Christian Church was filled for the wedding of Ellie Frasier and Glen Patterson. Glen had asked Cal to be his best man and Grady to serve as one of the ushers. Grady had agreed before he learned that he was expected to wear a tuxedo. He wasn't sure how a man could breathe with a shirt buttoned up that tight.

The main advantage of being in the wedding party was that Caroline was one of Ellie's bridesmaids. Grady had never realized that four women all wearing the same dresses could look so different. In his—admittedly biased—opinion, Caroline was the most beautiful. Savannah, of course, was a close second.

Since it was the hottest time of the year, Wade McMillen kept his sermon short. Ellie and Glen exchanged their vows as both their mothers sat in the front row quietly weeping. The Moorhouse sisters sobbed loudly, and Dovie Boyd dabbed at her eyes, as well. Even the coolly composed Dr. Dickinson, sitting beside Dovie, sniffled a bit as the *I do*'s were said.

Grady met Frank Hennessey's eye as they exited the church. Frank had his arm protectively around Dovie, and his expression seemed to say that he had plenty of years on Grady and he still didn't understand what made women weep at weddings.

The reception was held at the Grange hall and, on this Saturday afternoon, there were as many cars parked out front as the night of the big summer dance. The table closest to the door was stacked high with elegantly wrapped wedding gifts.

Grady ended up spending most of his time in the reception line, but once again he was compensated by having Caroline at his side.

"Ellie looks so beautiful," she said when the last guest had made her way through the line.

Grady's patience when it came to these formal affairs was limited. He felt tired and hungry. "Do you want something to eat?" he asked with a longing glance at the buffet table.

"I've got to help Ellie change out of her wedding dress," she told him.

"You mean we can take off these fancy duds?" He eased his index finger between the starched collar and his neck.

"Not us. Just Ellie and Glen."

"Not fair," he complained.

"Go help yourself to some dinner and I'll be back before you know it." She kissed his cheek, and while it was only a sample of what he wanted, he'd take what he could get.

"Where'd Caroline go?" Cal asked, coming up behind Grady in the buffet line.

"To help Ellie change out of her dress." Grady thought that made him sound like an expert on wedding etiquette, but he wouldn't have had a clue if Caroline hadn't told him.

"Who designed these starched shirts, anyway?" Cal muttered, "The Marquis de Sade?"

"I wouldn't doubt it." Grady reached for a plate. It'd been hours since he'd last eaten. Between that and the afternoon's exertions, he was starved.

"Glen's a married man now," Cal said as if it had only now hit him.

"Does that bother you?" Grady asked, thinking there'd be a big adjustment in Cal's life. Grady had heard, Glen was moving into town with Ellie; apparently, they'd put money down on a house.

"Doesn't bother me at all—but it would if he hadn't married Ellie. Those two are good together."

Grady felt the same way. Cal and Glen had been his neighbors all his life. Neighbors and best friends. The three of them were as close as family, and yet Grady had to wonder if he knew Cal as well as he thought he did. Again and again he'd mulled over the news that Cal had once dated Caroline, but he firmly believed Cal would have married her if he'd been the baby's father.

Grady had given up trying to work out who Maggie's father was. He felt certain it had to be someone he knew, perhaps trusted, otherwise she wouldn't hesitate to tell him. Whenever they were together he watched her struggle with herself. The one time she'd been ready to tell him, he'd stopped her. He wanted to kick himself for that now. This secret was tormenting her—and him, too.

Last Sunday on their picnic, he'd tried to reassure her that it didn't matter. He loved Maggie and he loved her. Apparently he'd failed, because she seemed more apprehensive than ever.

"Glen looks at Ellie the way you look at Caroline," Cal said casually.

"It's that noticeable, is it?"

Cal nodded. "You could say that."

They carried their plates to a recently vacated table in the far corner of the hall.

Grady stacked the empty plates to one side and pulled out a chair. Cal sat across from him. "I'm thinking of asking Caroline to marry me," he said, mentioning it in an offhand way. It was the first time he'd said it aloud. He watched Cal's reaction, closely.

"All right!" Cal grinned. "I wondered how long it'd take you. I've always liked Caroline."

"I love her." Grady had no problem admitting it, and if Cal had any leftover emotion for her, he'd rather they cleared the air now.

"Then what's the holdup?"

Grady felt a surge of anger, not at the question but at the answer. He stabbed his fork into a thick slice of ham as he waited for the bitterness to leave him. This was a day of shared joy, and he refused to allow his brother to ruin it.

Cal propped his elbows on the table. "My guess would be that Richard's got something to do with this. I thought he wasn't around anymore."

Without elaborating, Grady told him about the latest fiasco involving Richard. Cal and Frank Hennessey were the only two people with whom Grady would discuss his worthless brother. He supposed Cal had told Glen; that was only natural, and fine with him. Six years earlier, when Richard had disappeared with the inheritance money, Cal had advised Grady to press charges against him. Grady had agonized over it and in the end decided not to. Now he wondered if he'd made the right decision.

Few other people knew of Richard's treachery.

Savannah might have told Caroline, but he couldn't be sure. Of all the women in town, Caroline had been the most sensible about Richard and his attentions. Grady admired her for seeing through his brother and not being taken in by his easy charm. Nearly everyone had been deceived by his flattery and suave ways, but not her.

"Richard's gone," Grady said, answering his friend, "and yet he isn't. He left behind damn near eight thousand dollars in debts."

Cal gave a low whistle.

Grady told him how his brother had charged things on local accounts all around town. Clothes, liquor, food, even camping and ranch supplies, although God only knew what he intended to do with them. Frankly, Grady didn't *want* to know.

"They aren't your debts," Cal was quick to remind him. "The bills have Richard's signature on them."

"But he put them on the family accounts."

Cal sighed in resignation. "You paid them, didn't you?"

"I didn't have any choice." It was the Weston name that stood to be tarnished. Grady knew he wouldn't be able to look his friends and neighbors in the eye when his own brother had bilked them, unless he himself made good on the debts. Which he had. That eight thousand had nearly wiped out his savings, but he'd get by, just as he always had.

Earlier in the week he'd checked out engagement rings in the jeweler's window, and he'd realized he wouldn't be able to buy as big a diamond as he wanted for Caroline; he also realized it was more important to be debt-free.

Cal was about to ask him something else when Frank Hennessey abruptly pulled out a chair and joined them. He cast them a grateful look. "I'm safe for now," he said in a low voice.

"Safe from who?" Grady asked, puzzled. Frank normally didn't run from anything or anyone.

Frank threw back his head with a groan. "Dovie. The woman's got that look in her eye again."

Cal and Grady exchanged glances. "What look?" Cal ventured.

"Marriage. I . . . I've been telling her for the last ten years that one day I'd marry her. I meant it at the time, but I tell you, boys, the mere thought is enough to make my blood run cold. I can see now I'm not the marrying kind—I'm just not! I've got to get *her* to see that." He hunched forward. "But I don't want to upset her, either."

"I thought—assumed that you and Dovie had, you know, an understanding," Grady whispered.

"We do," Frank said. "But every once in a while she reminds me of that stupid promise and I find an excuse to delay it, and she's satisfied for another few months. Then we attend a wedding or one of her friends has an anniversary, and she brings the subject up again. You'd think after this length of time, she'd figure we've got a pretty good arrangement. You'd think she'd be willing to leave well enough alone." He gave a long-suffering sigh. "I'm crazy about Dovie, but marriage isn't for me."

Grady began to speak, but Frank cut him off. "Weddings are dangerous things, boys. Dovie took one whiff of those orange blossoms, and next thing I knew she had that look."

"Why does she want to get married?" Cal asked, voicing Grady's own thoughts. If she'd been content for ten years without a ring on her finger, she obviously wasn't as keen on marriage as she let on.

"Dovie says a ten-year courtship is long enough. Either I follow through or this is it." Frank shook his head sadly. "I should never have said anything to her about marriage," he muttered, "but I couldn't help myself. I thought I'd lose her if I didn't propose, so I . . . sort of . . . did. At the time I actually believed we could make a go of it. Now I know marriage just wouldn't work. Not for me, anyway."

"Give her time to accept reality," Grady suggested.

Frank shook his head in despair. "You don't know Dovie like I do."

"You're sure you don't want to marry her?" The question came from Cal. Cal's mother and Dovie were good friends.

"It isn't that at all," Frank said. "I don't want to get married, period. It has nothing to do with Dovie. She's the best thing that ever happened to me."

"But you told her you would."

"I know," Frank admitted. "The thing is, most of the time she's as happy with our arrangement as I am. We live separate lives. She has her shop and her interests, and I have mine, and we both like it that way. We see each other just about every day, and hell, she knows how I feel about her."

"But you won't marry her, no matter what?"

"I told you, marriage and I aren't compatible." Frank looked at them mournfully. "I like my life just the way it is." The sheriff slowly exhaled. "The two of you understand, don't you, seeing that neither one of you is married, either?"

Cal glanced quickly at Grady, eyebrows raised. "This isn't a good time to be asking Grady that," he said.

"What?" Frank said with a moan. "You aren't thinking about getting married, are you?"

"As a matter of fact, I am."

Frank swore under his breath. "Caroline, isn't it?"

Grady nodded, not hiding his grin.

"She's a fine woman, but damn it all, this is going to send Dovie into wedding overdrive."

"I haven't asked Caroline yet," Grady said.

"Thank God, because once Dovie learns you two got engaged, I won't hear the end of it."

"I can't guarantee Caroline's answer."

"Do you honestly think she'll refuse?" Frank asked in a way that said he knew the answer. "It's fairly obvious how you feel about each other."

"Naturally I'm hoping. . . ."

"Why borrow trouble?" Cal asked. "Of course she'll say yes. Why shouldn't she?"

TEN YEARS, Dovie mused darkly. She'd wasted ten years of her life on that ungrateful lawman. Arms folded, she paced her living room, back and forth, back and forth, trying to walk off her anger.

It wasn't working.

By the time they left Ellie and Glen's wedding reception, Dovie was barely speaking to Frank. He didn't have a lot to say, either—which was just as well. He'd proposed to her shortly after they'd met, and all these years she'd waited. All these years she'd believed in him and hoped and loved him.

Well, she'd better smarten up and accept the truth. Frank never intended to marry her, and really, why should he? He enjoyed all the delights of married life with none of the responsibilities. Twice a week he spent the night, and in the morning she made him breakfast and handed him his clean laundry and sent him on his way with a kiss.

No more.

There'd been only one other man in Dovie's life, and that was her husband. But Marvin had been dead thirteen years now. And for ten of those years she'd pined after a lawman who claimed to love her, but apparently not enough to marry her.

A light knock sounded on her back door. It had to be Frank Hennessey—the only person in the entire world who came to her in the dark of night. And Dovie knew why he'd come. Well, he could forget it. She had a thing or two to say to him.

She marched through the house and threw open the door, startling Frank.

"If you're here for the reason I think you are, then you can turn around and go right back home." She pointed in the direction of his parked car.

He blinked. "Dovie, sweetheart, you don't mean that." He removed his hat and wore the anguished look of a misunderstood and badly maligned male.

"I certainly do mean it, Franklin Hennessey." She would have slammed the door on him, but he'd stuck his foot in.

"We have a good life just the way it is," he said enticingly.

"If I'm so happy about our lives, then why do I feel this ache in my heart? Why can't I sit through a wedding without dissolving in tears? I want you to marry me, Frank."

The pained expression returned. "Oh, Dovie, I can't do that."

"Can't or won't, Frank?"

He didn't answer and she knew why.

"I love you, Dovie." The words were a low purr.

"You *say* you love me, but you won't do anything to prove it," she spit, folding her arms and refusing to look at him.

"I can't tell you how sorry I am. I always thought . . . I believed one day I'd be able to . . . to take the plunge. But I realize now that marriage would never work for someone like me."

"Then we're at an impasse. I guess the reality is that you won't marry me. Not now and not ever."

"But it's not because I don't love you!"

"So either I accept you the way you are or—"

"Our arrangement has worked so far, hasn't it, my love?" he asked his eyes pleading.

"Or I break off this dead-end relationship," she continued, ignoring his words.

Frank went pale. "Oh, Dovie, you wouldn't do that."

Dovie drew a deep breath and the anger vanished. A peace of sorts came over her, a calmness. "I have to, Frank—for my own self-respect, if nothing else."

He stared at her as though he didn't understand.

It hurt to say the words, but either she did this or she'd never be able to face herself in the mirror again. Squaring her shoulders, she smiled sadly and said, "It'd be best if we didn't see each other anymore."

The sheriff's mouth dropped open. "Dovie, please! Be reasonable about this."

"It's over, Frank." She straightened and looked him straight in the eye.

"Okay," he agreed, unmistakable regret in his voice. "If that's the way you want it."

Dovie's hand gripped the door handle. "Goodbye, Frank," she said.

"Good night, Dovie." As though in a daze, he turned and left.

Tears clouded her eyes, but she refused to let them fall. She'd loved Frank for ten years, and it would be a major adjustment to untangle her life from his, but she'd do it and be a stronger woman for it.

A loud knock on the windowpane of her back door made her jump. Dovie answered it to find a bewildered-looking Frank standing on the other side.

"I just want to be sure we understand each other," he said, holding his hat in both hands. "Are you saying you don't want me stopping by on Wednesday and Saturday nights anymore?"

She rolled her eyes. "That's exactly what I'm saying."

"I see." He seemed to ponder her words for a moment. "What about dinners on Sunday?"

"I think we should put an end to that, as well."

"Afternoon tea at your shop?"

"You can find some other woman to spend your afternoon break with," she suggested, even though the thought of him seeing anyone else nearly destroyed her.

"There isn't another woman in the world I'd rather be with than you."

A slow smile eased up the corners of her mouth. "Then the answer is simple. Marry me the way you promised."

Frank ground his teeth. "I can't, Dovie. I wish to hell I could, but it's impossible. I just can't do it."

"There are certain things I can't do, either, Frank." She softly closed the door.

CAROLINE KNEW this dinner was different the minute Grady phoned to invite her. He was formal and polite—as if he was planning something other than a casual evening out.

"He's going to ask you," Savannah insisted. "I'm sure of it." It'd been a week since Ellie and Glen's wedding, and the topic of love and marriage hadn't strayed far from her best friend's mind.

"Have you thought about how you'll respond when he does?"

Caroline had thought of little else for an entire week. Not her response, should he bring up the question of marriage, but *his* response once she told him the truth about Maggie. The conversation lay before her like a stretch of deep, treacherous water. They'd need to get through that before she'd be able to consider her reply.

She figured he'd introduce the matter of marriage over dinner. Everything pointed to that. Rumor had it that he'd been seen in the jewelry store earlier in the week. In fact, he'd made a number of trips into town.

He'd stopped by the post office three times, which was highly unusual. If she saw him in town even once a week that was a surprise; three times was almost unheard of.

Maggie was spending the night at Dovie's, so Caroline had the luxury of a free afternoon in which to indulge herself without the constant interruptions of a six-year-old. She soaked in a perfume-scented tub, painted her toenails and curled her hair with a hot iron, all the while praying everything would go smoothly.

This was supposed to be the night of her dreams. But by the time Grady arrived to pick her up, she was a nervous wreck. The hours of anticipating his reaction had left her tense and jittery. Not knowing how he'd feel, what he'd say, was almost more than she could take.

The doorbell rang precisely at six, reminding her that even in small things, Grady Weston was reliable, a man who kept his word. His eyes widened with appreciation when he saw her, and she realized every minute she'd spent in front of the mirror had been worth it.

"I didn't think it was possible for you to look more beautiful than you did at Ellie's wedding," he said with the sincerity of a man not accustomed to giving compliments.

"Thank you." She twirled around to give him a full view of her new dress. "Do you like it?"

"Oh-h-h, yes."

"Where's Maggie?" he asked, glancing around.

"With Dovie. She's spending the night."

He handed her a bottle of wine, as if he'd suddenly remembered it was in his hands.

"Shall I open it now?" she asked.

"Sure. If you want."

He followed her into the kitchen, and as she searched for a corkscrew, she saw him pacing the room, his lips moving.

"Grady?"

His head shot up and he looked startled.

"Did you say something?"

He shook his head in quick denial.

She found the corkscrew and gave it to him. While he wrestled with the cork, Caroline took out two wineglasses.

"This isn't going to work," he announced, and set the bottle down on the countertop, the cork half-out.

"That's the only corkscrew I have," she said.

"I'm not talking about the wine." He pulled out a kitchen chair and with both hands on her shoulders urged her to sit. Then he finished opening the wine, a white zinfandel, and poured them each a glass.

He drank down the first one in three gulps; after that, he immediately refilled his glass.

"If your parents were alive, I'd talk to them . . . but it's just you and me. So—I'll say what I have to say."

"What you have to say?" she repeated, her eyebrows arched. Despite her own anxiety, she couldn't help enjoying his discomfort. Just a little.

He pointed his finger at her as he struggled with the words. "I have to do this now. If I wait any longer, I'll say or do something stupid, and the entire evening will be ruined." His eyes were warm, openly revealing his love. "And that isn't what I want."

"What *do* you want, Grady?" she asked, in a soft voice.

He reached for his wine and took a deep swallow.

"Wine is usually sipped," she murmured.

"I know," he said, "but I need the fortification."

Caroline's heart swelled with emotion. "Oh, Grady, I love you so much."

He stared at her for a long wonder-filled moment. "I love you, too." He smiled then, sweetly. "I practiced this proposal a dozen times on the drive into town, and now I find myself completely at a loss. I don't know where the hell to start."

"The fact that you love me is a good opening."

"But I have to tell you so much more."

"Love is only the beginning . . ." This was where she needed to explain the past, but she couldn't. Not now, in the most wonderfully romantic moment of her life. Not when the man she loved with all her heart was about to ask her to share his life.

"I'm free to love you," he said.

"Free?" she repeated, not understanding.

"Richard's gone."

She frowned and felt a sudden chill race down her bare arms. "What does Richard have to do with this?"

"Everything." She could feel the anger coming from him. She swallowed, waiting for him to elaborate.

"Richard has been a thorn in my side for six long years. He's my brother, and for that reason alone, a part of me will always love him. But I refuse to allow him to dictate my life a minute longer than he already has."

"What . . . what do you mean?"

"I'm finished dealing with the problems my brother created. I refuse to pick up any more of the pieces, or accept any further responsibility for the disasters he's left in his wake. I'm not paying another debt of his. Every minute of the last six years has been spent struggling to regain ground Richard stole from me. I resent every one of those wasted minutes, and I refuse to deal with his mistakes anymore."

Caroline wasn't sure how she could remain upright in her chair, why she didn't pitch to the ground.

The harshness left Grady's eyes as he looked at her. "As I said, I'm no longer tied to Richard or his troubles, so I can tell you how much I love you. Maggie, too." The anger dissipated and his features softened with love. "I'm free to ask you to share my life, Caroline, if you'll have me."

He hesitated, and when she didn't immediately respond, he said gently, "I'm asking you to marry me."

The choking in her throat made it impossible to respond.

"Is the decision that difficult?" He sounded a little hurt.

"No . . ."

"I did it all wrong, didn't I?" he muttered. He thrust a hand into his coat pocket and produced a velvet ring case. "Give me another chance to do this the way you deserve."

"Grady—"

"No, don't say anything. Not yet." Then he opened the small velvet box. "It took me thirty-six years to find the woman I want to be with for the rest of my life, and that woman is you, Caroline Daniels."

She pressed both hands over her mouth, her eyes filled with tears.

"Would you do me the honor of becoming my wife?"

She tried to speak and found that she couldn't.

"Just nod," he suggested.

"I can't," she finally managed, her voice cracking.

"Can't nod?"

"I can't marry you . . ." She stood up, then walked to the sink and stared out the window. This was the most difficult thing she'd ever done, outside of burying her mother. Only now she felt as if it was her heart she was laying to rest. Her heart. And her future.

"You're saying no?" He was clearly shocked.

"I can't because . . ." She stopped, unable to continue.

"You *can't* marry me?"

"No."

"Is that your final answer?"

She dared not turn around and look at him. "That's my final answer," she said in a monotone.

She heard him retreat, his heavy steps taking him as far as the living room. Without warning, he rushed back into the kitchen.

"Just one damn minute," he shouted. "I don't accept that. You just finished telling me how much you love me!"

She couldn't deny it and so she said nothing.

"If you're going to reject my proposal, then at least have the decency to look me in the eye when you do it."

Slowly, her heart breaking, she turned toward him.

"Tell me to my face that you don't want to marry me," he demanded.

Her chin came up. "I won't marry you."

Grady's jaw was clenched. *"Why not?"* The two words were like knives.

"Because if you married me . . ." she began, gazing straight ahead. She couldn't go on.

"I'm not good enough for you, is that it?"

"No!" This was said with all the conviction of her soul.

"Then say it," he yelled. "Just say it."

"Because if you married me," she started again, "you'd be left to deal with yet another one of Richard's mistakes."

He frowned darkly. Then he understood, and a look of horrified disbelief came over him. "Are you saying that *Richard* is Maggie's father?"

Caroline hung her head and nodded.

Ten

Richard was Maggie's father. Nothing Caroline could have told him would have shocked Grady more. The news went through him like a bolt of lightning. He was speechless with surprise, then numb with disbelief. Richard? His no-good cheating irresponsible brother was the father of Caroline's child? It was more than he could take in. More than he could accept.

Once his mind had cleared enough to let him respond, he asked the obvious questions. "When were you lovers? I don't remember the two of you so much dating."

"We didn't, not in the normal sense." She reached for her wine. "I was in San Antonio in college, my senior year," she said, her voice low. "It was finals week. Knowing how crucial it was for me to do well, my mother didn't tell me what'd happened to your parents until after the exams. I felt horrible, sick to my stomach the moment she told me. I was furious with her for not letting me know. I'd always loved your mother. Your father, too." She inhaled deeply.

"You weren't at the funeral, were you?"

"No—because I didn't hear about it in time."

"Then how does Richard play into this?" He realized he sounded irritated; he couldn't help it. Damn it all, he was furious. Exasperated, too. The numbness was wearing off, and in its stead, a slow-burning anger began to build. Once again his brother had found a way to cheat him. Nothing in his life, *nothing*, was untainted by that bastard and his fiascos.

"San Antonio was his first stop after he took the money," Caroline continued.

Grady's eyes narrowed. "So you know about that? The theft?"

She nodded. "Savannah told me," she said. "Years later."

Grady pulled out a chair and sat down. He didn't think his knees would support him much longer.

"It was one of those flukes," Caroline went on. "I was gassing up at a service station and Richard pulled in. He didn't recognize me at first, but I told him how sorry I was about his parents." She looked away and took another steadying breath. "He seemed broken up about it."

"Broken up enough to walk away with the forty thousand dollars that was our inheritance," Grady mumbled.

"We had coffee together and he told me how he'd found your mother's and father's bodies."

"That's a lie!" Grady cried, knotting his fists in outrage. "Frank Hennessey found them and came and told us." How like Richard to seek all the sympathy!

"I know it's a lie now," she whispered, "but at the time I didn't have any reason not to believe him."

Grady vowed to stay quiet, seeing as every time he spoke, it interrupted the story, and this was one he very much wanted to hear.

"He broke into sobs and . . . and said he hadn't been able to bear the pain and after the funeral had blindly driven off, not knowing where he was going or how he'd gotten to San Antonio. He said he hadn't eaten or slept in days."

"And you believed him?" Grady shouted.

"He'd suffered a terrible loss." She raised her voice. "So, yes, I believed him."

Grady wiped a hand down his face. "I'm sorry, I didn't mean to yell."

"I . . . I didn't, either."

Despite the apology, he struggled with his temper. "It's something of a shock to learn that the woman I love has slept with my brother."

She didn't respond, but Grady could see that his words had hit their mark. He didn't want to hurt her, but he felt a sick ache in every part of his being, and lashing out was a natural response. Even when he knew he was being cruel and unfair. He hated himself for it, but couldn't seem to hold back.

To Caroline's credit she didn't retaliate or ask him to leave. He admired her restraint and wished his own response had been more generous, more forgiving. In time, perhaps, he could be, but not now. Definitely not now.

After a silence Caroline picked up her story. "He was an emotional mess and I took him home with me. We weren't in the house five minutes when he fell asleep on the sofa. I phoned my home and my mother confirmed that Richard had disappeared the afternoon of the funeral.

I . . . I didn't tell her he was with me. I should have. I realized that too late, but my sympathies were with Richard. He'd received a terrible shock and—"

"No less terrible than what Savannah and I suffered."

"I know, but he was with me and you were here in Promise." She clenched her hands in her lap. "Don't you think I've gone over this a million times since? Don't you think I have my regrets, too?"

He nodded, hating himself for being angry and unable to keep his emotions under control. Every time he thought about Richard being Maggie's father, a fierce kind of outrage gripped him.

"Do . . . do you want me to continue?"

"Yes," he replied, mentally preparing himself for what was to follow.

"According to Richard, he was overcome with grief, running from his pain and . . . and he'd found me."

"It was fate, right?" Grady's sarcasm was heavy.

"Yes . . ."

"He spent the night?"

"Yes." Her voice grew small. "I made up a bed in the living room for him, but in the middle of the night he came into my bedroom and said he needed someone to hold."

"And you let him?"

"Yes."

"I suppose he felt all better in the morning, then?"

"Grady, it wasn't like that."

Her voice grew strong, then defiant. He stared at her, and for a moment almost hated her. But it wasn't possible; he loved her too much. No one else possessed the power to hurt him like this. Loving Caroline and Maggie had brought him such joy, but it made him vulnerable, too. Vulnerable to pain and to anger. Vulnerable to a lot of emotions that were unfamiliar to him. Uncomfortable emotions.

He wasn't sure he wanted to experience them again, not if it made him feel like this.

All at once sitting became intolerable and he jumped to his feet. "Was it rape?"

She took a long time answering. "No. That's not Richard's way. But I was inexperienced and he . . . he used my naïveté."

It came to Grady, then, what she was telling him. "He seduced you, didn't he?"

"I was young and a virgin. I thought he was the most handsome man in the world. He was hurting—both his parents had died in a tragic accident—and he'd turned to me for comfort. I didn't mean to let him make love to me, but he was so convincing, and before I realized what was happening, he was in bed with me, kissing me, telling me how much he needed me to take away this terrible pain. I tried to tell him I couldn't do that, but he wouldn't listen and then . . . he climbed on top of me and—"

"How long did he stay at your place?" Grady asked, thinking how desperately he and Savannah had searched for Richard. His sister had been close to a nervous collapse those first few days following the funeral.

"I woke up alone the next morning." She swallowed and wrapped her arms around her waist as if warding off a sudden chill. "He was gone. Without a word, without a note. Gone."

"When did you realize you were pregnant?"

"Six weeks later. I didn't know what to do. I was in denial and then in shock. It was horrible enough knowing I'd slept with a man who didn't care about me, who'd used me for his own purpose. Later, after a doctor confirmed the pregnancy, I had no way of contacting him to let him know."

"Did you think he'd leap up and offer to marry you?" Grady knew he sounded sarcastic, but couldn't restrain himself.

"No . . . but I thought he should know."

Grady said nothing, not wanting to ask the obvious question, and then he found it impossible to keep silent. "Does he know now? Is that why he took Maggie? Because he learned he had a child?"

"No!" she cried. "He knows nothing. I didn't even put his name on the birth certificate."

"Why'd he bring her back, then?"

"How should I know? But I'm grateful, terribly grateful, that he did." So was Grady.

"Maggie's *my* child," Caroline said with open defiance. "There's none of her father in her."

Grady wanted to believe that. Now that he knew the truth though, it was obvious Maggie was his brother's child. Biologically, at any rate. Maggie had Richard's eyes and his dark hair.

"When he came back, did he try to pick up where you'd left off?" This was another one of those questions it hurt to ask because he feared the answer. And, he saw, another one of those questions that cut Caroline to the quick.

"No," she whispered. "When Richard first returned, I was terrified he'd figure out Maggie was his daughter and try to take her away from me. Don't you remember how I avoided the ranch after he first got home?" Her voice grew tight with remembered anxiety. "In the beginning I invented one excuse after another not to stop by. Every time I was near him I was afraid he'd say something about that night, and then I realized . . ." She paused, then covered her mouth with one hand and closed her eyes.

Grady's arms ached to hold her, but he remained where he was, steeling himself against her. "Realized what?"

"That . . . that he didn't even remember. I was just another face, another body. He'd used me the same way he'd used people his whole life. He might have suspected he'd . . . he'd been to bed with me, but he couldn't be sure, so he kept quiet."

"You're positive about that?"

"With Richard how can anyone be positive about anything? But it was just that one time and it was so long ago. I'm sure there've been a hundred women since."

They were silent for several moments before Grady spoke again. "Does anyone else know?"

She shook her head.

"Savannah?"

"I think she might have guessed, but we've never discussed the subject, and I've never come right out and told her."

"Then what makes you think Savannah's guessed?"

"I saw her look at Maggie once and then at Richard. Later I saw Richard's baby book in the kitchen and I knew she'd been comparing photographs."

So his sister knew, which left Grady to wonder how many other people in Promise suspected. How many others were laughing at him behind his back?

Grady decided it was time to leave. He'd heard everything he could bear to listen to for one evening.

"Thank you for telling me. I know this wasn't easy—and I appreciate your honesty. You needn't worry—your secret is safe with me."

"It wouldn't work, Grady," she said sadly, her eyes full of tears. "I can see that now. It just wouldn't work with you and me."

Then, weighed down by a sadness that seemed to encompass all the grief and despair he'd ever felt, he walked out the door. He had her answer. He loved her, had asked her to be his wife and she'd rejected him. Now he understood why.

"MOMMY," MAGGIE WHISPERED as Caroline lay on the living-room sofa, "are you sick?"

"I'm fine, honey."

"Then how come you're crying?"

"I'm sad, that's all," she said, discounting her pain for her daughter's sake.

"Why are you sad?" Maggie pressed.

"There's a pain deep inside here," she said, flattening her hands over her heart.

"It's not going to bleed, is it?"

"No." Although a physical wound would be easier to endure.

In two days she hadn't heard from Grady, but then, she hadn't expected to. Twice Savannah had phoned, but Caroline had let her answering machine take the calls. She wasn't up to talking, even to her best friend.

"Are you going to bleed?" Maggie asked her again, her small face stiff with fear.

"No, Maggie. What makes you ask?"

The child didn't answer and Caroline slid over on the couch to give her room to sit down. The little girl curled up with her, and Caroline held her tight. It took a long time for the tension to leave Maggie's body. Eventually she drifted off to sleep and that, in Caroline's eyes, was a blessing.

Such a release didn't come for her, but she longed for it. At least when she was asleep, Grady's face wasn't there to haunt her. Awake, though, she couldn't escape the image of his shocked expression when he'd learned the truth.

The accusation, the blame, the disgust. By the time he left, he could barely tolerate being in the same room with her.

Caroline hugged Maggie, and to her amazement soon found herself drifting off. She must have slept because the next thing she knew, Maggie was shaking her shoulder with one hand and holding the portable telephone with the other.

"It's Savannah," she said.

Caroline could see it would be impossible to delay talking to her friend any longer. She sat up and took the receiver. 'Hi," she said, still groggy and slightly confused.

"It's Savannah. Are you all right?"

"I'm fine," she lied.

"If that's the case, why haven't you returned my calls?"

"I'm sorry, but I just didn't feel like talking."

Savannah hesitated, then blurted, "Good grief, what's the matter with you two? You sound as miserable as Grady."

Caroline had nothing to add to that.

"I'm coming over," her friend announced.

"Savannah, no! Please." But the line had already been disconnected and Caroline realized there was no help for it. Savannah Smith was a woman on a mission, and she wouldn't rest until she'd done whatever she could to straighten things out between these two people she loved. Two people who loved each other, according to Savannah. Well, she was right. Caroline did love Grady and was confident he loved her. Just not enough.

Knowing Grady's sister was coming to visit, Caroline washed her face and applied fresh makeup. The last thing she needed was for Savannah to return to the ranch with tales of Caroline pining away for want of Grady—however true that might be. She changed into a fresh shirt and jeans, then ran a comb through her hair.

Savannah arrived less than an hour later, storming into the house like an avenging angel. Caroline was ready with a fresh pitcher of iced tea, waiting for her in the sunny backyard patio. Maggie played contentedly in her sandbox, building castles with imaginary friends.

"All right," Savannah said, the minute they sat down. "What happened?"

"You mean Grady didn't tell you?"

Savannah gave a soft snicker and rolled her eyes. "All he'd say was that what happened is between you and him."

"He's right."

"I can't stand this, Caroline! He asked you to marry him, I know that much."

"He told you?"

"He didn't have to—I saw the diamond. Which means if he has it and you don't, you must've turned him down. But that doesn't make any sense. You love Grady."

Caroline said nothing.

"You *do* love him, don't you?"

"Yes." But that wasn't the issue.

"Then, Caroline, why would you reject him? I don't understand. I know it isn't any of my business, but it hurts me to see two people so obviously in love this unhappy."

Caroline didn't mean to start crying. The tears embarrassed her and she blinked rapidly, praying Savannah wouldn't notice. But of course she did and wasn't about to pretend otherwise.

Leaning forward, Savannah placed her hand on Caroline's arm. "Oh, Caroline, please tell me. I want to help."

"You can't. No one can."

Savannah wasn't so easily dissuaded. "You helped me when Laredo left, don't you remember? When he went back to Oklahoma, I was in so much pain I didn't know if I'd survive it, and you were there for me. It wasn't so much what you said, although I recall every word. It was your love and friendship that helped me through a horrible time. Let me help you now."

Caroline cupped the cold glass of iced tea with both hands. "He did ask me to marry him, and you're right, I refused."

"But why?"

"He . . . he said he was free to ask me because he was finished dealing with his brother's mistakes. Finished cleaning up after Richard." She inhaled and didn't exhale for several seconds. "I had to tell him. He has a right to know."

"About Maggie?" Savannah asked gently.

As Caroline suspected, Savannah had guessed that Richard was Maggie's father. She nodded.

"But why did you refuse his proposal?"

"I love Grady, but I don't want him to consider Maggie and me a burden. Just one more responsibility he's dealing with because of his brother. Another screwup in a long list."

"Doesn't Grady understand that Richard used you, too?"

"I'm not sure he does," she breathed. "It was too much of a shock."

Savannah sat back in her chair and tapped her finger against her lips. "Well, this certainly explains a great deal."

"Grady would feel I'd broken a confidence by discussing this with you," she felt obliged to remind her friend.

"You needn't worry about that."

"Why not?"

Savannah grinned. "My brother isn't speaking to me at the moment."

"Oh, Savannah."

"Not to worry. He isn't speaking to anyone."

So Grady wasn't taking this any better than she was. "He growls when one of us even dares to mention your name. Oh, and I heard him on the phone the other day. Apparently he was talking to Frank Hennessey because he said—or rather, shouted—that he wanted his bastard of a brother brought to justice."

"I take it there's no word about Richard?"

"None." Savannah shook her head. "It's as if he's vanished off the face of the earth, and at this point I don't really care. Richard deserves what he gets, as far as I'm concerned. Especially after this latest fiasco."

Caroline frowned, not understanding. "What fiasco?"

Savannah sighed. "He didn't tell you, did he?" She didn't wait for a response. "Grady can be too noble for his own good sometimes. Richard charged eight thousand dollars' worth of goods on the family accounts."

"No." Caroline felt sick to her stomach just knowing their brother was capable of something this underhand and cruel. Richard was well aware how long it had taken Grady to regroup after the family lost its money. Money stolen by Richard. Then, just when Grady was financially able to get back on his feet, up popped Richard again. *Up pops the weasel.*

"He paid off every bill with his own money. Laredo and I wanted to share the expenses with him, but Grady refused. Seeing that we're newly married and building a home now, he wouldn't hear of it. Laredo wouldn't leave it at that—he said we're all partners and the money should come out of the business. But Grady said no. I don't have to tell you how stubborn he can be."

"You see?" Caroline said. "For the last six years all Grady's done is work to clean up Richard's messes. I'd just be one more."

"You don't honestly believe that, do you?"

"Yes, Savannah, I do."

"Then you don't know my brother." Savannah smiled slightly. "Give him time. Grady isn't that easily discouraged. He may need a few days to work things out, but he'll be back."

Caroline *wanted* to believe it, but she was afraid to hope.

"He loves you and Maggie. Mark my words, he isn't going to take no for an answer."

Caroline shook her head helplessly. She'd seen the pain in Grady's eyes, seen the shock and grief. She was just one more problem his brother had left behind, and he wanted out.

Caroline didn't blame him.

Eleven

Grady was in one bad mood. He'd been angry and cantankerous all week, to the point that he could barely stand his own company. Wiley said he'd rather chase strays than put up with Grady's foul temper and had left him to finish the repairs on the fence line by himself.

Grady had been doing the backbreaking work all afternoon, and although he'd managed to replace several rotting posts and make other fixes, his mind was a million miles away. Actually only about forty miles away. And while his hands were busy digging fence holes his thoughts were on Caroline.

"Damn it all to hell," he muttered and threw down the shovel. He'd finally finished for the day. Sweat poured from his brow, and his chest heaved from the physical exertion. "Damn it," he said again. He *should* be happy. The sale of the herd was scheduled and his financial problems would soon be over. Beef prices were up slightly. So why *wasn't* he happy? All he could think about was one headstrong woman who was too damn proud for her own good. What in the hell did she mean when she said a marriage between them wouldn't work? Why the hell not?

He could stand there stewing in the hot September sun or he could do something about it, Grady decided. Only he wasn't sure what. He tossed his tools into the back of the pickup, then drove at breakneck speed toward the house.

Savannah was working in her garden when he pulled into the yard. Her head was covered with a wide-brimmed straw hat, and she wore a sleeveless summer dress and an apron. The minute she spotted him she stepped out of the flower garden, a basket of freshly cut roses dangling from her arm.

"Grady?"

"Woman's a damn fool," he said, heading into the house. He took the porch steps two at a time. It didn't surprise him that his sister followed him inside; he would have been disappointed if she hadn't.

"I assume you're talking about Caroline," she said as she set the roses on the kitchen table.

"Is there anyone more stubborn than Caroline Daniels?" He paced the floor of the large kitchen, unable to stand still.

"Only one person I can think of," she said, smiling slightly. "And that's you."

"Me?" Grady considered himself a reasonable man. "Caroline rejected *me*. Not the other way around."

"Did she now?" Savannah removed a vase from the cupboard above the refrigerator. Grady recognized it as one that had belonged to their mother—crystal, sort of a bowl shape. He'd always liked it. Savannah began deftly arranging the roses.

"I asked Caroline to marry me," Grady said impatiently. He'd never intended to tell anyone what had happened, but the events of that evening burned inside him. It was either tell Savannah or scream it from the roof-top.

"So I understand," she murmured.

Grady had had it with women and their subtle messages. While he might normally have appreciated Savannah's reserved manner, it infuriated him just now.

"What exactly do you understand?" he demanded.

"Two hurting people, if you must know. Two people deeply in love with each other, neither one fully appreciating or—"

"She said no," he cut in. "She wasn't interested in being my wife—said it wouldn't work. Said it twice, as a matter of fact."

"Did she now?"

Grady slapped his hat against the edge of the counter. "If you have something to say, Savannah, just spit it out."

"Well, since you asked . . ." She gave him a demure smile. "It seems to me—and of course I could be wrong—that Caroline might have said no, but that wasn't exactly what she meant."

'I'm a simple rancher. If she said no and meant something else, then she should've come right out and *said* what she meant. I'm not a mind reader."

"Neither am I," Savannah stated. "But really, how else did you expect her to respond?"

"A yes would have sufficed."

"And what was she supposed to do then? Wait until your wedding day to casually mention that her child is also your niece?"

"No. It doesn't matter who fathered Maggie. I'm offering to be her daddy, to make her my own."

"Exactly!" Savannah rewarded him with a wide grin. "Bingo, big brother! Now collect your prize."

The woman was speaking in ridiculous riddles. "Damn it, Savannah, what do you mean by that?"

"You should be able to figure it out."

He frowned.

Savannah sighed loudly. "I believe what you said was, *It doesn't matter who fathered Maggie*. Now tell me, why is that?"

"Why?"

"Yes, why?" she repeated.

"Because I'm asking to be her father."

The smile was back in full force. "Very good, Grady."

His frown deepened.

"You're almost there, big brother." She added a long-stemmed yellow rose to the vase.

"Almost? I've been there and back a thousand times in my mind. Why do I have to fall in love with the most stubborn woman in the entire state of Texas? What did I ever do to deserve this?"

"I don't know, but if I were you, I'd thank God every day of your life for a woman as wonderful as Caroline."

He stared at her.

"*If* you're lucky enough to convince her to be your wife, that is," Savannah said.

"As far as I'm concerned she has to come to me now." A man's pride could only take so much, and Caroline had run roughshod over it one time too many.

Savannah shook her head. "Wrong."

"Wrong?" Grady didn't see it like that, but he was desperate enough to listen to his sister's crazy reasoning.

"You were doing so well there, too," she said with another sigh. "Grady, I've never known you to be a man who took no for an answer. It's just not like you to roll over and play dead."

"I'm not playing dead!"

"You're just acting that way?" She made the statement a question, which irritated him even more.

"Either you don't love Caroline as much as I believe, or—"

"I love her and I love Maggie, too. When Maggie was missing, it felt as if a part of me was gone. When I saw she was safe and sound, I damn near broke into tears myself."

Savannah, ever patient, ever kind, beamed him a dazzling smile. "I'm not the one who needs to hear this, you know."

"So you're telling me I should ask Caroline again." Even as he spoke, he was shaking his head. "Not in this lifetime." In his view, it was Caroline's turn to risk her pride. If she wanted to change her mind, she could let him know. He grabbed his hat and walked out the back door.

"Where are you going?" his sister asked.

Until that moment he hadn't been sure, then in a flash he knew. "I'm going to give Caroline a chance to change her mind."

EDWINA AND LILY MOORHOUSE had just stepped up to the counter when the door to the post office flew open and Grady Weston stepped inside.

The two elderly women turned to look at him; so did Caroline. He was staring straight at her, and she could tell he was breathing fire.

"Caroline—"

She instantly returned her attention to the Moorhouse sisters. "Can I help you?" she asked ever so sweetly, ignoring Grady. Her heart was pounding like a frightened kitten's, but she refused, *refused,* to allow Grady to intimidate her.

"You can talk to the Moorhouse sisters until Kingdom come, and it isn't going to help. Eventually you're going to have to speak to me, too."

Edwina's eyes rounded as she glanced at her sister. "It's Grady Weston again."

"I have eyes in my head, sister. I can see it's Grady."

"Fit to be tied, from the looks of him."

"Indeed."

Despite the way her heart raced, Caroline found herself smiling.

"I do think he's constipated again, sister."

Lily studied him, tapping her foot. "Prunes, young man, eat prunes. They'll do wonders for your disposition."

Grady scowled at her, but Caroline knew it would take a lot more than that to intimidate the retired schoolteacher.

"Listen here, Grady Weston, I wiped your nose in third grade, so don't you be giving me dirty looks. My, oh my, but you always were a headstrong boy."

It was clear Grady wasn't going to be drawn into a verbal exchange with the two women.

"In some ways," Lily mused, "your stubbornness was a characteristic I admired."

Edwina slapped a ten-dollar bill onto the counter. "We'd like a book of stamps, Caroline."

"Of course." Caroline handed her the stamps with her change.

"Good day."

"Good day," Caroline replied, watching them leave.

"Good day, young man," Edwina said as she passed Grady and winked.

Caroline wasn't sure what to make of the wink. If Grady noticed it, he didn't let on.

He touched the brim of his hat and stepped around the two women in his rush to reach the counter.

"Can I help you?" Caroline asked, lowering her gaze for fear of what he might read in her eyes.

"As a matter of fact you can." Grady's voice echoed in the room.

She waited, figuring he wasn't going to ask for stamps.

"I'm here to talk some sense into you."

"Grady, listen—"

"Hear me out first. The last time we spoke I asked you to marry me and you turned me down."

Caroline doubted he'd ever fully comprehend how difficult it had been to reject him. She'd wanted to say yes more than anything she'd ever wanted in her life. But no self-respecting woman willingly entered a marriage if she believed she'd be a burden to her husband. Even loving him the way she did, she couldn't do that to him. Couldn't do it to herself.

"Be warned," he said, lowering his voice.

"Warned?"

"This time I'm not taking no for an answer."

"Grady, please . . ." He made this so damned hard.

"Sorry, it's too late for that. I don't want anyone but you."

She looked away rather than meet his gaze.

"For the past six years I've worked day and night and done without— just so I could make up for what we lost because of Richard. He's stolen six years of my life, Caroline. He's robbed me and Savannah of too much already, and I'll be damned if I'll let him rob me of anything else."

"I . . . I don't understand."

"If you allow Richard to stand between us now, it'll be one more thing my brother's taken from me. But this time I'm not the only person he's hurting. He's hurting you and Maggie, as well. Is that what you want?"

"No." Her voice sounded weak, unconvincing.

"You appear to have doubts."

"I . . . There's more than just me to consider," she said.

"Okay, let's talk about Maggie."

Slowly Caroline raised her eyes to his. Her daughter had to come first. Always. "What about Maggie?"

"I love her, too." It was the first time Grady had mentioned his feelings for her child, the first time he'd said this. "I'm looking to be more than your husband, Caroline. I'm looking to be Maggie's daddy."

She bit her lower lip.

"My brother might have fathered this child, but I'll be the one to raise her, to love her, to kiss her skinned knee. I'll put her to bed at night, sit with her when she learns to read, teach her how to ride Moonbeam. Me, not Richard."

It was a long speech for Grady, and every word was heartfelt. Caroline knew that in her bones, sensed it deep inside. They were the words of a man who understood that fatherhood was more than biological. Much more.

"Oh, Grady . . ."

"Is that all you have to say?"

"I—"

The door opened and Nell Bishop walked in with Jeremy and Emma. "Hello," she said with a cheerful wave as she headed for her post-office box.

"Hello, Mr. Weston."

"Howdy, Jeremy."

"We're going swimming in the pool," Emma announced.

Nell sorted through her mail. "Come on, you two," she said, and steered her children toward the door. She paused to look back at Grady and Caroline. "Everything all right?" she asked cautiously.

"Yes," Grady barked.

Caroline nodded.

Nell, who'd been married to a man as stubborn and lovable as the one standing there in front of her, smiled. "Yes, I can see that everything is coming along nicely." Then she and her children left.

"What'd she mean by that?" Grady demanded.

Caroline shrugged. "You'll have to ask her."

"Well?"

The gruff question caught her by surprise. "Well, what?"

"Are you going to change your mind about marrying me or not?"

"I—"

"You're a fool if you turn me down."

"Honestly, Grady—"

"You aren't likely to get a better offer."

This last comment irked her no end. "What makes you so sure?" she snapped. "Look, Grady," she began before he could answer, "let me ask you a question. Do you love me?"

"You know I do."

"You might have said so."

"I did," he insisted.

"When?"

"The first time I proposed."

"Oh." Well, that *was* true. But everything hinged on how *much* he loved her. "I'm afraid we'd be a burden to you."

"How?"

Caroline swallowed. "Every time you look at Maggie—and me—you'll be reminded of Richard. That's what I'm afraid of. We'd be just another problem Richard left for you to fix."

"That's not the way I see it, Caroline. I told you, remember? I won't let Richard take another thing away from me. And you know what? For the first time in his life, my brother has given me something wonderful. He's hurt me, true, but he's also blessed me—in you. In Maggie."

"But—"

"Obviously the question is, do *you* love *me?*" he said. "You seem to be the one having trouble making up your mind."

"I love you so damn much," she confessed.

No sooner had the words left her lips than Grady reached across the counter for her. Their positions, the obstacle between them, made the kiss awkward. It hardly mattered. They'd kissed countless times by now, but no kiss had ever meant this much.

It was a meeting of their hearts.

His mouth was warm and urgent against hers.

"We're getting married," he whispered.

"Yes," she whispered back. She whimpered when he deepened the kiss, then wrapped her arms around his neck and invited the exploration of his tongue.

The sound of someone entering the post office broke them apart. Caroline looked up guiltily, feeling a little shy.

Dovie Boyd stood in the foyer. She nodded toward them. "Hello, Grady. Caroline."

"Hi, Dovie," Caroline said, grateful Dovie wasn't a gossip. She shuddered to think of the consequences if someone like Louise or Tammy Lee had happened upon them in each other's arms.

"You're the first to hear our good news," Grady said, taking Caroline's hand. He grasped it firmly in his own, then raised it to his lips. "Caroline has agreed to be my wife."

Dovie's eyes grew wide. "Congratulations! I couldn't be happier." She opened her purse and took out a linen handkerchief. "I really . . . couldn't . . . be . . . happier," she said, sniffling and dabbing at her eyes. "You're a wonderful couple and . . . and I think it's just wonderful, really I do." She turned abruptly and walked out, apparently forgetting what had brought her to the post office in the first place.

GRADY, CAROLINE and Maggie sat on the front-porch swing. "Will I call you Daddy?" Maggie asked Grady.

"Of course. If you want to."

She nodded. "Then I'll have a daddy, too."

"Yes, princess, you'll have a daddy."

"And Mommy will have a husband."

"And Grady'll have a family." He tucked his arm around Caroline's shoulder, loving her so much.

"Us," Maggie said, and tossed her arms in the air. "Your family is us."

"What do you think of that?" Caroline asked her daughter.

Maggie considered the question a moment, looked up at Grady and slowly grinned. "You don't do magic tricks," she said, "but I like you better 'cause you love me and Mommy."

"That," Grady said, kissing the top of her head, "is very true. You're both very easy to love."

"I'm glad you think so," Caroline whispered and leaned her head against his shoulder, utterly content.

DR. TEXAS

One

Texas is the only state big enough to hold your dreams. Someone had told Dr. Jane Dickinson that when she signed up for this gig. But whoever it was obviously hadn't lived in Promise.

With medical-school bills the size of the national debt, signing a three-year agreement to practice medicine in the Texas hill country in exchange for partial payment had seemed the perfect solution. Whatever romanticizing she'd done when she'd first thought about making the move from urban California to the heart of rural America had faded with the reality of her situation. Texas had bugs practically as big as pit bulls and she'd always been somewhat phobic about insects, whether they were of the crawling or flying variety. More serious, more disturbing, was the fact that she simply didn't fit in with this community. People were never less than polite, but they hadn't accepted her. They came to her as a last resort—if they couldn't cure whatever ailed them on their own—and then complained because she wasn't Doc Cummings. Being fresh out of medical school, female and a good fifty years younger than the beloved practitioner hadn't helped, either.

But although Jane was lonely and often at loose ends, she felt that she'd begun to make strides. Becoming friends with Dovie Boyd had a lot to do with that. The older woman owned an antique shop with the small Victorian Tea Room tucked in one corner, and she'd generously offered Jane not only friendship but advice. Life had taken a decided turn for the better since that first morning Jane had spoken to Dovie.

Her last scheduled patient for the day had left, and so had Jenny Bender, her receptionist. Jane sat at her desk, leaning comfortably back in her chair. The makeup she'd applied that morning had long since dissolved in sweat, and her feet ached. It'd been a busy day, which was a good sign. It meant that more people of Promise were coming to trust her skills.

Ellie Patterson was due to return from her honeymoon this week, too. Her second new friend was a local businesswoman. They'd recently met, thanks to Dovie. Jane liked Ellie's no-nonsense approach to life, her quick wit and down-to-earth attitude. After having lunch together, Jane could tell they had the potential to become good friends. She hoped that was the case, because at this point, she needed all the friends she could get.

A distinct noise in the outer office cut into her thoughts, and Jane stood up to investigate.

"Is someone here?" she called, walking out of her office.

Nothing.

"Hello," she tried again, wondering if she was beginning to hear things.

"Dr. Jane?" A child's voice came from the waiting room.

Jane found six-year-old Maggie Daniels standing just inside the clinic door. "Oh, hi, Maggie."

The little girl's pigtails fell forward as she lowered her head. "Hello."

Maggie's mother was Promise's postmistress, and the post office was next door to the health clinic. She'd talked to Caroline Daniels a number of times, and had heard just a day or two ago that Caroline and a local cattle rancher, Grady Weston, were now engaged.

"Where's your mother?" Jane asked. It was unusual for Maggie to come to the clinic by herself.

"At work," she answered, still keeping her head lowered. Her arms were wrapped protectively around her stomach.

Jane knelt down in front of her. "Are you feeling all right, Maggie?"

The little girl shook her head.

"Where do you feel sick?"

"My tummy."

Jane brushed the hair from the child's forehead and checked for fever. Maggie's skin was cool to the touch. "Does your mommy know you're here?"

Maggie's head flew up, her eyes wide with alarm. "No! Please don't tell her, okay?"

"But if she doesn't know where you are, she might worry."

"She said I could play while she finished work. Mrs. Murphy had to drop me off early today 'cause she had a dentist appointment."

Jane assumed Mrs. Murphy baby-sat Maggie after school.

"Is something at school bothering you?" Jane guessed, thinking this stomachache might be linked to an incident there. School had been in session a little more than two weeks. That Maggie didn't want her mother to know where she was aroused Jane's suspicions. Perhaps Maggie had gotten into trouble with her teacher and was worried about what would happen when her mother found out. Either that, or she suffered doubts or fears regarding her mother's recent engagement.

"I like school," Maggie said, and her face brightened. "I'm in first grade this year."

"But you're not feeling well?"

The little girl shook her head, sending her pigtails swaying. "My tummy hurts."

"Okay," Jane said. "Maybe we'd better have a look." She held out her hand to Maggie, who slipped her own small one into Jane's.

"You won't tell Mommy?" Maggie pleaded again.

"Not if you don't want me to," Jane said, although she wondered if it was wise to make such a promise. But it was clear the child was deeply upset about something. While Jane didn't have a lot of training in pediatrics, she suspected that if she hadn't reassured Maggie, the child would have bolted.

Playing the situation by ear, Jane led Maggie into the examination room and lifted her easily onto the table.

"Take off your backpack and I'll listen to your tummy," Jane instructed, picking up her stethoscope.

Slowly and with obvious reluctance Maggie did as she was asked, but when Jane went to move the backpack off the table, Maggie grabbed it back and clung to it. Jane realized immediately that whatever bothered the child was in that backpack.

"Is there something important in your bag?" Jane asked casually.

Maggie nodded. She tucked her chin tight against her chest. Finally, hesitantly, Maggie opened the zipper. Twice she paused and glanced up at Jane as if questioning the wisdom of continuing.

Jane allowed the girl to make the decision on her own. Apparently Maggie had decided to trust her, because once she had the bag completely open, she withdrew an old dilapidated-looking doll. It was either a replica of an antique or the genuine thing, although that didn't seem likely. Either way, the doll had seen better days. It was falling apart. The face appeared hand-stitched, the once red lips faded to a pale pink. The muslin dress had probably been white but was now a washed-out shade of yellow. The dull calico apron had frayed edges. Despite its condition, the doll had a certain appeal. At one time it must have been the much-loved toy of some young girl.

"I want you to keep it," Maggie said in a small tense voice as she held out the doll.

"But I couldn't do that," Jane protested.

"Please . . ." Big tears welled in Maggie's dark eyes. "I took it . . ." She clutched her stomach with both arms. "I'm sorry for taking her away from—" She stopped and her lower lip started to wobble, but she quickly pulled her emotions together.

"Can't you take it back to the person it belongs to?" Jane asked.

Maggie shook her head vigorously, the pigtails whipping about her face.

Jane frowned. "So you want me to keep her for you?"

Maggie nodded.

Perhaps that was the best solution. Again Jane followed her instincts, which told her that pressing Maggie to tell her anything more was a mistake. The little girl clearly regretted having taken the doll and wasn't sure how to handle the situation now.

"All right. I'll do that." She could display the old doll in her office in the hope that whoever owned it would come to her and ask. That would save Maggie the embarrassment of having to return it.

"I promise to take good care of your friend," Jane said solemnly. She helped Maggie down from the table. "Come on, let's find a new home for your doll." Perhaps later Jane could make a few discreet inquiries. Dovie might know something or have a suggestion, since she owned an antique shop—although the older woman seemed unusually distracted at the moment. Jane assumed it had something to do with Frank Hennessey, the local sheriff, who'd been Dovie's longtime male friend. Apparently they'd had some kind of argument and were no longer seeing each other.

Maggie slipped her hand into Jane's as they walked into the small office once occupied by Doc Cummings. The most logical place to set the doll was on the bookshelf, which looked out into the hallway. Anyone passing by was sure to see it.

Carefully Jane put the toy on the top shelf. "Okay," she said, and took a step back. "What do you think?"

The youngster smiled and released a great sigh. "My tummy doesn't hurt anymore."

"That's wonderful." A miracle cure, Jane mused; she must be a better doctor than she'd imagined. "If you want to come and visit your friend, you're welcome to do that any time," Jane told her.

Maggie shook her head, then whirled around. "Mommy's calling," she said. Racing down the hallway, she grabbed her backpack from the examination table and flew toward the waiting room. She paused abruptly and looked back. "Thank you, Dr. Jane."

"You're welcome," Jane said with a smile.

Then Maggie disappeared out the door.

If only dealing with her other patients was this easy.

DOVIE BOYD was miserable. She wandered between the lush rows of her garden, picking ripe tomatoes from her heavily laden plants. Her only consolation was that Frank Hennessey probably felt even worse than she did. For ten years they'd been friends. More than friends. During those years they'd talked frequently of marriage—with Dovie generally bringing up the subject. Frank had been a bachelor all his life; Dovie understood that marriage would be a big change for him and had been patient. No, she thought now, she'd been stupid. Although she loved Frank, she'd never been completely comfortable with their arrangement. He knew that, which must be why he'd made promises he didn't intend to keep. When she pressured him about it after Ellie Frasier and Glen Patterson's wedding, he owned up to the fact that he simply couldn't marry her. He loved her, he claimed, but he wasn't the marrying kind. He just couldn't do it.

The truth had been painful, but she'd lived long enough to recognize something else. Either she accepted Frank and their relationship the way it was or she broke it off.

She broke it off. Not that it was an easy decision. She missed him. Missed their afternoon chats over coffee, missed their romantic dinners and sitting on the porch gazing at the stars, sipping a nice glass of East Texas wine. She missed cuddling up with him at night, too. For the better part of nine years Frank had spent two nights a week with her.

Her twenty-six year marriage to Marvin had been a good one, although to her regret they'd remained childless. She'd loved her husband and grieved deeply for him when he died.

That was thirteen years ago. She'd still been young enough then to want a man in her life—was young enough still! Frank had courted her for two years before they'd become lovers. She would never have believed she'd allow a man into her bed without the benefit of a wedding band. But she had, trusting with all her heart that Frank would one day marry her. In retrospect she wondered how she could have let the arrangement continue this long.

In other years Dovie would pick two or three large green tomatoes for Frank; this year she left them to ripen on the vine. There wouldn't be any fried green tomatoes for Frank Hennessey. The thought saddened her, reminding her that there was a gap in her life, that she'd lost an important person. But this break, no matter how painful, was necessary, she told herself.

Just then Frank's patrol car rounded the corner and Dovie's heart accelerated. Although tempted, she looked away, pretending not to notice.

"Hello, Dovie," he called softly.

She glanced in his direction. He'd come to a stop and rolled down the car window.

"How are you?" he asked in that sweet seductive way he had. He'd always used that tone when he wanted Dovie to know how much he loved her.

Slowly she turned to look at him. "Very well. Thank you for asking," she said, then continued down the row, picking tomatoes. No sooner had the words left her lips when she heard his car door slam. It demanded an effort of will not to get up and move toward him. She fought a desperate urge to stare at him, to indulge her heart and her eyes. Frank was a fine-looking man even now as he neared retirement age. He'd maintained a trim physique and most people wouldn't guess he was sixty.

"Seems your garden has a lot of tomatoes this year," he commented. He remained on the sidewalk, following her from the opposite side of the picket fence.

"Seems that way," she said after a moment, wondering at the wisdom of allowing this conversation. All it did was remind her how unhappy she was without Frank, how much she missed him. From the glances he sent her, she knew he missed her, too. She also knew he was trying to wear down her resolve.

"How've you been?" Frank pressed when she didn't elaborate on the abundance of her garden.

"Wonderful." She prayed God would forgive her the lie.

"I'm afraid I can't say the same. I miss you, Dovie. Nothing seems right without you."

Nothing seemed right for her, either, but she wasn't about to admit it. What made this breakup so difficult was that she loved Frank. Despite that, she couldn't go on with their arrangement. It wasn't the life she wanted. She craved what most women of her generation did—and maybe most women, period. Commitment, emotional security, an open acknowledgement of love.

"I miss you, sweetheart," he said again, in a soft sad voice.

"Then marry me, Frank."

His eyes narrowed. "We've been through this a hundred times.

Dovie, you know how I feel about you. I'd give my life for you. You're the best thing that's ever happened to me. If I were to marry anyone, it'd be you, but I *can't* Dovie, I just can't."

It hurt to hear the words, but she was glad he'd said them because this forced her to remember that nothing would ever change between them.

"I love you, Dovie! I'm doing my damnedest to understand why everything's different and all because I told you the truth. None of this would've happened if I hadn't admitted I couldn't go through with marriage."

"We've already said everything that needs to be said," she told him, shifting the weight of the basket from one arm to the other.

"Let me help you with that," Frank offered. "That's much too heavy for you."

He was halfway to the gate before she stopped him. "I can manage on my own."

He gripped two pickets so tightly that his knuckles whitened. His blue eyes implored her. "Dovie, please."

Already she could feel herself weakening, and she forced herself to be strong. It'd been less than two weeks. Sooner or later Frank would understand. This wasn't a game, or an ultimatum or an attempt to manipulate him. They just saw things differently; it was as simple as that. He'd made his decision and she'd made hers. He would simply have to accept that she wasn't giving in or changing her mind.

"I need to go inside. Good seeing you again, Frank. I hope you have a pleasant evening." Then she headed toward the house and didn't look back.

After setting the tomatoes by the sink, Dovie reached for her phone and punched in her best-friend's number.

Mary Patterson operated the local bed-and-breakfast with her husband, Phil, and the couple had been friends of Dovie's for years. Although Dovie was well aware that others knew of her arrangement with Frank, the only person she'd actually confided in was Mary.

"Frank was just here," Dovie announced when Mary answered the phone. Her hand clenched the receiver and she closed her eyes, distressed by the brief confrontation. It had left her feeling weak and lightheaded.

"What did he say?" Mary asked.

"That he misses me and wishes things could go back the way they were before."

"You refused to listen, right?"

"Right," Dovie answered.

"Good!" Mary said with conviction. "That's exactly what you *should* do."

Her support was something Dovie badly needed just then. "He said he's miserable."

"As well he ought to be!"

"I am, too, but I suppose I'm more determined than I am miserable."

"Oh, Dovie." Mary's voice was full of sympathy. "I know how hard this is on you. But Frank's strung you along all these years, promising to marry you, and then he decides he can't go through with it. You should sue him for breach of promise."

"I wouldn't do that."

"I know."

"It's just that I feel so alone," Dovie confessed. "In some ways this is as difficult as when Marvin died."

"This *is* a death," Mary said compassionately. "The death of a relationship."

Her friend was right, Dovie realized sadly. She'd been able to bury her husband, lay him and their lives together to rest. She'd taken the time she needed to heal, the time she'd needed to grieve, and then, when the worst of the pain was over, she'd opened her antique shop. Starting the business had helped her get through the first lonely year. What she needed now, Dovie decided, was a diversion, something that would see her through the long difficult weeks ahead.

"I'm thinking of traveling," Dovie announced, although the thought had only just come to her.

"Traveling?" Mary echoed. "Where?"

"I'm not sure—possibly Europe. I've heard about the wonderful antiques you can get there. I'll make it a buying trip," she said, warming to the idea. Not only would it be her first trip abroad, she'd be able to write it off as a tax deduction.

"When?" Mary asked.

"I . . . I'm not sure yet, but I'll talk to Gayla Perkins at Adventure Travel in the morning."

"Dovie . . ." For the first time Mary hesitated. "This sounds drastic."

"I need to do *something* different," Dovie said. "Otherwise I'm afraid I'll give in to Frank."

"Will you travel alone?" Mary asked.

Dovie hadn't gotten that far in her planning. "It looks like I'll have to."

"Take a cruise, then," Mary advised.

"A cruise?" Dovie hadn't thought of that. "I don't know . . ."

"You might meet someone." Mary's voice rose with enthusiasm. "They have short ones, three and four days. I understand the prices are reasonable and there's plenty of single men."

Dovie didn't want any other man in her life.

"A cruise would be perfect for you," Mary went on. "I read not long ago about certain cruises that specialize in matching up singles. That'd be ideal."

"Oh, Mary, I don't know . . ."

"What's not to know? You want to travel, and if that's the case, then do it in style."

"A cruise," Dovie said slowly, letting the idea grow more familiar.

"Not just an ordinary cruise," Mary corrected, "but a short one especially for singles. Can you imagine how Frank's going to feel when he hears about that?"

Dovie figured she had no business caring about Frank's feelings one way or the other, but she did. A dozen times a day she had to remind herself that Frank Hennessey was no longer part of her life. They were no longer a couple. She had her own life to live, and the time had come for her to explore other possibilities. Yes, a singles cruise could be just the thing.

"I'll do it," Dovie said. "First thing tomorrow. I'll call Adventure Travel."

"You won't be sorry," her friend assured her.

Dovie had a strong feeling Mary was right.

THE ALARM WOKE Cal Patterson at the usual hour. He rolled out of bed and stretched his arms high above his head, yawning loudly. On his way into the bathroom, he caught his reflection in the mirror and stopped to stare at himself. Hmm. Not much to look at. He wondered at this sudden need to examine his features. Probably had to do with Glen and Ellie getting married, he decided.

He'd grown pensive since the wedding. He'd found himself entertaining a number of intriguing notions after Ellie and his brother had left on their honeymoon. Like the fact that he missed Glen. Really missed him.

Glen. Married.

Even after the wedding, it still didn't seem possible. They were brothers and partners in the Lonesome Coyote Ranch. Both had been born here, and as far as Cal was concerned he'd die here, too. The ranch was his life, his blood, his soul.

Glen was like him, a rancher at heart. Their ancestors had settled in Texas a century and a half before, and the family had been ranching one spread or another ever since. When the time was right, Cal suspected Glen would buy his own ranch, one closer to town since Ellie would need to travel in every day.

Cal had finished dressing when he heard a door close downstairs.

"Don't tell me you're still sleeping?" a voice called up. "What the hell kind of ranch are you running here?"

Glen? His brother was supposed to be on his honeymoon! Cal started down the stairs. "What are you doing here?" Cal shouted.

"I go away for a few days and this whole place goes to hell in a handbasket."

Cal reached the bottom of the stairs, and the two brothers stared at each other. It'd barely been ten days since the wedding and yet it felt as if they'd been apart for ten years. They hugged with the fierce love of brothers who were also close friends.

"How was the Gulf?" Cal asked, breaking away and moving toward the kitchen to make a pot of coffee.

"Terrific," Glen said, "although Ellie and I didn't get outside much."

Cal hadn't expected that they would, seeing as this was their honeymoon. "I didn't think you were due back for a couple of days yet."

"We weren't, but you know Ellie. She was worried about the feed store."

"And you were worried about the ranch."

Glen rubbed the side of his jaw. "Not . . . worried, exactly."

The two laughed and Cal grabbed a couple of mugs. "So, is married life everything you hoped for?"

"More," Glen said wistfully. "I knew I loved Ellie," he continued, his voice thoughtful, "but I didn't realize exactly how much until this past week. I feel like I'm the luckiest man alive. Hey, Cal? You might want to think about making the leap one day yourself."

Cal let the comment slide and poured them each a cup of coffee. He handed one to his brother. "Ellie is special," he said.

Glen sugared his coffee, and they talked business for the next forty minutes, then headed to the barn for the start of their day.

By the afternoon it was difficult for Cal to remember that Glen had ever been away. They'd worked together for so many years they didn't require words to communicate. As soon as they'd finished delousing the calves, Glen made a beeline for the barn and his favorite gelding, Moon-shine. He groomed the big bay, then washed up. "I'll see you in the morning," he said on his way out of the barn.

Cal grinned to himself at his brother's eagerness to hurry home to his bride. "Sure thing," he said, waving him off. Although Glen had spent most of his free time with Ellie before they got married, she'd often driven out to the ranch. Cal had enjoyed watching their exchanges, and he'd especially relished being the beneficiary of Ellie's delicious home-made dinners. She'd taken a few cooking lessons from Dovie, mostly in preparing basic meals, the kind Cal liked. Well, she could practice on him as often as she wanted. He wasn't much of a cook himself, but managed to fry up a decent steak every so often.

"Damn, I almost forgot," Glen said halfway out the barn door. "Ellie wanted me to ask if you had plans Friday night."

"Plans?"

"For dinner," Glen answered, as if that should be obvious.

"I don't have anything special going," he said. Already his mind was full of the meals she'd served in the weeks leading up to the wedding. Memories of her roast chicken and garlic mashed potatoes made his mouth water. "If she's thinking of inviting me over, you tell her I accept."

Glen looked surprised. "You sure about this?"

"Why shouldn't I be?"

"Well . . ." Glen's mouth widened in a grin and he slowly shook his head. "No reason. I'll tell Ellie to count on you for Friday night."

"You do that."

Cal walked his brother out. He stood there for a moment, watching the dust plume as Glen's truck barreled out of the yard and down the long driveway. Not for the first time in the past ten days Cal wondered what his own life would be like now if he'd married Jennifer Healy.

Two years earlier Cal had been engaged. But less than forty-eight hours before the wedding Jennifer had changed her mind and abruptly left town. She'd given him no explanation.

But Cal knew why she'd done it. She'd wanted him to be something he never could.

He'd loved her, or had convinced himself he did. But she'd had other plans for him, plans she didn't divulge until the wedding arrangements were made. Jennifer seemed to believe that once they were husband and wife, she'd be able to convince him to sell his half of the ranch to Glen. Her scheme included moving him to San Antonio or Houston. Even now, two years later, Cal couldn't imagine himself living in big-city America. It shocked him that a woman he loved, the woman he'd intended to marry, didn't understand that a city the size of Houston would slowly kill him. He was a country boy, through and through.

When he'd adamantly refused to give in to her demands, Jennifer had walked out, leaving him to deal with the embarrassment of canceling the wedding at the last minute. And yet—perhaps it was ego, he didn't know—he had the distinct feeling that if he'd asked, she might have stayed.

But he hadn't asked, hadn't believed the relationship was worth saving. Her preference for leaving the ranch, leaving Promise, would have always been an issue between them. She would have held his decision against him and they'd have argued about it again and again. So he'd let her go. He realized in that moment that he'd given his heart to a woman who would have abused his love.

After Jennifer left, his attitude toward women had undergone a swift change. He found them untrustworthy and deceptive. Glen and others had tried to convince him that not all women were like Jennifer. Deep down Cal believed that, but he wasn't willing to give anyone that kind of power over him a second time. He'd learned his lesson well.

His new sister-in-law was an exception. He'd always been fond of Ellie and was understandably proud that he was the one to figure out how Glen and Ellie felt about each other long before either of them had a clue. Actually, considering how anti-romance he'd become, that was little short of amazing.

Ellie was a sweetheart and Glen was a lucky man. His sister-in-law was an idealist, though. She firmly believed in the power of love. While that might prove true for others, it hadn't for him.

Cal never intended to marry. He was thirty-six and set in his ways. His life was full and he didn't have room in it for a relationship; he'd made damn sure of that. Whenever he was tempted to let his guard down and fraternize with the enemy, something would happen to remind him that women weren't to be trusted.

Given time, he thought cynically, ninety-nine percent of the female population would turn on a man. He'd seen it happen. Well, maybe not in Promise—not often, anyway. He could actually think of a few success stories. Glen, of course. His parents. Savannah Weston and Laredo Smith. And now his best friend, Grady Weston, was engaged to Caroline Daniels; he supposed their marriage stood a chance if anyone's did. But he was still convinced he was right. Anyway, Texas men weren't prone to "sharing their pain." You wouldn't find a cowboy crying his eyes out on some talk show about a woman who'd done him wrong. In Texas men sat around and drowned their sorrows in beer. If they mentioned their trou-

bles, it was in words no television channel could air. And ten to one, if a
man had problems, there was a woman involved.

Cal headed back to the house. He'd grab something easy for dinner
and then tackle some paperwork. Come Friday, Ellie would be cooking
up something memorable.

He paused in his tracks as he recalled that sly smile of Glen's when
he'd asked about Ellie's cooking.

Then it hit him like the proverbial bolt of lightning. Ellie had invited
him all right, but no one had said anything about her doing any cooking.
His brand-new sister-in-law intended to set him up with one of her girlfriends. She was fixing to play matchmaker.

It'd be a cold day in hell before Cal would sit still for that.

TWO

Jane was astounded—and delighted. Only two days home from her honeymoon, and Ellie Frasier Patterson had already dropped in to visit her. Jane was between patient appointments, so she and Ellie spent a few minutes catching up on news. Then Ellie announced that Jane would be joining her and Glen for dinner that Friday night.

"But—"

"You don't have an option here," Ellie said with a grin. "You need a Texas education and you're going to get it."

Jane took half a second to think it over. "I'll be there." She'd asked for help. Why turn it down when it was offered?

"Be at the Chili Pepper at seven Friday night," Ellie instructed on her way out the door.

Jane made a note in her weekly planner, then sat back in her chair with a triumphant smile. Finally, after spending six months in this town, she was making progress. This would be her first night out with people her own age, and she looked forward to it.

On Friday night she arrived at the restaurant precisely at seven. The place was packed. She glanced around and then saw Ellie wave her arm to get her attention. Ellie, her husband, Glen, and a man Jane recognized as Glen's brother were sitting in a booth in a far corner. Jane waved back and wove her way between the tables toward them.

"Hello," she said, raising her voice to be heard above the country-and-western tunes blaring from the jukebox.

"You remember Glen," Ellie said, indicating the man sitting next to her. "And my brother-in-law, Cal."

"It's good to see you both again," Jane said, smiling brightly.

The rancher stood—reluctantly, Jane thought—to allow her to slide into the booth next to the wall, opposite Ellie. It concerned her a little that Ellie hadn't said anything about this being a double date; Jane wondered if Ellie's brother-in-law had been kept equally in the dark. Probably, or he wouldn't be here. She'd seen him around before, and although she hadn't known his name until now, she thought Cal Patterson was one of the rudest unfriendliest men she'd ever *not* met.

He was good-looking, or could be if he bothered to smile. Tall and lean, he had that rough-and-tumble cowboy appeal.

One glance from Cal gave her the answer she'd suspected. He, too, had been duped, but judging by his fierce scowl, he thought she was in cahoots with Ellie.

Jane's high hopes for the evening died a sudden and painful death.

"I'm so glad you could make it," Ellie said, and handed Jane a menu. Cal sat next to her as stiff as new rope and about as welcoming.

The waitress brought over a pitcher of beer and four mugs. Willie Nelson's plaintive voice rolled from the jukebox just then, and Jane's mouth gaped in astonishment as the entire restaurant began to sing along with him. She would've joined them had she known the words.

"If you're going to live in Texas you gotta love Willie Nelson," Ellie informed her when the tune was finished.

"Not just Willie, either," Glen added, "but country music in general."

"I like Garth Brooks," Jane told them, although she was familiar with only a couple of his songs. "And Johnny Cash."

"That's a good start," Glen said, giving her a friendly smile. He lifted a mug to his lips, having waited for the froth to settle, and Jane reached for her own. She wasn't much of a beer drinker, preferring white wine, but when in Rome . . .

Cal sampled his beer, too. "If you're serious about living in Texas, then you'll need at least one button on your car radio set to a country-and-western station."

Jane was surprised by his remark. "I am serious," she told him. Other than an awkward greeting, this was the first time he'd spoken directly to her.

"She wasn't born here," Ellie said, smiling, "but she came as soon as she could."

Everyone laughed.

The waitress returned for their order—barbecued ribs, baked beans and coleslaw all around—and soon afterward brought a second pitcher of beer. Jane had yet to finish her first glass, but both men were ready for another.

"What else do I need to do?" Jane asked. "If I want to become a Texan, I mean."

"Clothes are important," Ellie said, "but I can help you with that later."

Jane smoothed her skirt. She'd already learned that lesson the hard way. She'd worn a business suit to a party soon after her arrival and had been sadly overdressed for the occasion. Most everyone else had been in jeans and tank tops. A couple of months later, she'd attended a dance and had dressed casually only to discover it was a formal affair. She'd felt like a fool and stayed no more than a few minutes, feeling completely out of place.

"That's where I've seen you," Cal said. "You were at the party Richard Weston threw for himself, weren't you?"

Jane nodded. She'd only been in town a few days when she'd met a handsome congenial rancher who'd invited her to a party. She hadn't known a soul in Promise, and his was the first friendly face she'd seen. Richard had stopped her on the street and insisted that anyone as beautiful as she was had to come to his party. She'd arrived terribly overdressed and hung around feeling unwelcomed and uncomfortable for more than an hour.

"Whatever happened to Richard?" Jane asked. "I saw him around town a few times, but not recently."

The other three went strangely silent and then exchanged looks as if they weren't sure how much to tell her.

Jane stared at them. "Did I ask something I shouldn't have?" Without knowing it, she'd apparently entered forbidden territory. She couldn't prevent a small sigh from escaping. It'd been this way from the beginning—like being in an alien culture, with no one to guide her or tell her the rules. Or explain the native customs, she thought wryly.

"It's just that Richard Weston is . . . a sad case."

"Sad?" she echoed dutifully.

"He's all foam and no beer," Glen said. "He's hurt a lot of good people, and worse yet, the ones he's abused most have been his own family."

"Richard arrived back in town after being away six years," Cal muttered. "He made a nuisance of himself and caused a lot of trouble for Grady and Savannah before he disappeared."

"I . . . I didn't know," Jane said. She'd talked to Richard briefly a couple of times. Their first meeting, when he'd invited her to the party, had been pleasant enough, but the subsequent encounter had left her with the distinct impression that the man was frivolous and irresponsible;

apparently her assessment hadn't been far off. She frowned, thinking through the relationships. Okay, Richard was the younger brother of Grady and Savannah, and Savannah was married to . . . Austin? No, Laredo Smith. Grady had recently become engaged to Caroline Daniels. Even after several months, Jane had a hard time keeping track of all the connections.

"Yeah. Richard disappeared not long ago," Ellie said.

"With Grady's truck," Cal added. "That's Richard for you." He shook his head as though the mere mention of the other man's name disgusted him.

"He stole his own brother's truck?"

"And a lot more." This from Cal, too.

"I don't think we need to worry about him coming back, though," Glen said, sounding sure of himself. "He's gone for good, and all I can say is good riddance."

The others nodded in agreement. A moment of silence followed.

"Do you know about the Bubbas?" Ellie asked, abruptly changing the subject. "Have you met any?"

"Just a couple of the youngsters I've examined who have that nick-name."

"There's much more to being a Bubba than a name," Glen told her, grinning once more. "You don't have to be *called* Bubba to be one. There's your basic Bubba, and then there are your different variations, according to what state you live in."

Jane was quickly getting lost. "Perhaps it'd be best if you defined what a Bubba is. A Texas Bubba," she qualified, not wanting to be confused by any other Southern Bubba-types.

"Well," Glen drawled, "that's not as easy as it sounds."

"Sure it is," Cal said. "He drives a beat-up truck with a rifle or fishing pole in the gun rack."

"And carries a fifty-pound sack of dog food in the bed of his truck," Ellie said, "which he probably bought from me."

"He's got a case or two of empty beer and soda cans rolling around on the floor on the passenger side of the cab."

"Is he one of those guys who wears a monster belt buckle?" Jane asked eagerly.

Glen and Cal glanced at each other. "All Texans wear giant belt buckles," Glen informed her kindly.

"Yes, I know, but Bubba buckles are smaller and their bellies are bigger."

"You got it!" Ellie and Glen chorused.

Ellie took a swallow of her beer. "So, Jane, you need a bumper sticker. It's not just a Bubba thing. Everyone in Texas has at least one. Three or four are better."

"Okay." This didn't sound difficult. "What should it say?"

"Touch my truck and you die," Cal suggested.

"I don't drive a truck," Jane said with a smile. "I could buy one, though, if I need to."

He grinned, too, and Jane was surprised by the way it transformed his features. Gratified, too. It made him as attractive as she'd guessed it would. "Buying a truck won't be necessary," he told her.

"Insured by Smith and Wesson," Glen said next.

Jane rolled her eyes. "I don't *think* so."

"Don't mess with Texas," Cal continued.

"I think I'd better start taking notes," Jane said in a mock-serious voice, reaching for her purse. This was fun, especially now that Cal seemed to have loosened up some. Was it the beer—or the company?

"She needs a hat," Ellie announced just as their dinner arrived.

"A hat?"

"A lady Stetson," Glen tossed in, and picked up a dripping barbecued rib with both hands.

"A hat doesn't mean a damn thing if she doesn't ride," Cal said as he offered the platter of ribs to Jane.

She helped herself to one, then carefully wiped her fingers on the rather inadequate paper napkin.

"Ride? As in horse?" She looked from Glen to Cal and then to Ellie.

"You're right, Cal," Ellie said, frowning thoughtfully. She nodded in Jane's direction. "You're gonna have to learn to ride."

Jane bit into the pungent smoky-tasting rib, enjoying it more than she would ever have believed. "You're sure about this?" she asked. "I have to ride?"

"Positive."

"Okay," Jane said with some reluctance. "Do you know of anyone who gives lessons?"

"Lessons?" Glen asked, and the three burst into spontaneous laughter.

Jane didn't know what she'd said that was so funny.

"Everyone around here grows up with horses," Ellie explained apologetically. "Most of us were sitting in a saddle before we could walk."

"Then what does someone like me do?"

The question appeared to give them pause. "I don't know," Glen replied at last. "Laredo Smith's raising quarter horses. He might agree to give you lessons."

"I doubt he has the time," Cal inserted. "Laredo and Savannah are building a house, and Laredo's trying to do as much of the work as he can himself. Last I saw they had a good start on it."

"Well, we need to come up with someone who can teach you to ride," Ellie said. She looked sharply at Cal, but Jane noticed that Ellie's brother-in-law was ignoring her. She had a feeling that Ellie'd hoped Cal would jump in and volunteer. Cal didn't, and Jane suspected he wanted nothing more to do with her. It was a pity, because she would have liked to know him better.

CAL HADN'T BEEN KEEN on this evening from the moment he'd realized Ellie wasn't cooking dinner at her own house—and even more so when he figured out she was matching him up with the town doctor. He would've put an end to her less-than-clever method of throwing Dr. Texas in his face if he hadn't worried about annoying his new sister-in-law. He'd known Ellie for years, but the relationship was different now, and he had to respect that. When the evening was over, he'd make sure Ellie understood he didn't appreciate her matchmaking attempts.

When Jane had first shown up at the restaurant, he'd been prepared to remain closemouthed and unfriendly. The last thing he'd wanted was to give the impression that he was interested in dating some city slicker. Far from it. But soon the beer had loosened his inhibitions and he'd begun to enjoy the lighthearted conversation. He considered Jane's eagerness to adapt to Texas downright charming. When she'd offered to buy a truck to go along with his suggestion for a bumper sticker, he found himself almost taken with her. Damn it, he liked her attitude. Despite appearances, she knew how to have a good time, and as for turning Texan, she was obviously willing to try.

The bill arrived for their dinner and Glen reached for it. "We'll split it," Cal said.

"How much do I owe?" Jane asked, bending down for her purse.

Cal placed his hand on her arm. "It's taken care of."

Ellie beamed him a smile dazzling enough to blind him. He wasn't sure what had made him offer to pay for Jane's dinner. This wasn't a date, wasn't even *close* to one. But hell, he figured he owed the woman that much after the unfriendly way he'd started off the evening.

"What do you want to do now?" Glen asked his wife.

"How about bingo?" Ellie suggested, looking at the others.

"Bingo?" Jane repeated.

"Sure. There's a game every Friday night in the room above the bowling alley," Ellie said. "You'll love it. Just consider it part of your Texas education."

"I . . . don't think I've ever played," Jane confessed. "But if you think I should . . ."

"Don't you worry," Cal said, impressed once more with her willingness to fit in. "It's not difficult to learn."

Since the bowling alley was only a couple of blocks away, they decided to walk. Cal wasn't sure why he tagged along. His intent had been to beg off after dinner and join his friends at Billy D's, the local watering hole. Of course Glen wouldn't be around, and probably not Grady, either. Jimmy Morris and Lyle Whitehead would be shooting the breeze as usual—not that Cal was a big fan of Lyle's. The guy was far too ready to take offense and want to settle things with his fists. Anyway, Cal realized that, when it came right down to it, he was enjoying himself with his brother and Ellie. Doc Texas wasn't bad, either, although he was determined to make sure she realized this wasn't a real date.

The upstairs room of the bowling alley was set up with tables and chairs for the twice-weekly bingo sessions. A concession stand in the back of the room sold cold drinks, popcorn and hot dogs. Lloyd Bonney, a retired rancher who'd moved into town a couple of years ago, called out the numbers from his position at the front.

They purchased three bingo cards each and were heading for a table near the electronic bingo board when Cal saw his parents. He groaned inwardly. It would be just like his mother to read far more into their little foursome than was warranted. Mary Patterson refused to accept that her oldest son wasn't interested in marriage. She kept insisting she wanted grandchildren and it was his duty to provide them. Cal was convinced Ellie and his brother would be more than happy to handle that task; he only wished she'd stop harassing *him* about it.

"You want to sit by Mom and Dad?" Glen asked after they'd waved to their parents.

Cal growled his reply and his brother laughed. "That's what I thought."

They located some space at one of the long tables, and the two women ended up sitting between the brothers, which was fine, Cal supposed—although to the casual observer it might look as if Jane was *with* him. He wasn't much of a talker and felt grateful that Ellie and Jane carried on a nonstop conversation. Cal shook his head, amused at the way women could chatter. He never did understand how they could have so much to say to each other.

Lloyd flipped a switch and the electronic board lit up. The air machine bounced the lightweight balls bearing the bingo letters and corresponding numbers.

Because Jane was new to this, Cal watched her cards for her during the first game, checking to be sure she caught the number on each of them.

"B-fifteen," Lloyd called.

Cal checked his own card and closed off the appropriate box. The other two didn't have fifteen in the B row. Once again he glanced over at Jane's row of cards and saw that she'd missed one. He pointed it out to her.

"Oh, thanks," she said, and smiled her appreciation.

A smile. Just a smile, and yet it warmed his heart. He was startled by his reaction. It was so . . . unexpected. Damn it, something must be wrong with him to take a smile, a simple expression of thanks, and make more of it than was warranted. Obviously he'd had one too many beers.

The evening wore on, and while Cal didn't have any luck, Glen bingoed once for a twenty-five-dollar purse. The last game was the grand finale, Blackout Bingo, where every number on the card had to be closed in order to win the two-hundred-dollar grand prize.

As he had all evening, Cal glanced over at Jane's cards after he'd checked his own numbers. Other than that one time, she hadn't missed any. Lloyd had called out forty-five numbers or so when he noticed that one of Jane's cards was nearly filled. She had four blank spaces compared to his best one, which showed at least ten. The next two numbers Lloyd called were both on Jane's card.

He could feel her excitement growing. Five numbers later she had only one open space. She needed O-sixty-four. Jane closed her eyes, propped her elbows on the table and crossed the fingers on both hands.

Two numbers later Lloyd called, "O-sixty-four."

Together Cal and Jane screamed, "BINGO!"

Cal hadn't meant to yell, but he was damn near as excited as Jane. She leaped to her feet and hugged Ellie and then Cal, as though this two hundred dollars was two hundred thousand.

"Congratulations," Cal said. He couldn't help being delighted. Jane's excitement was contagious.

"Two hundred dollars," she breathed, as if this was more than she'd seen in her entire life. Lloyd personally counted out the money, placing the bills in her hand.

Clutching them in her fist, Jane wildly hugged Ellie again.

Ellie laughed. "I told you that you'd like this game."

"I *love* this game." Jane pressed the money to her heart. "I'm gonna buy me a real Texas outfit. You want to come along and make sure I get what I need?"

"You're on," Ellie replied as Jane tucked the money into her purse.

Afterward Cal and Glen stopped and greeted their parents.

"Mom, Dad, this is my friend Jane Dickinson," Ellie said, saving Cal the embarrassment of introducing her and then explaining that technically she wasn't his date. He was grateful that Ellie had taken the initiative; otherwise his parents might get the wrong idea. His mother didn't need any encouragement to match him up.

"Good to see you dating again," his father said, blindsiding him.

He'd expected his mother to comment on Jane's being with him, but not his father. "This isn't a date," Cal felt obliged to correct him, and not entirely for his dad's sake, either. It saved Jane the need to correct his father's assumption.

"Congratulations on your win, Jane," Mary said. It was easy to read what his mother was thinking—from the look in her eyes, she was already envisioning grandchildren.

After exchanging pleasantries and saying goodbye to his parents, they walked back to the Chili Pepper where they'd left their vehicles. Glen opened the truck door for Ellie and helped her in.

"I had a wonderful time," Jane said, her blue eyes bright with pleasure. "My best since moving here. Thanks so much for including me."

"How're you getting home?" Glen asked when he apparently realized she hadn't come in a car.

"I walked. It's only a few blocks."

"Would you like a ride?" he asked. Cal probably would have offered but was pleased that his brother had done it first. If Glen hadn't, he'd be obliged, and he didn't want her to think he was seeking out her company.

"I appreciate the offer, but I feel like walking. Thank you, though."

Glen climbed into his truck and backed out of the parking space as Ellie waved farewell.

Cal opened his pickup door, prepared to leave himself. "Sure you don't want a ride?" he said, trying not to sound reluctant.

"Positive. Good night, and thanks for dinner. That was really sweet of you."

Cal stood waiting by the open door until Jane had crossed the main intersection. Only then did he climb into his truck and start the engine. Checking the rearview mirror for traffic, he caught sight of Jane ambling down the street. He sighed, silently cursing himself. He didn't feel right leaving her to walk home on her own. She might not be his date or even his friend, but damn it all, he felt responsible for her safety. Especially when she was walking around with her bingo winnings in her purse. Promise didn't have a crime problem, but it didn't hurt to be cautious.

Cal cut the engine and climbed out of his truck, then raced after her.

She glanced up at him in surprise when he reached her. "I'll walk you home," he said gruffly, matching his steps to hers.

She blinked as if she wasn't sure what to say. "Thank you."

He shoved his fingers into the small pockets at the top of his jeans. They walked in silence, neither of them making an effort to talk. Two blocks off Main Street, Cal was glad he'd decided to escort her home. The streetlight on Fourth Avenue had burned out, and the sidewalk was darker than a bowl of black bean soup.

"Perhaps you'd better give me your arm," Cal suggested halfway down the block.

She did, and he tucked her hand in the crook of his elbow. Oddly, he *enjoyed* doing this small thing for her.

"That's something you and Ellie and Glen forgot to mention," Jane said suddenly.

"What's that?"

"The men in Texas are real gentlemen."

"My momma didn't raise no Bubbas," Cal said, joking, and they both laughed. It felt good to laugh, and Cal had done more of that in the past few hours than he had in months.

"Listen," he said impulsively as they neared the small house behind the health clinic, "are you serious about learning to ride?"

"Very much so."

"All right, then I'll teach you."

"You will?"

Cal wasn't sure what had prompted the offer, but since he'd blurted it out, he couldn't very well back down now.

The light from her porch illuminated her face. She looked like the original California girl with her short sun-bleached hair and eyes as blue as the Pacific. Already Cal was calling himself a damned fool and he hadn't even given Jane her first lesson. Maybe someone should offer to give *him* a lesson—on how to keep his stupid mouth shut.

SAVANNAH SMITH had made the appointment to see Dr. Jane Dickinson Tuesday morning. She hadn't been feeling well the past few weeks and thought it was time for a general checkup. Besides, she had her suspicions.

In the past half year her life had undergone a number of drastic changes. First and foremost, she'd met Laredo; they'd fallen in love and were now married. About the time Laredo had come into her life, her brother Richard had reappeared after a six-year absence. Thanks to her influence, Grady had allowed Richard to stay at the ranch, which was more than charitable of him, seeing as their brother had stolen from them—and that Grady's inclination had been to turn him away. Apparently she'd still had some lessons to learn regarding Richard. Painful ones.

Savannah had desperately wanted to believe he'd changed, but then, so had Grady. Against his better judgment, her brother had given Richard opportunity after opportunity to prove himself. In the end, when he disappeared with Grady's truck, it was exactly what she'd learned to expect. Only this time he didn't steal only from them; he'd also charged thousands of dollars' worth of goods and services in town. It was a matter of pride and principle to Grady that those bills be paid.

The merchants in Promise had accepted the charges because of the Westons' good name, and Grady wouldn't let Richard disgrace it or ruin a hundred years of excellent credit. The money had come out of the profits from selling off the herd; it was money that could have been spent in other ways, money that would have benefited the Weston ranch, the Yellow Rose.

Savannah's bout of ill health had started shortly after Richard's sudden departure. She'd done her best to hide it from her husband, but Laredo knew something was wrong because he'd been the one to suggest she make the appointment. Sitting in the examination room now, Savannah silently prayed that the diagnosis was what she suspected.

The door to the examination room opened and Dr. Dickinson walked in. It was a bit unsettling to have a doctor younger than she was. Particularly after all those years of seeing old Doc Cummings.

"Hello," Dr. Dickinson said, smiling. She held out her hand and Savannah shook it. This must be a big-city thing, she thought, because generally women in rural Texas didn't shake hands.

"I'm pleased to meet you," Savannah answered. This was their first actual meeting, although they'd seen each other at various events.

The physician sat down on the chair across from her. "You haven't been feeling well?"

Savannah nodded. "My stomach's been queasy, usually in the morning and often late in the afternoon, too."

"Any other symptoms?"

"I'm so tired lately. The other night it was all I could do to stay up past eight, which is ridiculous."

The doctor made a notation on her chart. "Anything else?"

"Well . . . yes. My period's two weeks late."

This information was written on the chart, as well. "I understand you were recently married."

Savannah nodded. "In June."

"Are you using any form of birth control?"

Savannah found such talk excruciatingly embarrassing. "Uh, usually," she answered, blushing hotly.

"I'd like to do a urine test," the doctor said.

"Okay. So do you think I might be pregnant?"

Dr. Dickinson's answering smile was warm. "You're showing all the symptoms."

Savannah let out a deep breath as that confirmation settled over her. Pregnant. So soon? She'd known it was the likely reason for her nausea and tiredness—not to mention the missed period. But . . . pregnant? Somehow, it didn't seem possible, and yet she supposed it was inevitable considering their haphazard methods of birth control.

After a brief physical examination Savannah provided a urine sample. Waiting for the test results seemed to take forever when in reality it was only minutes. Savannah's emotions ran the entire spectrum. She felt mostly an overwhelming sense of joy—a joy so deep and profound it was difficult not to leap up and shout with it. Simultaneously she was aware that the timing could hardly be worse. She and Laredo had spent much of the summer drawing up plans for their own home. Every penny they'd managed to pull together had gone into the project. Now wasn't exactly the ideal time to announce she was going to have a baby.

The door opened and the doctor returned. "Congratulations, Savannah. You're going to be a mother."

Savannah's hands flew to her mouth and tears welled in her eyes.

"How do you feel about this pregnancy?" the physician asked.

"I . . . it's a surprise. I mean, it is and it isn't. I realize it shouldn't be, but . . ." She realized she was babbling. "I'm happy. Very happy."

"I'd like to set up a series of appointments for you, plus I'd like to start you on a regimen of vitamins."

"All right."

"Good," Dr. Dickinson said. "So I'll see you in a month." Then she gently patted Savannah's back and left to attend to the next patient.

Savannah's head continued to buzz as she drove back to the ranch. To her amazement Laredo was waiting for her when she pulled into the yard. He hurried over to the truck and opened the door the second she'd parked.

"What did the doctor have to say?" he asked before she had time to climb out. His eyes revealed his anxiety.

"Oh, Laredo, you aren't going to believe this. We're pregnant!"

"Pregnant?"

"Oh, please tell me you're glad. Because I am. I swear I could explode!"

They walked into the kitchen and Laredo pulled out a chair and sat down. "Pregnant," he said again, as if he couldn't quite believe it.

Savannah nodded, studying this man she loved beyond all reason. As she knew it would, a slow easy smile spread across his face. "Pregnant," he said more loudly this time. "My wife's going to have a baby! Just wait until my mother hears about this."

Savannah smiled. Their love was the most profound wonder of her life. And as she'd now discovered, it was only the beginning.

Her husband leaped to his feet and caught her in his arms. "We're going to have a baby!"

"I know the timing's bad . . ."

"The timing's perfect. You're perfect. Life's perfect." He threw back his head and laughed, and then he kissed her.

"Hey, you two," Grady said when he stepped into the kitchen. "What's going on?"

Three

For the first time since Jane had come to Texas, she felt a sense of belonging. Friends made all the difference. Her evening out with Ellie, Glen and Cal had cheered her immensely, and within a few days she'd followed all their instructions. She had a Texas bumper sticker, a Willie Nelson cassette in her car, and she routinely listened to the Brewster country-and-western station. A shopping spree with her bingo winnings plus a chunk of her savings had netted her an outfit Annie Oakley would've been proud to wear. Not only that, her first riding lesson was scheduled for Friday afternoon. If she got any more Texan, she wouldn't recognize herself!

Thursday-afternoon traffic in the clinic was slow; she hadn't seen a patient in more than two hours. Attaching her beeper to her waistband, she headed toward Dovie's antique shop, taking the rag doll Maggie Daniels had brought her. Every time she entered the office the old-fashioned doll smiled at her with its faded pink lips, looking somehow forlorn, as though it—she—wanted to pour out her sawdust heart. If anyone could help Jane locate the doll's rightful owner, it was Dovie.

Her friend seemed to be experiencing a lull in business, too. Dovie's face broke into a welcoming smile when Jane walked into the shop.

"Jane, how are you?" Dovie asked, rushing over to hug her. She had to skirt wooden tables and dressers and chairs, all draped and dangling with jewelry and scarves. Jane was impressed by the quantity and quality of Dovie's wares.

"I'm terrific," she answered.

Her arm around Jane's waist, Dovie led her to the Victorian Tea Room and poured them each a cup of fragrant lemon tea. When she'd finished, she asked about Friday night's dinner.

Jane talked nonstop for ten minutes, relating the highlights of the evening. She mentioned winning at bingo and that Cal had walked her home and volunteered to teach her to ride.

"Cal?" Dovie sounded shocked. "Cal Patterson?"

"I know. I was surprised myself. At first I could tell he wasn't thrilled to be paired up with me. He seemed to think I'd finagled this matchmaking myself, but after a while, he was fine." She grinned. "You could say he underwent an attitude adjustment." She considered Cal a gentleman in an age when chivalry was all but dead. He'd gone out of his way to escort her home, out of regard for her safety. That certainly hadn't been required, but Jane appreciated it. In the days since, she'd thought quite a lot about him.

Dovie's eyes twinkled with delight. "You're exactly what that young man needs."

"I met his parents, too."

"Mary and Phil are two of my dearest friends," Dovie told her.

Jane sipped her tea, then lifted the bag with the doll onto her lap. "Actually I have a reason for stopping by other than to let you know how everything went last Friday." She opened the bag and carefully withdrew the fragile toy.

Dovie's eyes widened when she saw it. "Where in heaven's name did you find that?"

Jane hesitated. "I'm not at liberty to say."

Dovie's brows rose a fraction of an inch.

"I will tell you that someone brought it to me—feeling a lot of guilt. Apparently this person took the doll and shouldn't have, and for reasons I can't understand is unable to return it. I was hoping you might know who the rightful owner is."

Dovie turned the antique in her hands and thoroughly examined how it was constructed. "I'd swear it's authentic."

"You mean this *is* a real antique?" Jane asked, wondering where and how six-year-old Maggie could have come by it.

"She's real, and probably worth quite a lot of money."

"You're joking." The doll was ready to fall apart.

"I'm not." Dovie gave the toy back to Jane with some hesitation. "Are you sure you can't tell me the name of the person who gave you the doll?"

Jane shook her head. "I wish I could, but I'd be breaking a confidence."

Dovie accepted her answer. "Do you have any idea where this unnamed person got the doll?"

"Didn't say." In retrospect, Jane realized there were any number of questions she should have asked Maggie. But the child had been in quite a state, sick with regret and worry. At the time it'd seemed more important to reassure the little girl than to worry about the doll's owner.

"There's only one place I can imagine finding anything like this," Dovie said, her look thoughtful. A frown slowly formed, furrowing her brow.

"Where's that?" Jane asked.

"It doesn't seem possible . . . but there's been talk about it lately and I have to wonder. The doll might have come from . . . Bitter End."

It was Jane's turn to lift her eyebrows. She'd never heard of the town and was fairly certain she would have remembered one with such an unusual name. "Bitter End?"

"That's the name the settlers chose more than 130 years ago, after the Civil War. If I remember my history correctly, the journey across Indian territory and through the war-ravaged South was harrowing. Not a family came through the trip unscathed. Parents lost children and children lost parents from Indian attacks and disease. By the time they reached the Texas hill country, their faith had nearly been destroyed."

"Times were so difficult back then," Jane said, remembering that the now-common childhood diseases were often the source of death.

"Those pioneers faced hardship after hardship," Dovie continued. "Overcome with bitterness, the town's founding fathers decided to name their community Bitter End."

"I've never heard of it."

"Few have," Dovie said. "It's a ghost town now."

"Really? You've been there?" Jane asked, her curiosity keen. She'd never dreamed something like that existed in this vicinity.

"Have I been to Bitter End?" Dovie's laugh was abrupt. "I'm sorry to say I haven't. I'd like to and perhaps one day I will. The only reason I even know about it is because of something my father said years ago."

"I'd like to go there," Jane said. She'd always been a history buff, and visiting a ghost town would be a wonderful adventure.

"Jane, I hate to disillusion you," Dovie said kindly, "but I don't even know if the old town is still standing."

"Could you give me directions?"

"If I knew where it was, possibly, but there are no paved roads. It's somewhere up in the hills. You need to remember this is a real ghost town."

"But what happened? Why did everyone leave?" Jane's mind filled with questions.

Dovie looked as though she regretted bringing up the subject. "I don't have a clue. No one does. At one time I believe the town was quite prosperous—a fast-growing community. My father said he'd even heard that the railroad was scheduled to lay track there, but all of that changed overnight."

"Overnight?" The details were becoming more and more intriguing. "Something drastic must have happened."

"A natural catastrophe, perhaps," Dovie suggested. "No one knows."

"That doesn't make sense," Jane said, thinking out loud. "Tornado, fire, flood—anything like that would have destroyed the whole town. There'd be nothing left. Anyway, why wouldn't they rebuild if that happened?"

"I don't know," Dovie murmured. "My father mentioned it twice in the years I was growing up. As I recall, he said everyone packed up and moved—no one knows why. They abandoned almost everything."

"Then there's a possibility the entire town's intact."

"Yes . . . I suppose there is," Dovie said.

"Do you know people who've actually been there?"

She took her time answering. "A few."

"Who?"

Dovie was about to speak when the bell above the front door rang, and Sheriff Frank Hennessey walked into the store.

It seemed to Jane that Dovie went pale. "Jane," she whispered, getting to her feet, "don't leave me."

Jane nodded.

"Hello, Sheriff," Dovie said. Her tone lacked its usual warmth.

"Dovie."

The sheriff glanced in Jane's direction, and his look made it clear he wished she wasn't there. In any other circumstances Jane would have made her excuses and left, but Dovie had plainly asked her to stay. However uncomfortable she was, Jane felt obliged to honor her friend's request.

"What can I do for you, Sheriff?" Dovie asked.

Frank Hennessey glanced at Jane again. "Dovie, in the name of heaven, this has got to end," he said in a low urgent voice. "We're both miserable."

"We've already been through this a thousand times. Nothing's going to change."

The sheriff's mouth thinned. "I love you," he whispered.

"So you say." Dovie began to move about the shop, rearranging things here and there. Frank Hennessey trailed behind her, looking lost and utterly wretched.

When his pleading didn't work, the sheriff tried a different tactic. "What's this I heard about you traveling?" he demanded as though he had every right to know.

"It's time I saw something of the world."

"A *singles'* cruise, Dovie?" His disapproval was evident.

Dovie sighed expressively. "Who told you?"

"Does it matter?"

"As a matter of fact it does, because I want to be sure that whoever it was has nothing more to report."

"You didn't want me to know?" The sheriff's tone had gone from irritated to hurt.

"What I choose to do with my life from here on out, Frank Hennessey, is *my* concern, and only mine."

He stiffened. "You don't mean that."

"Yes, Frank, I do." Dovie had completed one full circle of the shop. She stopped in front of the table where she and Jane had been drinking tea. "You remember Dr. Dickinson, don't you?"

The sheriff gave Jane little more than a perfunctory nod.

"Good to see you again, Sheriff Hennessey," Jane said, but she doubted he'd even heard.

His gaze remained on Dovie. "This has gone on long enough," he said, and he no longer seemed to care whether or not Jane was privy to their conversation. "I'm crazy about you. It's been damn near three weeks, and we're no closer to settling this than we were then. I need you, Dovie! It isn't like you to be unreasonable. I don't know who put this craziness in your head, but it's got to end, for both our sakes. Can't we resolve this?"

"Resolve this?" Dovie repeated as if she found the statement amusing. "What you mean is, can't I give in to you. It's not going to happen, Frank. You've made your decision and I've made mine, and that's all there is to it."

"Damn it, Dovie, would you listen to reason?"

"There's nothing more to discuss," Dovie said, not quite disguising the sadness in her tone. "I think it'd be best if you left."

Frank stared at Dovie in disbelief. Then, in an act of pure frustration, he slapped his hat against his thigh and stormed out of the shop, leaving the display windows shaking.

Dovie sank into the chair and Jane noticed that her hands were shaking. "I'm sorry to subject you to that, Jane," she said, her voice as shaky as her hands.

"Are you all right?" Jane asked, truly concerned.

"No," Dovie admitted, "but I will be in time."

"Are you really going away?"

"Yes. I've booked a three-day cruise, but not a singles' one. Mary Patterson suggested that, but I'm not interested in getting involved again—at least not this soon."

"You love Frank, don't you?" Jane probed gently.

"Yes, fool that I am. I do. But he's stubborn, and unfortunately so am I." She didn't elaborate, but Jane had a pretty clear picture of the problem. Dovie wanted a ring on her finger, and Sheriff Hennessey wasn't about to relinquish his freedom. From the looks of it, they were at an impasse.

"You'll enjoy the cruise," Jane said, wanting to encourage her friend in the same kindly way Dovie had encouraged her. "And it'll do you a world of good to get away for a while."

"I'm sure you're right." Dovie made an unsuccessful attempt at a smile. "I talked Mary and Phil Patterson into coming along with me, and by golly, we're going to have the time of our lives."

She said this, Jane noted, as though the person she most needed to convince was herself.

It CAME AS A SURPRISE to Cal to realize he was actually looking forward to seeing Jane Dickinson again. By Friday afternoon he was ready to teach that California gal everything she cared to know about the joys of riding.

From his brother Cal learned that Ellie and Jane had been shopping and Jane had purchased an entire Western outfit, complete with hat and cowboy boots.

They'd talked briefly by phone earlier in the week, and Cal had suggested Jane come to the ranch at five o'clock, since the days were growing shorter now.

Accustomed to women being late, Cal didn't actually expect her to show up on time. He was pleasantly surprised when her car turned into the yard at five minutes to five.

She parked, then opened the car door and gingerly stepped out. Her clothes were so new they practically squeaked.

"This really is very kind of you," she said, smiling.

Cal walked all the way around her, amazed by the transformation a few clothes could make. She looked great. Terrific. If he didn't know better, he'd have assumed she'd been born and raised in the great state of Texas. At least, until she opened her mouth, and then all doubt was removed. She didn't sound anything like a Texan—but he didn't feel he should hold that against her.

"What do you think?" she asked, holding her arms out at her sides.

"Your Wranglers seem a little stiff, but other than that, not bad. Not bad indeed!"

"Did you check out my bumper sticker?" she asked.

He hadn't, so he turned to look—and roared with laughter. Sure enough, she'd gotten a sticker. It read: *Texas Crude.*

"Not only that, I'm listening to Reba, Clint, John Berry and Alabama."

Cal loved it. "Wonderful."

She laughed and he discovered that he liked the sound of it. Soon he was chuckling himself, and for no damn reason that he could think of. Hmm. Something like this could ruin his reputation as a curmudgeon.

"You ready?" he asked.

"Ready as I'll ever be," she said, then exhaled a deep sigh.

Cal led the way. He'd already chosen Atta Girl for her and brought the horse out of the paddock. Atta Girl was a gentle chestnut mare who'd delivered six foals over the past ten years. Cal trusted her to treat the greenhorn with patience.

"This is Atta Girl," he said, rubbing his hand down the mare's neck.

Jane stood directly in front of the animal. "Pleased to meet you," she said with the same seriousness she might have used to address the bank manager.

"She isn't going to shake your hand," Cal said, struggling not to smile.

Jane gave him a glance that said she didn't find him all that funny, but he noticed she had a hard time containing her amusement, too. It'd been a long time since anyone had affected him this way.

"I thought we'd start with you learning how to saddle her," he said. Once she was familiar with the basics, he'd let her mount.

Jane nibbled her lower lip. "Before I put a saddle on her back, I thought maybe Atta Girl and I should talk this over."

He assumed she was joking, but it soon became obvious she wasn't. Apparently she intended to have some polite conversation with Atta Girl first.

"I thought you might like to get a good look at me," Jane said, just as if she were talking to a person. "It must be frustrating to carry someone around without being able to see who it is."

Cal tried not to roll his eyes, but didn't succeed. At this rate it'd take a month of Sundays to get her on Atta Girl's back.

"She can't really see you, anyway," Cal felt honor bound to tell Jane.

"Do you mean to say you gave me a blind horse?"

He shook his head. "Horses are notorious for having bad eyesight. You notice how far apart her eyes are? How they're on either side of her face?"

Jane looked at one side of Atta Girl's face and then the other.

"Because of that, horses have what you might call a broad view of things, and although they can tell when there's something approaching, what they generally see are shadowy figures."

"Oh," Jane said, and tentatively touched the mare's soft muzzle. "In that case, Atta Girl, you need carrots. Lots and lots of carrots. I'll bring you some on my next visit."

"While we're at it," Cal said, "it's probably not a good idea to approach a horse from the rear. It's an ugly way to die."

"How reassuring," Jane muttered.

"Not to worry, you're safe with Atta Girl."

"At least her name isn't something like Killer."

"That was her sire's name," Cal teased.

Jane placed her hands on her hips. "Are you trying to scare me?"

"Would I do something like that?" he inquired, the picture of innocence. While he had her attention, he told her a number of other facts she should know. Riding information, as well as bits and pieces of horse lore. She listened with complete concentration. Not until she'd grown accustomed to riding would she really experience the thrill of it. Nothing in life could compare with galloping through a field of wildflowers on a warm spring day with the wind in your face.

"What kind of relationship do you have with your horse?" she asked. "Do you think of him the way Roy Rogers thought of Trigger?"

"Probably not." He hoped he wasn't shattering any illusions. "Thunder's a loyal partner, but he's not my best friend. The tricks he knows aren't going to end up on any television show, but he cuts cattle better than any pony I've ever ridden." Cal paused, wondering whether to add the next part. "Also, I'm not having him stuffed when he eventually goes."

Jane looked startled, but recovered quickly. She asked a number of intelligent questions, which he answered to the best of his ability.

"You ready to saddle her up?" he asked.

Jane drew a deep breath and nodded.

Having been around horses his entire life, Cal had no fear of them.

Respect, yes, but not fear. Jane was intimidated; following his example, though, she refused to show it. Nor would she allow her intimidation to stop her from getting on with the lesson.

Cal brought out the brushes, a blanket, the saddle and tack. He taught her by demonstrating and then letting her do it herself. Atta Girl was everything he'd expected. To his amusement Jane stopped what she was doing several times, walked around to the horse's head and spoke to her. Anyone might have thought they were actually communicating.

"You're sure this isn't too much trouble for you?" she asked Atta Girl next.

"Jane," Cal muttered, thinking she was quite possibly the most sensitive person he'd ever met. Also the most ridiculous, but he found himself more entertained than annoyed.

By the time she had the saddle on, it was close to seven and twilight was beginning.

"We'll save the actual ride for another lesson," he said. "But it'd be a shame if you didn't at least mount her after all this."

Jane's expression was skeptical. "You think I should? Tonight?"

He nodded, then watched as she walked around to discuss the prospect with Atta Girl. "Does she have any objection?" Cal asked as a joke.

"She doesn't seem to," Jane said, apparently taking him seriously.

"I'll help you adjust the stirrups," he said. It was a skill that demanded experience and time. "You're doing great."

"I'll bet that's what they said to Custer before the Battle of Little Big Horn," she complained, then put her foot in the left stirrup and heaved herself up.

Apparently the cinch wasn't as tight as it should have been, because before he could warn her, the saddle slid sideways, sending her directly under Atta Girl's stomach. Jane let out a cry of alarm while Atta Girl pranced about in an effort to maintain her balance. Cal held his breath, fearing the mare would inadvertently step on Jane. To his amazement he watched her roll out from under the horse and leap to her feet. Indiana Jones had nothing on Dr. Texas!

"Are you okay?" Cal asked. Everything had happened so fast he'd barely had time to react. He took hold of Atta Girl's reins and quickly reassured the frightened mare by speaking gently to her.

"That does it," Jane said breathlessly, her hand over her heart.

"You're quitting?" Cal asked, not that he blamed her. She'd had quite a scare.

"No, I'm joining Weight Watchers. I damn near downed that poor horse."

Cal stared at her, then started to chuckle. The laughter came deep from inside him, and nothing could have held it back. Nothing. It was as though two years of fun and laughter had been confined inside him, waiting for precisely this moment. A few hours with Jane Dickinson, and all the pent-up enjoyment of life came spilling out of him in waves of unrestrained delight.

"Well, I'm glad you find this so funny," she said.

Tears ran down his cheeks and he wiped them aside with the back of his hand. "Damn, but I can't remember when I laughed so hard." Jane crossed her arms, and not wanting his reaction to offend her, he gave her a brief hug. "You're a good sport, Jane."

She muttered something unintelligible.

"And listen, there's no need for you to lose weight—you're perfect just the way you are. The saddle slipped because the cinch wasn't tight enough. It had nothing to do with your size."

She seemed none the worse for wear and within seconds she was smiling, too. "You're willing to give me another lesson?"

"You bet, Dr. Texas."

Her smile broadened.

In fact, Cal could hardly wait. This was the most fun he'd had in years. Even Jennifer, the woman he'd loved enough to marry, had never provoked this much reaction in him—apart from the anger and humiliation he felt when she'd dumped him.

"Next week?" Jane asked.

Cal nodded, but waiting an entire week for her second lesson was too long. He wanted to see her again soon.

"Can you make it Tuesday, Dr. Texas?"

She laughed. "You bet, cowboy—and at least my jeans are broken in now."

JANE RETURNED to her house, threw off her clothes and soaked in a hot tub. She couldn't very well claim she was saddle sore, seeing that she hadn't so much as managed to sit on a horse. But she'd taxed rarely-used muscles in her effort to avoid being trampled by Atta Girl.

All Cal had done was laugh, and while he might have been amused, she'd been frightened out of her wits. But all's well that ends well, she decided, not sure if it was the desire to learn to ride or her attraction to Cal that had prompted her to agree to a second lesson.

She liked him. A lot.

Climbing out of the tub, she dressed in a light robe, made some popcorn for dinner and settled down in front of the television with a rented video. The tape had just started when the phone rang.

It was so rare for her phone to ring that she stared at it for a moment. Any emergency calls came through her beeper. At last she picked it up.

"Hello?"

"Janey, it's Mom. How are you, sweetheart?"

"I'm feeling wonderful." She reached for the remote control and stopped the movie. Since her arrival in Promise she'd tried to hide her unhappiness from her parents. Now she was eager to share the good news of making friends and becoming part of the community.

"You sound terrific."

"Listen, honey," her father said, speaking from the extension, "your letter arrived this afternoon. What's all this about a ghost town?"

Excited after her discussion with Dovie, Jane had written home, elaborating on the story, adding bits of speculation and her decision to learn everything she could. From what Dovie had said, the frontier town was real; information had been passed down from one generation to the next. But still, a person could grow up believing in some historical "fact" and later learn it had been a legend with little or no basis in reality.

"Do you honestly believe there's such a place as Bitter End?" her mother asked.

"I don't know, but I'd like to find out."

"How do you intend to do that?" her father wanted to know. "You didn't tell us in your letter."

"I don't know . . ." Dovie had told her there weren't any roads leading to the ghost town, and a quick survey of an area map revealed a thousand spots where the old town might be.

"I'm as fascinated by all this as you are," her mother said. "I've always loved history, too."

"What interests me is the mystery involved," Jane said.

"You mean why everyone left the town?" her father said.

"Yes. If I understood Dovie correctly, the town was thriving. Then overnight everyone just packed up and moved away. Actually they came here, to Promise."

"And nobody knows why they abandoned one town and founded another," her mother said.

"That's right," Jane said. "No one seems to know. Dovie's never been there herself, but from what she told me there's a good possibility the entire town is still standing."

"But it's over a hundred years old."

"Over 130. As far as I've been able to find out from reading state history, the original settlers were probably a mixed bag of immigrants, outlaws and Southern sympathizers who'd lost everything in the Civil War. That was pretty typical of the people who came to Texas at that time. Most of them had packed up what was left of their worldly belongings and traveled here, hoping to put the war behind them."

"I'm fascinated," her mother said again. "I'll do some research and see if I can find any books that mention Bitter End."

"Thanks, Mom, that'd be great."

"It sounds from your letter," her father said, "that you're enjoying Texas. This last letter was a lot less . . . reserved than before."

Jane chuckled. "Well, I've got a complete cowgirl outfit now, and one of the local ranchers calls me Dr. Texas."

It was her father's turn to chuckle. "Don't let him give you any ideas. You're Dr. California, understand?"

She did. She was following in her grandfather's and her uncle Ken's footsteps. As soon as her student loans were paid off, she'd be joining her uncle's medical practice in Los Angeles. One day she'd inherit the practice. Uncle Ken claimed she was his favorite niece. While a couple of her cousins had shown an interest in medicine, she was the only one who'd taken it seriously. The schooling had been difficult, her internship and residency demanding. She'd given up every aspect of a social life and been left to deal with a huge debt.

Her parents had helped her out financially, but medical school was expensive. Her uncle had offered to help, too. Still, when the opportunity arose to wipe out most of her debt by working in Texas, she'd leaped at the idea. Three years was nothing. The time would pass before she knew it, or so she'd believed.

Her first six months in Promise had proved otherwise.

Until recently.

Until she met Cal Patterson.

Four

Late Monday night Frank sat in his patrol car outside Dovie Boyd's home, mulling over what he should do next. He was miserable, and he knew she was, too. He'd loved Dovie for a lot of years, but this was the first time he'd encountered her stubbornness. It was enough to drive a man to drink.

Louise Powell, dressed to the hilt in her Texas trash, complete with star-shaped sunglasses and a silvery hat with a rhinestone band, had approached him at the bowling alley café. She'd let it drop that Dovie had booked a singles' Caribbean cruise. Now if that didn't beat all. Louise had gotten the information from Gayla Perkins at the travel agency and had taken great delight in rubbing his nose in it.

It was downright embarrassing. Here was the town gossip, flapping her tongue all over the county, telling everyone who cared to hear that Dovie was seeking greener pastures.

His fingers tightened around the steering wheel as he reviewed his options. He'd tried, heaven knew he'd tried, but damn it all, he loved Dovie and he didn't want to lose her, especially to another man.

He checked his wristwatch and knew she hadn't gone to bed yet. He sighed deeply, remembering the times they'd cuddled up together on her big feather bed, watching television. She'd made the everyday routines of life special, adding her own little touches here and there. She sun-dried the bed sheets, then stored them with woven lavender wands so that when he crawled in beside her he felt their cool crispness and breathed in the light perfumed scent of summer.

Dinner, too, was something special. Dovie set her table with a linen cloth and napkins, using china and real crystal. She could serve home-baked macaroni and cheese with the panache of the finest restaurant.

Damn, but he missed her.

Swallowing his pride, Frank stepped out of the car and approached the house. He had to try one last time. If he couldn't get her to listen to reason tonight, then he'd have no choice but to accept her decision.

As was his habit, he parked the car around the corner, out of sight from the street, and approached through the backyard. He missed their night together more than he would've thought possible. He knew Dovie, and she was lusty and vital, a real woman with a woman's needs. It was a source of consolation to realize she must miss their nights together, too.

He knocked lightly on the back door and waited, hat in hand.

The porch light went on and he saw her pull aside the lace curtain and peek out. It was several long seconds before she unlocked the door and opened it.

"Hello, Dovie." He kept his gaze lowered. Coming to her like this wasn't easy.

"Frank."

He didn't speak, but merely raised his eyes to hers. He loved her, as much as he was capable of loving any woman. Surely she knew that! But he wasn't the marrying kind. He couldn't help it; he needed his freedom in order to breathe. Marriage, even to Dovie whom he adored, would feel like a noose around his neck.

Everything had been perfect. They'd each had their own lives and a life together, too. He had his house and she had hers. Two nights a week he joined her for mutual pleasure. He was willing to do whatever it took, short of marriage, to return to that arrangement.

"It's not true," she said, breaking the silence, "about the singles' cruise. I don't know who told you that, but I'm not looking for another man."

A weight seemed to lift from his shoulders. So she wasn't seeking out someone else. Although he was grateful, all he could manage was a nod.

"I've just decided to do some traveling," she told him.

"Why?" That was another thing he'd always loved about Dovie—she enjoyed the simple pleasures in life. She shunned luxuries, content with a walk in the moonlight when he would gladly have taken her out for an evening at a fancy restaurant.

"I've lived my entire life in Promise," she explained. "If I don't travel now, I never will. I understand the Caribbean is lovely and I've always dreamed of visiting the islands there. At one time I thought I'd see it with—"

"I'll take you." If all she wanted was a trip, a vacation away, he'd book their passage in the morning. No questions asked. Anywhere in the world she wanted to go.

"As your wife, Frank?"

The bubble of hope he'd felt burst with her words. "Oh, Dovie, you know I can't do that."

"Yes, I do know. That's why I'll be traveling without you."

The frustration was almost intolerable. "Don't you miss me?" he cried. He ached with the need to hold her.

She looked away but not before he saw the sheen of tears in her eyes.

"I miss you so much," she whispered.

"Oh, Dovie." He reached for her hand and kissed her palm. "Can't we work this out like two adults? I love you and you love me. It's all we need, all we've ever needed."

Her skin was silky smooth and touching it fired all his love, all his passion. "Let me spend the night." His eyes pleaded with her.

Her long hesitation gave him hope.

"No," she finally whispered.

"Dovie, you don't mean that!"

"I do mean it." She eased her hand from his grasp.

Frank couldn't believe this was happening. He'd come so close to convincing her—and he wasn't about to give up without a fight.

"I'm a man with strong needs," he said, hoping that would influence her.

"I love you, but I'm not sleeping with you again, Frank, not unless we're married."

"Dovie." He groaned her name. Damn it, the time had come to play hardball, acquaint her with a few facts. "There are other women in Promise who'd welcome my attention." He was a handsome cuss and he knew it, but there wasn't a woman in the world he wanted more than Dovie Boyd.

"Yes, I'm sure any number of them would," Dovie said.

Frank saw the hurt in her eyes and was furious with himself for suggesting he'd consider seeing anyone else. But he'd tried everything possible to get her to listen to reason.

"Perhaps another woman *would* be the best answer," Dovie murmured. She stepped back from the threshold.

He opened his mouth to tell her he'd been only bluffing, but he wasn't given the opportunity. Dovie's door was closed firmly in his face. He stared at it in stunned silence.

Hell and damnation, the woman drove him crazy! It'd serve her right if he did go out with someone else. Maybe then she'd realize what she was giving up; maybe then she'd come to her senses. Yup, that was what he'd do, Frank decided. She was taking a fancy cruise and plenty of eligible men were bound to come sniffing around. Well, he was entitled to some compensations, too.

Eventually, he hoped she'd accept that, even though he loved her with all his heart, he wasn't about to let her or any other woman maneuver him into marriage. In a few months he'd be sixty-one years old. He'd managed to avoid marriage so far. Why would he change now? Marriage was a trap, especially for a man like him—despite those sentimental beliefs of Dovie's.

But as soon as she learned he was seeing another woman, she'd be back. What had begun as a bluff now sounded like a good strategy. Dovie needed some competition; that way she'd realize how good they'd had it. One thing about Dovie, she was a fast learner.

Frank felt another faint stirring of hope. Before long, he told himself, Dovie would be begging him to come back.

EARLY TUESDAY AFTERNOON Ellie stepped outside the feed store and inserted a few coins in the pop machine. The morning had been hectic and she was grateful for this respite, however brief. She opened the can of soda and saw Jane Dickinson walking across the street.

"Jane," she called, raising her hand in greeting. "Come on over."

Jane returned the wave, glanced both ways, then crossed the street.

Ellie's father had recognized early in his career the importance of customer relations. He'd strived to make the feed store a friendly place in which to conduct business. He'd wanted to give ranchers and anyone else who dropped off an order a cozy place to sit and chat. The large shaded porch had been furnished with chairs and a pop machine for that purpose.

She and Glen had spent many an afternoon in this very spot. They'd been friends long before they'd fallen in love—a love it took them far too long to recognize or acknowledge. Even now, a month after their wedding, it astonished her that they could have been so blind to their feelings.

"Hi," Ellie greeted Jane. "I heard about the riding lesson," she said carefully.

Jane smiled and claimed an empty seat beside Ellie. "It went okay— I think. Cal's teaching me with Atta Girl, and other than damn near toppling the mare, I did fine."

Glen had told Ellie the story of the saddle slipping during Jane's first lesson. He reported that Cal had laughed so hard in his telling of the story he was almost incomprehensible. It'd taken Glen a while to understand what had happened.

"Actually I'm amazed you're willing to go back for a second lesson, seeing the way Cal behaved," Ellie said, wanting to kick her brother-in-law for his lack of manners.

At the mention of his name, Jane's face brightened. "He was great," she said. "Patient and gentle."

Ellie wondered if she was having a hearing problem. It wasn't possible that they were referring to the same person. *"Cal?"*

Jane eyed her. "Yes, Cal. He's the one who's teaching me."

"I've never heard him referred to as patient and gentle, at least not since Jennifer—" Ellie stopped abruptly.

"Who's Jennifer?" Jane asked.

Ellie sighed inwardly. She'd already mentioned Cal's former fiancée so she might as well continue. "She and Cal were . . . friendly at one time."

"Friendly?"

"An item."

"How much of an item?"

Ellie could see there was no help for it. "They were engaged."

Jane didn't respond right away. "I see."

Ellie wouldn't have said another word if Jane hadn't pressed. Would have preferred it that way. Apparently Cal was quite taken with the new doctor, and she didn't want to be responsible for upsetting this hopeful turn of events.

"Do you mind telling me what happened?"

That was difficult. If this had concerned anyone other than Cal, Ellie would have suggested Jane simply ask him. But for the past two years Cal had closed himself off from most people as a result of the broken engagement. And he'd rejected the possibility of any other relationship with a woman. Ellie didn't want to scare Jane off; if anything she wanted to encourage a romance between these two lonely people.

Glen had been shocked when he learned that Cal had offered to teach Jane to ride. Even Ellie had been surprised. And delighted. Naturally she'd *hoped* he'd volunteer, but she'd believed it'd take some champion finagling on her part. The last thing she'd expected was for Cal to volunteer on his own.

Ellie hesitated, wondering how much she should say. "There isn't really that much to tell."

"I don't mean to pry," Jane said.

"Well . . . you should probably know," Ellie said. "Cal never did tell us exactly what went wrong. He loved Jennifer. Anyone looking at the two of them could see the way he felt about her."

Jennifer, though, wasn't the type Ellie would have chosen for her brother-in-law, but then, Cal hadn't sought her opinion. Glen hadn't been impressed by Jennifer, either, but like Ellie, had kept his views to himself. Ellie had met Jennifer, who'd worked at a local branch of a large bank, in the course of business. She'd quickly decided Jennifer Healy was selfish and manipulative, an opinion shared by a number of other people Ellie knew.

"I gather they disagreed about something, and two days before the wedding," Ellie continued, "Jennifer called the whole thing off. She gave him back the ring and left town."

"Moved?"

"To Houston. Glen heard sometime later that she was living with a salesman."

"She walked out two days before the wedding," Jane repeated slowly.

"A big family wedding," Ellie elaborated. "Cal was stuck with phoning all the guests and telling them the wedding was off. He had to return gifts, cancel all the arrangements . . . . Humiliating, huh? Naturally, everyone speculated about what had gone wrong. But Cal didn't want to answer questions, so he retreated. Didn't come into town for months."

"It must have been a painful time for him."

Ellie nodded. "He wasn't the same afterward."

Jane's eyes asked the obvious question although she didn't voice it.

Ellie answered it, anyway. "He likes you, Jane. You know something? In two years you're the first woman he's done more than speak a few gruff words to."

"Me?" Jane flattened her palm against her chest.

"Yes. I know I'm right. He likes you."

Jane laughed and shook her head. "I don't think so."

"He's teaching you to ride, isn't he?"

"Yes, but I suspect that's because he felt sorry for me."

Ellie dismissed the excuse with a shake of her head. "You don't know Cal the way I do. Since Jennifer walked out on him, his attitude toward women has been less than charitable. Trust me, he's interested in you."

WITH ELLIE'S WORDS ringing in her ears, Jane headed out to Lonesome Coyote Ranch for her second riding lesson. It'd been four days since her last one and she was looking forward to learning more. About horseback riding, yes, but also about Cal Patterson.

Ellie had said it'd been two years since Cal's broken engagement. Two years since he'd participated in anything social. What her friend didn't know was that it'd been even longer for Jane. She was twenty-eight years old and couldn't remember her last real date. There'd been a few get-togethers with other medical students, but even these had been severely curtailed during her internship and residency. When it came to dating, high-school girls had more experience and finesse than she did.

Cal was already in the yard when she arrived. "Howdy," he greeted her.

"Hi." She walked away from her parked car. As she'd jokingly said on Friday, her jeans were less stiff this time. The boots, however, still felt awkward, but eventually she'd get used to wearing them, or so Max Jordan had assured her.

Cal's smile was warm. "I wasn't sure you'd show."

"Why not?"

He chuckled. "Ellie tells me it was exceptionally rude to laugh at your, uh, accident. She says I should apologize."

Jane shrugged off his apology, such as it was. "I'm willing to put the incident behind us if you are."

"I am." He led the way toward the barn. "Atta Girl's been waiting for you. She'd like a second chance, too."

The first part of the lesson went well, as they reviewed what she'd learned the last time. She saddled Atta Girl herself, making sure to check the cinch, then mounted the mare with a boost from Cal and a minimum of fuss.

"How does it feel?" he asked, taking the reins and leading Atta Girl into the corral.

"I didn't realize I'd be this high off the ground." She gripped the saddle horn with both hands. Once they arrived at the fenced area, Cal gave her the reins, and Jane held on for dear life.

Cal had her ease Atta Girl forward in a slow walk. Not bad, she decided. In fact, it was kind of exciting.

"This is great!" she called out. Some of her excitement must have communicated itself to Atta Girl, because the mare increased her speed.

"Ride the horse, not the saddle," he reminded her.

"I know," she shouted back. His advice, however, did little good. Try as she might, Jane felt her rear bouncing hard on the unyielding saddle. She'd bounce up and slam down against the leather with a force powerful enough to jar her molars. Fearing she was about to lose her hat, she held on to it with one hand.

"Are you sure I'm doing this right?" she shouted to Cal, certain she wouldn't be able to maintain her balance another minute. The ground looked a long way down.

Cal mounted his own horse and rode next to her, circling the corral. She envied the grace with which he rode; it was as if man and beast moved as one, just the way those cowboy books said. Jane attempted to work her body in unison with Atta Girl's movements, but couldn't find the appropriate rhythm, despite her efforts.

"How . . . am . . . I . . . doing?" Each word vibrated as she rebounded against the saddle.

"You're a natural," Cal assured her. He slowed the gelding's pace and Atta Girl followed suit. Jane's rear end was grateful, not to mention the rest of her. She would never have guessed that her *teeth* would hurt after a riding lesson.

"Will I ever feel as comfortable in a saddle as you?" she asked, envying his skill and grace. She marveled that he hadn't so much as worked up a sweat.

"Give it time," he said.

Together, side by side, they circled the corral, keeping to a walk. By the time Cal guided her to the gate and helped her dismount, she'd begun to feel like a real rider.

Except for the fact that her legs almost went out from under her when her boots touched the ground. She waited for the numbness to fade, adjusted her jeans and took her first steps. Once she was assured that her teeth were intact and her head wasn't in danger of falling off, she was able to talk.

"I hurt less after a forty-mile bicycle ride," she said, rubbing her derriere with both hands.

"You're still a tenderfoot."

"It isn't my feet that are tender," she countered.

Cal threw back his head and laughed, although she didn't think she'd been that funny. "I don't know anyone who makes me laugh the way you do," he said.

"I just speak the truth," she muttered, and he laughed again.

He helped her remove the saddle and rub down Atta Girl, then invited her to the house.

For a bachelor's place, the house was meticulous. The kitchen countertops were spotless. Either he didn't cook or he cleaned up after himself. Judging by the guys she'd known in medical school, he was a rare man if it was the latter.

"Thirsty?" he asked, opening the refrigerator. "Want a drink?"

"Please."

He took out a couple of cans of soda and handed her one. They sat at the kitchen table, Jane wincing as her rear end made contact with the hard wooden seat.

"You doing anything Friday night?" Cal asked casually, then took a deep swallow of soda.

"Nothing important," she said, thinking he was asking about her next riding lesson. "What time would you like me to be here?"

"Here?" He frowned. "I was inviting you to dinner."

At first Jane was too stunned to answer. Cal Patterson was asking her out on a date. A real date. It'd been so long since she'd been asked that she didn't even recognize it when she was. "I'd be—" she flashed him a smile "—delighted. I'll look forward to seeing you Friday night."

When he walked her to her car a few minutes later, he told her that her riding was progressing nicely.

She grinned. "That's because I've got a great teacher."

Cal opened her car door. "I'll pick you up at seven," he said. "That okay?"

"Seven," she agreed, and hoped he didn't hear the nervousness in her voice. She had a *date,* a real date. With Cal Patterson.

Maybe Texas wasn't so bad, after all.

FRIDAY NIGHT Cal shifted the hangers from one side of his closet to the other, looking for a decent shirt. He didn't know what in hell had prompted him to invite Jane to dinner.

Then again, he *did* know. He liked her. Fool that he was, he'd allowed her to get under his skin. He blamed Ellie for this. Blamed and thanked, depending on how he felt at any given moment.

He could add Grady Weston's name to the list of troublemakers. First, his brother decides to marry Ellie. Then not a month passes before Cal's best friend from childhood announces *he's* engaged, too. Grady was going to marry Caroline Daniels, the postmistress. Cal shook his head. The men in Promise were deserting bachelorhood in droves.

Cal had no intention of joining their ranks. Asking Jane to dinner might be misconstrued as romantic interest in the town's new doctor, but that wasn't the case. He liked her, enjoyed her company, but considered her safe. She was a California girl, born and raised. A city girl. In three years' time, she'd be heading back where she belonged, where she fit in. What appealed to him was the way she could make him laugh. And hell, stuck as she was in small-town Texas, he felt sorry for her.

That was it, Cal decided as he jerked a clean shirt off the hanger and put it on. He knew she was all alone down here; he was just being nice to an out-of-state girl, inviting her to share a meal and a few laughs. After that he wouldn't see her again, he vowed. Except for their riding lessons, of course.

He hadn't actually expected her to show up for the second lesson, not after the way he'd reacted to her fall off the saddle. A smile touched the corners of his mouth as he remembered her Butch Cassidy roll beneath Atta Girl's belly. My, oh my, could that woman move. Which led to thoughts he immediately censored. . . .

He fastened the shirt snaps and eased into a clean pair of Wranglers. He wasn't going to a lot of trouble for this dinner, no sir. Nor had he mentioned it to his brother. Glen would make more of it than was there, and he'd for sure tell his wife. Cal did *not* want Ellie to know about this.

A Johnny Cash tune drifted into his mind and he whistled along—until he realized what he was doing and abruptly stopped. He hadn't whistled in years. What the hell was happening here?

The forty-minute drive into town was accomplished in no time at all, or so it seemed. He'd take Jane to dinner as promised, then the minute they were finished he'd escort her home, head to Billy D's and meet up with his friends. On Friday night Billy's was always packed.

Another thing he'd do, Cal determined as he walked the short distance from the curb to Jane's front door, was have a little heart-to-heart with the doc. He had to explain that while this evening was a pleasant diversion, this was not a relationship with a future. It wasn't a relationship, period.

As gently as he could he'd tell her that he wasn't interested in her romantically. There wasn't any point in it, seeing that she'd be returning to California and he was staying here. Being the kind of guy he was, honest and straightforward, he didn't want to mislead her into believing something could develop out of this. It was just a dinner. One dinner.

He rang her doorbell and waited. He might even say something right away. Get it over with quickly.

The door opened and Cal's jaw dropped. Wow. Jane was beautiful. She wore a two-tone blue denim ankle-length skirt with a matching blouse. The buttons were big silver-dollar coins. With her sparkling blue eyes and short blond hair, she looked sophisticated. Western *and* sophisticated. Sort of L.A. meets San Antonio. It was all he could do not to slobber.

"I'll be ready in a moment," she said, holding open the screen door.

Cal removed his hat when he walked into the small house. He remained standing while she reached for her purse and clipped the beeper onto her black leather belt.

"I'm on call," she said, explaining the beeper.

"You clean up real good," he said once he found his voice.

She smiled. "You don't look so bad yourself."

"Any place special you'd like to eat?" he asked.

"You choose."

Not that there was much choice. The Chili Pepper was the best restaurant in town, but they'd eaten there the week before. The café in the bowling alley served damn good chow, but it wasn't the type of place to take Dr. Texas, especially with her dressed to the nines. That left the Mexican Lindo, which he suggested.

"I'm game," she said.

The restaurant was less than five blocks away and the weather was accommodating, so they walked. They were led to a corner booth and Cal felt grateful for that, since it afforded them a measure of privacy. They'd barely sat down when the waiter delivered a bowl of corn chips and fresh salsa. Jane glanced at the menu and quickly made her decision.

"Cheese enchiladas," she told him before he could ask.

Cal selected chili verde, one of his favorites.

He asked for a beer, and because she was on call, Jane ordered an iced tea. They were just beginning to relax when Jane's beeper went off.

She removed it from her belt and read the code. "There's an emergency," she said. "If you'll wait a couple of minutes, I'll phone the service."

"Sure." This was what he wanted, Cal tried to tell himself. She was offering him a perfect out, and he should be thankful. He hadn't stopped to think about the questions their being together was sure to raise. Lots of questions, especially from his family and friends.

Jane was gone only a couple of moments. "It's Jeremy Bishop," she said, hurrying back. "Nell thinks he's broken his arm. She's driving him to the clinic now."

"Is it bad?"

"I won't know until I see him. I'm sorry, Cal, but I have to go."

"I understand," he assured her.

Her eyes showed her regret before she turned and walked quickly out the door. As soon as she was gone, he realized she'd be alone at the clinic. Nell was an emotionally strong woman, but Jeremy was her son and she might need someone to talk to while Jane dealt with the boy's injury.

Cal signaled the waiter. "Can you bring me the bill?"

The young man was clearly flustered. "But you haven't eaten yet. If there's a problem . . ."

"There's no problem," Cal said. "Dr. Dickinson had an emergency and I've decided to leave myself."

The waiter nodded gravely. "Your order just came up. Would you like a takeout box?"

"Sure," Cal said. He hadn't thought of that.

When the waiter finished transferring the dinners to cardboard containers, Cal paid for them and made his way to the clinic.

He arrived at the same time as Nell, Jeremy, and Nell's other child, Emma. Nell looked pale and distraught. She'd wrapped Jeremy's arm in a pillow; he was obviously in pain and his face was streaked with tears.

"Hello, Jeremy," Jane said, taking charge immediately.

Cal wasn't sure she realized he was there until she turned. "Oh! Hi, Cal."

"I thought I'd keep Nell company in the waiting room," he said.

"Good idea." She thanked him with a smile. Cal put their dinners on the reception desk and guided Nell to a chair, while Jane slid an arm around Jeremy's shoulders and steered him toward the examination room.

"I want to be with my son," Nell insisted.

"I'll come for you in a few minutes," Jane promised, "but first I need an X ray to see what we're dealing with here."

Nell accepted the decision and sank into her chair. She stared straight ahead, her features sharp with fear. "I found him by the tractor," she whispered.

Cal wasn't sure she was talking to him, but he understood the significance of what she was saying. Nell had been the one to find her husband trapped beneath a tractor. The vehicle had turned over on him and crushed him, and she'd been powerless to do anything but hold his hand while he died.

"Jeremy climbed up on it even though I've warned him repeatedly to stay away."

"Seems to me he's learned his lesson," Cal said. "I don't think you'll have any problem keeping him away from now on."

Nell smiled, and Cal wondered if he should stick around or head over to Billy D's. To his surprise he discovered he had no real desire to join his friends. He'd much rather stay right where he was and help Nell—and Dr. Texas.

Five

"In a month you'll be husband and wife," Reverend Wade McMillen said, leaning back in his leather chair in the study.

It didn't seem possible, but the wedding date had sneaked up on her. Caroline had discovered that putting together a wedding, even a small one involving just family and a few close friends, had demanded every spare moment she had.

"A month," Caroline repeated, glancing at Grady. They'd been attending counseling sessions with Wade for the past few weeks. Even now, Caroline had a difficult time taking it all in. She'd loved Grady for years, but had hidden her feelings behind a prickly attitude. It used to be they couldn't stay in the same room without sparks flying and tempers flaring. They ignited fireworks now, too, but for other reasons.

"It doesn't seem possible," Grady said, his gaze holding Caroline's.

"You're as ready now as you'll ever be," Wade said, grinning at them. "I've counseled a lot of couples in my time. I often get a feel for the relationship before the vows are spoken. And I'm confident the two of you are going to have a strong secure marriage."

Grady reached for Caroline's hand and squeezed her fingers. "I feel that way, too."

Caroline nodded, her love for Grady clear to see.

"No problems with Maggie?" Wade asked.

"None." Caroline assured him. There'd been a time when the child had been terrified of Grady's booming voice, but no longer. Her six-year-old was enthralled with him. Caroline had no doubt of his love for her daughter. The day Maggie had disappeared, kidnapped by Richard Weston, Grady had proved how deeply he cared for the child. And for her.

"She isn't showing any bad effects from the time she was missing, then?" Wade went on.

"Not that we can tell," Caroline replied. "She seems to be sleeping better these days. She hasn't woken up with nightmares recently, either." Caroline frowned, shaking her head. "No matter how hard I tried, though, I couldn't get her to tell me about her dreams—or what happened when she was gone. Then overnight, the bad dreams stopped. She's her normal cheerful self again."

"She talks about me becoming her daddy and seems genuinely excited about it," Grady added.

Wade looked at him. "You were worried you were somehow the cause of Maggie's nightmares?"

"Yeah, but now she's more accepting of me and more affectionate than ever."

Caroline nodded; she was pleased that Grady had started the adoption process. "I'm convinced that whatever was troubling her is somehow connected to the time Richard had her."

"Richard," Wade repeated, his brow furrowed. "Has anyone heard anything from him or about him lately?"

"Not a word," Grady said. "I know the sheriff's pretty frustrated. It's like Richard's disappeared off the face of the earth."

A chill raced down Caroline's spine every time she thought about Grady's brother. He'd hurt a lot of people, but what infuriated her more than anything was how he'd used and abused his own family. He'd run off with the ranch assets the day the Westons laid their parents to rest, creating untold hardship for Grady and his sister, Savannah. Six years later he'd returned, down on his luck. Grady and Savannah had taken him back in, tried to help him, and once more Richard had proved he couldn't be trusted. After charging thousands of dollars' worth of goods, Richard had disappeared again.

Grady, being honorable and decent, had paid those bills himself rather than have the local businesses absorb the losses. While it meant they wouldn't be starting their marriage with any substantial savings, Caroline loved Grady for being the kind of man he was.

"Shall we schedule the wedding rehearsal?" Wade asked.

Brimming with excitement, Caroline and Grady nodded; soon after, their session was over.

Grady tucked his arm around her waist as they left the church and headed toward the parking lot.

"Have I told you today how much I love you?" Grady asked. He kissed her as he opened the passenger door.

"It's something I'm not going to tire of hearing," Caroline said. Grady's love was a blessing she hadn't expected to receive. She was coming to this marriage with a child and a lot of emotional baggage. Much of that was thanks to Richard, who'd fathered Maggie during a brief and ultimately meaningless liaison. So meaningless he didn't even remember it. Caroline had been terrified that this would make her and Maggie a burden for Grady, another mess of Richard's he had to clean up. She'd been convinced it would be better to let Grady walk out of her life—but he'd refused to let that happen. He loved her and Maggie. When she told him about Maggie's father, his initial reaction had been shock—because she'd kept the truth from him. But he'd recovered quickly and said that the man who raised and loved Maggie would be her *real* father, and that would be him. In the weeks since their engagement Grady had proved his devotion to her and to Maggie over and over again.

"Do we need to pick up Maggie right away?" Grady asked now.

Dovie Boyd had volunteered to baby-sit the little girl during the counseling sessions with Wade. "What do you have in mind?" she asked, leaning her head against his shoulder.

Grady started the truck's engine. "I was thinking we could stop at the bowling alley for a pizza." He glanced at her. "You game?"

"I'm game for anything with you," she assured him. "But I'll need to phone Dovie to make sure Maggie's okay first."

"No problem." He backed out of their parking space and they drove to the bowling alley.

After a quick phone call, Caroline joined Grady in a booth at the café. He got out so she could slip in beside him. Not so long ago, he'd have preferred to sit in the cold rather than share her company, Caroline mused. Now they could hardly bear to be separated by even a table.

"Everything all right with Maggie?" he asked.

"She's fine. Dovie said she's already asleep."

"Hey, first grade is a big step for a kid."

Especially when Maggie had only recently outgrown naps. She fell asleep before her eight o'clock bedtime most evenings.

"Dovie doesn't mind keeping her a bit longer?"

"Not at all," Caroline told him. She didn't mention that she was worried about her friend. Although Dovie hadn't said much about her breakup with Sheriff Hennessey, it had obviously been hard for her; a smile didn't come as easily and she seemed listless, depressed. From what Caroline had seen of the sheriff, he wasn't handling the situation any better.

Caroline wished she could help in some way, but experience had taught her that Frank and Dovie had to work this out themselves. She wasn't optimistic, though. Their relationship had been a long-standing one, and if they were going to reconcile, she suspected it would have happened by now.

"I talked to Glen yesterday and he told me something about Cal," Grady said after they'd ordered the mushroom-and-pepperoni pizza. "You'll never guess."

"When it comes to Cal, you're right—I won't guess."

"He's got a date."

"A date? Cal?" Caroline was shocked. "Who?"

Grady smiled. "The new doc."

"Jane Dickinson?"

"Right. He's teaching her how to ride."

This *was* news. "What possessed him to do such a thing? Cal, the woman-hater."

Grady shrugged. "Hell if I know. I gotta tell you it came as a shock to me, too." He leaned toward Caroline. "Cal didn't even tell his brother. Glen found out from his mother, who heard about it from Dovie, who heard from the good doctor herself."

"Typical," Caroline said with a laugh. "But still, it sounds promising."

Love would change Cal Patterson, and she was anxious to see it happen. Ever since his broken engagement, he'd shut himself off from any association with the opposite sex. Caroline suspected falling in love would have a positive powerful impact on him.

Caroline liked Cal and knew that his friendship was important to Grady. She was pleased that Grady had asked him to serve as best man at their wedding. In every way that counted, Cal was more of a brother to Grady than his own.

"I saw Cal's truck this evening," Grady said.

"Parked outside the health clinic," Caroline guessed.

He nodded. "I have a feeling about this."

"A good feeling, I hope."

"A very good feeling," he said, grinning.

THE CLOCK SAID almost ten before Jane had finished setting Jeremy Bishop's arm and securing it in a cast. After giving Nell instructions for the pain medication, Jane and Cal walked the family outside.

"You were a good patient, Jeremy," Jane told the boy. He'd been in a lot of pain, but despite that, he'd willingly cooperated with everything she'd needed him to do.

"He's got a lot of his father in him," Nell said, looking proudly at her son. She stood outside her car, drawn and tired from the ordeal. "Thank you both," she said. "I was pretty shaken when we first arrived. I'm afraid if I'd gone into the examination room, I'd have done something stupid— like faint."

Jane had thought the same thing. "You're his mother. It's to be expected."

"You were great with him," Nell told her. "I can't thank you enough."

"That's what I'm here for." It was helping people like Nell and her family that made Jane's job a pleasure. They hadn't really met before tonight, but she'd heard about Nell from Ruth Bishop, a heart patient. Nell was a widow and Ruth's daughter-in-law.

"Go home, get plenty of rest, and if the pain doesn't decrease, give me a call."

"I will," Nell promised, climbing into the car. "Thanks again."

Jane and Cal stood by the door of the clinic until Nell had pulled out of sight.

"You hungry?" Cal asked, his hand on Jane's shoulder.

"Starving," she confessed.

"Me, too."

They warmed the takeout in the microwave and sat side by side on the examination table, holding the cardboard containers on their laps.

"This tastes like heaven," Jane told him between bites. The enchilada sauce and melting cheese dripped from her plastic fork.

"That's because we're hungry."

"I'm sorry our dinner date was ruined." She did feel bad about that. Cal had been thoughtful and patient—bringing them their meal, comforting Nell, sitting here for hours—and she wanted him to know how much she appreciated it.

"I'm not," he surprised her by saying. Her reaction must have shown in her eyes because he added, "It was good to see you in action. You're a damned good doctor."

His praise flustered her and she looked away. "Thank you."

"You were great with the kid," he said, and hopped down from the table to toss the container in the garbage.

"I appreciated your help. Nell was frazzled and anxious." She crossed the room to discard her leftovers; when she turned around, she inadvertently bumped into Cal.

His arm shot out to balance her, although she wasn't in danger of falling. The move had been instinctive, but the moment he touched her, she froze. Cal did, too. It was a little thing, of no importance, but it caught her off guard. The shaken look on Cal's face told her he was equally affected.

Then before her instincts could warn her, it happened. Cal bent his head and kissed her. It was almost as though that, too, was an accident. The kiss was hard, quick, their mouths moist and warm. Then it was over.

Jane stared at him, unblinking. Cal stared back. They studied each other for a startled moment. He seemed about to apologize when he suddenly grinned, instead. It was one of the sexiest smiles she'd ever seen. Then he kissed her again.

As kisses went, this one was innocent. Simple. Yet Jane trembled with the aftershock. She'd been too long without a man, she decided. That was why this rancher had such a powerful effect on her senses.

Desperate to steer her mind away from what had just happened, she said, "I . . . I spoke with Dovie Boyd recently. She happened to mention a ghost town."

Cal frowned, but Jane wasn't sure his displeasure was the result of their kiss or her comment. Possibly both.

"Bitter End," Jane added. "Have you ever heard of it?"

He nodded and shoved his hands into his pockets.

He wasn't forthcoming with any more information. "Then there really *is* a ghost town in the area?" she prodded.

Cal shrugged.

Jane made herself busy about the room, putting away her supplies. "Have you been there?"

He didn't answer until she turned to face him, and even then his eyes avoided hers. "Once, as a kid."

Her excitement grew. "Will you take me there? I'd love to see what it's like now."

"Jane, I can't."

His refusal bewildered her. "Why not?"

"I don't even know if I could find it."

"But we could do that together. I'll be taking more riding lessons, and we've got to move me out of the corral at some point. This would give me a goal, some incentive."

"I don't think so."

"Why not?" Jane could tell he wasn't pleased with her persistence.

"It's dangerous there."

"All I want to do is see it," she said, unwilling to give up without an argument. "One time, that's all I'm asking."

"It's not a good idea."

It was his attitude that got to her—as if she were a child who had to settle for *because I said so* as an excuse. How could he kiss her one moment and insult her the next?

"Is there a reason for this?" she asked, her voice growing cool.

"A very good one."

She waited for him to explain himself, and when he didn't, she said it for him. "It's because I'm an outsider, isn't it? Because I wasn't born and raised here. It's all right for me to give three years of my life to this community, but I'll never be fully accepted." The strength of her feelings shocked Jane. It hurt that he'd categorically deny her the one thing she'd asked.

His features softened. "Jane, that's not it."

"Then what *is* it?"

"First, I don't know where Bitter End is. I really don't. Second, I've got better things to do with my time than wander around the countryside looking for some old town best forgotten."

This was quite a speech for Cal. "But you've already been there once."

"Years ago," he said, "when I was a kid."

"You should be able to find it again."

"Jane, *no.*"

The evening had started out with great promise; now this. What Cal Patterson didn't understand was that she was an old hand at getting what she wanted. She'd been forced to acquire the skills, to refine the tactics. Medical school had taught her that. She'd learned how to deal with older physicians who felt women had no place in medicine. She'd come face-to-face with the old-boy network more than once. People assumed this sort of outdated thinking wasn't prevalent any longer, but they were wrong. She'd seen it and dealt with it on a daily basis, and learned there was more than one way to achieve what she wanted.

"I'm sorry to hear you won't help me find the ghost town," she said softly.

"It's no place for a greenhorn."

"I see." Her tone was noncommittal.

He narrowed his eyes. "Why do I have the feeling I'm butting my head against a brick wall?"

So he knew. "I'll find Bitter End with or without you," she said matter-of-factly.

Cal's eyes closed for an instant. "And if I decide not to continue with the riding lessons, you'll have someone else teach you, too?"

"Yes." She wasn't going to lie about her intentions. That was exactly what she'd do if necessary—only she hoped it wouldn't be. "I'd much rather continue with you, though." She took a deep breath. "Cal, I'm not trying to be manipulative here. But I want to see this town. I'll admit I've become kind of obsessed with it. And I'll do whatever it takes to get there."

It was several moments before he responded. "It's not safe in Bitter End."

"So you said."

"The town's . . . evil."

"Evil? You mean there are *ghosts*?"

"Not that type of evil." He paced the room, as though it was impossible for him to stand still any longer. "Grady Weston, Glen and I found Bitter End a number of years ago. I must have been about fifteen at the time, high on adventure. Fearless, like all kids that age. Cocky, some might say."

"I wouldn't have thought that was so long ago," she joked.

He didn't crack a smile. "We searched for weeks, the three of us. It was summer and we went out looking every day we could. We studied maps, even checked out an old journal that had belonged to Grady's father and had a few cryptic hints."

"But you found the town," Jane said, her voice rising with excitement.

"Yes, eventually we located it."

"Did you explore? What was it like? I'd love to see it! Oh, Cal, please reconsider."

His sigh was deep and troubled. "You can't imagine how thrilled we were when we stumbled across it. We'd been searching all that time, and then one afternoon there it was. Surprisingly most of the buildings were intact."

"That's incredible!" Just wait until her mother heard this. She'd want to know every detail.

"But it wasn't what we expected," Cal told her, his eyes somber.

"How do you mean?"

"There's something wrong in that town. Like I said, something evil. We all felt it the moment we rode down the street. The horses felt it, too. The entire time we were there, they were skittish."

"Something evil?" This made no sense to Jane. "What exactly was the feeling like?"

"I've thought about it a lot in the last few months, ever since Grady told me Savannah's been out there."

"Savannah Smith?" Jane wondered if Cal realized he'd handed her a way of locating the town.

"She went there looking for old roses. According to what Grady said, she felt it, too. That same feeling."

"Well, what *was* it?"

Cal shook his head. "It's impossible to describe. I've never experienced anything like it before or since."

"Try," she pleaded.

"Like there's a rope tightening around my chest," he said, struggling to find the words. "A feeling of sadness. Loss. As though more than a century wasn't enough time to wipe out the grief or the agony of whatever happened."

"I'd still like to see it for myself," she told him.

"I figured you would." His tone was resigned.

"Does this mean you'll take me?" She clasped her hands, prayerlike. She didn't want another riding teacher. She liked the one she had. And she wanted Cal to be her guide to Bitter End; if there was danger in the town, she'd rather he was with her.

"All right," he finally agreed. "We'll go look for it."

Overjoyed, Jane threw her arms around his neck and hugged him. The next instant Cal wrapped his arms around her waist and pulled her against him. Without warning, his mouth crashed down on hers. The kiss was urgent. Exciting. Cal didn't give Jane an opportunity to break it off, not that she would have, but gradually, as though he realized what he'd done, he mellowed the kiss. He wove his fingers into her hair, then slowly, cautiously, they began to relax against each other. Jane moved her lips, opening to him—and the excitement built again.

Cal groaned. He twisted his mouth against hers, seeking more, and Jane was all too willing to comply. She wasn't sure a man had ever kissed her quite like this. With such need, such intensity.

When he broke away, they were both gasping. "I . . . I think I need to sit down," Jane said, reaching for the nearest chair and lowering herself into it.

"Me, too," Cal said.

Involuntarily she raised her hands to her lips. The kiss had been fierce. Wonderful.

"I didn't mean for that to happen," he said next. But instead of sitting, he stalked about the room.

"I know."

"I think you should realize I've already decided it would be . . . ill-advised for us to get involved."

He sounded so absurdly formal. Had she been in full possession of her wits, she would have challenged him, demanded to know his reasons.

But his kisses had left her senseless. Her own pride played a role in her reaction, too. She just looked at him, unwilling, unable, to respond.

"I don't mean to insult you," he added.

"You didn't," she was quick to assure him, then hesitated, more confused than offended. "Are you saying you want to put a halt to the riding lessons?"

"Not at all. When will you be ready again?"

From the intense look in his eyes, Jane had the feeling he was inquiring about a lot more than horseback riding. "Tomorrow?" She raised her eyes to his. She wasn't shy or cowardly or afraid of risks. Medicine wasn't a career for a woman who was weak at heart. If she had been, Jane wouldn't have lasted a month in medical school.

"I'll see you at three," he said on his way out the door.

"I'll be there," she called after him. It'd take more than stubborn pride to upset her. She had a strong feeling that Cal Patterson had met his match—and an even stronger feeling that she'd met hers.

RICHARD WAS BORED but he was smart enough to realize that the moment he left Bitter End, he'd risk being caught and hauled to jail.

By now, despite switching license plates, the truck he'd "borrowed" would be listed in a police computer as stolen.

Relieving his boredom by leaving the ghost town was a risk he couldn't afford to take, although it was damned tempting.

Leaning his chair against the side of the old hotel, he strummed a few chords on his guitar. Only, it wasn't nearly as much fun to play without an audience.

He reached for the half-empty whiskey bottle and indulged in a healthy swig. The liquor wasn't going to last, he could see that. He'd drunk twice as much as he'd estimated. His limited supply would need to see him through the next few months. A bottle wasn't much company on the long lonely nights, but it was all he had. Hell, a man took what he could get.

He strummed a few more chords on the guitar and sang halfheartedly. If his life had taken a different turn, he might have entered show business, made a name for himself. He would've enjoyed that.

He returned the bottle to his lips, shuddering at the potency of the drink. Enough liquor would help him forget. Or help him remember. Problem was, he couldn't decide which he wanted anymore.

He tipped back his head and shouted with everything in him, "Is anyone home?" He waited for a response and was both relieved and disheartened when none came.

Even a ghost might be some company.

According to the days he'd marked off on the calendar, this was Friday night. If he'd still been in Promise, instead of hiding up in this godforsaken ghost town, he'd probably be at Billy D's, drinking with the boys. Shooting the breeze, playing pool or maybe a game of darts.

He'd be singing, too, along with the jukebox. A little David Allan Coe, the ex-con turned singer. His music could get raunchy and off-color, but Richard didn't mind. It was just the thing for a Friday night at the saloon.

But this Friday—and how many others to follow?—Richard would be alone.

What he missed even more was female companionship. He could have had a cozy love nest here had he been thinking clearly. But everything had come down on him and there hadn't been time to find a woman to bring with him—or maybe two.

The loneliness wouldn't be half so bad with a couple of sweet young things to keep him occupied. Yeah, he could've convinced them this was an adventure. And he could've let them fight over him, which was guaranteed to be entertaining. Not too hard on his ego, either. Women didn't walk away when *he* was around. All except Ellie Frasier, now Ellie Patterson. Richard frowned. He didn't know what he'd done wrong. Her choosing Glen Patterson over him hurt his pride.

"She's a fool," he said aloud.

One day Ellie would regret her choice, Richard was sure of it. She could have married him, instead of that hick Patterson. Everything had gone downhill after that.

The creditors had started closing in and it'd become impossible to hide the charges he'd made on Grady's accounts. As soon as Grady learned the truth, he would have kicked him out. But Richard hadn't given his brother the chance; moving with speed, he'd left Promise before any of it came to light.

He'd carefully worked out every detail of his plan, stocking up on stolen food and supplies for weeks beforehand. It wasn't an easy task, but he'd been at his deceptive best. He was proud of the way he'd pulled it off, too, keeping his activities hidden from the family.

Grady and Savannah were pathetic, really.

As far as Richard was concerned, his brother and sister deserved everything they got. Anyone that trusting needed to be taught a lesson. Richard had burned them twice, and it hadn't been difficult. He wondered if they'd ever learn; he suspected they wouldn't. They weren't the type, neither one of them. He experienced a twinge of guilt, but refused to waste time on a useless emotion. Grady and Savannah were nothing short of gullible. He looked at it this way—he'd done them a favor. Taught them a life lesson. He couldn't help it if they were slow learners.

A shooting star blazed across the autumn sky and Richard raised his bottle in salute. He wished he had a woman on his arm, but okay, that wasn't possible. His little home away from home was a damn sight better than a jail cell, and that was where he was headed if the law ever got hold of him.

Life was much too complicated, Richard mused. What had started out as a simple transaction back in New York had gone sour. The bad taste of it lingered in his mouth, but there was no use fretting about it now.

In addition to his many talents, Richard Weston was a survivor. He might be down but he wasn't out, and once his current troubles came to an end, he'd be back on his feet.

If Ellie had married him, he would've used her inheritance to pay off some rather dangerous debts—and to grease the right palms. But she was with Glen. Stupid woman. She didn't know a good thing when she saw it.

He tipped back the bottle, took another drink and immediately felt worse. He was lonely and restless. All the self-talk in the world wasn't going to change that. While he might be safe, he wasn't happy.

Six

Jane removed the blood-pressure cuff from Ruth Bishop's upper arm and noted the reading on her chart. Ruth's diastolic and systolic numbers were well within the normal range, which was good. The medication was doing its job.

"Overall, how are you feeling?" Jane asked as she reached for her prescription pad to write a renewal.

"Good," Ruth said, after a short hesitation.

Jane looked up. "Is there anything else you'd like me to check? You're here now and I'd hate to have you think of something later." Jane held office hours on Saturday morning because it seemed a convenient time for a lot of people. If Ruth decided, once she got home, that she *did* have some other concern, Jane wouldn't be available again until Monday. Not only that, Ruth would have to make the long drive a second time.

Jane waited quietly for a minute or so.

Ruth finally spoke. "Actually it's my daughter-in-law," she said.

Jane sat down and made herself comfortable. It'd taken her a while to realize that, when it came to confidences, people shared at their own pace and in their own way. Not just the people in Promise, Texas, but people everywhere.

"Nell was in last night with Jeremy," Jane said, wanting Ruth to know she was familiar with her daughter-in-law.

"I know. Jeremy said that for a lady doctor you weren't half-bad."

Jane unsuccessfully hid a smile.

"He meant that as a compliment," Ruth said, her cheeks growing pink.

"Don't worry, Ruth, I hear that all the time."

"It's difficult for some folks to get used to the idea of a female doctor."

Ruth wasn't telling Jane something she didn't already know.

"I'm living with Nell," Ruth explained, "helping her out when I can. Encouraging her. It was a blow to both of us when Jake died . . . I never expected my son would join his father before me." Her eyes teared up, and Jane leaned forward to hand her a tissue. Ruth thanked her in a choked voice and dabbed her eyes.

"So . . . what about Nell?" Jane asked gently, giving the older woman time to compose herself.

"Early this morning I found her in the living room weeping. That's not like her. She's not a woman who shows her pain. When we buried Jake, it was Nell who remained strong, who comforted the family, who held us all together. I don't know what we would've done without her."

From her psychology classes, Jane remembered that in a family crisis there was usually one member who remained emotionally steady for others to lean on for support. She'd seen the truth of this time and again. Sometimes family members traded roles, almost taking turns, at comforting and helping one another through a crisis.

"Nell shed her share of tears, I know that," Ruth said, "but she did it privately. She loved my son, grieves for him still."

"I'm sure that's true," Jane said. She hardly knew Nell, but the widow was unmistakably a strong independent woman, someone she'd like to call a friend.

"Jeremy's broken arm shook her more than I realized. I wasn't home at the time. The Moorhouse sisters, Betty Knoll and I play bridge on Friday nights. Edwina and Lily bring out their cordial—same recipe Dovie uses—and we let down our hair and relax."

Jane could picture the four older women and suspected they were crackerjack bridge players.

"Nell told me Jeremy had climbed on the tractor. That he fell off and broke his arm." Ruth grew quiet for a moment. "You may not know this, but Jake died in a tractor accident. It must have been terribly upsetting for Nell finding Jeremy by the tractor. Especially since she's the one who found Jake. He was still alive and in shock, but was gone before help could reach him."

"I'm so sorry," Jane murmured. She could only imagine the horror of finding your husband trapped beneath a tractor. Nell had been pale and shaken when she arrived with Jeremy, Jane remembered; she must have been reliving that unbearable time. Thank heaven Cal had been at the clinic and was able to distract Nell while she dealt with the injured boy.

"It's been almost three years since Jake's been gone. It doesn't seem like it could be that long, but it is."

"It's a big adjustment, losing a son." Jane said softly.

"And losing a husband. Last night I found Nell sitting in her rocker by the fireplace," Ruth said, continuing with her story. "It was three in the morning, and when I asked her what woke her up, Nell told me she hadn't been to bed yet."

"Had she been up with Jeremy?" The question was prompted by Jane's concern that perhaps the pain medication hadn't worked adequately. After the shock of a broken bone, Jeremy needed his rest. His mother did, too.

"No. Nell was . . . remembering." Ruth fell silent for a moment. "I . . . I worry about my daughter-in-law," she admitted. "It's time she moved on with her life. Met someone else."

Jane said nothing, preferring to let the other woman speak.

"I don't think it's a good idea for her to spend the rest of her life grieving for Jake," Ruth said, her own voice trembling with emotion. "I know . . . knew my son and he wouldn't have wanted that."

"Have you told her this?" Jane asked.

"Oh, yes, a number of times. She brushes it off. Last summer, for the Cattlemen's Association dance, she received two invitations. I was ecstatic, thinking it was past time the men in this town paid her some attention."

Jane was thinking Nell had done better than she had herself. No one had asked her, but then, she'd been new to the community and hadn't met a lot of people yet. By that she meant Cal. He would've been her first choice had she known him.

"Nell turned down both offers," Ruth said, pinching her lips in disapproval. "No amount of coaxing could get her to change her mind, either." She exhaled noisily and Jane recognized Ruth's impatience with her daughter-in-law. "As it turned out, Emma had an upset tummy that night, so Nell made a quick appearance at the dance but came home within the hour. I was baby-sitting and I told her to stay as long as she wanted—have a good time, I said, but she'd have none of it."

It sounded to Jane as though Emma's upset stomach had been a convenient excuse for Nell to hurry home.

"How can I encourage her?" Ruth asked.

This was at the heart of her worries, Jane realized. "You can't," she said.

"But it's been almost three years," Ruth said again.

"Nell has to be the one to recognize when it's time. No one else can do that for her."

"I know, but I'd like her to get out more. Socialize. Spend time with her friends, but she hardly even does that. Nell works too hard and laughs too little."

"It's not something you can force," Jane said. "Nell will know when she's ready."

"I hope it's soon," Ruth murmured. "My son was a wonderful man, but she's too fine a woman to pine for him the rest of her life. Much too fine."

Jane was sure that was true.

STORM CLOUDS darkened the afternoon. Glancing toward the sky, Cal hurried outside. Electrical storms weren't uncommon in the Texas hill country, and he wanted his livestock in the shelter of the barn.

The dogs helped him and he'd gotten Atta Girl and a chestnut mare named Cheyenne safely into the barn when he saw Jane's car pull into the yard. Damn, with the approach of the storm, he'd forgotten about the lesson. Despite that, she hadn't been far from his thoughts all day. Not since the moment he'd first kissed her.

He didn't know what had driven him to do anything so foolish, especially after insisting there was no future in this relationship. Impulse, he supposed—an impulse he planned to avoid from now on.

Frightened by the thunder, Moonshine, Glen's favorite gelding, pranced about the yard, making him difficult to catch. He wouldn't have given Glen nearly as much trouble, but there was nothing Cal could do about that now.

The wind howled and the first fat drops of rain fell haphazardly from the sky. "Can I help?" Jane had to shout to be heard.

"Go in the house before you get soaked," Cal ordered. The rain was falling steadily now, and Cal knew it would only grow more intense.

"I can do something!"

He should've known she'd insist on helping him. Dr. Texas wasn't the type who took orders willingly. Cal groaned; he certainly knew how to pick 'em. He couldn't be attracted to a docile eager-to-please female. Oh no, that would be too easy. Instead, he had to go and complicate his life with a woman whose personality was as strong and obstinate as his own.

Against his wishes, Jane ran to the corral and stood on the opposite side, waving her hands high above her head. To Cal's amazement Moonshine had a change of heart. Either that, or the quarter horse was so unsettled by the sight of a California girl flapping her arms around, he figured the barn was the safest place for him. In an abrupt turnaround, the gelding trotted obediently into the barn, one of the dogs barking at his heels.

Cal followed him inside and out of the rain. He waited for Jane to join him before closing the door. The rain fell in earnest, a real downpour, pounding the ground with such force the drops ricocheted three inches upward.

Cal led Moonshine into his stall. "I didn't think you'd come, what with the storm and all," he told Jane.

"I wasn't sure I should."

It went against his pride to let her know how pleased he was she had.

"Do you want me to drive home?" she asked, sounding oddly uncertain and a bit defensive.

It was the way he'd feel had circumstances been reversed. "You're here now. The weather's a write-off but we'll make the best of it." Which shouldn't be too hard. Dr. Texas looked damn good in her hip-hugging jeans and boots.

He removed his jacket and handed it to her. "Let's make a run for the house." Opening the barn door, he looked out and cringed. The rain was still coming down in torrents and it was almost impossible to see across the yard. They'd be drenched to the skin by the time they reached the house.

Holding the jacket above her head for protection, Jane moved beside him to view the downpour. "My goodness, does it rain like this often?"

"Often enough," he muttered.

"I've never seen anything like it."

Seeing she'd been born and raised in Southern California, Cal could believe that. He'd read about small towns near Death Valley where the children had never seen rain at all.

"You ready?" he asked.

"Any time," she said, with a game smile.

Lightning flashed. Not willing to wait any longer, Cal offered Jane his hand. She clasped it tightly and held the jacket over her head with her free hand. They sprinted toward the house, sliding a bit on the muddy ground. He kept his pace deliberately even, fearing she might slip.

Breathing hard, they burst into the house together. Jane released Cal's hand immediately. The water dripped from him as if he'd just stepped out of the shower, and his clothes were plastered to his skin.

"You're drenched," Jane said, and gave him back his jacket. Despite the protection it had provided, her hair and face glistened with rain-water.

"So are you," he said, and for the life of him, he couldn't pull his gaze away from hers.

"Not like you." She moistened her lips with her tongue and that was Cal's downfall. He'd already promised himself there wouldn't be a repeat of the kiss they'd shared last night, but nothing could have stopped him from sampling her lips once more. He leaned forward and pressed his mouth to hers.

He wasn't sure what he expected, but not her sigh of welcome. Nor had he anticipated her stepping farther into his embrace. His breathing grew heavy and so did hers. The kiss deepened and she slipped her arms around his neck and moved even closer. The feel of her soft body against his was enough to make him weak at the knees.

He lifted his head. "I'm getting you all wet."

"I know."

"You shouldn't have come," he whispered, although his head and his heart waged battle.

"Do you want me to leave?"

"No." His response was instantaneous. Direct. Reluctantly he eased her out of his arms. "I'll go change."

"I'll put on a pot of coffee."

He nodded and headed toward the stairway, taking the steps two at a time. Every minute not spent with her felt wasted, and he was a frugal man.

He stripped off his shirt, then flung it aside, drying himself with a towel. He reached for a sweater and pulled it over his head. He'd just donned a clean pair of jeans and had stepped back into his boots when the electric lights flickered and went off.

The house was almost completely dark. Even though it was midaf-ternoon, the heavy black clouds closed out the light.

"Jane," he shouted from the top of the stairs, "are you okay?"

"I'm fine," she called back.

"I'll be right there." Cal draped his wet clothes over the edge of the bathtub and ran a comb through his hair before going downstairs. He got a flashlight from the hallway and found Jane in the kitchen standing next to the stove.

"I guess we'll have to do without the coffee," she said.

"Will wine do?" he asked.

"Great idea." His eyes were adjusting to the darkness and he saw her smile at him.

It would be easy to get lost in one of those smiles. "I'll get a fire going." He took her hand and led her into the living room. He knelt in front of the brick fireplace, arranged the kindling, then placed a couple of logs on top. The match flared briefly and ignited the wood. Soon a fire burned invitingly, its warmth spreading into the room.

"This is cozy, isn't it?" Jane said, huddling close to the fire.

"I'll be back in a minute with the wine." As it happened, he had a number of bottles left over from the wedding that had never taken place. He'd wanted Glen and Ellie to use the wine at theirs, but Glen had declined, insisting Cal save it for a rainy day. Like right now, Cal thought wryly.

He returned with a corkscrew, two goblets and a bottle of merlot.

He sat on the carpet with Jane, his back supported by the sofa, a glass of wine in his hand. Jane sat next to him, chin resting on her bent knees.

"I'm glad you're here," he said, not looking at her. It was a big admission, seeing as he'd told her—twice—she shouldn't have come.

"I'm glad I'm here, too."

He put his arm around her shoulders and she scooted closer to his side. She turned to him with another one of her potent smiles. It was an invitation to kiss her again, an invitation he wasn't about to ignore.

She wanted his kisses, her smile said. Cal had thought of little else from the moment they sat down in front of the fire. He'd attempted to discipline his response to her, but his resolve weakened by the moment, and he'd all but given up.

He lowered his head and watched as her eyes closed. He could deny himself no longer. The kiss that followed was intense and passionate. He hadn't meant it to be—but he couldn't help it, either. His mouth played on hers until he groaned.

Thunder exploded, and for an instant Cal thought it was the beat of his own heart. Jane had that kind of effect on him. He broke off the kiss and, closing his eyes, leaned his head back against the sofa. Drawing in several deep breaths, he struggled to find his equilibrium.

He couldn't make himself stop wanting her. But it wasn't right; he knew that. This relationship had no future.

At last he straightened and took a sip of his wine. Jane did, too, and he noticed that her hand trembled slightly. His was shaking, too.

He'd rarely been more unnerved. He thought of telling her about Jennifer, then changed his mind, afraid she'd read something more into the information than he intended. And yet he couldn't say what his intentions were.

"Are you cold?" he asked, diverting his attention from these dangerous thoughts.

"No. How about you?"

The wine had warmed him. The wine and her kisses. "I'm fine."

All of a sudden, they were shy with each other.

Probably in an effort to distract herself, Jane started a conversation, mentioning people in town she was beginning to know. Cal eagerly joined in, answering her questions, bringing up other names. At least when they were talking, he wasn't thinking about making love to her.

The hell he wasn't!

"This has got to stop," he said, and at her look of surprise, realized he'd spoken aloud.

"What's got to stop?" Jane asked.

Embarrassed, he couldn't think of a single response. "This," he said, setting his wineglass aside. The next moment she was in his arms again. The kiss started in hunger and progressed to greed. Her response was immediate and she went soft and pliable in his arms.

"Cal?" she whispered, gazing up at him.

"Mm?" He spread a row of moist kisses on her neck and jaw. She moaned softly and rolled her head to one side. His senses filled with the taste of her, the citrusy scent of her. He couldn't make himself quit, couldn't make himself *want* to quit.

She moaned again when he let his tongue slide along the hollow of her throat.

"You wanted something," he reminded her.

"Yes . . ."

"What?" He worked his way back to her lips.

He wasn't sure how it happened, but soon her head rested on his lap and he was bent over her.

"You're right—we should stop," she murmured with little conviction.

"I couldn't agree with you more," he said, and kissed her again.

She looped her arms around his neck and raised her head from his lap. They strained against each other, trying to get closer, closer. His thoughts—all the reasons kissing Jane wasn't a good idea—didn't mean a thing.

Jane's mouth parted for him and his tongue curled around hers. The next thing he knew, his hand had worked open the front of her blouse and slipped inside to cup a satin-sheathed breast. Her skin was warm to the touch.

This attraction was becoming increasingly dangerous. And harder to resist.

"What should we do?" he asked, needing her to say or do something to stop this.

"I . . . don't know."

He kissed her again, slowly, thoroughly. "You're a Valley girl."

"No, I'm not! Anyway, you're a rebel."

"You belong in California."

"You punch cattle for a living."

"There's no future in this."

"None whatsoever."

Cal frowned. "Then why do I feel like this?"

"When you know the answer, tell me."

To his dying day Cal wouldn't know what it was about this stubborn beautiful woman that made him laugh the way he did. He threw back his head and howled.

Jane apparently didn't find it all that amusing. She sat upright, then shocked him by climbing over him and straddling his lap. His eyes grew wide with surprise.

His amusement faded when she threw her arms around his neck and teased him with nibbling kisses that left him hungering for more.

"You taking me to find that ghost town, Rebel?" she whispered.

"Do I have a choice?"

"None whatsoever."

He muttered under his breath. "I'll do it, but I won't like it."

She grinned. "There'll be compensations," she promised.

"I'm counting on that."

And then she really kissed him. By the time she finished, he would have gladly taken her anywhere she asked.

FRANK FELT like a schoolboy as he splashed aftershave on his face and studied his reflection in the bathroom mirror. For the first time in eleven years he had a date with someone other than Dovie. He'd rather be with her, but they remained at an impasse and he was tired of fighting a losing battle.

It'd taken him three days to compile a list of candidates and then pare it down to one woman. His decision made, he'd phoned Tammy Lee Kollenborn and invited her to dinner and a movie. It helped soothe his wounded ego when she eagerly accepted.

Of all the eligible women in town, Tammy Lee was the most attractive. She was a fiftyish divorcée who wore a little too much makeup and was friends with Louise Powell; that was the downside. On the other hand, since Louise was the town gossip, word of his seeing Tammy Lee was sure to get back to Dovie.

Tammy Lee had been divorced for twenty years or more, Frank knew, and that was a factor in her favor. She'd dated a number of men in town and revealed no sign of wanting to remarry. Another plus. From what he heard, she received hefty alimony payments. She routinely traveled and had spent one summer in Europe, returning to Promise with some mighty interesting souvenirs. Apparently she'd brought back a giant round mirror festooned with romping nymphs and satyrs. Rumor had it she'd fastened it to the ceiling above her bed. In time, Frank might have the opportunity to investigate that particular piece of gossip for himself.

Frank didn't know Tammy Lee well, but she was exactly the type of date he was looking for. Once Dovie heard about this, she was sure to have a change of heart. If she didn't, well, that was that. He'd done everything within his power to get her to see reason. Short of marrying her, which he refused to do.

He reached for his jacket and headed out the front door, grateful the rain had ceased. He was starting slow, easing into this relationship. Dinner, followed by a movie. They could chat over the meal, get comfortable with each other. A movie was a good way to end the evening, no pressure to carry on a conversation.

Frank picked up Tammy Lee at her house. She opened the door and beamed him a broad smile. "I can't tell you how pleased I was when you phoned," she said, draping a fringed wrap over her shoulders. "The first person I called was Louise."

Louise Powell. Well, it was no less than he'd expected. Louise might be a blabbermouth, but this time, it was to his advantage.

"You look terrific," he said, thinking a compliment early in the evening would put them on a good footing. She wore a gold lamé jumpsuit with a jeweled belt that emphasized her trim waist and hips. He especially appreciated her high heels, found them sexy. Fewer and fewer women wore them these days.

Tammy Lee stopped and checked her reflection in the hallway mirror, then smiled. "What a nice thing to say."

Frank waited for her to return the compliment, but she didn't. He led her outside and opened the car door, wanting to impress her with his manners. Dovie had always enjoyed the little things he did to show her he cared.

"I'm a modern woman," Tammy Lee said after he'd climbed into the car and started the engine. "I can get my own door, but it's real sweet of you to do that."

"You don't want me to open your car door?"

"It isn't necessary, Frank."

He smiled and decided he was pleased. This was a woman who spoke her mind, who asked for what she wanted. He respected that.

They chose to eat at the Chili Pepper, and their appearance created something of a stir. Frank felt he should apologize for the attention they received.

"Don't worry about it," she said, graciously dismissing his concern. "I know what it's like when a longtime relationship ends. People are curious, wanting to know the details."

People like Louise Powell, Frank added silently.

Frank ordered a steak and a baked potato with all the fixings. He'd lost a few pounds pining for Dovie, and was ready to make up for lost time.

He was mildly disappointed when Tammy Lee asked for a plain green salad with red-wine vinegar.

"I'm watching my weight," she explained.

Frank guessed that her trim figure demanded sacrifice. He ordered a cold beer to go with his meal, while Tammy Lee ordered a highball, her first of three. He wondered about the calories in those, but didn't ask. At four-fifty a drink, she could have ordered the steak. She surprised him further when she asked to see the dessert menu.

"Every once in a while I allow myself a goodie," she said.

Frank never ate restaurant desserts. Dovie, when he could convince her to go out, refused to let him eat a pie baked in an aluminum-foil tin. She insisted she could outbake anything that came from a freezer. He'd never argued with her.

Tammy Lee ordered apple pie à la mode.

"Save room for popcorn," he told her.

She shook her head. "I don't touch the stuff."

"Oh," he said. That was his favorite part of going to the movies. Yes, the theater charged outrageous prices, but it was a rare treat and one of the few indulgences Dovie enjoyed, too. They bought the largest bag, with butter, and shared it.

"I was sorry to hear about your breakup with Dovie," Tammy Lee said, sounding anything but.

"Yes, well, these things happen." Frank wasn't willing to discuss Dovie with another woman.

"I've always liked her," Tammy Lee said.

That statement was patently insincere.

"She's a special lady," Frank said, growing uncomfortable with this conversation.

Tammy Lee frowned slightly. "I did understand you correctly, didn't I? You and Dovie are no longer seeing each other?"

Frank shifted in his seat. "Do you mind if we change the subject?" he asked pointedly.

"Of course not. It's just that, well, I know you and Dovie were . . . close, if you catch my drift."

Frank wasn't sure he did. "How do you mean?"

"Well . . ." Tammy Lee lowered her voice significantly. "I understand you spent the night with Dovie at least twice a week."

Frank opened his mouth to tell her it wasn't any of her damn business how close he and Dovie were, but she stopped him.

"The only reason I mention this, Frank, is that . . ." She paused and sent him a pained look. "This is rather embarrassing, and I do hope you'll forgive me for being blunt, but I'm in a position to help you through these difficult times."

"Difficult times?" What was she talking about?

"Physically," she whispered, beaming him another one of her smiles. "I'm currently without a man in my life and I'd welcome your attentions, Sheriff Hennessey."

He didn't think a woman had ever shocked him more. Frank shook his head in wonderment. Two years. It'd taken him two full years of courting Dovie before she'd allowed him into her bed. And even after all the time they'd been involved, she was uncomfortable making love without the sanction of marriage. Yet this woman was brazenly letting him know she'd welcome him to her bed on their first date. Sure, he'd admit to a mild fantasy about her supposed sensual bedroom—but checking it out on their first date? What in hell had happened to the world since he'd been out of circulation?

"Well?" Tammy Lee asked.

"Perhaps we should discuss this at a later time," Frank said.

"Have I shocked you, Frank?" she asked, then laughed coyly.

"Shocked me? What makes you ask that?"

"Your ears have gone all red." She snickered as if she found this highly humorous.

Tammy Lee's words irritated him, but he attempted to disguise his reaction. Frank was actually looking forward to the movie for the simple reason that they wouldn't be speaking. She said the most outrageous things, and he was getting tired of it.

The theater in Promise had only one screen. The seats were rather worn, but comfortable. The feature films weren't always first-run, but since it was the only show in town, few complained.

Frank purchased their tickets and was putting his change back into his wallet when Tammy Lee decided to get possessive. She rubbed his back affectionately and cozied up to his side, wrapping her hands around his upper arm. He shouldn't be surprised, he supposed; her actions were certainly in keeping with her conversation.

When he looked up, he saw the reason his date had started to cling to him like a blackberry vine. Standing only a few feet away from him was Dovie Boyd, holding a small bag of popcorn and a paper cup of soda. Her eyes widened with a flash of shock and pain. He feared she was about to drop her drink and admired her for her fast recovery.

Tammy Lee all but draped her arms around his neck, nuzzling his ear like some annoying insect he longed to bat away.

Dovie offered them both a brave if shaky smile. "Hello, Frank. Hello, Tammy Lee," she said. And then, with the grace of the lady she was, she turned and walked into the theater.

Seven

Jane saw Cal every day after their rainy afternoon. The riding lessons continued, but they found other reasons to be together, too. After their first date he no longer made an issue of their not becoming involved and she was glad. She particularly liked meeting him at the ranch, liked seeing him in his own world, which was new and strange and enchanting to her.

It was Sunday, two weeks after the storm. For her riding lesson that afternoon, they rode to the farthest pasture with Digger, Cal's dog, racing along beside them. The day was glorious, a perfect autumn day with temperatures still in the mid-seventies.

Jane had become almost comfortable in the saddle. Either she'd built up calluses on that part of her anatomy, she thought wryly, or she'd gained skill. Probably a combination of both.

Jane frequently mentioned Cal in her letters and phone calls home. She'd taken a great deal of ribbing from her father about this penchant she had for horseback riding. He told her he'd thought she'd outgrown it when she was thirteen. Like many girls, she'd been horse-crazy, reading horse stories and collecting figurines. In a way, what Cal had given her was the opportunity to live a long-ago dream.

"You're quiet this afternoon," Cal remarked when they reached the crest of the hill.

The view of the pasture below was breathtaking. Cattle grazed there, scattered picturesquely about the fields. Cal had explained earlier that most of his herd had been sold off now, and he was wintering a relatively small number of bulls and heifers.

"I'm thinking," she said, in response to his observation.

"I hope it isn't taxing you too much."

"The only thing that taxes me is you."

"Me?" He pretended to be insulted.

"You keep putting me off."

The laughter faded from his eyes. He knew exactly what she was talking about. She hated to be a pest, but she wasn't going to let him delay much longer. The ghost town beckoned her; she'd actually started to dream about it. Her mother had mailed her a thick book about Texas ghost towns, but Bitter End wasn't included. It amazed her that an entire town could be tucked away in these hills and so few people knew about it.

"I spoke with Grady and Savannah this afternoon," Cal told her.

"Why didn't you say something sooner?" she asked. It was what she'd been waiting to hear, as Cal knew very well. Savannah had been to the town earlier in the year and apparently found the most incredible old roses blooming in the cemetery. Having visited the town fairly recently, Savannah would be able to give her and Cal directions and save them the trouble of a long search.

When Cal didn't answer, she pressed, "Aren't you going to tell me what they said?"

"In a little while."

Jane was beginning to understand Cal. He didn't like being pressured and would eventually get to the point—but he preferred to do it without coaxing from her. Her patience was usually rewarded, and considering how good he'd been to her, how generous with his time, she could wait.

"This truly is God's country, isn't it?" she said. Cal had helped her develop a love of the land. He didn't preach or lecture about it. Instead, he allowed her to see and feel it for herself. He'd taught her to appreciate what it meant to be a real cowboy, too. Some people thought that cowboys were a dying breed, but for Cal, the work and the life were vital and worthwhile. There wasn't a task on the Lonesome Coyote Ranch he couldn't handle—branding cattle to breaking horses to birthing calves.

"Do you mean that, about this being God's country?" he asked.

"Yes." And she did. The land was astonishingly beautiful. What she'd come to love about it was what Cal referred to as "elbow room." The hill country was gentle rolling hills, and pastureland that was fresh, green, limitless.

Cal had told her he could ride as far as the eye could see, to the horizon and beyond, and not meet another soul. This was something she was only beginning to fathom. So much space!

"What about California?" he asked.

"It's beautiful, too, but not like this."

Cal shook his head. "Too populated. That stuff about earthquakes—it seems to me Mother Nature's saying there're just too many people living in one spot and she's just trying to shake them loose."

He glanced her way as if expecting her to argue with him. She merely smiled and shrugged. She had no intention of ruining a perfect afternoon by getting involved in some pointless argument. Not when the wind was gently blowing in her face and the sweet smells of earth and grass rose up to meet her.

The silence out here took time to accept. At first she'd felt the need to fill their rides with chatter, but as she spent more and more time around Cal, she'd begun to appreciate the lack of sound, to stop fearing it. Cal, by his own admission, wasn't much of a talker. He'd shown her that silence had its own sound, but with the frantic pace of her life, she'd been unable to hear it.

They dismounted, and the two horses drank from the creek. Jane walked over to an oak and leaned against the trunk, one leg bent. Cal picked a handful of wildflowers and handed her the small bouquet.

She rewarded him with a kiss on his cheek. From the way his eyes flared she knew he would've liked to kiss her properly. They'd done plenty of that lately, their attraction growing each time they met. Cal backed away from her now, as if that would help remove him from temptation.

"Tell me what it means to be a rancher," she said.

His gaze held hers. "In what way?"

"I want to know about cattle."

He frowned, then squatted down and plucked a blade of grass. "A good cowboy can tell just by looking at a cow if she's healthy. Her coat'll tell him if she's eating right. The eyes let him know if she's in any kind of trouble."

Jane gave him an encouraging nod. "Go on."

"It's gotten to the point where I can look at a heifer and know when she's ready to spill her first calf," Cal continued. "And one glance at a calf'll tell me if it's suckled that day or been separated from its mother."

Jane was fascinated. "Tell me more."

"It's said some folks don't forget a face. A good rancher doesn't forget a cow."

"You're joking, right?"

His smile told her he wasn't. "They have their own personalities, and they're as individual as you and me. I know that the old cow with the missing horn likes to hide in the willow trees, and the one with a patch of white on its backside is a leader. That one with a cut ear—" he pointed "—is likely to charge a horse and rider.

"My job, if that's what you're asking, is to care for the cows. The cows then tend the calves, and trust me, each cow knows her own calf. She can pick out her baby in a herd of hundreds."

Jane was amazed, but didn't doubt him for a second.

"Cows are constantly on my mind," he said, then cast her a look and added, "or used to be."

She felt a warm glow and smiled.

"I think about them morning, noon and night," he went on. "I watch them, study them, and work hard to improve the quality of the herd."

"How do you do that?"

"Every year is a gamble. Weather, disease, the price of beef. With so many things that can go wrong, I cut my losses early and often. If a heifer doesn't breed, she's sold, or if she calves late, she might not get a second chance. I expect a cow to deliver nine calves in nine years, and if she skips a year, I sell her. That might sound harsh, and I often agonize over these decisions. My cattle are more than a commodity to me. The future of Lonesome Coyote is based on the everyday decisions Glen and I make."

Jane had no idea ranching was so complicated. It was a consuming life that required not only hard physical work but research, complex decision-making and business skills.

"Glen and I, along with Grady, have been doing quite a bit of cross-breeding in the past few years, mostly with longhorns. Breeding exceptional cattle isn't as easy as it sounds. Despite the use of artificial insemination and genetics, it's an inexact science that relies on good stock, good weather and good luck." He grinned. "Hey, stop me if I'm lecturing. This is more talking than I normally do in a month."

Jane grinned back. "I hadn't realized there were so many breeds of cattle—although I guess I associate longhorns with Texas."

"At one time there were more than six million longhorns in Texas, but by the late 1920s, they were close to extinction."

"I read that they were making a comeback."

Cal nodded. "They are." He described his cross-breeding program in some detail, and Jane found herself listening avidly to every word. Biology had—naturally—always interested her.

"Cal, I've really enjoyed hearing all this."

His eyes narrowed as if he wasn't sure he should believe her.

"I'm coming to love Texas," she said happily. And Cal Patterson too, but she kept those feelings buried for now, fearing what would happen if she acknowledged how she felt.

"What about California?"

"It's my home—I love it, too."

"You'll go back," he said, his face tightening.

It seemed as if he was challenging her to deny it. Jane didn't, but every day California seemed farther and farther away. Her life was here in Texas now. After years of planning to go into partnership with her uncle Ken, she found the thought starting to lose its appeal. Promise needed her, and she was only beginning to understand why she needed Promise.

"It's time we headed back," Cal said, and went to collect the horses.

"What did Grady and Savannah say about Bitter End?" she blurted, anxious to know.

Cal stopped. "They both tried to talk me out of taking you there."

"Did they succeed?"

He took a long time to answer. "I know you. You're determined to find that town with or without me. You told me as much. And after what they said, I'm inclined to let you try."

"You will take me there, won't you, Cal?" she asked, nervous about his response.

He nodded. "When's your next day off?"

"Wednesday."

"We'll go then."

"Thank you. Oh, thank you!" She raced toward him, threw her arms around his neck and kissed him.

He groaned. "I swear you're going to be the death of me," he muttered.

"But I promise it'll be a great way to die."

THE ACHE INSIDE DOVIE refused to go away. When she hadn't seen or heard from Frank in several days, she'd been almost glad. Every time he came to visit her, it was more and more difficult to send him away. She was afraid that her resolve was weakening. She missed him, missed their times together and the companionship they'd shared. She'd never felt more alone, not even after Marvin had died.

Despite his talk, the last thing she expected Frank to do was go out with another woman, especially this soon. It told her everything she needed to know. Seeing him with Tammy Lee had been one of the most disheartening experiences of her life.

Dovie hated to think unkindly about anyone, but Tammy Lee and

Louise Powell were enough to try the patience of a saint. From the way Tammy Lee was clinging to Frank, massaging his back, rubbing her leg down his calf, Dovie realized they'd already become lovers. The thought cut with the sharpness of a knife, and she braced herself against the pain.

The fact that business was slow was a blessing in disguise. In her current state of mind, Dovie was practically useless. She wandered around her shop, unable to sit still, unable to think clearly. Her eyes would start to water for no reason, and somehow it always surprised her; she thought she'd cried all the tears left inside her.

Frank was out of her life once and for all.

The bell above the shop door tinkled and Louise Powell casually strolled in wearing a smug look.

Dovie groaned inwardly. "Hello, Louise," she said, determined to reveal none of her feelings.

"Oh, hello, Dovie." The woman bestowed a saccharine-sweet smile on her.

"Is there anything I can help you find?" she asked, silently praying that whatever Louise wanted was out of stock so she'd leave.

"I'm just browsing," Louise said, wandering from one display to another. She picked up a pair of Kirk's Folly earrings and held them to her face, examining her reflection in the mirror. "Nice," she said, then glanced at the price, raised a brow and set them back down.

"I don't suppose you have any of those rubber piles of dog do-do? They make the funniest practical jokes."

"I'm afraid not," Dovie said. As if she'd actually sell such an outrageous item!

"Hmm," Louise murmured. "So how are you doing these days, Dovie?"

"Wonderful." Dovie gritted her teeth.

"I understand you're leaving on your cruise soon?"

Dovie was looking forward to it more every day. "Yes."

"It must be coming up next week."

Dovie wondered how Louise knew this. "That's right."

"With Frank out of your life, I imagine you're hoping to meet another man."

Dovie said nothing.

"It's a shame, really," Louise said. "I always thought you and Frank made a handsome couple."

Again Dovie said nothing.

"But your loss appears to be Tammy Lee's gain."

Dovie's nails bit into her palms. "I wish them both well," she said.

Louise shook her head. "You're a marvel, Dovie, a real marvel. I don't know if I could be nearly as magnanimous. Tammy Lee was afraid you were offended about her going out with Frank, but I can see that isn't so. You're the picture of generosity."

Dovie forced a smile and hoped Louise didn't notice how brittle it was.

"Tammy Lee's without a man right now," Louise rambled on, "and she's thrilled to be dating Frank. He's such an attractive man."

"Yes, he is." Dovie eased her way toward the front door. Fortunately Louise followed.

"It was good seeing you again," Louise said.

"You, too," Dovie lied.

Louise left and Dovie sank into a chair. The knot was back in the pit of her stomach, and she wondered if it'd ever go away.

That evening Dovie fixed herself a salad but had no appetite. Her home, after thirty years in the same place, suddenly felt too large. Perhaps this was a sign she was ready for a change, a drastic one. She'd been born and raised in Promise, and she'd seen precious little of the world. The upcoming cruise would give her a sample of what life was like outside the great state of Texas, but the cruise was only a few days long. Afterward she'd be back dealing with people like Louise, who relished rubbing Frank's new relationship in her face.

Dovie didn't know if she could bear it. For the first time in her life she seriously considered moving. With the money from the sale of her home and business, plus what was left of Marvin's life insurance, she could live comfortably. Nothing else held her in Promise. She'd stay in touch with the friends she had and make new ones.

The phone rang. Absently Dovie reached for it, studying her home with fresh eyes, wondering how long it would take to sell.

"Hello, Dovie."

The shock of hearing Frank's voice was nearly her undoing. She grabbed hold of the kitchen chair, feeling as though she might faint.

"Frank."

The telephone line hummed with silence.

"How are you?" Frank asked tentatively, as if he didn't know what to say.

She was at a loss about how to respond and decided on a lie, doubting he wanted the truth. "Good, and you?"

"All right. Mostly I was phoning to see if you needed anything."

A new heart to replace the one you stabbed, she answered silently. "I . . . don't need anything," she said. "Thank you for asking."

Frank said nothing for a moment. "About the other night . . . I thought I should explain."

"Frank," she said swiftly, "please, there's no need to explain anything to me."

"But I thought—"

"No, please. I prefer not to know."

"But, Dovie—"

"Whom you date is none of my business. I knew when we parted—when we decided we were at an impasse—that you'd be seeking . . . companionship elsewhere." Only, she'd credited him with more taste.

"You're the one taking the cruise," he reminded her, the coolness in his voice testifying to his displeasure.

Dovie had nothing to say about her vacation plans, especially not to Frank.

"I've heard about those cruises," Frank continued. "I've seen reruns of 'Love Boat.' People book those fancy liners looking for romance."

"I'm sure that's true in some cases." Not in hers, however. Now seemed as good a time as any to put his mind to rest regarding the future. "I've been giving some thought to . . . to making certain changes in my life."

"I'm hoping you're about to tell me you want me back." His eagerness was certainly a balm to her wounded pride.

"No, Frank."

"You're going to be looking for another man, right?" he accused.

"No, Frank," she repeated. "I'm not seeking out a new romantic interest." *Unlike you*—but she refused to say it. "I'm thinking of selling the house and moving."

Her words were met with silence, then, "You don't mean it!"

"Yes, Frank, I do."

"But why?"

"You have to admit it's very awkward for us both. You're dating again now and—"

"One date, Dovie. I swear to you that's all it was."

"It doesn't matter."

"I don't even like Tammy Lee."

But there were bound to be others. Dovie didn't know if she had the strength to stand back and smile while the man she loved became involved with another woman. The only thing worse than seeing Frank with someone like Tammy Lee would be seeing him with someone who could be right for him. A woman who'd love him the way she did.

"What about your antique shop?" he asked. "You care about that store. It took you years to put everything together, and now you've added the Victorian Tea Room."

"I'll have to sell it—either that or close it down."

"But the women in town love your store!"

"Then perhaps one of them will be willing to purchase it."

"You don't mean it," Frank said again, his voice rising. "This is just another ploy to get me to change my mind and marry you."

That he would believe her capable of such a thing hurt. "No, Frank, it's not. I'm contacting the real-estate people in the morning. Perhaps I shouldn't have mentioned it, but I felt you should know. Goodbye, Frank."

"I'm not going to marry you or anyone," he shouted as if she was hard of hearing.

"Yes, you've made that quite clear." At this point, if he *had* experienced a sudden change of heart, Dovie wasn't sure she'd agree to marry him, anyway.

CAL WASN'T HAPPY with the idea of finding Bitter End and he wouldn't be going there now, but for Jane.

He drove into Promise, hoping that when he arrived she'd have changed her mind, but one look told him he might as well save his breath. Jane opened the front door, and when she saw him, practically launched herself into his arms.

"I'm so excited!" she said, hugging him.

It was beginning to feel damn good to hold her. Beginning, hell, it felt like this was exactly where she belonged. Once again Cal forced himself to remember that Jane would put in her stint here, but when her three years were up, she'd return to California.

"I spent part of the morning with Savannah," he said, and withdrew a slip of paper from his shirt pocket. "She drew me a map showing us how to get to Bitter End."

"That's wonderful!"

Cal didn't agree.

"You're sure you'd rather drive?" She sounded disappointed that they wouldn't be going on horseback.

"I'm sure." He spread the map on top of the coffee table for her to examine.

She pored over it and then smiled up at him with such enthusiasm it was difficult not to feel some excitement himself. The problem was, Jane didn't understand what she was asking of him, and he couldn't find the words to explain it.

He'd seen the ghost town once, and that was all it had taken for him to know he never wanted to go back there. As teenagers, he and Glen and Grady had happened to overhear a conversation between his parents and the Westons. They'd been intrigued. Just as Jane was now.

They'd come up with a scheme to locate Bitter End on their own. The adventure had appealed to them; the secrecy, too.

Cal remembered that he'd been the skeptical one of the bunch. He wasn't sure he believed such a place existed. Glen seemed convinced the ghost town was there. Grady was undecided.

In the end it was Glen who turned out to be right. The old town was hidden deep in the hills, just as his parents had said. At first the three of them had been ecstatic, jumping up and down, congratulating each other. Cal remembered thinking that someone would probably include their names in a history book or a magazine article—as the boys who'd found a lost ghost town. Someone might even interview them for television.

None of that had happened—and for a reason. Not one of them ever mentioned finding Bitter End to any of their peers and certainly not to their parents. In fact, they'd never mentioned it again—until recently.

It was almost as though they'd made a secret pact not to discuss what they'd found, but that hadn't been the case. They didn't talk about it because they weren't sure what had happened or how to explain it.

All Cal could recall was how uncomfortable he'd been. How the feelings, of fear and oppressiveness, had overwhelmed him. The others had reacted the same way. After less than ten minutes all three had hightailed it out of town as if the hounds of hell were in hot pursuit.

"Should I bring a sweater?" Jane asked.

"That's probably a good idea." Cal wished to hell he could talk her out of this, but since that wasn't likely, he was determined to be there with her.

"I brought along a camera, too," Jane said as she swung a backpack over her shoulder. "Mom asked me to get some pictures."

"You mentioned the town to your mother?"

"Wasn't I supposed to?"

Cal wasn't sure how to answer. "No one around here talks about it much."

"I know," she said with a certain exasperation. "I don't understand that."

"Perhaps you will once you've been there."

"I wish I knew why everyone's so secretive about this place."

Cal knew it wouldn't do any good to tell her. She'd soon discover the answer on her own.

The drive out of town went well enough. They discussed Savannah, who'd told Cal about her pregnancy. Cal was happy for her and Laredo. "I imagine Glen and Ellie will be thinking about children soon, too," he said. "I hope so."

"Cal, they're newlyweds."

"Yes, but if my mother'd had anything to say about it, Ellie would've gotten pregnant on their wedding night and delivered their first grandchild nine months and thirty seconds later."

Jane laughed softly. "Your mother is eager for grandchildren to spoil. So is mine."

Cal wasn't wading into those shark-infested waters, not for anything.

With the help of Savannah's map, they were able to locate the general vicinity of the town. It would have helped had the tire tracks not been washed away by the recent storm, but every now and then Cal recognized some landmark himself. It amazed him that the memory of these details hadn't been lost. Although it'd been years since his visit, Cal had repeated the journey in his mind many times since.

He parked the truck when they'd driven as far as possible.

"According to Savannah, we'll need to walk in from here."

"I'm ready."

Jane had dressed in khaki shorts, hiking boots and T-shirt; on his advice she'd also worn a hat. Cal held her hand as they climbed over the rocks and limestone ledge.

"There," he said, pointing as the town came into view below. Seeing it again stole his breath. The buildings, the way the streets were laid out, were almost exactly as he remembered, as though the years had stood still. The church, at the far end of town, still stood with its burned-out steeple. The graveyard was beside the church. Some of the buildings along the street were of sun-bleached wood, some of stone, now brown with age. Stores, a saloon, livery stable with a small corral, a mercantile and even a hotel. A corral was situated close to the hotel.

"This is incredible," Jane breathed, slipping the backpack from her shoulders. She pulled out her camera and began shooting. "I can't believe it's here like this. . . ."

Once she'd finished snapping pictures, Jane scrambled forward, bounding energetically over the rocks. Cal followed close behind, watching her, waiting for her reaction once she felt it.

He experienced the first sensation, a feeling of darkness and desolation, when they stepped onto the main street of Bitter End. Jane apparently did, too, because she stopped cold and slowly turned to face Cal. A puzzled frown appeared on her face.

"What *is* that?" she asked, lowering her voice to a whisper.

"What?" he asked, although he knew.

"This . . . this feeling."

"I don't know."

"You said this place was evil. I didn't know what you meant."

"I wasn't sure how to say it," Cal told her. But he could find no other word to describe what he and the others had experienced that day.

Jane's grip on his hand tightened as they made their way down the middle of the street. "It's growing stronger," she said in a weak whisper. "Do you feel it, too?"

"I feel it." The sensation grew heavier and more intense with each step they advanced.

"Look!" Jane said, gesturing at a rocking chair outside the saloon.

"What?"

"There's a guitar there."

"A guitar?" It took Cal a moment to see it, propped against the wall.

"That doesn't look like an antique, does it?" Jane said.

Cal went to investigate. He climbed the two short steps onto the boardwalk and reached for the guitar.

"Is it old?" Jane asked.

"This is no antique," Cal said, and frowned. Furthermore it was familiar. Where had he seen this guitar before? For the life of him, he couldn't remember.

"Cal, look!"

She was halfway down the street when Cal glanced up. He set the guitar down and raced after her. She was just outside what had once been the mercantile.

"What is it?" he asked.

She held up a half-full can of soda. "Someone's been here recently," she said.

He nodded. "Very recently." He was ready to leave even if she wasn't.

"Let's get out of here," Jane said.

Cal grabbed her hand and they turned to go back the same way they'd come in.

It wasn't until they passed the livery stable that they heard it. A moaning sound, coming from the hotel where Cal had stood only a minute or two ago.

Jane tensed and so did Cal. "What's that?" she whispered. "I didn't think I believed in ghosts, but . . ."

Cal had a sinking suspicion it wasn't a ghost. All at once he remembered where he'd last seen that guitar.

Bitter End didn't have ghosts, but it appeared to be populated by a single rat.

Eight

Savannah loved visiting Dovie's antique shop with its storehouse of treasures from earlier times. This particular visit was special for another reason—she planned to tell Dovie about the baby. Since Dr. Dickinson had confirmed her pregnancy, the knowledge that her child, Laredo's child, was growing inside her occupied more and more of her thoughts.

Dovie Boyd glanced up from behind the glass counter that displayed some of the shop's pricier antique china and jewelry.

"Savannah, my dear." Dovie's greeting held her usual graciousness and warmth. "It's good to see you."

"It's always a pleasure, Dovie." Savannah noticed that her friend was pale this morning. Come to think of it, she'd seemed tired and listless for a while now. Savannah assumed that had something to do with her separation from Frank Hennessey, although Dovie had never discussed it.

"Can I help you find something?" Dovie asked, stepping around the glass counter.

"I'm looking for something special," Savannah said, placing her hand on her abdomen, "for our baby's nursery." She waited for Dovie's reaction.

"I don't have much in the way of—" Dovie stopped midsentence and stared at Savannah, her eyes brightening. "So *that's* what's different."

"You noticed already?" Savannah was only about two months along. It didn't seem possible that anyone would be able to detect the pregnancy this soon.

"In your eyes," Dovie explained. "You're fairly glowing with happiness." She smiled. "I know it's a cliché—that pregnant women have a glow about them—but like most clichés it has a basis in truth."

Some days it was all Savannah could do not to burst into tears when she thought about all the wonderful changes that had taken place in her life this past year. The afternoon she'd found the ghost town and dug up the White Lady Banks roses in the church cemetery had forever changed her life. It was on the return drive that she'd seen Laredo Smith walking along the side of the road. To this day she didn't know what had possessed her to stop and offer him a ride. She'd never done anything like that before or since. Within a few months she'd become Laredo's wife and now they were expecting a child.

"I *am* happy," Savannah said.

"You're radiant." They hugged, and as the older woman pulled away, Savannah noticed again how drawn Dovie looked.

"You haven't been ill, have you, Dovie?" she asked, deciding she should ask, just to be sure.

"No. I just haven't been sleeping well." She managed a smile and continued, "I have some news, too."

Savannah had already heard that Mary Patterson had talked Dovie into a cruise; she was delighted. Dovie could use a vacation, however short, and her absence might clarify a thing or two in Frank's mind. Dovie was a remarkable woman, and if Frank Hennessey didn't realize it, then the sheriff was more of a fool than she'd thought. But she knew Frank almost as well as she did Dovie and suspected that the problem, whatever it was, would soon be resolved.

"I've decided to sell the house." Dovie's announcement was inflated with forced enthusiasm. "I'm going to be moving."

"Moving," Savannah repeated, trying to conceal her shock.

"I talked to a real-estate agent this morning and I'll be listing the house this afternoon. I'm . . . not sure just yet what I'll do about the business."

Speechless, Savannah needed time to recover.

"I know this comes as a surprise," Dovie said.

"Where will you go?" Savannah asked, when in reality her question should have been *why* Dovie would go. Why she'd consider leaving Promise. This was her home. She was an essential part of this community, loved by everyone here. Her shop was the very heart of the town, a mingling of past and present, a constant reminder of the heritage that made Promise special to those who lived there.

"I've decided to do some traveling," Dovie said, again with an eagerness that rang false. "I'm going to explore the world."

"The world . . ."

"The United States, at any rate. I understand that Charleston's lovely, and I've never seen New York. I've never seen the Rockies . . ." Her voice tapered off.

This was more than Savannah could take in. She felt the sudden need to sit down. "I realize it's a bit early for tea, but perhaps you wouldn't mind putting on a pot?"

"Of course."

While Dovie fussed with the tea, Savannah contemplated what she should say. She thought about her own relationship with Laredo, remembering how she'd felt when he returned to Oklahoma and she didn't believe she'd see him again. She'd made changes in her life, too, needing to do *something* to combat the terrible pain of his leaving. The changes hadn't been drastic, although Grady and a few others had behaved as though they no longer knew her. Cutting her hair was a small thing. Dovie planned on packing up her fifty-seven years of life and leaving everything that was familiar.

Savannah noticed that her friend's hand trembled as she poured the tea.

"Why would you leave here?" Savannah asked gently. "I'd like to know the real reason you'd consider moving away from Promise."

Dovie lowered her eyes and folded her hands in her lap. She didn't say anything for several tense moments. "Frank's dating Tammy Lee now and I can't bear—"

"Frank and Tammy Lee?" Savannah interrupted. She could hardly believe her ears. What man in his right mind would prefer that . . . that trashy Tammy Lee over Dovie?

"If it isn't Tammy Lee, it'll soon be someone else and . . . I can't abide seeing him fall in love with someone else." Dovie pulled a limp lace-bordered handkerchief from her pocket and dabbed her eyes.

Savannah leaned forward, hugging the woman who'd been both friend and substitute mother to her. She sympathized with the pain Dovie felt and wished there was something she could say or do that would ease her broken heart.

"Obviously I gave Frank more credit for intelligence than he deserves," Savannah snapped. The next time she saw him, she'd give him a tongue-lashing he wouldn't soon forget.

Dovie quickly composed herself, clearly embarrassed by her show of emotion. "It isn't such a bad thing, my leaving Promise," she said on a more cheerful note. "I'm actually looking forward to traveling. Eventually, I'm sure I'll find someplace in Montana or Colorado that reminds me of Promise. I'll settle right in and make a new life for myself." Her enthusiasm appeared more genuine this time. Savannah hated the thought of losing Dovie, especially for a reason as *stupid* as Frank Hennessey's stubborn pride.

She was about to say something else when an antique doll caught her eye. Faded and tattered, it sat on the edge of a dresser. Dovie's gaze followed hers.

"Do you recognize the doll?" Dovie asked. "Jane Dickinson brought it in and asked me about it. Apparently someone brought it into her office and asked her to find the owner. It's quite old and rather fragile. Have you ever seen it before?"

Savannah walked over to look at the antique doll. She picked it up and carefully examined its faded embroidered face. The button eyes seemed to stare back at her. "I've never seen anything like this."

"Me, neither." Dovie shook her head.

"But . . . it looks like something that might have come from Bitter End."

"Bitter End. That's what I thought," Dovie said excitedly.

"But how would anyone have gotten hold of it?" Savannah asked.

"Your guess is as good as mine." Dovie frowned. "Apparently whoever gave the doll to Jane—she couldn't tell me who—did so because he or she felt guilty about taking it."

"Why would anyone give it to . . ." Savannah paused.

"I suspect it was a child," Dovie said thoughtfully.

"I was thinking that very thing," Savannah murmured.

"It's highly unlikely that any child's been to Bitter End, though," Dovie pointed out. "Other than a handful of people, who even knows about the town?"

All at once everything fell into place. "*Richard* knows about Bitter End," Savannah said intently. "And he kidnapped Maggie for several hours, remember? What if he took her to Bitter End? He could've either given the doll to Maggie in an attempt to buy her silence or else Maggie took it without him knowing."

"Someone needs to ask Maggie about this," Dovie said.

Her thoughts were a reflection of Savannah's own. Maggie had refused to talk about the time she'd been missing, despite numerous efforts by a number of people, herself included. Even knowing what she did about her brother, Savannah couldn't believe Richard would intentionally take the child. Everyone had been terribly worried—no one more than Savannah, whose fears had been compounded by guilt. The child had been in her care when she disappeared, and Savannah had blamed herself.

Then early the next morning Maggie had come running down the driveway. For the rest of her life, Savannah would remember the way Grady had raced toward the child. At that moment she'd realized how much her brother had come to love Maggie. He might not have fathered her, but he'd always be a real father to the little girl. She'd long had her suspicions about Maggie's biological father, but had kept those to herself.

"Perhaps Grady should be the one to ask Maggie about the doll," Savannah said. The little girl had refused to discuss where she'd been or who'd taken her, but she trusted Grady now and seemed willing to confide in him. Since she hadn't been physically harmed, Frank had felt they should count their blessings and leave it. He doubted Maggie would be able to help them locate Richard, anyway. However, that was before they knew about the doll.

"Someone should bring Frank into this, too," Dovie said. "I understand there's a warrant out for Richard's arrest . . ." Her voice faltered and she looked away. Whether her reaction was because of Frank or Richard, Savannah couldn't say.

"I'll have Grady call him."

For the next couple of hours Savannah was involved in talking to people. She'd contacted Jane Dickinson's office and learned that it was her day off. Apparently she'd gone somewhere with Cal Patterson.

Caroline agreed Grady would be the right person to discuss the matter of the doll with Maggie. Sheriff Hennessey was brought in, as well, and suggested they talk to her at the ranch house.

Savannah returned to the ranch, baked bread and mulled over what she'd learned from Dovie. She was also worried about Richard. She knew he had a rifle, but didn't like to think that her brother would intentionally hurt anyone. After these past few months, though, she couldn't predict what he might do.

When Caroline and Maggie arrived late in the afternoon, they all gathered in the living room, together with Frank Hennessey. Maggie stayed close to her mother, glancing nervously about the room. Grady held his arms open and Savannah was gratified to see the child willingly sit next to him.

Grady opened the bag Dovie had given Savannah and withdrew the old tattered doll. "Do you recognize this?" he asked Maggie.

The little girl took one look at it and covered her face with both hands. Her shoulders started to shake. "I'm sorry I stole her! I'm sorry!"

"But the doll said she was glad." Grady spoke with such gentle concern that Savannah wanted to kiss him. "She told me how grateful she was that she had someone to love her."

Maggie lowered her hands and gazed at him with searching eyes. "She told you that?"

Grady nodded gravely. "She came from the ghost town, didn't she?"

Maggie's hands flew back to her face. "I'm not supposed to tell!"

"It's all right, Maggie," Grady continued. "You won't be punished."

"But Richard said Mommy would die if I told anyone. He said I'd never see her again and that she'd bleed real bad."

Frank muttered a curse under his breath, and while Savannah wouldn't have used that precise language, she was in full agreement. That her brother would knowingly frighten the child in this manner was inexcusable. His one redeeming act had been to bring Maggie back. He'd stolen another truck shortly thereafter, but at least Maggie had been safely returned.

"Sometimes people say things that aren't true." Grady placed his arm around the child's shoulders, both shielding her and comforting her at once.

Maggie kept her head lowered, as though she felt undecided about what to do.

"Is Richard at the ghost town?" Caroline asked softly.

"Will you die if I tell?" Maggie asked her mother.

"No, sweetheart, I won't die." Caroline linked her fingers with Grady's. "I'm going to marry Grady very soon and we'll all be very happy."

"Will you have other babies so I can be a big sister?"

Savannah watched as Caroline met Grady's eyes, then nodded. "Yes, sweetheart, you'll have plenty of opportunities to be a big sister."

"Can I really keep the doll?" Maggie asked next.

Grady raised the rag doll to his ear, his expression somber. Maggie watched his every move. Slowly, a bit at a time, Grady's mouth formed a smile. "She says she needs someone to love her and take care of her and be kind to her."

"I can do that," Maggie said with a questioning glance at her mother.

"She needs lots of tender loving care," Caroline added. "She's fragile and old."

"I'll take good care of her," Maggie promised. "I'll call her . . . Isabelle."

Grady handed her the doll, and Maggie pressed Isabelle against her shoulder and gently patted her back.

"I'm sorry Richard lied to you," Savannah felt obliged to say.

"I don't like Richard anymore," Maggie said.

"You don't need to worry about seeing him again," Frank Hennessey assured her. "Once I get my hands on him, he won't see the light of day for one hell of a long time."

"IN HERE." Cal's heart pounded as he peered into the hotel. The staircase had collapsed and he was able to make out a figure trapped beneath the boards. Richard Weston, he was sure.

Jane was a few steps behind Cal. They cautiously entered the hotel and began to approach the ruined stairs.

"Stand back," Cal ordered, looking up to make sure nothing else threatened to fall. As soon as he'd assured himself it was safe, he started to remove the boards.

It was indeed Richard, and his groans grew louder, more plaintive. He was in obvious pain and close to unconsciousness.

Jane checked his vital signs. "There's no telling how long he's been here."

"Two days," Richard whispered, his voice weak. "Am I going to die?"

"Not if I have anything to say about it," she said firmly.

Cal understood that to Jane, medicine was a passion the same way ranching was to him, and he respected her for it. *Loved* her for it. He loved her courage and her sense of humor, too, her honesty, her kindness. Why that realization should come to him at a time like this, he didn't know. He'd intended never to make himself vulnerable again after Jennifer had humiliated him in front of the entire town. But he loved Jane. He felt no doubt, not about her or his feelings.

He continued to lift the heavy pieces of wood that trapped the injured man. The way in which Richard's leg was twisted told him it was badly broken.

Richard was moaning for water. Jane carefully lifted his head and dribbled liquid between his parched lips.

"Don't let me die," Richard pleaded between swallows. "Tell my mother I'm not ready."

Jane raised her gaze to Cal's.

"His mother died more than six years ago," he told her.

"He's hallucinating," she explained. "We need to get him out of here. The sooner the better."

"How?" The truck was parked some distance away, and Cal was aware it would be nearly impossible to move him.

"He's lost consciousness," Jane said.

"His right leg's broken."

"I suspect internal injuries, as well."

"How are we going to transport him?" Cal asked, seeking her advice. His biggest fear was that moving Richard, especially in his frail condition, might kill him. Cal didn't need Richard Weston's death on his conscience.

"We have to get help," Jane said, and while her voice was calm, he sensed the urgency in her words. "Leave me here and go back to town. Have Sheriff Hennessey call for a medevac. His injuries are far too extensive for me to handle. He's going to have to be airlifted out of here."

"You'll be all right alone?" he asked, getting to his feet.

She nodded, then looked up at him. "Hurry," she said. "I don't think he'll last much longer."

Cal sprinted out of the hotel, running through the brush and up the hill as fast as he could force his legs to move. He didn't like the idea of leaving Jane in Bitter End, but he didn't have a choice.

By the time he reached the pickup, he was panting and breathless. Sweat poured off his brow as he leaped into the cab and fired the engine to life.

He drove to the highway at a speed far too great for the terrain, and the truck's jolting threw him repeatedly and painfully against the door. Bruises, however, were a small price to pay for saving a man's life.

No sooner had he reached the highway than two patrol cars came into view, their lights flashing. Cal pressed his hand on the horn and slammed on the brakes. He screeched to a stop, swerving partway into the other lane.

Frank Hennessey was out of his patrol car in seconds. "This damn well better be good," he yelled.

"Richard Weston," Cal said, hopping out of the pickup. "At Bitter End. He's injured badly."

To Cal's surprise Savannah and Grady got out of the patrol car, as well.

"So he's holed up in Bitter End?" The question came from Grady.

"Yes. Jane and I were there. We found him. Apparently he was on the stairway in the hotel when it collapsed. He's in bad shape—broken leg, internal injuries."

"Oh, no!" Savannah covered her mouth.

"We shouldn't try to move him. We'll need to arrange for a chopper—he's got to be airlifted out."

Frank was already reaching for his radio, barking out orders.

Cal felt Savannah studying him. All he could say was, "Jane's there. She knows what to do."

He wanted to reassure Savannah that everything would be fine, but he couldn't. He had no way of knowing what had happened since he left the town. From what he'd seen of Richard, and from what Jane had said, it didn't look promising. Cal knew that despite the things her brother had done, Savannah still loved him.

"How is he really?" Grady asked him privately.

"Not good." No point hiding the truth from Grady. They'd been friends since childhood, and Grady counted on him for the truth. "I don't know if he's going to make it, so prepare yourself for the worst."

Grady nodded and moved away. "Maybe it'd be best if we called in Wade McMillen," he said, wiping one hand down his face. "If there's time . . ."

Grady wanted to give his brother the chance to make his peace with God. Cal had his doubts. Richard had always been unrepentant. Worse, he was unconscious, possibly dying, and nothing short of a miracle would save him now.

Cal suspected that the following hours would repeat themselves in his mind for years to come. Because of the fresh tire tracks left in the soft ground, Cal was able to lead Sheriff Hennessey, Grady and Savannah to Bitter End. The second patrol car returned to Promise for Wade McMillen. If Richard wasn't in need of the pastor's comfort, then Savannah and Grady would be.

Cal's biggest concern wasn't for Richard. Instead, his thoughts were on Jane. He'd hated like hell to leave her, knowing how uneasy she'd felt in the ghost town. Damn Richard Weston. If he died, leaving Jane alone with a dead man in the middle of that empty town, he'd never forgive the bastard.

As it turned out, Richard was still clinging to life when they reached Bitter End. Grady and Savannah immediately besieged Jane with questions about their brother.

Cal stepped out of the way and watched as Jane skillfully reassured them. She'd been busy while he was away, Cal noticed. Even without medical equipment, Jane had worked to save Richard Weston's life. She'd created a makeshift splint for his leg and managed to shift him onto his side. She'd monitored his pulse and his breathing.

Frank put out a red flare for the helicopter, and it seemed no time at all before he heard the distinctive sound of the blades.

With Jane's help, the medics loaded Richard onto a stretcher and hooked him up to an emergency oxygen supply. Cal and Frank cleared a path, then Richard was carried to the helicopter.

His injuries were determined to be too extensive for the hospital in

Brewster, and he was transported to Austin, instead. If he lasted that long, Cal thought grimly. It would be touch and go.

Because of the limited space aboard the helicopter, Jane wouldn't be traveling with them.

They all stood back as the chopper rose, carrying Richard Weston away. Cal placed his arm around Jane's shoulders and felt her trembling.

"Whatever happens is out of my hands now," she whispered.

Cal pressed his chin against the top of her head. "You did everything you could."

"I know." She glanced up and down the streets of Bitter End. "I don't want to come back here," she said with vehemence. "Ever!"

Cal couldn't agree with her more.

IT WAS A DAY Frank Hennessey would long remember. Richard Weston, if he lived, faced twenty years behind bars without the possibility of parole. Richard deserved that prison sentence, but Frank felt badly for Grady and Savannah.

Wade McMillen had counseled both of them. Frank never had been one to attend church, but he liked and respected Reverend McMillen. As long as Wade didn't preach at him, then Frank wouldn't quote the law at him, either. In a situation like this, he figured, the reverend provided a service nobody else could. Including the sheriff.

Frank was with the brother and sister when the phone rang about eight that night. Grady leaped on it, and after the initial greeting, glanced across the room where Savannah sat with Laredo.

He nodded and murmured a handful of thank-yous before replacing the receiver. "That was the hospital in Austin," Grady announced. His words had everyone's attention.

"He's going to make it," Grady said, and his voice cracked. When Caroline put her arm around him, Grady clung to her tightly.

Savannah burst into tears and hugged her husband.

Frank didn't want to be the one to remind them that once Richard had recovered, he'd be placed in a maximum-security prison. If Frank hadn't disliked the man already, what Richard had said to Maggie to prevent her telling anyone where she'd been would have done it.

Since the deputy who'd driven Wade McMillen out to the Yellow Rose had already left, Frank drove the reverend back to town.

They chatted amicably, sharing insights and theories about the youngest Weston's personality. Frank dropped Wade off, then, on impulse, drove past Dovie's house.

He wasn't sure what he intended to do. Probably nothing. A few weeks ago he would've been spending this night with her. She would probably have waited up for him, brewing a pot of coffee in case he wanted to talk, which he almost always did. He missed those times with Dovie.

Despite everything, he missed her more rather than less with each day that passed. As he'd expected, her lights were out. She might be asleep—or on that cruise she'd mentioned. He'd forgotten the exact date she was supposed to go—although Louise Powell and Tammy Lee could no doubt have told him.

With a heavy heart he turned the corner, and that was when he saw the Realtor's sign. His heart felt as if it'd taken a ten-story tumble. She hadn't been bluffing when she said she'd leave Promise. He stared at the sign, shaken and hurt, trying to imagine Promise without Dovie.

Two days later Frank sat in the café at the bowling alley drinking a mug of coffee. His dour mood had kept his friends at bay. Anyone looking for idle conversation sought out someone else.

He noticed with something of a shock that Wade McMillen had slipped into the seat across from him.

Frank scowled. "I don't remember asking for company."

"You didn't, but I decided to join you, anyway." Wade raised his hand to attract the waitress's attention. Neither spoke again until she'd brought his coffee.

"Look, if you're interested in scintillating conversation, I'd be happy to steer you elsewhere. I'm not in the mood."

"So I noticed, Sheriff. Something on your mind?"

He had to give the preacher credit for guts. "As it happens, there is."

"Want to talk about it?"

"Not particularly."

Wade studied him. "I don't suppose this has something to do with Dovie Boyd."

"Why? Did she come and cry on your shoulder?" Frank muttered angrily.

"Nope. Dovie didn't say a word."

"Then how'd you know?"

Wade smiled, and it was the knowing grin of an observant man. "You might say *you* told me, Frank."

"Me?"

"You've been down in the mouth for weeks. The way I figure it, you can trust me enough to help or you can sit in the café and stare at the wall."

"Is it that obvious?"

"Yup."

Wade certainly didn't pull his punches, Frank thought. "It's not going to do any good to discuss it. My mind's made up. Besides, I already know what you're going to say."

"Do you, now." The knowing smile was back in place.

If Frank hadn't liked the other man so much, he might have been irritated. "You're a preacher."

"Yes, but I'm also a man," Wade told him.

Frank sighed deeply. "Dovie wants me to marry her."

"And you don't love her?"

"Wrong," he snapped. "I love her so damn much I can hardly think straight anymore. We had a good thing, the two of us. I spent the night with her a couple times a week, and we had one of the best damn relationships I've ever had. I always had this sort of vague thought that one day we'd get married—and then I realized I couldn't. I just could not go through with it," he said slowly, shaking his head. "As soon as I told her the truth, it was over. Just like that. Hell, if I'd lied to her, she'd never have known the difference. A lot of good being honest did me." He suspected his words had shocked the minister, and that was exactly what he wanted. To Frank's surprise Wade didn't so much as blink.

"You love her, but you don't want to marry her."

"Yes," Frank said more loudly than he intended.

"Any reason?"

"I've got a long list," Frank muttered.

"I'm not going anywhere," Wade said.

Frank wished he would. Wade McMillen wasn't going to tell him anything he didn't already know. He wasn't going to offer a quick solution to a complex problem. If anything, he'd make Frank feel even guiltier for not marrying Dovie.

"You enjoy your freedom," Wade said. "A man who's been a bachelor all these years is set in his ways."

"Exactly." Frank was impressed at Wade's understanding. "I happen to like the way I live, and much as I love Dovie, I don't want a woman messing with how I do things."

"I'm a bachelor myself," Wade reminded him.

"If I want to belch after dinner, I don't need to worry about offending a woman. I can hang around the house in my underwear if I feel like it. I can pile up all my papers and magazines and read them all at once without hearing about the mess."

"I know what you mean."

"If my dirty clothes litter the floor for a couple days, I won't have someone picking them up for me and then complaining about it."

"That's what I'm like, too," Wade said, "but it does get lonely every now and then."

"Damn lonely," Frank agreed. And nothing helped. The dinner date with Tammy Lee had been a disaster, one that wouldn't be repeated. The only woman he wanted was Dovie.

"I'm going to lose her, Wade," he said, staring into his coffee. "She's put her house up for sale."

"So I understand."

"There's no solution. Either I change who I am or I let her walk out of my life."

"And both of those prospects are making you unhappy. It's eating you up inside."

"I might as well be drinking acid," Frank confessed. The knot in his stomach had become permanent. Even when he went to bed at night, he couldn't make himself relax. He used to fall asleep the instant his head hit the pillow. No longer. His mind constantly churned with the two miserable alternatives—marriage or no Dovie.

"There's no solution," he muttered again.

"I wouldn't say that," Wade countered. "Sometimes people are so caught up in the problem the obvious answer escapes them."

Frank raised his gaze to meet Wade's.

"There's a reason I came to talk to you," Wade continued. "I've got an idea," he said, steepling his fingers in front of him. "One that'll give you both what you're looking for."

Nine

Dusk settled comfortably over the Yellow Rose Ranch. Caroline stood on the porch, savoring the beauty of the sunset and the peace of a Sunday evening. Within minutes the moon would rise to greet her, and a million twinkling stars would nod their welcome.

Grady joined her, standing behind her to slip his arms around her waist. In less than a week they would become husband and wife. As the wedding approached, Caroline tried not to become sidetracked by the events concerning Richard. He'd robbed her and Grady of so much already. All she wanted now was to blend her life with Grady's.

"I thought I'd find you out here," he whispered close to her ear.

She hugged his arms. "I needed a moment of solitude."

"We both do." Grady exhaled slowly. "So much has happened in the past few days it's hard to take it all in."

Savannah and Laredo had moved into their new home. At the same time, Caroline and Maggie had made the transition from their rented house in the city to the ranch house with Grady. They'd spent all day hauling boxes from one place to the other. Later in the afternoon Laredo and Savannah had driven to Austin to visit Richard and had yet to return.

"Maggie's asleep," Grady said, nuzzling her neck.

Caroline closed her eyes, cherishing these moments alone with the man she loved. It was a rare pleasure these last hectic days before the wedding.

"I'm looking forward to just the two of us being together," she told him. Away from the worries about Richard, the wedding, the hard work of merging one household with another. They'd decided to take a four-day honeymoon in New Orleans, and just then, getting away seemed to Caroline like a small slice of heaven.

"You're not the only one anticipating our honeymoon!" Grady chuckled softly. "It's beginning to feel like Grand Central Station around here."

"This time next week I'll be your wife."

"And I'll be your husband," Grady said, as if he still had trouble thinking of himself that way. "I swear there's something happening in Promise this year."

"How do you mean?"

"All the weddings." Grady sounded incredulous. "It started with Savannah and Laredo."

"Then Ellie and Glen."

"Now it'll be us."

"I have a sneaking suspicion who's going to be next." Caroline nudged Grady lightly with her elbow. "Cal and Jane." She'd watched them the day Richard was discovered in Bitter End and recognized the signs. She suspected they were only now becoming aware of their feelings for each other. Caroline had noticed something else, too—the rough edges of Cal's personality seemed to be wearing smooth. Perhaps even more telling were the changes Caroline had noticed in Jane. The California native had become one of them. A Texan at heart.

The last time Ellie had stopped by the post office to collect her mail, she'd mentioned that Cal was giving Jane horseback-riding lessons. Caroline would bet that the good doctor was becoming familiar with more than horses. Jane Dickinson had the look. "Yes," she said softly. "Cal and Jane."

"You're suggesting Cal's in love?" Grady shook his head. "No way!"

"We'll see," Caroline said confidently. "I wouldn't be surprised if they announced their engagement before the end of the year."

Grady responded by snickering in her ear. "Boy, are you off base with that one. Cal and I've been best friends for years. If he was thinking of getting married, don't you think he'd mention it to me?"

"Not necessarily."

"You don't know Cal and me—we're like this." He crossed two fingers and waved them under her nose. "Close."

"Uh-huh."

"So," Grady said with conviction, "if Cal was interested in a woman, I'd be the first to know. We don't have secrets from each other."

"Oh, really?" Caroline tried but couldn't keep the sarcasm out of her voice.

"Damn straight."

"Then answer me this," she said, smugly. "When did you tell Cal you were in love with me?"

His silence was answer enough.

"Well, I'm waiting." She turned to face him, hooked her arms around his neck and tilted back her head to get a good look at his face.

Grady's eyes avoided hers. "That's not a fair question."

"Why isn't it?"

"Because . . . well, because it took me a long time to figure out how I felt about you and even longer to act on it. That being the case, I couldn't very well say anything to Cal."

Caroline rolled her eyes for effect.

"Hey," Grady argued, "the man is always the last to know."

Her cocky grin was wasted on him. "My point exactly. Cal won't mention his feelings for Jane until he's ready to put an engagement ring on her finger. Trust me on this, Weston."

"Is that right," he muttered.

"That's right."

"And how did you get so smart?"

"Practice," she teased, and kissed the corner of his mouth. "Lots and lots of practice."

His eyes grew dark and sexy as he focused his gaze on her lips. Slowly he lowered his mouth to hers in a kiss that was open, purposeful and hungry.

The kiss was wonderful. Being right was nice—but not nearly as satisfying as two minutes in the arms of the man she loved.

JANE SAT AT HER DESK reviewing her appointment schedule for the following day. She was nearly finished and eager to escape the office for her next riding lesson. In truth it was Cal she really wanted to see, not Atta Girl, fond though she was of the horse. They'd been making steady progress, and when she arrived these days, it wasn't unusual for Atta Girl to gallop to the fence to greet her.

The time Jane spent at the ranch had lengthened to include dinner on her lesson days. Since Cal wouldn't accept payment for teaching her to ride, she'd taken it upon herself to cook his meal afterward. She experimented with traditional Texas recipes, but introduced some "California cuisine," too.

More and more Jane found herself looking forward to being with Cal. This evening she planned to create a special meal, complete with birthday cake and candles. Cal had no way of knowing it was her birthday—but he was the person she wanted to spend it with.

"Do you need anything else?" Jenny Bender, her receptionist, asked a few minutes later.

"Not a thing, Jenny, thanks—and thanks again for the flowers." How Jenny had learned about her birthday, Jane could only guess.

"I'll be heading out, then," Jenny said. "The answering service is on."

As soon as Jane was finished, she locked up the clinic and hurried to her house. The white lab coat was replaced with a freshly laundered snap shirt, and her skirt with comfortable slim-leg jeans. Cal had found an old pair of chaps and she strapped those on over the jeans, then reached for her hat and gloves. She was two minutes from walking out when she heard the doorbell.

Groaning inwardly at the delay, Jane answered the door.

"Surprise!" Her mother and father stood on the other side, their faces revealing guileless pleasure at surprising her.

"Happy birthday, darling," her mother said.

Jane stood there, too shocked to do anything more than stare.

"My goodness," her father said. "Look at you!"

Jane hugged her mother and kissed her father's cheek. "What do you think?" she asked, and whirled around to let them have the full effect of her transformation.

"I love it!" her mother cried.

"Cowboy chic," her father added with a grin.

Jane brought them both into the living room. "What are you doing in Texas?"

"Your father's attending a conference in Oklahoma City starting on Wednesday. We decided that since we were going to be this close, it'd only be a hop, skip and a jump to come by and surprise you for your birthday."

Jane had to admit she was surprised, all right.

"We've come to take you to dinner," her father said. He handed her an envelope, which she knew contained a check. "Happy birthday, honey."

"Thanks, Dad, Mom. I can't believe you're really here!" She took a deep breath. "Where are you staying?"

"Your father found a quaint little bed-and-breakfast place here in town."

"Cal's parents own that," Jane said excitedly.

"The same Cal you've been telling us about?" Her mother raised her eyebrows.

"One and the same. Mom, Dad, would you mind if I invited him to join us? I don't know if he can, since it's such short notice, but I do want you to meet him."

"A cowboy?" her father asked.

"One of the best you're likely to meet," she said. "A *real* cowboy."

"You're not falling in love with him, are you?"

"Dad, please! I'm a big girl now and I can make my own decisions."

"Fine, but remember you belong in California, not Texas."

Jane's excitement dimmed as she felt the pressure building inside her. From the time she'd been accepted into medical school, everyone had assumed she'd join her uncle's practice. Everyone including Jane. She wasn't so sure anymore. Cal had said that once her commitment to the government was satisfied, he knew she'd return to California. She'd neither confirmed nor denied it. She couldn't, because she didn't know herself. She knew what was expected of her, but her heart had begun to tell her something different. She loved her work at the clinic. It had taken time and effort to become part of this community, and now that she'd established friendships, she didn't want to leave. Nothing needed to be decided right now, she realized that. But the reminder was one she'd rather ignore, especially since she'd never mentioned her uncle Ken to Cal.

"Is this what you've been wearing for your riding lessons?" her mother wanted to know.

She nodded, proud of her accomplishments.

"Don't get too acclimatized," her father said in a heavyhanded attempt to humor that did nothing to disguise his message.

"Dad, would you stop? I'll be back in just a minute," she said. The phone in the kitchen offered some privacy. She punched out Cal's number and waited through four long rings before he answered.

"You're coming, aren't you?" he asked immediately.

"I can't."

"Why not?"

It thrilled her to hear how disappointed he sounded. "My parents arrived unexpectedly to take me to dinner. They'd like to meet you," she said, stretching the truth, but only a little. "Can you drive into town and join us at the Chili Pepper?"

He hesitated, then said, "I'll need an hour before I can get there."

"We'll wait," she promised, eager for her family to meet the man who'd come to mean so much to her.

When she hung up, Jane discovered that her mother had entered the kitchen. Impulsively Jane hugged her.

"You're happy, aren't you?" Stephanie Dickinson observed.

Jane knew that her parents had worried about her move to Texas, especially in the beginning before she'd made friends. It was the first time she'd lived more than an hour from her family home, the first time she'd been so completely on her own.

"I'm anxious for you to meet Cal," she said, clasping both her mother's hands. She wanted this meeting to go well on both sides, although she wasn't ready to share her feelings for Cal with anyone yet, not even her mother.

"Didn't you say his parents are the owners of the bed-and-breakfast? They certainly seem like nice people. They're packing for a cruise, and apparently they leave in the morning."

"They're wonderful." So was Cal, but she didn't mention that. Jane had met Mary and Phil the night she'd first played bingo and had seen them a number of times since. They were warm gracious folk whose personalities were perfectly suited to operating a bed-and-breakfast.

"You're not really serious about this cowpoke, are you?" her father asked, entering the kitchen.

"Daddy!"

"Don't go losing your heart to a cowboy," her father teased, kissing her soundly on both cheeks. "I can't get over the sight of you in all this cowboy gear. I don't know if I'd have recognized you."

Smiling, Jane went along with his silliness, realizing suddenly how much she missed her parents. She knew her dad could be a little too obvious in his remarks; she also knew he loved her and cared about her welfare.

After changing out of the riding clothes and into a skirt and sweater, she brewed a pot of coffee. The three of them sat in the living room visiting while they waited for Cal. Jane showed them her photographs of Bitter End, and they enjoyed a vigorous discussion of theories about its abandonment.

The instant the doorbell chimed Jane was on her feet. She was unaccountably nervous about Cal's meeting her parents.

"Hi," he said in his soft Texas drawl.

"Hi," Jane returned, and held open the screen door for him. Cal looked incredibly attractive, in jeans, polished boots, a white Western shirt and tweed jacket; she'd hardly ever seen him so formally dressed. Since their trip to Bitter End, her feelings for him had solidified. He'd been supportive and helpful, and later, after Richard Weston was airlifted to the hospital in Austin, he'd sat and talked with her. Among other things, he'd told her about Richard Weston's family history. His willingness to do this, to share a part of himself and his community, revealed that he'd come to trust her. It meant more to her than fifty riding lessons and a hundred bingo wins.

"Mom, Dad," she said, taking Cal by the hand and leading him into the room. "This is Cal Patterson."

Her father stood and the two of them exchanged hearty handshakes. Cal held a bouquet of flowers in his left hand, which he gave to her mother.

"You mean to say those aren't for me?" Jane teased, setting her hands on her hips in mock outrage.

Cal flashed her a sexy grin and she blushed. Jane could actually feel the heat enter her cheeks. Only one man was capable of doing this to her, and that was Cal.

"I thought we'd take Mom and Dad to the Chili Pepper," Jane said. "It's the best barbecue in town," she explained to her parents.

"Great. A chance to taste authentic Texas barbecue," her father said jovially.

"Do they have a low-fat menu?" her mother asked.

"No." Jane was adamant. "And don't ask for dressing on the side, either."

"But, Jane—"

"Mother, trust me on this."

"All right, all right," her mother said.

Although the restaurant was only a few blocks away, her father insisted on driving. Since Cal and Jane had been in to eat a couple of times, the hostess greeted them by name and led them to a booth.

"The music's a little loud, isn't it?" her father complained the minute they were seated.

"They like it that way here," Jane said.

"That country music's got a real twang to it." Her mother grimaced as if she could barely stand to hear it.

"I was afraid you were going to develop an accent," her father added, "and you'd end up sounding like that girl who's singing now."

Jane offered Cal an apologetic smile, trying to convey that her parents didn't mean to be condescending. He nodded reassuringly.

A Willie Nelson song came on, and as usual, everyone in the restaurant sang along, Jane included. Her parents lowered their menus and stared, transfixed by the boisterous songfest. The instant the tune ended, patrons and waiters went about their business again.

"This is Willie Nelson country," Jane explained.

"Everyone in California feels the same way about the Beach Boys," her mother said.

"Although I wouldn't call them *boys* anymore," her father put in, and this time Cal and Jane both laughed.

They ordered their drinks—beer for everyone except Stephanie who was having iced tea, "with fresh lemons," she'd specified.

"Can't decide, Mom?" Jane asked.

"It's all . . . so . . . ."

"Western," Jane supplied.

Her mother nodded.

"Mom, you aren't going to find nouvelle cuisine in Promise."

"Oh, all right," Stephanie Dickinson said with a sigh, closing her menu. "I'll have a salad. I just hope they serve a decent avocado."

It was all Jane could do not to groan out loud. Especially since she was uncomfortably reminded of her own attitude a few months ago.

Her father was the conversationalist in the family and he began telling a story about stopping at a service station in a small town outside San Antonio. "I asked this old geezer how far it was to Promise and he said—" her father paused for effect "—it was down yonder." He laughed until his eyes watered. "Then he corrected himself and said it was *way* down yonder."

Jane noted that Cal didn't laugh nearly as hard. "Dad," she said, "this *is* Texas."

"I know, I know. When in Rome—"

"Yes, Daddy."

Their meals arrived—three orders of barbecue and one green salad—and Jane relaxed as they began to eat.

"Did you know it's Jane's birthday?" her father asked when they were nearly finished.

"Dad!"

"As a matter of fact, I did," Cal said. He reached into his pocket and withdrew a small square box wrapped in white paper with a gold bow.

"Who told you?" Jane asked him.

He hesitated, then confessed, "Jenny."

"My receptionist," Jane told her parents.

"Aren't you going to open it?" her mother asked, eyeing the box.

"It's not an engagement ring, is it?" her father chided. "I don't want a cowpoke to steal my little girl's heart."

"Dad!" Jane hurriedly removed the paper. Inside the jeweler's box was a Black Hills gold necklace and gold chain. Jane lifted her gaze to Cal's. "Thank you," she whispered. "It's beautiful."

For a second it was only the two of them. His eyes held hers for the sweetest moment. "So are you," he said, for her ears only.

Jane removed the necklace from its cotton bed and Cal helped her put it on. When he'd finished, Jane noticed that her mother and father were watching them closely.

"So . . . you've adjusted to Texas?" her father asked unnecessarily.

"I like it here."

"Her attitude changed the night she won the Blackout Bingo jackpot," Cal told them.

"You played bingo?" Her mother looked aghast.

"We all do, just about every Friday night." Jane knew they didn't really understand that bingo was one of the few entertainment choices in a town the size of Promise.

"You're joking, I hope." This from her father.

"I bowl, too." Only once, but her family didn't have to know that.

Her mother gasped.

Jane laughed and squeezed Cal's hand. Oh, yes, their attitude was very much what her own had been like when she arrived here. She truly understood now, for the first time, why her reception in town had been cool. "It's another one of those when-in-Rome things."

"Just don't bring these Texas habits with you when you come home," her father said. "I can't imagine what Ken will think."

"Ken is Harry's brother," her mother explained. "Jane will be joining him at his medical clinic when she's finished her assignment here."

"Eventually he's going to make our little girl a full partner," her father said proudly, and smiled at her. Jane gave him a feeble smile in return, wishing they'd kept this information to themselves.

"I see," Cal said.

Jane felt him stiffen, and when she squeezed his hand again he didn't respond by squeezing her fingers back. She should have known this would happen, should have explained to Cal long before now about her uncle Ken. She would have, if she'd known what to say. Now he'd been hit with the information at the worst possible moment. She couldn't explain or reassure, not with her parents there. She'd lost her chance to tell him tactfully and in her own way.

They all rode back in the car to Jane's house, and her parents left shortly afterward, promising to stop by the health clinic the next morning, before they drove on to Oklahoma.

"I need to go, too," Cal said, disappointing Jane. She'd hoped they'd have some time alone together.

"You can't stay a few minutes?" she pressed.

"No."

"You'll phone later?" she asked as she walked him to the door.

"I'll try," he said noncommittally.

"I'd like to explain what my parents said about me joining my uncle Ken's medical practice. I apologize for not mentioning it sooner. Nothing's for sure yet, and—"

"We'll talk about that later."

"All right," she mumbled, her heart sinking. His look told her everything. He was angry now, and felt betrayed, and it would be best to let him sort through his feelings before they talked this out. "Thank you for the necklace," she told him, and despite his being upset with her, kissed him soundly on the lips.

HE REALLY KNEW how to pick 'em, Cal decided, not for the first time. Jennifer, and now Jane. He must have a weakness for deceptive city girls. At least he hadn't made the mistake this time of asking the woman to marry him.

From this point forward he was determined to avoid all women whose names started with the letter *J*.

Cal sat out on the porch in the moonlight and reviewed the evening. He'd been looking forward to meeting Jane's parents, but it hadn't taken him long to discover that the elder Dickinsons viewed him and the entire population of Promise as hicks. However, he could live with that. What he couldn't live with was Jane's plans to join her uncle's medical practice. She might have said something herself, and a hell of a lot sooner. He could only assume she'd kept the information from him on purpose. She intended to go back to California, just the way he'd claimed; it sounded as though her life was already planned for her. Planned years into the future, with no room for someone like him.

His forehead pounded with an increasingly painful headache. Cal walked inside and turned on the kitchen light. Obviously he needed to have his head examined. Not because of the headache, but because he was fool enough to make the same mistake twice. Only this time it hurt more.

This time his heart was fully involved and he'd started to dream again.

CAL EXPECTED Jane to show up the following afternoon and she did. A few minutes before five he heard the familiar sound of her car; fortifying himself, he stepped out of the barn, eager to get this confrontation over with.

"Hello," she called, closing her car door. She was dressed in her shirt

and jeans and looked as brightly beautiful as a rodeo princess. He
wanted to remember her like this.

"Hi," he said, keeping all emotion out of his voice.

"Thanks for being so patient with my parents last night," she said. "I
can't believe some of the things they said."

They stood a few feet apart, a little awkwardly.

She sighed and glanced sheepishly at him. "I realized I sounded just
like them not so long ago."

"You're right, you did." He wasn't going to disagree with her.

"But I came around, with a little help from my friends."

He nodded.

"Mostly from Dovie and you. Ellie, too."

He didn't respond.

"I'm here for my lesson," she said, as if she needed to remind him.

"I'm afraid there won't be one today."

Disappointment flashed from her eyes. "Oh."

"You should have phoned first."

"I . . . I . . ." She nodded. "You're right, I should have. Do you
have time for a cup of coffee?"

His initial thought was to refuse her and hope she'd be smart enough
to figure it out for herself. But he suspected it would take more than the
cold shoulder for a woman as stubborn as Jane to get the message.

"All right, I'll make time for coffee," he said, although he wasn't
happy about it. He wanted her off his ranch and out of his life *now*, while
he had the strength to let her leave.

He walked into the house, reheated the coffee and poured them
each a mug. He carried the mugs out to the porch; no need to sit inside
on an afternoon as pleasant as this.

"You didn't mention going into partnership with your uncle when
you finished your assignment here," he said bluntly.

"No," she said. "It's always been accepted by the family that I would
and—"

"It's all right, Jane, you don't need to explain it to me."

Her relief was obvious. "I should have said something much sooner,
I know, but I didn't want you to get the wrong idea."

He stared into the distance, training his eyes on the rolling hills
nestled against the horizon. It was either that or look at her, and he
didn't think he could do that and still say what he had to say.

"You're a very good doctor," he began, and the compliment was
sincere. "If I hadn't realized that earlier, you proved it the day we found
Richard Weston."

"Thank you."

"You'll be a valuable asset to your uncle's practice."

"I'm not quite sure that's what . . ." She faltered, and he could see she was having a difficult time.

"Listen, Jane, I've been doing some thinking and I believe it'd be best if we suspended our lessons."

His words were met with stunned silence. "You're serious, aren't you?"

"Very."

"Just because I *might* be joining my uncle's medical practice? I haven't even made up my mind about that! I wish you'd hear me out first."

"No." This was important. "Because you belong in California."

"Hogwash."

"You might adapt to life here in Texas for a while, but it isn't going to last. The writing's on the wall."

"And just when did you become a handwriting expert?"

"Last night."

She snorted. "Oh, come on, Ca—"

Cal interrupted her. "I was wrong. You aren't Dr. Texas, you're Dr. Big City. Big plans. Big bucks, platinum charge cards, high-powered friends."

Jane vaulted to her feet, spilling her coffee on the porch. "Don't give me that, Phillip Calvin Patterson."

He was surprised she knew his full name, but this wasn't the time to ask how come she did.

"You know what the real problem is, don't you?" She dragged in a deep breath, preparing to answer her own question. "You're a coward."

"I'm not going to trade insults with you, if that's what you're looking for," he said.

"I'm not stupid."

"I didn't say you were."

Hands on her hips, she threw her head back and glared at the sky. "You might as well have said it," she returned, calmer now. "I love you and I'm fairly certain you feel the same way about me."

"You're taking a lot for granted."

"Perhaps, I am," she agreed, "but if you're idiotic enough to send me away because you're afraid . . ."

His eyes flared at the word.

"Afraid," she repeated, "then you're a fool, as well."

"It might be best if you left," he said. His head was beginning to pound again. He wasn't up to dealing with a tirade.

"If that's what you want, I will. And I won't be back—"

"That's what I was hoping," he said, and hated himself for being so cruel.

"—unless you ask," she finished as though he hadn't spoken.

With her head held high, she walked in the direction of her parked car, then stopped halfway across the yard. For a moment he figured she was planning to argue with him some more, but he was wrong. Instead, she turned toward the corral where Atta Girl stood, her sleek neck stretched over the top rail.

Jane stroked the mare's nose and whatever she said apparently met with Atta Girl's approval, because the animal nodded and snorted. Climbing onto the bottom fence rail, Jane put her arms around Atta Girl's neck and hugged her. Then she leaped down, stroked Atta Girl's nose again and walked over to her car and climbed inside.

A minute later she was gone. She'd retained her dignity—and his heart.

Ten

Jane had called Cal Patterson a coward and a fool, and she'd meant it. Add to that stubborn, unreasonable, infuriating . . . and worse.

Dr. Big City. Big plans. Big bucks. Each time his words came to mind she grew more furious. After all the time she'd spent with him how could he know so little about her? That really hurt.

By Thursday she was exhausted. Sleep eluded her and she'd rarely been so frustrated or out of sorts.

Ellie stopped by the clinic late Thursday afternoon when the office was technically closed. Jenny led her back to the office, where Jane sat making a desultory attempt to organize the top of her desk.

"I take it this is a personal visit," Jane said after Jenny had left.

"Have you got a few minutes?" Ellie asked.

Jane nodded. "For you I do, but not if you're here to talk about Cal."

"Fair enough," Ellie said, entering the room. She sat in the chair across from Jane's desk.

"You know what infuriates me most?" Jane blurted, her anger spilling over. "It's that Cal didn't have the common decency to talk this over with me. Oh no, he just *assumes* I'm returning to California without so much as waiting to hear my side."

"Jane, I thought you didn't want to talk about him."

"Forget I said that." Jane shook her head. "And you know? That's not the worst of it," she went on. "Not only doesn't he hear me out, he sends me away like I'm a child he can order around."

"I'll admit—"

Jane interrupted her. "He was completely out of line in what he said. If he didn't want to see me again, fine, but to insult me—that was going too far."

"He insulted you?" Ellie sounded appropriately outraged.

"Tell me, do I look like a big-city doctor to you?" Jane demanded without expecting a response. "I don't even wear makeup any more. Well, maybe a little mascara and lipstick, but that's all. I haven't washed my car in months. I wear jeans practically all the time." She took a deep breath. "And when's the last time you saw a big-city doctor asking some disgruntled rancher to teach her how to ride? A rancher who implies that this supposed big-city doctor is only interested in money, by the way."

"He said that?" Ellie was clearly shocked.

"Sort of. And more—like it was time I left."

"Cal suggested you leave Promise?"

"No, the ranch, which I did, but not before I put in my two cents' worth."

"Good for you!"

"I told him he was a coward."

Ellie's eyes widened. "You told Cal *what?*"

"That he's a coward, and I said it to his face."

"What did *he* say?"

Jane paused and tried to remember. "Nothing."

"Nothing?"

"Nothing memorable, anyway."

Ellie clapped her hands, apparently enjoying the details of Jane's final skirmish with Cal. Her outrage, however, only helped so much. "I hope you're here to tell me how utterly miserable he is." It would boost Jane's deflated ego to learn he was pining away for her.

"Actually," Ellie said, her gaze warm with sympathy, "I haven't seen him, so I can't. But Glen has."

"Oh?" Jane's spirits lifted hopefully.

"Apparently Cal's been pretty closemouthed about you."

Those same spirits sank again, even lower than before.

"But Glen did say Cal's been in a bitch of a mood."

Jane couldn't have held back a smile to save her soul. So . . . the man was suffering. Good.

"I don't mean to be nosy—" Ellie's gaze shifted uncomfortably to her hands "—but what happened? Everything seemed to be going so nicely."

"You tell me!" Jane cried. "My parents arrived as a birthday surprise, and we went to dinner and Cal joined us."

"So he's met your parents."

"Yes, but I rue the day. No," she said, changing her mind, "I'm glad it happened before . . ." She hesitated. "Actually, it's too late for that."

"You're falling in love with Cal?" Ellie asked bluntly.

"I've already fallen." Might as well admit it. "I felt close to him—closer than I have to anyone. For the first time since my college days there was someone in my life who . . ." She let the rest fade.

Ellie was silent for a minute. "You weren't far off, you know."

"About what?"

"Cal being a coward. He *is* afraid."

"Of what? Me moving back to California? Give me a break, Ellie. I've been here less than a year and my contract's for three. Do I need to decide right this minute if I'm going to live in Promise for the rest of my life?"

"No."

Jane ignored the response, too keyed up to stop now. "He's being more than a little unreasonable, if you ask me."

"I agree with you."

"I'm not another Jennifer Healy."

"I know that. Glen knows that. You know that," Ellie said.

"But not Cal."

"Not Cal."

Jane brushed a stray hair from her face. "I told him I loved him," she said, revealing the most intimate and embarrassing part of their argument. She'd exposed her heart to him, and he'd not only dismissed *her* feelings, he'd denied his own.

"Oh, Jane, just be patient. He'll figure it out. Eventually."

"He might have offered me a reason to stay," she said, her voice little more than a whisper.

Ellie sighed expressively. "I don't know what it is about men in Texas. They're stubborn as the day is long."

"Proud, too," Jane added. "Way too proud."

"Impatient."

"Uncommunicative."

Ellie nodded, then sighed again. "Wonderful. Loving. Protective and gentle and passionate."

Jane closed her eyes, not wanting to confuse the issue with anything positive.

"Are you going to Caroline and Grady's wedding on Saturday?" Ellie asked her, abruptly changing the subject.

"Caroline asked me to cut the cake."

"Cal will be there," Ellie warned.

"Cal is Grady's best man." For half a heartbeat Jane toyed with the idea of finding an excuse to skip the wedding, but she refused to let Cal Patterson influence where she went or what she did. "I'd better get used to seeing him around town," Jane said, more for her own sake than Ellie's. "We won't be able to avoid running into each other now and then."

A saucy grin appeared on Ellie's face. "That's exactly what I was thinking. Cal's going to see you at the wedding. He'll see you at the grocery store and the Chili Pepper and bingo. And every time he goes to the post office he'll drive by the clinic."

"Heaven help him if he gets sick," Jane said.

"That would be horrible, wouldn't it?" Ellie said, sounding almost gleeful at the prospect.

"Absolutely horrible," Jane agreed.

Ellie shivered delightedly. "I can hardly wait."

Jane laughed for the first time in days. "I can't wait to give this stubborn Texas rancher a booster shot in places men don't like to talk about."

THE LAST NIGHT of the three-day midweek cruise, Dovie decided to join Mary and Phil Patterson in the lounge for drinks and dancing. Mary had been after her the entire trip to make herself more accessible to the single men on board, but Dovie couldn't see the point.

The music was from the forties and fifties, and judging by the crowd on the dance floor, the audience appreciated it.

"I'm so glad you decided to join us," Mary said, greeting Dovie at the door and leading her to a small table at the back of the room.

"I couldn't see spending our last night aboard doing something silly like sleeping," Dovie teased.

Mary patted her hand. "I wish you'd enjoyed the cruise more."

"But I did," Dovie assured her friend. It had been the perfect escape. Being away from Frank had given her some perspective on the relationship and on the difficulties she and Frank had encountered.

A waiter came for her drink order, and Dovie asked for a glass of white wine. Maybe what she needed was a little something to loosen her inhibitions. Actually she felt better than she had in weeks—although she still missed Frank.

"I couldn't believe the way you took to the water! I wouldn't have guessed you were that much of a swimmer."

It'd been years since she'd gone swimming, but Dovie'd had no intention of wasting an opportunity like this. For her, the highlight of the cruise had been snorkeling off the Yucatán Peninsula. Viewing the different species of colorful and exotic sea life was an experience she would long remember. She said as much to Mary.

"But your thoughts were on Frank," Mary replied.

Dovie couldn't deny it. Three days away, and she was dreadfully homesick, feeling more than a little lost and confused. Mostly she was angry with herself for having done something as foolish as putting her home up for sale. Promise was where she belonged, and she wasn't about to let Frank Hennessey chase her away. Dovie didn't blame Frank, but herself; she'd simply overreacted to his dating Tammy Lee.

The music started again and Phil stood, ready to escort his wife onto the dance floor.

Mary hesitated.

"Go on, you two," Dovie urged, her own foot tapping to the music.

To her surprise, no more than thirty seconds had passed before a distinguished-looking man approached her table. "Would you care to dance?"

Dovie stared at him as if this was the most complex question she'd ever been asked. "Yes," she said, deciding suddenly. She stood up and placed her hand in his.

"I'm Gordon Pawling," he said as he slid his arm around her waist and guided her onto the dance floor.

"Dovie Boyd," she said.

"I know."

She looked at him in surprise. "How?"

"I asked your friends the first night of the cruise."

Dovie remembered Mary mentioning a tall handsome man who'd questioned her about Dovie. While it had salved her ego to know that someone had asked to meet her, Dovie wasn't interested in a holiday romance. The only man she'd ever loved other than her husband was Frank Hennessey. She still did love Frank. She wasn't a woman who loved lightly or gave her heart easily.

The crowded floor forced Dovie and her partner to dance more closely than she would have liked. Gordon, too, seemed uncomfortable with the way they were shoved together, but as the dance went on, they both relaxed.

She liked him. He didn't talk her ear off with tales of how successful or well-known he was. He simply held her close. It surprised her how good it felt to be in a man's arms again, even if the man was little more than a stranger.

When the number was finished, Gordon escorted her back to the table. "Thank you, Dovie."

"Thank *you*."

Mary and Phil approached.

"He's a lucky man, whoever he is," Gordon said.

Dovie frowned, wondering how he knew she was in love with someone else. Mary must have said something.

"I see you've met your admirer," Mary said, dabbing her handkerchief on her damp brow. "Won't you join us—Gordon, isn't it?"

Gordon looked to Dovie to second the invitation.

She could see no harm in it. "Please," she said, and gestured toward the empty chair next to her own.

"Thank you."

Gordon bought a round of drinks.

"Phil Patterson," Phil said, stretching his hand across the table for Gordon to shake.

"Gordon Pawling."

"Where are you from, Gordon?" Mary asked.

"Toronto, Canada."

Phil nodded. "I understand that's a beautiful city."

"It is," Gordon agreed.

"We're from Texas," Mary said, and Dovie nearly laughed out loud. No one listening to their accent would have guessed anywhere else.

"A little town in the hill country called Promise," Phil put in.

"Promise," Gordon repeated.

"Dovie owns an antique store there." Mary's voice held a note of pride.

"And we have the bed-and-breakfast," Phil added.

"I'm a retired judge," Gordon said.

"A judge." Mary's eyebrows rose slightly as she glanced at Dovie. She seemed to be saying that Gordon was a catch she shouldn't let slip through her fingers.

"Retired," Gordon was quick to remind them. "I haven't served on the bench for three years now."

"Do you travel much?" Mary asked. "Is that how you're spending your retirement?"

"Let's dance, Mary," her husband said pointedly. He got up and didn't give his wife much of an option.

Mary's reluctance showed as she rose to her feet.

As soon as they were out of earshot, Dovie felt she should apologize for Mary's questions. "You'll have to forgive my friend," Dovie said. "It's just that Mary's encouraging me to see other men." Once the words left her lips, she realized more explanation was required. "I've been seeing someone . . . in Promise . . . for quite a few years. We had a difference of opinion and now he's dating another woman." It hurt to say the words even to someone she wasn't likely to see after tonight.

Gordon reached across the table and squeezed her hand. "I need to revise my opinion of your male friend. He didn't know a treasure when he found it."

Dovie smiled. "Have you been talking to Mary?"

Gordon's smile was gentle. "No."

Dovie looked toward the dance floor and smiled, too. "Shall we?" she asked, preferring that they dance rather than discuss her relationship with Frank.

"It'd be my pleasure." Gordon stood and offered Dovie his hand.

They danced every dance for the rest of the night. At midnight they attended the buffet. Dovie's appetite had been lacking; even the lavish display of pastries and other goodies hadn't tempted her. Not once during the three days had she stayed awake long enough to partake of the midnight buffet.

Tonight, however, she was famished. Gordon Pawling filled his plate, and Dovie wasn't shy about helping herself, either. Mary and Phil were right behind them in the buffet line.

"I'm going to have to diet for a month after this," Mary complained.

"Make that two," Phil teased, and Mary elbowed him in the ribs.

Too full to think about sleeping, Dovie gladly accepted Gordon's invitation for a stroll on the deck when they'd finished eating.

The night was beautiful. Out in the middle of the Gulf of Mexico, miles from land and the lights of the city, the stars blazed, filling the sky.

"I don't think I've ever seen so many stars," Dovie said, leaning against the ship's railing.

"In Northern Ontario," Gordon said, "in the dead of winter when it seems like spring is only a distant promise, the stars look like this. When a fresh snowfall reflects the moonlight and starlight, it's almost as bright as day."

"It sounds lovely," Dovie said wistfully. "I've never been to Canada," she confessed. "I'm afraid I'm not much of a traveler. This is my first cruise."

"Mine, too."

"I wouldn't have come if it wasn't for Mary and Phil. Mary thought it was what I needed—to get away for a time."

"Was it?"

"Yes," she admitted after a moment. "I think it was exactly the right thing to do."

"I came because of my son."

Dovie heard the smile in his voice.

"Bill seemed to think that two years was enough time for me to grieve the loss of his mother. He insisted I take a cruise, and when I balked, he purchased the ticket himself and presented it to me on my birthday."

"He sounds like a determined young man."

"Very much so," Gordon said. "He's a younger version of me, I fear. He followed in my footsteps and seems headed for the bench."

"Your wife's been gone two years, then?"

"Yes," he said, and sadness weighted his words. "I loved her for forty years and I don't know if it's possible for me to love anyone else."

"It is possible," Dovie told him. Her own experience had taught her that.

"I'm beginning to think you're right," he said.

They turned away from the railing and Gordon tucked her hand in the crook of his arm. They walked together in silence, their pace leisurely, and they spoke of their lives and marriages and dreams.

An hour later she still wasn't tired, but they'd be disembarking the next morning and things would be hectic. She knew she should get some sleep.

Gordon escorted Dovie to her cabin. "Thank you," she murmured. The night had been perfect in every way.

"All the appreciation is mine," Gordon said, then very slowly leaned forward and kissed her on the lips.

Dovie blinked back sudden tears.

Gordon reached into his suit jacket and pulled out a business card. "My home phone number is listed here," he said. "In case things don't work out with your friend . . ."

Dovie accepted the card.

"Will you call?" he asked.

"I . . . I don't know." She didn't want to lead him into believing something might come of this one night.

"I'm very grateful to you, Dovie Boyd," he said. "For this evening. And for showing me that my son might possibly be right."

But Dovie was the one who needed to thank him. She'd learned something, too.

Her life could go on without Frank. And in time, she might fall in love again. . . .

* * *

CAL WAS AWARE of Jane's presence the minute he escorted Savannah Smith down the church aisle. Grady's sister was serving as matron of honor to Caroline Daniels, and he was best man.

Every pew in Promise Christian Church was filled. It seemed as if half the town—and half the county—had come to Caroline and Grady's wedding. Being the postmistress, Caroline knew just about everyone, and they knew and liked her. Grady, too. The integrity with which he'd handled Richard's debts was no small thing, and the merchants of Promise felt both gratitude and respect. This was a chance for the townspeople and ranchers to show how much Grady and Caroline meant to their community.

Cal didn't see Jane, but he knew she was in the church. He *felt* her there, and as hard as he tried to ignore her, he found it impossible. After walking with Savannah down the aisle, Cal joined Grady, who stood next to the altar. The organ music swelled through the sanctuary as Caroline appeared at the back of the church.

Cal heard Grady's soft intake of breath as he gazed at his bride. Caroline looked lovely in her dress, complete with veil and a long train. Cal smiled as he glanced at Maggie, wearing a green velvet dress for her role as flower girl.

Then his eyes sought out Jane. She sat on the bride's side, wearing a pearl white suit with big gold buttons. Accustomed to seeing her in jeans and a Western shirt, he didn't recognize her for a moment. Damn, but she was beautiful.

Cal forced his attention away from her and looked at Caroline, whom Frank Hennessey was walking down the aisle. He soon found his gaze wandering back to Jane. Her eyes refused to meet his, which was just as well.

He regretted the way they'd parted. Both of them had been angry, saying hurtful things, things they didn't mean. He'd told himself that sometimes it was necessary to be cruel to be kind—only in this case he was the one who'd suffered. He'd been miserable and lonely since that day. He knew their confrontation hadn't been easy for her, either, but she certainly seemed to be faring better than he was.

She might still be angry, but after a while she'd see that this was for the best. When the time came, she'd return to the life she'd always known in California. Her career plans were already in place—and they didn't include practicing medicine in rural America. They didn't include falling in love with a rancher.

The organ music faded, and Caroline joined Grady at the front of the church. Wade McMillen stepped forward to preside over the ceremony, smiling at the happy couple.

Before Caroline and Grady exchanged their vows, Wade had a few words to say about love and marriage.

Since he intended never to fall in love again, Cal only listened with half an ear. It wasn't until Wade said, "Love doesn't come with any guarantees," that Cal paid attention.

That was what he'd wanted. A guarantee. He wanted Jane to promise she'd never leave him. He'd been waiting for her to assure him that her future would always include him.

Without that guarantee, he hadn't been willing to take the risk.

The remainder of the ceremony was a blur in Cal's mind. He handed Grady the wedding band at the appropriate moment and escorted Savannah back down the center aisle following the ceremony.

Later, at the reception, he stood in the receiving line and exchanged chitchat with the guests as they paused to greet the newlyweds and other members of the wedding party.

Grady and Caroline were ecstatic. Maggie was with them and proudly referred to Grady as her daddy. As Cal watched he felt a sharp emptiness in the pit of his stomach. Overnight Grady had a wife and a daughter, and he'd pledged his life to them with nothing to safeguard the future. He'd stood before his family, friends and God and promised to love Caroline for the rest of his life. Without knowing what the next day held, or the next year. Whatever the future might bring, he was willing to love Caroline and Maggie.

The emptiness inside Cal increased. He loved Jane, but unless he was offered a money-back guarantee, he hadn't been willing to risk his heart by telling her how he felt.

When he lost Jennifer, he'd simply stepped aside and let her walk out of his life without saying one word to stop her. He'd done the same thing with Jane, only this time he'd loved much more deeply. Because of that, he hadn't just let her go; he'd pushed her out the door with both hands.

He'd refused to commit himself to the love he felt. Not without reassurances first.

As the wedding guests progressed down the receiving line, Cal saw Jane moving toward him. His heart reacted immediately, leaping with a rush of excitement at the mere sight of her. His mind buzzed with ideas of what he should say. Something pithy, something profound; he couldn't decide what.

Before he had the opportunity to display his wit and charm, she was there, standing in front of him, her hand in his.

"Hello, Cal," she said. Her eyes seemed to sear right through him. Then without warning she proceeded to the next person in line.

Cal yearned to call her back, to say he deserved more than a casual greeting, but he couldn't. The next guests stood directly in front of him and he was obliged to greet them.

Cal continued to greet the wedding guests. Whenever he could, he sought out Jane with his eyes. He saw her serve wedding cake and chat with each person, joking and laughing. If she was miserable without him, he'd be hard pressed to prove it.

He recalled the first few months after Jane had moved to Promise and how the people in town had avoided her. The fault had been on both sides. Jane had arrived with her newfangled ideas and big-city attitude, and folks in town hadn't been too tolerant. There'd been some unwarranted assumptions made by Jane, but also by the people of Promise.

All that had changed in the past two months. Jane had mellowed, made new friends, gained the confidence of people here. He remembered the night Jeremy Bishop had broken his arm and the gentleness she'd displayed to both the boy and his terrified mother.

Little Maggie Daniels had brought her the rag doll because she knew Dr. Jane could be trusted.

Cal had seen for himself her passion for medicine and the way she'd squared off against death, fighting every way she knew how to save Richard Weston's life.

Damn it all, he was in love with her, and his feelings weren't likely to change. If he wanted a guarantee for the future, he wasn't going to find one. Not with Jane. Not with any woman.

He hadn't liked it when Jane called him a coward. Even now it wasn't easy to admit she'd been right.

The cake was almost gone before Cal found the courage to approach the table.

"Is there a piece for me?" he asked.

Jane glanced up and he could tell by the look on her face that she was surprised to see him.

"I believe there are a few pieces left," she said cordially enough, but she gave herself away when she refused to meet his eyes. She reached for a plate and handed it to him.

He cleared his throat and said, "You look very pretty."

"Thank you. I bought this suit in downtown Los Angeles."

Cal let the comment slide. "Something's wrong with Atta Girl." He said the first thing that came to mind.

That got her attention. "What?"

"It's nothing to worry about," he told her, then grabbed a glass of punch and walked away. That was a dirty trick, but he was willing to use whatever he had to.

Cal found a vacant table at the other end of the hall and sat down. He hadn't been there a minute when Jane pulled out a chair and joined him.

"What's wrong with Atta Girl?" she demanded.

"She misses you," Cal said between bites of cake.

Jane stared at him as if she hadn't understood a word.

"I miss you, too," he said, swallowing his pride along with the wedding cake.

"Oh, Cal."

"Do they have cattle ranches in California?" he asked.

Her brow puckered in a frown. "I don't know—I'm sure they must."

"Good. I was thinking of moving there."

"To California?" Her voice rose a full octave. "In the name of heaven, *why?*"

This was where it became difficult, but having made his decision, he wasn't going to renege now. "Looks like I'm going to have to if I want to be near you."

Jane was on her feet so fast the chair nearly toppled backward. "You're taking a lot for granted, Cal Patterson."

"Perhaps," he agreed, recognizing his own response the day they'd argued and she told him he loved her. "But the way I figure it, if we're going to get married and you've already agreed to join your uncle's medical practice, this is the only solution."

Jane glared at him as though it was all she could do not to slap him.

"You *are* going to marry me, aren't you?" he asked.

Eleven

Back less than twenty-four hours from her cruise, Dovie worked endlessly in the church kitchen, helping the women's group with Caroline and Grady's wedding. She had artfully arranged hors d'oeuvres on silver platters and set them on the counter to be picked up.

Actually Dovie was grateful to be in here, away from the reception, although it was considered the least enviable of the jobs the women's group performed for weddings and other social events. At least while she was here, she needn't fear seeing Frank dance with Tammy Lee or flirt with any other women.

She hadn't seen him since her return, but then, it was still early. She steeled herself for their next confrontation, dreading it already.

Humming softly to herself, Edwina Moorhouse entered the kitchen. "Pastor McMillen is looking for you."

"Me?" Dovie couldn't imagine what he wanted.

"He asked me to send you to his office."

"Really?" Dovie washed her hands and reached for a towel. "Did he happen to mention what this was about?"

"Not a word," the older woman said.

But Dovie noticed that Edwina's eyes were twinkling. If she didn't know better, she'd think Wade and the Moorhouse sisters had something up their sleeves.

Tucking a stray curl behind her ear, Dovie left the kitchen. Pastor McMillen's office was just down the hallway and around the corner. His door was closed and she tapped on it politely.

"Come in," he called.

Dovie opened the door, and the first person she saw was Frank Hennessey, rising to his feet from a chair opposite Wade's desk. The sheriff also stood when she entered the room, his eyes focused intently on her. Dovie's pulse accelerated to an alarming rate, and she was grateful when Wade motioned for her to take a seat.

"Hello, Dovie," Frank said.

"Frank." She nodded once, but avoided looking in his direction. He sat down when she did.

"Actually I need to get back to the wedding," Wade announced. "My purpose here is to bring the two of you together to talk this out." With that, he left the room.

Dovie was too shocked to speak.

"I asked Wade to bring you here," Frank explained.

"Why?"

"Well, because I didn't think you'd come if I asked."

"I mean, why did you want to talk to me? As far as I can see, everything's already been said. You're dating other women now."

"One date, Dovie, and that was a disaster." He got to his feet and walked across the room to stare out the window. "There's only one woman I love and that's you."

"That's all well and good, but it hasn't gotten us very far to this point, has it?"

"No," he agreed with a certain reluctance.

Dovie's mind whirled. She couldn't imagine that Wade McMillen, a man of God, would condone Frank and her resuming their previous relationship, especially considering its physical aspects.

"You talked to Wade about us?" she asked.

"Actually he came to me."

"Wade?" Dovie had never heard of such a thing.

"I've been feeling pretty down lately," Frank admitted. "I assumed that once you saw me with Tammy Lee, you'd realize how much you missed me and want me back."

Dovie's mouth thinned with irritation.

"I don't think any idea of mine has backfired worse. I accept the blame for that—it was a sign of how desperate I was without you."

It didn't hurt Dovie's feelings any to learn he'd had a miserable time with Tammy Lee.

"Then you left on the cruise and . . . and I worried the entire time that you'd meet someone else." He hesitated, then asked, "Did you . . . meet someone?"

"Yes, a retired judge. He lives in Toronto."

"Oh." Frank turned to face her, eyes narrowed. "Will you be seeing him again?"

"I . . . I . . ."

"Don't answer that," Frank said, holding up his hand. "It's none of my business. Like I started to say, while you were away, I was pretty miserable. But then, nothing's been right since we split. Wade and I had a long talk, and I told him about you and me."

Dovie could feel the color fill her face even before she asked the question. "You didn't mention anything about . . . spending the night at my house, did you?"

"Yes."

"Oh, Frank, how could you?" She covered her face with both hands.

"He isn't going to judge us, Dovie," Frank hastened to assure her. "It's not his job. He told me that himself."

It was one thing for Frank to refuse to marry her, but to embarrass her in front of the pastor was something else entirely.

"I explained to Wade why I've had such a struggle with this marriage idea."

She hoped he'd done a better job of it with Wade than he had with her. As far as she was concerned, telling her he wasn't "the marrying kind" was a mighty poor excuse!

"I've lived alone all these years, and a man grows accustomed to having things his own way—to certain freedoms." He paused and his eyes pleaded with hers for understanding. "These freedoms I'm talking about don't have anything to do with other women, either."

"We've been through all this before," Dovie said, tired of the same old argument. She didn't want to hear his excuses again, especially when she could practically recite them herself.

"I couldn't find any solution to it, either," Frank said, his voice gaining speed and volume. "But, Dovie, don't you see, that's been the whole problem."

"What do you mean?"

"Wade said we'd overlooked the obvious solution, and by God, he's right. We can get married and I can still have my freedom."

"How?" she asked incredulously.

Frank's smile lit up his entire face. "It's so obvious I can't believe we didn't see it earlier. I'll keep my house and you keep yours. Some nights I'll spend with you—and if you want, you can sleep over at my house, too."

Dovie's head came up.

"I won't feel the walls closing in on me, but at the same time you'd have what you want. You'd be my wife, Dovie."

If she was tongue-tied earlier, it didn't compare to what she was now.

Frank's eyes were bright with hope as he reached for her hands. "Dovie Boyd, would you do me the honor of becoming my bride?"

She blinked back tears and smiled so hard it hurt. "Oh, Frank, I love you so much. Yes, I'll marry you." It was all she'd ever wanted. It didn't matter what other people thought or said. This was a plan that worked for *them*.

She didn't know who moved first, but they were in each other's arms and kissing.

God bless Wade McMillen, Dovie mused as Frank's lips found hers.

IF CAL PATTERSON made her cry now, with half the town looking on, Jane swore she'd never forgive him.

He held her gaze, his feelings for her glowing in his eyes. "I'm asking you to be my wife."

She brought her hand to her forehead. "I heard you the first time." Which, she had to admit in retrospect, wasn't a very gracious thing to say.

"Do you want me to get down on one knee in front of all these people, Jane?" he asked. Cal was standing now, too.

"No." She shook her head and retreated a step.

"I've got an engagement ring. It's a good one, big diamond and only slightly used, but I'm afraid the damn thing's cursed. If you don't mind, I'd prefer to buy you a new one. I'm hoping Harley will take the other as a trade-in."

"You'd sell your share of the ranch?" she asked, afraid she'd been hearing things.

"If I had to."

"Why?" she demanded.

"Because I love you."

Damn, he'd done it to her. Jane could feel the tears welling in her eyes, threatening to spill down her cheeks.

"After what Wade said earlier, I've given up demanding guarantees. Like the preacher said, love just doesn't come with one. I don't know what the future holds for either of us. All I know about my future is that I want you in it."

Jane pressed her index fingers under her eyes in a desperate effort to keep the tears at bay. "You make me weep in public, Cal Patterson, and I swear you'll live to regret it."

"You'd cry for me?"

"Yes, you fool!"

His lazy grin spread from ear to ear. "That's the most beautiful thing you've ever said to me."

"Oh, puh-leeze!" She whirled around while she could still see straight and stormed across the room. She wasn't surprised to find that Cal had followed her.

The music started, and after Caroline and Grady had danced the first number, other couples stepped onto the floor.

"I'm not light on my feet, but I'd be willing to give it a try, if you are," Cal said, offering her his hand.

Jane didn't think she could refuse him anything at that moment. She placed her hand in his and nearly sighed aloud when he touched her. The sense of rightness she felt in his arms was . . . miraculous. Incredible. And so exciting.

Cal's chin rubbed the side of her face. "You love me, don't you?" he whispered.

"You know I do."

"I love you, too, Dr. Texas."

"You're serious about moving to California?"

"If that's what it takes to be close to you."

It astonished her that he'd agree to leave Promise. It shocked her, moved her deeply, inspired her. "As it happens, I love living here," she whispered, resting her head on his shoulder. She closed her eyes and savored the feel of his arms around her.

"You'd be willing to live here?" he asked.

"Promise needs a doctor, doesn't it? Everyone here feels like family. I enjoy the challenge of my job. It didn't take me long to realize that joining Uncle Ken wasn't really what I wanted." She shook her head. "Before I came to Promise, I just didn't have enough experience to know that."

"What about your uncle?"

"He'll be disappointed, but he'll get over it."

"Your parents?"

"Give them time and they'll learn to love Willie Nelson as much as they do the Beach Boys."

"And me?"

"That may take some doing," she teased. "However, if you promise to make them grandparents . . ."

His arms tightened about her waist. "I'm feeling this very strong urge to kiss you, and either I embarrass us both right here and now or we sneak outside."

Jane smiled softly, so much in love that the emotion burned inside her. "I don't know about you, but I could do with a bit of fresh air."

In the middle of the song Cal stopped dancing, clasped her hand and led her off the dance floor.

Ellie Patterson lifted her head from Glen's shoulder, looking worried. Jane smiled broadly and gave her a thumbs-up. Ellie signaled back with a wink and laid her head back on her husband's shoulder again.

Once they were outside in the shadows of the church, Cal pulled Jane into his arms. She went there without resistance. His mouth found hers and his tongue licked the edges of her lips. With a small sigh of welcome, she opened her heart and her life to him. They kissed with a need that was so deep she forgot to breathe.

"You'll marry me?" he asked, his voice a whisper.

"Yes." The decision had already been made for her the instant he asked. She'd known then that this was what she wanted, that Promise was where she belonged. This was her home now, with Cal.

"When?"

"You in a hurry?" she asked, grinning delightedly. She couldn't see any reason to wait, either, not when they both knew what they wanted. Even waiting another minute seemed too long.

"You're damn straight I'm in a hurry," Cal said. "Let's talk to Wade right now."

Jane laughed and hugged him close. "Just remember, the future has no guarantees, Rebel."

"Well, it does come with at least one," he said, lifting her several inches off the ground. "My love for you."

"And mine for you," she whispered before her lips met his.

NELL'S COWBOY

NELL'S
COWBOY

One

Nell Bishop barreled down the highway, heading home, racing against the approaching storm. The March winds whipped against the pickup as she hurried toward Twin Canyons Ranch, thirty-four miles south of Promise, Texas.

Her mother-in-law was with the children, but Jeremy and Emma would have difficulty getting the animals into the barn without help. Ruth would do what she could, but the older woman's heart wasn't strong and . . . Nell didn't want to think what might happen if she didn't make it back in time.

Her life had been on a fast-moving treadmill for the past three years, ever since her husband died in a tractor accident. Storms were the least of her worries, considering the financial challenges she'd faced working the ranch without Jake. Not a day passed that her husband wasn't in her thoughts. Twenty years from now, *forty* years from now, he'd still be a part of her.

Ruth and others had encouraged her to remarry, at least to date, but Nell had resisted. She never expected to love again—not the way she loved Jake. Their love was the kind that happened only once in a lifetime, and no other man could compare to her Jake.

Nell had always known she wasn't any candidate for homecoming queen, but Jake had made her feel like one. He'd understood what it was to be big-boned and just plain big. Dainty or elegant would never describe her; at six feet, Nell was as tall as most men. Jake had been six feet four inches by the time he was a high-school freshman, and the only boy in school taller than Nell.

They'd lived in the same town all their lives, but it wasn't until high school that she'd noticed him. The very first day of high school, as a matter of fact. She was a freshman to his senior, and the minute his eyes met hers as she walked down the hall, she knew she'd found her life's mate. He was the only boy she'd ever dated. When he enlisted in the army and became an Airborne Ranger, she'd written him every day. He served his time in the army and was discharged a week after her graduation. Despite her family's protests, she'd married Jake while still a teenager.

Neither was to know that ten years was all the time they'd have together. It was Nell who'd found her husband trapped beneath the tractor, Nell who'd held him in her arms as the life flowed out of him, Nell who'd screamed in anguish, helpless to do anything to save her husband's life.

Now it was Nell who struggled to hold on to Twin Canyons Ranch, tended what remained of the herd, raised their children and cared for Jake's aging mother. The ranch had been Jake's dream—and hers; it was a small spread that they'd bought together, shortly after their marriage. But she was so very tired, weary to the bone with her financial struggles and other worries. The past three years had drained her mentally, emotionally and physically. For that reason she'd sold off most of the herd and started a new venture. A dude ranch.

Bless Jeremy's heart. Her son had been the one to give her the idea. Last year, she'd promised him a reward for acing his spelling test and he'd chosen to rent a movie. Of all the movies available, he'd picked *City Slickers,* and to Nell it was like a revelation.

After seeing the movie, Nell hadn't been able to sleep all night. She was certainly familiar with dude ranches, but it had never occurred to her that this might be a solution to her own dilemma. She couldn't say she understood it, but people actually paid for the opportunity to eat food cooked in a chuck wagon, ride around on horses and drive cattle. Why these people would prefer to live in primitive circumstances when they could experience the luxury of some fancy resort for basically the same price was beyond her. Apparently she had a lot to learn—but learn she did. After months of research Nell was convinced that a dude ranch really was the answer. With a portion of her profits from the sale of last year's herd, she'd had brochures printed and she'd contacted several travel companies. Now she was almost ready for business, and in a couple of months she'd be entertaining her first bunkhouse full of greenhorns.

In many ways she was a natural for this kind of work. After these few years without Jake, there wasn't a ranching chore she couldn't accomplish with the speed and dexterity of a man. At this point, she knew as much about ranching as any cowboy. Not only that, she'd heard the great stories of Texas all her life—stories about the state's settlement and the

Alamo and the early cattle drives and many more. She'd always loved those stories, and if she could make money telling them now, romanticizing the Old West, all the better.

Heavy black clouds darkened the sky. Pushing thoughts of Jake from her mind, Nell focused her attention on the highway. Driving well above the speed limit, she rounded a turn in the road and saw a sports utility vehicle parked along the side.

Some damn fool had stopped to take pictures of the approaching storm. The man obviously wasn't a local. Anyone from Texas would know to take cover, and fast. Like the state of Texas itself, storms tended to make an impression, especially spring storms like this one.

Despite her hurry, Nell applied her brakes and pulled over. With the engine running, she leaped down from the cab. The wind slapped her long braid against her face as she raced toward the stranger.

The greenhorn lowered his camera. "Howdy," he greeted her cheerfully. He was taller than she was and clean-cut. His clothes were new-looking but rumpled.

"Listen, I don't mean to be rude, but any idiot knows to head for cover in a storm."

His smile faded to a frown.

"I don't know where you're from or where you're going," she went on, "but if I were you I'd get my butt back into that fancy car of yours and drive into town as fast as those tires will take you." Having done her duty, she started back to her truck.

"Hey," he said, "Got a minute? I have a few questions."

"I have to go." Nell didn't mean to sound abrupt, but she didn't have time to waste. She'd said her piece and whether or not he took her advice was completely up to him.

"Are you from around the area?" he called after her.

"Yes! Now listen, we get hail the size of golf balls and if you don't want to pay to have the dents removed, then I suggest you make tracks for town."

"This will only take a minute . . ."

"I don't *have* a minute, I've got horses and calves to worry about," Nell shouted into the wind. "And I don't have time to convince you a storm is about to break." She raised her hand toward the threatening sky. "It's going to cost you plenty if you don't get that vehicle under cover."

"I'm insured."

"Hail is an act of God." Whether he caught her last words or not she didn't know. Nell leaped into her truck and put the pickup in gear. One glance in the rearview mirror proved that giving this stranger advice had been a wasted effort. He hadn't moved. Furthermore, he wasn't snapping pictures of the dark horizon anymore; he was taking pictures of her!

Shaking her head in wonder, Nell dismissed him from her thoughts, and drove home at breakneck speed.

When she pulled into the ranch yard, she saw Jeremy chasing chickens in a futile attempt to lure them into the coop. Emma and Ruth led the horses toward the barn, yanking on the reins as the two geldings battled the wind. The scene right before the tornado in *The Wizard of Oz* flashed through Nell's mind.

She parked the truck near the barn, where it would be protected, and hurried toward her family. With her help, Ruth and Emma managed to secure the animals before the storm broke.

By the time they scurried into the house, the rain had started and they were breathless and excited.

"We did it!" Twelve-year-old Jeremy said, exchanging a high five with his sister. Unlike most siblings, Jeremy and Emma rarely fought. Sure, they squabbled now and then—all kids did—but these two were close in age and temperament. They'd also been through the devastating experience of their father's death, which had created a strong bond between them.

Jeremy was large for his age, like his father and Nell, too—big-boned, muscular and tall. Two years younger, Emma was small and delicate, resembling Ruth, her grandmother.

"I'm glad you made it home in time," Ruth said, pouring Nell a cup of hot tea before filling a second cup for herself.

Nell gazed out the kitchen window at the ferocity of the storm. The wind propelled the rain at an almost horizontal angle, pelting the trees and flowers. Smaller trees were bent nearly in half. Many a new crop would see ruin this afternoon.

Sighing, she turned away from the window. "I would have been a couple of minutes earlier if it hadn't been for some greenhorn," she said. "The silly fool stopped at the side of the road to take pictures."

"Anyone you recognized?" Ruth asked.

"Never saw him before in my life." Nell would have remembered him if she had. He was big like Jake, sturdy and broad-shouldered. Unfortunately—unlike Jake—he didn't seem to possess an ounce of common sense.

Ruth shook her head. "Probably one of those tornado chasers."

Nell frowned. "I don't think so." He wasn't the type. Too soft, she decided, and although it might sound unkind, not all that bright. Anyone with brains knew to seek shelter in a storm.

"What's for dinner?" Jeremy asked.

"Not chili," Emma pleaded.

Despite herself Nell laughed. "Not chili," she assured her. Her family had been good sports, sampling different variations of her chili recipe for the past few months. Nell was perfecting her recipe and had used her family as taste-testers.

The Chili Cook-off was being held that weekend as part of the Promise Rodeo. These festivities launched spring the way the big Cattlemen's Association dance in June signaled the beginning of summer.

Nell held high hopes that her chili might actually win this year. Her talents in the kitchen were legendary, and she believed she made a great pot of chili. For weeks she'd been combining recipes, adding this, subtracting that. After feeding her family chili twice a week, she was finally satisfied with her recipe.

"Are you going to win the cook-off?" Emma asked.

"Of course she is," Ruth answered before Nell could respond. "I don't see why she shouldn't, seeing she's the best cook this side of the Rio Grande."

Both children nodded enthusiastically, and Nell smiled. "How about porcupine meatballs for dinner?" she suggested. The meatballs, made with rice and cooked in tomato soup, were one of the children's favorites. Jeremy and Emma instantly agreed.

"I'll peel the potatoes," Ruth said. As usual her mother-in-law was willing to lend a hand.

The lights flickered just then, and the house went dark.

"That's okay," Jeremy said. "We don't need electricity. We can roast weenies in the fireplace, can't we?"

"Yeah," Emma seconded. "We could have hot dogs."

"Sounds like a good idea to me." Nell reached for a candle, grateful her children maintained a sense of adventure. They were going to need it when the first dude ranch guests arrived.

CAL PATTERSON shook the moisture from his jacket as he stepped inside out of the driving rain. He removed his Stetson and placed it on the hook just inside the porch to dry. He'd done what he could to protect his herd, gotten his horses into the barn and battened down the shutters where he could. Glen, his brother and business partner, had left for town early in hopes of beating the storm. Cal had worked alone, listening with half an ear for his wife's arrival. He didn't like the idea of Jane driving all the way from town in this kind of weather.

"Cal, is that you?"

His heart rate accelerated at the sound of her voice. "Jane? What the hell are you doing here? Where's your car? I didn't see it."

"I live here, remember?" she teased, joining him in the kitchen porch while he removed his boots. She'd obviously just had a bath and now wore a flannel bathrobe, belted loosely about her waist. "And I didn't park in my usual place because Glen's truck was still there."

"You should've stayed in town," he chastised, but he was delighted she'd managed to make it home. He didn't relish the idea of a night spent without her. Two months of marriage, and he'd grown accustomed to sharing his home and his heart with this woman.

"The clinic closed early," she informed him, "and I've got my beeper. Anyone can reach me in case of a medical emergency."

Cal shed his jacket and slipped his arms around her waist, pulling her close and urging her into the kitchen. His wife was the town's only physician, so there were constant demands on her time. "I don't know if I'll ever be able to stop worrying about you."

"Hey, I'm a big girl."

"Sure you are!" He was about to kiss her when the lights went out. Not that he minded. A romantic interlude wasn't unwelcome.

"I've got a fire going in the fireplace," she whispered, pressing against him, reminding him of the benefits of married life. She looped her arms around his neck and kissed his jaw.

Cal shut his eyes and inhaled her fresh sweet scent. This was about as close to heaven as he expected to get in his lifetime. "I don't suppose you're wearing that see-through nightie of yours?"

"No," she said, "but that could be arranged."

"Now you're talkin'."

Cal felt her smile against his skin. "I love you, Rebel."

Growling, he swung her into his arms and carried her into the living room. Sure enough, a small fire flickered in the fireplace. This had become their favorite room; he'd lost count of the number of times they'd made love in front of the fireplace. The room had a special significance for him, since it was here that he'd first realized how much he'd come to care about her. It was here in this very room that Dr. Texas, as he was fond of calling her, had taken his freeze-dried heart and breathed life into his lonely existence.

Cal was happier than he'd ever thought possible. With each passing day he loved Jane more. Their love had demanded plenty of adjustments on both sides. Sacrifices. But for everything he'd given up, he'd gained so much more.

The storm raged outside and a fair one was building on the living-room carpet when Jane's beeper went off.

Cal groaned and rolled onto his back, inhaling several deep breaths. "That damn well better be important," he muttered.

"Cal!"

"I want someone *real* sick."

Giggling, Jane scrambled for her beeper and read the message. "It's Laredo Smith," she said.

"Wanna bet he's phoning about Savannah?"

"She's just over eight months," Jane said, sounding concerned.

"But Laredo's acting like she's three weeks overdue."

"He's worried, that's all."

Cal figured he would be, too, in Laredo's situation. This was the Smiths' first child, and Savannah was over thirty; as well, Cal knew there'd been some minor complications with the pregnancy. Despite that—and unlike her husband—the mother-to-be remained calm and confident. Savannah had insisted on a home delivery, overriding Laredo's protests.

"This shouldn't take long," Jane promised. She hurried over to the hall phone.

Cal cupped his hands behind his head and watched his wife move through the room, bathed in firelight. Her hair was mussed and her bathrobe hastily tied—and he couldn't recall a time she'd looked more beautiful. It never ceased to amaze him that Jane had agreed to be his wife.

Cal had begun to wonder if someone had spiked the water supply last summer. In less than a year most of his friends had married. First, Savannah Weston had met a stranger to Promise named Laredo Smith and subsequently married him. His own brother had married Ellie Frasier, owner of the local feed store, last September. No sooner had *that* wedding taken place when Grady Weston asked the postmistress, Caroline Daniels, to marry him—all within the space of a few short weeks. Even Sheriff Hennessey had married his longtime sweetheart, Dovie Boyd.

It hadn't been long before Cal fell in love himself.

At one time Cal, Glen and Grady had been confirmed bachelors. With Cal, it had been a form of self-protection, he realized now. He'd been jilted by a former fiancée and the experience had left him bitter, determined never to fall for a woman again.

But that was before he'd met Jane. Their first date was arranged by Ellie. At the time Cal had been annoyed and frustrated that his brand-new sister-in-law was matchmaking. By the end of the evening, however, Jane had managed to pique his interest. To his surprise he discovered he was looking forward to seeing her again. Before he could help himself, he was deeply in love with her.

A city girl. Worse, one from California. If anyone had told him six months ago that he'd marry a woman like Jane, he would have run screaming into the night. Now he couldn't imagine living two minutes without her.

With the phone against her ear, Jane caught her husband's eyes and blew him a kiss. He grinned, content to wait. Relaxing on the rug, he listened to one-half of the conversation.

"Don't worry," Jane was telling Laredo, "you didn't interrupt anything important."

Cal sat upright at that, raising his eyebrows. *Didn't interrupt anything important?* He saw that his wife could barely hold in her laughter at his expression.

But her smile faded as she continued to listen to Laredo. "No . . . no you were right to phone. How long ago did you say her water broke?"

The smile left Cal's face, too. This was more serious than either of them had anticipated.

"How far apart are the contractions?" Jane reached for a pad and pencil and noted the information.

Cal had delivered enough calves to know the signs of imminent birth. Savannah and Laredo were about to have their baby during the worst storm of the year.

"I'll be there within the hour," Jane promised, and replaced the receiver. "Savannah's in labor," she told Cal.

"So I heard." He stood and she walked over to him and caressed the side of his face. "Looks like we'll have to put our romantic interlude on hold."

"I'm a patient man," he reminded her. He caught her fingers and pressed a kiss into her palm. "What time are we leaving?" he asked, snapping his shirt closed as he spoke.

"We?" Jane asked, arching her brows expressively. "I'm perfectly capable of delivering this baby."

"I never doubted it for an instant." He opened her bathrobe, kissed the valley between her breasts and refastened it.

"I can drive in a storm, too."

"I realize that," he said, "but how good are you at keeping two strong-willed ranchers out of your hair?"

"Two?"

"Laredo and Grady." Cal knew his best friend, and Grady would be as nervous as Laredo at the birth of his first niece or nephew. Jane was going to have her hands full, and it wasn't with Savannah or the baby, either. It wouldn't surprise him if father *and* uncle made damned nuisances of themselves. "Trust me, darlin', you'll thank me later."

"Oh, all right, Cal Patterson, you can tag along, too. Now I'd better go change."

He grinned, pleased he'd been able to convince her she was going to need him. Truth be known, he wouldn't miss this birth for anything. It was about time something good happened in that family, especially after Richard Weston's trial and sentencing.

A baby was just what the Westons needed to put their troubles behind them. Cal was determined to celebrate the blessed event with his friends.

TRAVIS GRANT rolled into Promise at precisely the moment the storm struck. He drove down Main Street, peering out between the constantly beating windshield wipers, but he couldn't locate a single hotel. Seeing as his last meal had been aboard a plane and hadn't amounted to much, he decided to stop for dinner and inquire about a place to stay. By the time he found a parking space and raced to the restaurant through the pounding rain, he was soaked to the skin.

He gulped down a glass of water and started on a bowl of tortilla chips with salsa before he even looked at the menu. His stomach growled and he ordered *arroz con pollo,* his favorite Mexican dish.

Gazing out the window, he decided the town was just the way Richard Weston had described it. This was something of a pleasant surprise. Men like Weston weren't exactly known for their truthfulness. Travis had interviewed him shortly after he was sentenced to twenty-five years in a New York prison. No possibility of parole, either. He wouldn't have talked to him at all if it hadn't been for his ex-wife, who'd been Weston's state-appointed attorney. As far as Travis was concerned, Weston was the ultimate sleaze—an opinion that the interview only reinforced.

Knowing his interest in Western ghost towns, Valerie had told him about Weston, a man who'd hidden from the law in an abandoned town buried deep in the Texas hill country. Weston had agreed to an interview—in exchange for certain concessions. The warden of the prison, however, hadn't approved of the idea that Weston should have a TV and sound system in his cell. Weston had consented to the interview, anyway—because it was another opportunity to be the center of attention, Travis figured. Their meeting continued to leave a bad taste in his mouth.

If it hadn't been for Valerie, Travis would have abandoned the entire project, but his ex-wife seemed to have a way with the man.

Valerie. Travis frowned as he thought about her. She'd dumped him and their marriage for another man five years earlier. His lack of malice seemed to disappoint his friends. Frankly, he considered life too short to waste on ill will. He'd loved her, still did, but as she'd so eloquently put it, she'd fallen out of love with him.

She'd remarried as soon as the ink was dry on their divorce papers and seemed content. For that matter, he was, too, although it had taken him longer to achieve peace and he hadn't become involved in another serious relationship. Also, to his friends' surprise, he and Valerie had stayed in touch.

The waiter, a kid of maybe eighteen, delivered a plate heaped with rice and chicken and covered with a thin tomato sauce and melted cheese. "Could you give me directions to the closest motel?" Travis asked him.

"Brewster's got a motel."

"Great." Travis reached for his fork. "How far away is that?"

"About a hundred miles."

He laid his fork back down. "You mean to say a town the size of Promise doesn't have a motel?"

"We've got a bed and breakfast."

"Fine." A bed was a bed, and at this point he wasn't picky.

The waiter lingered. "You might have trouble getting a room, 'cause of the big festivities this weekend."

"Festivities?"

"The rodeo's coming, and then there's the big chili cook-off. I thought that was why you were here."

Apparently the town was small enough to recognize him as a stranger. "Where do the rodeo cowboys stay while they're in town?"

The youth stared at him as if the answer should be obvious. "Motor homes."

"All of them?"

"Unless they got family close by."

"I see," Travis murmured. He hadn't considered that there wouldn't be a motel—but then that was one of his problems, according to Valerie. He didn't think ahead.

"If you'd like, I could write you out directions to the Patterson's B and B."

"Please." Famished, Travis dug into his meal, devouring it in minutes. He'd no sooner finished when the waiter returned with a hand-drawn map listing streets and landmarks. Apparently the one and only bed and breakfast was off the beaten path.

Thunder cracked in the sky, followed by flashes of lightning. No one seemed to pay much heed to the storm until the lights flickered. Everyone in the restaurant paused and waited, then sighed with relief when the lights stayed on.

The storm was bad, but he'd seen worse off the New England coastline five years before. Holed up in a rented cottage in order to meet a deadline, Travis had watched storms rage as he fought his own battles. It'd been shortly after the divorce.

He thought of that sassy ranch woman who'd spoken to him today and wondered what she'd say if she knew he'd stood on a rocky bluff overlooking the sea, with the wind and rain pounding against him, and openly defied nature.

Remembering the way she'd leaped out of her truck, eyes flashing with outrage, brought a rare smile to his lips.

She'd been an attractive woman. Practically as tall as he was and full-sized, not some pencil-thin model. A spitfire, too. Definitely one of a kind. Briefly he wondered if he'd get a chance to see her again and rather hoped he would, just so he could tell her he'd managed to survive the storm.

Following the directions given him by the waiter at the Mexican Lindo, Travis drove to Pattersons' Bed and Breakfast, which turned out to be a large older home. He rang the doorbell.

Almost immediately a tall gray-haired lanky man opened the door and invited him inside. "Welcome to Promise." The man extended his hand and introduced himself as Phil Patterson.

"Travis Grant. Do you have a room for a few nights?" he asked, getting directly to the point.

"Sorry," Phil told him. "We're booked solid."

Travis had left New York early that morning and didn't relish the thought of traveling another hundred miles through a storm to find a bed for the night. "I'm tired and not difficult to please. Isn't there any place that could put me up for a few nights?"

Phil frowned. "The rodeo's coming to town."

"So I understand."

"I doubt there's a room available in Brewster, either."

Travis muttered a curse under his breath.

"Phil." A woman's voice called out from the kitchen. "You might try Nell."

"Nell?"

"Nell Bishop."

Phil sighed. "I know who Nell is."

"She's opening her dude ranch in a couple of months, so she's probably got rooms to rent."

Phil's face relaxed. "Of course, that's a great idea."

Travis's spirits lifted.

"I'll give her a call." Phil reached for the phone, punched in the number and waited. After a minute or two he covered the receiver. "Nell's busy, but her mother-in-law's there and she said you'd be welcome to drive out, but she feels obliged to warn you there's no electricity at the moment."

"They have a bed and clean sheets?"

"Sure thing, and Ruth—that's her name—said she'd throw in breakfast, as well."

He named a price that sounded more than reasonable to Travis. "Sold."

Phil relayed the information, drew him a map, and soon Travis was back on the road.

Patterson had told him that the ranch was a fair distance out of town; still, by the time Travis pulled off the highway and onto the gravel drive that led to Twin Canyons Ranch, he suspected he was closer to Brewster than Promise. Approaching the front door, he felt as though his butt was dragging as low to the ground as his suitcase.

A kid who looked to be about twelve answered his knock and stared blankly at him while Travis stood in the rain.

"Hello," Travis finally said.

"Hello," the boy answered. A girl two or three years younger joined him. Good-looking children, but apparently not all that bright.

"Most people come to the back door unless they're selling something, and if you are, we're not buying."

Despite feeling tired and cranky, Travis grinned. "I'm here about a room."

The two kids exchanged glances.

"Who is it?" He heard an older woman's voice in the background; a moment later, she appeared at the door. "For the love of heaven, young man, come out of the rain." She nudged the children aside and held open the door.

He stood in the hallway, which was all gloom and shadows except for the light flickering from a cluster of candles. Travis glanced around, but it was impossible to see much.

"Mom's in the barn," the boy said.

"I know that," the older woman told him. She put the candle close to Travis's face. "You look decent enough."

"I haven't eaten any children in at least a week," he teased, eyeing the two kids. The little girl moved a step closer to her brother.

"I'm Travis Grant," he said, turning his attention to the woman.

"Ruth Bishop, and these two youngsters are my grandchildren, Jeremy and Emma."

"Pleased to meet you." He shifted the suitcase in his hand, hoping Ruth would take the hint and escort him to his room. She didn't. "About the room . . ." he said pointedly.

"You'll need to meet Nell first."

"All right." He was eager to get the introductions over with so he could fall into bed and sleep for the next twelve hours straight.

"This way." She led him through the house to the back porch, where she pulled on a hooded jacket. Then she walked down the back steps and into the rain, holding her hand over the candle to shield the small flame.

Travis wasn't enthusiastic about clumping through the storm yet again, but didn't have much choice.

"Ruth?" a new voice called into the night. A low pleasant voice.

"Coming," the grandmother answered.

They met halfway across the yard in the pouring rain. "I got us our first paying guest," Ruth announced, beaming proudly. "Travis Grant, meet my daughter-in-law, Nell Bishop."

It took Travis no more than a second to recognize Nell as the woman who'd called him an idiot.

He liked her already.

Two

Nell located an old-fashioned lantern for Travis Grant. It had probably been in the family for fifty years and was nothing if not authentic. Next she gathered together fresh sun-dried sheets, a couple of blankets and a pillow. She tucked everything inside a plastic bag and raced through the storm, holding the lit lantern with one hand. When she arrived at the bunkhouse, Nell discovered Travis sitting on the end of a bed, looking tired and out of sorts.

The initial group of tourists was scheduled to show up the first week of May, and almost everything in the bunkhouse had been readied. It was primitive, but then this was the real thing. A genuine ranch, complete with enough cattle to give would-be cowboys the experience of dealing with a herd, horses for them to ride and plenty of land. Nell was as determined as Curly in the movie *City Slickers* to make real wranglers out of her guests. It was what they were paying her big bucks to do, and she firmly believed in giving them their money's worth.

"Thanks," Travis said when he saw her. He stood up to remove the bag from her arms, and she placed the lantern on a small wooden dresser opposite the bed.

"I realize this isn't the Ritz," she said as she spread the crisp sheet across the thin mattress.

"Hey, beggars can't be choosers," her guest reminded her. "I'm grateful you're willing to take me in at all."

Actually no one had thought to ask her. It was her mother-in-law who'd agreed to put him up for the night when Phil Patterson phoned. But to be fair, Nell suspected she would have agreed herself.

"With the rodeo coming, the Pattersons didn't have any vacancies," he explained unnecessarily, leaning over to help her with the top sheet and blanket.

The lantern actually gave a fair amount of light, much to Nell's chagrin. She chose to pretend she didn't recognize him. And either he was too tired to remember the way she'd harangued him at the side of the road or he'd decided to forget. Whatever the case, she was grateful.

"Does the Texas hill country generally get storms like this?"

"This one's worse than some," she told him, lifting the edge of the mattress to tuck in the covers. Given his size, she wondered if the bunk would be big enough for him. Well, there was no help for it, since this bed—or another exactly like it—was the only one available.

"What about losing your electricity?"

"Happens now and then," she said, not looking at him. She reached for the pillow and stuffed it inside the case, then plumping it up, set it at the head of the bed. "Is there anything else I can get you?" she asked, ready to return to her family.

"Nothing. I appreciate your putting me up," he said again.

"No problem."

"Mom." Breathless, Jeremy burst into the bunkhouse, his face bright. He carried a blue-speckled tin coffeepot in one hand and a matching cup in the other. Emma followed with a covered plate.

"Grandma sent us over with hot chocolate and—"

"—one of Mom's cinnamon rolls," Emma finished for her brother. Travis could see a black-and-white dog waiting patiently at the door.

He took the pot and cup from Jeremy and set them on the night-stand. "Hey, no one said anything about room service. How'd I get so lucky?"

Emma handed him the plate. "My mom's the best cook in the world."

Nell grinned and put an arm around each of her children. "Now probably isn't the time to mention we roasted hot dogs in the fireplace for dinner."

"Are you staying for the chili cook-off?" Emma asked their guest.

"I wouldn't miss it for the world." Travis sat on the side of the bed and poured himself a mug of steaming cocoa.

Nell wasn't sure how Ruth had managed to heat the cocoa—the fireplace, she supposed—but was pleased her mother-in-law had made the effort.

"Mom's going to win. Her chili's the best."

"Emma's opinion might be a little biased," Nell said, steering the two children toward the door. "Let us know if you need anything."

"I will. Good night," Travis said as they left to go back to the house.

Nell turned and smiled when she saw that he'd already started on the cinnamon roll with the appreciation of a man who rarely tasted anything homemade.

The children ran across the yard ahead of her. Lucky, their border-collie mix, followed at their heels. Ruth waited for Nell in the kitchen, holding the candle and looking inordinately pleased with herself.

"Travis Grant seems like a nice young man," she said the moment Nell entered the kitchen.

"He's from New York City," Nell said, wanting it understood right then and there that he was a big-city boy and only drifting through Promise. It just so happened that he'd ventured into a strange town and needed a place to sleep; there'd be plenty of guests just like him in the months to come.

"We have a big day tomorrow," Nell said. "It wouldn't hurt any of us to get to bed early for once."

As she'd expected, her children put up token protests, but they didn't argue long. Both were tired and, without electricity, there was little to entertain them. The lights probably wouldn't be coming on soon, especially with the rain and the wind still so intense.

"Did our guest mention what he's doing in Promise?" Ruth asked. She held her hand protectively in front of the flame of the candle she carried and led the way across the living room.

Nell wondered, too. "He didn't say."

"You could've asked."

"Well, I didn't. That's his business, not mine."

"Weren't you curious?"

"A little." A lot actually, but Nell wasn't willing to admit it.

"He's probably here for the rodeo," Jeremy suggested, heading up the stairs, Lucky at his side.

"Maybe, but I don't think so." Nell wasn't sure why she thought that, but she did. Her guess was that when morning came Travis Grant would pack up his bags and leave.

"He reminds me of someone," Emma said, and yawned.

"Me, too," Jeremy murmured.

Jake. Nell had seen it, too, not in looks but in build. Travis Grant was a lumberjack of a man, just the way her beloved Jake had been. Sadly the children's memories of their father had dimmed with time into vague recollections.

The family stood at the landing at the top of the stairs, where they exchanged good-night hugs and kisses. Even Jeremy let his mother and grandma kiss him tonight. Ruth guided the children to their bedrooms while Nell retrieved a candle for herself.

Once everyone was in bed, she undressed and put on a full-length white cotton nightgown. She unbraided her hair and brushed it out, the thick dark tresses reaching halfway down her back. Jake had loved her hair, had often gathered it in his huge hands and run it through his fingers. Nell missed those moments, missed everything about Jake.

Time, she'd discovered, was a great healer, just as Pastor McMillen had told her. The grief became duller, less acute, with every month and year that passed. But it was still there, always there. Now though, her grief shared space with all the good memories, the happy moments they'd had together.

Nothing would ever erase those ten wonderful years she'd shared with the man she loved.

Setting her hairbrush aside, Nell pulled back the covers and climbed into bed. She leaned against the headboard, her back supported by two pillows, and opened the drawer in her nightstand. She took out a pen and her journal.

By the light of a single candle, she wrote down the events of the day, pausing now and then to collect her thoughts. When she'd finished, she reread what she'd written, something she rarely did, and was surprised to note she'd mentioned Travis Grant in the first line. It didn't take her long to figure out why.

It was because he was like Jake and meeting him had shaken her. Not the first time on the road into town, when she'd stopped and read him the riot act, but later. It hadn't hit her until they stood across from each other to make the bed. He was the same height as Jake.

Nell reached for the framed photograph of Jake taken on their wedding day. It was a rare shot of him without his Stetson. Fresh from the military, his hair had been cropped close. He looked strong, capable—and oddly vulnerable.

Her heart clenched as it always did when she studied the photograph, but the usual tears didn't come.

"Good night, my love," she whispered, and placed the photograph back on her nightstand. As she did, Nell saw a light come on outside the window. Tossing the blankets aside, she peered out and noticed a bright even glow coming from the bunkhouse. The electricity was back on.

"I don't know how much longer this is going to take," Laredo Smith said as he reappeared to give another update on Savannah's progress. He'd practically worn grooves in the carpet from the bedroom to the living room where the men had gathered. Rain continued to beat against the window and there were occasional flashes of lightning, although the storm had begun to let up.

Grady smiled indulgently at his brother-in-law, grateful that the electricity was back on. "Babies take as long as they take," he said wisely. He reclined in the leather chair and laced his fingers behind his head, rather pleased with his insight.

"That's easy for you to say," Laredo snapped in a rare display of temper. "It's not *your* wife in there giving birth to your child. Let's see how calm you are when Caroline delivers."

The grin faded from Grady's face. Laredo had a point.

"Birthing babies is a whole lot different from bringing calves into the world," Cal said. Grady's best friend leaned forward and rested his arms on his knees, then glanced at his watch.

Grady was surprised when he checked the time. It was already past midnight, and it could be hours more before Savannah's baby was born. Not one of the assembled group showed any sign of being tired, much less leaving. Caroline and Jane were with Savannah, and his daughter was in bed upstairs. Six-year-old Maggie had tried to stay awake but fell asleep in his arms around ten.

Laredo had been with Savannah from the first, but returned to the living room periodically to make his reports. Grady watched his brother-in-law with interest. Laredo was so pale he looked in danger of passing out.

"I had no idea it would be like this," Laredo mumbled, ramming all ten fingers through his hair.

"That it'd take this long?" Grady asked.

Laredo vigorously shook his head. "No—that I'd feel this scared, this nervous. Savannah and I must've read ten books about pregnancy and birth, and I thought I was ready. Hell, man, I've been around horses and cattle all my life, but this is nothing like I expected."

Those books were the very ones Grady and Caroline were reading now. His wife was two months pregnant. Grady had been walking on air from the moment she'd told him. He'd thought about the baby a lot, his excitement building as he watched his own sister's pregnancy progress. He and Caroline had told only a few people, since she was months from showing.

To Grady, his wife had never looked more beautiful. Maggie was pleased and excited at the prospect of becoming a big sister. What Grady hadn't considered was this strange emotion Laredo exhibited.

Fear.

He hadn't thought of his child's birth as a frightening event. He'd imagined himself a proud father, holding his infant son or daughter. He enjoyed the prospect of people making a fuss and giving their opinions on which parent the baby resembled. Friends would come to visit and it would be a time of celebration and joy.

But tonight Laredo had destroyed his illusions. In his imaginings, Grady had glossed over the actual birth. Until now. Beyond any doubt, he knew that when it was Caroline's time to deliver their child, he'd be as bad as Laredo. Pacing, worrying, wondering. Praying.

"I'm going back in there," Laredo announced as though he couldn't bear to be away from Savannah a moment longer.

Grady stood, slapped his friend on the back to encourage him, then sank into his seat again.

"We're going to be just like him, you know," Cal said.

Grady nodded in agreement. "Worse, probably."

Cal grinned. "When's Caroline due?"

"The end of October."

"You two certainly didn't waste any time, did you?" Cal teased.

"Nope." Their wedding had been the last week of October, and Caroline was pregnant by the first week of January. They'd hoped it would happen quickly, seeing as Grady was already well into his thirties and Maggie was going on seven. It made sense to start their family early.

As the wind howled, Cal looked out the window. "Why is it babies are always born during a storm?"

"It probably has something to do with barometric pressure."

Cal scratched his head. "You think so?"

The hell if Grady knew, but it sounded good. The phone pealed in the kitchen and the two men stared at each other.

"It's probably Glen and Ellie again," Cal said.

Cal's brother and his wife lived in town and would have been with them, Grady suspected, if not for the storm.

Grady answered the phone. "Nothing yet," he said, instead of his usual greeting.

"Why didn't anyone phone me?" Dovie Boyd Hennessey demanded. Dovie and Savannah had been close since the death of Savannah's mother, Barbara, seven years earlier. Dovie owned and operated the antique shop, which sold everything from old scarves and jewelry to valuable china cups and saucers, all arranged around antique furnishings. The women in town loved to shop at Dovie's; she was universally admired and treasured by the town.

"Savannah's in labor and I only *now* find out," Dovie said, as though she'd missed the social event of the year.

"Who told you?" Grady asked. The women in Promise had a communication system the CIA could envy.

"Frank, naturally," Dovie told him. "I guess he talked to Laredo earlier this evening. He just got home." She paused for breath. "Has the baby come yet?"

"Nope, and according to Jane, it could be hours before the blessed event."

"How's Savannah?"

"Better than Laredo," Grady said.

Dovie's soft laugh drifted over the line. "Give her my love?"

"Of course."

"And call me the minute you hear, understand? I don't care what time of day or night it is."

"You got it," he said on the tail end of a yawn.

"Don't let me down, Grady."

"I wouldn't dream of it," he assured her.

By the time he returned to the living room, Cal had picked up a magazine and was flipping through the pages.

"You read that one an hour ago," Grady reminded him.

"So I did."

A few minutes later Caroline came into the room, and Grady leaped to his feet. "Sit down," he urged his wife. "You look exhausted." She should have been in bed hours ago, but he knew better than to suggest it. Caroline was as stubborn as they came, but then so was he. They understood each other, and he could appreciate her need to be with her best friend.

"It won't be long now," she told him as she slid her arms around his waist. "The baby's crowned."

Grady nodded. "Wonderful. How's Savannah?"

"She's doing well."

"And Laredo?"

"He's holding Savannah's hand and helping her with her breathing." Grady sat down, pulling Caroline onto his lap. She pressed her head against his shoulder, and he kissed her temple.

Grady glanced in Cal's direction and found he'd folded his arms and shut his eyes. Caroline's eyes were closed, too, and Grady decided to rest his own. Just for a few minutes, he told himself.

An infant's cry shattered the silence. Grady jerked awake and Caroline jumped to her feet and shook her head. "Oh, my goodness!" she gasped.

Grady hadn't a clue how long they'd been out. Cal straightened and rubbed his eyes with the heels of his hands.

"The kid's got one hell of a pair of lungs."

A few minutes later the bedroom door opened and Laredo emerged, carrying a tiny bundle in his arms. Grady noted that his friend's eyes were bright and his cheeks tear-streaked.

"We have a daughter," he said, gazing with awe at the baby he held. "Laura Rose, meet your family," he whispered to the newborn. "This is your uncle Grady and aunt Caroline."

"Hey, don't forget me," Cal said, stepping over to gaze down at the baby.

"That's Cal," Laredo continued. "His wife's the one who coaxed you into the world." Laredo gazed at the small group gathered around the baby. "Isn't she beautiful?" he said. "Doesn't she look like Savannah?"

Grady studied Laura Rose carefully and decided she looked more like an alien, but he certainly didn't say so.

Another hour passed before Grady and Caroline were in their own home and their own bed. Fortunately the rain had ended. Grady had carried a sleeping Maggie from Savannah's place to the car and then into her room; she never did wake up. He was exhausted, too. This had been a night to remember. His sister was a mother, and for the first time in his life he was an uncle. Damn, but it felt good.

Caroline pulled back the covers and joined him. She sighed as her head hit the pillow. "Did anyone phone Dovie?" she asked.

"I did," Grady said as he reached for the light.

"Good." Caroline rolled onto her side. "I think I could sleep for a week," she mumbled.

Grady drew his wife close, cuddling her spoon-fashion. His arm went around her and he flattened his hand against her stomach and grinned, feeling extraordinarily happy. Soon Laura Rose would have a cousin.

TRAVIS AWOKE and lay in the warm bed, unwilling to face the bright morning light. Not just yet, anyway. Something warm nestled against his feet, and he was content to stay exactly as he was for a few more minutes.

Despite his exhaustion, he'd had a hard time falling asleep. It didn't help that his legs stuck out a good six inches over the end of the bed. Those cowboys must've been pretty short guys, he thought wryly.

His eyes flew open as his toes felt something damp and ticklish. He bolted upright to find a goat standing at the foot of the bed, chewing for all it was worth. It didn't take Travis long to realize that the animal had eaten the socks clean off his feet. All that remained were a few rows of ribbing on his ankles.

Obviously, once he'd fallen asleep, he'd slept deeply—the sleep of the jet-lagged. He laughed and wiggled his toes just to be sure the socks were the only thing the goat had enjoyed. So far, so good.

"Yucky, what are you doing in here?"

The door flew open and Nell's boy—Jeremy, if Travis remembered correctly—rushed inside.

The boy planted his hands on his hips and glared at the goat.

"Morning," Travis said.

"Hi." Jeremy smiled and must have noticed Travis's feet for the first time because he burst out laughing. "Yucky ate your socks!"

"So I noticed."

"Sorry," Jeremy said, sounding anything but. He covered his mouth to hide a giggle, which made the situation even more amusing. "Mom said to tell you breakfast will be ready in twenty minutes if you're interested."

Travis didn't need a second invitation. His stomach growled at the mere mention of food. If the cinnamon roll the night before was any indication, Nell Bishop was one hell of a cook.

Travis dressed, showered and shaved, entering the kitchen just as Nell set a platter of scrambled eggs and bacon on the table.

"Morning," he greeted her.

"Morning," she returned, and poured him a mug of coffee.

Travis gratefully accepted it and pulled out a chair. Nell joined him and the children, and the three bowed their heads for grace. The instant they were through, Jeremy reached for the platter.

His mother sent him a warning glance and Jeremy immediately passed the platter to Travis. "Here," the boy said. "You're our guest. Please help yourself."

Travis was impressed with the boy's manners. So many children didn't seem to have any these days. He forked some fluffy scrambled eggs onto his plate and took a piece of toast from a bread basket in the center of the table. He gave Nell a sidelong glance as she buttered her own toast. She was obviously doing her best to be a good mother. The owner of the B and B had told him Nell was a widow, and he admired her for the loving manner in which she schooled her children.

"You collected all the eggs?" Nell asked Emma, interrupting his thoughts.

"Yes, Mama."

"Did you check under Bertha?"

The little girl grinned and nodded.

"I understand," Nell said, turning to Travis, "that we owe you a pair of socks."

He glanced up from his plate and saw that her mouth quivered with the beginnings of a smile.

"Best darn pair I owned."

"Your feet must've been pretty ripe to attract Yucky's attention," Jeremy said.

Travis couldn't help it; he burst out laughing. Nell, however, didn't take kindly to her son's comment. Jeremy read his mother's look and mumbled an apology.

Breakfast was wonderful, the food even better than he'd expected and the company delightful.

As soon as the kids had finished, they excused themselves and set their plates in the sink, then rushed out the back door.

"The children have animals to tend before they catch the school bus," Nell explained before he could voice his question.

"I see."

"Jeremy's got rabbits. Then there's Yucky, whom you've already met."

"We have a close and personal relationship," he said, leaning back in his chair, savoring the last of his coffee.

"Currently we have twelve horses, but I plan on buying several more. Jeremy feeds them grain and alfalfa, and Emma makes sure they have plenty of water. I'll be mucking out the stalls later this morning."

Travis could see that they had their chores down to a science and admired the way they all worked together. Briefly he wondered about Ruth, but guessed she reserved her strength for later in the day.

Nell cleared the remaining dishes from the table. "Take your time," she said as she put on a sweater and headed toward the door.

"Can I help?" he asked.

"Not at all. Just enjoy your coffee."

Travis did as she suggested and watched from the window as Nell and the children worked together. They were a real team, efficient and cooperative. Half an hour later Jeremy and Emma raced into the house and grabbed their lunch boxes from the counter.

"We gotta go to school now," Emma said, staring at Travis as though she'd much rather spend the day with him.

Jeremy was on his way out when he paused. "Will you be here to-night?"

Travis had to think about that. "Probably."

"I hope you are," the boy said. "It's nice having another man around the place." And with that, he flew out the door.

Travis rinsed his mug and set it beside the kitchen sink. He met Nell as he left the house. "Do you mind if I plug my computer into an outlet in the bunkhouse? I want to get some work done while I'm here."

"Not at all," she said, her smile congenial.

Whistling, Travis returned to the bunkhouse and retrieved his portable computer from his bag. With a minimum of fuss, he located an outlet and set up shop. The computer hummed its usual greeting as the screen saver reminded him that he was one hell of a good writer—a message he'd programmed in to battle the deluge of self-doubts all writers faced.

The note was just the boost his ego needed before he dug into his latest project. He'd achieved indisputable success with his series of Western stories for preadolescents and young teens. The book he planned to write next might possibly be his best; he could feel that even before he wrote the first word. A mainstream novel set in a Western ghost town— his editor had been ecstatic over the idea.

Travis never did the actual writing while he was on the road, but he wanted to document facts about the storm from the night before. One of his characters was sure to lose his socks to a hungry goat, too. He prided himself on the authenticity of his details, although in his past books, most of that background had come from research.

Rarely did anything happen to him that didn't show up in a book sometime, one way or another. He used to think he kept his personal life out of his work, but that was a fallacy. Anyone who really knew him could follow his life by reading his books. The connections weren't always direct. Take the end of his marriage, for example. Of the two books he'd written the year of his divorce, one took place in Death Valley and the other on the River of No Return. Those locations had corresponded to his emotional state at the time.

He didn't want to stop and analyze why a ghost town appealed to him now. Maybe because his life felt empty and he struggled with loneliness. Travis realized without surprise that he envied Nell her children.

He entered notes about Texas, the drive from San Antonio, his impressions of the landscape and the people. The storm was described in plenty of detail. He made notes about Nell and her children. Ruth, too.

The next time he glanced up, he was shocked to discover it was midmorning. He stored the information onto a computer file and headed for the kitchen, hoping Nell kept a pot of coffee brewing during the day. He didn't expect to see her, since she had stalls to muck out and plenty of other chores, many of which he knew next to nothing about.

He was pleasantly surprised to find her in the kitchen.

"Hello again," he said.

"Hi."

The spicy aroma of whatever she was cooking made him instantly hungry, despite the fact that he'd enjoyed one of the finest breakfasts he'd eaten in years.

"What are you making?" he asked. He noticed a can of beer sitting by the stove at—he glanced at his watch—10:35 a.m.! He wondered with some concern if she was a drinker . . . but then he saw her add it to whatever was in the large cast-iron pot.

"It's chili," she said. "Would you like a taste?"

"I'd love it."

Nell dished up a small bowl and brought it to the table where Travis sat. "This might sound like a silly question, but did you happen to mention to Ruth how many nights you intend to stay?"

He delayed his first sample, wondering if Nell was looking for a way to get rid of him. He'd be keenly disappointed if that was the case. He happened to like Twin Canyons Ranch. His visit would add texture and realism to his novel. And being here was so much more *interesting* than staying at a hotel, or even at a bed and breakfast.

"I'm not sure yet," Travis said in answer to her question.

He tried the chili. The instant his mouth closed over the spoon he realized this was the best-tasting chili he'd ever eaten, bar none. The flavors somersaulted across his tongue.

"What do you think?" she asked, her big brown eyes hopeful.

"If you don't win that prize, I'll want to know why." He scooped up a second spoonful.

"You're not just saying that, are you?" Her eyes went from hopeful to relieved.

"If I was the judge I'd award you the prize money without needing to taste anyone else's. This is fabulous."

Nell's freshly scrubbed face glowed with a smile. Travis had seen his share of beautiful women, but he felt few would compare with Nell Bishop and her unspoiled beauty. The kind she possessed didn't require makeup to enhance it. She was as real as a person could get.

"I made a terrible mistake when I saw you on the road yesterday," she said, suddenly frowning a little.

"How's that?"

"I implied you were . . . not too bright." She pulled out a chair and sat across the table from him. "I was wrong. You're obviously very bright, indeed!"

Three

"**H**ow come *you* were asked to be one of the judges for the chili cook-off?" Glen asked Ellie as they walked toward the rodeo grounds. The air was charged with excitement.

"Just clean living," his wife replied, and did her best to disguise a smile. Actually it had more to do with her participation in the Chamber of Commerce. But her husband had done nothing but complain from the moment he learned she'd been asked to judge the chili. It was a task he would have relished.

"I'm the one who happens to love chili," he lamented—not for the first time.

Unable to help herself, Ellie laughed out loud. "If you want, I'll put your name in as a judge for next year," she said, hoping that would appease him.

"You'd do that?" They strolled hand in hand toward the grandstand. Luckily the ground had dried out after the recent rain. The rodeo was one of the most popular events of the year, along with the big summer dance and the Willie Nelson Fourth of July picnic. The town council always invited Willie to the picnic, but he had yet to accept. With or without him, it was held in his honor, and his music was piped through the park all day.

"Sure will. I'll let Dovie know you want to be a judge next year," Ellie promised. "Consider it just one of the many benefits of marrying a local businesswoman."

Glen wrapped his arm about her waist and gave her a squeeze. "I know all about those benefits," he said, and kissed the top of her head.

He raised his hand so that it rested just beneath her breast. "Glen," she warned under her breath.

He sighed and lowered his hand to her waist.

Ellie saw Jane and Cal and waved. Dr. Texas immediately returned her wave, and the two couples sauntered toward each other.

"So you're going through with it," Glen said when he saw his brother.

"I can't talk him out of it," Jane said, rolling her eyes.

"I've competed in the bull-riding competition for ten years," Cal argued. "Besides, if I'm injured, I know one hell of a fine physician who'll treat me with tender loving care." He winked at his wife.

From the look Jane tossed her husband, Ellie suspected she'd be inclined to let him suffer. Grinning, she reflected on how well her matchmaking efforts had worked. She gladly accepted credit for pairing Cal with Jane; the match had been brilliant, if she did say so herself. Jane had moved to Promise as part of a government program in which she agreed to work for three years at the community health clinic in exchange for payment of her college loans.

Cal, of course, had been burned in the romance department several years earlier when his fiancée had dumped him a few days before their wedding and skipped town. In addition to the hurt and rejection he'd suffered, Cal had been left to deal with the embarrassment and the questions that followed. For years afterward he'd refused to have anything to do with women.

Until Jane.

She'd moved to town after living her entire life in California. Poor Jane had been completely and totally out of her element until Dovie took charge. One of the first things Dovie had done was introduce her to Ellie.

In the beginning Ellie wasn't sure it was possible for them to be friends. Jane had an attitude about all things Texan, and it rubbed her— and just about everyone in town—the wrong way. Everything she said and did had an air of superiority.

Jane's start had been rocky, that was for sure. Ellie smiled as she remembered that first lunch in which she'd suggested Jane take her wine-sipping, quiche-eating butt and go back where she'd come from. She was grateful now that Jane had decided to stick it out.

When Ellie set up the date between her distrustful brother-in-law and the doctor-with-attitude, she knew she was taking a chance. It would have been just like Cal to take one look at the setup and walk out of the restaurant. He hadn't. In fact, he'd shocked both Glen and Ellie when they discovered that he'd agreed to give Jane horseback-riding lessons.

They were married within six months and Cal was happier than she could ever recall seeing him. He hardly seemed like the same person.

"I have a feeling I could win this year," Cal said.

"He's been claiming that every year since he first entered," Glen muttered just loudly enough for everyone to hear.

"I'm gonna win," Cal insisted, defying his brother to challenge him.

"This is a man thing," Ellie explained to her sister-in-law. "Glen competes in the calf-roping event."

"I have the *blue* ribbons to prove it."

Cal winced at the small dig. "Ouch, little brother."

"Calf roping I can tolerate, but watching Cal on those huge bulls is something else again." Jane looked at her husband, and Ellie saw a spark of genuine fear in her friend's eyes. She had to admit she was grateful Glen wouldn't be competing on the bulls.

"I've done everything I know to talk him out of this," Jane confided as the two women made their way to the grandstand and found seats in the second row. Both men were by the chutes, chatting with their friends and making small talk with the professional rodeo riders.

Jane clenched her hands in her lap.

"It'll be fine," Ellie assured her. "Cal's no fool."

"How can you say that?" Jane said, biting her lip. "Only a fool would risk his neck riding an ill-tempered beast who weighs as much as the state of Texas."

Ellie laughed.

"If . . . if Cal happened to get hurt, I don't know if I'd be able to treat him."

"You love him that much?" Ellie asked.

"Yes, but that's not the reason. I don't think I could stop myself from clobbering him for worrying me like this."

Ellie laughed outright, although she understood.

The grandstand quickly filled to capacity as the competition time neared.

"I heard a wild rumor," Ellie said, hoping to distract Jane from her worries. "Someone told me Willie Nelson might make a surprise appearance at the dance later this evening."

"You're joking!"

She shook her head. "I don't know if it's true, but that's what people are saying."

"That would be wonderful. What brought it about?"

"I've heard he likes surprising people now and then." She gave a slight shrug. "He knows this is Willie country and he's never been able to come to our Fourth of July picnics. Maybe that's why."

"My parents went to hear him recently," Jane said. "They said he isn't going to replace the Beach Boys in their eyes, but the music was entertaining."

"Give 'em time," Ellie said.

The calf-roping event was one of the first on the program, and Ellie wasn't surprised when Glen took first place. She loved the way he raced after the calf, roped him on the first try and maneuvered the animal onto its back. He made it all look so easy. But when he tied the animal's legs, then tossed his hands in the air and leaped back, his eyes didn't go to the time. Instead, they zeroed in on Ellie and he'd smiled that secret little smile meant for her alone. Only then did his gaze go to the clock.

When his time was announced, Ellie jumped to her feet and applauded loudly. Pursing her lips around her index finger and thumb, she released a piercing whistle. Jane stood with her and the two of them made several victory punches in the air.

"How long before Cal rides?" Jane asked after they sat back down.

"Pretty soon."

Jane placed her hands between her knees and took several deep breaths. Ellie gently patted her shoulder. "Hey, it's only eight seconds."

"A bull like that could kill him in one."

Ellie let the comment slide. "Cal knows what he's doing."

Jane nodded, but she looked pale. Ellie realized how difficult this was for her. Not having been raised around cattle ranches, Jane must view these competitions as barbaric. Ellie decided she hadn't given her sister-in-law the credit she was due for marrying into this whole new way of life.

When the competition had begun and Cal's name was announced, Jane bit her lip and closed her eyes. Cal sat high in the chute on the bull's back, his concentration intense. The door opened, and man and beast plunged forward. The bull snorted, shaking his massive head, determined to dislodge his rider.

Jane leaped to her feet and covered her mouth with her hand. Ellie had just stood up, too, when Cal went flying off the bull's back. There was a collective drawing in of breath as the crowd waited for him to jump out of the bull's way. The clowns diverted the bull's attention, but Cal remained on the ground.

"Dear God!" Jane cried. "He's hurt. I knew it, I knew it." She was already stumbling past everyone in the row, Ellie right behind her. "I swear if that fall didn't kill him, I will."

By the time they made it down to the steps, Cal had been carried off the grounds on a stretcher. Just as they reached him, they heard the final contestant's name being called.

Glen, who was with his brother, took Ellie's hand. Jane knelt beside her husband, tears in her eyes.

"It's all right, honey," Cal said, clutching his ribs. He gave her a smile but was clearly in pain.

"He's had the wind knocked out of him," Glen said.

Jane began to unfasten Cal's shirt.

"Jane—not in front of all these people," Cal said in a feeble attempt at humor.

"Be quiet," she snapped.

"Best not to cross her in this frame of mind," Cal said, then groaned when Jane lightly pressed her fingertips against a rib.

"I'll need X rays, but my guess is you've broken a rib."

"It won't be the first."

"But it'll be the last one you'll ever get riding bulls," Jane said in a voice few would question.

"Whatever you say."

"You might want to take this with you." Max Jordan, a local business owner, hurried over to join them.

"Take what?" Glen asked.

Max grinned broadly and handed Cal a blue ribbon. "Congratulations, Cal! You stayed on longer than anyone."

Despite the pain it must have cost him, Cal let out a loud triumphant cry.

TRAVIS HAD BEEN WRITING for years. He'd researched rodeos and even written about them—but this was the first one he'd actually attended. Jeremy and Emma had volunteered to be his guides, and he welcomed their company. Nell was busy adding the final touches to her chili; judging would take place later in the afternoon. The last time he'd seen Ruth, she'd introduced him to two friends, Edwina and Lily Moorhouse, sisters and retired schoolteachers. One of them had mentioned something about cloves—cloves?—a special cordial, and the next thing he knew, all three women had disappeared. Made no sense to him.

Now that the rodeo was over, Jeremy and Emma decided it was time to show Travis the booths. It seemed everyone in town had something on display. All new to Travis. The closest thing New York had to this was the farmers' market, in which everything from rip-off brand-name running shoes and "real" French perfume to home-grown vegetables and spicy sausages was sold.

Travis and the kids wandered by the long tables where the chili was being cooked. "Hi, Mom," Emma called.

At the sound of her daughter's voice, Nell turned. She wore a pretty blue cotton dress with a white bib apron over it.

"I wondered where you two had wandered off," she said.

"The kids are playing tour guide," Travis explained. "They're doing a good job of showing me the ropes." He ruffled Jeremy's hair, and the youngster grinned up at him.

"I hope they aren't making a nuisance of themselves."

"On the contrary." They were likable kids, and seeing the rodeo and other festivities through their eyes had been a bonus.

"I'll get my purse so you can buy your lunch," Nell told her children.

"That's all right, Mom," Emma said. "Travis already fed us."

Nell's gaze briefly met his.

"We didn't ask," Jeremy added, apparently recognizing the look in his mother's eyes.

"It was the least I could do," Travis said, not understanding why she'd be disturbed about something so minor.

"My children and I pay our own way, Mr. Grant," she said before he could say anything else.

"It was my pleasure, Nell—honestly. Without Jeremy and Emma, I would've been lost." Both kids had taken delight in tutoring him in each of the rodeo events. They'd also shared tidbits about the community and its traditions, and the education he'd gained had been well worth the price of a couple of hamburgers and ice-cream bars.

"When are the judges going to be here?" Emma asked.

Nell glanced at her watch. "Not for another hour."

"You're gonna win," Jeremy said with confidence.

"I'm crossing my fingers for you, Mom." Emma held up both hands to show her.

"Good luck," Travis tossed in.

"We're headed for the carnival now," Jeremy said. "I promise I won't spend all my allowance."

Nell nodded and glanced at Travis. "Listen, everyone, I'm sorry, I didn't mean to snap at you earlier. I guess I'm more nervous than I realized about this contest."

"That's all right, Mom."

"No apology necessary," Travis said, thinking it was unusual these days to find anyone willing to apologize. It was a sign of maturity and inner strength, and he admired her for it. In fact, there seemed to be quite a bit to admire about Nell Bishop. . . .

"Have fun at the carnival," she said, stirring her chili.

"We will."

"If they don't mind, I'll tag along just for the fun of it," Travis said to Nell. He couldn't recall the last time he'd been on a Ferris wheel—probably when he was younger than these two; and maybe he could convince Jeremy and Emma to go on it with him.

He'd never spent much time around kids, although his books were geared to them. Life was full of ironies such as this, he reflected. Valerie used to say he related to children because he'd never grown up himself, and he supposed it was true. She'd meant it as an insult, but Travis had considered it a compliment.

They had a wonderful afternoon on the midway, and he loved every minute. He let Jeremy and Emma spend part of their allowance, but he paid for most of the rides. They went on the octopus, a ride he remembered from his boyhood, and Emma covered her eyes, screamed the entire time, then insisted they do it again.

"Don't spend all your money on us," Emma said when he bought them each a huge cotton candy.

Travis was half-tempted to say there was plenty more where that came from, but decided it would be a crass comment. "Don't worry . . ." he began.

"Be happy," Jeremy completed for him.

"Right," Travis said, and chuckled. He enjoyed children, always had. That was one reason he'd chosen to write for the age group he did. His overwhelming success had surprised even him.

"In that case, could I have some popcorn, too?" Emma asked.

Laughter bubbled up inside him. Both of these children were forthright and honest, hardworking and appreciative—and they had a sense of humor. It would be unfair to compare them to children in New York, since he knew so few, but he was sure these two were special. As special as their mother.

"Have you met Dovie?" Emma asked a short while later between mouthfuls of popcorn.

Dovie—not dove. A name. "No, I haven't."

"You gotta meet Dovie," Jeremy said, directing him away from the carnival rides.

They led him to a large booth set up close to the chili cook-off area. A friendly slightly rotund older woman stood in front of a colorful patchwork quilt.

"Hi, Dovie," Jeremy said.

"Hi, Dovie," Emma echoed.

"Hello, Dovie." Travis figured he didn't want to be left out.

Dovie looked at him and blinked, as if she was afraid she should've recognized him and hadn't. Jeremy and Emma burst out laughing.

"This is Travis," Emma said, and reached for his hand. It was an innocent gesture, but it tugged at his heart.

"He's staying at the ranch," Jeremy added.

"From what I hear, I'm the first paying guest," Travis explained.

"Pleased to meet you," Dovie said, holding out her hand. "I don't mean to be rude, but I'm wondering if I could interest you in a raffle ticket for this fine quilt."

"Of course." Travis reached for his wallet.

"The Dorcas Group at church is raffling it off to raise money for missions."

"How much?"

"A dollar each, or six for five dollars."

Travis pulled a ten from his wallet. "Give me twelve tickets."

Dovie flashed him an appreciative smile.

"He's a good guy," Jeremy said proudly.

"I like him, too," Emma added.

Travis tucked the ticket stubs securely into his hip pocket and wished Dovie luck with the quilt.

"Thank you. How long will you be in town?" she asked.

It'd been a common question all day. "I'm not sure yet."

"I hope you enjoy yourself."

Emma took his hand again. "You ready?" she asked. "For the chili judging?"

"Sure," he returned.

"Is it time?" Jeremy asked.

Emma nodded.

A crowd had gathered around the chili cook-off area and the judges, five of them, stepped forward to do their taste tests. The samples were numbered so it was impossible to tell who had cooked which chili.

"That's Ellie Patterson," Jeremy whispered. "She owns the local feed store." A pretty brunette sampled the first taste and nodded in approval.

"I hope that was Mom's," Emma said.

So did Travis. The taste she'd given him the day before was fabulous and nothing like any chili he'd tasted before. He'd accidentally discovered her secret ingredient was beer but had been sworn to secrecy.

In his short visit he'd learned quite a bit about Texas chili, which was different from anything he'd tasted in New York City or on his previous travels. In Texas the chili was thick with meat and spices and it wasn't made with beans.

"That's Mr. Jordan," Jeremy said, identifying the next judge. "He owns the Western-wear shop."

Someone called Billy D, owner of the local tavern, and Adam Braunfels, a restaurateur, tasted next.

The last one to try the chili samples was a large rancher type.

"Who's that?" Travis asked.

"Pastor McMillen," Jeremy whispered back.

That surprised Travis. The man looked like he'd be more comfortable on a horse than in a pulpit.

After all the judges had sampled the entries, they cast their votes. The crowd grew quiet with anticipation as the town sheriff, Frank Hennessey, stepped forward with the results of the voting.

Emma stood next to Travis with her eyes tightly shut, her hands raised and fingers crossed.

Sheriff Hennessey cleared his throat. "It was a difficult decision this year, but it appears that one entry stood out as the most flavorful. The voting is unanimous. The winner is—" the faint sound of a drumroll could be heard in the background "—number five."

Travis frowned, not knowing who the winner was until he noticed Nell. She stood there as though in a daze.

"Nell Bishop," Frank Hennessey shouted cheerfully as a stunned Nell moved slowly toward the microphone. "It gives me a great deal of pleasure to present you with this check in the amount of five hundred dollars."

Nell might be in shock, but Travis noticed that she snapped out of her stupor fast enough when it came to reaching for the check. The crowd loved it.

Following the competition, spoonfuls of chili, dished up in small paper cups, were left for the crowd to taste. People surged toward the table that held the samples labeled "number five."

"Yay, Mom!" Emma said, rushing forward and hugging her mother.

"This is really cool," Jeremy said. He exchanged a high five with his mother.

Travis barely knew Nell Bishop, but he was as thrilled that she'd won the cook-off as if the success had been his own.

NELL WAS EXHAUSTED. Exhilarated but exhausted. Adam Braunfels, one of the judges and the owner of the Chili Pepper, the best restaurant in town, pulled her aside when the competition was over. He told Nell her chili was the best he'd ever tasted and that he'd like to talk with her later about the possibility of buying her recipe. He wanted to serve it in his restaurant. Nell could hardly believe her ears.

Following their conversation, Adam handed her a ticket for a free meal and suggested she stop off at his booth for dinner. Nell sat at one of the picnic tables at the far end of the rodeo grounds and savored a barbecued-beef sandwich and a heaping cup of coleslaw. It was the first time she'd eaten all day; she'd simply been too nervous before.

Jeremy and Emma were with their grandmother, who'd taken them home. The kids had chattered incessantly about Travis Grant. Apparently he'd shown them the time of their lives and they sang his praises to all who'd listen.

"Do you mind if I join you?"

Her thoughts seemed to have conjured up the man. Travis stood directly across the table from her, holding a cup of coffee.

"Please." Nell gestured toward a chair, and Travis sat down.

"Congratulations again," he said.

"Thank you." She was dying to tell someone about her conversation with Adam Braunfels, but held her tongue. Nothing was definite, and she didn't want to say anything until the details were settled.

"From what I understand, I owe you a debt of thanks," Nell said. "The kids told me this was the best rodeo of their lives, and all because of you."

"I was just about to thank you for sharing them with me. They're terrific kids, Nell."

"I think so, too."

She pushed aside the rest of her dinner and reached for her coffee. After being on her feet all day, she was grateful to be sitting. "Ruth drove them home," she said unnecessarily. She'd stayed to clean up the kitchen area and talk to Adam, but was so relaxed now she wasn't sure she'd find the energy to move.

"I heard someone say Willie Nelson was coming for the dance later," Travis mentioned.

"Don't believe it." Nell hated to be the one to disillusion him. "This is Willie Nelson country. We love him, and we send him an invitation to a picnic in his honor every single year."

"He's never come?"

"No, but then, we don't really expect he will. He's got bigger and better places to perform. We understand that and love him, anyway." Whether or not Willie showed, the people of Promise would continue to enjoy his music. Willie Nelson represented everything they loved about country music.

"Tired?" Travis asked.

"A little." An understatement if there ever was one.

"Too tired to dance?"

It took a moment to understand the question. Travis Grant was asking her to dance with him. She stared at him, unsure how to respond. It was kind of him, offering to be her partner. With anyone else she would have found an immediate excuse to decline. Not with Travis. For one crazy moment she actually considered it.

"Thank you, but no," she finally said.

If she'd disappointed him, Travis didn't let on.

Nell checked her watch, thinking it was time—past time really—to head home. The band, a popular local group, was playing in the background. The stage wasn't in sight, but well within listening range.

"They sound good," Travis said.

They did. Much better than Nell remembered, but then, it'd been more than three years since she'd stayed for the evening festivities.

All at once a crazed cheer rose from the audience and the announcer's voice came over the microphone. "Ladies and gentlemen, it's a pleasure to introduce the good people of Promise, Texas, to *Willie Nelson*."

Nell's gaze flew to Travis. "This has got to be a joke," she said.

But even before the words were out, the opening strains of "Whiskey River" echoed across the grounds.

Her fatigue gone, Nell leaped to her feet and hurried toward the dance area. So did everyone else within shouting distance. Travis was right behind her.

Nell and Travis never did get to see him. The crowd grew so thick they couldn't do more than listen. Willie sang three numbers to wild applause, then suggested everyone dance. The music flowed, smooth and easy. People around her paired off, even though they weren't anywhere near the dance floor.

Travis smiled down at her. "Shall we?" he asked, stretching out one hand.

Nell couldn't stop looking at him long enough to decline. It wasn't that Travis was a handsome man. His face was too angular, his features too rugged to be considered pleasing.

He took her lack of response as answer enough and slipped his arm around her waist. His hold was loose and gentle. A lifetime ago Nell had loved to dance. Jake had possessed two left feet, but he'd made an effort for her sake.

Travis danced as if he knew exactly what he was doing—and as if he enjoyed it. What surprised her was how well they moved together, how gracefully.

"Don't look so shocked," he said with a laugh. "Big men aren't all klutzes."

"The same applies to big women."

"You're not big," he countered. "In fact, I'd say you're just about perfect." He brushed a stray lock of hair from her forehead, and his fingertips lingered a moment longer than necessary.

Nell didn't know what madness possessed her, but she closed her eyes and allowed herself to indulge in a fantasy. She didn't pretend that the man holding her was her dead husband. That would have been too painful. Instead, she fantasized that she was a different kind of woman, willowy and lithe, petite and beautiful. Like the young Audrey Hepburn of *Sabrina,* a movie Nell had loved all her life.

It was the night for such dreams.

The dance ended almost as soon as it had begun. Too soon. Nevertheless, she didn't dare to continue. Didn't dare to indulge in any more fantasies.

"Thank you," she whispered. "I've never enjoyed a dance more."

"Me, neither," Travis said, his voice low and sounding vaguely unlike him.

Of one accord they turned and walked across the grounds, toward the parking area.

"Nell." He stopped her in the shadow of the grandstand.

"Yes?"

"Don't be angry."

"Angry? Whatever for?"

"For this," he whispered. He turned her around to face him, then lowered his mouth to hers.

Four

His kiss left Nell feeling lightheaded, as if she'd been out in the sun too long. His lips lingered on hers, his arms firm about her waist. He would have kissed her a second time, she sensed, if she hadn't moved her head just then. She needed a moment to compose herself, to gain perspective and deal with what had happened—what she'd allowed to happen. At any point she could have stopped him . . . and hadn't.

"I . . . wish you hadn't done that." Her voice trembled, shaky with shock and wonder. What astounded her as much as his kiss was how much she'd enjoyed it.

"Are you looking for an apology?"

His voice was close to her ear and she realized that he still held her.

"I could give you one if you wanted," he went on, "but it wouldn't be sincere."

She smiled at his words and eased away from him. There was definitely something in the air tonight that had caused her to behave so completely out of character.

"It's because of today," she said aloud. "The whole day." One of the best days she'd had in three years of grief and struggle.

"The day?" Travis repeated, walking at her side as they continued toward the parking lot.

She glanced at him, surprised she'd spoken aloud. Since she had, she couldn't very well leave him in the dark. That would be rude and unnecessary. If he was to continue paying for room and board, then she had best set boundaries between them now. Kissing was definitely *out* of bounds.

"Naturally I'm flattered that you'd want to kiss me."

"I'd like to do it again, if you're not opposed."

She shook her head. "I'd rather you didn't."

He was quiet after that, but not for long. "What did you mean when you said it was because of *today?*"

She exhaled slowly. "Winning the chili cook-off. The kids having such a wonderful time. Willie Nelson showing up like that. Dancing in the moonlight . . . I wasn't myself. I wasn't thinking—otherwise that kiss would never have happened."

"How weren't you yourself?" he prodded.

Nell was much too tired to endure an inquisition. "I just wasn't."

"How?" he pressed.

"I was happy, excited . . ."

He couldn't seem to leave it at that. "You aren't normally?"

"No," she returned shortly. "Not for the last three years."

A silence followed her words. Nell heard his sigh.

"You must have loved him very much."

She didn't hesitate. "More than life itself. In many ways I died with my husband. Nothing will ever be the same again."

They paused in front of her battered pickup. The Dodge was well past its prime. It'd been ready for the scrap heap when Jake was alive, but Nell had coaxed three more years from it; she prayed the truck would last another year.

"I disagree," he said.

His words cut into her thoughts. She raised questioning eyes to him. "What do you mean?"

"You loved Jake, and it's obvious you two shared something very special. But you didn't die with him. The woman I kissed is alive and healthy. She's vital and lovely and passionate." He raised his hand as if to touch her face, but changed his mind and slowly lowered it. "I felt your heart pound against mine. The woman I kissed is *alive,* Nell. She has a lot to live for."

"I—"

"You might prefer to think of yourself as dead, but you aren't."

His words surprised her more than his kiss. She didn't know how to respond, how to react. Ruth had been saying the same thing to her, but in different words. All this time she'd resisted, afraid she'd lose even more of Jake than she already had. This was dangerous stuff, too dangerous to think about right now. She'd leave it for another time.

"You haven't dated since Jake died?" Travis asked.

She shook her head.

"What's the matter with the men in this town?" he asked in a way that suggested they were idiots.

"Grady Weston asked me to the big summer dance last year."

"And?"

"And I turned him down. Glen Patterson, too."

"Nell, no." He planted his hands squarely on her shoulders. "Wake up. Look around you. Breathe in the cool night air and let it fill your lungs. Let yourself *feel.*"

He spoke with such intensity all she could do was stare at him.

"You don't believe anything I've said, do you? I can see it in your eyes."

Instantly she lowered her gaze. "I'll never have with anyone else the kind of love I had with Jake."

"Of course you won't," he said.

The man said and did the most shocking things.

"Jake was Jake," he continued. "Any relationship you might have with another man will be different from your marriage to Jake because that man will be different from Jake." He paused. "The problem, Nell, is that you haven't seen it this way. The way you see it, any other man is destined to fall short because he can never be a replacement for the original."

She had to admit Travis made sense. It was exactly what Ruth and Dovie and several others, Savannah included, had been trying to tell her. Either she hadn't fully understood or she hadn't been ready to listen.

It hit her then that Travis spoke as if he was familiar with this type of loss. "You lost your wife?" she asked him.

Now it was Travis who looked away. "In a manner of speaking."

"What manner?" He'd prodded and pried, now she did the same.

"I'm divorced."

"You loved her?"

"Very much," he said, "and I assumed she loved me. But apparently I was wrong."

Nell waited for him to go on, and after a moment he did.

"She met someone else." Travis buried his hands deep inside his pockets as though he felt a need to suppress his anger, even now. "Someone who could give her the things she needed, the things I couldn't—and I'm not just talking about money." He sounded philosophical, but beneath his matter-of-fact statement, she recognized his pain. Recognized it because she'd experienced a similar pain.

"Tony, Val's new husband, sets her on fire," he said, his voice dripping with sarcasm. "I didn't."

Nell might have accepted the words at face value if not for one thing. He'd held her and kissed her. There was definitely fire in him, and it was burning strong. Maybe his ex-wife hadn't provided enough kindling, she mused—and felt some amazement that such a thought had occurred to her. "Bitterness wouldn't solve anything, so I decided to do what I could—go on with my life, put the past behind me."

"Have you?"

"I like to think so." He said this as if he expected her to challenge him. "How is it we're talking about me? You're the one who's still living in the past, not me."

"Really?"

Travis chuckled and held up his hand. "Enough. Your point is well taken. We're both among the walking wounded."

Nell smiled. "Perhaps we could learn from each other," she suggested.

Travis nodded. "Perhaps we can."

They drove back to the ranch in separate vehicles. Travis pulled into the yard seconds behind her.

"Good night," she called, offering him a friendly wave as she headed toward the house. A single light shone above the back porch door. In all likelihood Jeremy and Emma were sound asleep; it would surprise her if Ruth was still up.

" 'Night, Nell."

Once inside the house, she climbed up the stairs to her room, undressed in the dark and sat on the edge of her bed, reviewing the events of the day. When she turned on the bedside lamp and took out her journal, it wasn't the five-hundred-dollar prize money she thought of. Instead, she found herself writing about Travis's kiss and the discussion that had followed.

JEREMY AND EMMA had been up for at least an hour by the time Nell got out of bed. Sundays were just as hectic as schooldays because chores needed to be finished before they left for Sunday School and church.

Nell had coffee brewing and was cracking eggs for French toast when the kitchen door opened and Travis strolled casually inside. "Morning" he said, helping himself to coffee.

"Good morning," she said, whipping the eggs into a frothy mixture before adding the milk. The griddle was ready and she had six slices of egg-soaked bread sizzling in short order.

"You coming to church with us?" Jeremy asked as he and Emma dashed in.

"Ah . . . ." Travis glanced at Nell.

"It's the Lord's day," Emma said severely, as if there should be no hesitation on his part.

"You're welcome to join us if you wish," Nell said.

He didn't show any sign of reluctance. "I'd enjoy that."

At breakfast Jeremy sat on one side of Travis, Emma on the other, the children accepting him as easily as they would a much-admired uncle.

"We're lucky Mr. and Mrs. Patterson didn't have any rooms left to rent," Jeremy said.

"Real lucky," Emma agreed.

"With the rodeo over, the Pattersons should have plenty of room," Ruth muttered as she walked into the kitchen, yawning.

The news landed like a bombshell in the kitchen. The children stared at each other as though they'd just learned the horrible truth about Santa Claus. Nell felt an immediate sense of disappointment, but Ruth was right. Phil and Mary would have space available for Travis now, and the accommodations would be far more comfortable than a too-short mattress in the bunkhouse. At Phil and Mary's, Travis wouldn't need to worry about a goat eating the socks off his feet, either.

"That's true. Mr. Grant could move into town," Nell said, trying to sound as though it made no difference to her. It shouldn't, but hard as she tried to convince herself it would be best if Travis left, she hoped he wouldn't.

Every eye went to their guest. "Move into town?" he repeated, glancing at each in turn. "Would anyone mind if I stayed on here? Your goat and I have recently come to terms. It would be a shame to leave now."

She shouldn't be this happy, Nell decided, but she was. She really was.

"WHAT TIME IS IT?" Frank Hennessey mumbled as he rolled over in the large feather bed and stretched his arms to both sides.

"Time for you to be up and dressed," Dovie said. "Church starts in less than thirty minutes."

"Church," Frank groaned. "Dovie, you know how hard it is for me to sit through Sunday service." But he eased himself up in bed to enjoy the sight of his wife fluttering about the room, hurriedly dressing. Dovie was a fine-looking woman and he took pleasure in watching this woman he loved.

It'd taken him long enough to make the leap into marriage. Not many men waited until they were sixty years old—maybe that was why the decision had been so hard. He might have remained single all his life if not for a woman as wonderful as Dovie. Their arrangement was perfect, he'd thought. Twice a week he spent the night. Two of the best nights of any week.

Dovie, being the kind of woman she was, had wanted them to get married. He'd led her to believe that eventually he'd be willing, and for ten years he'd believed it himself. Then all at once Promise experienced a rash of weddings and Dovie became possessed by the idea of marriage.

That was when he'd realized he simply wasn't the marrying kind. Painful though it was, he'd confessed to Dovie that he just couldn't do it—and she'd promptly ended their relationship. Those weeks apart had been agonizing for him.

He loved her, but he'd broken his word to her, and although he hated himself for hurting the woman he adored, he couldn't give up the comforts of his life as a bachelor. For instance, the fact that his house was a mess. It was *his* mess, though, and he knew where things were. Dovie wouldn't tolerate the unsightly stack of magazines by his recliner or the pile of laundry beside his bed.

Marriage meant more than making a commitment to her, he'd thought; it meant he'd be forced to alter his entire life. At sixty such a drastic change didn't come easy.

Things had looked hopeless—and grew even worse when he made the mistake of taking Tammy Lee Kollenborn out one evening. That was the night he'd known he could never love anyone but Dovie. Afterward, when Dovie had gone away on a short cruise, he'd been terrified she'd meet another man. It seemed inevitable that he was going to lose her, and the knowledge was destroying him.

The solution had come from an unexpected source. From the man he'd assumed would be the least understanding. Reverend Wade McMillen. Frank owed him big time. The local preacher had suggested that Frank and Dovie get married but maintain separate households, the same as they were already doing. Then they could both have what they wanted. What they needed. Dovie had the commitment she craved, the wedding band on her finger. And Frank was free to eat baked beans out of a can in front of the television, wearing nothing but his underwear, if he so desired.

"Dovie," he whispered softly, watching a silk slip float down over her breasts and hips. "Come here, love."

"Don't you use that tone of voice with me, Frank Hennessey. I'm running late as it is."

"Dovie," he coaxed, and sat up. He held out his arms to her. "How about a good-morning hug?"

"Not now."

"No?" Frank was surprised. Dovie rarely refused him anything, especially when it came to what she called "the delights of the flesh." He'd never met a woman like her. Dovie was a lady to the core, but when it came to lovemaking, she was both lusty and generous.

"It won't stop with a hug and you know it," she chastised.

He did know it, and he sighed deeply.

Dovie disappeared into her closet.

"Where are you going now?" he called.

"Out of sight, out of mind," she called back, giggling.

Frank tucked his hands behind his head and closed his eyes. He didn't bother to tell her it didn't work that way, at least not with him. The time they'd been apart, he'd done nothing but think of her. Thoughts of Dovie had tormented him day and night, until he was sure he'd lost his mind.

"Do that again," he said, savoring these moments in bed.

"Do what?" came her muffled question.

"Giggle."

"That's a silly thing to ask." But she did.

Frank loved the sound of it. He had to smile every time he heard her giggle. Or laugh. Or just heard her, period.

Dovie reappeared a minute later in a royal blue dress that buttoned up the front and belted at the waist. She braced one hand on the bed post as she slipped into her pumps.

"I'm going to do something with my hair and then I'm heading for church."

"No hug?"

One outraged glance answered the question. Frank laughed.

"I'm driving out to see Savannah, Laredo and the baby after church," she said.

"Do you mind if I tag along?" he asked.

Apparently his question caught her by surprise because she abruptly stopped brushing her hair and met his gaze. Her eyes softened. "You want to see the baby?"

Frank nodded. "That surprises you?"

"Yes. Do you like babies?"

"Actually I'm quite fond of children." It was his one regret in life. He'd give anything to have met Dovie as a young man and had children with her. She would have been a wonderful mother, just as she was a fabulous wife. "I would have liked kids of my own," he confessed with a hint of sadness.

She continued to stare at him and he noticed a sheen in her eyes—as though she was about to weep.

"Dovie?" he asked gently. "What's wrong?"

"Oh, damn," she said, sniffling. "I'm going to ruin my makeup and I don't have time to fuss with it now."

Frank climbed out of bed and reached for his robe. "What is it, Dovie?" he asked again.

"I always wanted children," she whispered. "So badly."

"I assumed you and Marvin decided not to have a family," he said. They'd never discussed the subject, and it seemed strange to be doing so now.

"We couldn't have children," Dovie said. "Marvin . . . had the mumps as a teenager. I never complained, but . . ."

"Couldn't you have adopted?"

"Marvin wouldn't hear of it. I asked him to reconsider many times, and he refused. As much as I wanted to be a mother, I couldn't bring a child into our home when my husband felt the way he did."

"I'm so sorry, Dovie."

She attempted a smile. "It was a long time ago. I don't even know why I'm crying. But when you said how much you regretted not having children, I realized . . . why I love you so much."

The hug he'd been longing to collect all morning was now given with spontaneity. Frank held her tight and closed his eyes.

"Perhaps Savannah and Laredo will allow us to be substitute grandparents for Laura Rose," he whispered.

"I was thinking the same thing," Dovie said. She cradled his face and smiled, her eyes bright with unshed tears. "I love you, Frank Hennessey."

"I wish we'd met years ago," he said, voicing his earlier thoughts.

"We met at exactly the right time," she told him. "Any sooner and I would've been married."

"Any later, and you might've been with that judge you met on the cruise. The Canadian guy."

"Perhaps," she admitted, but skeptically. She dabbed at her eyes. "Frank, I really must rush. You know how compulsive I am about being on time."

Frank checked his watch and knew if he hurried, he'd have time to dress and join her.

"I'll go with you," he said.

"Any reason?" she asked.

"Several reasons—but if I take the time to list them, we'll be walking in during the middle of Wade's sermon."

* * *

TRAVIS WAITED until Jeremy and Emma had left for school on Monday morning before he approached Nell, who was in the barn. "Ruth said I'd find you here," he said, feeling a bit awkward.

She was busy tending a newborn calf, but glanced up and smiled when he entered the barn. Kneeling in the straw, feeding the animal with a large baby bottle, she explained that the calf was one of twins and had been rejected by its mother. Once again Travis found himself admiring her compassionate capable nature.

They exchanged a few pleasantries as she worked, and when she'd finished, he opened the stall gate for her.

"Thanks," she said, walking over to the barn faucet where she washed and dried her hands. "So what can I do for you?"

"Do you have time to talk for a few minutes?"

"Why?" she asked bluntly.

"Well, I'm a writer," he explained, "and I'm working on a project that has to do with this area."

"All right," she told him, "but I haven't got time to stop now. I need to go out and check the fence line. Tag along if you want."

"I'd enjoy that."

It wasn't until Nell led a gelding out of his stall that he realized she didn't intend to use the truck. Travis had ridden before—in Central Park. Years ago.

"You're going on a horse?" This probably wasn't the most intelligent question he'd ever asked. But he had to weigh his decision; on the one hand, he wouldn't mind some Western riding experience and it would be a chance to talk to her. On the other, he didn't want to risk looking like an idiot in front of a woman he found *very* attractive.

"You don't ride?" she asked in a voice that suggested she should have thought of that herself. She expertly placed the saddle on the gelding's back.

He hesitated before he answered. "A little."

"You're welcome to join me if you want. I've got Jake's saddle and you'd fit that comfortably."

"Is Jake's horse still around?" He figured that would have to be an older horse, which could only help his situation.

"Yup."

"Does he take to strangers?"

"Some."

"That's encouraging."

Nell tossed back her head and laughed, her long braid swaying. "Come on. It'll be fine."

Within minutes she'd brought a huge quarter horse out of his stall. Travis watched her saddle him, amazed at her ease with animals.

"Twister, meet Travis," she said, handing him the reins.

Travis found it amusing that she'd introduce the horse to him and not the other way around.

She led the two geldings outside into the sunlight. With a swift graceful motion, she mounted. "Do you need help getting up?" she asked when he stood there, unmoving.

He tried to look as if the question had insulted him; actually he wouldn't have objected to her holding the reins while he swung his leg over the saddle. With a mighty effort he did manage to scramble onto Twister—appreciating the fact that Nell didn't laugh at him.

As they started out, she set a slow easy pace, for which Travis was grateful.

"You wanted to ask me about the area?" she reminded him.

"Yeah," he said jerkily as his butt bounced against the saddle. "Te-ll m-e wh-at you kn-ow abou-t the gh-ost town."

Nell eased to a stop. "Ghost town?" she asked, frowning.

Twister, following the other horse's lead, stopped, as well. "If I remember correctly, it's called Bitter End."

"That's why you're here?" she asked. "Why you came to Promise?" She nudged her horse into a trot. "I thought you were a writer!"

"Yeah." Travis managed to keep pace with her, but not without a price. If he survived this with all his teeth intact . . . "I am. And I w-want to—"

"Who told you about Bitter End?" she asked, stopping her horse again. The warmth she'd shown him had cooled noticeably. "You're from New York," she said. "You know Richard Weston, don't you?"

"I met him once, yes, but, Nell—"

"What did he tell you about Bitter End?" she demanded. "We were afraid of this," she muttered, not looking at him. "Everyone was."

"Afraid of what?"

"It doesn't concern you."

"Nell, if you'd give me a chance to explain." He shifted in the saddle, wishing he could touch her, reassure her in some way.

"You've already said everything I need to know. You're a friend of Richard's—"

"No, I'm not! Don't even think that. I met the man *once*, Nell. Just once. For a couple of hours. But it only took me a couple of minutes to see the kind of person he is."

That brought her up short. Her gaze returned to him, cautiously, as if she wasn't sure even now. But he could see she wanted to believe him, wanted to trust him. He yearned for that as much as he did her kisses.

"Valerie, my ex-wife, defended him—his state-appointed attorney. Richard mentioned the ghost town to her, and she told me. I was intrigued. A ghost town from the Old West, one that's basically undiscovered and hasn't been commercialized. I wanted to see it for myself, as background for a project I'm working on."

Nell said nothing. Then she said, "So you came all this way because of Bitter End?"

"That's what initially brought me here. Yes." But he liked the people of Promise, especially Nell and her family.

"Now I suppose you're looking for someone to take you there?"

"Yes—I want to see the town." He wanted to learn the history behind it, too. It was more than just a ghost town, if what Weston said was true, and Travis was hoping to unravel its secrets, include them in his book.

"I'm afraid you've made a wasted trip."

Her unwillingness to help him took him by surprise.

"I won't take you to Bitter End. And no one else will, either."

She sounded stubborn about it, but he could be stubborn, too. "I'm going there," Travis said. "I'll find it, Nell. Others have and so will I. But I'd rather we did it together."

"I can't . . . I won't. You don't understand."

"Then explain it to me."

"That town has done nothing but bring Promise grief. We just want to forget about it."

"What aren't you telling me?" he asked.

His question seemed to catch her off guard. She was silent for a long time; when she spoke again, it was with the seriousness of a woman who knows more than she wants to. "Nothing good has ever come out of that place. Nothing. The best thing for you is to forget you ever heard it mentioned."

"You've been there?"

"No," she admitted reluctantly.

"Then how do you know? Who told you? How many people have actually been in the town?"

Nell shrugged, not answering him.

"Then how can you be so sure if you've never been there yourself?"

"Everyone knows," she whispered.

"But you've found out where it is?"

She hesitated. "I have a vague idea where it might be."

"Where?"

Nell made a sweeping motion with her arm. "It's out there somewhere. Exactly where, I couldn't tell you."

"And even if you could, you wouldn't."

She nodded.

"This is a historic site. Doesn't anyone understand that?"

"Bitter End?" Nell laughed without amusement. "Why is it so important to you?" she asked again.

"Curiosity, mainly," he told her. "Like I told you, I'm a writer and I'm using a ghost town in my book. I wanted to make it as authentic as possible. I'm also intrigued by the mystery."

"Well, you'll have to ask someone else to take you, because I won't."

"Who, then?"

"I doubt that anyone will. But you might try Grady Weston."

Richard Weston's brother, Travis remembered.

"I wish you well, Travis. If you ride back to the house, Ruth will give you the Westons' phone number." Having said that, she galloped off, leaving him to make his own way back to the barn.

"All right, Twister," Travis said, doing his best to sound calm. "It's you and me, boy. We're friends, right?"

He pulled on the reins to reverse their direction. "See the barn, Twister?" He pointed toward it. "Let's walk there . . . slowly." Apparently the horse didn't care for Travis's tone of voice, because he took off at a gallop. It was all Travis could do to stay in the saddle.

When he reached the barn, he managed to dismount, then, legs shaky, succeeded in removing the saddle; the bridle he left for Nell. He coaxed Twister into the stall with his name on it, then tottered back to the house.

That afternoon when he phoned Grady Weston, he learned Nell wasn't the only one with strong feelings about Bitter End. It took him several hours to reach the other man; once he did, Weston practically bit his head off. In no uncertain terms, he made it clear that he'd have no part in satisfying Travis's curiosity. Travis supposed Grady's aggression could be attributed to his negative feelings about his brother.

Nell sought him out in the bunkhouse an hour or so later. "Did you speak to Grady?" she asked, her mood more conciliatory, or so it seemed.

"Briefly."

"And?"

"And he isn't willing to show me where Bitter End is, either. Just like you predicted."

She nodded. "You'll be leaving, then?"

"No."

It wasn't the answer she'd expected; he could tell by the way her eyes widened. "No?"

"I'm going to locate Bitter End, Nell, with or without this town's help."

Five

Nell was furious with Travis, but she didn't know why. That morning, as she'd ridden across her property, checking the fence line, she'd thought about him. And she'd thought about Bitter End.

Just when she was beginning to like Travis, really like him, she'd discovered that he had an ulterior motive. He'd made friends with her children, kissed and flattered her, pampered Ruth. All this because he wanted her to take him to Bitter End.

He'd been open enough about telling her he was a writer. Now everything was beginning to fall neatly into place. His job was what had brought him to Promise, probably with all expenses paid by his publisher. She should have suspected he had an ulterior motive for befriending her and her family. He was planning to write about Bitter End—although she didn't really know why. He'd told her he was working on a book. What kind of book? she wondered, and what, exactly, did he hope to achieve?

What *really* infuriated Nell was his comment about Bitter End being a historical site. He seemed to be implying that Texans were a bunch of hicks who didn't appreciate their own history. Well, that was the furthest thing from the truth! She knew as much about this state's history as anyone around here. In fact, she thought grimly, maybe she respected history *more* than that . . . that Easterner. That wannabe cowboy. Because at least she recognized that the past still had power over the present—the way Bitter End had power over Promise.

Everything she'd ever heard about the town had been negative. Her family's roots went back to the original settlement, which had been founded shortly after the Civil War; so did Jake's. Something ugly had happened there, something horrible. Whatever it was, it'd been disturbing enough to cause everyone to vacate the town. No one knew why, and for years and years the town was rarely mentioned. When people did discuss Bitter End, they spoke in hushed whispers. Now some ignorant Yankee wanted to turn it into a historical site!

When Richard Weston was fleeing the authorities, he'd holed up in the town, and that made sense. He belonged there, if anyone did. Richard had figured out where the town was partly because of Savannah. Despite Grady's objections, she'd explored the countryside to find Bitter End in her quest for lost roses.

Nell had asked Savannah about it, and she'd watched a shiver move down the other woman's arms as she recounted her visit. Savannah had mentioned an impressive find in the cemetery—Nell had forgotten what the roses were called. Savannah had gone on to describe the eerie feeling that had come over her; she'd hurriedly taken the rosebush and left.

Later, convinced she'd allowed her imagination to run away with her, Savannah had returned, hoping to rescue other roses. She'd told Nell the most astonishing fact. Nothing grew inside the town. Not even a weed. The town was completely without life.

Yet all Travis saw was a money-making opportunity. He'd come to Promise to dig up information about a place best forgotten. Despite everything she'd said, everything Grady had told him, he'd insisted he was going to find Bitter End. Then he'd write about it and attract more people, strangers, to the town. Soon tourists would pour into Promise and their lives would no longer be their own. No one here knew why the settlers had abandoned Bitter End—and Nell thought it was better to leave things that way, to let whatever secrets were buried there lie forgotten. She wasn't the only one to feel this way.

She wished now that Travis had chosen to move into town, to the bed and breakfast. Phil and Mary would know better how to handle his curiosity.

Nell closed her eyes and groaned at the memory of how pleased she'd been when he decided to stay on at the ranch. She felt lost and inadequate; worse, she felt foolish for having allowed this man to weave his way into her life.

She understood now that he had his own reasons for kissing her, for encouraging her kids, for staying at her ranch.

Reasons that had nothing to do with *her*.

SAVANNAH HAD JUST PLACED Laura in her crib when someone knocked on the back door.

"Anyone home?" Unexpectedly her brother stepped into the kitchen.

"Grady, come in." Savannah didn't bother to hide her surprise. It was unusual for him to drop by the house on his own. Her home was only a short distance from the ranch house, and while Grady visited often, it was almost always with Caroline and Maggie.

"How are you feeling?" he asked.

"Wonderful." The birth had been the most incredible experience of her life. Savannah had known there'd be pain and had prepared as best she could for labor. What she hadn't known was how she'd feel afterward—that sensation of stunned joy and amazement, that surge of accomplishment and pride.

In her arms she'd held living proof of her love for Laredo. Together they had created this new life, this beautiful child.

"I was just about to have a cup of tea," Savannah said, crossing to the stove. "Would you care to join me?"

Grady removed his hat and set it on the oak table. "Sure."

He'd get around to explaining his visit in his own time. Savannah could see no need to rush him.

She filled two cups and carried them to the kitchen table, then sat across from him. He asked her a few questions about the baby, but she noticed that he wasn't really paying attention to her responses. He was thinking, weighing his next words, wondering if he should approach her about whatever he'd *really* come about. After living with Grady all those years, Savannah knew him well, better than he realized.

"Nell's guest called me," he said casually as he stirred a second spoonful of sugar into his tea.

Nell's guest! That was the reason for this visit. The sugar had given him away. Grady seldom added sugar to anything, and two teaspoons was particularly telling.

"I don't believe I've met him," she said.

"His name's Travis Grant. Seems nice enough—Caroline and I met him at the rodeo."

"Oh?"

"Like I said, he phoned yesterday."

"Really?" She remained calm, unaffected.

"He knows Richard."

The words hit her without warning and Savannah stared at her brother. A sinking sensation came over her, and a deep sadness. Her younger brother had been sentenced to twenty-five years in prison without parole. It hurt to think of Richard locked behind bars. She'd written him twice, once shortly after he'd been taken back to New York to stand trial and then after he'd received his sentence. He hadn't answered either letter.

"Actually it was Grant's ex-wife who introduced him to Richard," Grady added. "Apparently she was the court-appointed attorney who defended him."

"Did this Travis Grant tell you what he wanted?" It went without saying that if Richard was involved, their brother was looking out for his own selfish interests.

Savannah often wondered what had turned Richard into a man who acted without conscience or compassion. Her heart ached every time she thought about him. *Why?* She would never understand why he'd used his family, why he'd betrayed good people, why he'd exploited the vulnerable.

Twice he'd stolen from her and Grady. The first time had been the day they'd buried their parents. While Grady and Savannah stood beside the grave, Richard was sneaking away with the forty thousand dollars in cash left them by their father. Six years later he'd returned with a hard-luck story, needing a place to stay.

Savannah blamed herself for what happened next, since she'd been the one who convinced Grady to let him stay. But Grady wouldn't let her accept the blame. He insisted they were equally at fault because he'd known what kind of man Richard was and had closed his eyes to the obvious. Both of them felt an obligation to family, and they both wanted to believe their brother had changed.

Within a few months of arriving back in Promise, Richard had charged thousands of dollars at various stores in town, using the Weston accounts, the Weston name. When it was all uncovered, Richard had conveniently disappeared, leaving Grady to foot the bill. Only after he was gone did Grady and Savannah learn the whole truth. Richard had been on the run—from his unsavory creditors and "partners" and from the law. The New York City DA's office had a list of charges long enough to put him behind bars until he was an old man.

What hurt Savannah most wasn't the fact that Richard had destroyed her faith in him; it was learning that her brother was guilty of bilking immigrants. He'd helped get them into the country illegally, then forced them to live and work in deplorable conditions. If that wasn't bad enough, he'd confiscated their money. He'd been one of several men accused and convicted of a crime so heinous she cringed every time she thought about it. That her own flesh and blood had hurt innocent people in this way had devastated her. Men, women and children had suffered because of her brother.

"Richard told Travis about Bitter End," Grady continued.

Savannah exhaled a deep sigh. "So Travis is here to find it?"

"That's what he says."

"For what purpose?"

"I don't know for sure. He's a writer, so I imagine he's doing research for an article about Bitter End."

Savannah thoughtfully replaced her cup. "What did you tell him?"

Grady scowled, then met her eyes.

"Grady Weston, what did you do?"

He gave her a wry smile. "Now I know where Caroline gets that tone of voice. I should have recognized it was from my very own sister."

"You were rude, weren't you?"

He shrugged. "I told him to mind his own damned business. I said there wasn't a soul in this town who'd help him, and advised him to give up his search now."

"Oh, Grady."

"I don't think he's going to take my advice."

Savannah mulled over this information for a couple of minutes. "I'm beginning to think it might be a good idea to put the past to rest."

"What do you mean?"

"No one knows what happened in Bitter End," Savannah reminded him. "No one's sure why the entire town up and moved. It almost seemed to take place overnight. From what Ellie told me, there were still cans on the shelves in the mercantile store. People left furniture, clothing, all kinds of valuables behind. They were in such a hurry to leave they couldn't get away fast enough."

"It was probably some disease or something to do with the water," Grady reasoned.

"Perhaps. I'm sure there's a logical explanation for what happened. All I'm saying is it's time to find out what went wrong and why. And who better than a writer? Someone who knows how to research and how to separate fact from legend. A stranger. Someone who can approach this without the emotions and fears we all have about Bitter End."

Grady didn't look convinced. "As far as I'm concerned, it's best not to disrupt the past."

Savannah considered her brother's words. "A year ago I would have agreed with you."

"But not now?" he asked, sounding surprised.

"Not now," she said. "Having Richard home was a painful and bitter lesson. It taught me that turning away from the truth, ignoring trouble, is a dangerous thing to do."

"It isn't like we're hiding anything," Grady insisted. "No one knows what went wrong in Bitter End."

"Then don't you think it's time we did?"

"Why?"

"Because, as the Bible says, the truth shall make you free."

"I'm free now," Grady said. He stood up and walked over to stare out the window above the sink.

"We aren't free, Grady," she offered gently. "Otherwise we wouldn't be this afraid."

"I'm not afraid," he countered sharply.

She didn't contradict or challenge him, but she knew that wasn't entirely true. Whatever had happened all those years ago in Bitter End still haunted them. In Savannah's opinion, it was time to bring it into the light, expose it and deal with the consequences. Each generation has been influenced by Bitter End, whether they admitted it or not.

Savannah recalled the first time she'd heard about the ghost town. Grady had been the one to tell her. He'd heard their parents talking when he was a teenager, discussing this secret place and its mysterious past. Afterward Grady, Cal and Glen had decided to find the town and, in the manner of boys, went about making it their own private adventure. Savannah had wanted to join them, but they didn't want a girl hanging around.

She would have gone to look for it on her own, except that Grady had said he'd take her to Bitter End once he knew where it was. Naturally she had to promise not to tell anyone, especially the Patterson brothers.

The three boys had eventually located the town. But Grady never did take her there; it was the first and only time he'd broken his word. All he'd tell her was that something horrible must have happened in that place. She remembered how he'd closed his eyes and shivered, and vowed he was never going back.

His words had remained with her for a long time.

About a year ago she'd sought out the town herself. According to an article she'd read, abandoned cemeteries and homesteads were often a good source of nineteenth-century roses. That motivation was strong enough to let her put aside her apprehensions about the place. After weeks of searching, she'd stumbled upon the town, hidden deep in the hills. Only then did she understand what her brother had meant.

The instant she'd stepped onto the main street of Bitter End, a feeling had come over her, an eerie sensation of anxiety and dread. And yet she couldn't have named the reason, couldn't have said what she feared.

Afterward she managed to convince herself that she'd imagined the entire episode. So she returned. But she'd been right the first time. Something was there—not a ghost, but a persistent feeling of intense sadness, a haunting sorrow.

"Let him do it, Grady," she said, releasing a pent-up sigh. "Let him find out what happened in Bitter End. Let Travis Grant expose whatever wrongs were committed there."

"You think a stranger can do that?"

"He can start."

Her brother pondered her words, his face thoughtful. Then he slowly shook his head. "It isn't often I disagree with you, but I do now."

"You're not going to help Travis find Bitter End?"

"No."

She accepted his decision, but deep down, she wondered how long it would take him to change his mind. Grady was having second thoughts already; otherwise he wouldn't have come to her in the middle of the day. Especially during the busiest time of the year.

Savannah knew she was right, and she knew Grady would eventually see it. Beneath his doubts he, too, felt a need to lay this matter to rest once and for all.

TALK ABOUT STIRRING UP a hornets' nest, Travis mused as he sat and stared at his blank computer screen. Nell had avoided him all day. And after speaking to Grady Weston, it wouldn't surprise him if the other man was busy rounding up ranchers to tar and feather him. All this because he'd asked a few questions about a ghost town. Why were they so intent on keeping this secret, whatever it was?

He wondered if the people here even knew what had happened in that town. Perhaps they were being influenced by fears and vague suspicions rather than facts.

Travis preferred to face problems, not let them fester. He believed in knowledge and the power of truth. Shutting down the computer, he leaned back in the chair, hands behind his head, reviewing his options. Soon, however, he discovered that his thoughts weren't on Bitter End anymore.

Instead, he was thinking about Nell. Despite her disapproval of his plans, he admired her strength and courage. He was attracted to her, he admitted that, and he sensed she felt the same way. Even if she preferred to ignore it.

Travis decided to get a breath of fresh air and he reached for a sweatshirt. He walked out of the bunkhouse and around the yard, stopping to say hello to Yucky. As he neared the front of the house, he was pleased to find Ruth sitting outside in a rocker, crocheting.

"Travis," she said with a friendly smile. "Come join me."

After Nell's silence and Grady Weston's explosive anger, Travis was more than grateful for a cordial greeting. He climbed the steps and leaned against the porch railing.

"Was that you I saw on Twister yesterday morning?" Ruth asked.

"Yeah," he said, not mentioning that he considered himself lucky to be in one piece.

"That gelding's got a mind of his own."

"So I discovered."

Ruth laughed, and he grinned himself. The older woman's fingers agilely worked the yarn, never slowing. It amazed him that she could carry on a conversation without disrupting her work.

"What are you making?" It wasn't what Travis wanted to ask—he had questions about Nell. However, any inquiries would have to be a natural part of the conversation. Unobtrusive.

"An afghan," she answered. "I find crocheting relaxes me."

He started to comment, but Ruth broke in. "You're curious about Nell, aren't you?"

Her directness surprised as much as pleased him. "I won't deny that I am."

Ruth nodded. "She's interested in you, as well. I haven't lived with her all these years not to understand the way she thinks. Have you kissed her yet?"

Slightly embarrassed, Travis laughed. "Yes."

"And?"

"And it was very good."

"You plan on bedding her?"

"That's none of your business," Travis said. He wasn't accustomed to discussing his love life with elderly women, or with anyone else, for that matter. However, he'd certainly fantasized about making love to Nell. She was a passionate woman. Their one kiss had given him a glimpse of that. She was also a woman who didn't believe in half measures; it was all or nothing. He knew that when it came to love, loyalty or friendship, she held nothing in reserve.

For that very reason, she was reluctant to become involved with another man. The potential for pain was too great.

That was something Travis understood. The breakup of his marriage had been one of the most painful ordeals of his life. He'd loved Valerie and been stunned to learn that she wanted out of their marriage, that she'd viewed their lives together as a temporary thing until someone "better" came along.

She'd been intrigued with Travis because he was a writer. Later she'd urged him to give it up and get a real job. Everyone knew there wasn't any real money in publishing. Not unless you were Stephen King. She'd been scornful about his financial prospects.

The irony was that she'd left him too soon. Not long after their divorce, he'd hit it big and his books had been selling almost as fast as the publisher could print them. She laughed about her lack of insight now. Once, a year before, she'd tried to lure him into bed, saying she'd made a terrible mistake and wanted him back. It'd flattered his ego, but in the end he'd told her he wasn't interested in sleeping with a married woman.

In the years since the divorce Travis had rarely dated. Friends had tried to match him up and he knew he was considered a catch. But he preferred the comfort of solitude; being alone was better than being with the wrong person.

The next time he fell in love, it would be with a woman who loved him back, heart and soul. A woman willing to make as strong a commitment to him as he did to her. In the years since Val had left him, he hadn't met such a woman.

Until Nell.

"She's a bit prickly at the moment," Ruth said, and for the first time since he'd joined her, the older woman's fingers paused. "Did you two have a spat?"

"Not really," Travis said. He didn't bring up the ghost town for fear Ruth would respond the same way Nell and Grady Weston had.

Ruth scowled. "I don't know what's wrong with her, then, but she'll come around. Be patient, you hear?"

Suddenly the screen door burst open and Nell stuck her head out. "Ruth, have you seen—" She stopped midsentence when she noticed Travis.

"Seen what?" Ruth asked, looking almost gleeful at Nell's reaction to him.

"My kitchen scissors."

"Top drawer, left-hand side. Look under the church directory."

"Afternoon, Nell," Travis said.

"Oh—h, Travis."

It shocked him how his heart raced, how exhilarated he was by the sight of her.

"I'm putting a chicken on to roast," Nell said, her voice unmistakably nervous.

"Let me help," he insisted, and didn't give her a chance to object.

"Yes, let Travis help," Ruth murmured, sounding as if she was about to burst into laughter. "Nell's never cooked a chicken in her life."

Nell marched into the kitchen with Travis following, and just the way she walked told him she wasn't pleased. "I don't need any help roasting a chicken," she announced brusquely.

"I didn't think you did. I just wanted to talk to you."

"If it's about Bitter End, there's nothing to say."

"At least explain to me why everyone reacts this way the minute I say the name."

"I already have."

"Tell me again."

"No." She paused. "Bitter End's the only reason you came here, isn't it?"

"Yes." He wasn't going to lie.

"Then there's nothing to talk about."

"There's everything to talk about."

She stared at him, her expression wary.

"I want to know what it is about this ghost town that evokes this type of response. Don't you want to find out what caused everyone to leave? Aren't you curious?"

"I don't need to know—no one does," she said, then dragged in a deep breath. "You don't understand."

"Then explain it to me."

"I'm afraid," she admitted reluctantly. "Afraid it'll be like opening Pandora's box. I really believe that in this case, ignorance might be bliss."

He frowned.

She shook her head. "Leave it, Travis . . . please?"

"Fine. I'll leave it—but just for the moment." He lowered his voice. "Right now I'm more concerned with settling this matter between you and me. We were on the brink of getting to know each other."

"No, we weren't," she denied vehemently. "You're reading more into one kiss than you should . . . You caught me at a weak moment."

"I want to catch you again."

"No," she said with such force she appeared to surprise herself. "Don't even try."

It took a moment for her words to sink in, and when they did, a slow satisfied smile appeared on his lips. "You liked it that much, did you?"

"No!" she said. "I . . . I wish it'd never happened."

"It frightened you half to death, didn't it?"

She shook her head, which sent her braid flying. "This is the most ridiculous conversation I've ever had. It'd be best if you left now."

"Not on your life. Oh, Nell, sweet Nell, don't you realize I felt it, too?"

"There was nothing to feel, dammit!" She whirled around and headed for the sink. A chicken rested in a pan on the countertop. Reaching for it, she thrust it under the faucet.

"It's only natural for you to be afraid," he said in low soothing tones as he slowly advanced toward her. He rested his hands on her shoulders, but the instant she felt his touch, she jumped.

"Nell, sweet Nell," he whispered, and kissed the side of her neck.

"Don't do that!"

"Then what about this?" He ran his tongue around her ear and felt a sense of triumph at the almost imperceptible sound of her moan.

"Not that, either," she said, obviously struggling to put some starch in her voice.

"And this?" he asked as he wrapped his arms around her middle.

The chicken fell unheeded into the sink.

"No one's going to help you . . ."

"Help me what?"

"Look for the town."

"Fine, I'll look for it on my own." He spread a series of nibbling kisses along her neck.

"You won't find it."

"That's okay, because I've found you."

A shiver moved through her. "I think you should go."

"Where?" He was far too involved in kissing her neck and her ear to pay much attention. Her words said one thing and her body another. Her hands hung idle at her sides and she let her head fall back, exposing her throat to his mouth.

"Somewhere else . . ." Her words were barely audible.

He turned her carefully to face him and smiled at her tightly shut eyes. "Open your eyes, Nell," he instructed. "I want you to know who's kissing you."

"I don't want you to . . ."

He laughed softly and cupped her face with both hands. "I'd expect you to be honest, if not with me, then with yourself."

She opened her eyes, and he knew his words had hit their mark. "Good, very good," he whispered, and gently lowered his mouth to hers.

His lips had just made contact when the phone on the kitchen wall rang. The sound startled them, broke them apart.

Travis groaned. Every nerve, every sense had been readied to enjoy their kiss.

After two rings, Nell answered it. "Hello," she said, her voice trembling, but only a little.

It surprised him how close to normal she sounded. Travis wasn't sure he could have pulled it off nearly as well.

He watched as her gaze revealed surprise. "It's for you." She handed him the receiver.

"Me?" Only a few people knew he was in Promise. "Travis Grant," he said into the mouthpiece.

"This is Grady Weston."

Grady Weston. Travis didn't think victims were normally contacted in advance of a tar and feathering.

"I've changed my mind," the other man said gruffly.

"About what?"

"Taking you to Bitter End. Be ready by noon tomorrow."

"Fine . . . Great!"

Travis replaced the receiver. Nell stood a few feet away, with arms crossed, her eyes worried.

"Grady's decided to help me find Bitter End, after all," he said.

Six

Only eleven-thirty. Travis glanced at his watch, pleased that Grady Weston had agreed to show him the way to Bitter End. He wasn't sure what to expect once they got there, especially considering people's reactions every time he mentioned it.

Killing time, he walked over to the paddock outside the barn where Jeremy's horse, Dot Com, ran free. Earlier, Jeremy had told him proudly that he'd come up with the name himself. Now Travis stood and watched the young animal racing back and forth, kicking up his hind legs, running for the sheer joy of it.

The air was clear and Travis inhaled deeply. Until now he hadn't spent much time in Texas other than book signing and media tours in cities like Dallas and Houston. He'd written several stories set at least partly in Texas, but his research had been limited to libraries. The greater his success, the tighter his schedule and the less time he had for personal investigations. A shopping center in San Antonio or an airport in Dallas hadn't prepared him for what he'd discovered here in the hill country. He found the vast openness awe-inspiring and the life so dissimilar from his existence in Manhattan he felt as though he were visiting an alien planet.

The silence was perhaps the most profound difference. Without even realizing it, Travis had grown accustomed to city noise. Taxis honking, buses, shouting, street musicians, the clang and clatter of vendors. He'd lived in Manhattan for almost fifteen years now and hadn't realized how loud it could be. These few days in the country with Nell and her family had changed his whole perspective.

To his surprise he'd slept all night, every night. He never drafted his books while on the road, but the tranquility here had both relaxed and inspired him, and he was overwhelmed with ideas. He'd started to jot

THE HEART OF TEXAS COLLECTION

down a few thoughts on his laptop last night, and before he knew it four hours had passed. It'd felt like fifteen minutes.

His great-grandparents had been farmers, he remembered. He wondered if he'd inherited some of his ancestors' love of the land, though he'd never experienced country living. His parents had divorced when he was young, and he'd lived in New York state for most of his life.

He heard a sound behind him and glanced over his shoulder. Nell. A smile automatically came to his lips. He was convinced she didn't have a clue how beautiful she was. His attraction to her was as strong as anything he'd known; it still surprised him.

Ruth's probing questions of the day before hadn't helped, either. Thoughts of making love to Nell had begun to fill his dreams, and while the physical attraction was intense, he found Nell compelling in other ways. He loved her determination, her sense of family, her pride in the ranch and the sheer grit it'd demanded to keep Twin Canyons afloat.

"Do you have a few minutes?" she asked, coming to stand beside him.

"For you, always," he said.

She rested one arm on the top rail of the paddock fence and studied Dot Com as though she needed to compose her thoughts before speaking.

"Problems?" he asked.

She shook her head, and the long braid swung back and forth.

One day he'd enjoy undoing that braid of hers, letting her hair slip unrestrained through his fingers. He imagined filling his hands with it and drawing her face to his and kissing her.

"I . . . I don't know if Jeremy and Emma know about Bitter End," she said, her voice low. "Naturally there was some talk after Richard was found, but mostly everyone kept it as hush-hush as possible."

"And you're afraid I'm going to tell them?"

"Yes."

"I take it you'd rather I didn't?"

"Please . . ."

But as she spoke, Travis noticed the hesitation in her voice, as though she wasn't sure this silence would be right for her children.

"You really feel it's right for them not to know?"

A small smile trembled at the edges of her mouth. "Am I that readable?"

"No." He placed his boot on the bottom rail next to hers and, leaning forward, rested his arms on the top one. "I'm beginning to know you."

She smiled. "You think so, do you?"

Her eyes went serious then, and Travis knew this matter of the ghost town and whether or not her children should know continued to bother her.

"They'll hear about Bitter End one way or another," he said.

"The children and I have never discussed it," Nell told him, "although I'm almost convinced they heard something about it after Richard's accident. But they didn't ask and I didn't volunteer any information. For all I know, Jeremy and Emma know everything there is to know about the town."

"I won't say anything in their presence if that's what you think is best." He wanted to reassure Nell that he was worthy of her trust, that her confidence in him was well placed.

"There's something else," Nell said, her expression growing truly somber now. She turned and looked away, as though she found Dot Com's antics of sudden interest.

"You can speak to me about anything you want, Nell."

"I have no right to ask you this."

"Ask me, anyway," he insisted gently. He suspected she was wondering about his divorce. She glanced at him, and he saw the gratitude in her eyes.

"It's natural to be curious about me," he encouraged. "I feel the same way about you. I like you, Nell, a great deal, and I'd welcome the opportunity to deepen our friendship."

She hung her head, and he was sure he'd embarrassed her.

"Ask me," he urged.

"Travis . . . please, don't go. That's what I'm asking."

"You don't want me to go to Bitter End?" He couldn't fathom why, after everything that had been said.

"I've never told anyone this—not even Jake." She faced him, meeting his eyes steadily. "Once, as a child, I heard my parents talking about the town. I was young and impressionable, and I've never forgotten it."

"What did they say?"

She shook her head. "I don't recall exactly. All I can remember is they were worried that one day I'd ask questions about it and find it myself. They'd decided not to mention it until I came to them."

"Which is what you've planned to do with your own children."

Apparently she hadn't made the connection because her eyes widened as she recognized the truth. "You don't understand, Travis, my father was a big man. Nothing intimidated him—but he was terrified of Bitter End."

"He'd been there?" Travis asked.

Nell nodded. "Once, with a bunch of his friends. Whatever he saw or experienced disturbed him, and he was anxious to protect me."

"Is that what you're trying to do for me, Nell?"

She nodded, then shrugged. "You're from New York City—what do you know about the Old West? There are dangers you wouldn't understand."

"I'll be with Grady."

"Yes, but . . ."

"Does this mean you care about me?" He wanted to hear her admit it.

"Of course I care about you," she returned impatiently. "I care about everyone."

"It'd do wonders for my ego if you'd admit you cared for me in a more . . . personal way," he said, loving the way her cheeks instantly filled with color.

She frowned, dismissing his remark. "Call Grady and tell him you've changed your mind," she pleaded urgently.

It hurt Travis to refuse Nell anything.

Her eyes held his, and her fingers squeezed his arm.

"I have to go," he told her with genuine regret. "I'd do almost anything for you, but what you ask is impossible." Even as he spoke, he knew he'd disappointed her.

Another woman might have responded with anger. That had been Val's reaction when she didn't get her way. Not Nell's. Instead, she offered him a resigned smile, as though she'd expected him to refuse. He could tell from the closed expression on her face that she'd retreated emotionally.

He was about to argue, explain himself, when the screen door opened and Ruth appeared, holding the cordless phone.

"For you, Travis," she said. "It's Grady Weston."

Travis took the phone and lifted it to his ear. "Hello," he said crisply, damning the other man's timing.

"Problems," Grady said, skipping the usual chitchat. "I've got a water pump down. Which means I'm not going to be able to take you out to Bitter End this afternoon."

Damn, Travis thought. It wasn't Grady's fault, but his time here was limited; not only that, he felt as though he'd just fought—and won—a dreadful battle asserting his need and his right to go there, and now the opportunity had been snatched away.

"Savannah's been though," Grady continued.

Travis was shocked. Surely Grady didn't expect a new mother to go traipsing all over the countryside!

"She could draw you a decent map," Grady said, "and give you some directions. Then you could find it on your own."

Travis's sagging spirits buoyed. "Good idea. I'll give Savannah a call."

"I apologize if this puts you out any."

"I'll find it on my own, don't worry."

They ended the conversation in the same abrupt way they'd started it.

Ruth and Nell were both watching him when he finished. "Grady's got problems with a water pump."

"But you're going, anyway," Nell said, and her lovely face tightened.

"Yes, I'm going, anyway."

Nell nodded sadly, then turned and walked away.

GRADY WAS LATE getting back to the ranch for dinner, and Caroline found herself glancing out the window every few minutes. Shortly after she'd arrived home from the post office, Savannah had phoned, explaining that a water pump had broken. Both Laredo and Grady were working on it, and neither man was likely to be home soon.

Caroline hadn't been a rancher's wife long, but she'd lived around cattlemen most of her life. Caring for the herd took priority over just about everything. The herd was the family's livelihood and their future.

Savannah had mentioned something else, too, and that was the reason Caroline awaited Grady's return so anxiously. Her sister-in-law had told her Nell's dude-ranch guest knew Richard.

Caroline was astonished by the apprehension those few words could bring her. She hadn't realized Richard held such power over her. It'd been months since they'd last heard news of him. Richard had been nothing but a source of heartache for the family—and for her.

The fact that Nell's would-be cowboy was an acquaintance of Richard's explained a great deal. Grady had been restless and short-tempered the night before, tossing and turning. Caroline had awakened around two and found him sitting on the porch in the very spot his father had once favored. He hugged her close, kissed her, then after a few minutes, sent her back to bed.

Caroline had known something was troubling him, but not what. He'd tell her, as he always did, when he was ready. That was how Grady operated. But now she had reason to suspect that his recent bout of restlessness was somehow connected to Richard.

At six Caroline ate dinner with Maggie and put a plate aside for Grady. Maggie was playing with her dolls in her bedroom when Grady and Wiley, their foreman, rode into the yard.

Caroline moved onto the porch and savored the sight of her husband, sitting his horse with natural ease. His dog, Bones, trotted along behind. Bones was the grandson of Grady's beloved old dog, Rocket, who'd died the previous year. He looked a great deal like his grand-daddy. The minute he'd been born, Grady had picked him out of the litter and trained him personally.

Her heart swelled with pride and love as she watched her husband dismount and head into the barn.

"Welcome home," she said when he returned a short time later. His steps were slow and heavy and she knew how tired he must be.

Grady's face revealed his pleasure at being home and finding her waiting for him. Caroline held her arms open. Grady didn't hesitate to walk into them and hold her tight.

"The pump's working?" she asked.

"Good as new," he said as he released her.

"You hungry?"

"Starving," he growled.

"Then wash up and I'll warm dinner for you."

When he came back into the room he seemed revived. Wearing a lazy grin, he said, "Maggie's decided on a name for the baby."

Months earlier Grady had allowed the child to name a new born colt—which he'd subsequently given her for her sixth birthday—and she'd chosen Moonbeam. When they learned Caroline was pregnant, Maggie had assumed she'd be naming her little brother or sister, as well. No amount of explaining could convince her otherwise.

Caroline could just imagine the name her daughter had chosen. "I'm afraid to ask."

"For a boy, she's decided on Buckwheat."

"Buckwheat?"

"And for a girl, Darla."

"Ah." Caroline understood now. The television had been on earlier that afternoon and Maggie had been watching reruns of "Our Gang."

"I'll talk to her again," Caroline promised, thinking she'd let Maggie go through the baby-name book with her. She wanted her daughter to feel part of things, but Maggie needed to understand that the ultimate decision rested with her and Grady.

"I don't know," Grady said with a thoughtful look. He pulled out a kitchen chair and sat down. "Buckwheat has a nice ring to it, don't you think? Buckwheat Weston. And we wouldn't need to worry about any other kids in his class having the same name."

"Grady!"

Her husband chuckled, reaching for his fork.

Caroline poured herself a glass of iced tea and sat down across from him. "I talked to Savannah this afternoon," she said, hoping he'd bring up the subject of Richard.

Grady didn't so much as blink as he took his first bite of pork chop. If anything bothered him, he didn't show it. Nothing, it seemed, would deter him from enjoying his meal. A man had his priorities, thought Caroline with wry amusement. He'd wait until he'd finished his meal.

"Did Savannah mention that Travis Grant knows Richard?" he finally asked.

Caroline nodded.

"You weren't going to say anything?" He regarded her quizzically, as though her silence had surprised him.

"I knew you'd mention it eventually."

Grady reached for his coffee and held the mug between both hands. "It bothers me knowing my brother's in prison," he admitted. "God knows it's what Richard deserves . . ." He leaned forward, set the mug aside and reached for Caroline's hand. He looked into her eyes and she felt his love, stronger than anything she'd ever known.

"I couldn't sleep last night," he told her.

"I know."

"I didn't understand it, not at first. Every time I closed my eyes, Richard was there. Dammit, this is my brother, my little brother. Mom and Dad would have wanted me to look out for him, but—"

"No." Caroline shook her head and tightened her fingers around his. She believed that Grady's parents would have wanted Richard to accept responsibility for his own actions. She told him so.

"Deep down I realize that," Grady said, and released a deep sigh. "But last night I realized something else." He lowered his gaze. "I'm afraid of Richard."

"Afraid?"

Grady nodded. "It's idiotic, I know, but those fears seemed very real in the dead of night."

"But why? He's locked away. He can't hurt us or—"

"My greatest fear," Grady said, interrupting her, "is that one day he'd try to take away what is most precious to me. You, Maggie and the baby."

"Oh, Grady, it'd never, never happen."

"I know it doesn't make sense. But remember that one of Richard's great pleasures was grabbing whatever he thought anyone else wanted," he said bitterly. "Especially something that was important to me."

"Grady, don't you know how much I love you?" she demanded. Had the situation been reversed, though, she suspected she'd feel exactly the same. All she could think to do was reassure him.

Standing, Caroline walked to the other side of the table and sat on his lap. She draped her arms around his neck, then lowered her mouth to his. Their kisses grew in length and intensity, stoking fires of need.

"I've changed my mind," Maggie announced as she stepped into the kitchen. She clutched some small stuffed animals in her arms. "Buckwheat is a dumb name for a boy."

Caroline sighed and pressed her forehead against Grady's shoulder.

"I was just getting attached to it," he said, sounding almost like his normal self. "Do you have any other ideas?"

"Beanie," the six-year-old suggested next. "We're gonna have our own Beanie baby."

Caroline groaned and Grady chuckled.

DINNERTIME CAME and went and Travis had yet to return. Nell did the dishes, but kept her eye trained on the dirt road that wound down from the two-lane highway. He'd been gone the better part of seven hours.

"Are you worried?" Ruth asked as Nell dried her hands on a dishtowel.

"About what?" she asked, pretending she didn't know what Ruth was talking about. She hated being this transparent, but she couldn't stop worrying about Travis. He'd gone in search of Bitter End all on his own, despite her request that he give up this stupid search. It hurt that he'd refused to heed her advice. It'd taken every ounce of pride she possessed to ask him to stay away.

Now this.

"You've been looking at the clock every five minutes," Ruth pointed out. "Travis will be back any moment—there's no need to worry."

"How can you be sure?" Nell asked in a rare display of temper. Anything could have happened. Anything. The scenarios that flashed through her mind saw him dead and bleeding at the side of the road. Or inside a collapsed building, like Richard.

"Did you phone Savannah and Grady?" Ruth returned.

In her panic Nell hadn't thought to contact them. It made all the sense in the world that Travis would stop off and discuss what he'd discovered with Grady. She was surprised she hadn't thought of it herself. Foolish, that was what she'd been. Foolish and histrionic.

Her heart leaped with renewed hope. Casting her mother-in-law an apologetic glance, Nell reached for the cordless phone. Caroline answered on the second ring.

"Hi, it's Nell," she announced cheerfully. "I don't suppose Travis Grant is there?"

If Caroline was surprised to hear from her, she didn't let it show. "No, Nell, we haven't seen him."

"Not at all?" Nell couldn't hide the apprehension in her voice.

"Is everything all right?" Caroline asked.

"I'm sure it is," Nell replied, making light of her concern. By sheer willpower she forced her pulse to return to normal. This not knowing was hell. *Hell!* "I expected he'd be back before now, that's all. I'm sure everything's all right."

They chatted a few minutes longer and Nell promised she'd phone back if Travis hadn't shown up at Twin Canyons by nine.

Nine o'clock. Nell glanced at the clock on the stove. Two more hours. The day's light was already beginning to fade. She didn't know what Ruth thought when she said she was going out to look for him herself. But she figured she'd go stir-crazy waiting another minute; another two hours was out of the question.

She grabbed the truck keys off the peg on the back-porch wall and was out the door. A sense of urgency filled her, a combination of anger and fear.

If anything had happened to him, she swore she'd give every pair of socks he owned to Yucky. The man was a fool to traipse across unfamiliar territory.

It wasn't until she was at the top of the drive, the truck's headlights stretching across the paved highway, that she remembered she didn't know where Bitter End was or how to get there. Making a quick decision, she headed south toward the Weston spread. From what Caroline had just told her, Travis had gone to Savannah for directions.

Nell left the engine running when she arrived at Savannah and Laredo's home. She leaped out of the cab and raced across the yard.

Savannah met her at the door and said, "Caroline phoned and said no one's heard from Travis."

"Not a word?"

"No. But I drew him a map," Savannah said.

"Can you draw me one, too?" Nell asked.

"Of course." Savannah led the way into the kitchen.

Nell followed, her heart pounding.

"You're worried, aren't you?" Savannah asked.

Nell nodded, afraid if she said anything, her voice would crack. Dammit, she was beginning to really care about that greenhorn. Which infuriated her, because she didn't *want* to care about him. He'd drifted into their lives and would drift out again. A few weeks after he left, Jeremy and Emma would probably have trouble remembering his name.

Not Nell. It would take her much longer to forget Travis Grant.

"That map took a long time to draw, and I don't want to keep you waiting," Savannah said, reaching for a pad and pencil. "I'll have to give you a rough sketch." She bent to her task, and in a minute the job was done. "You should be able to figure it out from this."

Savannah's hurried map wasn't ideal, but it gave Nell something to go on.

"Would you like me to come with you?" Laredo asked, joining the two women.

"No." Nell couldn't see any reason to drag him into the night.

"You're sure?"

"Positive. Thanks for your help," Nell said. She bounded out of the house and back into the truck.

Savannah and Laredo came to stand by the back door silhouetted in the light that spilled from the kitchen. Nell realized she hadn't been able to hide her feelings from them any more than she'd concealed them from Ruth. Heart still pounding, she waved goodbye, then turned back up the drive.

In situations like this, she knew she had to face her worst fear. Recognizing what it was came easy because she'd encountered it once before.

Her greatest fear was finding that Travis had been hurt or killed.

"Dear God, no," she pleaded aloud, her mouth dry with horror. *Not again.* Finding Jake crushed beneath the tractor had forever changed her. It had nearly destroyed her, too.

The tears gathering in her eyes infuriated her, and she roughly swiped them away with the back of her hand.

She came to a juncture in the road and checked her map to choose which way she should turn. According to the directions, Bitter End was inaccessible by car. Which made sense, otherwise the town would have been found and explored much earlier.

If the makeshift map was at all accurate, Bitter End wasn't anywhere close to the road, and the turnoff point was some distance yet. She inhaled deeply, forcing herself to remain calm and in control of her emotions. As she drew near the section of highway where she'd need to drive onto unpaved land, she slowed to a crawl.

Her heart flew into her throat when she saw tire tracks that turned off the road. She was sure they were made by the vehicle Travis had rented.

She remembered again what had happened to Richard. Cal had found him in Bitter End, near death, half-crazed from thirst and his injuries. A stairway had collapsed on him, and he'd been two days without water or medical attention. It was described as a miracle that he'd survived. He'd been airlifted to Austin and hospitalized.

Nell shook off the memory and concentrated on driving. The terrain was hilly and uneven and the truck pitched and heaved first one way and then another. Fortunately it was a clear night and a bright three-quarter moon had risen; at least she could see where she was going.

Why Travis was in such an all-fired hurry to find the town she'd never know. He was probably on deadline. Here she was, desperately worried about a man who was no doubt planning to make a laughingstock out of the entire community.

He'd urged her to see the town herself, and now he was getting his wish. Nell slowed, squinting into the distance, convinced she'd seen a flash of light.

She eased the pickup to a stop and opened the door. Standing on the narrow running board, she peered in the direction she'd seen the light. It wasn't visible now.

"Travis," she yelled at the top of her lungs. She waited for a response and thought, just for a second that she'd heard one.

Getting back into the truck, she sped ahead, heedless of the terrain. Sure enough the light reappeared.

"Travis! Travis!" She slammed on the brakes when he was caught in the farthest reaches of her headlights.

Jumping out of the cab, she shouted. "Travis?"

"Here!" As he raced toward her she stumbled in his direction.

He held a flashlight, which he dropped when she neared. He threw open his arms. She wasn't sure which to do first, kiss him or slug him.

She fell into his arms with a force that might have knocked a slighter man to the ground. All at once nothing mattered, except that he was alive, uninjured, and she was in the warm security of his embrace.

"What happened? Where were you? Dear God in heaven, did you have any idea how worried I was?"

He shut her up with a kiss, then explained everything in five simple words.

"I ran out of gas."

Seven

"**Y**ou ran out of gas?" Nell shrieked.

Travis felt foolish enough without her yelling at him, then figured it was what he deserved. He didn't know how he could've let something like that happen. His only excuse was his unfamiliarity with the vehicle—pretty lame as excuses went.

"I'm sorry," he told her.

"Sorry—all you can say is you're *sorry*?"

To her shock and dismay, Nell broke into sobs. She covered her face with both hands and half turned from him. Stunned that he'd driven her to tears, he moved to reach for her, but stopped, not sure how she'd react to being held when she was in such distress. The sight of her weeping was more than he could bear. He gently drew her to him, comforting her, holding her loosely. She struggled at first and he let her.

"You're right, Nell, sorry just doesn't cut it," he whispered soothingly.

"You're a fool," she told him, wiping the tears from her face.

"I know."

"You're not supposed to agree with me."

He cradled her face between his hands. "You were worried sick, weren't you?"

Even in the dark, with only the headlights behind her and the glow of the moon, he read Nell's fear.

"I . . . I was the one who found Jake," she said. "I was so afraid you . . . ."

She didn't finish; she didn't need to. Travis wrapped his arms completely around her, his heart pounding with an emotion so overwhelming it made him weak in the knees.

"I'm fine. A little chagrined but fine."

"I'm not," she said, and clung to him.

Holding her like this was worth every moment of anxiety he'd endured, every second he'd floundered around, hoping he'd headed in the right direction. Common sense said he should have remained with the vehicle, but he'd felt compelled to make his way back to the road. Back to Nell.

She sniffled and raised her head to gaze up at him. Their eyes met, and something warm and wonderful passed between them. A recognition, an acceptance, a consent.

It was a profound moment.

Travis lowered his mouth to hers, and when their lips met, he barely managed to stifle a groan, it was that good. His lips lingered on hers as he prolonged the kiss, not wanting it to end.

She slipped her arms around his neck. He'd been the one to initiate the few kisses they'd exchanged to this point. She'd allowed his kisses, even enjoyed them, but she'd always remained slightly aloof, tentative.

That restraint was gone now. Her fingers were in his hair and her mouth clung to his, warm, demanding, erotic. By the time the kiss ended, Travis felt weak, drained—and at the same time exhilarated.

"Nell . . . sweet Nell." His voice was barely audible.

As she buried her face in his shoulder, he closed his eyes and breathed in her scent, the scent that belonged only to her. Equal parts soap and hay . . . and Nell. A cool breeze rushed against his face, and he silently prayed it would clear his head. At the moment all he could think about was making love to Nell. Not here, he told himself. The timing, the location, everything was wrong, but his body seemed intent on convincing him otherwise.

"Let's talk," he murmured.

"What do you want to talk about?"

"I have a few thoughts I want to discuss with you."

"Now?"

He nodded. "It won't take long."

He slid an arm about her waist and they walked toward the pickup. Nell turned off the engine and lowered the tailgate. They sat on it side by side.

Now that he had her attention, Travis wasn't sure where to start. He reached for her hand and held it between both of his; unable to resist, he kissed her knuckles. A heavy sigh worked its way through his chest as he gathered his thoughts.

"Travis?"

"First of all," he said, "I'm sorry I worried you."

She made a small sound as if to say now that he was found, all was forgiven.

"You came looking for me." His respect for her multiplied a hundredfold, especially now that he knew she'd been the one to find her dying husband. She'd had no idea what to expect tonight, but she'd put aside her fears and gone in search of him. "I don't think I've ever met anyone braver than you."

"Me?" She laughed softly. "I'm the biggest coward who ever lived."

"Not true."

"If I was as brave as you suggest, I wouldn't have asked you to stay away from Bitter End."

He smiled, following her thoughts. It didn't surprise him that they aligned with his. "That leads nicely into what I wanted to discuss with you."

"Bitter End?"

He felt her stiffen and searched for the words to reassure her.

"Did you find it?" she asked.

"Unfortunately, no. I got lost. My map-reading abilities leave much to be desired. I haven't a clue how close I was or wasn't."

She made no comment.

"Next time I want you to come with me."

"This is a joke, right?" she burst out.

He shook his head. His hands continued to hold hers. "You came looking for me—"

"Yes, but . . ."

"Don't you realize how much courage that took?"

"But I couldn't bear not knowing—"

"You also need to know what happened in Bitter End. You and everyone else in this community. The truth is long overdue. It's time to uncover the past, place it in the proper perspective, stop pretending Bitter End doesn't exist. Once everyone knows what happened there, the allure will be gone. You won't need to worry about Jeremy and Emma sneaking away to find it on their own."

"They wouldn't do that," she insisted weakly.

"Didn't you say your own father did? And Grady and the Patterson brothers searched for it when they were kids."

"Who told you that?"

"Savannah," he said. "This afternoon. They aren't the only ones either."

Nell turned away from him.

"Why me?" she asked, her voice weary.

"I need someone who knows the history, someone who'll help me understand it. According to Savannah, your family was among the original settlers. All I know is what Richard Weston told me and—"

"I wouldn't believe a word that snake said!"

"Right. So will you help me?" he asked quietly. "Come to Bitter End with me. Together we can solve this mystery once and for all."

Nell's shoulders rose with a sigh. "I . . . need some time to think it over."

"All right." He suspected that in the end she'd agree.

"You ready to go home now?" he asked.

"Home," she repeated. "Yes." She glanced at him. "We'll get your car tomorrow."

When they were in the truck cab and Nell had started the engine, it suddenly occurred to him that he'd referred to Twin Canyons as home.

Home. That was how it was beginning to feel.

RUTH SAT IN HER ROCKER and worked the crochet hook and yarn. While her fingers were busy with their task, her mind sped off on its own course. Nell had been gone more than two hours now, worried sick about that tenderfoot.

The children were upstairs asleep and the house was quiet. Calm. A cat nestled in Nell's chair, and Lucky, Jeremy's dog, slept on the braided rug in front of the fireplace. Yet Ruth's mind raced.

She'd been a youngster herself, about Emma's age, when she first heard the rumors about Bitter End. She remembered a schoolmate had told her about the mysterious ghost town, hidden in the hills. She was convinced it'd all been a lie, a story her friend had concocted. Then, years later, when she was wise and mature and all of thirteen, she'd overheard Edwina and Lily Moorhouse mention a ghost town.

Ruth trusted the Moorhouse sisters and had asked them about it. They, too, had claimed it was real and explained that the history of Promise was tied to the forgotten town. Only a few people knew about it, and even fewer knew where it was situated.

Ruth sighed and her hands went idle in her lap. Only one other person had shared her secret—which was that she'd been to Bitter End herself—and he was long dead. At eighteen she'd decided she would find this town. Cocky and self-confident, she'd gone in search of it.

That was how she'd met Jerome Bishop—her Jerry. He was older and had fought overseas toward the end of the Second World War, coming home a decorated hero.

She remembered how curious she'd been about him, how interested.

But he was nearly thirty and she was still in her teens. He'd encountered her riding on his land and asked her a few questions. She didn't dare tell him the truth, so she'd fabricated something and prayed he'd believe her.

He hadn't, but said if she was a cattle thief, she was by far the prettiest one he'd ever seen.

Ruth smiled at the memory. A few days later she was back, certain she wasn't anywhere close to Bishop land. But Jerry found her, and in her rush to get away and avoid his questions, she'd let her horse escape and twisted her ankle as she tried to catch the reins.

In his concern about her injury Jerry hadn't plied her with questions, but carefully examined her foot, his touch gentle for such a big man. She'd been half in love with him following their first meeting, but after this, her heart was forever lost.

Naturally such a romance was impossible. He was older, more worldly; she was just a schoolgirl. He didn't kiss her, nor did he chastise her. Instead, Jerry had rounded up her mare, then escorted her almost the entire way home. She'd been too shy to talk much, giving one-word replies to his questions. Before he'd left her, he asked her to forget the ridiculous notion of finding Bitter End on her own—not that she'd ever admitted she was looking for it. He'd gone so far as to suggest she stay home in the afternoons and read books or talk on the phone with her friends. Ruth had smiled politely and said she'd take his advice under consideration.

The next evening he'd stopped by the house to discuss ranching with her father. Ruth had been involved in helping her brothers with their homework. She felt Jerry's eyes on her, and through the whole evening, she feared he'd mention her afternoon horseback excursions. He didn't.

The next time she ventured out horseback riding, Jerry was waiting for her.

"Are you meeting a lover?" he'd demanded.

"No." She'd been appalled that he'd even think such a thing.

She doubted he believed her, but she couldn't bear letting him think she loved another man. Instead, she'd broken down and told him she was attracted to someone who felt he was too old for her. If he'd guessed she meant him, Jerry never said. When he couldn't convince her to forget about finding the lost town, he'd reluctantly agreed to accompany her.

The day they'd stumbled upon the ghost town was one she would long remember. That was when Jerry had first kissed her. Ruth wasn't sure which had excited her more—his kiss or locating the town.

But it was the only time they'd ever been to the town. High on exhilaration, they'd walked down the center of the deserted main street.

Soon they realized something was very wrong. It was spring and the hills were blanketed with bluebonnets, yet Ruth noticed not a single flower in Bitter End.

The place was bleak, dark. A huge blighted tree stood at one end of town. Everything was dead.

But that wasn't what had kept them from returning. It was the ugly feeling, the sensation of dread that pressed against her heart, making it almost difficult to breathe. Jerry had kept her close to his side and mumbled something about the town reminding him of the feeling he'd had when he came upon battlegrounds during the war. It felt like death, he'd said.

Whatever had happened was horrible enough to cry out from the land, from the buildings and everything around them. Whatever it was had killed this town and forever marked it for ruin.

They'd never gone back. Never wanted to. Finding the lost town had been their secret, a silent bond they'd shared. To the best of Ruth's knowledge, they'd never spoken of it again.

Afterward there'd been no reason for them to meet. Ruth had missed Jerry more than she could say, but if he missed her, he didn't let on. They met in passing twice—both times in Promise—and exchanged little more than casual greetings. Ruth was miserable, loving him the way she did, and she was sure he cared for her, too. So she decided to take matters into her own hands. It was a brazen thing she did; she smiled at the memory of it and the shocked look on Jerry's face the day she rode over to his family's ranch. She'd figured she had nothing to lose. Her ostensible reason was that she'd be graduating from high school within a few weeks and needed the advice of an older more experienced person about her best course of action.

He'd asked about her options and she'd mentioned two: marrying him or moving to Dallas with a friend and finding work there. Jerry's face had tightened, and then he'd suggested that marrying him was probably the better of the two ideas, but he preferred to do the asking.

She granted him that much and waited impatiently for him to make his move. The day she graduated from high school he stopped by the family home with a diamond ring. Afterward they'd argued amiably about who'd proposed to whom; it was a private joke between them.

A few years after they were married, Jerry's mother had died and they'd inherited the chest.

The very chest that sat in the attic of this house, Jake and Nell's place. She'd gone through the contents once. To a historian the chest would have been a treasure trove, filled with bits and pieces of life in the nineteenth-century hill country. But it was more than that. Ruth had recognized almost immediately that some of the things packed in the cedar-lined chest had come from Bitter End.

She'd looked them over, then closed up the box and never investigated it again. Ruth supposed it was because she'd been so young at the time, and that one visit to the town had continued to haunt her. She'd wanted nothing more to do with Bitter End. No link to it. If she couldn't throw out the chest—and she couldn't—then she'd hide it away, obliterating from her mind any memory of that horrible place. Jerry must have agreed, because once he knew the contents, he'd never asked about it again.

The time had come, Ruth believed, to reopen that chest. They had to disclose what was known about the town, discover its secrets, undo whatever damage they could. She was too old now for such a task. But it seemed somehow fated that Travis Grant had arrived when he did.

She would talk to him, show him the chest, whether Nell wanted her to or not.

That decided, Ruth picked up her crochet hook and started back to work. The clock chimed nine; Nell would be returning with Travis soon. She had a good feeling about those two. They were well matched, the way Nell and Jake had been.

Yes, the more she thought about it, the more fated Jake's appearance began to seem.

THE FOLLOWING MORNING, Nell was in the kitchen preparing the children's breakfast when Ruth came downstairs.

"I take it you found Travis," her mother-in-law said, with a slight smile.

"I found him," Nell confirmed.

As if to verify her words, the back door opened and Travis stepped inside. He looked fresh from the shower, his hair wet and recently combed. His gaze searched out Nell's and he smiled. "Morning, everyone."

"Morning, Travis," both Jeremy and Emma said at once, and their faces brightened at the sight of him.

"Where were you last night?" Jeremy asked. "I asked Mom, but she said she wasn't sure."

"I wasn't sure, either," Travis replied.

Nell cast him a warning glance. He'd already promised he wouldn't tell the children about Bitter End, but she feared he'd forgotten his word.

"I got . . . lost," Travis said, keeping his gaze on her. When she stopped stirring the oatmeal long enough to glare openly at him, he winked.

Nell felt the color rush to her cheeks and prayed her children wouldn't notice, but her prayer didn't reach heaven fast enough to include Ruth. She noticed her mother-in-law grinning as she took her place at the table, obviously pleased.

When the oatmeal was ready, she served it with brown sugar and raisins. The toast was from a loaf of the homemade bread she'd baked the evening before. She'd kneaded away her worries about Travis on the dough, and it was some of the lightest fluffiest bread she'd ever baked.

The grandfather clock in the living room chimed eight, and the children leaped up from the table, grabbed their lunches and dashed out the door.

"You finished with your chores?" Nell shouted after them.

They both assured her they were.

"What are your plans for the day?" Ruth asked, directing the question to both Nell and Travis.

Travis glanced at Nell. She dragged in a deep breath. "I'm driving Travis back to where he left his car. We're taking along a five-gallon can of gas," she explained.

"You going anyplace else?" her mother-in-law pressed.

"I've asked Nell to help me find Bitter End," Travis said.

"Will you, Nell?" Ruth searched her face.

"I'm not sure."

"I think you should," Ruth said unexpectedly.

For a moment Nell was too shocked to respond. "You want me to find Bitter End?"

"That's what I said." The older woman nodded. "And once you've located the town and walked through it, come back and tell me. Don't dawdle, either. There's something I have for you—both of you. Something that's been in the attic all these years."

"Ruth?" Nell asked in hushed tones, bending over her mother-in-law. "What is it?"

"Ruth?" Travis knelt down in front of her.

The older woman smiled and gently touched his cheek. "Find the town," she said softly. "Just find the town."

Travis helped Nell clean up the kitchen, then loaded the can of gas in the back of the pickup. She was already in the cab when he climbed inside.

"Thank you," he said.

The man could unnerve her faster than anyone she'd ever known. "For what?"

"For coming with me."

In the light of day Nell was annoyed for responding to Travis's kisses the way she had. It was because of her relief at finding him safe; it must be. She simply hadn't been herself—except she'd used that excuse before.

Despite Ruth's encouragement, she intended to tell him she refused to look for the town. She didn't want to know what was there, didn't care to find it.

"Losing your nerve, are you?" Travis asked.

"No," she denied heatedly, then added, "I'm a rancher, not a . . . historian."

"And a—"

"Coward," she finished for him. Her fingers ached from her death grip on the steering wheel. What it came down to was fear. Everything she'd ever heard about the town rang in her ears—rumors, warnings, advice. And it all seemed to whisper *Keep away*.

"What's Ruth talking about?" Travis asked once they were on the road.

"I . . . I don't know," Nell said, which was only partially true. The attic was full of forgotten treasures from the Bishop family. Old clothing, furniture, letters and memorabilia. Seeing that Jake's family, like her own, had been among the original pioneers, it was quite possible that something stored in the attic had come from Bitter End. Anything her parents might have had, however, had been taken with them when they retired to Florida.

"Won't you come with me, Nell?" Travis coaxed.

It took a long time, but reluctantly she decided Travis was right. She had to confront whatever was there, not just for her own sake but that of her family. Her friends. The people of Promise. It sounded melodramatic to put it in those terms, but then it was a melodramatic situation. Certainly an extraordinary one.

"All right," she finally whispered.

"Thank you," he said again.

Had they been anywhere else, not tearing down the road in her pickup, Nell was convinced Travis would have gathered her in his arms and kissed her. Had they been anywhere else, she would have let him.

That was quite an admission for her, she realized. Despite her reservations and doubts, she was falling in love with this greenhorn. Every unmarried rancher in the area had asked her out at some point since

Jake's death, but who did she fall for? A writer. A man who was going to break her heart, one way or another.

Nell let Travis do the driving after a while, and an hour later, with Savannah's map spread out on her lap, Nell suddenly cried, "Here!" She pointed to a grove of trees on the right.

Travis brought the truck to a stop.

"We go on foot from this spot," Nell said, rereading Savannah's instructions for the tenth time.

"So I was close," Travis muttered to himself.

They left the truck and started out on foot. Nell could already feel her heart pounding, and not from physical effort, either. It seemed to thunder, *Keep away, keep away,* with every beat.

"Are you okay?" Travis asked her a few minutes later.

"Sure," she lied. "What's there to fear?"

"We don't know that yet, do we?" he said, his expression serious.

They didn't speak for a while as they made their way through heavy brush and over rocky, treacherous ground. When they reached a limestone outcropping, Nell paused to look over the small valley below—and gasped.

She pointed a shaking finger at a charred steeple in the distance. The church was the tallest structure, but she could see others, too.

Travis's gaze followed the direction of her finger. "Bitter End," he whispered.

Nell studied the cluster of buildings. From her vantage point she could look down at them, could see the whole town laid out. Bitter End was divided by one main street with buildings on either side. The church and cemetery were at one end of the town, a corral at the other. Some of the buildings were constructed of stone, others of wood. It surprised her how well preserved everything seemed to be.

"So far, so good," Travis said.

Nell wordlessly agreed and breathed in deeply before they scrambled down the hill and into the town. They arrived near the corral. As they progressed, Nell experienced a feeling of heaviness, of being weighed down, that reminded her of how she'd felt those first few months after Jake's death.

She didn't say anything, but wondered if Travis felt the same thing.

"What is it?" he asked in a hushed tone.

They were on the main street now, their hands tightly clenched. With each step they advanced into the town, the feeling intensified. The weight pressing on Nell's heart grew stronger and stronger until she slowed her pace.

"I . . . I don't know."

"What's that?" Travis pointed to the saloon and the rocking chair that sat in front of it. Something leaned against the building.

"It . . . looks like Richard's guitar," she said. "He hid here for weeks before he was found."

"How could he have stood it?" Travis wondered, his voice low and hoarse.

"I don't know." Nell didn't understand why they felt compelled to speak so quietly. He squeezed her hand, and by tacit agreement they moved from the street onto the boardwalk. Savannah was right, she thought with a shudder. There was nothing living here—except the ceaseless wind.

She paused and looked inside the mercantile. A half-dozen bloated cans of food were scattered on the shelves. An old cash register stood on the counter, its drawer hanging open.

"Someone was looking for spare change," Travis remarked.

"Probably Richard." Evidence of his presence was everywhere.

They located the room in the hotel where he'd been sleeping and carefully skirted past the area where the stairs had collapsed. The wood floors were stained with his blood. Debris and empty bottles appeared here and there; magazine pages and food wrappings were blown against the sides of buildings.

"What are you thinking?" Travis asked as they neared the end of the street.

"That I want the hell out of here."

He chuckled, but the sound was uncomfortable. "Anything else you want to see?"

"No." She slid her arm through his and stayed close to his side. The oppressive sensation remained, reminding her even more forcibly of the horrific grief she'd suffered after Jake's death. It had become a part of her, something she lived with day and night. When it finally did ease, it went a little at a time. Slowly she could laugh again, then dream again. She was only now discovering she could love again. She stopped, suddenly struck by an idea.

"Hold me, Travis," she said urgently. They were near the church.

"Now?" He seemed surprised.

"Please."

He pulled her into his arms and she spoke into his ear. "I'd like to try an experiment."

"Okay. What do you need me to do?"

"Nothing," she said, then thinking better of it, added, "much."

She felt his smile against her skin.

Easing away from him, she placed her hands on both sides of his face and touched her lips to his. The kiss was deep, involving, as intense as the kisses they'd shared the night before. When she drew back, she studied his face.

"I like this kind of test," he told her flippantly. "Am I being graded?"

"No."

"Why not?"

"Travis, this is serious."

"I am serious."

She sighed expressively. "All right, I'll give you a B-plus."

"Why not an A?"

"Travis, you won't get an A until you answer my question."

"Fine. What's the question?"

"The feelings. Have they lessened?"

"I'm feeling all sorts of things just now. Which feeling do you mean?"

"The one we felt when we entered the town."

"I won't know until you kiss me again."

"Quit joking! This is important."

"I wasn't joking. I can't tell."

"Never mind."

"Why?"

"I have my answer."

"And?"

"It *has* lessened," she said. "I'm sure of it."

He nodded. "You're probably right."

Holding hands, they walked out of Bitter End. As they approached the outskirts, she felt a sudden sense of release, as though the bonds that constrained her had gone slack. A few steps outside the town, the feeling had all but disappeared.

After that, they concentrated on the arduous trek back to the road and said very little for some time.

"Are you okay?" Travis asked once.

"Fine. What about you?"

"Fine."

Travis followed her in his rental car as she drove back to Twin Canyons Ranch. Ruth sat on the porch with the rocking chair positioned to face the road; she stood and put away her crocheting as soon as she saw them.

"Did you find the town?" Ruth asked when they entered the kitchen.

"We found it," Nell told her.

She nodded. "I figured you would," she said softly. "Travis, would you follow me upstairs? There's something I'd like you to bring down."

Eight

Travis had one hell of a time bringing the cedar chest down from the attic. It almost seemed as though it was reluctant to give up its secrets, he thought, knowing how whimsical that sounded. Then he needed all his strength to pry up the lid.

Nell stood back, while Ruth edged close to him, firm and purposeful.

With the chest finally open, the first thing Travis noted was how neatly packed it was. The top layer was folded clothes, which Ruth carefully removed and set aside.

They found an old family Bible beneath the dresses and men's shirts. Ruth held it respectfully with both hands. "It's exactly like the one Ellie has," Nell breathed. "Ellie Patterson—used to be Frasier," she explained to Travis. "Ellie owns the feed store in Promise. Her family came here when mine did, and Jake's."

Travis could picture her easily. Ellie, as he recalled, had judged the chili cook-off.

"Ellie found the Bible while she was sorting through her father's things after he died," Ruth said. "She used the Bible for her wedding ceremony. I was touched that she had, since she was so close to her father." Carefully Ruth folded back the leather binding and examined the title page. "It says this Bible belonged to Joseph Savage."

"Jerry's great-great—there are too many greats for me to remember," Ruth said, "but the family's directly descended from Joseph's, that much I know."

"I'm sure this Bible is identical to the one Ellie owns," Nell said, moving in close and running her finger down the page.

"It wasn't unusual for a salesman to come into town and sell any number of the same item," Travis said. "My guess is that's the case here." In his research he'd come across references to old-time peddlers who rode from one town to the next selling their wares. More often than not, the men who sold Bibles were itinerant preachers, too, performing marriages, conducting funerals and preaching fire-and-brimstone sermons.

The next thing Nell extracted was an aged cardboard box. "Probably more clothes," she suggested. "Someone's wedding dress?"

"Open it," Ruth said.

Nell set the box down and with trembling hands removed the lid. She was wrong; it wasn't a wedding dress, not even an article of clothing, but parts of a quilt made of a cream-colored muslin.

"What is it?" Travis asked.

"The backing and some squares for a quilt, from the looks of it," Ruth said. "Apparently someone started the project years ago and never finished it."

"It's not any pattern I've ever seen," Nell said. "Most quilts have an overall design."

And most were a great deal more colorful than this one, Travis mused. The squares lacked the vivid and varied colors of others he'd seen.

"It looks like each square's a picture of some sort," Nell said, and held up one with an oak tree embroidered in the center. The detail was impressive, the stitches minute. She squinted and stared at the square, then shook her head. "I think there's something carved into the side of the tree," she said.

Ruth looked at it and shook her head. "My eyes aren't what they used to be."

Travis took a turn, as well, and after staring at it intensely, was able to make out the letters. "It seems to say, 'cursed'."

"Cursed?" Nell repeated. "Weird." She set the square back in the box. They studied the other squares, but again didn't find them particularly attractive. Each had a different image, although it wasn't always clear what that image was meant to be.

Nell returned the pieces to the cardboard box and set it aside. Leaning over the chest, she reached in and said, "Doesn't this beat all?"

"What is it?" Travis asked.

"It's a doll." Nell pulled out an obviously old rag doll, stuffed tight with a hand-stitched face. It had been made of white linen that had faded to a dull yellow, not unlike the color of the quilt squares. The red calico apron added a splash of brightness.

"I've seen one like that before," Ruth said, frowning in concentration. "Oh, yes! Dr. Jane had one exactly like that in her office not long ago."

"Dr. Jane?" Nell asked. "That seems odd. Are you sure?"

"Positive. She had it sitting on a bookcase. I remember seeing it the last time I was in for my physical. You remember, Nell? You drove me into town yourself. I needed my blood pressure medication renewed."

"How would Dr. Jane come by something like this?" Nell asked. "She's from California."

Travis listened to the conversation and shook his head. A doll identical to one that had come from Bitter End was owned by a California native? He agreed with Nell; it didn't make sense.

"Let's ask her about it," Travis suggested.

"Can't hurt," Nell said, and Ruth nodded.

The rest of the chest's contents consisted of old newspapers from the 1920s through the assassination of President Kennedy in 1963, army discharge papers and the like. Those, too, were neatly filed in cardboard boxes.

As Ruth carefully repacked the chest, Travis helped Nell finish the chores around the ranch. And then, together, they drove into town.

"This is probably a wild-goose chase," Nell said.

"Probably," he agreed, wondering if she'd had second thoughts about pursuing the significance of their discoveries.

They parked in front of the medical clinic, and once again he noted Nell's hesitation. "Nell," he said softly, "what is it?"

"Nothing," she insisted.

Travis stared at her. Ever since they'd returned from the ghost town, she'd been quiet, withdrawn, speculative. He didn't know what to make of it.

Dr. Jane was with a patient. They sat in the waiting room, and Travis flipped through magazines until the receptionist led them back to Jane's office. Travis glanced around; he noticed no antique doll on her bookcase now.

Jane entered briskly and took a seat at her desk. "Good to see you, Nell," she said. "Hello," she added, nodding in his direction.

Nell introduced Travis and they shook hands. Dr. Jane Patterson's lovely blue eyes revealed a genuine pleasure at seeing Nell—and open curiosity about him.

"Ruth mentioned noticing a rag doll in your office a few months ago," Nell said, getting immediately to the point of their visit.

"Doll?" Jane frowned as if she'd forgotten, but then apparently remembered, because she smiled. "As a matter of fact, I did, but I . . . no longer have it."

"Would you mind telling us where you got it?" Travis asked.

Jane studied them both. "Is there a particular reason for these questions?"

Nell and Travis exchanged glances. "We found a doll very similar to the one Ruth saw here," Nell explained.

Jane reached for a pen and started making small circles. "Can I ask where you found this doll?"

"Have you been to Bitter End, Dr. Patterson?" Travis asked abruptly. Then he remembered she *had* been. Jane was the one who'd found and treated Richard Weston.

He felt Nell's displeasure with him at the bluntness of his approach. But his curiosity was at a fever pitch. He was looking for answers, and the only way to get them was to ask the right questions. A growing sense of excitement filled him.

The doctor surprised him by asking a question of her own. "Have *you* ever been to Bitter End?"

Nell and Travis looked at each other.

"We were there this morning," Travis answered.

"Did you find the doll there?"

"Not exactly," Travis said. "It was in an old chest in Nell's attic."

"I see." Jane folded her hands and leaned back in her chair. "I don't suppose it would do any harm to tell you how I came to have that doll. Maggie Weston brought it to me."

"Maggie?" Nell sounded shocked.

"This was months ago, before Caroline and Grady were married and he legally adopted Maggie. You might not be aware of this, but Maggie disappeared the same time Richard Weston did. As far as anyone can figure, Maggie must've been hiding in the pickup Richard stole from the Yellow Rose Ranch. For a whole night, Caroline and Grady didn't know where she was. Sheriff Hennessey's the one who put two and two together."

"It must have been hell for Caroline," Nell said in sympathy.

"I'm sure it was. The following morning Maggie reappeared as mysteriously as she'd vanished. She wouldn't say where she'd been, but the sheriff thinks Richard brought her back."

"Thank God!"

"He'd taken her to his hiding place, then—in the ghost town?" Travis asked. His jaw tightened at the thought of a five-year-old in Bitter End.

"Apparently so," Jane said. "No one knows exactly what Richard said to the child to convince her to keep his secret. But considering the type of person he is, it's not too hard to guess."

"Prison's too good for the likes of Richard Weston," Nell muttered.

The more Travis learned about him, the more inclined he was to agree.

"While she was in Bitter End, Maggie found the doll and tucked it in her backpack. Later it worried her that she'd taken something that didn't belong to her. She developed stomachaches, and that was when she brought the doll to me."

"And the reason you had it on your bookshelf," Nell added.

"Exactly! I didn't know at the time that the doll was from the ghost town. I'd hoped the rightful owner would see it in my office so I could simply return it without mentioning Maggie's name."

"Where's the doll now?" Travis wanted to know.

"Maggie has it. Once the truth came out, Grady and Caroline decided Maggie could keep it."

"The memory of how she got it doesn't bother her?" Nell asked.

"It doesn't seem to. She believes she saved that doll. So her feelings about it have become quite positive."

"Good," Nell said. "I'm glad such a horrible experience ended well for her."

Jane smiled, then her gaze swung to Travis. "You're visiting Nell?"

"Actually I'm doing research for a story."

"He's my first guest," Nell explained. "The dude ranch hasn't officially opened, but he needed a room and Mary and Phil suggested my place."

Travis didn't like the classification. A guest—a paying one at that. She'd said it as though there was nothing between them, as though their kisses meant nothing. Despite her tone, Travis couldn't make himself believe it.

"I see," Jane said, sounding a little unsure.

She wasn't the only one. "Nell and I are finding out everything we can about Bitter End," Travis explained. "It's time the mystery of that town was solved."

Jane nodded. "I couldn't agree with you more. My fear is now that the word's out, someone else is going to decide to hide there. If something isn't done soon, there's every likelihood people will get hurt again. Some of those buildings aren't safe for people to explore. It's a wonder they've stood all these years as it is."

"The entire town should be destroyed," Nell said, her voice raised.

Travis disagreed with a sharp shake of the head. "Bitter End is an important part of Texas history. Why would anyone want to destroy it?"

Nell didn't answer.

* * *

CAL AND GLEN took a long-overdue lunch break, letting their horses graze near Gully Creek while they ate their sandwiches. The morning had been spent vaccinating cattle. Cal felt they both deserved a respite while the crew, who'd lunched earlier, finished up.

Although Cal saw his brother every day, they rarely had a chance to talk anymore. Especially now that they were both married. Glen was busy with his life in town; he and Ellie had bought a run-down Victorian that they were fixing up. Cal and Jane were still newlyweds, still learning about each other. A lot had happened in the two men's lives in the past year, more than Cal could adequately take in.

Glen finished his lunch first, then stretched out on the cool grass, shading his eyes with his Stetson.

"Jane mentioned something interesting the other day," Cal said, leaning back and resting his weight on his palms.

"What?"

"Nell Bishop was in to see her with that city slicker guy from New York."

"I wouldn't say that to his face," Glen said, lifting the Stetson and grinning. "I think he wants to be a cowboy. Besides, the guy's bigger than you."

"So what? Hey—I'm a Texan!"

"He went to see Jane? What's the matter," Glen joked, "is he having trouble with the drinking water?"

"No, he's been to Bitter End."

If Cal hadn't gotten his full attention earlier, he had it now. Glen sat up and looked at his brother. "Is that for real? How the hell did he find it?"

"Grady and Savannah drew him a map."

"You're kidding!"

"Nope."

"What gives *him* the right?"

Cal smiled, remembering that his initial reaction had been similar to that of his brother. "He thinks it's time someone solved the mystery."

"Really?"

"I tend to agree with him."

"Fine, but it should be one of us, then, someone from Promise. Don't you think?"

"Why?"

"Because it's *our* town. Our history. Personally I don't like the idea of some city slicker poking around in affairs that aren't any of his damn business. If he wants to uncover a few skeletons, I say let him open his own closet."

"You willing to do it or not?"

"Dig up the dirt about Bitter End?" his brother clarified.

"Yup." Cal studied his brother. "You know—figure out what went wrong. And why."

Glen expelled a long breath. "I say let sleeping dogs lie. Frankly I don't need to know."

"That's the way I felt, too," Cal told him. "Until recently."

Glen broke off a long blade of grass and stuck it between his teeth. "What changed your mind?"

"Richard Weston."

"What about him?" Glen asked, sounding disgusted.

Cal didn't hold any more affection for Grady's brother than Glen did; Richard had done nothing but embarrass the family and the community. It wasn't common knowledge that he'd stolen from his family not once, but twice—and, as they'd since learned, he'd victimized a lot of vulnerable people in a really nasty scam back East. The news about his arrest and prison sentence had been the talk of the town for weeks. Some people had difficulty believing Richard was capable of committing such crimes. Cal had no such problem. Richard was a lowlife and deserved every day of the twenty-five-year sentence he'd received.

"Richard being airlifted out of Bitter End brought up a lot of questions about the town. Quite a few folks had never heard of it. Others had and wanted to know more. I think it's time we put an end to this speculation and settle the past once and for all."

"Grady agrees with you?"

"He'd planned to personally take Travis Grant there, until his water pump broke. Even then, he had Savannah draw Travis a map. From what Jane told me, Nell's involved in this, too."

Glen continued to chew on the stem of grass. His hands were tucked behind his head and he stared up at the blue sky. "Maybe you're right."

"What can we do to help?" Cal asked after a silence.

"You and me?" Glen seemed surprised.

"We're among the few who've actually been to the town."

Glen closed his eyes. "Don't remind me."

Glen had been there once, Cal twice—most recently with Jane, who'd insisted she wanted to find the town. He'd finally given in and agreed to accompany her, knowing that otherwise she'd search for it on her own.

As it happened, their going into the ghost town precisely when they did had saved Richard Weston's life. The events of that day had shaken Cal considerably. He was accustomed to being in charge, knowing what to do, but if it hadn't been for Jane and her medical expertise, he could have done little but watch Richard Weston die.

"I'm trying to remember what I know about Bitter End," Glen said, cutting into his thoughts. "What do you think Nell and her friend might want to know?"

Nell and her friend. Cal ignored the question and concentrated on the picture that formed in his mind. He'd seen Travis and Nell dancing at the rodeo not long ago. It had been a shock to see her in the arms of a man, especially since she'd always refused dates and invitations. Once the shock wore off, he'd felt pleased. She'd been completely absorbed in the guy, hadn't even noticed him and Jane.

The ribs he'd injured in the rodeo had been hurting like hell, but he'd managed to talk Jane into staying for the dance. The pain was worth it, seeing as Willie Nelson had unexpectedly shown up. Jane still talked about it; she'd been thrilled.

"A penny for your thoughts," Glen teased. "If they're worth that much."

"I was just thinking about Nell and Travis Grant. . . ."

"What about them?"

"There's a romance brewing."

"So?" Glen said.

"So, I think it's a good idea. I liked Jake—he was one of my best friends—but I'd hate to see Nell grieve the rest of her life away. Jake wouldn't have wanted that, either."

"Is she interested in this Travis character?"

"Seems to be." More than that, Travis Grant was obviously taken with her. Whatever was happening there, Cal hoped it would work out for Nell. She was in line for a bit of happiness.

JEREMY LIKED Travis Grant—so much that it actually worried Nell. Her son was enthralled with him. Several times now she'd been forced to talk to Jeremy about giving Travis time to himself. Like this afternoon, for example. She knew Travis was writing, but the minute her son returned home from school, he'd raced out to see Travis. She didn't know what they'd talked about, but Jeremy had been wearing a silly grin ever since. As if he knew something she didn't.

She'd chastised him soundly for not doing his chores, and he'd left the house in a temper. At dinnertime, when she couldn't find him, she knew where he was likely to be. She hurried over to the bunkhouse and knocked at the door.

"Yeah?" Travis called.

Apparently this was how New Yorkers said, "Come in."

Nell opened the door and was surprised not to see her son there, making a pest of himself despite her scolding. "Have you seen Jeremy?" she asked.

"Not lately." Travis was sitting in front of his computer screen, his brow burrowed.

"I hope I didn't interrupt anything," she said, feeling badly to have barged in on him, considering she'd admonished her twelve-year-old for doing the same thing.

"No problem, Nell." He seemed abstracted and barely glanced away from his work.

She quietly closed the door. Jeremy sometimes liked to escape to the hayloft and read, especially if he was angry with her. She headed in that direction next, hoping to make peace with him.

"Jeremy." She stood in the middle of the barn, staring up at the loft.

"Yeah." Her son peeked over the ledge.

Yeah. Just like Travis. She swallowed the urge to correct him and said, "Time to wash up for dinner."

"Already?" he groaned. He climbed down from the loft and followed Nell back to the house, dragging his feet. He didn't mention the incident earlier that afternoon, and because he hadn't, she didn't, either.

"What are you reading?" his grandmother asked him.

"A book," he said, and set it on the kitchen counter. "When will Emma be back from Girl Scouts?"

Nell glanced at her watch. "Any minute. Kathy's mom is dropping her off. Would you kindly tell Travis dinner will be ready in ten minutes?" She didn't need to make the suggestion twice; Jeremy was out the door as fast as a cartoon character racing across the screen.

"He seems to like Travis," Ruth commented.

"I noticed."

"That worries you?"

It did, Nell thought. Once Travis left—and he *would* leave—her son might well feel abandoned. Initially she hadn't been concerned, but Jeremy's liking for Travis had recently grown into full-scale adulation.

And what about her own feelings? Travis had shaken up her emotions, made her feel all kinds of things she'd shut herself off from. Like attraction. And . . . desire.

"Yes," she answered her mother-in-law. "I'm worried he likes Travis too much."

"You seem to like him yourself," Ruth added slyly.

Nell bit her lip, unable to explain or confide.

"Something happen you want to talk about?" The older woman studied her closely.

Nell just shook her head. Fortunately Ruth left it at that, giving her a hug before pitching in to set the table.

Dinner consisted of meat loaf, scalloped potatoes, homemade bread, corn, green salad and fresh rhubarb pie. Emma ran in the back door, shucking off her jacket, just as they were about to sit down.

As usual, dinner conversation settled around the children and school. This evening Nell was more than grateful to let her two youngsters do the talking. Particularly since her adventures with Travis in Bitter End wouldn't have been an appropriate subject. Nor did she want to discuss their trip into town and the chat with Dr. Jane.

"What's that book you were reading earlier?" Ruth asked when there was a lull in the conversation.

"*Prairie Gold,* by T.R. Grant," Jeremy said. His gaze briefly flew to Travis before he helped himself to a second slice of bread. "He's a great writer."

"You've read enough of his books," Nell said in a conversational tone as she passed the butter to her son.

"You heard of him?" Emma asked Travis.

Jeremy burst into giggles and Nell quelled him with a look.

"You could say we're friends." Travis smiled at Emma, and Nell wondered if he was teasing her daughter. She certainly wouldn't appreciate it if he was.

"I've read all his books," Jeremy stated proudly.

"Every one of them," Nell testified.

"Do you *really* know him?" Emma asked, returning to Travis's earlier statement.

"Travis is a writer," Nell said. "He probably knows lots of other writers." She didn't want to put him on the spot.

Once more Jeremy burst into giggles.

"What's going on here?" Nell demanded.

"Mom, have you ever wondered what the T.R. in T.R. Grant stands for?"

"No," she said. She hadn't given the matter a moment's thought.

"Travis Randolf," Travis supplied slowly, holding her gaze and refusing to let go.

Nell dropped her fork with a clatter.

"Nell?" Ruth said, her eyes showing concern.

"You're T.R. Grant?" Nell whispered, finding it hard to speak and breathe at the same time.

Travis grinned. "At your service."

Nine

"**I** told you I was a writer," Travis explained, as though the logic should have been obvious.

"I figured it out this afternoon!" Jeremy exclaimed excitedly.

"But you didn't say *what* you wrote," Ruth said, frowning.

It just so happened that one of the most popular children's authors in the entire country was sitting at this very table, was sleeping in their bunkhouse. Was kissing her senseless every chance he got.

"Nell?" Travis's gaze continued to hold hers. "Maybe you and I should talk about this privately after dinner."

The idea of being alone with him for even a minute was too much. She shook her head vigorously. "That won't be necessary."

Before Travis could comment, Jeremy and Emma immediately bombarded him with questions. At any other time Nell would have cautioned them to mind their manners. But not tonight.

After dinner Ruth went into her bedroom to watch "Jeopardy" on her television set. Protesting loudly, Jeremy and Emma were sent upstairs to do their homework, while Nell cleaned the kitchen.

She scrubbed the dishes, rinsed them, dried them. She didn't turn around, but she knew Travis was still in the kitchen long before he spoke.

"You might have said something," she told him in a deceptively mild voice.

"Well, I didn't exactly hide it, but I didn't shout it from the rooftops, either." He paused. "Does it change who I am?"

"Yes . . . no."

"I'd rather you got to know me for who I am first—without muddying the waters with my success."

Although she understood, it hurt that he hadn't trusted her with the truth. But it was just as well. This simply reinforced what she already knew—that she shouldn't expect anything from him.

"You wanted to ask me something?" she said pointedly.

"I want to go back to Bitter End in the morning."

"Why?"

"We're missing something important there, Nell. I can feel it, but I can't put my finger on it."

"I don't have time to waste. I've got work to do around here."

He hesitated. "I need you."

"Why?" she cried again, standing with her back to him. "You know the way now. You *don't* need me."

"I do," he said softly. "But I'll leave it up to you." Having said that, he quietly left.

WHEN MORNING ARRIVED and the children were off to school, Nell had a change of heart. This, she promised herself, would be the last time. From then on, Travis was on his own.

"I'm glad you're coming," he said, smiling as she climbed into the sports utility vehicle beside him.

"We ran into a dead end," she muttered. "And if it were up to me, we'd drop the entire project now."

"You don't mean that."

It was true she didn't, but she refused to admit it.

They parked the same place they had before and made their way into the ghost town. Even before they reached Bitter End, Nell could feel the sensation approaching. Gradually it descended on her, the intensity mounting with each step she took.

"What are we looking for?" Nell asked in a whisper, standing close to his side. She'd prefer to keep her distance, but the town frightened her.

"I don't know yet," he said, his voice low.

As they stood in the center of the street in the middle of Bitter End, Travis surveyed the buildings. "Does anything strike you as familiar?" he asked after a moment, his voice slightly raised.

"No." Nothing had changed from the day before except her anxiety to leave, which had only increased.

"The tree!" he shouted, pointing down the street. He started for it, leaving her behind.

He stopped some yards from the large dead oak with its gnarled, twisted limbs.

"Wh-what about the tree?" she asked, breathless from running after him.

"Nell, don't you remember the quilt? That's the tree! You can tell by the trunk."

Travis walked slowly toward it. "Look. Nell, look."

He ran his finger over the rough crude letters in the dead wood.

Nell's swift intake of breath was the only sound.

There, carved into the side of the tree, was the word "cursed."

IT CAME TO TRAVIS then, in a blinding flash. The quilt squares they'd found so puzzling held the key to whatever had happened in Bitter End.

"The quilt," he said. "The squares tell what happened to the town."

"A story quilt! I hadn't even thought of that." Nell's eyes went bright with excitement. It was all Travis could do not to kiss her right then and there. He resisted, with difficulty.

He might have kissed her, anyway, if he hadn't felt her withdrawing from him. The fact that he was a successful novelist had come to light at the worst possible moment. In retrospect, he realized he should have told her much sooner, but he'd enjoyed the anonymity. He appreciated being accepted and liked for the man he was and not for what he'd achieved.

Then, too, her unawareness of his identity, his success, had given him a chance to know her. His career hadn't intruded on their relationship. They'd simply become friends. Well, more than friends if he had his way.

Unfortunately he'd felt Nell retreating emotionally as soon as she'd learned the truth about him. She believed he'd misled her and he supposed he had, although he hadn't meant to. He'd planned to tell her in his own time. And now . . .

"Think," Nell said, biting her lower lip. "What else was on those quilt squares?"

Travis tried to remember, but his thoughts were on Nell, not on the quilt. There'd only been a handful, five or six squares. Obviously they weren't enough to complete the entire quilt, which meant some squares were missing, maybe forever lost.

"Okay, the oak tree. And one of the squares showed a grave marker," Nell said, counting them on her fingers.

"One of them showed something that resembled a dry riverbed," he recalled. "But there's no river around here."

"Gully Creek isn't far," she said with a thoughtful frown.

"It isn't unheard of for creeks to run dry," he added.

"What else?" Nell asked.

"A frog?"

"Yes, but a frog doesn't make sense," Nell said.

"If there was a creek here, there could have been frogs."

"Yes, but . . ." She shook her head. "The quilt sounded promising at first, but I'm beginning to have my doubts—especially about the square with a hangman's noose. What could that possibly mean?"

"I don't know," Travis admitted. Like her, he was feeling some reservations. "You said one of the squares was a grave marker, right?"

She nodded.

"Do you remember what it said?"

"Yes." Nell answered and took a deep breath. "It said Edward Abraham Frasier and there was a Bible reference."

"I don't suppose you remember the Bible reference."

She nodded. "Matthew 28:46."

It didn't mean anything to Travis. They'd have to wait until they were back on the ranch and had access to a Bible.

" 'My God, my God, why have you forsaken me?' " Nell quoted in a soft voice.

Travis was impressed. "Great," he said, and reached for her hand, squeezing it gently. He intended to check out the cemetery next to see if they could find the grave marker.

"I . . . read that passage frequently after Jake's death," she whispered.

Travis remained silent, knowing this was a difficult moment for her.

"Let's go look at the markers in the cemetery here and see if we can find that name," she finally said.

The graveyard was behind the church, surrounded by a sun-bleached cedar-rail fence. Several markers still stood, crude crosses, a few headstones.

Travis wandered among the graves, but found nothing.

"It's impossible to read the names," Nell protested. "Something might have been etched into the wood, but you can't read it anymore."

Travis knelt in front of one headstone, choosing it randomly. A rosebush bloomed nearby. The irony of it didn't escape him—the only living plants in this town were in the cemetery. God had a great sense of humor.

He could see that a name had once been visible on the simple stone marker, and not knowing what else to do, he ran the tip of his finger gently over it. After a moment he could make out the first letter.

"W," he said aloud.

"Did you say something?" Nell asked, strolling toward him. She stood at his side while he continued to kneel in front of the marker.

"A," he said, his enthusiasm growing. "L . . . T, I think . . . E . . . R.''

"Walter?"

"That was his name." Travis glanced up at her. "Try pressing your finger over the inscription," he said.

Nell did as he suggested, kneeling in front of another grave, close to Travis. It wasn't easy; her hands were callused from ranch work while his were more sensitive. The most strenuous activity he used his hands for was tapping computer keys.

"A!" she shouted triumphantly.

"Wonderful," he said. He removed a small notebook and pen from his pocket. Walter E. Bastien was the first name he entered. If he read the dates correctly, Walter had died at age three.

"D . . . E . . . L . . . E," Nell completed excitedly. "Adele!"

Travis moved on to the next marker. They were able to read nine names before they found Edward Abraham Frasier. He'd died at age five. Of the ten names they'd recorded, Travis noted that eight were children, who'd all died before the age of seven.

"Life was hard in those days," Nell said soberly. "My great-grandmother was one of ten children and only five survived to adulthood."

"A fifty percent mortality rate."

"I couldn't bear to lose a child, not after . . ." She didn't need to complete the thought.

"Well," Nell said abruptly, sitting back on her haunches, "this is all very interesting, but what does it mean?"

Travis didn't know and merely shrugged.

"How can we solve anything? We need to know what happened! Okay, so the quilt is somehow tied in to the town's history, but what does it tell us? Bitter End does indeed have a tree with the word 'Cursed' carved in the wood. And we found the grave marker for Edward Frasier, who's got to be an ancestor of Ellie's but it doesn't mean anything if we don't know all the facts."

"The tree's dead," Travis murmured.

"What else is new?" she said, sounding almost flippant. "Everything in this town is dead."

"I want to know why. What happened here? At one time this was a prosperous enough community, but something went very wrong. Something that no one's ever written about, so we're stuck with no documentation. Except . . . what about old newspapers?"

"If Bitter End ever printed a newspaper, whatever copies were published disappeared a long time ago."

"We don't know that." His research skills were beginning to kick in. "I'm thinking that if something horrendous happened, it would be reported elsewhere."

"Like where?"

"Perhaps in the Austin newspaper. Maybe San Antonio. It wouldn't do any harm to check it out."

"But how in heaven's name would we ever find that? Travis, it would take weeks of looking through microfilm."

"My dear," Travis said, slipping his arm around her waist, "haven't you ever heard of the Internet?"

ELLIE WAS BUSY reading a cookbook when Glen walked into the kitchen, fresh from the shower. He skidded to a stop when he saw her and pretended to be terrified, shielding his face with both arms.

"All right, all right," she said dryly. "Very funny. But I'm not planning to poison you, if that's what you're thinking." Ellie's limited culinary skills had become a shared joke. She'd learned a few recipes but rarely ventured into new territory.

"Honey, I don't mind cooking."

Ellie knew that was true, but Glen's repertoire consisted primarily of roast beef, beef stew and spaghetti with meat sauce, except that he added ingredients not generally associated with those dishes—jalapeños, green olives and walnuts. He was also inventive when it came to salads.

"Where did you get the cookbook?" he asked.

"The library," Ellie said. She couldn't see investing a lot of money in the project until she was sure she was up to the task.

"Do I dare inquire what's for dinner?"

"Tamale pie, cooked in a kettle." She had all the ingredients assembled on the kitchen counter. Her sleeves were rolled up and she'd tucked a towel into her waistband. If she *looked* capable and in control, she figured she might *feel* that way.

"That's your first mistake," Glen said knowingly.

"What?"

"Following a recipe. Use your instincts."

"I don't have any," Ellie muttered. Her upbringing hadn't been traditional. From early childhood, it was understood that she'd be taking over the family business. Instead of spending time in the kitchen with her mother learning the conventional domestic skills, she'd been with her father learning about types of feed and tools and worming medications.

"You've got instincts," Glen insisted. "You just don't know it yet. Here, let me read the recipe."

"Glen . . ." she protested, but knew it would do no good. In the months since their marriage, she'd managed to acquire a few skills. Dovie had given her cooking lessons and taught her the basics. Still, Glen continued to tease her.

"Tamale pie," he read over her shoulder. "Look at this," he said with disgust. "There's no mention of jalapeños."

"There's chili powder in the sauce."

"Instincts, Ellie, instincts."

"I'll add jalapeños as soon as I develop some," she said. "Instincts, I mean." She booted him firmly out of the kitchen. "Scoot. Go read the newspaper. Watch television. Worry about the price of beef—whatever—but leave me to my own devices."

He gave a disgruntled shrug, then did as she requested. She'd purposely chosen this recipe because it looked simple enough even for her. If all else failed, she had a frozen entrée tucked away in the freezer.

After reading the recipe twice, she started her task, remembering what Dovie had taught her. One step at a time. Everything went smoothly and she was beginning to think that there might be some Martha Stewart in her, after all. She'd actually enjoyed this, although the kitchen was a disaster. For now, she planned to bask in her success and leave the dirty dishes for later.

The beauty of this recipe was that the entire dinner was cooked on the stove. The cookbook warned against removing the lid and checking on the cornmeal topping until the required time had passed. While she waited, she glanced through the other recipes, finding three or four casseroles that looked tempting. Glen would eat his words, or more accurately, he'd eat her tamale pie and rave about it.

"How much longer?" Glen shouted from the living room.

"Not long."

"Are you making a salad?"

"I was thinking about it."

"Want any help?"

"Oh, all right." She sighed as though she'd made a major concession. In truth, she was pleased. Glen used his much-vaunted instincts to concoct salads, and tossed together the most amazing creations. He started with the traditional lettuce and tomatoes, then added whatever else he could find, including cheddar cheese, shredded carrot, sliced Bermuda onion and even seedless grapes.

"Cal mentioned something interesting the other day," her husband said, his head stuck inside the refrigerator. He reappeared, loaded with ingredients, both plain and exotic.

"Cal is always interesting."

"He said Nell and that reporter friend of hers are looking into solving the mystery of Bitter End."

This was news. "How?"

"He didn't say. At first I was opposed to the idea and said so."

"I'd rather they bulldozed the entire town and set it on fire," she said, not realizing until now that her feelings ran this strong. She'd been there once with Richard Weston, and that had been enough to last her two lifetimes. Never, ever would she return. Of course it didn't help that her companion had done his best to scare her half to death.

Richard had started by blindfolding her for the drive so she wouldn't be able to find the way on her own—as if she'd want to. When they arrived, he'd promptly disappeared. Then he'd popped up in front of her, frightening her so badly she'd nearly fainted.

"At first I felt it was best just to let things be," Glen said.

"You've changed your mind?"

He washed the lettuce and patiently tore it into small pieces. "Cal's right about Bitter End." His tone was thoughtful. "Ever since Richard was airlifted from the town, there's been plenty of speculation about it. Not many people had heard of it, before, but more and more have learned it's there. Because of Richard."

"So we have another thing to thank Richard Weston for," Ellie said sarcastically. It infuriated her to remember she'd actually dated that lowlife. He'd pretended to be enthralled with her, had even proposed marriage. On the other hand, though, if it wasn't for Richard, Ellie doubted she would have recognized how much she loved Glen.

Her husband had been equally blind. When he did finally figure out he was in love with her, he'd managed to humiliate her in front of the entire town. Naturally Richard had encouraged that. Even worse, he'd succeeded in convincing Glen that Ellie was going to marry *him*. That Glen actually believed it was a huge affront to her pride. But in the months since, he'd more than made it up to her.

Glen was a good husband, and when the time came, he'd make a good father. She loved him immensely, and her love grew stronger every day.

"In this instance," Glen said, "I do think we should thank Richard. Bitter End has been a blight on our history for a lot of years."

"Something horrible happened there." One trip to that awful town had proved it. Just thinking about it made her skin crawl.

"But what?" Glen asked in challenge. "Isn't that the real mystery?"

"Yes," she agreed, but stopped herself from saying more. The timer on the stove went off, signaling dinner was ready. She cast an eye to her husband and sincerely hoped this meal turned out to be as appetizing as the cookbook had promised.

Glen finished preparing his salad, adding last-minute touches of almond slivers, cilantro and goat cheese, tossing everything together with a panache she'd never possess. They carried the meal to the kitchen table, and for a while were too busy eating to bother with conversation. Her tamale pie was pronounced an unqualified success and Ellie was thrilled.

"Aren't you the least bit curious about Bitter End's history?" Glen pressed.

"Yes," she admitted with some reluctance, "but at the same time I'm afraid."

"Of what?"

"Unearthing skeletons I'd prefer remained buried," she murmured. "Suppose it was my ancestors who were responsible? I'd never be able to hold up my head again."

"No one's going to blame you for something that happened over a hundred years ago."

"Don't be so sure."

"It could have been my family," Glen said, resting his fork beside his plate. "Or the Westons. Whatever made Richard the kind of person he is—well, that had to come from somewhere. There could be a whole lot of dirt disclosed."

"You still feel Nell and her . . . friend should go ahead with this?"

"Yes," he said, "for a lot of reasons. I'd rather deal with some embarrassment than have a kid get hurt out there because he's curious about the mystery." His voice grew uncharacteristically serious. "Secrets are dangerous, Ellie. They lead to fear and repression. Remember what the Bible says—'The truth shall make you free.'"

"The Bible," Ellie repeated. She'd found one among her dad's things. When she opened it, she'd read the names handwritten in the front. She'd studied the births and deaths that had been listed. One death had occurred in Bitter End. A boy of five, Edward Abraham Frasier. It was what had drawn her to the ghost town. She'd wanted to find his grave, but the markers had been impossible to read. Richard had lost patience and she'd given up, eager to escape the town and the dreadful feeling that had come over her while she was there.

"I found something else in my father's things," she said. "I don't think I showed it to you. A six-inch square of material fell out of the Bible."

"What kind of square?"

Ellie shrugged. "At first I thought it might be part of a quilt, but no one would make a quilt with this picture on it."

"What was it?"

"A giant grasshopper," she said. "Huge. The stitching was all very tiny and neat, but frankly it was quite ugly. For a while I thought of having it framed, seeing as it's so old, but eventually I decided against it. A grasshopper isn't something I want hanging in our bedroom."

"I don't know," Glen said, with a teasing glint in his eyes. "I find it rather romantic."

"Romantic?"

"I'm buggy over you."

Despite herself, Ellie laughed.

Glen laughed, too, but then his expression sobered. "I wonder if you should tell Nell and her writer friend about this."

Ellie wasn't sure yet if that was something she wanted to do.

NELL SQUINTED at the computer screen, amazed that something smaller than a board game was capable of such magical feats. Travis had brought his laptop into the house, and by plugging in a few wires had connected it to her kitchen phone. Afterwards he'd reached the web site for one of the state universities and begun reviewing the files on state history.

After an hour she'd taken over the task. Sitting at the kitchen table, she'd become fascinated by what she was reading. So much information available with such little effort! It astonished her. She had to force herself to remember what they were looking for. She feared that even if she did find the answer, she wouldn't recognize it.

"Mom." The back door swung open and Jeremy appeared. He stopped short when he saw Travis, his delight unmistakable. "Travis!"

"Jeremy, my man, how's it going?" Travis held out his palm, and Jeremy slapped it.

Nell rolled her eyes. Before she could comment, the door opened again and Emma burst in. Seeing Travis, she squealed with pleasure and raced toward him. He lifted her into his arms and hugged her.

In less than three weeks' time, Travis Grant had worked his way into their hearts. And hers.

"I told my teacher who you really are," Jeremy announced on his way to the refrigerator.

"And?"

If Jeremy didn't notice the hesitation before Travis spoke, Nell did.

"She didn't believe me. That's the thing about teachers," her son said with all the wisdom of his years. "They get jaded because so many kids lie these days."

"Give me her name and address, and I'll have my publisher mail her an autographed book."

"Would you?" Excitement flashed in Jeremy's eyes.

"Will you mail one to me?" Emma asked.

"Sure," he said, putting her down.

Jeremy tossed her an apple, which Emma deftly caught. "You want a cookie?" he asked Travis. "They're some of Mom's best."

"Of *course* I want a cookie."

Emma brought a pitcher of milk from the refrigerator.

Soon the three sat at the table, chatting. They were so involved in their conversation, Nell thought she might as well be invisible. She smiled to herself. Despite her fears about Travis's leaving, she'd learned something this afternoon. A lesson from her own children.

Both Jeremy and Emma accepted that eventually he'd return to New York. Instead of fretting about it or complaining that he'd disrupted their lives, they were grateful for his visit. Grateful to have met him.

Nell, too, had plenty of reasons to be grateful to Travis. Not only had he pulled her out from her protective shell, he'd also warmed her heart. She knew what it was to feel passion again, to feel that quickened interest in life. To feel what a woman felt when she was falling in love with a man. Nell didn't flinch from the thought.

Another thing: her children's reactions to him revealed how much they needed a father figure, a male role model. For years she'd been bogged down in her grief and refused to see what should have been directly in front of her.

Dinner that night was an informal affair. Ruth was in town with friends playing bridge, and the kids were content with leftovers. While she assembled sandwiches, Travis showed Jeremy how to play a couple of computer games.

"I want to learn, too," Emma insisted impatiently.

"Wait your turn," Jeremy muttered, not removing his gaze from the screen.

Nell thought to remind both kids that there would be no computer after Travis left, in case they thought she'd run out and buy them one. Fortunately she stopped herself in time. Perhaps in a year or two, when the dude ranch was successful, she'd be able to afford a computer. The technology was fast becoming part of everyday life, and she would need one as her business grew. That, and a dishwasher.

Following dinner, Jeremy and Emma, with their usual protests, went upstairs to do homework. Nell was left alone in the kitchen with Travis. He sat at the table with the laptop while she washed up the few dishes they'd used.

"I owe you an apology," she said, surprising herself.

He lifted his eyes from the screen and she gave him a feeble smile. "I've had a rotten attitude recently."

"I need to apologize myself," he said. "I should've mentioned sooner exactly what kind of writer I am."

"That's your business, Travis, and none of mine. As you said the other night, it doesn't make any difference to who you are as a person." She turned and reached for another dish, drying it by hand. "I want to thank you for being so good with the kids. It's no wonder they enjoy your books so much."

"They're delightful kids."

"I think so," she said.

He pushed back his chair, scraping it against the floor. "You're delightful, too," he said, coming to stand beside her. He removed the plate and dish towel from her hand.

"Travis?" She looked up at him, not knowing what to expect. Then again, she did.

He kissed her just the way she knew he would and she allowed herself to be consumed by it. His hands were in her hair, his fingers buried in her braid.

He sighed heavily when he lifted his lips from hers. "Kissing you could become addictive."

"That's what you said about my cookies earlier." Her small attempt at humor was a gentle reminder that this kiss—in fact, everything between them—was to be taken lightly. As soon as they had the information they needed, they'd be able to work out the details regarding the events in Bitter End. And once the mystery was solved, Travis would return to New York.

And she'd return to life as she knew it, a little smarter and a little more capable of coping with the future.

He continued to hold her until they heard the sound of footsteps racing down the stairs. They broke apart like guilty teenagers.

Jeremy walked into the kitchen, stopped and looked at the two of them. "Am I interrupting anything?"

Nell denied it with a shake of her head.

"I came for a glass of water," he said. A minute later he was gone.

Travis sat in front of the computer again. Nell sat next to him, reviewing the notes he'd taken and rereading her own. They'd found a number of references to Bitter End, but nothing concrete that pertained to the mystery.

Not yet, at any rate. Nell had a positive feeling, though; she was really beginning to enjoy this.

"Nell," Travis said, holding his finger against the computer screen.

"What is it?"

"This newspaper article from the *Brewster Review*—it's from 1879."

"But that's a year before Promise was founded."

"My point exactly." He got out of his chair. "Read it for yourself."

Ten

Nell slid onto the chair Travis had vacated and stared at the computer screen. Excitement bubbled up inside her. Was it possible Travis had stumbled onto the answer already?

As she scanned the first paragraph of the newspaper article, her spirits sank. Travis was looking too hard for a connection. She hated to be discouraging but could see nothing relevant.

"All this reports is the wrongful death of sixteen-year-old Moses Anderson in Bitter End."

"Continue reading," Travis said.

Nell returned her attention to the screen. "It says Moses was defending a saloon girl from an abusive drunk." Nell glanced up at him, a puzzled expression on her face.

"Read on."

Nell did so, mumbling a couple of lines aloud. "And the other men in the saloon sided with their friend." She gasped as she read the next paragraph. "The drunk and his friends dragged the young man outside and—" she looked up at Travis "—hanged him." Nell sighed at the brutality of such a deed. The boy was only sixteen. Nevertheless she didn't see how this one act of mob rule was connected to the troubles in Bitter End.

The question must have shown in her eyes because Travis asked, "Did you notice the teenager was a preacher's son?"

"Yes, but what makes you think this has anything to do with what happened to Bitter End?"

Travis's smile was wide. "The quilt. We were right, Nell—the mystery is linked to those quilt squares. Who better to curse a town than a man of God? The tree had the word 'Cursed' carved into it, remember?"

Of course she did. "Wasn't there another square with the hangman's noose? Maybe that's the connection—Moses being hanged." Nell's enthusiasm mounted. "Let's look at those quilt pieces again!"

"Good idea."

Travis followed her into the living room. She opened the cedar chest and removed the cardboard box. Nell set aside the folded sheet of muslin and placed the squares on the coffee table.

"What in heaven's name do a frog and a word carved in an oak tree have in common?"

Jeremy came down the stairs. "What are you doing?" he asked.

"Unraveling a mystery," Nell explained absently as she continued to study the quilt pieces.

"Why not put Moses Anderson's name on the tombstone, instead of Edward Abraham Frasier's?" Travis added, as though he was beginning to doubt his own theory.

"Who's Moses Anderson?" Jeremy asked, leaning forward to get a better look at the embroidered squares.

"Travis found a news article about him in an old newspaper," Nell murmured, concentrating on the squares.

"Off the Internet? Mom, I'm telling you, we gotta get a computer."

"Someday."

"Aw, Mom . . ."

"The river scene without a river," Nell muttered listening with only half an ear to her son's pleas.

"Did you notice that the stitching on the riverbank's sort of a rusty red?" Travis asked.

"Soil in the area is iron-rich," Nell explained, dismissing any significance in the choice of color.

"Moses turned the water into blood, remember," Jeremy commented. "We read about it in Sunday School last week."

"Moses did indeed," was Nell's vacant reply.

"Moses and his brother Aaron."

"That's it," Travis shouted, and threw his arms in the air. "Jeremy, you're a genius, a living breathing genius. That's it, that's the key." He gripped the boy's shoulders to hug him wildly. Then he reached for Nell, laughter spilling from him like water.

Jeremy and Nell stared at him as if he'd suddenly gone weak in the head.

"What are you talking about?" Nell demanded.

"The curse!" he shouted.

"What's Travis so excited about?" Emma asked from halfway down the stairs.

"I don't know how we could have been so blind." Now that Travis had stopped laughing, he clasped Nell around the waist and danced her about the room. Jeremy and Emma clapped and laughed.

"Travis, for the love of heaven, stop! Tell me."

Breathing hard, he draped his arms over her shoulders and rested his forehead against hers. "I can't believe we didn't see it sooner."

"See *what?*" she cried, growing more and more frustrated.

Travis turned her around so that she faced the coffee table. "Look at the quilt pieces again."

"I'm looking."

"What was the preacher's son's name?"

"Moses," she said.

"After his son was murdered, the preacher cursed the town."

"Yes." Her gaze went to the square with "Cursed" carved in the tree.

"Now look at the frog."

"I'm looking, I'm looking."

"Jeremy, bring me your Bible," Travis instructed.

The boy raced out of the room.

As soon as Travis mentioned the Bible, Nell understood. "Moses and the plagues."

Jeremy returned with his Bible and handed it to Travis, who started flipping pages in the Old Testament.

"Somewhere in the first part of Exodus," Nell said, fairly certain that was where the story of Passover was told.

"Here," Travis said, running his finger down the seventh chapter. First there's all this business about turning staffs into snakes, then Moses and Aaron did as the Lord commanded and hit the surface of the Nile with a rod, and the river turned to blood."

"Gully Creek became bloody?" That sounded a bit far-fetched to Nell.

"Maybe the water went bad and they couldn't drink it," Jeremy suggested.

"Or dried up," Travis said.

"What else happened in the Bible that ties to Bitter End?" she asked, eager now, reading over his shoulder. Travis skimmed through several chapters, listing the plagues that had befallen Egypt. The death of cattle, flies, hail and lightning, locusts, boils, crop failures were the ones described first.

"What was the one that came after the river turning into blood?" Jeremy asked.

"Frogs," Travis said triumphantly. "The land was covered with frogs."

"Not if the creek dried up." Someone had to show a little reason, Nell thought.

"I don't think we'll ever completely understand the dynamics of what happened."

"The grave marker," Nell said excitedly. "The five-year-old boy, remember?"

"Abraham Edward Frasier."

"Remember, it was the death of the firstborn sons that convinced Pharaoh to let the Israelites leave Egypt," Nell said.

"The children." Travis's voice was low. "Of the ten graves we were able to identify, eight were children." He paused. "The last plague was the death of the firstborn sons," he said slowly.

As a widow, Nell knew she could survive any financial trial, bad weather or crop failure, if she still had her home and her land. The one thing she wouldn't be able to stand was losing her children. If *they* were at risk, nothing else mattered.

"That's why everyone left the town," she said confidently. "Their children were dying. The community had withstood everything else—the river drying up, the pestilence, the other trials. But no land, no town, no community was worth the loss of their children."

The phone rang just then and Emma ran to answer it. "Mom," she shouted as though Nell was in the barn, instead of the next room. "It's Ellie Frasier."

WADE MCMILLEN sat at the desk in his study and tried to ignore the bright sunshine flooding the room. The most difficult part of his week was writing the Sunday sermon. While he enjoyed preaching, even enjoyed the research demanded in his work, he wasn't particularly fond of the effort that went into composing his sermons. Especially on a day as glorious as this one.

Putting aside his notes, he rose and walked over to his study window, gazing at the tree-lined streets of Promise. It was a changed town from the one he'd come to serve five years ago. And this past year had seen the most dramatic of those changes.

There'd been a number of weddings, sure to be followed by a rush of births. Just last week he'd been out to visit the Smiths' baby girl for the first time. Wade had watched Laredo, as the new father, rock Laura to sleep, crooning cowboy songs, instead of lullabies. The memory of that scene brought a smile to his lips even now.

Recently Grady Weston had proudly told him Caroline was pregnant. Wade was pleased; this was exactly the kind of happy news he'd been waiting to hear. Maggie would make a wonderful big sister. It would be nice, too, for the Smiths' daughter to have a cousin around the same age. Wade recalled how close he was to Les McMillen, a cousin only three months younger than he was. They'd been inseparable. In many ways he was closer to Les than his own brother, who was four years his junior.

It wouldn't surprise Wade any if Ellie and Jane, the wives of the Patterson brothers, showed up pregnant—and soon. He knew from the hints he'd heard Mary and Phil give their sons that the boys' parents were more than ready to become grandparents. Wade didn't think they'd need to wait much longer.

With his thoughts full of weddings and babies, Wade didn't realize he had visitors until he heard the voices outside his door. His secretary buzzed him on the intercom.

"Nell Bishop and Travis Grant are here to see you," Martha announced.

"Show them in." Wade knew Nell had a paying guest staying at Twin Canyons. Nell had briefly introduced him after service a couple of Sundays ago. Jeremy and Emma had been full of chatter about their guest the past few weeks, as well, but Wade hadn't met him yet.

His first sight of Travis Grant revealed a large man with a kind face.

"Wade McMillen," Wade said, and the two men exchanged handshakes. Wade gestured for Nell and Travis to sit down, which they did. Maybe he was getting to be an old hand at such things, but Wade felt he knew the reason for this unexpected visit.

One glance told him they were in love; he knew the signs. It was early, probably too early, for them to think about marriage. If that was what they were here to discuss, he'd feel obliged to suggest a long engagement. Nevertheless, Wade was pleased for Nell, very pleased indeed.

"What can I do for you?" Wade asked, leaning back in his leather chair.

"We've come to talk to you about Bitter End," Nell said.

Wade frowned. That was the last subject he'd expected her to mention. The ghost town that had been the cause of so much trouble lately, what with Richard Weston having holed up there. Sheriff Hennessey and the town council had combined their efforts to keep things quiet, but information always seemed to leak out, anyway.

"You do know about the ghost town, don't you?" Travis asked.

"Yes. Have you been there?" The question was directed at Travis, but Nell answered.

"We both have. Twice," she added.

"Actually three times."

Nell nodded. "Three times."

Good grief, they already sounded like an old married couple.

Nell looked at Travis and her eyes sparkled with excitement and happiness. "We think we've solved the mystery of why everyone left Bitter End."

"The town was cursed," Travis explained.

"Cursed?"

"By a preacher whose sixteen-year-old son was hanged when a mob of rowdy drunks got out of hand."

Wade hated to discourage them. In the Wild West it wasn't uncommon for a preacher to be credited with the ability to rain fire and brimstone down upon the backs of sinners. There were usually logical reason for these supposedly supernatural events, but they were cheerfully overlooked.

"His name was Moses," Nell supplied.

"The preacher's?"

"No, the teenager who was hanged."

The violence of the Old West never ceased to distress Wade, but then all he had to do was take a walk through an inner-city slum to appreciate that, in certain ways, humanity hadn't advanced much.

"When the mob of drunks hanged the boy, the preacher came to the town and cursed it with the plagues of Egypt," Nell said.

"That's our theory, anyway," Travis added.

Wade was willing to listen, but he didn't hold out much hope that this was really the reason the town had been abandoned all those years ago. "How do you know about the plagues?"

"From the story quilt."

Nell and Travis glanced at each other as if to decide who should explain the role played by this quilt. Apparently it was decided that Nell would, because she continued. "Ruth had a cedar chest in the attic that was given to her after her mother-in-law died almost fifty years ago. Inside it, we found the makings of a quilt. The backing was intact, but there was only a handful of completed squares."

"We found only six, but we knew there had to be others."

"There were," Nell said, her face glowing with enthusiasm. "Ellie Frasier phoned and told us about an embroidered square she'd found in her father's Bible."

"One with a giant grasshopper," Travis explained.

"Locusts," Wade murmured.

"Exactly."

"We're convinced," Travis said, pausing to look at Nell, who nodded eagerly, "that the final plague, the one that drove the families away from Bitter End was some kind of epidemic that killed their children. By now, the residents had endured one tribulation after another—bugs, weather problems, failed crops . . ."

"The quilt told you all this?" Wade asked.

"Yes," Nell said, "it explained everything. Well, almost everything."

"Go on." Wade motioned to Travis. "I didn't mean to interrupt you."

"When the children started dying, the people who were left panicked, packed up everything they owned and moved. Canned goods still remain on the store shelves, so my guess is they had a big meeting and made the decision to get out together immediately."

"Drought, disease, pestilence," Wade murmured. "I'd leave, too."

"It's an incredible story," Nell said, and glanced at Travis, her pride evident. "Travis is going to write about it."

"This is exactly the type of story I've been waiting to find. For years I've been writing for juveniles and I've searched for the right vehicle to cross over from children's books to adult fiction."

"You aren't going to stop writing for kids, are you?" Nell asked, looking distressed.

"No, they're my audience, and I'll always write for them. But the story of Bitter End gives me an opportunity to make my mark with another readership."

This exchange was lost on Wade. He knew Travis was a writer, but had assumed he wrote for a newspaper. Rather than ask a lot of questions, he narrowed it down to one. "Was there something you needed from me?"

The two of them stared at him as though they'd forgotten he was there. "We want you to bless Bitter End," Nell said.

"Bless it?"

"That's what the town needs," Travis interjected. "And according to what Nell tells me, Promise will benefit from it, too."

Wade wasn't sure there was anything to this curse business. All the disasters Travis and Nell had described were probably nothing more than an unfortunate set of coincidences. Superstitions ran deep back then, and people put credence in matters they shouldn't. But it wouldn't hurt to bless the town. He'd be happy to do it.

* * *

THREE DAYS LATER, Wade stood in the middle of Bitter End. With him were several members of the town council, Sheriff Frank Hennessey, the Patterson brothers and their wives, Grady and Caroline Weston, Nell Bishop and her writer friend, and Laredo Smith. It was unlikely this many people had congregated here in more than a hundred years. Each had come for his or her own reasons. And almost everyone who'd accompanied Wade was related to the original settlers in one way or another.

Bitter End. Not exactly a promising name for a frontier settlement. As Wade remembered it, the town had gotten its name from the first settlers, who'd arrived by wagon train. The journey had been long and arduous, but eventually they'd reached the land of their dreams. Unfortunately, due to the hardships they'd suffered on the journey, many of their dreams had turned bitter.

As soon as he set foot in the town, Wade had felt a gloom and a darkness settle over him, even though the day was bright and sunny. He tried to ignore it and proceeded with the ceremony.

Once everyone was gathered around him, he opened his Bible and read a passage. As he spoke the words, he felt the oppression loosen its grip on him.

If the preacher a hundred years ago had used the Old Testament, filled with its judgments and laws, to curse the land, then he'd bless it from the New Testament. Freedom from bondage and judgment would be his prayer.

Wade's voice rang loud and clear down the lifeless streets. When he'd finished reading, he bowed his head. The others followed his lead. Wade prayed that God would smile down on this land once more and make it a place of love, instead of hate, a home of joy, instead of sadness.

A chorus of amens followed when he finished.

Laredo Smith stepped forward, carrying a bucket, shovel and a budding rosebush. "Savannah couldn't be here today, but she wanted me to plant this close to the tree where the boy was hanged."

"That's a wonderful idea," Nell said. Then she pointed to the charred marks on the church steeple. "That was one of the plagues— lightning and hail."

Wade was fast becoming a believer of this incredible tale. He'd studied the quilt pieces—including a seventh one that had been found by Dovie, an illustration of lightning striking a church. And he'd checked out the Internet sites identified by Travis. The more he read and heard about Bitter End, the more everything added up.

"The feeling's not as strong," Wade heard Ellie Patterson murmur to her husband.

"I noticed that, too," Dr. Jane added.

Wade smiled to himself as the assembled group headed back to the highway where the cars were parked.

Wade enjoyed the way these friends talked and joked with each other, but he noted that Nell Bishop and Travis Grant appeared strangely quiet. They were the ones who deserved the credit for solving this mystery. Over the past few days, they'd been the center of attention, and while Nell seemed to be uncomfortable in the limelight, Travis was clearly in his element.

It was often that way with couples, Wade had observed. One shy, the other outgoing. One sociable, the other private. The law of opposites—the wonderful balance that brought stability into a relationship.

As they approached their vehicles, Travis stepped up to Wade. "I'd like to thank you again for all your help."

"The pleasure was mine," Wade said, and meant it.

"I'll be leaving Wednesday morning, and I wanted to take the opportunity to say goodbye," Travis went on.

That explained Nell's dour look. Travis was returning to New York City, a city far removed from this land of sagebrush and ghost towns and tales of the Wild West.

"The best of luck with your book," Wade said. "Keep in touch."

Travis glanced in Nell's direction and responded with a noncommittal shrug.

Wade couldn't help wondering what had happened between the two. Whatever it was, he felt saddened that they didn't have more of an opportunity to explore their love. Although he was far from an expert in the area of romance, Wade had sensed they were well suited.

"You're leaving?" The question came from Grady Weston.

Travis nodded. "I've been away far longer than I expected as it is."

"You're not going to let him drive off into the sunset, are you?" Caroline pressured Nell.

It seemed every eye turned to the widow. "As Travis said, he needs to get back." Her tone was stiff. Then she turned away.

TRAVIS STUFFED a stack of shirts in his suitcase, not showing any particular care. He was a patient man, but he'd been tried to the very limits of his endurance. Beyond!

Nell acted as though his return to New York was cause for celebration. She'd gone so far as to throw him a farewell dinner party. She'd invited her friends, and the last he heard a dozen people had promised to show.

All day she'd been in the kitchen, cooking up a storm, baking, chopping, sautéing. His last hours in Texas, and the woman he loved had her head buried in a cookbook.

Not that he didn't appreciate the effort. It was a kind gesture, but spending the evening with a crowd wasn't how he wanted it. He'd hoped to have a few minutes alone with Nell, but that wasn't to be. In fact, she'd made it quite plain that she *didn't* want to be alone with him. Fine. He was a big boy; he knew when he'd worn out his welcome.

"Do you need any help?" Jeremy asked as he came into the bunkhouse.

Travis zipped up his bag. "Thanks, but I've got everything packed."

The boy at least had the common decency to show some regret at Travis's departure. Emma, too, had moped around the house from the moment she walked in the door. She followed her brother into the bunkhouse.

"Hey, Emma," Travis said. "Why the sad face?"

Her lower lip quavered. "I don't want you to go."

"He *has* to go," Jeremy answered on his behalf.

"Do you?" Emma asked, her eyes wide and forlorn.

Travis opened his mouth to answer, but Jeremy beat him to the punch. "That's what Mom said, remember? His work and his whole life are in New York." Jeremy sounded as though he'd memorized his mother's response. A very reasonable response, he had to admit—but it wasn't what he wanted to hear.

"Mom said we're going to have lots of guests in the next few weeks," Emma told him.

"She's right," Travis said. Nell would have the dude ranch in full swing before long.

"We're bound to get attached to lots of folks," Jeremy said, again echoing his mother's words, Travis suspected.

Attached. Nell thought the relationship he shared with Jeremy and Emma was just one in a long list of attachments. The woman didn't have a clue, he thought angrily. He loved those kids! Her, too.

And all she saw him as—or *wanted* to see him as—was a paying customer at Twin Canyons Ranch. Which made him the first of many wannabe cowboys.

All he needed was some encouragement from Nell. Then he'd stay. Just one word of encouragement. Two at the most. *Don't go* would have sufficed. Instead, she was so pleased to see him off she was throwing a party. It was hard for a man to swallow.

The dinner guests started arriving at five. Nell had the front yard set up with tables and chairs. In addition to all the food she'd been cooking, her friends and neighbors bought over a variety of tasty dishes—salads and casseroles, pies and cakes.

Once dinner was served, they seated themselves at the tables and ate. Ruth sat next to Travis. He almost had the impression that she was waiting for him to do something—but what? After the meal Travis went around to pay his respects to the people he was just beginning to know. He seemed to hit it off with Grady Weston best. It was a shame to call a man a friend in one breath and tell him goodbye in the next.

Travis didn't know what Nell found so all-fired important, but he didn't see her the entire meal. As far as he could figure, she'd hidden herself in the kitchen where she'd been all day.

Before he could do anything about it, Grady joined him, and they exchanged pleasantries for several minutes. Then Grady grew strangely quiet. "What time are you going back to New York?"

"First thing in the morning," Travis said. His flight was late in the afternoon, but he had a three-hour drive ahead of him, plus the rental car to return.

"Do you . . . anticipate seeing Richard again?"

So that was where this conversation was headed. "I don't expect I will."

Grady nodded, his look grave.

"Would you like me to check up on him now and again?" Travis offered.

"He's a criminal and he's paying for his crimes, but dammit all, he's still my brother." Grady's voice dropped.

"Hey, no problem, and I don't need to say I'm there on your behalf."

"It isn't on my behalf, so to speak," Grady was quick to correct him. "I just want to be sure—I guess I'm looking for a change in him."

"Is it possible?"

"I pray it is," Grady said. He stood, patted Travis on the back and left the table to return to his wife.

The laughter and chatter continued for a while, and then people packed up their leftovers and were gone. Travis was grateful. Nell couldn't avoid him forever. He gathered up the serving dishes and carried them into the house.

Nell was washing dishes, her arms elbow-deep in soap suds.

"That was a wonderful dinner," he said.

"Thank you."

"I don't think anyone's ever gone to so much trouble to send me off." He realized he must have sounded a little sarcastic, but if she noticed, she ignored it.

"It wasn't any trouble," Nell countered. "Besides, the community owes you a debt of thanks. If it wasn't for you, no one would know what happened in Bitter End."

"You worked just as hard."

"You dragged me kicking and screaming into this project, remember?"

That wasn't *exactly* how Travis recalled it. She'd been reluctant, true, but had willingly enough accompanied him. They'd made a great team.

"I'm going to miss you," he said, and wished to hell she'd turn around so he could look at her. Instead, she stood with her back to him and revealed none of her thoughts.

"Me and Emma got all the trash picked up," Jeremy called from the living room.

"It's bedtime," she told them. "Go upstairs and wash."

"Aw, Mom."

"You heard me."

Nell must have removed the plug from the kitchen drain because he heard the water swish and gurgle. She turned to reach for a towel and beamed him a smile so dazzling it startled him.

"What time are you leaving?" she asked.

"Around six."

She nodded. "I probably won't see you, then."

He was hoping she'd suggest they have coffee together before he left. Just the two of them. No kids. No Ruth. Just them.

She didn't offer.

Travis forced himself to smile. "I guess this is it, then."

"This is it."

They stood and stared at each other for an awkward moment.

"It's been . . . great." Nell said at last.

He nodded. "I'd like to kiss you goodbye, Nell," he said.

She hesitated, then floated easily into his arms. When their mouths found each other, the kiss was a blend of need and sadness, of appreciation and farewell.

When she slid out of his arms, Travis was shocked by how much he missed her there. He might as well get accustomed to it, for she gave no indication that she cared to see him again. Not one word, not one sign.

"You'll keep in touch?" he asked, hoping she'd at least be willing to do that.

"The kids would love to hear from you."

Her words hit their mark. "But not you?"

"I didn't say that."

"Would *you* enjoy hearing from me?" It was damn little to ask.

She lowered her gaze and nodded.

"Was that so hard, Nell?"

She looked up at him and he was surprised to see tears glistening in her eyes. "Yes," she whispered. "It was very hard."

Eleven

It did no good to pretend anymore. Nell sat out on her front porch, watching the sunset. Travis had been gone a week and it felt like ten years. She'd fallen in love with a greenhorn. Travis Grant might know everything there was to know about computers, but he'd barely figured out which side of a saddle was up.

"A writer," Nell muttered, staring at the sky. She was thoroughly disgusted with herself. Everything she'd ever wanted in this life she'd had with Jake. But he'd died, and she was so lonely. She hadn't even realized *how* lonely until that New Yorker kissed her. All the men who'd pestered her for a date in the past couple of years and she hadn't felt the slightest interest. Then Travis came into her life and before she knew it she was in love. It felt like she'd been sucker-punched.

"Are you thinking about Travis again?" Ruth asked, standing just inside the screen door.

"No," Nell denied vehemently, then reluctantly confessed. "Yeah." *Yeah.* Now Travis had her doing it. If he'd stayed much longer, she'd sound just like a Yankee.

"You gonna write him?"

"No." Of that much Nell was sure.

"Why not?"

"I can't see where it'd do any good."

"Oh, Nell."

"He's from New York. He wouldn't be happy in Promise and this is where the kids and I belong." The situation was impossible, and the sooner she accepted that, the better it would be for everyone. Travis Grant was a writer who lived in the center of the publishing world. He'd come to Texas to research a book, not find himself a wife and take on a ready-made family.

She was convinced that in time she'd fall in love with someone from around here. Someone who stirred her heart. Travis had shown her it was possible; now all she had to do was find the right man.

"Nell, dear, I still think you should write him a letter." Ruth sat in the rocker next to Nell and took out her crocheting.

Even if she did write Travis, Nell mused, she wouldn't know what to say. Really, what was there to write about? Besides, he might misread her intent and assume she was asking something of him.

Eventually she'd get over him and her heart would forget. Any night now she'd stop dreaming about him. Any day now he'd fade from her thoughts.

No, she most definitely wasn't going to write. If he wanted to continue the relationship, then he'd have to contact her first.

Well . . . maybe just one letter, she thought. Just to be sure he arrived home safe and sound. And she could always ask him about the book. One letter, but only one.

That couldn't do any harm.

TRAVIS SQUINTED at the computer screen, then yawned and pinched the bridge of his nose. He'd been home all of eight days and he'd already written the first fifty pages of his new book—the book for adults. The words seemed to pour out of him. He couldn't get them down fast enough.

But then, he'd always been able to escape into a story when his life was miserable. It was one of the blessings of being a writer—and one of the curses. His stomach growled in angry protest and he realized it'd been twenty-four hours since his last meal.

He walked barefoot in the direction of his kitchen, surprised to realize it was morning. It was 6 a.m. according to the clock on the mantel. From the view through the windows in his high-rise apartment, he saw that the city was just waking up. In Texas Nell would be—

He stopped, refusing to think about Nell, or Jeremy or Emma. They were out of his life and that was the way it had to be. The way *she* wanted it. That had been made more than clear before he left Promise.

Promise. Yeah, right. They should have named the town Heartache.

His stomach growled again, more insistently this time, and Travis headed toward the refrigerator. It shouldn't have come as any surprise to find nothing he'd seriously consider eating. He was rummaging through his pantry shelves when the apartment intercom buzzed. He muttered under his breath as he heard his ex-wife's voice. Still muttering he waited at the door to let her in.

"You've been home for a week and I haven't heard from you," she said accusingly. "I thought I'd stop by on my way to work to greet the prodigal son." She'd always been an early riser, like him, and generally got to the office before seven.

"I've been working." He might not have been as friendly if she hadn't come bearing gifts. She carried a sack from his favorite bakery and a takeout latte. At the moment he would have thrown his arms around a terrorist offering food.

"You eating?"

He reached for the sack. "I am now."

Valerie chuckled and followed him into the kitchen. She was a lovely-looking woman, but Travis was now immune. Unfortunately she was cold and calculating, and about as different from Nell Bishop as a woman could get.

"So what'd you find out about that ghost town?" Val asked.

Travis quickly devoured two jelly-filled doughnuts, pausing only long enough to inhale. His stomach thanked him, and he settled back with the latte. Between sips, he filled in the details, casually mentioning Nell. He acknowledged her help in solving the puzzle and said nothing about his feelings toward her.

Valerie might have remarried, but she tended to believe that Travis remained stuck on her. He couldn't be bothered setting her straight.

"Who's this Nell?"

Damn, but it was impossible to hide anything from her! "A woman I met."

"You in love with her?"

Leave it to Val to get directly to the point. "Maybe." He licked the jelly from his fingertips rather than meet her gaze.

"Travis," she chided. "I know you, and 'maybe' isn't in your vocabulary."

"She was a . . . nice diversion," he said, evading her question. If he was truly in love with Nell, he'd walk on hot coals before he'd admit it to his ex-wife. The one who deserved to know first would be Nell. However, at this point, it seemed unlikely that their relationship would go any further.

"Did you meet Richard Weston's family?" Val asked.

Travis nodded. "They're good people."

"Actually Richard's not half-bad himself."

Travis's gaze narrowed. He was surprised she didn't recognize Weston for the kind of man he was. He'd credited her with better judgment. "What's going on?" he asked.

Val shrugged. "Nothing. How can it? He's behind bars."

"You actually like this guy?"

Val crossed her legs and smiled. "I know what he did, and while he isn't exactly a candidate for a congressional medal of honor, I find him rather charming."

Snakes could be charming, too. Frankly Travis didn't like hearing her talk this way. Recently Val had implied that she and husband number two weren't getting on, but surely she wouldn't get mixed up with a prisoner. "Time for a reality check, Val."

Her eyes flared. "You're one to talk," she snapped. "You're in love with some cowgirl widow."

"I didn't say I loved her."

"You didn't have to. It's written all over you."

Travis exhaled sharply. He had better things to do than get involved in a useless argument with his ex-wife. "All I'm saying is be careful with Richard, all right? He's a user."

"Of course," she said, and gave Travis a demure smile. "We both know I'm too self-centered to do anything that's ultimately going to hurt me." She stared at him. "You, on the other hand, might be tempted to do something foolish about this cowgirl of yours."

"She isn't mine." Travis didn't want to talk about Nell.

"Have you heard from her since you left?"

He sighed. "Do you mind if we talk about something else?"

Val's delicately shaped eyebrows lifted. "You really are taken with her, aren't you?"

"So what if I am?"

"Are you going to leave it at that?"

"Probably," he said, his control slipping.

"You could always write her. Or call."

"And say what?"

"Don't look at me—you're the one who works with words. Seems to me you should have plenty to say." She glanced at her wrist and leaped to her feet. "Gotta run. Court this morning. 'Bye darling." She kissed his cheek and was out the door.

He wasn't going to write Nell, he decided. He would if there was anything to say, but there wasn't. It'd be a cold day in hell before he let another woman walk all over his heart. And really, when it came right down to it, he and Nell didn't have a thing in common. Not one damn thing.

Well . . . maybe one letter to ask about the kids and Ruth. And he did plan to send Jeremy and Emma autographed books. He'd keep the letter short and sweet, thank her for putting him up, that sort of thing. One letter wouldn't hurt. But only one.

NELL'S GAZE fell on the calendar hanging on the bulletin board by the phone. If she'd calculated right, her letter to Travis should arrive in New York City that day. She'd agonized over what to say and in the end had made it a chatty friendly letter. At least that was what she hoped. Her one fear was that her real feelings shone between every line.

Ruth walked into the kitchen. "I picked up the mail while I was in town," she said as she set down her purse and a shopping bag. "Do we know anyone in New York City?" she asked coyly.

Travis. Nell's heart thumped. Because she didn't want Ruth to know how excited she was, she casually reached for the stack of mail, sorting through the various solicitations and bills until she found the envelope. It *was* from Travis.

She stared at it so long Ruth said, "Well, for heaven's sake, girl, open it."

Nell didn't need to be told twice. She ripped open the envelope, her hands shaking with eagerness. Her eyes quickly skimmed the first typed page and glanced at the second. Once she saw how much he'd written, she pulled out a chair and sat down. She read slowly, wanting to savor each word, treasure each line. Like her, he was chatty, personable, yet slightly reserved.

"Well?" Ruth said.

"You can read it if you want."

Ruth looked downright disappointed. "Are you telling me he didn't say anything . . . personal?"

"Not really." Then again, he had, but it was between the lines, not on the surface. His letter really said that he missed her. That he was thinking of her, working too many hours, trying to get on with his life. Nell identified all this because she'd conveyed identical things to him—in what she'd written and what she hadn't.

"There's a package here, as well, for Jeremy and Emma," Ruth said.

In her rush to read Travis's letter Nell hadn't noticed.

"Are you going to write him back?" Ruth asked.

Nell nodded, but she'd wait a couple of days first. It might look as if she'd been anxious to hear from him if she replied too soon. Despite that, she sat down at the dinner table that night and wrote him a reply. The kids each wrote a thank-you note for the autographed books, and it didn't seem right to delay those. Since she was mailing something to him anyway, and her letter was already written, she sent it off the next morning. It wasn't a special trip into town; she had other errands so it worked out conveniently. Or so she told herself.

Ruth was standing on the porch grinning from ear to ear when Nell returned. "You've got company," Ruth called when she climbed out of the pickup. She glanced at the dark sedan parked near the bunkhouse.

Ruth's smile blossomed as Travis opened the screen door and joined her on the porch.

"Hello, Nell," he said, grinning.

He wore a Stetson, faded blue jeans and rich-looking cowboy boots. He might not be a working cowboy, but he was the best-damn-looking one she'd seen in a very long while. It took all the restraint she could muster not to run straight into his arms.

"Are you surprised?" he asked.

She nodded, afraid she couldn't say anything intelligible.

"I'll leave you two to sort everything out," Ruth stated matter-of-factly, and started toward the house.

Her eyes pleaded with Ruth not to leave her, but the older woman was oblivious to her silent cries for help. Nell didn't know what to think, what to say. Her heart raced, but she was afraid to read anything into Travis's unexpected visit. Maybe he was in the area for more research or for business or . . .

She walked over to the porch and sat down on the top step.

"Mind if I join you?" he asked before he sat down next to her.

"Of course not."

"You look wonderful," he said softly.

She nodded her thanks for the compliment. "Were you in the area . . . ?" She had to ask.

"No."

"I . . . I got your letter." She wanted to tell him how excited she was when she saw it, but couldn't manage the words.

"I got yours, too. That's the reason I'm here."

"My letter?" He must have booked the flight out of New York a minute after he'd read it.

"You love me, Nell don't you?"

She nodded slowly.

"I love you, too," he whispered, and reached for her hand.

"But—"

"Hear me out," he interrupted. "You're about to list all the reasons it's impossible for us to be together, but there's nothing you can say that I haven't thought of myself. We're different, but it's a good kind of different. We're good together, a team."

"But—"

"Together we solved a hundred-year-old mystery. There's a lesson in it, too. The people who left Bitter End were looking to make a new life, a new start, and put the pain of the past behind them. I'm offering you the same opportunity—and taking advantage of it myself. We belong together, Nell. You and me and Ruth and the kids."

"But—"

"I'm almost finished," he promised, and drew in a deep breath. "It'll be a new life for all of us. I love you, Nell. I want to marry you."

"I can't live in the city," she blurted.

"You won't have to."

"You mean that?" It was almost more than she dared believe.

"Not if you don't want to. I can work anywhere, you know. One of the benefits of being a writer." He paused. "So?"

"I'll marry you." She'd known that the minute she saw him standing on the porch.

"You don't have any questions?" He seemed almost disappointed that she wasn't going to argue with him.

"Yeah. One." She smiled. "Just how much longer do I have to wait for you to kiss me?"

Within a single beat of her heart, Travis had wrapped her in his arms. His mouth was hard and hungry over hers, and Nell let herself soak in his love. He loved her, really loved her! And he was right that it was time to put aside the past and start again.

"How soon can we arrange the wedding?" he whispered against her throat.

"Soon," she said.

Travis chuckled. "But not soon enough to suit me." Then he kissed her again.

LONE STAR
BABY

LONE STAR
BABY

One

Amy Thornton was out of money, out of luck and out of hope. Well, she had a little cash left, but her luck had definitely run out, and as for her reserves of hope—they were nonexistent. When the Greyhound bus rolled into the bowling-alley parking lot in Promise, Texas, she stayed in her seat. Disinterested and almost numb, she stared out the window.

Promise seemed like a friendly town. June flower baskets, filled to overflowing with blooming perennials, hung from the streetlights. People stopped to chat, and there was a leisurely, almost festive atmosphere that Amy observed with yearning. Smoke wafted from a barbecue restaurant, and farther down the street, at Frasier Feed, chairs were set up next to a soda machine. A couple of men in cowboy hats and boots sat with their feet propped against the railing; they appeared to find something highly humorous. One of them threw back his head, laughing boisterously. His amusement was contagious and Amy found herself smiling, too.

A couple of people boarded the bus. As soon as they'd taken their seats, the bus doors closed. "Next stop is Brewster," the driver announced.

"Excuse me!" Amy cried, and surprised herself by leaping to her feet. "I want to get off here."

"Here?" The driver looked at her as if he thought he'd misunderstood. The bus had sat there for fifteen minutes without her saying a word.

"Yes," she said, as though Promise had been her destination all along. "I'll need my suitcase."

Muttering irritably under his breath, the driver climbed out of the bus, opened the luggage compartment and extracted her travel-worn case.

Five minutes later, choking on the bus's exhaust, Amy stood in the parking lot, wondering what madness had possessed her. She was home-less, without a job and nearly six months pregnant. She didn't know a soul in this town, yet she felt compelled to start her new life here. Away from her mother. Away from Alex. Away from all the unhappiness that had driven her out of Dallas.

Austin had been her original destination. Her mother's cousin lived there—not that Beverly Ramsey was expecting her. But she *was* the only other family Amy had. Moving to Austin had seemed preferable to stay-ing in Dallas, and despite the pregnancy, she'd felt confident she could find employment fairly quickly, if not in an accounting office, then per-haps as a temp. Anything would do for now, as long as she managed to meet her expenses until she located something more permanent. Natu-rally she'd hoped that Beverly would invite her to stay until she found an apartment. Two weeks, she'd promised herself. No longer. Just until she was back on her feet. Yet the thought of calling her mother's cousin mortified Amy. Her mother had sponged off Beverly's kindheartedness for years. It went against everything in Amy to ask for help. She'd rather make it on her own.

If only she knew what to do.

Promise, Texas. Holding her suitcase with both hands, she glanced down Main Street again. If ever she'd needed a promise, it was now. A promise and a miracle—or two.

The baby kicked and Amy automatically flattened her hand against her stomach. "I know, Sarah, I know," she whispered to her unborn child. She hadn't had an ultrasound but chose to think of her baby as a girl and had named her Sarah. "It's not the smartest move we've made, is it? I don't know a soul in this town, but it looks like the kind of place where we could be happy."

Her stomach growled and she tried to remember the last time she'd eaten. A small poster advertising $1.99 breakfast special showed in the bowling-alley window. Apparently there was a café inside.

The small restaurant was busy; almost all the seats were taken, but Amy was fortunate to find an empty booth. A waitress handed her a menu when she brought her a glass of water and glanced at her suitcase.

"You miss the bus, honey?" she asked. "You need a place to wait?"

"Actually I just got off," Amy said, touched by the other woman's concern. "I'll take the breakfast special."

"It's the best buy in town," the woman, whose name tag identified her as Denise, said as she wrote the order down on her pad.

Seeing that the waitress was the friendly sort, Amy asked, "Do you happen to know of someone who needs a competent bookkeeper?"

Denise gnawed thoughtfully on her lip. "I can't say I do, but I'm sure there's a job for you in Promise if you're planning to settle here."

The news cheered Amy as much as the welcome she felt. Already she was beginning to believe she'd made the right decision. Promise, Texas, would be her new address—the town where she'd raise her baby. Where she'd make a life for them both. "I can do just about anything," Amy added, not bothering to disguise her eagerness, "and I'm not picky, either."

"Then I'm sure all you need to do is ask around."

A rancher sitting at a table across from Amy caught Denise's eye and lifted his empty coffee mug. "Be right with you, Cody," she said, then looked back at Amy. "Tex will have your meal out in a jiffy."

"Thanks for your help," Amy said, grateful for Denise's encouragement and kindness. As she waited, she found herself fighting the urge to close her eyes. She staved off a yawn as her meal arrived.

The eggs, toast and hash browns tasted better than anything she'd ever eaten. She hadn't realized how hungry she was and had to force herself to eat slowly. When she'd finished the meal, Amy left her money on the table and included a larger than usual tip in appreciation for Denise's welcoming helpfulness.

As she stood up to leave, the rancher Denise had called Cody sent her a curious glance. He smiled in her direction until he noticed the slight rounding of her abdomen, then his eyes widened and he abruptly turned the other way. Amy shook her head in amusement.

Taking Denise's advice, she walked down Main Street and looked for Help Wanted signs posted in store windows. She saw none, and it occurred to her that it might not be a good idea to apply for a position, suitcase in hand. Her first priority was finding a place to live. Besides, her feet hurt and the suitcase was getting heavier by the minute.

That was when Amy saw the church. It could have appeared on a postcard. Small and charming, it was built of red brick and had wide, welcoming steps that led up to arched double doors. They were open, and although she felt silly thinking this, the church seemed to be inviting her in.

Amy soon found herself walking toward it. Lugging her suitcase up the stairs, she entered the vacant church and looked around. The interior was dark on one side, while rainbow-hued sunlight spilled in through stained-glass windows on the other.

Silently she stepped inside, slipped into a back pew and sat down. It felt good to be off her feet and she gave an audible sigh, followed by a wide yawn. She'd rest a few minutes, she decided. Just a few minutes . . .

The male voice that reached her came out of nowhere. Amy bolted upright. Her eyes flew open and she realized she'd fallen asleep in the pew.

"I beg your pardon," she said, instantly feeling guilt. It took her a moment to discern anything in the dim interior. When her eyes had adjusted, she saw a tall rugged-looking man standing in the church aisle, staring down at her. He resembled a rancher, not unlike the one she'd seen in the café, except that he wore a suit and a string tie.

"Is there a problem?" he asked, his voice gentle.

"No." She shook her head. "None." Flustered, she stood clumsily and grabbed for her suitcase.

"My sermons might be boring, but people generally wake up before Thursday afternoon." His smile unnerved her.

"I didn't mean to fall asleep. I closed my eyes and the next thing I knew, you were here." She glanced at her watch; she'd drifted off for at least twenty minutes, although it felt more like twenty seconds.

"You don't have anything to apologize for," the man told her kindly. "Are you sure there isn't anything I can do to help?"

"How about a miracle or two?" She hadn't meant to sound so flippant.

"Hey," he said, dazzling her with a wide Texas grin, "it just so happens miracles are my specialty." He held his arms open as if to say all she needed to do was ask and he'd direct her request to a higher power.

Amy looked more closely at this man, wondering if he was real.

"Wade McMillen," he said, offering her his hand. "Reverend Wade McMillen."

"Amy Thornton." She shook hands with him and withdrew hers quickly.

"Now, what kind of miracle do you need?" he asked, as if rescuing damsels in distress was all part of a day's work.

"Since you asked," Amy said, slowly releasing her breath. "How about a place to live, a job and a father for my baby?"

"Hmm." Reverend McMillen's gaze fell to her stomach. "That might take some doing."

So he hadn't noticed the pregnancy before, but he did now. "Some miracles are harder than others, I guess." Amy shrugged, figuring it was unlikely he'd be able to help her. But she got into this predicament on her own, and she'd get out of it the same way.

"But none are impossible," Wade reminded her. "Come with me."

"Where are we going?"

"The church office. I'll need to ask you a few questions, but as I said, miracles are my specialty."

DOVIE BOYD HENNESSEY stepped back from the display she'd been working on and studied it with a discerning eye. The pine desk was a heavy old-fashioned one. She'd placed a book next to the lamp, with an overturned pair of old wire-rimmed spectacles on top. A cable-knit sweater was casually draped over the back of the chair, as if someone was about to return. The knickknacks, a quill pen and ink bottle along with a couple of framed pictures gave it a well-used comfortable feeling.

The effect was all she'd hoped for. Her shop had enjoyed a rush of business in the past few months, and the antiques were moving almost as fast as she could get them in the door. Just last week she'd sold a solid cherry four-poster bed that had been in inventory for the better part of eighteen months. Dovie was thrilled. Not just because of the sale, but with the bed gone, an entire corner of the shop would be freed up, allowing her to create a brand-new scene.

Designing these homey nooks was what she loved best. If she'd been thirty-five years younger, she'd go back to school and study to be an interior decorator. Her skills were instinctive, and she loved assembling furniture and various bits and pieces to create the illusion of cozy inviting rooms. But with Frank talking about retiring and the two of them traveling, she probably wouldn't be as involved in the running of her store as she'd been in years past.

As if the thought had conjured up the man, the bells above her door chimed and Sheriff Frank Hennessey walked into the shop.

"Frank!" She brightened at the sight of him. They'd been married nine months now—and he could still fluster her! He was a striking man for sixty, handsome and easy on the eye.

"Travis Grant come for that cherry bed yet?"

"Not yet," Dovie told him, wondering at the question.

Frank smiled—and it was a saucy sexy smile she knew all to well. "Frank, don't be ridiculous."

"We're married, aren't we?"

"It's the middle of the afternoon—good heavens, someone could walk in that door any minute." She edged protectively to the other side of the desk.

"You could always lock the door."

"Frank! Be sensible."

He walked toward the desk.

Giggling like a schoolgirl, Dovie moved beyond his reach. "What about the display windows?"

"Draw the shades."

He had an answer for everything.

"Frank, people of our age don't do this sort of thing!"

"Speak for yourself, woman," he said, racing around the desk.

Dovie let out a squeal and fled with her husband in hot pursuit. He'd just about caught up with her when the bells above the door chimed. Frank and Dovie both froze in their tracks.

Louise Powell, the town gossip, stood just inside the doorway staring as if she'd caught them buck naked on the bed. Her head fell back, her mouth dropped open and her eyes grew round as golf balls.

"Well, I never," she began.

"Maybe you should," Frank suggested. "I bet Paul would appreciate a little hanky-panky now and then."

Dovie elbowed her husband in the ribs and heard him swallow a groan. "Is there something I can help you find?" Dovie asked with as much poise as she could muster. A loose curl fell across her forehead and she blew it away, then tucked it back in place.

"I . . . I came to browse," Louise muttered. "It's Tammy Lee's birthday next week and . . ."

Dovie couldn't imagine there being anything in this store that Tammy Lee Killenborn would find to her liking. The inventory included classy pieces of jewelry, subtly elegant clothing and delicate figurines. Nothing she sold had sequins—which was more Tammy Lee's style—but Dovie would never have said so.

"I think it might be best if I came back another time," Louise said, mouth pursed in disapproval. She marched out of the store.

Dovie turned to glare at her husband. "You can bet that five minutes from now everyone in town is going to know my husband's a sex fiend."

Frank grinned as though nothing would please him more.

"Have you no shame?" she asked, but had a difficult time holding in a smile.

Her husband took one look at her and burst out laughing.

Dovie soon joined him.

He locked his arms around her and hugged her close. In all her life Dovie had never been loved like this. For twenty-six years she'd been married to Marvin Boyd; while she'd loved him she hadn't experienced this kind of happiness.

"I don't think you need to worry that Louise will return," Frank assured her. "She isn't going to find something for Tammy Lee here—because, my beautiful wife, you don't sell Texas trash."

"Frank, be kind." Dovie's own opinions made her no less guilty, but she was unwilling to confess as much.

"Hey, I'm just being honest."

Dovie went to the small kitchen off the Victorian Tea Room and reached for two mugs. "Do you have time for coffee?"

Frank nodded. "Actually, I have a reason for stopping by."

"You mean other than seducing me in the middle of the day?"

His grin was full of roguish humor. "Wade McMillen phoned a little while ago."

The pastor was a favorite of Dovie's, and Frank's, too. It'd been Wade who'd suggested a solution to their dilemma. As a lifelong bachelor, Frank had feared he was too set in his ways for marriage, but Dovie had found it impossible to continue their relationship without the emotional security and commitment of wedding vows.

Wade had come up with the idea of their getting married but maintaining separate households.

In the months since their wedding Frank had been gradually spending more and more of his evenings with her. In recent weeks the nights he slept at his own house had become few and far between. He'd lived exclusively with her for most of a month now and showed no signs of leaving, although the option was available to him. Once or twice a week, he'd stop off for his mail or an item of clothing, and he'd check on the house, but that was about it.

"Wade's helping an unwed mother who needs a place to live and I think we can help out."

"Us?" Dovie asked. Frank was by nature generous, although few people realized it.

"I had an idea," he said with a thoughtful look, watching her, "but I wanted to talk it over with you first."

"Of course."

Frank carried their coffee to one of the tables, and she followed with a small plate of freshly baked peanut-butter cookies. She noticed her husband's hesitation.

"Frank?"

"I did a background check on this woman. She's clean. I was able to talk to her landlord and her former employer. From everything they said, she's responsible, hardworking and decent. Her employer said her ex-boyfriend was a jerk. Apparently he hounded her day and night, insisting she get an abortion. From the sound of it, he made life so uncomfortable she quit her job and told everyone she was moving in with family."

"Where's her family, then?"

Frank's gaze held Dovie's. "From what I could find out, she doesn't have anyone to speak of her. Her mother's a flake, her father's dead and apparently that's just about all there is."

"The poor thing."

"I was thinking . . ." Frank hesitated. "My house has been sitting empty the last month and, well, it probably wouldn't hurt to have someone house-sit. I don't need the rent money, and it'd be a help to me, too."

It took Dovie a moment to understand what he was telling her. "You want to move in permanently with me?"

"For all intents and purposes, I'm living with you now," he said. "There's fewer and fewer of my things at the house. Some old clothes and my furniture. But I won't do it, Dovie, if you object, although I'd like to help Wade and this woman if I could."

"Object?" She all but threw herself into his arms. "Frank, I'm positively delighted!"

"You are?"

She couldn't have hidden her happiness for anything. "I love having you live with me."

"I'd like to keep my house."

"Of course."

"But if it's going to sit empty ninety percent of the time, it makes sense to have someone living there."

"I couldn't agree with you more." This was better than she'd hoped, better than she'd dreamed.

"Naturally, it's only on a trial basis."

"You could move back to your own place anytime, Frank, you know that."

"I wanted to talk to you about it first, but it does seem that letting this young lady stay at the house would help her *and* me. It's a win-win situation."

"It does seem like that, doesn't it?" He sounded as though he'd thought this through but wanted her either to concur or talk him out of it. "Are you sure you're comfortable having a stranger live in your home?"

"Why not? Anything of value has long since gone to your place."

"Our place," she corrected softly. "My home is your home. You're my husband." She said the word with pride and a heart full of love. For eleven years they'd dated and during that time he'd come to her back door. Twice a week, regular as taxes. As her husband, there was no need for him to worry about avoiding gossip, no need to conceal his love. No reason for her to pretend, either.

"And you're my wife." He clasped her hand and squeezed gently.

"Do you want to call Wade now?"

"I think I will." He scooped up a couple of peanut-butter cookies and headed toward her office in the back of the store.

Dovie took a cookie and relaxed in her chair. She had yet to meet this young woman of Wade's, but she liked her already. This unwed mother had helped Frank make a decision he might otherwise have delayed for months—if not years.

WADE HAD BEEN JOKING when he told Amy Thornton he was a miracle worker. But it was clear from the moment he saw her that she was in serious distress. Her face was drawn and her large dark eyes were ringed with shadows. When he found her in the church, she'd looked embarrassed and apologetic. Before he could stop her, she'd grabbed her suitcase and clung to it like a lifeline.

Wade persuaded her to come into the office, where he introduced her to his secretary, Martha Kerns. While the women talked, he made several discreet phone calls from his study. He heard Martha suggest a cup of herbal tea, and a few minutes later her footsteps as she left the room. Interrupting his phone calls, Wade peeked out the door to see how Amy was doing. To his surprise, she was sound asleep, leaning to one side, head resting against her shoulder, eyes closed.

As unobtrusively as possible, he lifted her feet onto the sofa and she nestled against a pillow. He paused to study her. In the short walk from the church to the office, she'd told him she was twenty-five, a full eight years younger than he was. Never had eight years seemed so wide a gulf. She was pretty, with thick shoulder-length auburn hair, pulled back and clipped in place. Her skin was naturally pale and wonderfully smooth. Had he touched her cheek, he was certain she would have felt like satin.

Martha returned from the kitchen with two mugs and set them down on the corner of her desk. "She looks a little like an angel, doesn't she?"

Wade didn't answer, but not because he didn't agree. Amy did indeed look angelic. Removing his sweater from his closet, he covered the sleeping woman's shoulders.

While Amy continued to doze, he made a few more phone calls and finally managed to reach Frank Hennessey. Within the hour Frank called him back.

"I'm over at Dovie's," the sheriff announced. "We think we've come up with a solution to the housing problem."

"You know of someone willing to give her a place to live for a few months?" Wade's original thought had been to hook her up with one of the local ranchers as a cook or other part-time helper, but he'd soon realized that her pregnancy would restrict her activities. From there his thoughts moved to the idea of her working as a live-in nanny. In March Savannah Smith had delivered a beautiful baby girl, and Caroline Weston was due in three or four months. Weddings and babies. Wade had been witness to them all.

"Actually I was thinking she might be willing to house-sit for a while."

"Excellent idea." Wade wished he'd thought of that himself. "But who?"

Frank cleared his throat. "Uh, Dovie and I talked it over, and we were thinking maybe she could watch my place."

It didn't take Wade long to understand the implications. "That's an excellent idea," he said again.

"I did a background check on her," Frank said. "Talked to her former employer, too. From everything he said, she's a good person who's been put in a difficult position."

"I don't know what she can afford for rent."

"I don't plan on charging her any," the sheriff said. "She'd be doing me and Dovie a favor. Besides, she has other expenses to worry about."

"That's very kind of you," Wade said. So Frank had made inquiries concerning Amy. It was all Wade could do not to interrogate him. Sleeping Beauty was in his outer office, and he wanted to know more about her. *Much* more. She didn't fit the homeless helpless mode. He wondered why she'd decided to come here, where she had no friends or relatives, no prospects of work or accommodation.

"I have a line on a job for her," Wade said, feeling downright proud of himself.

"Wonderful. Who?"

"Ellie Frasier," he said, forgetting that the feedstore owner was a Patterson now. Glen and Ellie were married last September; he'd officiated at the ceremony himself.

"The feed store?" Frank didn't sound as if he approved of the idea.

"As a bookkeeper," Wade told him. "I told Ellie up front that she's pregnant, but she didn't seem to mind. Ellie said she'd like to meet Amy first and interview her. She's been looking for someone to come in part-time and take up the slack. She could occasionally use help in the store, too." Wade was beginning to feel like the miracle worker he'd confidently proclaimed himself to be. He grinned, thinking all his miracles should be this easy.

"Dovie and I would like to meet her, too."

"Of course." It stunned him that Frank would open his home to a stranger like this. Frank and Dovie knew next to nothing about Amy Thornton, other than what her former employer had said. Yet they felt comfortable enough to invite her to live in his house. Wade wasn't sure he would've been as generous or as trusting. However, Frank was a lawman—a sheriff who'd seen plenty of reason to distrust his fellow man—and if he trusted Amy, Wade could do no less.

They ended the conversation by arranging that Wade would bring her over to the shop in an hour or so.

Wade returned to the outer room. Amy stirred then and sat up, looking disoriented, as if she wasn't sure where she was. "Oh, my," she whispered, pushing the hair away from her face. "I'm so sorry. I don't know what's wrong with me. I . . . I can't seem to get enough sleep."

"Don't worry about it," Wade said, and Martha added, "You need extra sleep right now."

"There are some people I'd like you to meet," Wade told her.

"I don't mean to cause you a lot of problems, Reverend McMillen," she said as she handed him his sweater.

"You're not a problem, Amy. Besides, didn't I tell you miracles were my specialty?"

"Fortunately Mr. Miracle Worker here has a lot of helpers in the community," Martha said with a smile.

Wade couldn't have agreed with her more. He led Amy out of the office and to the curb where he'd parked his Blazer. A soft breeze rustled the leaves of maples and oaks, the faint scent of roses and jasmine perfumed the air.

"I'm taking you to Dovie's place first," Wade said, starting the engine. "Frank and Dovie wanted to meet you—and discuss an idea."

"An idea?"

"I'll let them explain."

The Hennesseys were waiting for them. He watched Amy's face when she walked into Dovie's antique store. She paused as if it was too much to assimilate. He'd felt much the same way when he'd first seen the sheer *number* of things in her store. He'd been impressed by Dovie's displays, though. They were so attractive he couldn't help feeling they belonged in a magazine. When she opened her Victorian Tea room, it'd fast become the gathering place for women all around town. Dovie used only the finest linens, the best crystal and bone china from her stock. At first Wade had felt as awkward in her store as he would in a lingerie shop, but Dovie had quickly put him at ease.

"You must be Amy," Dovie said, crossing the room to greet them. "Welcome to my shop."

"It's . . . beautiful." Amy couldn't stop looking around.

"I've made us tea," Dovie said, and they followed her to a table at the far side of the room.

Frank watched Amy carefully and Wade saw her meet his gaze without flinching or visible discomfort. He sensed she had nothing to hide, and for that Wade was grateful. Situations such as this held the risk of problems; one of his fears was that Amy was running away, possibly from the father of her unborn child. But despite the potential for trouble, he wanted to help her.

Frank waited until everyone had a cup of tea before he mentioned his idea.

"You mean to say you'd let me live in your home?" Amy sounded incredulous. "But you don't even know me."

"Are you hiding something? Is there anything in your background we should know?" Frank asked.

"No," she was quick to inform them, her eyes wide and honest.

"I didn't think so." Frank's features relaxed into an easy smile. "Actually, having you stay there helps us, too. I won't need to worry about the house sitting empty, and you'll have a place to live until you've sorted out your life and made some decisions."

"I . . . I don't know what to say other than thank you."

Wade could see that Amy was overwhelmed by the Hennesseys' generosity and trust.

"I won't disappoint you," she said as if making a pledge.

"Just so you'll know exactly what's expected of you, I thought we should sit down and put everything in writing. I don't want there to be room for any misunderstanding."

"I'd like that," Amy concurred.

"Do you want to see the house?"

"Please."

Wade stood and checked his watch. "Give us thirty minutes. Amy needs to talk to Ellie first."

"Fine, I'll see you then."

Wade escorted Amy out of the shop and down the street to Frasier Feed. Ellie's father had died the year before, and Ellie had taken over the business. He knew that Glen had been helping her with the paperwork, but it had become an increasingly onerous task. Ellie was finding that it required more time than she could spare.

Ellie met them on the sidewalk outside the store.

"This is Amy Thornton," Wade said, introducing the two women. "Amy, Ellie Patterson."

"Hi," Ellie said, her greeting friendly. She gestured to the chairs by the soda machine. They all sat down, although Wade wasn't sure he was really needed for this interview.

"If you don't mind, I have a few questions," Ellie said.

"All right." Amy stiffened a little, as though unsure what to expect.

Ellie asked about job experience and Wade was glad of the opportunity to listen in. He was pleased to learn Amy had worked for the same employer for almost seven years. She'd started with the company as part of a high-school training program and had stayed on after graduation.

Wade remembered Frank telling him that her former employer had given her a glowing recommendation.

"Seven years." Ellie seemed impressed. She asked a series of other questions and took down references and phone numbers. Wade watched in amazement as almost instant rapport developed between the two women.

"Could you start on Monday?" Ellie asked.

"You're offering me the job?" Amy's voice quavered. "Now? Already?"

"Does that surprise you?"

"I'm . . . shocked. And thrilled. Thank you. Thank you so much." Tears gathered in her eyes and she stopped for a moment to compose herself before she continued. "Your store," she said, having a hard time getting the words out. "It's one of the reasons I got off the bus."

"I don't understand," Ellie said.

"It looked so friendly, like your customers were also your friends."

"My customers *are* my friends," Ellie said. "I'm hoping we can become friends, too."

A smile lit up Amy's face. "I'd like that very much."

Wade grinned in delight. This was working out perfectly. Within hours of arriving in Promise, Amy Thornton had a job and a place to live. Frank, Dovie and Ellie reaffirmed his belief in the basic goodness of most people.

Once they were back in the car, Wade drove to Frank's house and pulled into the driveway.

Amy glanced at him. "This is the house?"

Actually it was more of a cottage, Wade thought. Cozy and comfortable-looking.

"You really are a miracle worker, aren't you?" she said in apparent awe.

"A place to live and a job. Hey, no problem," he said, snapping his fingers like a magician producing a rabbit in a hat. "No problem at all."

"I don't think finding a father for my baby is going to be as easy," she said, climbing out of the vehicle.

A father for her child. Wade had forgotten about that.

TWO

Dr. Jane Patterson had a gentle way about her, Amy thought as she dressed. The examination had been her most comfortable to date. From the moment she learned she was pregnant, Amy had faithfully taken her vitamins, made regular doctor's appointments and scrupulously watched her diet. Her one fear was that her baby would feel the tension and stress that had been her constant companion these past six months.

There was a light tap on the door, and Dr. Patterson entered the examination room.

"Is everything all right with the pregnancy?" Amy asked immediately.

"Everything looks good. From what I could tell, the baby is developing right on schedule," Dr. Patterson said. "I don't want you to worry. Continue with the vitamins and try to get the rest your body needs." She sat down across from Amy, leaned forward and gave her a reassuring pat on the hand. "I'm going to be starting a birthing class in the next couple of weeks and was wondering if you'd care to join."

Amy bit her lip. She'd like nothing better than to attend this class, but it probably required a partner, someone who'd be willing to coach her through labor and birth. Unfortunately, being new in town, she didn't know anyone she could ask.

"There are several women in the community who are entering their third trimester," the doctor went on.

"Will I need a partner?"

"It's not necessary," she said, and Amy saw compassion and understanding on the doctor's face. "You don't need to decide just yet," she added. "As I mentioned, the class won't start for a couple of weeks, but if you're looking for a partner, I suggest you ask Dovie Hennessey. She took me under her wing when I first arrived in Promise. I didn't know anyone and had trouble making friends."

"You?" Amy could hardly believe it.

Dr. Patterson laughed lightly. "Oh, Amy, you wouldn't believe all the mistakes I made. I felt so lost and lonely. Dovie made me feel welcome and steered me toward the right people. She's wonderful."

Amy lowered her gaze, embarrassed that she was reduced to accepting charity and relying on the kindness of strangers. "Did you know I'm staying in Sheriff Hennessey's house?" she asked.

"I heard you're house-sitting, if that's what you mean."

It puzzled Amy that she could have stepped off the bus in a town she didn't know existed and be welcomed as though she were long-lost family. Half the time she was left wondering when she'd wake up to reality. Wade McMillen had jokingly said he was a miracle worker, and so far, he'd proved himself to be exactly that. A week later, her head still spun at the way he'd gone about finding solutions to her problems.

"Would you like me to put your name down for the birthing class?" Dr. Patterson pressed.

"Yes, please," Amy said. It seemed that the people of Promise, Texas, had made room for her in their community and in their hearts. "I'll think about asking Dovie . . ." She hated to request yet another favor. Besides, she couldn't see what would prompt a busy woman like Dovie to agree, especially when she and her husband were already doing so much for her. Dr. Patterson seemed to think it was a good idea, though, and Amy wouldn't mind becoming friends with the older woman. Everyone she knew was back in Dallas. Her friends, her colleagues and of course her mother. Alex hadn't liked her seeing anyone else, even girlfriends, and over time she'd lost contact with quite a few people.

"Dovie will be thrilled if you ask her," the doctor was saying.

Amy stared at her. "Dr. Patterson, I don't know—"

"We don't stand on formality here," the other woman interrupted. "You can call me Jane—Dr. Jane if you prefer." The accompanying smile was warm.

"You'll let me know when the classes start?"

"Jenny has the sign-up sheet out front. Give her your name and she'll make sure you're notified before the first class. And while you're speaking to Jenny, go ahead and schedule your next appointment for two weeks."

"Two weeks?" The doctor in Dallas had seen her only once a month. "There's something wrong you're not telling me about, isn't there?"

"Relax, Amy, everything looks perfectly fine. You're healthy and there's nothing to indicate anything's wrong with the baby."

"Then why?"

"You're entering the third trimester, and it's normal procedure to see a patient every two weeks until the last month, when your visits will be weekly."

Amy relaxed. Generally she didn't panic this easily, but so much had already happened that she couldn't help worrying.

"I'll talk to Jenny on my way out," she promised.

"If you have any questions, I want you to call me day or night, understand?" Jane wrote the office phone number on a prescription pad and handed it to Amy. "This is my pager number if the office is closed and it's not an emergency."

"Thank you." Amy's voice shook. She felt overwhelmed by the fact that strangers cared about her and her unborn child when her own mother's reaction had been just the opposite. She'd called Amy ugly horrible names. Alex, the man she was convinced she loved beyond life itself, had shown exactly the kind of person he was when she told him about the baby. He didn't want his own child! People she loved, trusted, had turned their backs on her, and instead a community of strangers had welcomed her with open arms, taken her in, given her the help she needed.

"You'll talk to Dovie then?" Jane said as Amy prepared to leave.

Amy inhaled a stabilizing breath and nodded. "I'll do it right away." Before she lost her nerve or changed her mind.

Since she wasn't expected at the feed store until noon, Amy walked over to Dovie's after she'd left the doctor's office. She tried to convince herself that what Jane had said was true—that Dovie would be delighted to attend the classes with her.

Birthing classes. In three months Sarah would be born. Three months! This shouldn't have come as any shock. But it did. She had so much to do to get ready for the baby. She hadn't even begun to buy the things she'd need. Baby clothes, a crib, a stroller. Her heart started to pound at the thought of everything that had to be done and the short time left in which to accomplish it all.

Amy pushed open the door to Dovie's store and the bells above the entrance jingled lightly.

"Well, hello, Amy," Dovie greeted her from across the room. She was arranging freshly cut red roses in a crystal vase. "Aren't these lovely?" she murmured, pausing to examine one bud more closely. "Savannah Smith came by with Laura earlier this morning and brought me these."

"They're beautiful." Amy swore that if Dovie hadn't been alone just then, she would have abandoned her mission.

"How are you feeling?" Dovie asked.

"Great. I'm enjoying working with Ellie."

"From what Ellie said, you're doing a fabulous job."

Amy was unable to stifle a smile. She'd started her job that Monday afternoon and had spent the first two days organizing Ellie's desk. It was abundantly clear that Ellie had been putting off too much of her paperwork. This job wasn't a fabricated one; Amy was convinced of that. Frasier Feed genuinely needed a bookkeeper and more. Her organizational skills had given her the opportunity to show Ellie how much she appreciated the job.

"Ellie's a wonderful employer."

"After your first day she told me she wondered why she'd delayed hiring someone."

Amy had wondered that herself, but didn't think it was her place to ask. If anything, she was grateful Ellie had waited; otherwise there wouldn't have been an opening for her.

"I just finished seeing Dr. Patterson for the first time," Amy said.

"Isn't Jane terrific?" Dovie's question was asked in an absent sort of way, more comment than inquiry. She added another perfectly formed long-stemmed rose to the arrangement.

"Yes . . . She mentioned she's starting a birthing class in a couple of weeks."

"Caroline Weston's due around the same time as you."

Amy wasn't entirely sure who Caroline was. A friend of Dovie's apparently.

"I'm going to need a birthing partner," Amy blurted out, thinking if she didn't ask soon, she never would. "Dr. Patterson . . . Dr. Jane assured me I could attend the class alone, but then she suggested I ask you to be my partner." She dragged a deep breath into her lungs and hurriedly continued, "I realize it's an imposition and I want you to know that I . . ." She let her sentence drift off.

Dovie's hand stilled and she glanced up, her eyes wide. With astonishment? Or perhaps it was shock; Amy didn't know which. Her initial reaction had been accurate. Asking something this personal of someone she barely knew, someone who'd already helped her so much, was stepping over the line.

"An imposition," Dovie repeated. "Oh, no, not to me. Not at all. I'd consider it an honor."

"You would? I mean, Dovie, you and Frank have done so much for me and the baby. Letting me stay in his house . . . I can't tell you how grateful I am. Thank you. Thank you." If she didn't leave soon, Amy feared she'd embarrass herself further by bursting into tears.

"Just let me know when the first class is scheduled, all right?"

Amy nodded. "Jenny said she'd have all the information for me at my next appointment."

"We'll make a great team." Dovie's eyes gleamed with confidence; she gave every indication of being delighted that Amy had asked her. Just like Dr. Jane had said.

Amy had almost stopped believing there were good people left in this world, and then she'd stumbled on a whole town of them.

DENISE PARSONS HAD NEVER BEEN friendly with Louise Powell. The woman enjoyed gossip and meddling far too much. The minute Louise entered the café, Denise could tell she wanted something—and she sincerely doubted it was the French-dip luncheon special.

Sighing with resignation, Denise filled a glass of water and reached for a menu, then approached the booth.

"Hello, Denise," the other woman purred.

Yup, she was after some juicy gossip all right, but Denise hadn't a clue what it might be. Well, whatever Louise hoped to learn had brought her into the bowling alley on a Thursday afternoon, which was highly unusual.

"Hello." She returned the greeting with a certain hesitation. She didn't enjoy being a party to Louise's type of friendship. "What can I get you?"

"Coffee would be great."

"Would you like anything with that?" Tex had been after her to push desserts. With one of the ranchers she might have suggested a slice of rhubarb pie, but personally she preferred to have Louise in and out of the café in record time.

"I understand you were the first one to speak with that new gal in town," Louise said, instead of answering Denise's question.

Denise wasn't sure who she meant.

"The pregnant one."

So Amy Thornton was the reason for this visit. Denise hadn't noticed Amy was pregnant until she'd stood up to leave. Louise stared at her, anticipating an answer. "Yes, I talked to her." She couldn't see any point in denying it. "Did you say you wanted anything with the coffee?" she asked again.

"Nothing." Louise righted her mug and gazed up expectantly.

Denise wasn't about to let the town busybody trap her into a lengthy and unpleasant conversation; she promptly disappeared. She was back a minute later with the coffeepot and a look that suggested she didn't have anything more to add.

Oblivious to anything but her own curiosity, Louise was ready and waiting. "What did she say?"

"Who?" Denise asked, playing dumb.

"That unwed mother," Louise snapped.

"She asked about the breakfast special."

Louise's eyes narrowed. "Did she mention the baby's father?"

Setting the coffeepot down on the table, Denise leaned closer as though to share a secret. "She did say something interesting."

The rhinestones in the older woman's hat sparkled as she scooted closer to the end of the booth. "What?"

"She asked . . ." Denise paused and looked both ways.

"What?"

"If we served sourdough bread."

The keen interest in Louise's eyes changed to annoyance. Her back went stiff and she straightened, moving away from Denise, implying that it didn't do her image any good to be seen associating with a waitress. "I can see we have nothing more to discuss," Louise said primly. "And furthermore, this coffee tastes burned."

"I made a fresh pot less than thirty minutes ago." Denise had a son in junior high, a kid with attitude. If she wanted someone to insult her and question her abilities, she could get it at home; she didn't need to go to work for it.

With her lips pinched, Louise scrambled out of the booth. She slapped some change down on the table and walked out the door, leaving it to swing in her wake.

"What'd that old biddy want?" Tex shouted from the kitchen.

"She's trying to make trouble, is all." Denise put the coffeepot back on the burner. "Asking about Amy." The unwed mother was fair game in Louise's eyes, Denise realized sadly. The poor girl was doing the best she could and Denise hoped everything would work out well for her and her baby.

"Did you tell her leave the kid alone?" Tex demanded, none too gently.

"I did," Denise shouted back. In her own way she'd given Louise as good as she got, and she felt a small but definite sense of triumph.

WADE HAD KNOWN Amy was scheduled to visit Jane on Thursday morning, so he waited until later that evening to visit her. The last time they'd talked had been Sunday morning.

He'd be lying if he didn't admit how pleased he'd felt when Amy showed up for church services. Frankly he'd been more than a little surprised. In his years of serving as a pastor, he'd learned a number of lessons about human nature, not all of them positive—and as a result he'd suffered his share of disappointments. He sincerely hoped Amy wouldn't turn out to be one.

Richard Weston had certainly tested his faith in people. The youngest of the Weston family had shown up in Promise after a six-year absence and taken advantage of the kindness and goodwill of the community. Just when his underhandedness was about to be exposed, he'd disappeared. Eventually he was found—hiding in a nearby ghost town—and returned to New York to stand trial on charges stemming from a scheme that had involved cheating and abusing immigrants. Wade had spent many an evening with Grady Weston and his sister, Savannah Smith, helping them come to terms with what their brother had done—to them and to others. Richard was serving a twenty-five-year prison sentence, and it was unlikely he'd ever come back to Promise. Not that anyone wanted him to.

His experience working as a pastor had given Wade a sixth sense about people. He'd seen through Richard Weston almost immediately, but unfortunately had been unaware of the man's schemes until too late. Even knowing Richard for what he was, Wade had been shocked by the extent of his perfidy and the horror of his crimes.

He liked Amy and trusted her, not that he was looking for her gratitude. Actually he'd done little more than point her in the right direction. Ellie hadn't hired her simply because she needed a job. And rightly so. She'd hired Amy because of her qualifications.

Home and job—everything had fallen neatly into place. Then on Sunday morning Amy had arrived in time for the morning service, looking almost afraid. Her expressive brown eyes told him she was expecting someone to tell her she should leave. Expecting someone to tell her she didn't belong in a house of God. Wade swore if anyone had so much as tried, he would . . . He stopped, not realizing until that very moment the depth of his feelings.

He was proud of the way his flock had welcomed Amy Thornton into the fold. Proud of each and every one of them, even Louise, who—so far, anyway—had shown more curiosity than malice.

Wednesday morning Ellie Patterson had phoned Wade to thank him for finding such a whiz of a bookkeeper. Wade couldn't accept full credit; he'd had no idea Amy was a gifted organizer. He smiled, pleased that everything was working out so well.

He rang the doorbell and waited. It might have been best had he phoned first, but he'd learned early on in his pastoral career that if he did phone, most people invented excuses to keep him away. He'd never understood what they feared. Women seemed convinced he'd march right into their kitchens and inspect the inside of their ovens. Men seemed to worry that he might catch them enjoying a bottle of beer—when in reality he'd have been happy to join them.

Involved in these thoughts, Wade stepped back in mild surprise when the door opened and Amy stood on the other side.

"Hello," she said, brightening when she saw who it was.

He wasn't accustomed to people actually being pleased to find he'd unexpectedly dropped by. "I thought I'd see how the doctor's appointment went this morning," he said.

Amy held open the screen door for him. "Come in, please. I just finished making a batch of sun tea. Would you care for a glass?"

"Sure."

Amy had been living at Frank's house for only a week, and already Wade saw subtle changes. She'd draped a shawl over the back of Frank's shabby recliner, and a vase of fresh-cut flowers rested in the center of the coffee table. The wooden floors shone, the windows sparkled; the books were dusted and straightened. A women's magazine lay open on the sofa.

"Make yourself comfortable," she said, and disappeared into the kitchen. She returned a couple of minutes later with two glasses of iced tea. She explained that it was a lemon herbal tea to which she'd added a sprig of fresh mint.

"I hear you were in to see Dr. Jane."

Amy nodded, then sipped from her glass. "She's wonderful."

"We think so."

"I was a little worried, because I was a couple of weeks overdue for an exam, but she assured me the pregnancy is progressing nicely."

Wade noticed how she pressed her palm against her abdomen as she spoke. It was an unconscious movement, he suspected. If he hadn't known about the pregnancy, he probably wouldn't have even guessed her condition. The swelling was slight and could almost be attributed to body type.

"I've signed up for birthing classes and Dovie has agreed to be my partner."

"Dovie," Wade repeated. "That's great." She was a perfect choice. Dovie loved children; a couple of months ago she'd surprised him when she volunteered to teach Sunday-school class for two-and-three-year-olds. What amazed him even more was that Frank had joined his wife one recent Sunday. It'd been difficult enough to get Frank Hennessey to darken a church door—but teaching Sunday school to a group of preschoolers? That had left Wade with his mouth hanging open in shock. Frank Hennessey seemed full of surprises lately, attributable, no doubt, to Dovie's influence. She'd be good for Amy, too, he mused. And vice versa . . .

"It all seems so real now," Amy was saying. "Dovie seemed pleased about going to the birthing classes with me."

Wade sat back on the sofa. "Have you decided what you're going to do about the baby?" he asked. This was a difficult subject, but one that needed to be addressed.

"How do you mean?" Amy asked.

"Have you made any decisions about the baby's future?"

"Are you asking me if I've decided to put my child up for adoption?"

He was pleased she understood his intention without his having to spell it out. This was such a delicate subject. Emotions could be volatile and he wasn't trying to steer her in one direction or another. At twenty-five Amy Thornton was perfectly capable of making up her own mind.

"I'm not here to pressure you in any way," he told her.

"In the beginning I considered all my options." She paused and he saw the muscles in her throat work as she struggled within herself. "The man I loved . . . who I thought loved me . . . wanted me to end the pregnancy. My mother, between calling me names, wasn't willing to offer any type of support. She said she wanted nothing to do with me again." Amy regarded him steadily. "Thank you, Wade."

"You're thanking me?"

"You're the first person in nearly six months to ask what I want for my child."

He noticed the sheen in her eyes. "So, what have you decided?"

Her hand went back to her abdomen. "I'm an adult and I have good job skills. Ellie seems to think the part-time position will develop into full-time employment. While I don't have a lot of discretionary income and finances will be tight, I've decided to raise my baby myself."

The decision hadn't been easy, Wade knew. He could tell from the look on her face. She was afraid, vulnerable and alone, but she seemed to have found peace with that. It was everything he needed to know.

"I left Dallas because of my baby," Amy said. "The baby's father . . . well, let me just say that he's out of my life and there's no possibility we'll get back together." She paused and then, unable to hide the pain in her voice, she whispered, "My mother has disowned me." Her voice grew stronger. "The baby and I are a package deal, and seeing that I've already made two rather unpleasant stands on Sarah's behalf, I figure I'll stick it out for the long haul. I'm very much looking forward to being a mother." This part was added with a smile and something more. Inner peace.

Amy Thornton hadn't come to this decision without struggle, Wade realized. It wasn't one she'd made lightly.

"I don't understand the question, though," she said, her mood abruptly shifting into amusement.

"What do you mean?"

"I thought you were the miracle man, Reverend McMillen."

"Well, yes . . . I suppose, but . . ."

"Don't go backing out on me now," she said, placing her hand on her hip in mock outrage. "The first time we met, you made it quite clear that you were capable of producing whatever I needed."

"Hey, I found you a house and connected you with Ellie, didn't I?"

"Yes, you did and don't think I'm ungrateful. But if you'll remember, you also promised to find me a father for my baby."

DOVIE POSTED the notice for the big Grange dance in her shop window. Next to the rodeo and chili cook-off, this function, sponsored by the Cattlemen's Association, was one of the biggest social events of the year.

At the dance the previous summer Glen Patterson had made a fool of himself over Ellie. It was one of the incidents that had led—indirectly—to their marriage. Glen had been a little slow to figure out how he felt about Ellie, and Richard Weston had leaped into the breach. Which had helped Glen clarify his own feelings. Certainly Richard was none to happy when Ellie chose to marry Glen, but Dovie strongly suspected Ellie's recent inheritance had been the key to Richard's interest.

Vulnerable as she'd been at the time, it was little wonder Ellie hadn't seen through Richard the minute he started showering her with attention. Eventually she had of course—with no help from Glen, Dovie mused.

She finished taping up the notice for the dance, then stepped outside to make sure it was positioned straight. The day was lovely, the mid-

morning still cool with a slight breeze. The reader board at the bank
alternated the time and the temperature, and Dovie noted it was seventy-
four. By late afternoon it'd be close to ninety.

A great many changes had come about since last year's dance. Several marriages, births, including Savannah and Laredo's daughter. Caroline Weston, the town's postmistress and Grady's wife, was showing
nicely now and was as pretty as Dovie had ever seen her. She all but
glowed with happiness. It wouldn't have surprised Dovie if Ellie or Jane
decided to start their families soon, too. Those stubborn Patterson men
had waited until their midthirties to get married. Better make up for lost
time, Dovie thought with a wicked grin.

"What's that?" Amy Thornton asked, startling her as she walked up
behind Dovie and read the sign.

"The Cattlemen's Association puts on a big dance at the Grange hall
every year."

"Oh." Amy sounded sorry she'd asked.

"You're going, aren't you?"

Amy shook her head. "Not like this."

"Like what?" Dovie challenged.

The younger woman cradled her protruding stomach. "In case you
hadn't noticed, Dovie, I'm six months pregnant."

"What's that got to do with anything?"

Amy shook her head. "I couldn't attend a dance."

"Why not, in heaven's name?"

"I . . . just couldn't."

"If you're worried about having something appropriate to
wear . . ."

"I don't have anything appropriate, but that's only part of it. I realize
these are modern times, but I'd still need a date."

Dovie smiled. "No, you wouldn't. My heavens, plenty of ranchers
attend the dance without a partner, and gals, too. Don't you worry, you'll
have more men buzzing around you than a can of fresh cream."

"I wouldn't feel . . . right."

"And why not?" Dovie demanded.

"I . . . don't know anyone," Amy said.

Dovie studied her for a long minute. "I can't think of a better way
for you to get to know the people here, and for them to know you."

Still Amy hesitated.

"Will you at least think on it?" Dovie pressed. Going to the dance
was the best way for Amy to meet other people close to her in age. It'd
help if she did have someone to escort her, but she was too new in town.

"I'll think about it," Amy said, "but I'm not making any promises."
Dovie patted her elbow, pleased Amy had agreed to at least consider
it. "Good girl."

Amy flushed and looked slightly embarrassed. "I wanted you to
know that the birthing class starts a week from Monday. We're meeting
at the health clinic between seven and eight-thirty."

"I'll be there with bells on," Dovie promised. Excitement bubbled
inside her at the prospect of sharing the moment Amy gave birth to her
baby.

They exchanged a few more pleasantries, then Amy continued down
the street. Feeling motherly, Dovie wandered back into her shop. She'd
bonded with Amy Thornton, she thought, nodding in satisfaction. The
girl was like a lost waif, in need of love and nourishment. Not physical
nourishment, but emotional. Even as little as a week had shown a vast
improvement in her appearance. She wasn't nearly as pale, and the dark
shadows under her eyes had all but disappeared.

Dovie strongly suspected this was the first time since she'd learned
she was pregnant that she was getting proper rest. In thinking over Amy's
story, Dovie was appalled. The young woman had hastily gotten off the
bus without knowing a soul in Promise. When questioned, all she'd say
was that she'd looked down Main Street and thought it might be a
friendly town.

While Promise was indeed friendly, it wasn't unlike a dozen other
communities Amy had traveled through on her way to Austin.

Dovie wouldn't say anything to Frank, and possibly not even to
Wade, but she had the distinct impression that Amy was *supposed* to get
off that bus when she did. There was a reason she was in Promise. Dovie
wasn't sure what it was just yet, but time would eventually reveal it.

"I can't believe the dance is almost here."

The deep male voice behind her took Dovie by surprise. She gasped
and placed her hand over her heart. "Reverend McMillen!"

"Sorry, Dovie, I didn't mean to frighten you."

"I was lost in thought and I didn't hear you sneaking up behind me.
Didn't even hear the bell!"

He laughed and handed her the Sunday-school material he'd promised to deliver at the beginning of the week.

"The big dance is scheduled for the twenty-seventh this year," Dovie
said. "You're going of course."

"Of course."

Not that Dovie remembered him doing a lot of dancing in years past.
Mostly Wade hung around with the ranchers. The thing was, he fit right

in. Tall and broad-shouldered, the preacher looked and acted as though he'd be at home on a horse or roping a calf. It often took people aback when they learned the only herd Wade managed was a church full of stubborn humans.

"Remember last year?" Wade asked.

"I'm not likely to forget," Dovie told him.

"Glen was fit to be tied when he found Ellie dancing with Richard."

Dovie had been thinking the same thing herself only a few minutes earlier. "It was a turning point in their relationship."

"Not that the road to romance was smooth for either of them," Wade reminded her.

"The dance was a turning point for Caroline and Grady, too."

This small bit of information appeared to surprise the reverend. "What do you mean?"

"Savannah and I were the ones who encouraged Caroline to ask Grady when Pete Hadley announced a ladies' choice."

"She did, too, didn't she?"

"Yup, and I think that was what woke Grady up to the fact that she's a woman."

Wade rubbed the side of his face. "Seems the dance is responsible for a lot more romances around here than I realized."

That was when the idea hit Dovie—and hit her hard. Actually it was the perfect solution and she wondered why she hadn't come up with it sooner. My, oh my, it *was* just perfect.

"You've got that look in your eye, Dovie," Wade said, and he stepped back warily.

"I do?" she asked, feigning surprise. She'd already concluded that it was no fluke Amy had chosen to settle in Promise, and now she thought she knew why. She blurted out her idea. "I think you should take Amy to the dance."

"Me?" he cried. "Oh, no, you don't! My job description *doesn't* include escorting lonely hearts to dances!"

Three

Amy stopped at Dovie's house to pick her up for the birthing class far earlier than necessary. She'd been looking forward to this ever since Dr. Jane had first mentioned it. Waiting another fifteen minutes seemed more than she could stand.

Dovie was in her garden when Amy approached.

"Oh, my, is it that time already?" Dovie asked the instant she saw her. Flustered, she glanced at her wrist.

"I'm early," Amy apologized.

"Don't let her kid you," Frank said, joining his wife. "Dovie's been on tenterhooks all evening. I don't think I've ever seen her more excited about anything."

It warmed Amy's heart that her friend was looking forward to coaching her through labor and birth. The thought of having to go through the birth alone had weighed on her mind for months. The wrenching sense of loneliness had virtually disappeared since her arrival in Promise. She marveled anew at these wonderful people.

"I'll just be a moment," Dovie promised, and rushed toward the house.

"There's no hurry," Amy called after her.

Frank sauntered over to the gate and opened it for Amy. "You might as well sit a spell." He led her past the large well-groomed garden toward the wrought-iron table and chairs on the brick patio.

"Dovie's got quite a garden, doesn't she?"

"It's like this every year," the sheriff said. "Heaven only knows what she's going to do with twenty-five tomato plants, but she always seems to know someone who could use them."

Fresh tomatoes were a particular favorite of Amy's. One day she'd like to plant her own garden . . . Perhaps next year.

"Do you think Dovie would mind if I looked at her plants?" Amy asked, noticing the small herb garden next to the tomatoes.

"Go right ahead. Dovie's garden is her pride and joy. If you want to wait a few minutes, she'll give you the grand tour herself." It seemed to Amy that Frank was just as proud of her accomplishment.

Dovie appeared almost immediately afterward, wearing pressed navy blue trousers and an attractive cotton knit sweater in a lovely rose. Just as Frank had predicted, she was more than willing to walk Amy through her garden. "I seem to have a green thumb," she remarked, shrugging in an offhand way.

"She could coax orchids into blooming in the Arctic," Frank murmured.

"Now, Frank, that's not entirely true," Dovie said, as she slid her arm through Amy's. They strolled down the narrow garden rows, commenting on this plant and that one. The corn was almost knee-high, and the pole beans and other vegetables were well under way.

"I've always wanted a garden," Amy said, and realized how wistful that must have sounded.

"Well, I could certainly use help in mine." Dovie smiled. "Of course it'd be a little awkward for you this year, but perhaps next."

"I'd like that," Amy said. She'd never known people could be this open and generous.

"Shall we head on over to the health clinic?" Dovie asked.

The walk didn't take more than a few minutes. Amy's hands had grown damp with nerves by the time they arrived. She suspected she'd be the only pregnant woman attending without a husband, and she was right. Three other couples were already inside the clinic waiting. Dovie played hostess, greeting each one and then introducing Amy. Caroline Weston looked to be about six months pregnant, as well, and she and Amy were soon talking comfortably. She was pretty, Amy thought, with her dark brown eyes and soft brown hair. Until now they hadn't been formally introduced, but Amy had chatted with her at the post office when she'd gone to apply for a post-office box.

"Dovie was thrilled you asked her to be your birthing partner," Caroline told her. She sat next to her broad-shouldered rancher husband, Grady Weston.

"I'm the one who's grateful." Amy didn't mind saying so, either. "Being new in town, I was afraid I'd be going through labor alone."

"That would never have happened," Caroline said with confidence. Their eyes met and briefly held. "I wasn't married when I had Maggie," she said softly. "My mother was my labor coach. Jane would have made sure someone supportive was with you."

Caroline was telling Amy far more than the words themselves conveyed. She was saying that at one time she'd walked in the same shoes as Amy. She understood what it meant to stand alone and was offering her encouragement and support. Caroline was married now, and from the tender looks she shared with her husband, it was obvious they were deeply in love.

The class lasted ninety minutes, and the time flew. During the first half hour, everyone spoke for a few moments; Amy, feeling shy, said very little. Then Dr. Jane showed a thirty-minute video of a birth and answered questions. The film had been an eye-opener for Amy. Unlike the others, she hadn't been raised in a ranching community and had never been around farm animals. The baby stirred and kicked as she watched; and Amy felt a surge of pure excitement. The final thirty minutes were spent explaining the breathing techniques used during the early stages of labor.

The key, Amy discovered, was finding a comfortable position. Caroline sat on the carpeted floor and leaned her back against Grady's bent knees and pressed her hands against her stomach. The most comfortable position Amy found was lying flat on her back, knees drawn up. She stared at the ceiling and concentrated on practicing her deep breathing.

Dovie sat by her head and brushed the hair from Amy's brow. Surprisingly Amy discovered that she'd relaxed to the point of nearly drifting off to sleep.

Grady and Caroline offered Dovie and Amy a ride home, but Amy preferred to walk. Dovie did, too.

"Thanks for the offer," Amy said. She was looking forward to the next class—in part because she felt that she and Caroline could easily become friends.

"If I don't see you before, I will at the dance Saturday night," Caroline told Dovie as she climbed inside the car. As if she'd forgotten something important, she poked her head out the open window and gestured to Amy. "You're coming to the big dance, aren't you?"

Amy froze. Dovie had mentioned it earlier, and she'd hoped to avoid the subject altogether. Perhaps—like planting a garden—next year would be better timing.

"Amy?" Dovie urged, apparently waiting for her to respond to Caroline's question.

"I . . . don't think so," she mumbled, flustered and unsure. She longed to go, but it was impossible. Next year, she thought, when she felt confident again. When she felt like a contributing member of the community. When she was slim again. No man would find her attractive now with her rounding stomach and her ankles swollen by the end of the day. When the time was right—well, she had a man in mind. . . . It was, admittedly, much too soon to be thinking along those lines, but Wade McMillen was by far the kindest man she'd ever met. Not to mention one of the most attractive!

Caroline waved when Grady pulled the car away from the curb, and Amy waved back.

"So you've decided not to attend the dance," Dovie said, and did nothing to disguise her disappointment.

"I can't," Amy insisted.

"And why's that?"

"A number of reasons."

"The decision is yours, of course," Dovie said, but it was plain the older woman wanted her to reconsider. "However, I think it would do you a world of good to get out and mingle with people your own age. The dance would be the perfect opportunity to do that."

"Next year," she said, but if she'd hoped to appease Dovie, she failed.

"I want you to give me one good reason you feel you should wait."

Obviously Dovie wasn't about to drop the subject with her usual grace. If anything, she sounded more adamant than she had earlier.

"Oh, Dovie, I wish I could go, but—"

"That does it," Dovie interrupted, cutting her off even before she could complete the thought.

"Does what?"

"You're attending the dance, and I refuse to take no for an answer."

Amy laughed at her friend's stubbornness. "You seem mighty sure of yourself."

"I am." Dovie flashed her a smile that could only be described as smug. "Since I've taken on the role of your fairy godmother, all I need to do now is find the dress and the prince. The dress is simple, and as for the prince—" she giggled with sheer delight "—I know just where to look."

WADE DIDN'T GENERALLY avoid people, especially members of his own congregation, but Dovie Boyd Hennessey had been after him all week to take Amy Thornton to the big dance. He'd given Dovie a flippant response when she first proposed the idea, but the truth of the matter was he *did* like Amy. He admired her courage and determination, her grit.

And it didn't hurt any that she was easy on the eyes. When he was with her, Wade forgot he was a pastor and remembered he was a man. He wasn't sure he liked that feeling. He happened to enjoy his life exactly the way it was. Besides, if he was going to ask Amy out, then it would be when he felt ready and not because Dovie Hennessey thought he should. He didn't appreciate being pressured; no one did. So he avoided her.

"I'm not asking you to take Amy as her pastor," she muttered the one time she did manage to catch him—outside the post office. "For the love of heaven, open your eyes, Wade McMillen! Amy's a beautiful young woman."

"My eyes *are* open," Wade said. Far wider than he cared to admit.

Dovie's face relaxed into a knowing grin. "Then the matter's settled."

"Dovie, it isn't a good idea." Wade wasn't about to let her maneuver him into this craziness. At least not without putting up a struggle. "I'm sure once people meet Amy there'll be plenty of men wanting to date her. It wouldn't be fair to saddle her with me so soon after she's arrived."

"That's just an excuse and you know it!"

"I'll tell you what," he said, willing to bend, but only a little. "If no one else has asked her by Friday, then I'll take her myself."

"And insult her like she's some . . . some castoff. I think not."

There was no satisfying the woman. "Someone else will ask her," he muttered, and left it at that.

Dovie's eyes grew hot enough to cause a nuclear meltdown, but she said nothing more.

Wednesday morning Wade had just ordered the breakfast special at the café in the bowling alley when Sheriff Hennessey slipped into the booth across from him. He righted a coffee mug and motioned to Denise.

"I take it you're avoiding my wife," Frank Hennessey said.

"Can you blame me?" Wade asked.

Frank's tanned face broke into a grin. "I tell you, when Dovie's got a bee in her bonnet, nothing distracts her from getting what she wants." He paused. "I actually feel sorry for you."

Wade had gone over the last conversation with Dovie a dozen times and didn't see how he could do more than he already had. He'd given her his best offer and the woman had insisted he was insulting Amy. This was what made dating hazardous. He saw offering to escort Amy to the dance if no one else invited her as a gesture of kindness. According to Dovie, that wasn't the case. Well, as far as he was concerned, the best thing to do was avoid the dance issue entirely, avoid Dovie, avoid the attraction he felt for Amy—avoid it all.

Denise brought over his breakfast and filled Frank's mug with fresh hot coffee.

"Dovie's talked Amy into attending that dance without a date, so you don't need to worry about her chasing you down any longer."

Wade was relieved and he suspected he had Frank to thank for this unexpected reprieve. "Amy isn't going to have a problem attracting men," Wade said. She was attractive and sweet, and he had no doubt others would soon notice that, too.

A part of Wade, one he didn't want to face, was pleased no one had asked her. He wasn't sure how he'd feel about Amy dating one of the local ranchers, and yet . . . that was exactly what he wanted, wasn't it?

"Amy's *real* pretty," Frank agreed with him.

Wade didn't appreciate the reminder. "It's just that . . ."

"Yes?" Frank urged.

Wade longed to explain himself, but he couldn't seem to do it. He didn't understand his own reluctance to invite Amy to the dance, so he said the first logical thing that popped into his head. "I just don't think it's a good idea for a pastor to be romantically linked with an unwed mother. People might get the wrong idea."

Frank held the mug with both hands. He nodded slowly. "I suspect you're right. People are funny about that kind of thing."

Perhaps there was more truth to his words than he realized; Wade no longer knew. Rarely had he felt so confused. It made sense not to complicate his relationship with Amy. For one thing, some folks were sure to make more of a simple date than was warranted. Louise Powell, for instance.

Frank relaxed, leaning back against the red vinyl upholstery, and continued to sip his coffee. "This reminds me of a situation I read about not long ago."

"What situation?" Wade asked.

Frank chuckled. "Dovie's got me reading the Bible these days. She said if I was going to be helping her teach Sunday-school classes, I'd better know what I was talking about."

Wade reached for a slice of bacon, his attention more on his meal than on Frank. "Good idea."

"That's what I thought, too. But there are definite similarities."

Wade was afraid to question too much.

"Between you and that man named Joseph." Frank leaned forward and rested his elbows on the table.

"Joseph?" The bacon had yet to touch his lips.

"You remember him, I'm sure. The one who was engaged to a virgin named Mary. It must have been embarrassing for him, too, don't you think? Here's the woman he's agreed to marry, and she unexpectedly turns up pregnant. Now he loves Mary, but he knows that kid in her belly doesn't belong to him. He also knows that if he continues with the engagement, everyone will believe the worst of him and his bride-to-be."

Wade set the bacon back on his plate.

"Not that I'm suggesting Amy's any virgin, mind you," Frank said.

Wade's appetite had been keen five minutes earlier; now, what little breakfast he'd managed to swallow sat like a lump of day-old oatmeal in the pit of his stomach. He glared across the table at the sheriff.

"Something wrong, Pastor?" Frank asked. His face broke into a grin. A wide one.

"That was below the belt, Frank."

"How's that?"

"Quoting scripture to a pastor."

"I didn't quote scripture."

Wade pushed his plate aside, appetite gone. "You didn't need to."

"You taking Amy to the dance?"

And Wade had thought that Dovie was less than tactful. He was beginning to understand that husband and wife made one hell of a team. "All right, all right," he said ungraciously, "but I want you to know right now that this is the end of it, understand?"

"Fine. If that's the way you want it."

"I do."

Frank's eyes flew to his. "I do? Isn't that what a groom says when he speaks his vows?" Chuckling, Frank slid from the booth and swaggered out of the café.

Wade was still glaring.

AMY WOULD HAVE BEEN kidding herself if she said she wasn't excited about her date with Wade McMillen.

"Date" might be too strong a word. Two days earlier Wade had phoned and invited her. Amy strongly suspected it was a pity invitation, but at this point pride was no longer as important as it had been. Rather than question what had prompted the invitation, she'd simply accepted.

The instant she got off the phone, Amy had phoned Caroline Weston. While she barely knew her, she felt Caroline was someone she could speak to openly.

Within an hour Amy had received two phone calls. The first one was from Dovie, who promised to bring her the perfect dress. Almost immediately, another call came from Savannah Smith, who was delighted to hear that Wade had asked Amy to the dance. More than delighted. She said it was about time Reverend McMillen realized he was a man, as well as a minister.

The afternoon of the dance, the three women descended on Amy like a swarm of bees.

"Dovie says she's your self-appointed fairy godmother," Caroline remarked as she walked into the house.

"Just consider us Dovie's assistants." Savannah Smith followed her into the living room, carrying a sleeping baby in an infant seat.

Dovie was the last one to enter the house. She carried a lovely antique white gown in her arms. "Ellie and Jane are coming, too, but they might be a few minutes late."

Amy wasn't sure what to make of all this.

"The way I figure it," Caroline said, studying her watch, "we have approximately two hours."

"Two hours for what?"

Caroline looked at her as though the answer was obvious. "To help our dear pastor realize something he's chosen to ignore for too long."

"Oh . . ." Amy recalled Savannah's words about Wade. But she didn't understand what, exactly, it had to do with her.

Before Caroline could explain further, the doorbell chimed again.

"Are we too early or too late?" Ellie Patterson asked. Dr. Patterson—Jane—was with her.

"Your timing's perfect," Caroline assured them both.

"What's going on?" Amy asked, still wondering what Caroline and Savannah had meant about Wade. While she appreciated all the attention, it certainly didn't take five women to deliver a dress. Then, suddenly, Amy understood—these women were here to give her a makeover. Apparently she looked worse than she'd realized.

Sagging onto the sofa, she brushed her shoulder-length hair back from her face, using both hands. "I'm hopeless, aren't I?" she said, staring up at the women who crowded her living room.

"Hopeless?" Dovie repeated.

The five women burst out laughing.

"Oh, Amy," Dovie said gently, "it's just the opposite." She sat down next to her and reached for Amy's hand, holding it between both of her own. "We're not here to make you beautiful. You already are."

"Then why . . . ?"

Caroline and Savannah exchanged glances as if to decide who would say it.

"We're here to bring Wade McMillen to his knees," Caroline said.

"But he's been wonderful to me!"

"He'll be more than wonderful once we get finished with you," Ellie insisted.

The other women appeared to be in full agreement.

"What do you think of this hairstyle?" Savannah flipped open a magazine for Amy to inspect. The picture revealed an advertisement for cosmetics with a pencil-thin model wearing a black evening gown. There was a slit in the dress that stretched all the way up her thigh and her hair was a mussed flock of red curls. She clutched a strand of diamonds to her nonexistent breasts and threw back her head in laughter.

Not in two lifetimes would Amy resemble this model.

"Do you like the hair?" Savannah pressed.

"The flat stomach appeals to me a whole lot more."

"In time," Savannah promised.

If Laura's mother was an example, then Amy had hope. The infant, asleep in the portable carrier, wasn't more than three or four months old, and Savannah was as trim as a teenager. Amy had begun to wonder if she'd ever get her shape back.

Every day she discovered that more clothes no longer fit. She wore her jeans with the zipper open and a large sweatshirt pulled over them. Even the elastic bands around her two skirts had been stretched beyond recognition.

"I brought a few maternity clothes I thought you might need," Savannah whispered. "I figured we're about the same size. Unfortunately Caroline's too tall to wear anything of mine. Use them if you want and pass them on when you're through."

Then the transformation began. While Savannah brushed her hair, Ellie did Amy's nails and Caroline applied her makeup. When she'd finished, she started on her own.

Amy felt her eyes smart with tears and quickly blinked them away. "Why would you all do something so kind for a stranger?" she asked.

"A stranger?" Ellie squeezed Amy's hand. "You aren't a stranger."

"But I could rob everyone blind," she said, tossing out her arms. "I could run away in that dress."

"But you won't," Dovie said confidently.

"What makes you so sure?"

Dovie paused and gave a casual shrug. "After all these years, I think

I've become a good judge of people. You, Amy, are one of the special ones."

"Don't you even think about crying," Caroline said, waving a mascara wand in her right hand. "You'll ruin your eye makeup."

Amy blinked furiously and the six of them broke into peals of laughter.

"Actually," Jane said, flopping down on the sofa, "let's be honest here and admit the truth. We like you, Amy. You haven't lived here a month, and already you're one of us."

Amy smiled, because that was the way she felt, too.

"Now let's be even more honest," Jane said. "We're here on account of Wade."

The others were quick to agree.

"Wade?" Amy repeated.

"Wade," they said in unison.

"I'm afraid," Dovie said kindly, "that our dear pastor needs to be brought down a peg or two, and we've decided you're the one to do it."

"What has he done?"

"He's gotten . . ." Jane searched for the right word.

"Smug," Ellie supplied. "Set in his ways and too damned sure he's got everything in his life all figured out. He needs a bit of shaking up."

The others nodded. "He's a little too arrogant," Savannah said.

"About the church?" That didn't sound anything like the Wade Amy had come to know.

"No, not with the church," Savannah replied, looking thoughtful.

"We're talking about . . ."

None of her friends seemed to want to say the word. They glanced at one another.

"Romance?" Amy finally suggested.

"Exactly," Dovie said, rubbing her palms together. "He's gotten rather . . . stodgy when it comes to matters of the heart. He's a little too sure he doesn't need love and marriage—that they don't fit with being a pastor."

"And we felt it was time someone opened his eyes."

"You think I'm the one to do that?" Amy found the suggestion highly amusing.

"You're not taking us seriously, are you?" Caroline asked.

"How can I?" Amy giggled. "Have any of you happened to notice I'm pregnant?"

"All the better," Ellie muttered. "Wade McMillen is about to get a crash course."

"You ready, girls?" Savannah asked, and pulled a hair dryer from deep inside the diaper bag.

"Ready," came a chorus of replies.

For the next while Savannah worked endlessly getting Amy's thick hair to curl like the redheaded model's in the magazine. Amy wasn't allowed to look in a mirror. While Savannah worked on her, Caroline painted her own nails and Ellie stood in front of the living-room mirror and tested a new brand of eyeliner.

"I don't think Frank ever dreamed his house would turn into a women's dressing room," Dovie teased.

They laughed again. When Laura awoke and wailed for her mother, Amy was sure the infant hadn't been asleep more than a few minutes. She was astonished to realize it had been two hours.

"My goodness, where did the afternoon go?"

"Are you ready to take a look in the mirror?" Jane asked.

Amy considered the question and nodded. The others instructed her to close her eyes, then the six of them trooped into the bedroom. Jane guided Amy to a spot in front of the full-length mirror.

"Okay, open your eyes."

The first thing Amy saw was the five women gathered around her, all smiling gleefully. Her own reflection stunned her. The transformation was complete. She'd never looked more glamorous, more lovely. Amy felt like Cinderella.

"What do you think?" Caroline asked.

"I . . . don't know what to say."

"You're gonna knock him for a loop," Jane said confidently.

"And the best part is," Ellie said, standing next to her sister-in-law, "we're all going to be there to see it happen."

WADE MCMILLEN muttered under his breath as he slipped the string tie with the turquoise clasp over his head. He adjusted it and headed for the front door.

He wasn't sure how he'd gotten roped into this date. This would be the first time he'd taken anyone to the big dance. He wasn't sure it was a precedent he wanted to set. Not only that, he'd been finagled into the date and it didn't sit well with him.

Amy was a sweet kid. *But that's exactly what she is,* he reminded himself. *A kid.* Twenty-five was far too young for a man of thirty-three. If he was going to become romantically involved, then it would be with . . . Unfortunately no one came to mind.

He blamed Frank for this whole thing, right along with Dovie. The two people he'd helped out when they'd reached an impasse several months back. And this was the thanks he got.

Wade closed his eyes and groaned. Amy was young and pretty. Young enough and pretty enough to set Louise Powell's tongue wagging, that was for sure. Well, let the troublemaker talk all she wanted. She would, anyway, and anything he said in his own defense was sure to be misconstrued.

So he'd take Amy to the Grange hall tonight, and he'd dance with her, too, if that was what she wanted. But he fully intended to introduce her around. Charlie Engler might be interested. Steve Ellis, too. Both owned smaller spreads seventy or eighty miles outside Promise. They usually drove into town on Friday afternoons and split their time between the feed store and drinking beer at Billy D's. Lyle Whitehouse was often with them, but Wade wanted to steer Amy away from him. Lyle had a temper and tended to enjoy his liquor a little too much.

What Charlie and Steve needed, Wade figured, was a stabilizing influence. A wife and ready-made family would go a long way toward setting either man on the right path.

That decided, Wade reached for his Stetson, then locked the front door. He whistled as he drove toward Frank's old house. He hadn't thought to get Amy a corsage and stopped at the local Winn-Dixie on his way. Nothing fancy. He couldn't see investing a lot of money in a bunch of dyed blue carnations that were sure to get squashed when she danced. Besides *he* wouldn't be the one to smell their fragrance. Charlie would. Maybe Steve.

He parked his Blazer at the curb and hopped out. His smile was already in place when he rang the doorbell. Knowing Dovie had helped Amy find a decent dress, he wanted to be sure he complimented her on how pretty she looked.

He pressed the doorbell with one hand and held the flower in the other.

An inordinate amount of time passed—at least two minutes—and Wade pressed the bell again. The door opened just then and a fashion model stood before him. His mouth must have dropped open; all he could do was stare. This had to be a joke and if so he wasn't amused.

"I'm here for Amy," he said, wondering who was behind this scheme.

"Wade, it's me," she said, and laughed softly.

Four

Nell Bishop felt like an entertainment director aboard a cruise ship. Her dude ranch was in full operation now, and the second group of cowboy wanna-bes had thought it would be great fun to end their adventure by attending the dance put on by the local Cattlemen's Association.

There were four men and two women, all gussied up in their finest Western gear. She'd driven them to the festivities in the used minivan she'd bought at the first of the month. So far, her plan to turn Twin Canyons into a dude ranch, complete with a trail drive and sleeping under the stars, had been an unqualified success.

Of course Nell had gotten plenty of help along the way. Her mother-in-law, Ruth, and her children, Jeremy and Emma, had been indispensable; so were the two hands she'd hired.

The crazy part was that after spending a year and a half planning and developing her idea, she was ready to abandon everything—for love. Travis Grant was to blame for this sudden change of heart.

Nell remained on the edge of the dance floor, watching old Pete Hadley, who stood on the stage, a fiddle tucked under his chin, accompanying a country-and-western band. Couples formed uniform rows and performed the latest in line dances.

Men and women alike slid across the polished wood floor, looking like a scene out of a 1930's Hollywood musical, and all Nell could think about was how much she missed Travis. The engagement ring on her finger was testimony of his love. Although they spoke daily by phone, it wasn't enough. They were eager to marry, eager to start their lives together.

Unfortunately planning a time for their wedding wasn't a simple matter. Nell had obligations, and so did he. Because of the dude ranch, she was forced to stay in Texas. A summer in New York would have been a fabulous cultural experience for Jeremy and Emma, but it wasn't possible. Not this year.

Nor could Travis just pack his bags and move to Texas. Not yet. Like her, he had commitments. Speaking engagements, an author tour, followed by a research trip that had been booked for more than a year. Being apart like this wasn't what he wanted, either, but it couldn't be helped.

Three months, he'd told her, and then they'd be together for the rest of their lives. It hadn't sounded so bad when he first outlined his schedule. The weeks would fly by, he'd said, and they had. It was almost July now, and soon August would arrive and before she knew it, September. On the first Saturday of September Travis and Nell would become husband and wife.

"Nell." Caroline Weston stopped in front of the punch bowl beside Nell. "My goodness, I can't remember the last time I saw you. You look fantastic. How are you?"

"Wonderful," Nell told her friend, which was the truth. But if anyone looked fantastic, it was Caroline. Her pregnancy was obvious now and she literally glowed with an inner contentment. "You must be so happy." Nell was pleased that Caroline had found her cowboy at last. Grady Weston might be stubborn and quick-tempered, but he was a man who would love and honor his wife.

Caroline's face flushed with pleasure as she rested her hands on her stomach. "I've never felt better."

Grady joined his wife. He stood behind Caroline and caressed her shoulders. "Good to see you, Nell. How's the dude ranch going?"

"It's keeping me busy," she said. Her gaze wandered to the dance floor, and she was gratified to see that her guests were enjoying themselves. Two couples and two male business executives made up her current group. They were a good mix; everyone had gotten along well. Nell didn't expect that to be the case with every two-week session and considered herself fortunate.

"My feet need a rest," Caroline announced, and Grady led his wife to a row of chairs that lined one wall. A number of spectators sat there, visiting with one another.

Nell watched as Grady and Caroline joined them. Once she was comfortable, Grady brought his wife something cool to drink. Nell smiled absently and tapped her foot to the music. A year earlier, Grady had unexpectedly phoned and invited her to this very dance. She'd gotten two invitations, in fact—one from Glen Patterson, as well—and now, a brief twelve months later, both Grady and Glen were married.

The ache of loneliness inside Nell increased. Travis Grant was a city slicker, her first guest on the dude ranch, and she'd fallen head over heels in love with him. And he with her. Both had been married before. Nell was a widow, and Travis was divorced. Neither had any intention of falling in love again. But they'd been thrown together working to solve the mystery that surrounded Bitter End, the ghost town situated outside Promise. Eagerly on Travis's part, reluctantly on hers. But after research and much conjecture, they *had* solved it. In the process they'd fallen in love.

At first a lasting relationship between them had seemed impossible. Travis had returned to New York, and she'd resumed the business of her life, starting a new venture and raising her two children. But she'd been miserable. Travis, too. It wasn't long—less than two weeks—before they both realized they belonged together. They'd intended to get married right away. So much for best-laid plans. September had never seemed as far away as it did right that minute.

The music slowed and couples moved into each other's arms. Nell missed Travis so much that watching the dancers was almost painful. She was about to turn away when someone tapped her shoulder.

"I believe this dance is mine."

She instantly recognized the rich resonant voice. *Travis.* But that wasn't possible. He was touring on the East Coast and not due back in New York until Sunday. Not due in Texas until right before their wedding.

Nell whirled around, convinced her heart was playing tricks on her. "Travis?" Her shocked afraid-to-believe gaze met his. After a second of stunned wonder, she hurled herself into his arms.

Travis clasped Nell around the waist and, in his joy, half lifted her from the ground. Without caring about an audience, she spread kisses all over his face. "Travis, oh, Travis."

She didn't know how he happened to arrive in Texas for this dance or how long he could stay. None of that was important just then. Being in his arms was.

"Let's dance," he whispered, and reached for her hand.

Numb with happiness, she blindly followed him onto the floor.

Dancing was little more than a convenient excuse to continue holding each other. Nell closed her eyes as she moved into his embrace, listening to the slow mellow music. With her arms around his neck and her face against his shoulder, she clung to him and he to her. All too soon the dance ended, long before Nell was ready, and from the reluctant way he released her, she knew Travis wasn't ready, either. With no other choice they broke apart and applauded politely.

"How . . . When?" she asked as they walked off the dance floor. In her shock, she had trouble getting the words out.

Travis took her hand and led her to a quiet corner, away from the festivities. They sat facing each other, so close their knees touched.

"I phoned late yesterday afternoon," he began. "You weren't there. I was feeling miserable without you and exhausted from the tour. I was scheduled to fly back to New York last night."

Nell knew that much already.

"All at once I realized I didn't give a tinker's damn if I ever saw the New York skyline again. Everything that's important to me is right here in Promise."

"Why didn't you let me know . . . ?"

He grinned and touched her cheek as if he couldn't believe, even now, that they were together. "Ruth answered the phone and we talked. She told me you'd been working too hard."

"I haven't, it's just that— Oh, Travis, it's so wonderful to see you." If they'd been anyplace other than a crowded dance with half the town looking on, she would've kissed him senseless. She had so much to tell him, so much she wanted to ask in the little time they had before he left again. His promotional tour might be over, but he was scheduled to leave almost immediately on a research trip deep in the interior of Mexico.

Travis touched her face and his eyes brightened with intensity. "I'm not taking that trip."

"But Travis, you've been planning it for so long."

"I'll go someday, but when I do it'll be with you. I didn't know it was possible to feel this strongly about someone. As far as I'm concerned, the entire book tour was a waste. My publicist said that next time the publisher plans anything like this, they'll gladly pay to have you fly with me. I wasn't worth a damn. Look what you've done to me, Nell."

She smiled. "How long can you stay?" she asked.

Travis glanced at his watch and Nell realized he'd probably need to be back on the road by morning.

"Does the next forty years suit you?"

"What?" His response completely unsettled her.

"I want us to get married."

"Now?"

"As soon as we can set it up with Wade," he said. "We'll leave on our honeymoon right away. Somewhere wonderful, anywhere, I don't care as long as we're together."

"But I can't go now." Nell's heart sank. "I can't leave the ranch." Although her guests were due to depart the next morning, a fresh batch was scheduled to arrive first thing Monday.

"It's all been arranged," Travis insisted.

"Arranged? What do you mean?"

"Actually this was all Ruth's idea. She asked me to remind you of a surprise birthday party you threw for her last year. Well, this little surprise is her doing." Travis grinned. "Ruth's got your bags packed and says she refuses to listen to any excuses."

"What about—"

"It's covered, sweetheart. Ruth got two of her retired friends to come in and ride roughshod over the next bunch of greenhorns. Everything's under control, so don't worry."

"But—"

"We're getting married, Nell, no ifs, ands or buts!"

"Yes, oh, Travis, yes." Nell was overcome with gratitude—and with joy—that he was here and she was in his arms . . . and they were getting married!

"I knew you'd agree once you heard my plan."

Smiling through her tears, Nell hugged the greenhorn who'd captured her heart. Ruth had said that one day she'd give her a surprise as big as the birthday party Nell had thrown for her. Nell had never dreamed it would be something this wonderful.

"I'm crazy about you," Travis whispered.

Wonderful, indeed.

AFTER ACTING like an idiot at Amy's front door, Wade had quickly recovered his composure by making some ridiculous comment about the sunlight blinding his eyes.

He'd been blinded all right, but it wasn't by the sun. Just then he suspected it had been his own stupidity that had done him in.

The Lord had quite a sense of humor, Wade reflected. He considered what happened a sort of a divine-induced attitude adjustment. From the way he'd behaved, anyone might have thought that taking Amy to this dance was a burden. An unpleasant chore. He'd done everything but hide in an effort to avoid it. In reality, he was so calf-eyed over her it was all he could do to keep the drool off his chin. What he'd needed was a good swift kick in the rear. And Amy had provided it.

The minute they'd arrived, Amy had received more attention than a Smithsonian exhibit. Single ranchers had immediately flocked around her; two hours later, they still did. Wade had never seen anything like it.

No sooner had they stepped into the hall than Steve Ellis had asked for a dance. The guy had his nerve! Wade hadn't seen any of the other men stopping and requesting a dance from someone else's date. What really stuck in his craw was that the evening was half over and he had yet to dance with Amy.

He couldn't get close enough to ask.

Okay, okay, so this was probably what he deserved. He was the first to admit his attitude had been all wrong. He'd made a mistake in not owning up to the way he felt about her. A big mistake—but it seemed he wasn't going to get the opportunity to undo it.

This sudden interest was due to more than simply the fact that Amy was a beautiful woman. Anyone looking at her could see that. On the drive to the dance he'd struggled to keep his eyes on the road and not on her. So, okay, he was attracted to her. He liked her, too. Really liked her, and had from the first.

But he'd been afraid of what people would say if he pursued a relationship with her. A romance. Fear had dominated his actions.

Sheriff Hennessey had tried to talk sense into him. Unfortunately Wade's stubborn pride had prevented him from hearing the message. He resented being manipulated, and he'd focused on that, instead of his feelings for Amy.

From this point forward he refused to allow what others thought to dictate his decisions. He wanted to get to know Amy better. If she wasn't ready to date, then he'd start by being her friend. She was a generous person and he hoped she'd be willing to give him a second chance. That was, if he could manage to break through the throng of men vying for her attention.

At social events such as this, Wade made a point of dancing with the older single women, widows and the like. Women his mother's and grandmother's ages. Tonight, however, he couldn't make himself do it. The only person he wanted to hold in his arms was Amy Thornton—his date. So far, unfortunately, he'd only seen her from a distance.

"Are you enjoying yourself?" Dovie sneaked in the question as she danced past him on Frank's arm. The smile in her eyes told Wade she was well aware of how miserable he was.

Dovie Boyd Hennessey had a mean streak in her, he thought grimly. One that cut to the bone.

"Pretty as a picture, isn't she?" Frank asked as they glided past him a second time.

Wade didn't need to ask who they meant, either. But then he'd made it fairly obvious. He hadn't been able to take his eyes off Amy all night.

He was about to turn away and bury his sorrows in a plate from the buffet when the dance ended. Whether by luck or design, Amy stood next to him. She slid her arm through his and gave a deep sigh.

"I've got to sit down for a bit," she said to him. "My feet are killing me."

Here she was, the woman he'd been patiently waiting to dance with all night, and for the life of him, Wade couldn't think of a sensible thing to say.

She gazed up at him as though she'd been anticipating this moment the entire evening. "I hope you don't mind."

"No, ah . . . sure." His tongue refused to cooperate and work properly. He glanced over his shoulder and saw Grady and Caroline seated close by. Caroline's feet rested in his lap and Grady was rubbing her nylon-covered toes. The scene was intimate, the husbandly gesture loving and thoughtful. The ache inside Wade caught him unawares. In the last year a number of his friends had married, and while he was happy for them, he didn't feel the need for a wife and family himself. He'd always seen his life as complete, viewed his pastoral duties as too demanding for marriage. His satisfaction came from his work, and it was enough—or so he believed. In that moment, however—and other moments like it—he felt keenly alone.

"We can sit here," he said, finally clearing his head. He escorted Amy to an empty section of seats and sat down next to her.

"Thank you," she whispered, and sent him a warm smile.

Wade nearly drowned in her beautiful eyes. He saw her slip out of her shoes and wiggle her toes a couple of times. Then, feeling remiss, he asked, "Would you like something to drink?"

She nodded, her eyes grateful. "That would be wonderful, but nothing alcoholic."

Wade wanted to kick himself, convinced that the minute he left someone would take his seat. He'd been waiting for an opportunity like this and now he was going to lose it.

Sure enough, as soon as he reached the punch bowl, Lyle Whitehouse was standing beside her, leaning against a chair. He looked like he was about to sit down when he suddenly stared over at Wade. Then he nodded and after a couple of seconds walked away.

Wade made it back in record time, nearly stumbling over his own feet in his effort to get to her before some other rancher did.

"Here you go," he said, handing her the plastic cup. "Uh, how do you like the dance so far?" he asked, trying to make small talk.

"I'm having a wonderful time."

No doubt, Wade mused darkly, seeing as she'd danced every dance, and each one had been with a different partner. *Not* including him. But when Pete Hadley and the band started a favorite song of Wade's from the movie *Dirty Dancing,* "She's like the Wind," it was impossible to hold still.

"I know your shoes are off," he said, "but would you care to take a spin?"

Wade wasn't sure what he expected, but not such a quick agreement. "I'd like that."

She slipped her feet back into her shoes and he extended a hand to help her up. They walked onto the dance floor and he took her in his arms. She was tiny, eight or nine inches shorter than he was, which put the top of her head level with his shoulder. Yet they fit together nicely.

Wade wasn't exactly light on his feet, but he could manage a simple slow dance. Amy followed his lead as though they'd been partners for years. He hummed along with the song and was surprised when her soft voice joined his, harmonizing. They smiled at each other, and he gathered her closer.

That was when it happened. The baby kicked. Wade's eyes widened at the strength of the movement. "I didn't realize I'd be able to feel the baby," he said with awe. "That's really something."

"I think she likes the music."

"She?"

"Or he, but since I don't know, I decided to call the baby Sarah."

"And what if she's a he? Do you have a boy's name picked out?"

"Joseph."

That was appropriate, he thought, remembering what Frank had reminded him of the biblical story of Joseph and Mary. Appropriate and a little uncanny.

"A good solid name," he murmured, trying not to let his reaction show.

The song ended far too soon to suit him. He hated to ask Amy to dance again, knowing how worn-out she was, but he couldn't resist. "One more dance?"

She looked up and nodded. He might have been mistaken, but she seemed pleased that he'd asked.

AMY KNEW HOW CINDERELLA must have felt the night of the ball when she first danced with her prince, because that was exactly how she felt just then. All evening she'd waited for Wade to ask her; when it seemed he never would, she gave up. Then the minute she sat down he'd asked.

This was quite possibly the most wonderful night of her life, she mused as Wade held her close. The baby had decided to take up marching and was halfway to Pretoria when she did a swift about-face and kicked Wade. To Amy's delight, he'd been fascinated.

Her fairy godmother, in the guise of Dovie Hennessey, caught sight of her on the dance floor with Wade and winked. Amy winked back and managed to stifle a laugh.

Never in all her life had Amy been this popular with men. From the moment she arrived, she'd been bombarded with requests to dance. When she was first approached, she'd hoped Wade would explain to the others that she was his date. He hadn't done that. Amy knew he hadn't been excited about taking her to the dance and so, rather than burden him with her company, she'd accepted. But truth be known, Wade McMillen was the man she wanted to dance with, more than anyone.

He'd stood by most of the evening, watching her with everyone else, and that had been a bitter disappointment. Only she wasn't disappointed now.

Once they were on the dance floor, Wade didn't seem eager to leave. Amy didn't want to, either. If she closed her eyes, she could pretend that the man who held her was in love with her and wanted this baby. It was a silly fantasy, born of her need to create a secure happy world for her child.

She'd loved Alex with all her heart, but she'd been foolishly blind to his selfishness. For most of her life she'd been more parent than child to her own mother. It had come as no surprise that her mother cut herself off from her just at the time she'd needed her most. Disappointed though she was, Amy could handle the rejection because it was such a familiar experience. Even an expected one.

But Alex had lied to her and hurt her. Deeply. That was one reason this attraction to Wade had surprised her. Now that she was in his arms, even if it was on a dance floor, she couldn't make herself think of him as her pastor. He was a man. Vital, real and handsome.

The baby kicked again, harder this time, and Amy heard Wade chuckle.

"She's got good taste in music," he whispered close to her ear.

"Her mommy's fond of Roy Orbison, too."

"Would you mind if I . . ." Wade paused as though he wasn't sure he should proceed.

"You'd like to feel the baby?" she asked, tilting her head up just enough to look into his eyes.

"If you don't mind."

"I don't." She took his hand and pressed his palm against her stomach, holding it there. Sarah cooperated beautifully and Amy watched as his face took on a look of reverence and surprise.

"My goodness," he whispered. "That really is something," he said again.

"You should feel her from my end," Amy teased.

His expressive eyes brightened and he broke into a full smile.

"What took you so long?" she asked, feeling content. "The evening was half over before you even asked me to dance."

"I'm a fool. But—" he grinned sheepishly "—I'm a fast learner."

"Good."

The rest of the evening passed far too quickly for Amy. She could have danced with him all night, especially those slow, languid dances. What pleased her the most, perhaps, was how comfortable she felt with Wade. For a few hours it was as though all the worries and problems she'd carried alone all this time had been lifted from her shoulders.

Reality would return soon enough, but for now it was easy to pretend, easy to push her troubles aside and concentrate, instead, on the handsome prince smiling down on her.

Then it was midnight and time to head home. Following the dance, Wade and Amy were invited to a party at Glen and Ellie's place. Amy would have liked to go, but realized Wade had church services early the next morning. It didn't seem fair to keep him up half the night simply because she was in a party mood.

They sang along with the radio on the ride back into Promise. The drive out had been spent in silence, and while they'd done little real talking that evening, Amy felt they'd reached a tacit understanding. She felt they'd achieved an appreciation and acceptance of each other that had been missing previously.

Wade parked under the large weeping willow in front of the house. Moonlight filtered through the branches and cast a silvery glow about them.

Amy reflected on her unexpectedly wonderful evening. Her magical evening with Wade McMillen. Dancing with him, being held by him, was everything she'd known it would be. And she knew with certainty that this was the kind of man she wanted as a father to her child, the kind of man she wanted one day to marry. She'd given up thinking men like him still existed.

"I can't thank you enough," she said, leaning back against the seat and closing her eyes. "Oh, Wade, I had such a lovely time."

"I enjoyed myself, too."

She sighed, her heart full of joy and, yes, gratitude.

"The Fourth of July will be here before we know it," he said.

Amy had heard about the annual Willie Nelson Fourth of July picnic. The community faithfully invited Willy every year, but he'd never managed to come—and then he'd shocked everyone by showing up last spring for the annual rodeo and chili cook-off.

"Do you have any plans?" Wade asked.

"For the Fourth? None." Her hopes soared; surely he'd mentioned the holiday as a preamble to inviting her to join him. It was crazy to think this way, for a lot of reasons. She suspected he was reluctant to become romantically involved, because of his work. But she couldn't keep her heart from hoping . . . And for her, the timing was difficult, to say the least.

"I understand the community has a big picnic every year in the park," she added, encouraging him to continue.

"I've never been."

"You haven't?" Amy couldn't imagine what had kept him away.

"My family has a big get-together every year. It's quite a shindig."

Amy envied him his family.

"I was just thinking," he said, "that maybe you'd like to come this year."

"With you?"

"Unless, of course, you'd rather attend the community festivities."

Amy was afraid to reveal how eager she was to go with him. "No, I'd rather . . . I—thank you." She smiled tentatively. "I'd enjoy meeting your family." The baby stirred and Amy bit her lip. In retrospect, perhaps now wouldn't be the best time to meet Wade's parents. She could only imagine what they'd think when their preacher son arrived with a pregnant woman. That gave new meaning to the words "family outing."

As a child Amy used to wonder what it would be like to be part of a traditional family. A real family, where people cared about each other, where they shared things and celebrated together. A mother and father, brother and sister, grandparents. She'd experienced none of that, and she longed for it.

"Are you sure you want me to meet your parents . . . like this?" she felt obliged to ask.

"I wouldn't have asked you otherwise," Wade told her with a sincerity that couldn't be questioned.

They sat side by side, talking quietly for another five minutes before Amy yawned. She didn't want this incredible evening ever to end, but her eyes were closing despite her resolve.

"Let's get you inside," Wade suggested. He had his car door open before she could protest.

Reluctantly Amy straightened and let him help her out of the car. At the beginning of the night she'd felt young and full of energy. Six hours later, her feet hurt, her legs were weak and shaky, and she was more exhausted than she could remember being in her entire life. Exhausted . . . but happy.

Wade placed his arm around her as they walked up the sidewalk toward the small house. Until they reached the front porch, Amy hadn't given the matter of a good-night kiss a single thought. Now she turned to Wade, wondering what he'd do. He seemed as uncertain as she was.

"Well," he said, taking a step back. "I had a great time."

So he'd decided against it. That was fine; she understood. Perhaps next time, even if she felt a little disappointed now.

"Thank you for taking me to the dance," Amy said formally, opening her handbag to search for the key.

"Amy?"

She glanced up, and when she did, she realized that he intended to kiss her. And she intended to let him.

Five

Wade had officiated at a few hurried weddings, but none in which the bride had less than forty-eight hours to prepare. The bride and the entire community. The first Wade had heard of Nell and Travis's wedding was Sunday, after services. Travis announced they'd be applying for the license Monday morning and would greatly appreciate it if Wade could marry them that same evening.

Sure enough, Monday evening the couple stood before him, surrounded by family and friends. In his years as a minister, he'd performed dozens of marriages. Most engaged couples attended several weeks of counseling first. Generally he hesitated to marry people who were in too much of a rush. Nell and Travis hadn't taken his counseling sessions, but he'd talked extensively with them both when they became engaged. They showed all the signs of making their marriage strong and lasting. They were committed to each other and to their relationship. While deeply in love, neither was ruled by passion. Both were mature adults who were accepting and encouraging of each other.

Outwardly their differences seemed overwhelming. Travis lived in New York City and Nell single-handedly managed a cattle ranch near Promise. Travis was a well-known author and Nell a struggling businesswoman. But Wade soon realized their differences were superficial; what they had in common was far more important. They shared not only a deep love but a goal, a vision for the future. A vision that had to do with creating a supportive and loving home for each other and for Nell's family. Wade didn't have one qualm about this rushed wedding.

Nell might have had only forty-eight hours to prepare for her wedding, but the church was as lovely as he'd ever seen it. The sanctuary had been decorated with roses and candles whose flickering light cast an enchanted glow over those who'd gathered to share the moment with

Travis and Nell. Savannah Smith had supplied armloads of red roses, arranging them in glittering crystal vases. Wade couldn't recall seeing any roses lovelier than the ones from Savannah's lush garden, certainly none with a more glorious scent.

Wade smiled at the couple. Given that the wedding was being held with little prior notice, no invitations had been mailed. But word had been passed on the street. It surprised Wade that so many people had come tonight to share in Nell's joy. Then again, it didn't. The folks in Promise admired Nell, so they wanted to stand with her as she pledged her heart to Travis. Grateful for the role he'd played in resolving the mystery of Bitter End, the town had accepted Travis as one of their own. People were happy for the couple and looked to show their support.

After a few introductory words Wade opened his Bible. When he'd finished, he glanced up, prepared to ask Nell and Travis to repeat their vows. As he did, he noticed Amy sitting next to Dovie and Frank.

He'd seen her briefly following the Sunday service, but she'd slipped away before he was able to seek her out. The night of the dance had been a revelation to him; he'd finally acknowledged how he felt about her. Finally acknowledged that he felt an attraction to Amy—that he wanted to pursue a relationship with her, even if it threw his whole life into chaos. Which it would.

When they danced, he'd felt her baby move against him and an unfamiliar emotion had stirred deep inside him. Later, he'd placed his palm over her extended stomach and it was as though her child had leaped to greet him. Then, he'd brought her home and kissed her good-night. The moment had been fleeting, but her kiss had stayed with him for hours afterward. Was with him still. In the two days since, he'd thought of little except Amy and her child. He wondered if she'd been thinking of him, too. And hoped she had. Even now, in the middle of a wedding, it was all he could do not to stare at her.

He hadn't expected Amy to be here tonight, but he was glad she'd come—if for no other reason than he could see her again.

"Travis, do you take . . ." Wade continued speaking, the words as much a part of him as the scripture passage he routinely read in the marriage ceremony. Yet, again and again, his attention wandered back to Amy, as if drawn to her by an invisible force.

After the ceremony the congregation applauded loudly. Travis kissed Nell, and when they broke apart, Nell's face was flushed with happiness. She hugged her children as Ruth, her mother-in-law, dabbed at her eyes with a handkerchief.

Beaming, Travis pumped Wade's hand, then hugged Jeremy and

Emma, Nell's son and daughter. Wade laughed outright when Travis kissed a flustered Ruth on the cheek.

Dovie had baked a wedding cake and that, along with coffee, was being served in the church hall immediately afterward.

Wade waited until the church was empty, blew out the candles and followed the crowd to the reception. He found himself standing next to Amy, who was eating a thin slice of cake.

"That was a beautiful ceremony," she said.

"Weddings and baptisms are my specialties."

She patted her stomach. "Sarah's pleased to hear that."

"Has she been marching around much today?"

"Like a drum majorette."

Wade chuckled. He finished his cake and set the paper plate aside. "I wanted you to know how much I enjoyed the dance on Saturday night."

"I did, too." Her cheeks went pink. "I'm looking forward to spending the Fourth of July with you and your family."

There was no further time to talk; Travis approached them, thanking Wade jubilantly. He also thanked Amy for coming to share in their happiness.

Forty minutes after the ceremony Nell and Travis were gone and the hall had emptied. Dovie and a couple of other women from the church had stayed behind to clean up. Amy was with them, ready to pitch in and do what she could.

Wade made his way back to the sanctuary to turn out the lights and lock up the church for the night. The peaceful silence was a distinct contrast to the noise and merrymaking of the reception. He slipped into a pew; he liked to check in with the "Boss" now and then when something was weighing on his mind.

Wade leaned forward, bracing his elbows on his knees. "Okay, okay, so I'll admit it, I'm attracted to her. There, I said it, are you happy? If you were sending me a wake-up call, then I received it loud and clear. I like her—and I liked kissing her. You've got my attention." He raised his head. "Now what?"

Why a scene from the church dinner nearly a year ago would flash into his mind just then, Wade couldn't say. It was one of the biggest social functions held by the church, and he remembered how difficult it'd been to find a place to sit. His friends were all busy with their wives or lady friends. It was one of the only times Wade could remember feeling alone. Shortly afterward he'd given some thought to seeking a romantic relationship. He'd gone so far as to make up a list. He'd completely forgotten that or where he'd placed it.

His Bible.

He reached for the leather-bound volume at his side and found the tattered slip of paper tucked under the fly leaf. What he read was:

1. A woman who loves God as much as she does me.
2. A woman as interested in a family as I am.
3. Long legs.

He laughed out loud at the last request. His smile slowly faded and it seemed as if the voice in his heart wasn't as still or as small as it had been in the past.

"Amy?" he said aloud. God had sent Amy for him?

Sighing deeply, Wade leaned back against the wooden pew. An argument rose fast and furious within him, then died just as quickly. The strength of the attraction he felt for her had overwhelmed him the night of the dance. Afterward, too.

Questions crowded his heart. "I don't mean to complain, Lord, but are you sure you sent me the right woman?"

Silence.

"All right, all right, I get the message. I asked. You sent. I shouldn't complain. It's not that I object to Amy, mind you," he whispered, "it's just that . . ." What? "Just that . . ." he began again, and realized he was afraid. Not of falling in love. He was ready for that; he'd come to terms with the prospect of upheaval in his life—had even begun to look forward to it. But he was afraid of what he didn't know. He didn't want to demand answers or pry into her life, but it wasn't as if he could ignore the pregnancy, either.

He was afraid of making an emotional commitment to her and her baby, and then watching her walk out on him. Afraid of loving her and risking his heart.

Amy Thornton had come into his life, looking for a few miracles. What he hadn't understood at the time was that she might accomplish a few miracles of her own.

GRADY WESTON's long hard day had been spent driving his herd of stubborn cattle from one range to another. The sun beat down on him with an intensity that was a prelude of what would come later in the summer.

He felt good. About life. About love. About his family. In about three months he and Caroline would be parents for the second time. Maggie was his daughter in every way that mattered. The father's name had been left blank on the birth certificate, so he'd been able to adopt her shortly after he married Caroline. But this pregnancy would be the first time he'd experienced all the emotion and joy that came before the actual birth.

Boy or girl, as far as Grady was concerned he'd be happy with either. Even without knowing, he loved this child with a fierceness that was equaled only by his love for Maggie.

He recalled the night his sister had given birth to Laura Rose. Laredo had been hopeless, barely able to function. Grady had found his brother-in-law's actions somewhat amusing, but as Caroline's time drew near, Grady suspected he wouldn't be much better. Already he worried about her. He wished he could talk her into quitting her job at the post office early, but she was determined to work until the last minute. Whether or not she'd return to work after the baby was born was entirely up to her. She'd mentioned she might take a few years off and go back once their youngest had reached school age. He hoped she would; for her own sake more than his.

Grady looked up and was surprised to see someone approach. He strained his eyes, not recognizing the rider until he came closer. It was Wade McMillen. He couldn't imagine what the reverend might want, unless it was to announce some kind of trouble. Studying the rider, however, told him that wasn't the case. Wade rode with an easy grace, instead of the urgency a crisis would demand.

"Howdy," Grady called out, touching a finger to the brim of his hat.

"Howdy," Wade returned. "Laredo said I'd find you out here. Hope you don't mind that I borrowed one of your geldings."

"I don't have the slightest objection." Wade was a fine rider; if he hadn't become a preacher, Grady figured he would've made one hell of a rancher.

"Have you got a few minutes?" Wade asked.

"Sure."

Wade regarded him seriously. "What I wanted to discuss is private. I'd prefer that it stayed between you and me."

Grady nodded. "If that's the way you want it, then that's how it'll be."

"I appreciate it." Wade met his eyes. "This is difficult to talk about," he began. "I never asked Caroline about the father of her child."

Grady felt his anger rising. "For all intents and purposes, I'm Maggie's father. That's all anyone needs to know."

"I realize that, Grady, and I certainly don't mean to imply anything by asking—but she has a birth father."

"Yes," Grady admitted reluctantly. He couldn't love his six-year-old daughter any more than he already did.

He remembered his initial shock when he'd learned his no-good brother, Richard, was her biological father—when he'd learned that Maggie was the result of a liaison Richard had apparently forgotten. But none of that mattered. Maggie truly was the child of Grady's heart.

There was a time when she wouldn't even look at him, preferring to hide her face in her mother's skirts. Having little experience with children, he'd been unintentionally gruff and impatient with her. But eventually Maggie had been won over—not without determined effort on his part and not without a crisis first. In retrospect he was pleased that winning Maggie's heart had been so difficult. When they'd finally made their peace, he'd experienced a sense of exhilaration and triumph.

"Why all these questions about Maggie?" Grady asked.

Now it was Wade's turn to grow silent for a long moment. "Did you meet Amy Thornton at the dance Saturday night?"

"Amy Thornton," Grady repeated. He frowned. "Isn't she the gal taking the birthing class with Caroline and me?"

"She's the one," Wade said, nodding.

"Dovie's her partner?"

"Yes."

Grady eyed the reverend. "The pretty little gal."

Wade nodded again.

Grady understood now why Wade had come to him. "Are you planning to ask her to marry you?" he asked bluntly.

Wade eye's widened at the directness of the question. "I can't answer that . . ."

"But you're thinking about it?"

"Not yet, but . . . well maybe," he admitted.

For a man contemplating marriage, Grady noticed that Wade didn't seem too pleased. Time for a man-to-man discussion, as his father used to say. That being the case, they might as well sit down and let the horses rest. He headed Starlight in the direction of the creek.

A silent and obviously troubled Wade followed him over the crest of the hill. Willow trees bordered the slow-moving water, their long supple branches dipping lazily in the cool water. Grady dismounted and led Starlight to the creek's sloping bank. He sat on a large rock and waited until Wade was comfortable before he resumed the conversation. "Okay, let's talk this out," he suggested.

"The thing is," Wade said, "I don't *know* anything about Amy."

"Do you love her?" It was a bold question, but Grady couldn't see skirting around the subject when that was all that truly mattered.

Wade's head came up. "I think so . . . Yes." He closed his eyes. "I don't know why I do or how it happened. A week ago I was doing everything I could, short of leaping off a bridge, to get out of taking her to the dance."

Grady laughed. "I seem to recall Caroline mentioning a certain reluctance on your part."

"You mean Amy knew?"

"I think she might have."

Wade groaned aloud.

"What caused this sudden change of heart?"

The question went unanswered for a moment. "I'd tell you straight if I could. When I went to pick her up for the dance, I felt as if . . . as if someone had stuck me with a cattle prod. I'd noticed her before, plenty, but I don't know . . . I was afraid, I guess. Afraid of exactly what's happening now. She's beautiful, but I don't want you to think that's the only reason I'm attracted to her."

"Well, it doesn't hurt any."

"True, but it's much more than that," Wade said. He reached for a long blade of grass and peeled off a strip. "I've only kissed her once, and as far as kisses go, it was pretty chaste."

"But you enjoyed it."

Wade's tight face broke into a grin. "I damn near blew a fuse."

Grady laughed, remembering the first time he'd kissed Caroline. It had left him reeling for days. All he could think about was kissing her again. Judging by the desperation and yearning on his face, Wade was obviously experiencing the same reaction.

"Then Monday night at Nell's wedding . . ."

"Yes?" Grady prodded the minister.

"I . . . I had the strongest sense—" he glanced at Grady, then quickly averted his gaze "—that Amy and I were meant to be together." He paled slightly. "I barely know her and I know almost nothing about her past."

"You mean, who's the father of her baby and why isn't she with him?" Grady believed in plain speaking.

Wade shrugged, and again he hesitated. "It's just that . . ."

"Just what?"

Wade tossed the blade of grass aside and then, as if he needed something to do with his hands, removed his hat and held it by the brim, slowly rotating it. "I'm worried," he admitted.

"Falling in love isn't always easy," Grady said, feeling adequately knowledgeable on the subject. "Especially when there's a child involved. That complicates things. But you have to be willing to love the kid as if she's your own—or he, of course. And you have to trust the woman you love. . . ." His own romance with Caroline had gone through its share of difficulties. In truth, he'd been a stubborn fool, and it'd probably help Wade if he shared that, but Grady preferred to let Wade think him wise and perceptive.

"There's a lot of unknowns with Amy."

That would worry Grady, too. It'd been different with Caroline. Grady had known her almost all his life, not that he'd paid her any heed until recent years, when she'd become friends with Savannah.

"You might just ask her," Grady said. "I find the direct approach less confusing and troublesome myself."

"I could do that," Wade agreed, but he didn't sound confident about it.

"You don't want to ask her a lot of questions," Grady said.

"I'd rather she volunteered the information."

Grady didn't blame him for that. They sat there a good ten minutes without either one of them speaking. Grady was a patient man; he didn't mind waiting.

But when Wade continued to brood in silence, Grady finally asked, "What can I do to help you?"

Wade seemed to slowly shake himself free of his thoughts. "I guess I want you to tell me I'm not acting like a fool," he said in a low voice. "And that there's a chance for me with Amy—and her baby. That I'll say and do the right things."

Grady stood and slapped the minister on the back. "You'll know what's right when the time comes."

Wade exhaled. "I expect I will. Thanks for the pep talk."

"No problem. Come to me for advice anytime you want. I'm not exactly an expert on romance, but I'm willing to help." He actually felt sorry for the poor guy. He'd known Wade for a long time now and had never seen him looking so confused and unsettled.

Falling in love wasn't all starlit nights and picnics and romantic moments; it was also pain and uncertainty and risk.

Wade had just found that out.

AMY AWOKE BEFORE DAWN on the Fourth of July, excited about spending this day with Wade McMillen.

Admittedly part of her excitement was due to the fact that she'd been invited to join his family's celebration of the holiday. In their brief conversation she'd learned that Wade was the oldest of three. His younger brother and sister were both married and each had two children. His mother apparently doted on her grandchildren.

The thought produced a small stab of pain. Amy's mother had wanted nothing to do with *her* grandchild. With effort Amy pushed away all thoughts of her. Alicia Thornton's life had been ravaged by drugs, alcohol and an endless series of disastrous relationships; she'd never functioned with any adequacy as a parent.

From the time she was able to make sense of her own life, Amy had been determined not to make the same mistakes her mother had. Until recently she'd done a good job, behaving responsibly. Then she'd met Alex.

He was another person she preferred not to think about.

Wanting to contribute something to the festivities, Amy tied an apron around her nightgown. "Okay, Sarah," she said, "we're going to bake Wade an apple pie." Dovie had told her Wade had a sweet tooth and one of his all-time favorites was apple pie. She'd even provided Amy with a recipe from her grandmother's cookbook. A crust made with buttermilk, and a few chopped dates added in with the apples.

Feeling ambitious, Amy baked two pies. One apple and one strawberry-rhubarb. Both turned out beautifully. She left them on the kitchen counter to cool, then showered and dressed for the day.

Her wardrobe was limited, but Savannah had given her a few clothes that fit perfectly. She chose a pair of shorts and a sleeveless top, then glanced at herself in the full-length mirror on the bedroom door.

"Oh, my, Sarah Jane," she whispered when she viewed her reflection. "We look *very* pregnant."

Well, there was no help for that. It wasn't as if she could hide the pregnancy; anyway, Wade was well aware of her condition when he invited her. If he'd had second thoughts, he would have said something before now.

No sooner had she finished curling her hair and applying her makeup than the doorbell chimed.

Wade stood there, looking about as handsome as a man had any right to be. She felt a jolt of pleasure at the sight of him.

"Come on inside," she said, unlatching the screen door. "I'm almost ready."

"I'm a few minutes early."

Amy hadn't noticed. "All I need to do is load up the pies."

"Pies?" He quirked one eyebrow.

"Strawberry-rhubarb and apple."

He groaned. "Apple's my favorite."

"That's what Dovie said."

"Did she also tell you what she discovered with Frank—that the way to a man's heart is through his stomach?"

Amy unsuccessfully hid a smile. "She might have mentioned something along those lines." She found a cardboard box in which to transport the pies. Wade moved to help her, and before she understood what he was doing, they bumped into each other.

His arm went out to balance her and she froze when his skin touched hers. Slowly she raised her eyes to his. Her breath jammed in her throat at the look of naked longing on his face. And she realized that same longing was reflected on her own.

Without conscious decision—Amy was convinced of that—they reached for each other. Her arms circled his neck and she stood on her toes, offering him her mouth. Wade kissed her with a thoroughness that left her grateful she was supported by his embrace.

"I've been dreaming of kissing you again since last Saturday."

"I . . . have, too," she whispered. Her eyes were closed. She was afraid to open them, afraid reality would ruin the moment and she couldn't bear that.

"I've thought of nothing but you all week."

"Oh, Wade, are we crazy? I hardly know you. You hardly know me. And yet . . . it's as though we're . . . supposed to be together."

She felt his chest lift with a sharp intake of breath and instantly regretted having spoken. It was true; she'd thought of him all week. But it'd been more than that. Something had changed the night of Nell and Travis's wedding.

Something had happened. Even though Amy didn't really know the couple, she'd let Dovie persuade her to attend the ceremony. Dovie had explained how Nell and Travis had met and fallen in love, and she'd mentioned the ghost town. Amy had found their story inspiring and romantic. She had to admit she was intrigued by Bitter End, too. To think the town had been forgotten all those years!

But as she sat in the church, her attention focused on Wade, and she suddenly had the most intense feeling of *connection*. She was going to love Wade McMillen, she knew it, and he was going to love her. She couldn't explain where this certainty had come from, but she'd definitely felt it. And so, she thought at the time, had he.

However, having recently demonstrated her poor judgment when it came to men, Amy wasn't inclined to believe in what had happened.

Later she'd managed to convince herself that it had been a form of self-hypnosis. Dr. Jane had said that because of the pregnancy, her emotions might be off-kilter.

That was it, Amy was sure. All these mixed-up feelings had been a fluke. Until now, she'd been able to believe that.

"I'm sorry," she whispered, mortified to the very marrow of her bones. "I didn't mean . . ."

Wade cradled her face between his hands and gazed into her eyes. "You felt it, too, didn't you?"

She lowered her lashes rather than admit the truth.

He kissed her as though to remove all doubt. This time their kisses were neither patient nor gentle, but fiery. Urgent. She wasn't sure if those kisses were meant to deny what they felt, to prove it false—or the opposite.

The baby stirred and Wade must have felt the movement because he abruptly broke off the kiss. Speechless, they clung to each other.

"We'd better go," he finally said. "We have a long drive ahead of us, and Mom and Dad are waiting."

Amy envied him his fast recovery. By the time the effect of their kisses had worn off, Wade had loaded the pies into his vehicle. Amy grabbed her purse and a sweater and locked the house.

Once they were on the road, Wade turned on the radio and they sang along to a Willie Nelson ballad at the top of their lungs. There was something exhilarating about speeding down the highway on a perfect July morning. Amy felt a delicious sense of anticipation, a quivery excitement.

"Tell me about Bitter End," she said when the song was over.

He seemed surprised that she knew about the abandoned town. "It was settled, oh, about 130 years ago, after the Civil War, by families hoping to make a better life for themselves," he said. "Then . . . there was some kind of crisis. Nell and Travis found out there'd been an unjust hanging. A preacher's son. Afterward the town was said to be cursed by the preacher, and everyone moved away."

"I'd like to see it."

"I'm sure you will someday."

"It must be an incredible sight," she said, remembering what Dovie had told her, although her friend hadn't actually been to the town herself. Ellie had, but wasn't inclined to speak of it. "Perhaps we could explore it together," Amy suggested.

"Perhaps," he said noncommittally.

"Tell me more about your family," she said next.

"Mom's a housewife-turned-shop-owner," he told her. "After all the years of staying home for us kids, she started her own yarn shop when Janice Marie went away to college. She's always loved to knit, and this seemed a perfect outlet for her creativity. I don't think anyone's more surprised at Mom's success than she is."

"I don't know how to knit."

"Then my mother would love to teach you—whether you want to learn or not," he said with a chuckle. "Dad's a retired insurance broker, but he's busier now than he ever was working. He volunteers at the grade school tutoring children at risk. Last I heard, he was coaching Little League, too. He told me he simply hasn't got time to work, not when he's having this much fun."

"It sounds like you have a wonderful family."

"Just wait until you taste the barbecue. That's Dad's real speciality. He won't let anyone near the grill, not even my mother. He takes real pride in his slow-grilled ribs." Wade went on to describe the apron and hat his father would be wearing. A complete wardrobe reserved for the Fourth of July.

Amy's laugh was carefree. "Now what about your sister?"

"She's mean and ugly."

"Wade!"

"Well, she was when she was twelve and if she's changed I haven't noticed."

Amy didn't believe him for a minute.

"I can't understand what prompted André to marry Janice Marie."

"It might've had something to do with love."

Wade snickered. "It might, but I doubt it. Janice Marie bakes the world's best applesauce cake, and André has a weakness for it."

Amy rolled her eyes.

"Hey, he confessed it to me himself."

"What about your brother?"

"Larry? He's spoiled rotten. Both him and Janice. I'm the only one who turned out decent."

"Yeah, right." She grinned. "I can't wait to ask your mother the *real* story. You know, I'm so looking forward to meeting them." She paused. "What did they say when you told them you were bringing me?" She leaned back, patting her rounded stomach.

"They don't know you're coming."

Amy's amusement died. "What do you mean, they don't know I'm coming?"

Wade didn't appear to notice how upset she was.

"I didn't tell them. Hey, it's no big deal."

"Yes, it is," she said, her panic rising. "Take me back to Promise," she demanded. "I can't—I *won't* meet your family. Not like this. Not without them knowing . . ."

Six

Wade pulled over to the side of the road. Amy looked as if she was about to burst into tears. And he had no idea what he'd done wrong.

"Amy?"

She was breathing hard and tears welled in her eyes. She opened the car door and leaped out.

"What is it?" He followed her, not sure what to do.

"You didn't even tell your parents you'd invited me to the family get-together?"

He gave her a puzzled look. "We often invite impromptu guests. Mom prepares enough food to feed a small army. You're welcome with or without my parents' knowledge."

"Then they don't know I'm pregnant, either." She folded her arms and glared at the sky. "That was a stupid question, seeing they don't even know I exist!"

"My parents aren't going to judge you," Wade promised. "They'll be thrilled I'm bringing you."

She didn't seem convinced.

"All right, all right," he said. "If it's that important, then I'll use my car phone and we'll call them from here."

He watched her shoulders rise and then fall with a deep troubled sigh. "Are you going to tell them I'm almost seven months pregnant, too?"

"Ah . . ." He hesitated, not sure how to answer. If he admitted he was, Amy might find fault with him for warning his parents. If he reassured her he wasn't going to say a word, she might accuse him of setting them up for a shock. Either way, he feared he'd end up with just enough rope to hang himself. "What would *you* like me to say?" he asked.

"Tell them," she said, then chewed on her lower lip.

"Okay." He sat back in the car and reached for the phone.

He'd punched out four numbers when she cried out, stopping him. "No, don't!"

Wade replaced the receiver. "Maybe we'd better go over exactly what you do want me to say. Rehearse it in advance."

Amy climbed back into the Blazer and sat there, arms crossed. After a long tense moment she glanced at him. "Do you have any suggestions?"

"I could tell them we met in church."

"Well . . ." Her beautiful eyes smiled once again. "Isn't that a bit deceptive?"

Wade grinned. "It's the truth—sort of."

The amusement fled from her face. "Oh, Wade, I don't know what we should do."

"Couldn't we simply enjoy the afternoon?" That seemed the obvious solution to him.

"But I'll be self-conscious the entire time."

"Because you're pregnant?"

Amy covered her cheeks with both hands. "I can only imagine what your family will think of me."

"What makes you assume they're going to think anything?"

"Because people do. It's only natural."

"Then they'll think I'm the luckiest man alive to have convinced such a beautiful woman to share the Fourth of July with me." His mother and father were kindhearted generous people, but she wouldn't know that until she'd met them. Never in all his life had he seen either of his parents intentionally shun or hurt anyone. They just weren't like that. He wanted to tell Amy, but feared she wouldn't believe him.

"They'll think I'm one of your charity cases," she muttered.

Wade didn't mean to laugh, but the idea was so ludicrous, he couldn't help it.

"I'm glad you find this funny," she said. "Unfortunately, I don't."

His laughter died, and Wade turned to grasp her by the shoulders. "Oh, Amy, you're about as far from being a charity case as it's possible to get."

She blinked. "How do you mean?"

"Every time I look at you, I have to remind myself that I'm a pastor."

She frowned, and he released her.

"Don't you know?" he asked. "Every time I'm with you, I end up fighting with myself because I want . . ." He dared not finish the sentence, afraid he'd reveal the depth of his feelings. "Every time I'm with you I want to kiss you again," he said, his voice dropping to a whisper.

"Oh, Wade, how can you find me attractive with my stomach like this and . . . and my feet swollen?"

He smiled, wondering if she honestly didn't know. She was beautiful, so damned beautiful—inside and out. "I've never been more attracted to a woman than I am to you right this minute," he confessed. Gently he brushed the hair from her cheek.

Not to kiss her then would have been a travesty. Before he could question the wisdom of it, he leaned across the seat and pulled her forward for a slow deep kiss. Amy sighed, and her arms went around his neck and she melted against him. Kissing Amy was pure emotion, pure sensation . . . pure ecstasy. Because he was a minister, he sometimes forgot he was a man, with a man's needs and desires. That was the real reason Dovie had wanted him to start seeing Amy. He understood that now, although he hadn't appreciated her interference at the time. At the moment, however, he didn't need any reminders of his humanness. None whatsoever.

They kissed again and again, until he felt his control slipping. "Amy . . ." he groaned, needing to break this off while some shred of sanity remained. Already his thinking had become clouded by desire. He pulled away and cleared his throat. "I'm taking you to meet my parents," he said.

Amy didn't argue and Wade was grateful. He started the engine, and after glancing in the rearview mirror, edged the Blazer back onto the highway. "You don't have anything to worry about," he assured her, reaching for her hand. "Mom and Dad are going to love you."

Amy said nothing, but gave him a worried look.

"All I ask . . . ." He hesitated.

"Yes?" she prompted.

"Just remember this is my mother. She's proud of me . . ."

"Then she won't appreciate someone like me messing up your life. That's what you're trying to tell me, isn't it?"

The pain in her voice hurt him. "No, I was about to ask you not to listen to her tales of how well I took to potty training. That kind of thing."

Obviously relieved, Amy laughed. "She wouldn't say anything like that, would she?"

"I'm afraid so."

The tension eased from her face, and the beginnings of a smile took over.

"Mom dragged out my baby book the last time I brought a woman home for her and Dad to meet. You can't imagine how embarrassing it is to have a woman I'm dating examine naked baby pictures of me."

Amy cast him a skeptical glance. "You do this often, do you? Bring women home for your family to meet?" Her eyes held a teasing glint.

He'd walked into that one with his eyes open. "Well . . . not exactly."

"When was the last time?"

This was a test of Wade's memory. "It must be four or five years ago."

She raised her eyebrows as though she wasn't sure she should believe him.

"It's true," he insisted. "You can ask Mom yourself if you like." He wanted to let her know how special she was to him.

After almost three hours' driving, they reached Wade's hometown just outside Houston, a small community not unlike Promise.

The second Wade pulled into the driveway, the screen door opened and both his parents came out. His nieces and nephews, whom he loved beyond measure, followed right on their heels.

Wade squeezed Amy's hand. "You're going to be great. You don't have a thing to worry about."

Her smile was brave as Wade helped her out of the car. His parents hugged him briefly, then stepped back and waited for an introduction. Wade scooped up his two nieces and hugged them both, then gave his attention to the two boys.

"Mom, Dad, this is Amy Thornton," he said, his hand on her shoulder. "Amy, my parents, Charles and Karen McMillen."

Both his parents smiled and at precisely the same moment, as though rehearsed in advance, they lowered their eyes to Amy's stomach.

"That's either Sarah or Joseph," Wade continued.

"Good classic names," his mother said, recovering first.

Maybe he should've given them some warning, after all.

"Amy, this is Peter, Paul, Margaret and Mary," Karen McMillen said, gathering her grandchildren around her. "Welcome to our home."

Amy's hands trembled with nerves, Wade saw, but she smiled politely and extended her hand.

"We don't stand much on ceremony here," his mother said. Putting an arm around Amy's waist, she led her toward the house. "Come on inside and I'll introduce you to the rest of the family. Janice and her husband and Larry and his wife are already here."

Wade couldn't remember a time he'd loved or appreciated his

mother more. As soon as his mother and Amy were out of earshot, his father cornered him.

"She's pregnant."

Wade grinned. "So I noticed."

"Does someone intend to make an honest woman of her?" his father asked.

Wade's gaze followed Amy and he experienced a rush of emotion. "She's already honest—but I think I'm going to love her and her child."

His father nodded his head vigorously. "Good answer, son. No need to say more."

AMY HAD NEVER KNOWN a family like this, so close and fun-loving, generous and expressive. Because she was new here and still self-conscious, she felt most comfortable observing their interactions from a distance. Everyone treated her in a warm, genuinely friendly way. The kids were full of questions about her and Wade. She answered the ones she could and referred the ones she couldn't to him. Amy immediately liked his brother and sister, especially Janice, who was quick to point out that her name wasn't Janice Marie but Janice Lynn. Apparently only Wade called her Janice Marie. As a six-year-old allowed to help choose a name for his baby sister, he'd been adamant that his parents use Marie. Lynn, he'd insisted, sounded too much like a last name. Wade's younger brother didn't look at all like Wade. He was shorter and heavier set, while Wade was tall and lean. Larry was an insurance broker like his dad had been, and Janice ran a graphic-design business from her home.

More than once Amy found herself drawn into the family's activity, not because anyone tried to persuade her but because of the sheer fun they were having. Karen's grandchildren couldn't wait for dark before lighting their fireworks, so she gave them each a sparkler. Mary, who was just five, was terrified of the sparks and the sputtering, but refused to allow her brother and cousins to know it. She held her arm out as far as possible and squeezed her eyes shut as if she expected the sparkler to explode any second.

Midafternoon Charles McMillen donned his apron and chef's hat and began his stint at the barbecue. He was definitely in charge and very serious about it, too. But he allowed Amy to assist him with basting the ribs and the chicken. She had a wonderful time as they exchanged outrageous jokes and silly remarks. To have had a father like this . . .

Once dinner was ready, it lasted a full hour. Wade hadn't been exaggerating when he claimed his mother prepared enough food to feed an army; they needed two picnic tables to hold it all.

What amazed Amy most was the laughter and the noise. She didn't know families had this much fun together. The kids raced around the backyard, chasing each other, and if not each other, then butterflies. Games followed, croquet and a hotly contested game of basketball between Wade, his brother and brother-in-law.

"They used to play as boys," Janice said, sitting next to Amy. "Mom used to have to drag them off the court when it was time for supper."

Late in the afternoon Wade and Larry set up a badminton net and insisted everyone had to participate. Amy wasn't sure she'd be an asset, but Wade convinced her to join in.

"But I'm not any good at this." It was too humiliating to confess she'd never played.

"It's easy," he insisted. "Besides, I'll cover for you." He winked as he said it, as though he could actually manage to be in two places at once.

"All right, but don't be mad if I lose the game for us."

"Not to worry, I won't let that happen."

"What line of bull is my brother feeding you?" Janice shouted from the other side of the net.

"My advice is not to listen to him," Wade's brother declared.

Once the game started, Amy was delighted by how much fun it was. They played a sort of free-for-all style, with the children running furiously after each serve, shouting and laughing. The birdie apparently had a mind of its own and flew in every which direction except the one intended. It wasn't long before everyone dissolved into giggles.

At one point the birdie came right toward Amy. Every time it was anywhere close to her, Wade stepped forward and returned it with surprising ease.

Not this time.

"Get it, Amy," he shouted from behind her.

"Me? You want me to get it?" Even as she spoke, she raised her racket. Her shoe must have slid in a damp spot on the grass because her foot went out from under her and she dropped to her knees. Nevertheless, she returned the birdie, but in her enthusiasm lost her balance and fell forward, landing on her chin. The shock was softened by the soft ground, but it jarred her for a moment.

"Amy!" Wade was at her side in an instant. "Are you all right?" He dropped his racket on the grass and helped her sit up.

Amy was shocked to see the fear and concern in his eyes. "I'm fine . . . really. There's nothing wrong."

"What about your chin? The baby?"

"Everything's fine, Wade." Using his shoulder for leverage, she got back to her feet and reached for her racket.

"I think we should call it quits," Wade said.

His words were followed by a loud chorus of objecting voices, Amy's included.

"We're not going to quit," she insisted. "Not when we're down by two measly points."

"Yeah," ten-year-old Peter said. "I'm not a quitter."

"Me, either," Paul added.

"We're actually ahead?" Larry asked as if this was news to him. "Maybe it isn't such a bad time to quit, after all."

Janice and Larry's wife started swatting him with their badminton rackets, but it was all in fun. The game ended in a tie a few minutes later, and they all stopped when Karen called them back to the table for dessert.

"Who brought the apple pie?" Larry asked. Everyone turned to look at Amy in response to Larry's question. She wasn't sure what to say or do.

"It's the best apple pie I've ever tasted," he said, saluting her with his fork. "The crust is fabulous."

"You're eating my pie!" Wade accused him. "Amy baked that for me."

"You aren't going to eat a whole pie," his brother said confidently.

"Who says?"

"Boys, boys," their mother chided.

"I'll bake another," Amy offered.

That seemed to appease Wade. "All right," he said, and sat back down.

"For Larry," Amy added, and the entire family burst out laughing.

All too soon the day was over. Because of the long drive back to Promise, Wade and Amy left before the big fireworks display.

Amy hugged both of Wade's parents on her way out the door. Neither one had asked her embarrassing questions. Instead, they'd opened their home and their hearts to her without making judgments, with acceptance and love.

"Well?" Wade asked, once they were on the road.

She knew what he was asking. "Your family's . . . wonderful." No single word adequately described the experience of being with such warm gracious people.

"I told you so, didn't I?"

Amy rested her head against the back of the seat. "You're one of those, are you? An I-told-you-so guy."

"Hey, when a man's right, he's right and he deserves to make sure everyone knows it." He growled a he-man sound that made Amy laugh. She felt content and utterly relaxed.

An easy silence fell between them.

"I love it when you laugh," he said after a few moments.

Amy smiled at his words. There'd been precious little laughter in her life. She wanted to tell him about her childhood, about the things she'd seen, the ugliness she'd experienced. The bare cupboards and drunken men. . . . But the day was too beautiful to ruin with talk of such memories.

"I like your sister," Amy said, instead.

"Janice Marie . . ."

"She said that isn't her name."

"Well, that's the name I'd picked out if Mom had a girl. When they decided against it, I was downright insulted. What kind of name is Janice Lynn, anyway?"

"It's lovely," she said, thinking how pleased she'd be to have a friend like Janice. "Your dad's a hoot, too."

"He takes after me," Wade teased.

They chatted for the next hour, laughing frequently. The ride home was punctuated with plenty of washroom breaks—which Amy found she needed these days. They were stopped at a rest area when she first noticed a flash of color in the night sky.

"Look!" she cried, pointing.

"That's the fireworks from Brewster," Wade commented. "Would you like to watch for a while?"

"Please."

Wade helped her onto the hood of his Blazer and joined her. Before long the heavens were bright with bursts of color and exploding stars. Amy oohed and aahed at each one. Wade tucked his arm around her shoulders and she leaned against him. They stayed there watching the fireworks until the very end.

It was almost midnight by the time Wade pulled up in front of her house. She struggled to keep her eyes open, yawning as he escorted her to the door.

"That was the most marvelous day of my life," she said. It was the plain and simple truth, although he had no way of knowing that. "Oh, Wade I'm so glad you insisted I meet your family. They're wonderful."

"Hey, what about me?"

"You're not so bad yourself."

Moonlight dimly lit the small porch, and when Wade smiled down on her she realized how much she wanted him to kiss her. How much she needed his touch. It would be the perfect ending to a perfect day.

It seemed he was thinking the same thing, because he reached for her. Amy closed her eyes and sighed. His kisses were slow and leisurely, expressions of comfort and contentment rather than passion. When it was time for her to go inside, Wade unlocked the door and handed her back the key. Then he smiled at her in the moonlight.

"Thank you, Amy, for spending the day with me."

"No, thank *you*," she said. He'd given her so much.

DOVIE LOVED attending the birthing classes with Amy. She'd learned to breathe right along with her younger friend, and they occasionally practiced together in the evenings or on a slow Sunday afternoon.

"You're getting mighty close to Amy and her baby, aren't you?" Frank said one night after dinner. He carried the dirty dishes to the kitchen counter, then poured them each a cup of freshly brewed coffee.

"Does that worry you?" Dovie asked, joining him at the table. She doubted she could hide the truth from her husband. He knew her far too well. Besides, he was right. If she'd had a child of her own, she would have wanted a daughter like Amy. As the weeks went on Amy had come to trust Dovie more and more. Slowly she'd revealed bits and pieces of her past life; this trust had been extended to others, as well. Wade McMillen had a lot to do with the transformation in the young woman, Dovie felt. They were falling in love and it was wonderful to behold.

Poor Wade, Dovie mused. She almost felt sorry for him. He was so enthralled with Amy he could barely think straight. Amy was no different.

"How many classes do you have left?" Frank asked.

"Just a couple more." Dovie knew he found it difficult that she was away every Monday night, but he'd been a good sport about it. She put dinner in the oven and he ate alone, but when she returned from class, she was eager to share her experiences. He listened patiently while she chatted on and on about what she'd learned.

"When's the baby due?"

"Middle of October," Dovie told him. "And you know that as well as I do."

"Everything's fine with the pregnancy, isn't it?"

"According to Jane, everything appears to be normal. Fortunately Amy's young and healthy."

"Good."

Dovie grinned. Frank had taken a liking to Amy, too, although he wasn't as prone to discuss his feelings as she was.

"It seems to me that Amy should start thinking about getting the nursery ready."

"She's doing the best she can," Dovie said, quick to come to her friend's defense. "Denise Parsons is lending her a bassinet."

"What about a crib?"

"Wade's got that covered."

"Wade's buying her a crib?" Frank sounded shocked.

"Not exactly. He found a used one at a garage sale a couple of weeks ago and he's refinishing it."

"Our pastor?"

Dovie couldn't have disguised her delight to save her soul. "Although when it comes to Amy, I sincerely doubt Wade is thinking of her in terms of being her pastor." Dovie finished her coffee. "And I, for one, am thrilled."

"Uh, Dovie, not everyone appreciates Amy the way you and I do," Frank said, not looking directly at her.

"You mean there's been talk about Amy and Wade?"

Frank gave a noncommittal shrug. "Some."

Dovie was furious. "I can't just imagine who's responsible for *that,*" she muttered. No one got her dander up faster than Louise Powell. Try as she might to maintain a Christian attitude toward the other woman, Dovie was confronted again and again by her vicious tongue. "What's Louise saying?"

"Well, according to her, there are plenty of women without a questionable past. Wade could be dating them."

Dovie rolled her eyes rather than dignify such a statement with a response.

Frank grinned. "What's fun is watching Louise try to turn folks against Amy. People refuse to listen. They change the subject or make comments like how nice it is to see Wade so happy."

Dovie was proud of their townsfolk, too. "I'm having a baby shower for Amy next week." Everyone she'd called had been eager to participate. "It's a surprise, Frank Hennessey, so don't you let the cat out of the bag, understand?"

"My lips are sealed."

Dovie stood, and her husband grabbed her around the waist and pulled her into his lap.

Dovie put up a token protest, which he ignored.

"Is Amy going to ask us to be the baby's godparents, Dovie?"

"That's up to her." But Dovie strongly suspected she would. Twice now Amy had asked Dovie about the responsibilities entailed and hinted that Dovie and Frank would make wonderful godparents.

Dovie loved Amy's unborn baby as if Sarah or Joseph were her own grandchild. The closer Amy's due date drew, the more excited Dovie became. Already she'd knitted two blankets and one cap-and-bootie set. Her fingers weren't as nimble as they'd once been, but that didn't stop her.

"Sometimes I think . . ." Dovie paused.

"What?"

She wasn't sure she should say it aloud, but she'd ventured this far. "Sometimes it feels as if Amy is *our* child. She needs a family, and we have all this love to share."

Frank's arms tightened around her waist. "I'm beginning to believe the same thing."

WADE HAD NEVER BEEN good at carpentry. He still recalled his school shop project—a birdhouse. It had been a disaster. Give him a textbook and a room full of students any day of the week. He could teach them the principles of architecture, but he couldn't tell a screwdriver from a wrench.

He didn't know what had made him think he could refinish a crib, but he'd taken on the task with enthusiasm. Amy only worked part-time at the feed store, so once she'd paid her utility bills and bought groceries, she didn't have a lot of money left. The crib was his contribution. His own personal "welcome to the world" gift.

While the refinishing job might not win any awards for skill, he figured he should get an *A* for effort. He'd originally intended to give the crib to Amy at the surprise baby shower Dovie was throwing that afternoon. But it didn't make sense to haul the crib over to Dovie's and then back to Amy's place.

So he did the logical thing. He pretended to know nothing about the shower and dropped it off at her house directly.

Fortunately the contraption folded and fit in the back of his Blazer. Amy was busy washing dishes when he arrived. She wore the same shorts outfit she'd worn the Fourth of July, which produced a rush of warm memories.

"Hi." He kissed her lightly, then followed her inside. "I've got something for you."

"You do?" She smiled with anticipation.

"Sit down and close your eyes." He nudged her into a living-room chair.

Amy sat there quietly, eyes closed as he requested, and while she waited, he returned to the Blazer and carried the crib into the house.

"Okay, you can look now," he said, standing proudly by his work.

Amy stared up at him and then at the crib. Her eyes grew huge. "Oh, Wade." Her hands flew to her mouth.

"I refinished it myself." He realized he sounded like a Cub Scout boasting about his latest achievement badge, but he couldn't help it.

"Now all I need is a screwdriver to, uh, finish tightening the rails." Did that make any sense? He wasn't sure.

"I . . . don't know if I have one," she said.

Wade let her go through the motions of searching. He'd made darn sure she *didn't* have one before he'd brought the crib over. It was all part of the elaborate plan to get Amy to Dovie's place for the shower.

"Frank must have a screwdriver," he said, reaching for the phone. He went through a little performance at his end—quite convincing if he did say so himself—then hung up. "He wants us to come over."

"When?" Amy asked.

"Now."

She sighed, and he was afraid she might decline with some excuse. "Come on," he urged. "It'll do you good to get out of the house."

She didn't seem to believe him, but finally she nodded and got her purse from the bedroom. At almost eight months pregnant, Amy didn't move around as quickly or comfortably these days.

He helped her into the Blazer and closed the passenger door. He wanted to suggest that she run a comb through her hair or add a touch of lipstick, but didn't dare for fear she'd guess something was up.

"What are all the cars doing at Dovie's house?" she asked.

"I think one of her neighbors is having a Tupperware party," Wade said. Okay, so he was known to stretch the truth now and then. Hey, he wasn't perfect.

He rang the doorbell and stepped aside so Amy would enter the house first.

The instant she did, a loud chorus of "SURPRISE!" greeted her.

She gasped and stumbled back, crashing into him. "You knew?" she asked, twisting around to look at him. Shock and delight flashed from her eyes.

She shook her head. "No one's ever done anything like this for me before," she said, and burst into tears.

Seven

Four weeks. One month. And then, this tiny being in Amy's womb would be in her arms. It didn't seem possible.

Dressing for her appointment with Dr. Jane, Amy rubbed body lotion over her extended belly. It seemed to stretch halfway across the room. Studying her reflection in the mirror, Amy felt grotesque and misshapen, barely able to believe that this would soon be over. That soon, she'd be holding her baby.

She'd just finished pulling on a dress and slipping into her shoes—she'd long since lost sight of her feet—when the doorbell rang. Wade had wanted to take her to the doctor's appointment. He was even more attentive now, more solicitous. Increasingly Amy had come to rely on him. He was so gentle with her. Lately when they kissed, he restrained himself with two or three chaste kisses. If it wasn't for the yearning she read in his eyes, she might have assumed he no longer found her attractive. His gaze told her otherwise.

"You ready?" he asked, and walked into the living room.

"I'll only be a moment," she promised. "I want to put on some lipstick."

"You're perfect just the way you are."

Amy found his words touching. "You must be at the age where you need glasses, Wade McMillen."

"My eyesight is twenty-twenty," he countered. "I happen to recognize a beautiful woman when I see one."

Amy didn't know what she'd done to deserve someone like Wade in her life. She knew she'd fallen deeply in love with him, and it had become more and more difficult to hide the depth of her feelings. They hadn't spoken of love. Not once. And seeing that she was about to give birth to another man's child, Amy didn't feel she was in any position to discuss her feelings.

"Mom phoned last night," Wade told her. "She wanted to see how you're feeling. She asked me to give you her love."

"I hope you gave her mine," she said on her way into the bathroom.

"I did," Wade called after her.

Amy stood in the front of the mirror and applied a pale rose shade of lipstick. It never ceased to amaze her that a woman who was little more than a stranger would send her love, while her own mother had abandoned her. At no time in the past three months had Alicia Thornton made any attempt to contact Amy. Her mail continued to be forwarded and other than a couple of cards from people at her old job, there'd been nothing. No one had tried to reach her. Not her mother. Not Alex.

Which was just as well. She'd left Dallas wanting to escape their influence and make a new life for herself and her child. She liked the people of Promise and they had welcomed her with kindness and generosity. In only a few months Promise felt more like home than any place she'd ever lived.

DR. JANE PATTERSON'S office had grown steadily busier over the past two months; today the reception room was almost full. Jenny asked Amy to have a seat and Wade sat with her, holding her hand. Her free hand rested on her stomach.

"Would you like to go for lunch later?" he asked.

As often as they saw each other, they rarely went out on what would be considered a date. "I'd like that," Amy said.

"Any cravings?" he murmured. "Pickles? Ice cream?"

"Cheese enchiladas."

"Done. The Mexican Lindo has some of the best."

Amy didn't realize how hungry she was until he'd mentioned food, and then it was all she could think about.

Jenny appeared a minute later. "Amy, Dr. Jane will see you now."

Amy stood. "I'm sure this won't take long," she told Wade.

Jenny took her blood pressure and pulse and entered the numbers on her chart. Amy sat on the end of the examination table and waited.

Dr. Jane came into the cubicle and read the chart. "How are you feeling?" she asked.

"Ambitious," Amy said. She'd gotten the bedroom ready for the baby in the week since her last visit. The gifts from the baby shower had spurred her into activity. Everyone had been so generous.

"Ambitious," Jane repeated. "That's a promising sign. Are you experiencing any problems?"

"You mean other than rolling over in the middle of the night? I feel like a turtle who's been flipped onto its back and can't get up."

Jane grinned. "Other pregnant women have told me the same thing." She checked the swelling in Amy's ankles and after a brief physical exam asked her to make an appointment for the following week.

"Everything okay?" Wade asked Amy once they were outside.

"Perfect," she assured him. Other than feeling ungainly, she'd rarely been in better shape. This could be attributed to the care she'd taken with diet and the number of hours of sleep she seemed to require every night. In addition, Wade and Dovie had pampered her at every turn. Their emotional support and friendship had made a world of difference to Amy, and to the pregnancy.

"You've got my mouth watering for Mexican food," he said, holding her hand firmly in his.

"Mine, too."

They entered the restaurant in a festive mood, and the proprietor himself escorted them to a table. Amy barely had time to open her menu when the waiter appeared with chips, salsa and glasses of water.

"I don't know why I'm bothering to read this," she said. "I already know what I want."

For a moment Amy didn't think Wade had heard her. His attention was focused on the booth directly across from them. Amy's gaze followed his to two middle-aged women, both of whom were more than a little overdressed for the restaurant. One wore a shiny silver running outfit with high heels and star-shaped sunglasses. The other seemed decked out for the beach, in a halter top, panama hat and short shorts. She recognized the woman in silver by sight. Louise Somebody. Dovie had pointed her out; she'd said little, but Amy could tell from her tight-lipped expression that this Louise was not a person she liked or respected.

The waiter returned, ready to take their order and it seemed no time at all before he was back with their meals. Amy forked up a mouthful, for her first taste. The enchilada was full of spicy refried beans and melted cheese. Mmm. She took a bite, expecting to be transported to culinary heaven. But as soon as her mouth closed around the fork, those expectations were shattered by the conversation at the booth across the aisle.

"It doesn't seem fitting, does it, Tammy Lee, to have our pastor—a man who's supposed to be above reproach—dating an unwed mother."

"Yes, I would've thought Reverend McMillen would show a bit more discretion," the other woman said.

Amy saw Wade stiffen.

"This food is wonderful," Amy said, hoping to distract him and at the same time hide how much those cruel words hurt.

Wade's attention returned to her. "Ignore those two."

"I will if you will," she whispered back.

He nodded.

"She looks like she's about to pop any minute," the one in the beachwear said, just loudly enough to be heard.

"Personally I think Wade's involvement reflects poorly on the entire church." The woman in the running suit didn't bother to hide the fact that she was staring in their direction.

"I'm sure more than one person has questioned his priorities lately."

"Just who is she, anyway?"

Amy set her fork aside, certain she wouldn't be able to swallow another bite. The food that had been so appealing had little flavor now. What the woman said was true—and something Amy had chosen to overlook all these many weeks. Wade was a minister, a man of God; he had a reputation to consider, and his affiliation with her was hurting him in the eyes of his community.

"It's just not what you'd expect from a pastor."

"It makes you wonder . . ."

Wade slammed his fork down on the table. "I've had enough," he told Amy.

"No, please!" She was embarrassed enough. Anything he said or did would only add to her humiliation. And his own.

Amy had never seen him angry, not like this. His face was white, his fists clenched, as he got out of the booth and approached the two women.

"Good afternoon, Louise. Tammy Lee."

Both women nodded coolly.

"I couldn't help overhearing you just now."

"You heard?" Louise murmured as though she felt shocked by that—although she'd obviously intended it all along. But why? Amy wondered. Why would she purposely set out to embarrass Wade?

"You were talking about Amy Thornton and me. Have either of you met Amy?"

Amy felt their eyes shift to her. She smiled weakly and nodded in their direction.

"No . . ." one of them said.

"I can't say I've had the . . . pleasure," the other said.

"I already knew the answer before I asked," Wade confessed wryly, "because if either one of you had made the effort to know Amy, you'd realize something very important."

Both women stared at him.

"Amy is one of the kindest women I've ever known. She'd never go out of her way to embarrass someone—unlike certain others I could mention."

Louise pursed her lips at this.

"Furthermore," Wade continued, "I happen to be very much in love with Amy Thornton."

The shocked gasp, Amy realized, came from her.

"It hurts me that two women who are part of my church family would be this thoughtless, this judgmental. I hope that, in time, you'll both come to know and care about Amy, too."

Amy didn't hear the rest of the conversation. Her thoughts whirled around in her head. *Wade loved her.* He'd admitted it to those two women. But it troubled her that his love for her was damaging his reputation.

She folded her arms beneath her breasts, cradling her child, protecting him or her from the harsh judgments of the world. This matter of seeing Wade socially had worried her before, but they'd never discussed it. She'd been afraid to confront the issue, afraid that once she did, everything would change. Now she saw that her selfishness had hurt him. These women, gossipmongers or not, were members of his church, and it wouldn't be long before word spread throughout the congregation, possibly the entire town.

Reverend Wade McMillen was in love with an unwed mother.

Her thoughts distracted her, and she didn't even notice that Wade had returned to the booth.

"I apologize, Amy," he murmured. "I wish I could have spared you that."

She tried to reassure him with a smile, but was unable to muster even a token effort.

"I'm the one who should apologize."

"Nonsense."

She couldn't stop looking at him, couldn't stop hearing his words. "You love me?" she asked, her voice more breath than sound.

He reached for her hand. "Funny I should admit how I feel about you to someone else first, isn't it?"

"No." Her throat felt thick, clogged with tears, making it difficult to speak. She lowered her head, trying to clear her thoughts.

"I didn't intend to ask you to marry me like this."

Amy slowly raised her head. "Marry you? But . . . you don't know anything about me, about my family—about my background."

"I know everything I need to know."

"What about . . . Sarah? You don't know about her—about the man who fathered her." Amy hadn't mentioned a word about Alex, not to Wade, not to Dovie. Not to anyone. As much as possible, she tried to push every thought of her ex-lover from her mind and heart. One night just recently she'd found herself pretending Wade was Sarah's father, but decided that was a dangerous game.

"I love you, Amy."

"No." She shook her head vigorously. "You don't know what you're saying. You . . . We've been seeing too much of each other," she said, struggling to hide the panic rising inside her.

"I've never been more certain of anything in my life."

"Oh, Wade." She took her napkin and crumpled it with both hands.

"I want us to get married. Soon, too, so I can be Sarah's daddy."

Amy gave up the effort. She covered her face, reminding herself that her hormones were all askew and not to worry if she was more emotional than usual.

"Is that a yes or a no?" he asked with such gentle concern it made her want to weep.

Fighting for composure, Amy swallowed back tears and inhaled deeply. "I don't know what to say," she managed once her throat muscles had loosened enough for her to speak.

"Say you'll marry me."

"I . . . need time."

"Darling, I hate to pressure you, but all we've got is a few weeks before we're parents."

She'd love Wade McMillen to her dying day, Amy decided right then and there, for declaring himself Sarah's father.

"I promise to think about it," she told him. For now, that was all she would do. Think. Try to figure out what was best for her and for the baby. And what was best for Wade.

GRADY, CAL AND GLEN met on the border of Grady's property and the Patterson's ranch, in the same spot they'd often congregated as teenagers. Those days were long behind them now.

"What's this all about?" Cal asked, dismounting as he spoke.

"I assume there's a *reason* you wanted us to meet you here," Glen added, sliding down from his horse, a high-spirited gelding who pranced in place.

While he might sound like he was complaining, Grady could see that his eyes were alight with interest.

Grady grinned at his two best friends. "Actually there *is* an important reason. I want the three of us to return to Bitter End."

"But why? We were there not long ago. Wade was with us, remember? We had a little ceremony, prayed and everything. I'd hoped that was the end of it."

"This is a joke, right?" Glen said irritably.

If Grady hoped to get his friends' attention, he'd achieved his goal.

"No joke," he insisted. "The three of us need to go back."

"I'd like to remind you again that we were just there," Cal muttered.

Grady knew what his friends were thinking, because the same thoughts had been going around in his mind for a number of weeks now.

"Prayer or no prayer, I've seen enough of Bitter End to last me a lifetime," Glen said. "Far as I'm concerned, someone should burn that place to the ground before anyone else gets hurt."

"Then cover it with sulfur," Cal put in.

No one had come away from Bitter End with pleasant memories, not in more than a hundred years. Through research and a good deal of luck, Nell and Travis had uncovered the source of the trouble. Together they'd learned that Bitter End had been cursed by a preacher whose son had been wrongfully hanged. No one had paid much attention to the preacher, but then the town was beset with plagues of the sort brought down on Egypt thousands of years before. The citizens of Bitter End had endured it all—drought and locusts, sickness and hail—until the death of their firstborn children, and then they'd scattered in panic. A number of families from Bitter End had become the founders of Promise.

"Bitter End is a piece of Texas state history," Grady told his friends. "It's a part of who *we* are, as well."

Neither Cal nor Glen was as quick to argue now, and Grady knew it was because they recognized the truth of what he'd said.

"You want us to go back and . . . and confront the past, don't you?" Cal asked.

"That's my thought," Grady admitted. "I want us to stand in the center of that town and face whatever's there." Grady felt instinctively that this was necessary, although he couldn't really say why.

"We stood there with Wade," Glen pointed out.

"I know . . . but this is different."

"How?" Cal demanded. Even as he argued, he remounted Thunder, ready to follow through with the idea.

"I want to declare this land free of the curse."

"Like anyone's going to listen to us," Glen said.

"Any*thing,* in this instance," Cal added.

"Whatever." Grady had thought long and hard about this moment. He'd been one of the people who stood with Wade McMillen in the center of Bitter End. One of the men whose roots were buried deep in the history of this forgotten settlement. He wanted whatever was there, the curse, to leave.

They rode in silence, the three of them, like gunfighters heading for a high-noon shoot-out.

The town lay nestled in a small valley below a series of limestone outcroppings. Buildings, both stone and wood, stretched on both sides of the main road. The tallest structure was the church with its burned-out steeple. The wooden two-story hotel, rotting from years of abandonment, leaned precariously to one side, as if the next windstorm would send it toppling. His brother had nearly died in that hotel not many months ago. A sadness came over Grady when he thought of Richard, but he refused to allow his plans to be sidetracked.

By tacit agreement the three men stopped outside the building that had once been the mercantile. The horses shifted restlessly, their acute senses responding to the mysterious atmosphere.

"It's dead here," Glen commented. Nothing grew in town. Bitter End had died all those years ago.

"Do you feel anything?" Cal asked, whispering.

"I'm not sure," Grady said in a normal voice. He refused to give in to whatever was here, refused to bow to his fears.

Glen just looked around, his horse making an abrupt circle as if to check behind himself.

As boys, when they'd first happened upon Bitter End, they'd felt a sense of great sadness, a sense of unease, a tension that manifested itself in the physical. The oppressive silence had frightened them so badly it'd taken them twenty years to venture down these streets again.

The horses seemed incapable of standing still. All three men had trouble restraining them.

"I don't know what I feel," Grady reported. The first time around there'd been no question. The sensation had been overwhelming, unmistakable.

"That feeling of . . . grief. It's still here," Glen said, glancing over his shoulder. "But not nearly as strong as before."

"I feel it, too." This came from Cal.

"Are you ready to go back now?" Glen's question was directed at Grady.

He nodded, wishing he knew what to do. He'd hoped . . . hell, he wasn't sure what he'd been hoping for. He supposed he'd wanted to find something different, discover that the town had miraculously changed. That it had—somehow—come back to life.

WADE HAD BEEN looking forward to this for two weeks. Grady and Caroline had invited Amy and him to dinner at the Yellow Rose Ranch. Unfortunately he suspected that if they hadn't already agreed to this, Amy would've found an excuse to decline.

She hadn't been herself since the confrontation with Louise Powell and Tammy Lee Kollenborn in the Mexican Lindo. For the past few days, she'd been quiet and withdrawn, and he knew she was disturbed by what had happened. He didn't blame her.

It didn't help that his marriage proposal had come about the way it had. He'd been trying to work out the best approach all week, but then the incident at the restaurant had forced his hand. It wasn't how he'd wanted to ask her—and he couldn't help feeling some resentment, unchristian though he knew that was, toward those two meddling women.

He glanced at Amy as he drove to the Yellow Rose Ranch. She looked half-asleep, and while he knew she was tired, he also knew she was using her fatigue as an excuse to avoid a certain subject. His proposal. He'd waited a long time to find the woman he wanted to marry, and now he had, he wanted to marry her. The sooner, the better, for the baby's sake, as well as his own.

He wouldn't pressure her into a decision. When she was ready, she'd tell him; until then he'd be patient.

Amy straightened when he turned off the highway and into Grady's long drive. "We're going to have a good time tonight," he promised, leaning over to squeeze her hand.

Amy smiled. "I hope Caroline didn't go to a lot of trouble."

Wade knew Amy's due date was only a week earlier than Caroline's. The two women had become friendly and often met for lunch. He was well aware that Amy admired Caroline and relied on her advice, which Wade saw as a good thing.

Grady stepped onto the porch when Wade steered the Blazer into the yard, and Caroline appeared at her husband's side almost immediately afterward. She hugged Amy, then greeted Wade with real warmth. He gave her the flowers he'd brought in appreciation for the dinner. No wine, not until after the babies were born. He hoped there'd be many more such evenings—some of them at his house. His and Amy's.

It would be just the four of them tonight, since Maggie was spending the night with Savannah.

"Everything's ready," Caroline told them, "so we can eat anytime."

"I'm dying to see your nursery," Amy said.

The two women disappeared, but Wade wasn't fooled. Amy might want to look at the baby's room—he was sure she did—but the real reason she'd gone off with Caroline was to talk to her, perhaps seek out her advice about his marriage proposal.

Wade trusted Caroline to encourage Amy to marry him. If she mentioned what had happened with Louise and Tammy Lee, then Caroline would tell her those two didn't speak for the community. With few exceptions, the entire town had rallied around Amy. Caroline knew that as well as anyone.

In every problem is a gift, his grandfather had told him years ago, and Wade remembered it now. The gift Louise and Tammy Lee had given him was the courage to admit, openly and publicly, that he loved Amy.

Dinner proved to be both relaxing and fun. Caroline was an excellent cook and the prime rib, accompanied by garden fresh broccoli, a green salad and mashed potatoes, was one of the best Wade had tasted. This night out was exactly what he and Amy needed. Conversation was mostly light and entertaining, although they talked about Bitter End and answered Amy's questions. She asked about visiting the town, but both Grady and Wade discouraged that.

While Caroline and Amy cleared the table, Wade and Grady had time to talk privately on the porch.

"Speaking of Bitter End, I was there this week," Grady surprised him by saying.

"What made you go back?" Wade asked, taking a sip of his coffee.

Grady shrugged. "I don't know, but I felt I had to—that there's something unfinished there."

"What?"

"I don't know," Grady said. Then he changed the subject abruptly. "How are things between you and Amy?"

"I love her." Wade had already admitted it once and found it easier the second time.

Grady gave him a slow satisfied smile. "I guessed as much."

"Oh, yeah?"

" 'Fraid so, Preacher."

"I've asked her to marry me," Wade confessed.

"Is she going to?"

"I don't know." Wade had promised himself he wouldn't pressure her, but he had a feeling deep in his gut that told him the longer she kept him waiting, the less likely she was to agree. His chest ached at the thought of what his life would be like without her. Every conscious reflection included her. She'd become a big part of his world, of the way he planned his future.

Grady commiserated, but had no advice to offer other than "Don't give up."

At the end of the evening, Amy hugged both Caroline and Grady to thank them for dinner. "I've enjoyed myself so much," she said with such sincerity that no one could doubt her. Least of all Wade.

"Dinner was superb," Wade told Caroline. "Great food, terrific company." Because he was single, he was invited out to dinner quite a bit. No fool he, Wade often accepted. But this evening had shown him what his life would be like if—when—he was married.

Wade waited until they were back on the road before he broached the subject of marriage. "I wasn't going to say anything," he began, keeping his eyes on the road.

"About what?" Amy asked, then turned to him, eyes filled with alarm. "If you let me sit through the entire evening with a piece of broccoli stuck between my teeth, I swear I'll never forgive you."

Wade chuckled. "It isn't that." His humor quickly faded. "I wanted to ask if you're still thinking about . . ."

"If I'll marry you," Amy finished for him. "That's what you want to know, isn't it?"

"I love you, Amy. I want to marry you."

She was silent for so long he wondered if he'd blown it entirely. "Say something," he urged, trying not to sound as anxious as he felt.

"His name's Alex Singleton," she said, her voice low. "We met, of all places, in the grocery store."

Wade gripped the steering wheel hard. He wanted to tell her it didn't make a bit of difference who'd fathered her baby. It wasn't a detail he considered necessary. He loved her and he loved her baby. That was the only fact she needed to consider.

It hurt, too, to hear about another man wanting her, making love to her. But he kept his mouth shut, knowing Amy needed to tell him. In some ways this wasn't for him as much as it was for her.

"He asked me out for coffee. I said no, but he was charming and funny and persistent, so I agreed. The store had a deli, and we sat there. We . . . talked so long that the ice cream in my cart melted." She smiled at the memory. "He was sophisticated and wonderful. I thought I was in love that first day."

Wade found that listening was more difficult by the minute.

"Because he often went away on business, we weren't able to see each other more than once a week. I . . . I lived for those weekly dates. Regular as clockwork, he arrived every Wednesday evening and took me out to dinner. We ate at the most wonderful restaurants. Small upscale places."

"So he had lots of money."

"Oh, he had more than that, Wade." Her voice hardened. "He also had a wife and two children."

Eight

Thursday afternoon, Ellie Patterson left the feed store early. George, her assistant, would close up and Amy would help him. Amy had been taking on more responsibilities of late, and Ellie was grateful. She hadn't been feeling well the past couple of afternoons but suspected she knew why—especially since the home pregnancy test had been positive. Seeing her sister-in-law would confirm what she already knew.

Jenny Bender, Jane's receptionist, was just leaving when Ellie entered the health clinic.

"Jane's in her office," Jenny told her, motioning beyond the reception area.

"Thanks."

Sure enough, Jane sat at her desk making notations on a chart. She glanced up when she heard Ellie come in, and her tired face brightened. "Hi, there."

"Hi." Ellie threw herself into the chair nearest Jane's.

"Long day?" Jane asked sympathetically.

"Exceptionally long."

"You're looking a little peaked."

"I feel a little peaked."

Jane studied her. "Do you think you picked up a bug?"

A slow happy smile came from deep within. "The nine-month variety."

Surprise showed in Jane's face. "You're pregnant?"

Ellie nodded. "The little stick turned blue."

Jane clapped her hands in delight. She closed the chart she'd been working on and relaxed in her chair. "Does Glen know?"

"Not yet." Ellie hadn't meant to keep it a secret from her husband, but she didn't want him to be disappointed if it turned out, for some reason, to be a false alarm. "I thought I'd have you verify my condition first."

They chatted for a few minutes, laughed about the things they always did and made plans to spend a weekend in San Antonio later in the month. They talked with the easy familiarity that had developed between them since they'd married the Patterson brothers. Not until after Jane had examined her did Ellie grow quiet.

Jane didn't press her, but Ellie knew her sister-in-law was waiting for her to speak. "I'm afraid, Jane," she confessed. Her emotions had never been this muddled. Intertwined with the joy were all the fears she'd tried to ignore and couldn't.

"It's normal to be anxious. This is your first child, and your body's experiencing quite a few changes, right now. That can be confusing and stressful. Let's talk about it."

Ellie took a deep breath. "Mostly I'm worried that I'll be like my mother. She didn't have an easy pregnancy with me—that's basically why I'm an only child. And she never seemed to *like* having a kid around." Ellie hadn't been close to her mother, but the bond she'd shared with her father had been strong and special. It was the reason his death the previous year had shaken her so badly.

"You're not your mother," Jane assured her.

Ellie relaxed a little. "In other words, don't borrow trouble?"

"That's a good place to start."

Ellie nodded. "You're right. And I don't think my mother ever wanted a child, whereas I do." She gave Jane a tremulous smile. "Glen and I talked about starting our family soon. That's the reason I went off the pill when I did," she confided, "but we didn't think it'd happen so quickly."

"So you're not sure you're ready for this."

Ellie thought about that for a moment. "No, I'm ready," she said decisively. "I just hadn't expected to be this . . . fertile."

"I imagine Glen's going to gloat to Cal," Jane said with a manufactured groan.

"Have you and Cal decided when you're going to get pregnant?" Ellie felt it would be nice if their children were close in age. Her own cousins, who'd lived in Brewster, were twins, two years older, and when they were around, it was almost like having brothers. Her mother blamed her tomboy attitudes on Rick and Rob, both of whom had gone on to make the military their career. They'd missed her wedding, but had written to congratulate her and Glen.

"Before Cal and I can think about a family, I need to fulfill my contract here at the clinic," Jane said with a show of regret. "Don't misunderstand me, I love my work. It's just that we're eager to become parents. We're hoping I'll get pregnant about this time next year."

"That'd be wonderful."

"Mary's going to be pleased when she hears your news," Jane said, referring to their mother-in-law.

Glen's parents were looking forward to becoming grandparents, and it went without saying that they'd be ecstatic.

"I want you to start prenatal vitamins right away—"

"Jane, Jane." Ellie held up her hand. "Don't treat me like a patient. I'm your sister-in-law."

Jane laughed. "You're right. Congratulations!" She stood up and hurried over to Ellie to share a heartfelt hug.

FRIDAY MORNING Wade knew he should be working on his sermon, but he couldn't focus his thoughts. Every time he started to write down an idea, all he could think about was Amy. He worried about her, worried that she wasn't eating properly or getting enough rest. He wished she could take a few weeks off before the birth. He wondered what plans she'd made for child care once her maternity leave ended.

Now that her due date was so close, his worrying had become almost obsessive. If she wouldn't marry him, then he hoped she'd at least allow him to be with her when Sarah was born.

When he'd spoken to her on the phone recently, she hadn't sounded particularly interested in his company. But that could be his own doubts talking, because when he showed up at the house yesterday, she'd seemed genuinely pleased to see him.

Wade stared down at his sermon notes and, feeling uninspired, decided to take a break. His first inclination was to head for the feed store, check up on Amy, but he refused to make a pest of himself.

The one person who was sure to understand how he felt was Dovie Hennessey. Dovie was close to Amy, her birthing partner. He had another reason for visiting Dovie's store; he wanted to buy a gift, for Amy, a robe for after the baby was born. Something lovely and feminine.

He walked from the church into town, stopped to chat with the Moorhouse sisters en route. He arrived at Dovie's to find her, as usual, doing a robust business. She acknowledged his presence with a nod and continued to help Betty Bonney, who was considering an antique bowl and pitcher for her guest bedroom.

Wade was a patient man. While he was waiting, he wandered around Dovie's store, picturing Amy wearing this necklace or that scarf, imagining her on the brocade-upholstered love seat, holding her baby. With him beside her. . . .

A while later Mrs. Bonney left smiling and Dovie turned her attention to Wade. "This is a pleasant surprise," she said. "What can I do for you, Pastor?"

"It's about Amy," he replied, feeling a bit self-conscious. "I wanted to buy her something to wear after the baby's born. A robe. Or whatever you think would be appropriate." Actually this was all mildly embarrassing. He could just imagine what Louise Powell would say if she heard about this. If the woman thought it improper for him to have lunch with Amy, what would she think about his buying her nightwear? It didn't *matter* what Louise thought, he chided himself. She was an uncharitable and narrow-minded woman, and her opinions were of no consequence.

"A robe is an excellent choice." Dovie beamed him an approving look. "It's both practical and luxurious."

He nodded. "I want it to be special—not the type of robe she'd wear every day . . . if you know what I mean."

"I do. In fact, I have something in mind," Dovie said with a satisfied smile. "I was actually thinking of giving this to Amy myself." She led him to the far side of her shop. A selection of old-fashioned wardrobes dominated one corner. The doors of one wardrobe were open to reveal a number of party dresses and nightgowns on scented hangers. She reached inside and pulled out a soft pink satin robe, its long sleeves and collar edged in lace. It was exactly what he'd hoped for. Simple, elegant, beautiful.

"It's new—not vintage," Dovie explained. "But it's modeled after a 1930s pattern." She watched for his reaction. "What do you think?"

He swallowed hard and nodded. The vision of Amy in that robe did funny things to his insides. "It's perfect."

"I agree," Dovie said. "It's utterly feminine and I know she'd treasure it."

Wade touched the sleeve, intending to look at the price tag, but changed his mind the instant his hand made contact with the rich smooth fabric. His gut clenched. Amy, wearing this. Lying in his bed . . .

"I'll take it," he said quickly.

"Don't you want to know the price?" Dovie asked.

"Not particularly."

Dovie's grin spread across her face.

Wade took out his wallet as he and Dovie walked toward the cash register. She wrapped the robe in tissue paper and placed it carefully in a gift box, which she tied with a pink ribbon. When she'd finished, she glanced up at him. "Amy told you about Alex, didn't she?" Her gaze held his.

"Yes."

"She only told me this week, you know. She's shared very little about the baby's father."

"It's not important." He wanted Dovie to know he hadn't asked. In fact, he'd almost rather Amy hadn't told him.

"After the birthing class this week, I brought her home for tea. She cried her eyes out."

"Amy was upset?" He wasn't sure what unnerved him more—Amy's being distressed enough to cry or her choosing to weep on Dovie's shoulder and not his.

"Yes. She told me about Alex—and about her relationship with you. She said you'd been wonderful."

That reassured him a little; Amy must still care for him, still trust him. Her story had broken his heart. Yes, she'd been foolish and naive, but she wasn't the first woman who'd learned such lessons the hard way. Not the first woman who'd been lied to by a married man—and fallen in love with him.

"You love her, don't you?" Dovie asked, then laughed at her question. "You must. No man pays $125 for a satin robe otherwise."

Wade gasped in mock outrage. He would gladly have paid twice that.

"Do you want me to keep it here at the store for you until the baby's born?" Dovie asked after he'd paid for the robe.

"Please."

They talked a while longer, and then another customer came in and Wade knew it was time to leave. He walked to the town park and sat on a bench, watching the children at play, listening to the sound of their laughter.

Amy had told him about Alex and what had happened once she learned he was married. It wasn't until after she'd broken off the relationship that she'd discovered she was pregnant. Although she'd only mentioned her mother in passing, Wade surmised that they didn't get along and that her mother had provided absolutely no emotional support.

In the days since she'd made her revelations, he'd forcefully pushed all thoughts of Alex and Amy's affair from his mind. It was just too painful to think about Amy loving another man.

He knew that Alex had been afraid she'd come to him and demand child support, so he'd insisted on an abortion. When she refused, they'd had a horrible fight, in which her mother had somehow become involved.

She'd also told him, Wade, her mother had come up with an entirely unacceptable suggestion.

Wade could well guess. Six or seven years back, when he worked as a youth pastor in Austin, he'd been approached by a childless couple desperate to adopt a baby. Because of the limited number of available infants and the high number of applicants through legitimate agencies, Wade had been solicited by this couple, who hoped he could arrange a private adoption. They'd made clear that price was no object; in fact, the husband had bluntly spoken of "buying" a baby. While Wade appreciated how frustrating such situations could be, he referred the couple to an adoption agency with which he was familiar.

He could only assume that Amy's mother saw her daughter's baby as a profit-making opportunity.

Amy had been calm and collected while she'd relayed the details of her unhappy romance. Too calm, he recognized now. From what Dovie had said, she'd gone to a woman friend the following day and wept bitter tears.

It made Wade wonder why she'd remained so stoic with him. She'd spoken almost as if this had all happened to someone else.

Feeling a strong impulse to straighten things out with Amy, Wade walked over to the feed store. It wasn't the ideal place for such a talk, but this wasn't something they could ignore. They had to have an honest no-holds-barred discussion. And soon. Then he had an idea—he'd invite Amy to dinner. Tonight. At his place so they'd have the privacy they needed.

Never mind that he was absolutely devoid of any cooking talent. Hey, he'd barbecue a couple of steaks, throw some fresh corn in a pot of boiling water. Couldn't go wrong there.

Ellie was nowhere in sight and George was busy with a customer when Wade entered the store. A couple of local ranchers were hanging around the place, as well. Clyde Lester and James Ferguson sat on the front porch drinking cold sodas.

"Afternoon, Reverend."

"Afternoon," he returned, and went in search of Amy.

He found her in the back of the store with Lyle Whitehouse. Lyle seemed more interested in talking than in buying. Amy didn't see Wade and he suspected Lyle didn't either. He moved closer, not to eavesdrop on the conversation but . . . All right, he couldn't help being curious.

". . . like to get to know you better," Lyle was saying.

"Thank you, but as I said, this saddle soap is the best one on the market."

Irritation edged her voice. It was all Wade could do not to interfere, but he knew Amy wouldn't appreciate that.

"I noticed you first thing the night of the big dance."

Amy replaced the soap on the shelf. She didn't respond.

"I was thinking you'd be a lot of . . . fun."

"Is there anything else I could interest you in?" she asked coolly. The minute the words left her lips, her cheeks flushed red. "You know what I mean . . ."

"Sure thing," Lyle said with a laugh. "And you know what *I* mean."

"If George or I can be of any service, please let us know."

Wade glanced around and wondered what had happened to Ellie; generally, as owner of the store, she was highly visible. He frowned. As far as he knew, Amy had been hired as a bookkeeper, not as a salesperson. He wondered when she'd started dealing with customers and why she hadn't told him about the additional duties Ellie had given her.

"As a matter of fact," Lyle said with a sly grin, "there *is* something you can do for me."

Amy regarded him warily and Wade could see that the ranch hand's proximity made her uncomfortable.

"What's that?" she asked politely.

"As it happens I'm looking for a date Saturday night. Rumor has it you're single."

"I appreciate the offer, but I'm busy."

"Not *too* busy though, right?"

"Yes. Far too busy, I'm afraid."

Amy was about to move away when Lyle placed his hand on her shoulder and stopped her, pinning her against the wall. His oversize belt buckle nudged the mound of her stomach, and Wade felt revolted.

His hackles went up. He couldn't tolerate the idea of any man touching a woman without her consent. As far as he was concerned, Lyle had stepped way over the line. But rather than make a scene, he decided to wait for a few more minutes and let Amy handle the situation herself.

"Ah, come on, Amy," Lyle urged.

"No, thank you."

"What am I missing that the preacher's got?"

"Good manners for one thing," Amy said, trying to get past Lyle. But he held on to her, his grip tightening.

"We could have a lot of fun together," he said. "And once the kid's born you and me could—"

"Let me go!" she demanded.

Wade couldn't remain silent any longer. "I suggest you do as the lady asks," he said, stepping closer.

Lyle snickered and met Wade's look head-on. "What lady?"

Amy closed her eyes as if she'd been physically slapped. Without even knowing what he intended, Wade stormed forward and grabbed Lyle by the shirtfront and half lifted him from the floor.

"I believe you owe the *lady* an apology," he said from between gritted teeth.

"This ain't none of your business, Preacher."

"Wade, please," Amy pleaded.

Wade ignored her. Nose to nose with Lyle, he said, "I'm *making* it my business."

"Is that your bun she's baking in her oven, too?" Whitehouse sneered.

"We're taking this outside, you bastard."

"No!" Amy cried.

"Fine by me, Preacher man. I'll be happy to kick your butt for you."

Wade released him, and Lyle eased his neck back and forth a couple of times. "Anytime, Preacher man," he muttered. "Any time."

"Right now sounds good to me."

"Wade, don't." Amy grabbed hold of him, her fingers digging into his upper arm. "It's all right, please. I don't want you getting hurt on my behalf."

"I can hold my own," he promised her. He turned and followed Lyle out the front door.

Lyle had his fists raised by the time Wade got outside. He squinted his eyes against the bright sunlight as he rolled up his sleeves.

"What's going on here?" Clyde Lester asked.

"Preacher and I have something to settle man to man," Lyle answered.

"Wade, you wanna fight this guy?" Clyde was clearly shocked.

He raised his own fists. "You're damn right I do."

The older rancher looked flustered and unsure. "George," he shouted, "we got trouble here."

George called out to Wade, who turned at the sound of his voice. He didn't even see the fist coming. Lyle's punch hit him square in the jaw. Unable to stop himself, he staggered a couple of steps sideways.

Clyde and his friend cried out that Lyle had cheated. But Wade figured he'd deserved that sucker punch. It would be the last swing Lyle took at him, though.

Wade let out a roar and surged toward Lyle, tumbling them both onto the ground.

Snatches of speech made it into his consciousness. He heard Amy pleading with someone to stop the fight. Clyde was still yelling that Lyle was a cheat. Then George shouted that he was phoning for the sheriff. Soon afterward he heard Lyle grunt with pain. Or perhaps he was the one grunting. Wade didn't know anymore.

High school was the last time Wade had been in a fistfight, but he was strong and agile, capable of moving fast. And he wasn't a coward. Some things were meant to be settled this way, although he generally avoided physical confrontation. But no one was going to insult the woman he loved.

He got in a couple of good punches; so did Lyle. They circled each other like angry dogs and were about to resume fighting when Sheriff Hennessey arrived.

Frank leaped out of his patrol car and stared at Wade as if he couldn't believe his eyes. "What the hell's the problem here?" he said, pulling his nightstick from his belt.

"This is between Lyle and me," Wade said, pressing his finger to the edge of his mouth. His jaw ached, and one eye felt like it was already swelling. Lyle's face looked as if he'd been put through a garbage disposal. Wade figured he didn't look any better.

"Lyle, what happened?" Seeing he wasn't going to get anywhere with Wade, the sheriff tried the other man.

Lyle held Wade's look. "Nothing we can't settle ourselves."

"Well, I don't happen to like the way you two decided to settle it. I could haul you both into jail for disturbing the peace. That what you want?"

"It was my fault, Sheriff," Amy cried, stepping between Wade and Lyle. "Wade thought I needed help . . ."

Sheriff Hennessey glared at Lyle.

"Were you bothering this young lady, Whitehouse?" the sheriff demanded.

A truck pulled up beside the patrol car and Ellie got out. "What's going on here?"

"Seems like the preacher and Lyle here didn't see eye to eye," Frank explained.

"I didn't do anything but talk to the little lady," Lyle muttered. "Seems the preacher thinks he's got squatter's rights with her. He's—"

"Leave it right there," Frank said, stepping closer to Lyle.

"Are you going to arrest anyone?" Ellie asked.

Frank gave Lyle and Wade a hard look. "Is this over or not?"

Wade narrowed his eyes, which caused him more than a little pain. "If he's willing to let Amy alone, then I'm willing to call it quits."

"Lyle?" Frank focused his attention on the other man.

"All right," he growled, reaching for his hat. He shoved it on his head and stalked toward his truck.

"I think we've seen everything there is to see here," Frank said to the small crowd of curious spectators. He glanced at Wade and his expression said he was disappointed.

Wade wasn't particulary proud of himself at the moment, either. All he'd done was embarrass Amy and himself. He rarely let his temper get the better of him like this. It was a primitive response, he thought grimly. A primitive male response. He'd been in such a rage he hadn't been able to control himself, but damn it all, he was supposed to be an example to the entire community.

"Oh, Wade." Amy gazed up at him with tear-filled eyes. She raised her hand to his mouth.

He winced when her gentle fingers touched the corner of his lips. The taste of blood was in his mouth and his head pounded. His left eye was swollen almost shut.

"I've got a first-aid kit in the back of the store," Ellie said.

Amy and Wade followed her to the office, where she took the kit out of the drawer, then left them. Wade was grateful until he saw the tears running down Amy's face.

"Amy, darling, it doesn't hurt."

Her hands trembled as she tore open a gauze package. "Fighting! Oh, Wade, how could you?"

"I don't know exactly how that happened. Things just escalated. In retrospect, I agree it wasn't the best way to settle this, but I can't change that now."

"I'm perfectly capable of taking care of myself."

"I know, I know." Just then he didn't want to argue the right or wrong of it. He'd much rather Amy held him.

"Sit down," she said curtly. He did, and she dabbed at the cut on his lip. "What do you think people will say when they hear about this?"

"Yeah, well, it can't be helped."

"All I've done is hurt you," she said in a broken whisper.

He wanted to protest, but she touched an especially sore spot just then. He jerked back from her and brought his finger to the edge of his mouth.

"I think you should see Dr. Jane," she murmured.

"I'm not that badly hurt."

"No, but you need your head examined."

Wade laughed and winced anew. "Ouch! Don't make me laugh." He reached for her hand and held it in both of his. His knuckles were swollen, he noted, and the skin torn. "A kiss would make everything feel better," he told her, only half joking.

Very carefully she bent down and tenderly pressed her lips to his.

The kiss left an ache inside him that made Lyle's brutal punches seem insignificant. He loved Amy. He wanted her for his wife, wanted her to share his life and his bed. He stood up and wrapped his arms around her waist, burying his face in her shoulder.

As she hugged him close, he breathed in her warm womanly scent.

"This can't continue," she whispered, and broke away from him.

Wade wasn't ready to let her go. "What do you mean?"

"I'm hurting you," she said, her voice gaining strength.

She didn't seem to understand the joy and wonder that loving her had given him. He wanted to tell her, but she spoke again.

"Your credibility with the people in your church is going to be questioned because of this fight."

"That has nothing to do with you. I'll deal with that myself."

"Your reputation with the community—"

"Amy, stop."

"No. I won't stop. It's over, Wade, right here and now."

He couldn't believe what he was hearing. "What do you mean, over?"

She seemed to have steeled herself, because she didn't so much as blink. "Over, as in we won't be seeing each other again."

Lyle's sucker punch had surprised him less. "You don't mean that!"

"I do. It was inevitable, anyway," she said.

"What do you mean, inevitable?" He barely recognized the sound of his own voice.

"You and me," she whispered. "I'd need to tell you soon, anyway."

"Tell me *what?*" Although he asked the question, he already knew the answer. Amy had decided to reject his marriage proposal.

"I . . . can't marry you, Wade."

He sank back down in the chair, crushed by the weight of his pain and disappointment.

"The fact you asked me to be your wife is one of the . . . the greatest honors of my life. I want you to know that. I didn't make this decision lightly. I've been trying to find a way to tell you all week."

He was a man of words. A man who loved language, who knew how to use it and could respond to any occasion; it was part of his job, of who he was. But Amy's rejection left him speechless. All he felt was an encompassing sadness. And bitterness.

"What about Sarah?" he asked, unable to hide his anger. He felt she was being selfish, putting herself first. He'd offered to be more than her husband; he'd wanted to adopt her child.

"I'll raise her on my own. It was what I intended from the first."

He got to his feet. "You need to do what you think is best."

"That's exactly what I am doing. Thank you," she said, and her voice wavered slightly.

Wade ignored the emotion she revealed and struggled to contain his own. "I apologize for the embarrassment I caused you this afternoon."

"Oh, Wade."

"I won't bother you again." Having said that, he walked out of the office.

Nine

Preaching Sunday's sermon was one of the most difficult tasks Wade had ever performed during his entire time in the ministry. Word of the altercation between him and Lyle Whitehouse had spread like wildfire through Promise, gathering other rumors and ugly speculations. As he entered the sanctuary Sunday morning, he noticed that he'd drawn a record crowd. The church was filled to capacity, and the overflow had collected in the rear of the room. He'd certainly hoped to pack the pews, but not for a reason like this.

Curiosity seekers had come to see his cut lip and his black eye. They'd come to hear his explanation. He hated to disappoint all the good people of Promise, but he had no intention of offering excuses or justifications. He stood before them as a man who'd made a mistake. One he deeply regretted. He wasn't perfect and didn't pretend to be, but he was ready to accept the consequences of his actions—if it came to that. He hoped it wouldn't, but the choice wasn't his.

The choir opened the service with a favorite hymn of Wade's, written by Fanny Crosby a century earlier. Although it hurt his mouth, his voice joined theirs as he sang, *"This is my story, this is my song . . ."*

Rather than keep everyone in suspense, Wade approached the lectern when the hymn ended. "Good morning," he said, and managed a painful smile.

His words were enthusiastically echoed back. Several people craned their necks to get a better look at him. It was a wonder Louise Powell didn't topple into the aisle, considering how far she leaned sideways.

Wade didn't blame his parishioners for being curious. His reflection in the mirror told him far more than he wanted to know. He was a sight with his obvious injuries. The swelling in his jaw had gone down, although an ugly bruise remained. If his mother could see him now, she'd box his ears but good.

"Before I begin my sermon," he said, gazing out over the faces he knew so well, "I hope you'll indulge me while I take a few moments to discuss the rumor that I was involved in a fistfight with a local ranch hand."

A low hum of whispers followed.

"What you heard is correct. I was in an altercation this week."

Again he heard whispers, as though his ready admission had shocked certain people, although from his face it should have been obvious that at least some of the rumors were true. "I don't have any excuses or explanations." He cast his eyes down. "As members of this church, you have a right to expect—to demand—that your pastor's behavior be exemplary, above reproach. I have failed you. I've failed myself. I can only offer you my sincerest apology." His hands gripped the podium, his fingers white from the pressure.

"Seeing that such an action might raise a question in your eyes about my suitability as your pastor, I've asked the elders to pass out ballots for a vote of confidence. If you're still willing to have me serve you in the capacity of pastor, then I'll do so with a grateful and humble heart. If not, I'll leave the church. The decision is yours."

He sat down, and the elders moved through the church, passing out the ballots.

Somehow, Wade managed to finish the service. As soon as he'd given the benediction, he retired to his office while the votes were being counted. Alone with his worries and fears, he tried to imagine what his life would be like outside the ministry. With his emotions muddled, his heart broken and his career badly shaken, Wade desperately needed the affirmation of his church family. Without it . . . well, he just didn't know.

Max Jordan knocked politely on his office door.

"Come in." Wade stood, bracing himself for the news.

Max entered the room and set the ballots on the edge of his desk. "The vote is unanimous. The members of Promise Christian Church want you to stay on as our pastor."

Wade sank to his chair in a rush of relief.

"Quite a few of our members have written you notes we thought you should read. You've done a lot for the people in this town, and we aren't about to forget it."

Wade released his breath in a slow sigh. Even Louise Powell had voted that he stay on. Now *that* said something.

"We're not looking for a saint to lead us, Reverend," Max added. "As you said, what you did was wrong, but you were willing to get up in front of everyone and say so. It's reassuring to know you face the same struggles we do. It isn't always an easy thing, holding one's temper in check. You did the right thing, admitting you'd made a mistake and reminding us that violence isn't a solution.

"Today's the best sermon you've ever preached because we could see you'd reached that conclusion the way we have ourselves. The hard way—through experience."

Wade nodded, in full agreement.

"We want you to stay, Wade. Each and every one of us."

Wade took hold of Max's hand and shook it. "Thank you," he said.

"No, Pastor, thank *you.*"

Wade had never felt so humbled. His congregation had taught him a lesson in forgiveness that he wouldn't soon forget.

DOVIE HAD RARELY SEEN two people more miserable than Amy and Wade. It was clear to her that Amy was deeply in love with Wade and he was equally crazy about her.

"We have to do something," she told her husband early Monday afternoon. Frank generally stopped by the shop at some point for coffee. It was a habit established long before they were married and one she enjoyed to this day.

"You mean about Amy and Wade?" he asked, helping himself to an extra cookie. The peanut-butter cookies half dipped in chocolate were his favorites.

"Who else would I be talking about?" she snapped. She reached for a cookie, too, although she'd recently made a resolution to avoid sweets. But the situation with Amy and Wade had bothered her since Sunday-morning service.

"I don't think I'll ever forget Wade standing up in front of the church and apologizing like that." It'd demanded every ounce of self-restraint Dovie possessed not to leap to her feet and shout that she'd have punched Lyle Whitehouse out herself had she been there.

Wade had offered no justifications or excuses. She knew the details of the fight only because she was married to the town's sheriff. Although Frank hadn't been all that forthcoming.

"I respect Wade for doing that," Frank said. "But we can't go sticking our noses in other people's business, Dovie, no matter how much we care."

"But, Frank, this isn't just *anyone.* It's Amy."

Her husband sighed. "I know that, too, sweetheart, but we can't live their lives for them. Amy's old enough to make up her own mind."

"But she's miserable."

Frank hesitated. He and Dovie had grown to love the young woman who'd come into their lives so recently. It was as though they'd been given a daughter to love and cherish. They'd established a closeness that answered needs on both sides; Amy yearned for a family, and Dovie and Frank each had a heart full of love to share. It was almost as though her arrival in Promise had been ordained.

"I love Amy as though she were my own child," Dovie told her husband.

"I know, sweetheart. I do, too."

"Can't we do *something* to help her through this?"

Frank mulled over her question for a moment. "I don't know what we can do other than give her our support."

Dovie sighed, at a loss as to how to help her friend. She longed to wrap Amy protectively in her arms and keep her safe.

Frank left a few minutes later, and she carried their dishes to the tiny kitchen at the back of the shop. Her gaze fell on the beautifully wrapped gift she was holding for Wade. His eyes had shone with emotion—with love for Amy—the day he'd come into the shop and purchased the robe. He'd been almost giddy with happiness—a far cry from the way he'd looked on Sunday.

Amy had skipped church, not that Dovie blamed her. Under the circumstances staying away was probably for the best. Dovie could well imagine Louise hounding her with questions following the service; at least Amy had been spared an inquisition.

On impulse Dovie grabbed the gift and headed out the front door. She turned over the Open sign to read Closed, and walked toward Ellie's feed store with the purposeful steps of a woman on a mission.

Ellie met her out front and waved in greeting. "Hi, Dovie!"

"Is Amy around?" Dovie asked, breathless from her brisk walk. She felt a certain urgency to give Wade's gift to Amy now, despite the fact that it was early afternoon, Amy was at work and she herself had a business to run.

"She's at home." Ellie glanced down at her clipboard.

"She's not ill, is she?" Dovie was instantly concerned.

"I don't think so," Ellie said. She looked up again, meeting Dovie's eyes. "Has she asked you about Bitter End?"

Dovie frowned. "Yes, but not recently." The ghost town wasn't an ominous secret the way it had been in years past, but it wasn't a topic of everyday conversation, either. "What makes you ask?"

"She's been openly curious for some time," Ellie told Dovie. "I might be off base, but she was full of questions this morning, and then she asked for the afternoon off. She borrowed the truck for a few hours, too."

"You don't think she'd actually consider going there, do you?"

"I certainly hope not." But Dovie could tell Ellie was worried.

"When I questioned Amy about her plans, she hedged—as though she didn't want to tell me."

"Then I'll find out myself," Dovie said, and headed toward the small house where Frank had once lived, the gift box tucked under her arm. As she'd expected, Ellie's truck was parked in the driveway.

Amy answered Dovie's knock; her eyes widened when she saw it was her friend. "Dovie," she said, "come in."

Dovie took one look at Amy and instantly knew that Ellie's fears were well grounded. She was dressed in loose-fitting slacks, a sweatshirt and ankle-high boots. "You're going to Bitter End, aren't you?" Amy couldn't very well deny it, dressed as she was. "Amy, for the love of heaven, you can't just go traipsing around the countryside!"

"Why not?"

"Well, for one thing, you're pregnant—and . . . and it's dangerous."

"Then come too."

"*Me?*" Dovie brought her hand to her throat, taken aback by the suggestion.

"Yes, *you.* You've never been, have you?"

"No," Dovie admitted reluctantly. It wasn't because she didn't want to see Bitter End herself. She did, but Frank had put her off for one reason or another. She didn't think he'd purposely kept her away, just that he believed it wasn't anyplace for her. But she had roots there, too, and was curious about the old town.

"Aren't you interested?"

Dovie had to admit she was. "Even if I was willing to join you, I couldn't," she said. "I don't have any directions . . ."

"I have a map," Amy said, and led her into the kitchen. "Nell drew it up for me some time ago and I've been studying it."

"You're serious about this, aren't you?" Dovie said, as she gazed at the map.

"Very much so."

"But why now?"

"I . . . I don't know. I woke up this morning and I felt this . . . this burning need to do something, go somewhere. I need to get away for a while, I guess. I know it's silly, I know I probably shouldn't, but I want to see Bitter End. I'm prepared to go alone, but I'd rather someone was with me."

It went without saying that if things had been different, Wade would be taking her. Half an hour earlier, Dovie had been looking for a way to help Amy and Wade, and now it came to her that this would offer the perfect opportunity to talk. She and Amy would be spending time alone, and if ever Amy would confide her feelings it'd be now.

"I'll go."

Amy stared at her. "Are you *sure*, Dovie?"

She nodded. "I'll close up for the day, then call Frank and let him know what we're doing."

"He'll try to talk us out of it," Amy said, sounding as though she feared he might succeed.

"I won't let him."

"But . . ."

"I'll tell you what," Dovie said, thinking fast. "I've got a cellular phone and I'll conveniently forget to call him until we're there."

"Oh, Dovie, are you sure? He might get terribly upset with you."

"I'm sure he will, but Frank needs to know I have a mind of my own," she said firmly. "I've been wanting to visit that ghost town myself." If they were going to find it that afternoon, there were several things she needed to do. First she had to close the shop, then change clothes and leave a written message, as well as pack her cellular. "I'll be back in half an hour," Dovie promised. "Oh," she said, almost forgetting the purpose of her visit. "The package is for you."

Amy glanced at the beautifully wrapped box. "Another shower gift? Dovie, people have been so generous already. I don't know how to thank everyone."

"This isn't a shower gift," Dovie said. "It's from Wade."

At the mention of his name, Amy's head went back as if hearing it brought her pain. "Wade?" she whispered.

"He was in last week—before the fight—and bought it for you."

"But he . . ."

"He asked me to give it to you after the baby was born."

Amy frowned, obviously wondering why Dovie had brought it to her now.

Dovie shrugged. "I thought you might want to open it."

Amy looked at the box for a long time without moving toward it.

"I'll be back before you know it," Dovie said, suddenly excited by this little adventure. She felt that Amy knew her own limitations; if she wanted to visit Bitter End, then far be it from Dovie to stop her.

AMY LEFT THE PACKAGE sitting exactly where Dovie had left it. But not for long. She couldn't resist knowing what he'd bought, or why Dovie had felt compelled to give it to her now.

She fingered the large pink bow. Dovie had specifically said Wade had purchased the gift for *her*. Not for the baby, but for her.

The look in Dovie's eyes had told Amy something else, too. The gift had been purchased with love. Amy didn't know how to deal with the kind of love she'd found in Promise; it was all so unfamiliar. Frank and Dovie had been incredibly generous and kind. Caroline had become a good friend, and Ellie, in addition to giving her a job, was her friend, too. Dr. Jane had been wonderful, encouraging her, befriending her.

And Wade . . .

She tried to squeeze out the memory of the hurt she'd seen in his eyes when she said she wouldn't marry him.

She placed the box on her lap and carefully removed the ribbon. When she'd finished peeling away the paper, she set the box on the table, again. She hesitated, afraid that if she opened it, she'd be overwhelmed by a rush of emotion and pain. She hadn't seen Wade since the day of the fight and sincerely doubted she would. He might eventually come to visit her and see the baby, but Amy didn't expect to have more than casual contact with him following Sarah's birth. It hit her then how very much she was going to miss him. How very much she already did. This sudden need to do something, to get out and explore the ghost town, was a symptom of how she'd been feeling since she'd broken off their relationship. Restless, dispirited, lonely. Dovie was right; it was ridiculous to visit the town now, but that wasn't stopping her.

Finally Amy could stand it no longer and lifted the lid.

She gasped.

The robe was stunning, beautiful beyond anything she'd ever owned. She put the lid aside and reached for the robe and held it against her. Burying her face in it, she felt surrounded by Wade's love.

She heard Dovie's car just then, surprised it had taken her so little time. Amy glanced out the window and, sure enough, saw Dovie parked in her driveway. She waved, grabbed a sweater and hurried out the front door, map in hand.

"You ready?" she asked.

"Ready, willing and able," Dovie said with a conspiratorial grin.

Dovie drove while Amy navigated. The instructions were clear and it wasn't difficult to find the spot where Nell said to turn off the highway. The terrain was rough after that, but Dovie drove slowly and cautiously, winding around one hill and then another for what seemed forever.

Luckily a number of other cars had followed the same route in recent months, and their tires had worn a narrow path in the hard ground. It seemed incredible to Amy that anyone had ever found this place. They followed the route as far as it took them and stopped by a high limestone ledge.

"This is where the path ends," Dovie said.

Amy continued to study the map. "Nell says we'll need to go on foot from here."

"Down there?" Dovie questioned, sounding unsure.

"Yup," Amy confirmed. She opened the car door and climbed out, then walked to the edge of the limestone outcropping. Nestled in a small valley below was Bitter End. She saw stone and wood structures lining both sides of a main street. A church with a burned-out steeple and fenced graveyard stood at the other end. A corral and livery stable. A two-story hotel. From this distance, the buildings looked intact, as though the years had stood still. Amy sucked in her breath and glanced over her shoulder for Dovie. The older woman came to stand beside her.

"My goodness," she whispered.

The sight was oddly impressive, Amy had to admit. "Let's go see it up close," she said, reaching for Dovie's hand.

Dovie hesitated, studying the rock-strewn descent. "Amy, do you really think we should?"

"I haven't come this far to stop now."

"I know. Should you be climbing down this bluff in your condition?"

"Probably not."

"But you're going to do it, anyway?"

Amy nodded. "We'll help each other."

"If you're sure," Dovie said, and slipped her arm through Amy's.

The trek down wasn't easy. Not with Amy this close to her due date, and Dovie unaccustomed to this type of activity. But they took it slow and easy. Still, by the time they reached the town, both were breathless from exertion and excitement.

"Wow. We're really here," Amy said, taking her first tentative steps into the town.

Dovie's grip tightened on Amy's arm. "Frank would have a conniption if he could see us."

"Let's check it out," Amy said.

"I don't think it's safe to actually go inside any of the buildings, do you?"

"The stone ones look pretty solid," Amy said, surveying the street. This was an absolutely remarkable experience. She couldn't believe she was actually in Bitter End . . . and only wished Wade was here, too.

Together they explored from one end of town to the other. They identified the old tree, and after some investigation found the word "Cursed," which had been carved into the wood more than a century ago.

"This takes my breath away," Amy said, marveling anew as she traced the letters with her fingertip.

Dovie explained the curse. "I don't think anyone would have understood how this all came about if it wasn't for Nell and Travis. They were the ones to unravel the mystery."

"It's so . . ." Amy couldn't think of the right word.

"Barren," Dovie supplied.

"Exactly." Nothing grew in Bitter End. The town and everything around it had died. Bitter End had once held such promise . . .

Her thoughts skidded to a halt. Her relationship with Wade had been filled with promise, too, but that was dead now too, like this town. *Stop it,* she told herself. *That's a ridiculous comparison.* She was annoyed by her self-indulgence and embarrassed that she'd been so melodramatic. Wade deserved better from her. If only he was here . . .

As if in protest the baby moved. The pain was fast, sharp, sudden. "Ooh," she said involuntarily, wrapping her arms around her stomach.

"Amy?" Dovie's voice rose with concern.

"The baby just kicked," she said, making light of it.

"You're not in labor, are you?"

"No . . . no. It's three weeks yet. There's nothing to worry about." No sooner had the words left her mouth than warm liquid gushed from between her legs.

Her water had broken.

"Amy, what's happening?"

She heard the panic in Dovie's voice and reached out to take the other woman's hand. "We have a small problem here," she admitted in a shaky voice. "It looks like no one told Sarah she wasn't due for another three weeks."

"Your water broke?" Dovie asked. "Are you in pain?"

"It's not too bad." Amy was more frightened than anything.

"Let's not panic," Dovie advised, although her voice was shrill with nerves. She carefully led Amy to the rocking chair outside the hotel and sat her down. "Let's think this through."

"All right," Amy said, clinging to Dovie's hand.

"Frank. I should call Frank." She said this as if it were divine inspiration.

"What about Dr. Jane?"

"He can phone her," Dovie said. "For now, it's more important that you be comfortable and relaxed."

Amy clasped her abdomen. "I'll be fine as soon as . . . as soon as this pain passes." She closed her eyes, taking a deep calming breath. After a moment she opened her eyes again to find Dovie gazing at her, lines of worry between her eyes.

"Frank will have my head," she muttered as she punched out the number on the small cell phone and waited. It seemed an eternity before Frank answered. Amy watched Dovie's expression as she explained the situation, then saw her eyes widen. She held the phone away from her ear as Frank's voice gained volume.

"You can yell at me later, Frank Hennessey, but right now there are more important concerns."

The conversation between the two continued, but Amy concentrated on timing her contractions and heard little more of what was said. Dovie started pacing. She'd been off the phone only a minute before it rang, the sound cutting through the still afternoon like a fire alarm. Dovie answered immediately and talked for several minutes.

"That was Dr. Jane," she said when she finished, "but I lost her. My phone's dead. Frank knows exactly where we are, though. He'll see to everything."

Amy was in the middle of a contraction and she closed her eyes, counting the seconds the way she'd learned in class.

"Are you all right?" Dovie asked.

"The pains," Amy whispered.

"They're bad?"

"I didn't think they were supposed to be this intense right away."

Dovie squatted down beside her. "Not to worry. We'll get you to the hospital in Brewster in no time."

"I'm not ready! There's so much to do yet," Amy protested, more confused than frightened. She'd assumed she had three weeks. When she awoke that morning, she'd felt better—physically—than she had in days. But not emotionally. That afternoon she'd experienced almost a compulsion for physical activity. She'd hoped that exploring Bitter End would be an interesting distraction.

Like so much else lately, her adventure had backfired.

"Everything's going to be fine," Dovie murmured.

"I know. It's just that I shouldn't be here . . . Oh Dovie, how could I have been this foolish?"

"We both were, but everything's going to be fine," she said again. "Frank's on his way and he'll get you to the hospital in plenty of time."

"Thank you," Amy whispered. She closed her eyes to keep her thoughts focused on what was happening to her and the baby. She tried to remember everything she'd learned in the birthing classes, her breathing exercises and the importance of remaining calm and composed. It had all sounded manageable when she was in class; reality was a different matter. She knew she dared not climb back up the steep incline to the car. With her water broken, it could be dangerous for the baby.

Dovie comforted her and counted with her, encouraging her to breathe through contractions.

Finally, what seemed hours later, she heard the sound of someone approaching.

"Thank God," Dovie said. "It's Frank. And Wade."

"Wade?" Amy's eyes flew open. "You knew he was coming, didn't you?" she accused.

"Frank couldn't have kept him away," she said, pleading forgiveness with her eyes. "He was with Frank when I phoned." Dovie regarded her expectantly, as if seeking absolution for not telling her earlier.

"It's all right," Amy said. In truth she was glad he was there. She was afraid and, heaven help her, she needed him at her side.

Wade raced down the hill and into town well ahead of Frank, slowing down only when he reached the hotel steps. His eyes searched hers, his love visible enough that her chest tightened with pain.

"How are you?" he asked.

She smiled. "I've been better."

He clasped her hand in his and kissed her fingers. "I'm coming with you to Brewster. Please don't say no, Amy."

She smiled weakly and nodded. He knelt down in front of her, brushing the hair from her temples.

"Sarah's doing great, I think," she said, gripping his hand.

"What about you? What's the pain like?"

"Like nothing I can describe."

A contraction took hold of her just then and she drew in a deep breath and bit her lower lip. "Oh, Wade," she gasped.

Her hand tensed in his. She didn't mean to be so dependent on him, but now that he was here, she couldn't help it. She needed him. "Count," she instructed. "Please count."

"One, two, three . . ."

"Slower."

"One . . . two . . . three . . ." He continued until he'd reached twenty and she told him to stop.

She took several big breaths and opened her eyes. "The pains are much more intense than I expected." If they were this strong now, she couldn't imagine what they'd be like later.

"Let's get her to the car," Frank suggested.

"I'm ready," Amy said, and the two men helped her stand. Dovie stepped back and watched, her face taut with concern.

They'd gone only a few feet when another contraction ripped through her, nearly doubling her over. She moaned and clutched her stomach.

"Stop!" Dovie shouted.

"Stop?" Frank repeated, then stared at Dovie. "What's happening?"

"We aren't going to make it to the Brewster hospital in time, not with her contractions two minutes apart."

"What do you mean?" Wade demanded, although her words were perfectly clear.

Frank Hennessey studied him with a shocked white face. "Tell me, Preacher, how much do you know about delivering a baby?"

Ten

Sheriff Hennessey couldn't have called at a worse time. Max Jordan's pacemaker had gone haywire, and Jane dared not leave him, so she'd sent Frank on to Bitter End with specific instructions to phone the clinic as soon as they arrived in Brewster. The rest of her afternoon had been hectic, with the phone ringing off the hook. When she'd finished sewing up Wiley Rogers's sliced thumb and setting Walt Wilson's broken leg, she sorted through the messages and realized she hadn't heard back from Frank.

She was about to call Brewster Memorial to check when Ellie burst through the door.

"It is true?" Ellie asked, her face bright with excitement as she hurried into Jane's office.

"If you're asking about Amy, yes, it's true," Jane said. She stood in front of her file cabinet and slipped a chart back into place. She felt a rush of excitement herself. "Amy's about to have her baby. It turns out she went into labor in Bitter End."

"Why didn't somebody tell me sooner?" Ellie demanded. "Every tongue in Promise is wagging, and I'm the last person to hear what's happening with my own employee." Disgruntled, she flopped down on the chair and stretched out her legs.

"How'd you find out?" Jane asked, curious. The nuances of small-town life continued to fascinate her. Having been born and raised in Southern California, she never failed to be astonished at the lightning-quick way word traveled in Promise.

"George."

"Who told George?" Jane asked, shaking her head in wonder.

"Pete Hadley, who heard from Denise down at the bowling alley. According to Pete, Denise has a real soft spot for Amy."

A lot of people had a soft spot for Amy, Jane reflected. The young mother-to-be had captured the town's heart. Sunday, when Wade had stood before the congregation and asked for a vote of confidence, the people had given him their overwhelming approval. But their votes hadn't been cast for Wade alone. They were showing support and approval for Amy, as well.

Jane suspected there was even some sneaking admiration over the fact that he'd been defending her against the likes of Lyle Whitehouse. Given the circumstances, a lot of the men in the congregation would have done the same thing.

She didn't think Lyle would be showing his face round town anymore. Billy, the owner of Billy D's Tavern, had suggested the ranch hand take his business elsewhere. Feelings ran high when it came to looking after one of their own. Wade McMillen was highly respected, and folks tended to feel protective toward Amy, too.

"You know who's kind of a gossip?" Ellie said, waggling her eyebrows as if this was an interesting tidbit of information.

"You mean other than you?" Jane teased.

"Me!" Ellie pointed to her chest in mock outrage. "I'm the picture of discretion."

"If you say so." Struggling to hold in a smile, Jane closed the file drawer and waited. "Well, don't keep me in suspense. Who?"

"Martha Kerns."

"The church secretary?" Jane had trouble believing it.

"How else do you think word got around so fast?"

"Hold on here," Jane said, stopping her sister-in-law. "What's Martha got to do with any of this?"

"She was working in the church office when Wade suddenly rushed in and said he was leaving with Sheriff Hennessey."

"Okay, got you," Jane said. It made sense now. Wade had told Martha and word had spread from there. She opened the small refrigerator in her office and removed two bottles of spring water, holding one out to Ellie. "No caffeine," she said.

"Thanks." Ellie reached for it, popped open the top and sank back into her chair. "Do you think Amy's having a boy or a girl?" she asked after a moment of silence.

"Girl," Jane predicted. "After a while a doctor gets a feel for these things. A sixth sense."

"Really?" Ellie sounded impressed.

Jane hadn't a clue which sex Amy's baby was, and as for any measure of shrewd intuition, well, that was a joke. She didn't think she'd be able to carry on this nonsense much longer and abruptly changed the subject. "Have you told Glen you're pregnant yet?"

Ellie leaned forward and set the bottle on Jane's desk.

"From that grin on your face, I'd say he knows."

"He does."

"And he's happy?"

Ellie giggled. "You'd think he was the first man ever to get a woman pregnant. All this strutting around the house like a rooster."

Jane shook her head. That sounded just like her brother-in-law.

Although Cal and Glen were brothers, their personalities were vastly different. Jane's husband was quieter, more intense than his fun-loving brother. When she got pregnant herself and the time came for her to tell him, she could predict Cal's reaction. He'd grow quiet, and then he'd gather her in his arms and tell her how much he loved her. He'd pamper and spoil her, and they'd spend long quiet hours making plans for their baby. Glen might pamper Ellie, too, but he'd joke boastfully about it and be sure folks knew what a great husband he was. His high energy and good humor would make him a wonderful father.

"We're telling Mary and Phil tomorrow night," Ellie said.

"They'll be so thrilled." Jane took a long swallow of her drink. "If this keeps up, Promise is going to have a population explosion," she said. First Savannah Smith, then Caroline, Amy and now Ellie. She knew from talking to Nell that she and Travis hoped to add to their family, too. It'd been ten years since Nell had given birth to Emma, but Jane could find no reason for her to experience any difficulty in getting pregnant again. Because Nell was in her midthirties, Travis had voiced his concerns about the risks to her and the baby, but Jane had reassured them.

"Twins run in my family," Ellie said absently.

Jane couldn't help smiling. She could just imagine how her brother-in-law would react to twins.

"Do you think Amy might have had the baby by now?" Ellie asked. She straightened and leaned forward, anxious to hear the latest word.

"I was about to phone Brewster Memorial when you arrived," Jane told her.

"Go ahead. I'd love to be the one to give George the update."

Jane took another drink and flipped through her Rolodex for the phone number.

Just as she'd punched in the number, Jenny entered the office.

"Jane's phoning about Amy," Ellie whispered.

"Oh, good, I was about to ask."

"Dr. Jane Patterson," Jane announced. "I'm calling to check on one of my patients." She asked to speak to the nurse on the maternity floor, then placed her hand over the receiver. "They're transferring me."

"I have a sneaking suspicion Amy's having a boy," Jenny said.

"It's a girl," Jane said confidently.

"Boy," Jenny whispered back.

Jane rolled her eyes and pointed to her small refrigerator. "Help yourself."

"Thanks," Jenny mouthed.

"This is Dr. Jane Patterson from Promise," she said again, launching into her explanation about Amy.

"We're admitting someone now, but I don't have the paperwork yet," the on-duty nurse said. "If you wait, I'll get that information for you."

Once more Jane put her hand over the mouthpiece. "She's arrived safe and sound."

"What took her so long?" Jenny asked, checking her watch.

"Frank probably took extra time not to upset her," Ellie suggested.

Jane frowned. According to her brief chat with Dovie before the cell phone went out, Amy's water had broken and she was experiencing some hard labor pains. She'd expected them to have arrived at the hospital much sooner than this.

"Everything's all right, isn't it?" Jenny asked, her gaze holding Jane's. "They got there okay?"

"With Frank driving, did you have a doubt?" Ellie asked, and drank the rest of her water.

In other circumstances Jane would have traveled with Amy, but that was impossible today. Amy was with Frank, Dovie and Wade McMillen. Unless the mother chose a home delivery as Savannah had, most of the babies in the county were born at the hospital in Brewster.

The floor nurse came back on the line. "What did you say your patient's name was again?"

"Amy Thornton."

"She hasn't been admitted yet," the nurse said matter-of-factly.

"Pardon me?" Jane asked. Although she felt an immediate sense of panic, she remained outwardly calm. "I'm sure there's some mistake. Could you check again?"

"Please hold the line."

Ellie stood. "There's an easy way to settle this. Frank drove in his patrol car, didn't he?"

Jane nodded.

"All we need to do is phone the sheriff's office and ask them to radio Frank."

"Good idea." Jane relaxed while Ellie and Jenny disappeared into the outer room to use the second phone.

The nurse from Brewster Memorial returned to the phone. "I'm sorry, no one in Admitting has talked to or seen anyone named Amy Thornton."

Jane replaced the receiver as Ellie and Jenny appeared in the doorway.

Ellie's face revealed her anxiety. "Something's wrong."

"The hospital has no record of Amy," Jane said.

Jenny chewed on her lip. "I phoned the sheriff's office," she explained, "and they radioed Frank."

"And?" Jane asked.

"There's no response. Apparently he isn't in the patrol car."

"Then where is he?" she demanded.

"That's the problem—no one seems to know," Ellie said. "They've been trying to reach him for the last thirty minutes."

"How's SHE DOING?" Wade asked, unable to hide his anxiety. He no longer cared if Frank or Dovie knew how concerned he was. A rain squall had hit them soon after they'd decided not to carry Amy to the patrol car. They couldn't stay outside with Amy about to give birth; they had to find someplace safe and dry.

Bitter End was the last place he felt was safe for Amy. He blamed himself for this situation; she'd asked him about the town and he'd put her off. He didn't like the idea of her in this dead town, and the thought of her giving birth here sent chills down his spine.

With Amy moaning in pain and Dovie calculating the time between contractions, he felt panic rising inside him. All four of them were already soaked to the skin. The only structure in the town where Amy wouldn't have to lie on the floor was the church with its hard wooden pews, and with the two men supporting her, she managed to make her way inside. There were still some provisions from Richard's stay in the town, including towels, blankets and pillows.

Dovie cleaned a pew while Frank searched for anything else that might be of use. She and Wade helped Amy onto the pew, and then Dovie went off to give Frank a hand. Wade refused to leave Amy's side. He hadn't attended a single one of the birthing classes, and he didn't know if he was helping or hindering, but she seemed to want him there, and God knew he had no intention of leaving her. Not then. Not ever.

Again and again he counted the seconds as her body was gripped by contractions. Each one seemed to grow in length and intensity. He felt as if his heart would break at the agony she was suffering.

Then Dovie returned with Frank, each of them carrying a tarpaulin and some other supplies. Rain pounded against the roof and leaked into the center of the church where lightning had once struck. It astonished him that the building had survived the wear and tear of the elements all these years.

"Relax," Frank advised, squeezing his shoulder. "Everything's going to be fine." He'd found a lantern—obviously left there by Richard—and lit it. The immediate warm glow filled the dim interior.

"I'll relax once I know everything's all right with Amy," Wade told the other man, too tense to do anything but worry.

After maybe ten minutes, the rain stopped as suddenly as it'd come. Wade couldn't remember seeing a cloud in the sky, and then all at once they'd been trapped in the middle of a torrent.

Now that they'd made the decision to stay in Bitter End, it seemed fitting that Amy's child be born in a church, even one as dilapidated as this. Someone had been inside recently, and he doubted it was Richard Weston. Probably Travis Grant. He and Nell were back from their honeymoon and apparently he'd made a number of research trips to the old town.

"Is everything all right here?" Frank asked nervously. He pulled Wade aside, and Dovie took his place. Amy lay on a pew, a pillow beneath her head and as comfortable as they could make her.

"As far as I know," Wade assured him.

Frank nodded abruptly. "I'll be right back," he said.

"Where are you going now?" Dovie asked.

"To the patrol car. I want to radio the office. Tell 'em what happened and where we are."

"I wish I'd thought to charge the batteries in my phone," Dovie said with an apologetic expression.

"So do I," Frank muttered as he headed out of the church. "I'll get Amy's suitcase while I'm at it. We picked it up before we came out here."

Amy moaned, and Wade knelt down on the floor next to her.

"Oh, Wade, it hurts so much," she whimpered.

"Do you want me to rub your back?" Dovie asked.

"No . . . no." Amy stretched out her hand to Wade.

He clasped it in his own. Wanting to help as much as he could, he reached for the cool washcloth Dovie had brought in and wiped her brow.

The pain seemed to ease and so did her fierce grip on his hand.

"Have you ever delivered a baby?" Dovie asked him, looking paler by the minute.

"No," he said.

"Me, neither."

"I'm not exactly a pro at this myself," Amy said weakly in what he sensed was an effort to insert a bit of humor. A pain must have overtaken her again because she closed her eyes and started to moan.

"Do something," Wade pleaded with Dovie, who took her position by Amy's feet.

"The baby's fully crowned," Dovie whispered, glancing up at Wade.

Amy's answering smile was weak. "She's coming, Dovie, she's coming." With that she began to bear down.

"Pant!" Dovie instructed. "Pant."

Amy did, and Wade encouraged her with a stream of praise and reassurance.

"The suitcase," Dovie said. "We'll need the suitcase."

"It's in the car," Wade remembered. "Why the hell isn't Frank back? I'll go get it." He loosened his grip on Amy's hand but she refused to release his.

"No! Wade, Wade, please don't leave me."

Wade met Dovie's look.

"I'll go," she said, and hurried from the church.

Wade held Amy's hand against his heart. "I love you."

"I know. I love you, too. So much." Tears slipped from the corners of her eyes and rolled toward her ears. She sniffled once and started to moan again.

"Wade!" she cried. "The baby's coming!"

A calmness came over him, and he moved to the end of the pew, taking Dovie's role. The first thing he saw was a full head of wet dark hair. Amy panted, and the baby's head slipped free. Wade supported the tiny head, which fit perfectly in his large hands. The baby's small eyes were squeezed shut and she didn't look the least bit pleased with this turn of events.

It seemed that no time had passed before Dovie and Frank burst into the back of the church. Frank carried the suitcase.

"We need a baby blanket," Wade called.

Frank knelt down and opened the suitcase, and Dovie rushed forward just as Amy gave a shout and half rose. As she did, the baby slid into Wade's waiting arms. He gazed down at this perfectly formed miniature human being and experienced such a rush of love and joy it was all he could do not to break into sobs himself.

"Is it a girl?" Amy asked, crying openly.

"No, a boy," Wade said as the infant wailed loudly. The cry pierced through the church and Wade swore it was the most beautiful sound he'd heard in his entire life.

"An aid car's on the way," Frank told them. "I'm going to meet them by the highway."

"Go," Dovie said, and waved him off. She took the baby from Wade and wrapped him in a blanket, then handed the bundle to Wade, while she tended to Amy, who had delivered the afterbirth.

"A boy," Amy said, half sitting to look at her son. Tears streaked her beautiful face.

Tears of his own blurred his eyes as he stared down at the incredibly tiny being. The immediate sense of love he felt for this child was beyond comprehension. It took a real effort of will to hand him to his mother, but at last he laid the baby on her abdomen.

Amy gazed upon her son and lovingly kissed his brow. "Welcome, little Joseph Gair."

The baby screamed, as if he was protesting the rough treatment he'd already received from life.

"Gair—that's my middle name," Wade choked out. It had been his grandfather's first name.

"Your mother told me."

Wade reached out his finger and Joseph immediately clenched it with his hand. The connection was one that would last all his life. Wade was sure of it.

While Dovie finished with Amy, Wade sat at the far end of the pew holding Joseph. The child's eyes opened briefly and he looked up at Wade in the soft light and stopped crying. Within a minute he was sound asleep.

A boy. Not Sarah, but Joseph. "Sleep, darling boy, sleep," Wade whispered, and kissed his brow.

"Is everything all right?" Amy asked, twisting around to see Wade and her son.

"Perfect," he whispered. "Perfect."

Tears glistened in Amy's eyes, and he didn't know how she knew what he was thinking, but she did. He saw it in her look, in everything about her.

"Marry me," he said softly.

"Honestly, Amy, put that boy out of his misery and marry him," Dovie pleaded.

Wade could have kissed Dovie. He'd never been more convinced of anything than the rightness of marrying Amy and making Joseph his son. The moment the infant had entered life, he'd come into Wade's hands— to guide, to love, to support. This was his son, born of his heart. This was the woman he would love and cherish all his life.

"I love you so much," Amy whispered.

"Does that mean yes?"

"Yes." Her whispered response was half laugh and half sob.

This was the way it was meant to be. Amy and Joseph and him, and whatever other children might be born in the years to come.

"The aid car's here," Frank announced from the back of the church.

"Already?" Dovie sounded as though she didn't believe him.

"It was dispatched earlier," Frank said, walking toward them. "Apparently when we didn't show up at the hospital, Jane called the office and they radioed ahead for an aid car."

"It might have helped if they'd arrived ten minutes earlier," Dovie muttered.

Wade knew better. The aid car had arrived right on schedule.

AMY HAD NEVER SLEPT like this. The hospital room was dark, and she sighed and smiled as she reviewed the events of the day before. It didn't seem possible that she'd actually given birth in Bitter End. Things had gone crazy all at once, but she'd always be grateful for the way they'd happened. Otherwise Wade wouldn't have been there, and she couldn't imagine what Joseph's birth would have been like without him at her side.

If she'd ever doubted his love, he'd proved it ten times over in those few hours. She closed her eyes and recalled the incredible sense of rightness that she'd felt when she agreed to marry him. All her doubts and fears had melted away. Instinctively she knew it was what she had to do.

All her reasons for declining earlier remained, but after Joseph's birth, those reasons didn't seem nearly as important. Her greatest fear was that she'd be a detriment to Wade and his commitment to his church. Wade deserved someone better. It was what she'd sincerely felt, but all that had changed when she realized how much Wade loved her and her child. How much she loved him.

Content, she smiled, and for the first time noticed a shadow in the corner. Sitting upright, she saw Wade sprawled asleep in a chair. He'd stretched out his feet and slouched down, his arms flung over the sides.

"Wade," she whispered in astonishment. "What are you doing here?"

He awoke immediately, saw her and smiled softly. Sitting up, he glanced around the room. "What time is it?"

She looked for a clock but didn't see one. "I don't know."

"Oh." He glanced at his watch. "It's 4 a.m."

"Have you been here all night?" she asked.

"Guess so—it sure feels that way." He rubbed the back of his neck and rotated the stiffness from his shoulders.

"You must have been so uncomfortable." Amy couldn't believe that he'd been with her all this time.

"I'll live," he said. "How are you feeling?"

"Starved," she admitted.

He stood and shook out his legs. "I'll see what I can do about scrounging up something to eat."

"Don't go," she begged him, and held out her hand.

He walked over to her side and she lifted her arms to him. They kissed, and it was beautiful, sensual, intense. It felt good to be in his arms again, to recognize that sense of belonging.

"How did you happen to spend the night?" she asked.

She felt Wade's smile against her face. "They let me into the nursery to help with Joseph. I was there, Amy, when they weighed and measured him and washed him for the first time. He doesn't take to baths well." He paused to smile and their eyes held a long moment.

"Oh, Wade, I'm so happy."

"He's a beautiful baby boy," he told her.

"I'm having a little trouble adjusting to the fact that Sarah's a boy!"

"He's got a fine pair of lungs on him, too."

"I heard, remember?"

"Dr. Jane was by, and Ellie and Glen stopped in, too, and there are quite a few floral arrangements. The nurses kept them by their station because they didn't want to disturb your sleep."

"Everyone's been so good to me."

"It's because you're loved."

Amy felt that love. It overwhelmed her that the people of Promise would be this kind. That they would accept a stranger the way they had.

"Everyone was full of questions, too."

Amy could well imagine that.

"I must have been asked a dozen times how you ended up giving birth in the ghost town."

"I guess people think it was foolish of me to go there so close to my due date."

"I don't," Wade countered. "I'm convinced it was exactly where we were supposed to be."

She smiled and understood what he was saying. There was a rightness to her being in Bitter End, as if all this had been ordained long before.

Wade yawned loudly and covered his mouth.

"You must be exhausted," she said.

"I am," he told her. "It isn't every day a man delivers a son and convinces a gal to marry him."

"I should hope not," Amy said, and kissed the back of his hand.

Eleven

"**D**ovie," Frank called, hurrying from room to room to search for his wife. He could hardly wait to tell her the latest about little Joe.

"I'm in the garden." Dovie's melodic voice drifted into the house from the backyard.

Frank walked onto the back patio to discover his wife picking ripe red tomatoes from her ever-abundant garden. She wore a large straw hat and, in his view, had never looked lovelier.

"I saw Amy and Joseph this afternoon," he said, and laughed at the immediate flash of envy he read in her eyes.

"Frank Hennessey, why didn't you come and get me?"

"I would have, but it was a chance meeting. I'll have you know that little tyke smiled at me."

"He didn't."

"Dovie, I swear it's the truth. He looked up at me with his big beautiful brown eyes and grinned from ear to ear."

Dovie added a plump tomato to her basket. "He was probably pooping. He's only two months old. That's far too young to be grinning."

"Hey, I'm his godfather. I know these things."

She gave an exaggerated sigh. "And I'm his godmother and I know about these things, too."

"You're jealous because he didn't smile for you first."

"Well, I have news for you, Frank Hennessey. Little Joe most certainly did smile for me." The moment the words left Dovie's mouth, she snapped it closed, knowing she'd said more than she'd intended. Frank recognized that look of hers all too well.

"You've been to see him again," he charged. "I suppose you bought him another toy."

"I didn't," she denied.

The flush in her cheeks claimed otherwise. "All right, all right, I bought him a designer bib. Oh, Frank, it was the cutest little thing you've ever seen."

His eyes narrowed as though he disapproved, but in reality, he was having the time of his life spoiling this youngster, too. Amy and Wade had made him and Dovie the official godparents—and little Joe's unofficial grandparents. Christmas was a month away, and they'd already bought him more presents than Santa delivered to the entire state. They seemed unable to stop themselves. It was as though an entire new world had opened up to them with the birth of this child. They were crazy about the baby and crazy about each other, too.

"The bib was a policeman's uniform complete with badge," Dovie told him. "You aren't *really* angry, are you, sweetheart?"

How could he be? Frank loved this child as though he were his own flesh and blood. He suspected a great deal of this was the result of being present at little Joe's birth, but that was only part of the reason.

Frank had waited until he was sixty years old to marry, and once he'd committed himself to Dovie he wanted to kick himself for leaving it this late. He recalled with clarity the talk he'd had with his wife some months previously. Dovie had lamented the fact that they would never be grandparents.

He hadn't been much of a churchgoer, but after he'd married, he'd started attending services with her. He remembered one of Wade's sermons about Abraham and Sarah becoming parents well after their childbearing years. In some ways the story reminded him of what had happened to him and Dovie. Amy had arrived in Promise needing a family, and she'd adopted them and they'd adopted her. All the love they had in their hearts was lavished on Amy, Wade and little Joe.

"He's an incredible baby," Frank said.

"Incredible," Dovie echoed.

Frank slipped his arm around her waist. "You're pretty incredible yourself, Dovie Hennessey."

"So I've been told."

He threw back his head and hooted with laughter.

Dovie set her basket of vegetables aside and threw her arms around his middle. Her eyes sparkled with joy as she gazed up at him. "I'm happy, so very happy."

"I am, too." The transition to married life had been much easier than Frank had suspected. He'd fought long and hard, convinced he was too set in his ways to give up bachelorhood—and his stubbornness had nearly cost him the only woman he'd ever truly loved.

Frank hugged Dovie close. "We're going to spoil that baby rotten!" he declared.

"But, Frank, we're going to have so much fun doing it."

Frank could see that once again his wife was right.

THREE MONTHS after Christmas Savannah Smith ventured into Bitter End. What she found caused her to race back to the ranch and breathlessly inform her husband. Laredo suggested she tell Grady and Caroline that same afternoon, which she did. The news burst from her in a rush of excitement.

"You're sure about this?" Grady asked.

"Grady, I know what I saw."

Caroline and five-month-old Roy came to visit the following day. "You went to Bitter End?" her best friend asked. "Good grief, Savannah, what would ever make you go back there?"

"The anniversary of my first visit. It was two years ago, March twentieth, and I wanted to see if the rosebush I'd planted in the cemetery had survived."

Savannah's whole life had changed that day two years earlier when she found a weary cowboy walking down the side of a country road and offered him a ride. She'd never done anything like it before and she never would again. For the first and only time in her life, she'd picked up a hitchhiker, and before the year was out she'd married him. She and Laredo Smith had become partners in the Yellow Rose Ranch and partners for life.

"Grady phoned and told Cal," Caroline said, cradling her son in her arms.

"I talked to Nell and Travis, too," Savannah said.

"Someone must have phoned and told Wade."

"Glen and Ellie, I think," Laredo suggested.

"Wade suggested we all meet out there first thing in the morning."

"You're going, aren't you?" Caroline asked.

Laredo and Savannah looked at each other and nodded. "We wouldn't miss it," he told her.

Fourteen of them planned to gather in the ghost town and see the strange phenomenon for themselves. Each one had been to the town at some point or other in the past two years. Each for his or her own reasons.

Savannah felt a certain responsibility to be present, since she was the person who'd started it all two years ago when she'd gone to Bitter End in search of lost roses. She was also the person who'd stumbled upon this latest wonder.

They met and parked their vehicles outside the town. Then each couple walked down the steep incline onto the dirt road that led into the center of town.

Savannah watched and smiled at their reactions, knowing that the same sense of astonishment must have shown on her face twenty-four hours earlier.

Grady's arm was around Caroline's shoulder. Roy was asleep in his carrier. Little Joe, too. Savannah knew that in the years to come these two boys would be best friends. Much the same way Grady and Glen and Cal had been from grade school onward.

"It's true," Ellie whispered. Her pregnancy was obvious now. Glen's hand held hers.

"It's a miracle," Nell whispered, gazing around her.

All around them, in every nook and cranny, against the corral, by the old water trough and even near the large rock, roses bloomed. Their scent wafted about, perfuming the air, their muted colors bringing life and beauty to a once dead place. Pansies winked from small patches of earth—gardens a century ago—and bluebonnets covered the hillside, waving bright blue petals in the breeze.

Perhaps most incredible of all was the dead tree in the center of town. Up from the trunk had sprung new life, green shoots. In time the new tree would overshadow the old; life would vanquish death.

"Who can explain such a thing?" Frank asked, awestruck.

Savannah understood his awe; she felt the same way herself. Naturally there'd be a logical explanation for what had happened if they sought one. Most likely a freshwater spring had broken free.

"I don't know that I can explain it," Travis said, looking thoughtful. "But I can speculate about what might have caused this."

Everyone turned to him. "Bitter End's come full circle now," he said.

"Why now?" Ellie wanted to know.

"Well, keep in mind that I'm a writer—a storyteller—and I like events to have a structure. I like a sense of completion." Travis smiled at Amy and Wade. "But if my guess is right, we have little Joe to thank for all this."

"Joe?" Amy gazed down on her sleeping son.

"Amy, too," Dovie added, slipping her arm around the young mother's waist.

"A preacher's son died in Bitter End all those years ago," Travis said.

"And now a preacher's son has been born here. So, like I said, everything has come full circle."

"Full circle," Savannah whispered, knowing instinctively that this was indeed what had happened.

"The curse is gone."

Savannah smiled. "And in its place is a profusion of beauty."

A town in bloom, filled with promises for the future. Promises for life.

Dear Friends,

Lone Star Baby wraps up the Heart of Texas series. Everything's coming up roses in Bitter End, and Promise is about to experience a population explosion. My stubborn cowboys have all met their matches in love and in life. I'm sorry to leave my friends in Promise behind, but . . . new friends and adventures are beckoning me.

No project this involved can be accomplished without a lot of help from quite a few talented people. First and foremost, my editor, Paula Eykelhof. No writer works with a better editor than I do. Paula has my unfailing devotion for the long hours she put into every stage of Heart of Texas. Again, I was fortunate to have Maryan Gibson as copyeditor on this series. Andrea Szego, editorial assistant, was an invaluable asset to both Paula and me. And proofreader Peter Cronsberry, who expertly read through the entire Midnight Sons series, also worked on Heart of Texas. Rick Lovell painted the beautiful cover illustrations, and Lorraine Paradowski was the creative art editor on this project. Thanks to everyone for a terrific job!

Only the author's name appears on a book cover, but I wanted you to realize that no author stands alone, and the team I work with is the best!

As always, my notes of gratitude wouldn't be complete if I didn't mention my readers. Your letters and inquiries about the Texas series were just the incentive I needed. Thank you.

Now, Savannah, Ellie, Caroline, Jane, Nell, Amy and Dovie have something they wanted me to say. Together they've published a pamphlet they'd like to share with you. It includes recipes, household hints, gardening advice and more, with each woman drawing on her own expertise. If you're interested in receiving a copy, you can write to me at P.O. Box

1458, Port Orchard, Washington 98366. A stamped, self-addressed envelope would be appreciated.

Thank you again for joining me in Promise. Hope you enjoyed the visit!

Warmest regards,

Debbie